MVFOL

AN EXCLUSIVE MESSAGE TO BOOK CLUB MEMBERS
FROM LUANNE RICE:

When I was young, I grew up thinking of summer as a wonderful time to read—and to write. Every chance I got, I would grab a book and sit under the oak tree in our yard, or down on a towel at the beach, getting lost in stories. There is something about the freedom of summer—along with the sunlight, breezes, and (for me) salt air, that makes my imagination that much more active. My mother would take advantage of that by encouraging me and my sisters to write poems and stories nearly every day of vacation.

Those old habits are deeply ingrained, because summer isn't summer for me without new books. This year, there are two—*Summer's Child* and *Summer of Roses*. I've never written linked books before—two novels joined by a single story. Over the years I've written many novels set at Hubbard's Point, a magical community on the Connecticut Shoreline. There are rocky promontories, salt-water bays, golden marshes, graceful cottages, and people whose families have been summering there for generations. The characters there seem real to me, and I bring them back in book after book.

But this project is different. The story begins in *Summer's Child* with a shocking incident, a "ripped from the headline" event that is all the harder to accept because it happens in such a "normal" neighborhood, to such a nice family.

To tell this story, the novel moves from coastal Connecticut to the wilds of Nova Scotia. It explores love, fear, birth, death, secrets, betrayal, best friends, white whales, rose gardens, sharks, heartbreak—of a very real and literal nature, northern lights, an Irish Ceili, and two fiddle-playing sisters. I fell in love with the characters as I followed their lives, and the most amazing thing for me as a writer was this: it wasn't until I'd reached the last page of *Summer's Child*, after I wrote "The End," that I realized the story was really just beginning . . .

To finish it, I had to spin back in time, look into the bright beginnings and dark corners of these characters' stories. They unfold in *Summer of Roses*. This novel has threads reaching back into the past, weaving details together in order to understand the hopes and dreams that motivated these people to make the choices they did.

The two summer novels begin with a single mystery—a young woman, eight months pregnant, walks out of her grandmother's rose garden on the longest day of the year, and seems to fall off the face of the earth.

She has a devoted husband, a grandmother who adores her, best friends who would do anything for her, close ties to Hubbard's Point. The entire town begins to search for her. They hold a candlelight vigil.

The idea of such a beloved woman disappearing from such a safe place is almost beyond belief.

The local police take the case very seriously—and personally. Every one of them cares about the woman and her family. She reminds them of their wives, sisters, and daughters. One detective in particular, Patrick Murphy, makes the case his own. He follows every lead, gets involved with the family, spending so much time that his own relationships suffer in the process.

I wanted to explore the idea of romantic happiness—what looks beautiful, even enviable, from the outside can sometimes hide dark secrets. Even with close friends or family members, no one really knows what goes on within a couple except for the people involved.

Haven't we all known couples who seemed perfect? We'll see them at parties, or church, or at the soccer field, happy and smiling and obviously in love—seeming to have what everyone wants, leaving us to look at our own relationships and wonder if they measure up. But then something happens—the golden couple breaks up. Perhaps they divorce; worse, there are rumors of something sinister. What *really* happened behind the picket fence and lace curtains?

The books are full of women friends, old and new, people who care about each other and will travel to the ends of the earth—almost literally—to help. There's a couple who comes together after a long friendship; from that perspective, I wanted to write about second-chance love—which I think of as really grown-up love—after mistakes have been made, hearts broken, a few mysteries solved, and, especially, after a few things have been understood and forgiven.

For me, the story that runs through these two novels is a lot like the rose garden in which it begins and ends: the stony soil of winter yields green shoots, sturdy stems, delicate leaves, and a season's worth of roses by summer's finale.

Happy summer, and happy reading, to you all!
Luanne

Summer's
Child

Summer
of
Roses

Also by LUANNE RICE

Silver Bells
Beach Girls
Dance With Me
The Perfect Summer
The Secret Hour
True Blue
Safe Harbor
Summer Light
Firefly Beach
Dream Country
Follow the Stars Home
Cloud Nine
Home Fires
Blue Moon
Secrets of Paris
Stone Heart
Crazy in Love
Angels All Over Town

LUANNE RICE

Summer's
Child
&
Summer
of
Roses

BANTAM BOOKS

SUMMER'S CHILD AND SUMMER OF ROSES
Bantam Books

Published by Bantam Dell
A Division of Random House, Inc.
New York, New York

This is a work of fiction. Names, characters, places, and
incidents either are the product of the author's imagination or are used
fictitiously. Any resemblance to actual persons, living or dead, events, or
locales is entirely coincidental.

Bantam Books and the rooster colophon are registered
trademarks of Random House, Inc.

ISBN 0-7394-5514-1

Printed in the United States of America

Summer's Child

To Amelia Onorato

Acknowledgments

Thank you to Irwyn Applebaum, Nita Taublib, Tracy Devine, Betsy Hulsebosch, Cynthia Lasky, Barb Burg, Susan Corcoran, Carolyn Schwartz, Jim Plumeri, Kerri Buckley, and everyone at Bantam Dell for celebrating summer with me; Mia and the BDG; Sarah Walker; Paula Breger; Kim Dorfman and Mika and Alek Glogowski; everyone from the SoundHound sessions: Jeff Berman, Tom Spackman, Frank Cabanach, James von Buelow, Melissa Lord, Teresa Wakabayashi, Lori McCarthy, Melissa Rivera, Michelle Lewy; and the friends I saw in Phoenix: Jocelyn Schmidt, Mary McGrath, George Fisher, Lane Rider, Phil Canterbury, Greg Bresson, and Steve Maddock.

Prologue

At the time, it was the biggest story in the state. Every newspaper covered it on the front page. Her face was as well known as the governor's—and much more beloved. The excitement in her blue eyes, the enormous smile, the shimmer—yes, that's what it was—the way she positively shimmered with life, radiated goodness. She looked like everyone's favorite sister, best friend, and girl next door, all rolled into one.

The fact that she was pregnant when she disappeared gave the story an extra, terrible jolt. When you looked at her photo, now you saw her joy—as if you were right there with her. You imagined how thrilled she was to be having a baby, and you knew that she would be a wonderful mother. Some people hide their feelings, keep them inside for no one to see—not Mara. She'd never hidden anything. You just looked at her picture and knew—that smile and the brightness in her eyes left no doubt at all.

She was right there, smiling into the camera with the same degree of love and presence that she brought to everything in her life. *I love you—you know that, don't you? Take the picture so we can save it forever, put it into the baby book and prove how excited we were to know our child was on the way.* . . . Did Mara actually say those words, or were they just a trick of memory?

Being so open requires a sort of innocence. A hope—no, more than a hope . . . a conviction that the world was safe, that people were good. That life was a gift, and nothing moved except as a positive power. Bad things happened—attacks, violence, crimes—yes, unfortunately they did. But they could always be explained and therefore, eventually, understood—so they wouldn't have to happen again. So the people who did them could be helped, and could change.

Those were Mara's beliefs. Or they had been, back in the days just before her picture appeared on the front page of every paper in Connecticut. She had been an only child; her parents were dead. Perhaps that was why the whole country adopted her, searched for her, and grieved for her as they would have their own daughter, sister, or friend.

The anniversary of her disappearance always brought a new flurry of stories. TV stations ran recaps of old video shots, endless loops of her smiling, waving, holding the yellow watering can and wearing a pair of matching buttercup-yellow rubber rain boots in the garden. Newspapers reran the story every June 21, the anniversary of her disappearance and the longest day of the year, to remind readers of what had captivated the country so many years ago now. . . .

On the first night of summer, adorable five-foot-nothing, pregnant-as-could-be Mara Jameson went out to water the garden. Whether she hitched a ride and changed her identity, walked into the hands of a brutal stranger, or was already dead at the hands of her husband has never been known. Her body was never recovered; she was never seen again. No baby was ever born—or at least not with a mother named Mara Jameson listed on the birth certificate. The only clues were the yellow rain boots, left neatly standing next to the trickling hose.

The articles were grave, somber, but oddly wistful. They added up to a life never lived—a mystery never solved. What could have happened that would make her stop watering the garden and walk away? Who could ever forget that smile?

That smile that would never be smiled again. . . .

Chapter 1

Being retired had its pluses. For one thing, it was good to be ruled by the tide tables instead of department shifts and schedules. Patrick Murphy kept the small *Hartford Courant* tide card tacked up by the chart table, but he barely needed it anymore. He swore his body was in sync with the ebb and flow of Silver Bay—he'd be pulled out of bed at the craziest hours, in the middle of the night, at slack tides, prime times to fish the reefs and shoals around the Stone Mill power plant.

Stripers up and down the Connecticut shoreline didn't stand a chance. They hadn't for the two years, seven months, three weeks, and fourteen days since Patrick had retired at the age of forty-three. This was the life. This was *really* the life, he told himself. He had lost the house, but he had the boat, the truck. This was what people worked their whole lives for: to retire to the beach and fish the days away.

He thought of Sandra, what she was missing. They had had a list of dreams they would share after he left the Connecticut State Police: walk the beaches, try every new restaurant in the area, go to the movies, hit the casinos, take the boat out to Block Island and Martha's Vineyard. They were still young—they could have a blast.

A blast, he thought. Now—instead of the fun he had thought they would have together—"blast" made him think of the divorce, with its many shocks and devastations, the terrible ways both lawyers had found to make a shambles of the couple they had once been.

Fishing helped. So did the Yankees—they had snapped their losing streak and just kept on winning. Many the night Patrick combined the two—casting and drifting, listening to John Sterling and Charlie Steiner call the game, cheering for the Yanks to win another as he trolled for stripers, as his boat slipped east on the current.

Other things pulled him out of his bunk too. Dreams with dark tentacles; bad men still on the run after Patrick's best waking efforts to catch them; a lost girl; shocks and attacks and bone-rattling fears that gave new meaning to Things That Go Bump in the Night. Patrick would wake up with a pounding heart, thinking of how terrified she must have been.

Whether she was murdered, dead and buried all these years, or whether something had happened to drive her from her house, her grandmother's rose garden, to someplace so far away she had never been seen again, her fear must have been terrible.

That's the thing he could never get out of his mind.

What fears had Mara Jameson felt? Even now, his imagination grabbed hold of that question and went wild. The case was nine years old, right at the top of his unsolved pile. The paperwork had been his albatross, his constant companion. The case was the rock to Patrick's Sisyphus, and he had never—not even after it promised to ruin his marriage, not even after it made good on that promise, not even now, after retirement—never stopped pushing it up the hill.

Mara's picture. It sat on his desk. He used to keep it right beside his bed—to remind him of what he had to do when he got up. Look for the sweet girl with the heartbreak smile and the laughing eyes. Now he didn't really need the picture. Her face was ingrained into his soul. He knew her expressions by heart, the way other men knew their wives, girlfriends, lovers. . . .

She'd be with him forever, he thought, climbing out of bed at five-thirty A.M. He had only the vaguest idea of what his dream had been—something about blood spatter on the kitchen floor, the spidery neon-blue patterns revealed by the blood-detecting luminol, trickles and drops . . . spelling, in Patrick's dream, the killer's name. But it was in Latin, and Patrick couldn't understand; besides, who could prove she'd been killed when her body had never been found?

He rubbed his eyes, started the coffee, then pulled on shorts and sweatshirt. The morning air felt chilly; a front had passed through last night, violent thunderstorms shaking the rafters, making Flora hide under the bed. The black Lab rubbed up against him now, friendly bright eyes flashing, knowing a boat ride was in their future.

Heading up on deck, he breathed in the salt air. The morning star blazed in the eastern sky, where the just-about-rising sun painted the dark horizon with an orange glow. His thirty-two-foot fishing boat, the *Probable Cause*, rocked in the current. After the divorce, he'd moved on board. Sandra had kept the house on Mill Lane. It had all worked out fine, except now the boatyard was going to be turned into condos. Pretty soon all of New England would be one big townhouse village, complete with dockominiums . . . and Patrick would have to shove off and find a new port.

Hearing footsteps on the gravel, he peered into the boatyard. A shadow was coming across the sandy parking lot; Flora growled. Patrick patted her head, then went down below to get two mugs of coffee. By the time he was back on deck, he saw Flora wagging her tail, eyes on the man standing on the dock. Angelo Nazarena.

"Don't tell me," Patrick said. "You smelled the coffee."

"Nah," Angelo said. "I got up early and saw the paper; I figured you needed company so you wouldn't get drunk or do something really stupid. Longest day of the year's tomorrow, and the articles are starting already. . . ." He held the *Hartford Courant* in one hand, but accepted the heavy blue mug in the other as he stepped aboard.

"I don't drink anymore," Patrick said. He wanted to read the story but didn't—at the same time. "As you well know. Besides, I'm not speaking to you. You're selling my dock."

"Making millions in the bargain," Angelo chuckled. "When my grandfather bought this land, it was considered crap. The wrong side of the railroad bridge, next to a swamp, stinking like clam flats. But he was smart enough to know waterfront is solid gold, and I'm cashing in. Good coffee."

Patrick didn't reply. He was staring at Mara's picture on the front page. It had been taken in her grandmother's rose garden—ten miles from here, at her pretty silver-shingled cottage at Hubbard's Point. The camera had caught the light in her eyes—the thrill, the joy, that secret she always seemed to be holding back. Patrick had the feeling he so often had—that if he leaned close enough, she'd whisper to him, tell him what he so desperately wanted to know. . . .

"These papers really get a lot of mileage out of nothing," Angelo said, shaking his head. "The poor girl's been gone nine years now. She's fish food, we all know that."

"Your Sicilian lineage is showing."

"She's gone, Patrick. She's dead," Angelo said, sharply now. He and Patrick had gone to school together, been altar boys at St. Agnes's together, been best man at each other's wedding. He and Patsy had introduced him to Sandra.

"The husband did it, right?"

"I thought so, for a long time," Patrick said.

"What was his name, though . . . he had a different last name from Mara. . . ."

"His name is Edward Hunter. Mara had her own career. She kept her own name when she married him."

And now Patrick saw Edward Hunter's handsome charm-boy face, his stockbroker's quick, sharp smile—as wide and bright as Mara's, but without one ounce of her heart, soul, depth, integrity, authenticity, spark. . . . As a state cop, Patrick had encountered smiles like Edward Hunter's thousands of times. The smiles of men pulled over for speeding on their way home from places they shouldn't have been, the smiles of men at the other end of a domestic violence call—smiling men trying to convince the world they were better than the circumstances made them seem and reminding Patrick that "smile" was really just "slime" spelled sideways.

"Everyone thought so—not just you. But the bastard didn't leave a body behind. So you can't try him, and it's time for you—"

"We could have tried to pull a Richard Crafts," Patrick said, naming Connecticut's infamous killer convicted of murdering his wife, whose body was never found, on the basis of a few fragments of hair and bone discovered in a rented wood chipper. "But we didn't even have enough for that. I couldn't even find enough evidence for that."

"Like I was saying, it's time you moved on."

"Okay, thanks," Patrick said, his expression saying *why didn't I think of that?*, his Irish rising as he faced his friend Angelo—who had brought over the morning paper with Mara's face on the front page, who was about to sell his boat slip right out from under him. Flora had gone for a run around the still-deserted parking lot, and now she leapt back aboard the boat.

"What I mean is . . ." Angelo said, trying to find the words to fill the hole he'd opened up.

"What you mean is, it's time I got a life, I know," Patrick said, giving his old friend an old-friends glance—the kind of look that tells them they know you better than anyone, that you take their point, that they were right all along, when what you really want is to just shut them up and get them off your case.

"Yeah. To be honest, that's what I mean," Angelo said, chuckling with relief even as Patrick was folding up the newspaper and tossing it through the hatch—purportedly for disposal but actually to save forever.

As he saved all of Mara's pictures.

Because, he thought as he started up the engine and Angelo cast off the lines, as they headed out to the fishing grounds, it was one of the ways he had found to keep her alive. That, and one other way . . .

The whole world assumed that Mara Jameson and her unborn baby had died all those nine years ago, and they still did. Patrick thought back to his Catholic childhood, that phrase in the Creed: *We believe . . .*

in all that is seen and unseen. It was pretty much impossible to have faith in what you couldn't see. And the world hadn't seen Mara in over nine years.

Backing out of the slip, hitting the bow thrusters, he eased into the channel. The boat chuffed through the deepening water as gray herons watched silently from shadows along the green marshy shore. The rising sun shone through scrub oaks and white pines. Bursts of gold glittered on the water ahead.

The dead never stayed hidden. The earth gave them up, one way or another. Patrick knew they were relentless in their need to be found. The Tibetan Book of the Dead described the hungry ghosts, tormented by unbearable heat, thirst, hunger, weariness, and fear. Their realm seemed familiar to Patrick; having spent his career investigating homicides, he believed that the dead had their own emotions, that they haunted the living until they were found.

And Mara had never been found.

After all the work he'd done on her case, Patrick believed he would know—deep inside his own body—if she were dead. He felt Mara Jameson in his mind, his skin, his heart. He carried her with him every day, and he knew he'd never be able to put her down until he knew for sure what had happened to her. Where she was . . .

The birds were working up ahead, marking a school of blues just before the red nun buoy. Angelo got the rods ready. Flora stood at Patrick's side, her body pressed against his leg as he hit the throttle and sped toward the fish and tried in vain to escape the thoughts that haunted him wherever he went.

And he knew that when he got back, he'd be ready to write her this year's letter.

Ah, it was about to start again. As it did every year at this time. Just as the last traces of New England's long chill were gone from the air, just as the birds had returned north from their winter's journeys, just as the roses were coming into bloom and the gardens were awash with color, just as summer solstice was upon them, with its gift of the longest day . . . the time had come around again.

Maeve Jameson stood in her garden, pruning. She wore a wide straw hat, white linen shirt, and hot-pink garden gloves. In spite of all the cover-ups, she also wore sunscreen. They hadn't known about sun damage when she was a girl—they had all thought the sun was the great healing force—the more of it the better.

But she'd had a small skin cancer removed from her cheek last year, and was determined to do her best to keep it from happening again, to stay as healthy as she could, to stay alive until she knew the entire truth.

She had always been fastidious about putting lotion on her granddaughter. Mara had had such fair skin—so typically Irish, pale and freckled. Her parents—Mara's, that is—had been killed in a freak ferry accident on a trip to Mara's mother's hometown in the west of Ireland.

Maeve had taken over raising their daughter, their only child; every time she'd ever looked at Mara, she'd seen her son, Billy, and she'd loved her so much, more than the stars in the sky, more than anything—because she was a direct link to her darling boy, and she'd dutifully put sunscreen all over her freckled skin before letting her go down to the beach.

"You have the soul of your father in your blue eyes," Maeve would say, spreading the lotion.

"And my mother?"

"Yes, Anna too," Maeve would say, because she had loved her Irish daughter-in-law almost as if she'd been her own child. But the truth was, Mara had been all-Billy to Maeve. Maeve couldn't help herself.

So now she just stood in her garden, clipping the dead heads from the rosebushes. She tried to concentrate on finding the three-leaf sets, but she was distracted by the two newspeople standing out by the road. They had their cameras out, clicking away. Tomorrow—the anniversary of Mara's disappearance—the headlines would no doubt read, "Grandmother Still Waiting after All These Years" or "Roses for Mara's Remembrance" or some other malarkey.

The local newspeople had always made a cartoon of the situation—tried to boil everything down into an easily palatable story for their readers to understand. When no one knew the whole truth—except Mara. Edward had played his part in the terrible drama, and Maeve knew some segments, but only Mara knew it all.

Only Mara had endured it.

The state police detective had learned some of it. Patrick Murphy, another Hibernian, although not in the tradition of Irish cops that Maeve remembered from growing up in the South End of Hartford. Those fellows had been tough, all steel, no nonsense, and they'd seen the world in black and white. Everything was one way or another. Not Patrick.

Patrick was different. Maeve had taught school for fifty years, and if she had ever had Patrick Murphy in her class, she knew that she would never have pegged him to be a police officer. Not that he hadn't done a thorough investigation—if anyone could find Mara, Maeve knew it would be Patrick. But there was something in his makeup that reminded Maeve of Johnny Moore, an Irish poet she had once known.

She had seen it the day he had come here to Maeve's house, held her hand as they sat in rockers on the porch, and told her about the blood they had found on Mara's kitchen floor. Maeve's heart had frozen. It really had. She had felt her heart freeze and constrict, felt the muscle shrink, pulling all her blood back from her face and hands, so that her head had dropped down on her chest.

And when she'd come to, just a second or two later, Patrick was kneeling in front of her, with tears in his eyes because he was thinking the same thing she had so often feared would happen—that Mara was dead, the baby was dead, that Edward had killed them both.

Maeve had only to think of the tears in Patrick Murphy's blue eyes to feel her heart twist now, again, as she snipped away at the tangled rosebushes. She knew that he would come by—sometime in the next week or so—to check on her.

Maeve held the green plastic-handled garden shears in her pink-gloved hand, clipping her rosebushes. Cutting far enough down, right to the place where new life in the form of tiny green leaves emerged from the stem. Her arthritis was acting up.

She could almost feel the photographers wanting to ask her to go get the yellow boots and watering can, stage the yard as it had been that day nine years ago tomorrow.

"Hello, Maeve."

Looking up, she saw her neighbor and lifelong best friend, Clara Littlefield, coming through the side yard. Clara carried a wicker picnic basket overflowing with French bread, grapes, Brie, saucisson, and a bottle of wine.

"Hi, Clara," Maeve said. The two women bumped straw hats as they kissed.

"The roses look so beautiful this year," Clara said.

"Thank you . . . look at Mara's beach roses—they've really come into their own, haven't they?"

"They have," Clara said, and the two women admired the full bushes, lush with pink blooms, planted by Mara the year her parents drowned. So many years ago, meant to cherish her parents' memory, and now they were all Maeve had of Mara herself. Maeve's eyes filled with tears, and she felt Clara's arm slip around her.

"You brought us a picnic?" Maeve asked.

"Of course. I can't come to stay at your house without bringing food. It's like those sleepovers we had sixty years ago, when we'd take turns providing the s'mores."

"The sleepovers continue," Maeve said, smiling. "No matter how old we are . . ."

Clara laughed, hugging her again, almost making Maeve forget the reason for this particular sleepover, this picnic. Every June for the last eight years, Maeve's best friend had come over to stay, to spend the night before that day when Mara put down the green garden hose and yellow watering can, slipped off her yellow boots, and walked out of her grandmother's yard forever.

Forever was such a long time.

But, Maeve thought, holding Clara's hand as they walked into the kitchen to delve into the picnic basket, it went by just a little easier when you had a best friend by your side.

Chapter 2

The two girls had missed the bus, so they walked home from school, kicking a pebble ahead of them on the bumpy road high above the Gulf of St. Lawrence. They took turns. First Jessica would give it a good smack with her sneaker, send it bouncing along. When they caught up to the stone, Rose would take her shot. In between kicks, they walked and talked.

"Favorite color," Rose said.

"Blue. Favorite animal," Jessica said.

"Cats. Favorite book."

"*The Lion, the Witch, and the Wardrobe.*"

"Mine too." Rose laughed as she kicked the pebble and got air, sending it in a long arc down the middle of the road. "Did you see that?"

"Okay, you get the gold medal," Jessica said. "Back to Question Time."

"We've played this before," Rose said. "We already know the answers to all the questions."

"Not *all* the questions," Jessica said mysteriously. "We've only been friends since I moved here in April. I'll bet you don't even know where I'm from."

"Boston," Rose said.

"That's just what we tell people," Jessica said. She had a pretend-scary look on her freckled face. "But there are secrets that even my best friend won't know—*until she asks me . . .*"

Rose giggled. She and Jessica were almost nine, and it felt delicious to imagine that her new friend had deep dark secrets—and to know that to find out about them, all she had to do was ask. Mulling that over, she walked in silence. Off to the left, the Gulf of St. Lawrence stretched on forever. It was very calm and bright blue, with just the finest of haze spread like a silk scarf over its surface. Rose knew, when she saw haze like that, summer was almost here. She scanned the bay, in search of Nanny . . . when summer came, so did Nanny.

Jessica mis-kicked the pebble into the weeds, so she started over with a new one. Rose inched a little way down the bank to find the old stone; something made her want to keep it, so she put it in her pocket. By the time she looked up, Jessica had disappeared around the bend. Rose skipped a few steps. When she broke into a run, her heart fluttered like a trapped bird.

"Don't you want to know?" Jessica asked, dribbling the pebble the way she did a soccer ball on the field.

"Sure," Rose said.

"Then ask," Jessica teased. "Go on—I'll give you a clue. Ask me my real name."

"I know it—it's Jessica Taylor."

"Maybe it is, maybe it isn't. Maybe Taylor is my stepfather's name, or maybe we decided to name ourselves after James Taylor. We love his music."

"So do my mother and I!"

"My real father saw him in a concert once. At Tanglewood."

"Your real father?" Rose asked. She wanted to ask more, but something about the look on Jessica's face made her hold back. Stress pulled her eyes tight and made her jaw square. It only lasted a moment, was gone in a flash, but Rose had seen. The words "your real father" slashed between them; Rose felt them in her heart, like another trapped bird.

"The air sure is clean up here," Jessica said, changing the subject as they started walking again. "It's the reason we moved to Cape Hawk, so far from pollution and junk in the air. Or, at least, that's what my mother tells everyone. But maybe . . ."

"Maybe what?" Rose asked.

"Maybe the real reason we moved here is another scary secret!" Jessica said. She tugged on one of Rose's braids, then pointed up at the mansion on the hill. Deer tracks led through the thick brush, into the pine forest surrounding the great big stone house where the oceanographer lived. "Let's go up there and spy on Captain Hook."

"I don't think that's such a good idea," Rose said, feeling the strange flutter again. "Considering he's our friend and my mother has her store right next to his office."

"Yes, but that's way down at the dock," Jessica said. "She probably has no idea what goes on inside his big, crazy house. What if he's a mad scientist and we have to save her? What if he's a real pirate, with a name like Captain Hook?"

"His name is Dr. Neill," Rose said. She knew the kids called him

Captain Hook, but she never did. Rose knew that people were different, in all sorts of ways. She loved the things she and Dr. Neill had in common, and it made her sad when kids made fun of him. He was so tall and quiet, with that dark hair and deep-set eyes, and a thin mouth that never smiled. Except when he was near Rose and her mother.

"I feel bad that your mother's beautiful shop has to be right next door to him," Jessica said. "Any one-arm guy who spends his life chasing *sharks* . . ." She shivered. "When the rest of his family is so nice, with their whale-watch boats."

"My birthday party's going to be a whale watch," Rose said.

"I know, I can't wait. Because it's my birthday too."

"No! You're kidding!"

"Maybe I am . . . and maybe I'm not."

Rose pictured their classroom, with one bulletin board decorated with colorful squares, showing all her classmates' birthdays. Jessica's was in August.

"You *are* kidding," Rose said. "Because it's August 4—right up there on the board."

Jessica smiled. "You caught me. Well, only one of us gets to celebrate on Saturday. You, lucky girl!"

"I just hope Nanny's back by then. She's always here for my birthday."

"Who's Nanny?"

"You'll meet her."

"Will we really see whales?"

"Yes," Rose said. "They come back here every summer. This is their home, just like it's ours."

"Is that why the Neill family is so rich? Because they have all those whale-watching boats?"

"I guess so." Rose's fingers began to feel numb. She felt prickles race across her lips. The road inched upward, toward the eastern curve. Once they got to the top, they could start down. They were almost to the pinnacle.

"My stepfather says whales are just overgrown fish and people who pay good money to see them are suckers. He had an ancestor who got rich from whaling."

"Whales are mammals," Rose said, concentrating on every step. "They breathe air, just like us."

Tall rock cliffs ringed the town—from behind the big white hotel out to headlands jutting into the protected bay, which led into the Gulf of St. Lawrence. The icy Lyndhurst River flowed down, cutting a jagged path through the steep rock and forming a fjord. Rose had learned in school that this whole area had been formed by the Ice Age—that the rocks were from the glacier, and that the river flowing into the bay attracted fish and was the reason this spot was so popular with whales and seals.

"Come on," Jessica said suddenly, grabbing Rose's hand, tugging her toward a deer track leading up to Dr. Neill's house. Rose lifted her eyes. The sturdy Nova Scotia pines seemed to somehow elevate the stone house, hold it up above their branches toward the sky—sunshine glanced off the vast slate roof. She heard songbirds—just back from their long migration to the south—singing in the trees. Even with the glinting sunlight and the birdsong, and the hope of seeing Dr. Neill, the path was just too steep.

"Are you coming?" Jessica prodded.

Rose leaned forward, hands on her knees, resting a little. "Let's go down to my mother's shop instead, okay? She'll give us a snack, and maybe she'll teach you how to needlepoint your initials."

"You're just chicken!" Jessica said. But Rose noticed that Jessica actually looked relieved that they didn't have to go up the dark and spooky hillside. Rose shrugged, pretending to agree. She stayed there, leaning on her knees, conserving her strength.

"Okay, then," Jessica said. "We're soccer players. I'll pass you the ball, and let's see you take it down the field."

Jessica kicked the pebble her way, expecting her to dribble it the way she had. Rose started, but the walk home had been so long, and the trapped-bird feeling was getting worse. She glanced down at her hands, and saw Jessica follow her gaze. Her fingers were blue, and the expression on Jessica's face was pure shock.

"Rose!"

"I'm just cold," Rose said. "That's all."

"But it's hot out!"

Feeling panicked, Rose kicked the stone into the bushes—as if by accident. Jessica whooped with disbelief, then began to run down the hill toward the harbor.

"Come on," she called.

Rose wanted to sit down, but she couldn't bear for Jessica to see. Jessica was her new friend, and she didn't know. . . . *It's all downhill,* she told herself. *I can do it.* . . . She scanned the harbor town, fixed her eyes on her mother's store. Then she took a deep breath and began to walk.

Cape Hawk was not the sort of fishing town lined with elegant houses once occupied by sea captains. Its sidewalks were not of brick and they were not shaded by graceful elms. These wharves were not magnets for long white yachts and the people who sailed them. There was one beautiful hotel and a small campground for travelers. The nicest houses in town were owned by one family, the same people who ran the hotel and owned all the whale-watching boats.

This small northern outpost of Nova Scotia's herring fleet had four roads, called Church Street, School Street, Water Street, and Front Street. Frost heaves kept buckling the sidewalks, and the sea winds were so constant and relentless that only the sturdiest pines and scrub oaks could withstand the battering. No sea captain but one had ever made enough real money from the hard life in these waters to build houses worth commenting on, and he had built three—for himself and his children. That man was Tecumseh Neill.

This particular house, down by the quai, had been built in 1842, after Captain Neill's third voyage around the Horn aboard his ship, the *Pinnacle*. Town legend had it that he had been in pursuit of a single whale during the last years of his life, but three trips previously he had successfully caught whales and sold their oil in New Bedford and Halifax before building his house in Cape Hawk.

Glistening white clapboard with black shutters and a red door, his "downtown" house rose three stories to a widow's walk overlooking the Gulf of St. Lawrence. This structure, like the others he had built, had never left Captain Neill's family, having been passed down through the generations. For two centuries it had been occupied by his descendants, but this generation had split it up and rented it out—the top two floors being apartments, and the ground floor divided in half for commercial space. The house had wide granite steps, a wide front porch with white railings, and a red door.

Once inside the door, visitors stood in a small common space, the front hall. Captain Neill's original chandelier hung over the staircase. Lily Malone, the woman who rented one of the two first-floor stores, had tried to make the center hallway welcoming by hanging needlework done by herself and other women from the town. She had also hung some of her daughter Rose's paintings.

Lily Malone sat in the back of her shop, finishing up the party favors. She had sixteen pink paper bags lined up under her worktable, hidden from view, in case one of the intended recipients happened to wander in. So far today she had had five customers, three of them Nanouk Girls—members of Lily's needlepointing, hanging-out, and support club. She had also received two deliveries of thread and yarn, including the much-sought-after French-Persian wool-silk blend that everyone had to have, in rich, wonderful colors ranging from morning clover to sunset mesa.

Her store, In Stitches, had two big windows overlooking the dock, the whale-watch boats, and Cape Hawk harbor. Needlework was her shop's focus, and she carried threads for embroidery, cross-stitch, and needlepoint, a garden of colors in cotton, silk, wool-silk, French wool, Persian wool, and metallic fibers. The colors were varied and gorgeous—she had twenty-two shades of pink alone: shell pink, sand pink, lollipop pink, dawn pink, geranium pink, old rose pink, sweetwilliam pink, and many more.

On a symbolic level, she liked the idea of stitching things together, making something beautiful one tiny stitch at a time. On a practical level, it put food on the table. This gorgeous place happened to be about a million miles from absolutely anywhere. The women of the region flocked to her door. Some spent money they didn't even have. Lily let them buy yarn and canvas on credit; she collected big-time in terms of free babysitting and casseroles.

The hotel was also a great boon for business—at least in the summer months. Lily glanced out the window, up the hill. The sprawling, elegant, three-story white building sparkled in the sun, like a citadel of the northlands. The roof was bright red, topped by an ornate cupola emblazed with the name CAPE HAWK INN. Two rambling wings curved outward around perfectly manicured gardens of roses, zinnias, marigolds, larkspur, and hollyhocks. Camille Neill knew how to grow flowers—Lily gave her that.

Just then the school bus rumbled down the wharf. Lily pulled back the lace curtain to watch the last kids get off. She felt a small, almost imperceptible, wash of relief: if the bus was here, it meant Rose was home. It was silly, and she knew it. Rose was almost nine years old, so bright and self-sufficient and constantly reminding Lily that she could take care of herself.

Suddenly the door opened, and two women walked in. They were regular customers, Nanouk Girls. Marlena was local, but Cindy was from Bristol, forty miles away. Lily smiled and waved.

"Hi, Cindy, hi, Marlena," she said. "How are you?"

"Great, Lily," Cindy said. "I finished needlepointing my last dining room chair seat, and I'm finally ready to move on!"

"She's been at this project now for, what—three years?" Marlena asked.

"Did you bring one for me to see?" Lily asked. She kept her ears tuned for the phone to ring—either she or Rose always picked up the phone to call each other after school. Cindy dug into her satchel, pulled out two needlepoint squares—elegant bargello patterns, fine flame stitches done in autumn shades of deep red and gold.

"They match her dining room perfectly," Marlena said.

"They're wonderful," Lily said, examining the perfect stitches. "I remember when you started the first one, in the club. And you did six of them?"

"Eight," Cindy said proudly.

Lily laid the squares out on the desk. They were skewed slightly out of shape, like all needlepoint worked in hand. The canvas was fine, ten-mesh; the very edges, once white, were slightly gray from months of being handled. No matter how carefully a person washed her hands, skin oils transferred to the work and pulled dirt into the yarn.

"I know it's time to wash and block them," Cindy said. "What do you recommend?"

"Horse soap," Lily said, placing a pint jug of equine wash on the desk. "It's gentle and cheap, and it will do the trick. I'm undercutting the tack and feed store."

The women chuckled, and Lily glanced at the telephone—it still hadn't rung. She heard herself explaining how to block the work—get it back into a perfect square after all the pulling exerted on the canvas. Wash it, roll it in a towel to absorb the excess water, work it into shape using a T square, and pin it to the ironing board using stainless steel pins.

Cindy paid for the equine soap, while Marlena browsed through Lily's hand-painted needlework canvases. Lily picked up the phone; she'd make a quick call, just to make sure Rose was okay. But then Marlena leaned over.

"This is wonderful," Marlena said, holding up a canvas depicting a house by the sea, with window boxes cascading with petunias and ivy, and a sailboat in the distance. "Are there more of this series?"

"I sold out," Lily said.

"You do land-office business," Cindy said. "And well deserved. You're the only real needlework place within fifty miles of this godforsaken place, and you do the circle besides. . . . I swear I'd have left my husband three times over if I didn't have the Nanouk Girls to talk to."

"And I got over mine leaving me for the same reason, talking to all of you," Marlena said, placing the last of Lily's "Home Sweet Home" needlepoint canvases on the counter.

"Are you coming on the cruise?" Lily asked, laughing as she rang up the purchase.

"For Rose? And with everything we have to celebrate? You betcha!"

"We wouldn't miss it," Cindy said.

"See you Saturday, then," Lily said. "At the dock. We've chartered the *Tecumseh II*—the best boat in the fleet."

"Nothing but the best for us Nanouks! See you then!"

The minute they left, Lily reached for the phone and dialed. She got the machine. Rose's recorded voice came on: *Hello, we're not home right now. . . .* As soon as she heard the beep, Lily said, "Rose, are you there? Pick up?" But no one replied.

Footsteps creaked on the front porch. Lily pulled back the white lace curtain expecting to see Dr. Liam Neill, the oceanographer who kept his office across the hall. He was descended from the sea captain, Tecumseh Neill, the house's original owner. Instead of fishing or whaling like the rest of his family, he spent his life researching fish—sharks, specifically. Moody, elusive, the man spent more time with sharks than people—what more needed to be said?

But it was just the FedEx man, dropping something off at Liam's office.

Lily hung up the phone. She sat and picked up her own needlework—the habit had always soothed her—and took a few stitches. Rose might not have heard the phone. She could be outside, feeding her ducks. Or possibly she had gone to someone's house and forgotten to call. There were so many normal explanations. . . .

When the door to her store opened, she turned with a start. It was Jessica. Rose's age but so much taller, standing in the doorway in her blue plaid pants and yellow shirt, her mouth just slightly open, beckoning to Lily.

"What is it, Jessica?" Lily asked, already on her feet. "What's wrong?"

"It's Rose, something's wrong with Rose, she can't walk, her fingers are blue, and she had to sit down!"

"Where is she?"

"She's in the square, by the stone fisherman," Jessica said, and she started to cry, but Lily couldn't stay to comfort her as she ran out of her store as fast as she could.

Rose sat on the wall, leaning against the fisherman statue. The effort to hold her head up was too much, so she rested her forehead on her knees. Her chest felt tight, and every breath made her lungs burn, as if she were drawing air through a straw. Even before Jessica's footsteps faded, Rose heard someone big running over, and staring down at the ground, she could tell by the big heavy boots that it wasn't her mother.

"Rose, your mother's on the way. Your friend just ran to get her."

It was the oceanographer, Dr. Neill; his boots were glittery with fish scales. The sunlight made them look like bits of broken crystal, all bright fire and rainbows. He crouched down, and Rose felt his hand on the back of her head. "You're safe, your mother's on the way. Just relax and try to breathe, okay, sweetheart?"

Rose nodded and opened her mouth, taking in air. She knew the moment would pass, and she would be fine; she always was, but it was alarming when it happened. Her mind raced ahead to what would happen next. She pictured doctors, Boston, the ER. Yes, her day in the ER was coming again, it was. She wasn't even nine yet, but she could almost write her own medical chart.

Dr. Neill touched her forehead. She closed her eyes. His hand felt cool. Now she felt his hand move down to her wrist; she knew he was taking her pulse. Maybe he was scared by what he felt. Rose knew that some people were. She looked up at him. People were scared of him too. They had that in common. He wasn't smiling, but then, this wasn't something to smile about.

Once a teacher had pushed her down so hard, making her lie down even though all Rose needed to do was wait where she was. Another time a girl's mother had panicked and driven her all the way to the clinic in Telford, no matter that Rose told her she shouldn't go there. The oceanographer didn't do any of those things. He seemed very calm, as if he knew that some things couldn't be fixed so easily.

He sat on his heels and held her hand.

She stayed calm. Their eyes stared into each other as she breathed. She didn't even want to blink, but just keep looking into his deep blue eyes. Sharks swam in water as dark as his eyes, but she wasn't scared. He blinked once, twice, but he didn't smile.

"Don't go away," she said.

"I never would," he said.

"I want my mommy."

"She's on the way. Just another minute . . ."

"I want Nanny."

"We all love Nanny," Liam said. "And she's coming. She gave me a ring this morning, to let me know she's on the way."

"For my birthday?"

Dr. Neill gave a start, and his eyes flashed at the mention of her birthday. His family owned the boats, and in spite of the fact that the party was going to be all girls, Rose wanted him to be aboard. She knew that he didn't usually run the whale-watch boats, but maybe he could make an exception. She wanted to ask him, but she felt too weak.

"Yes, Rose. For your birthday. Just keep your head down. That's my girl. Just breathe."

There were so many things Rose wanted to say; she wanted to invite him to her party, wanted to ask him if it hurt when he lost his arm, wanted to tell him she was sorry he had had to go to the hospital and have surgeries, the way she did. But she couldn't do it. . . .

Now her mother came—Rose could feel her presence even before she heard or saw her. Her mother came across the square and suddenly was right there—Rose knew before she said a word. The oceanographer kept holding her hand. When he let go, he gave a slight squeeze. Rose squeezed back.

"I'm here, Rose," her mother said.

Rose felt her arms around her shoulders and knew, in a different way, that everything was going to be fine.

"We walked home," Rose said. Her mother held her so lightly, not wanting to press against her heart or lungs. Rose concentrated on breathing, getting oxygen. She stared at Dr. Neill's prosthetic arm, his hand—when he was young, he had had a hook, and the town kids had called him Captain Hook. The mean nickname had stuck. Now she looked down at her own hands. Her slightly clubbed fingertips were still blue, but less so than they had been a few minutes earlier. She was breathing better now and started to push herself up.

"Why don't you stay there for another minute?" Dr. Neill suggested.

"Thank you for helping her," Rose's mother said.

"No problem. I'm glad I was here."

"You knew what to do. . . ."

He didn't reply. Rose glanced up and saw him looking at her mother—their eyes met for a second, and she saw her mother blush. Maybe because she thought she'd said something stupid. Of course he knew what to do; he'd known Rose all her life. Rose stood up and saw tiny stars.

"I'm better now," Rose said, ignoring the pricks of light.

"Give it another minute," her mother said, but Rose shook her head vehemently.

"I'm fine—and we *don't* need to go to Boston today. We can wait till we're supposed to."

"You missed the bus?" her mother asked, ignoring Rose's mention of Boston.

Rose didn't even have to nod. Her mother knew her so well.

"You could have called me."

Closing her eyes, Rose thought of Jessica. Her new friend didn't know everything, hadn't watched Rose miss every tryout, every team meet, every soccer game. She didn't know that Rose got driven door-to-door—unlike the other kids, who were dropped off at convenient intersections or waypoints.

"You walked the whole way here? From school?"

"Yes," Rose said. Her breath was coming back. Dr. Neill had been standing right there, but suddenly he backed away—as if he didn't want to embarrass Rose further by hearing her mother scold her. Rose looked up, but he had already turned his back. "Mom," she said.

"It's okay, Rose."

"I can still have my party, right?"

"Rose's birthday," Dr. Neill said. "That's a red-letter day if ever there was one."

"Thank you, Liam," her mother murmured, with a funny, bright look in her eyes.

"No problem. Take care, Rose."

"You too," she said, and watched him go. White clouds moved across the blue summer sky, and seagulls circled above the docks. When she looked down, she saw some rainbow fish scales lying on the ground. Very carefully, she put them in her pocket with the first stone she and Jessica had been kicking. He had called her birthday "a red-letter day."

"A man of few words," her mother said, the way she made comments about people she didn't like much or didn't understand.

Rose's shoulder leaned firmly against the stone fisherman. While her mother stared after the oceanographer, Rose lifted her head and looked straight up at the statue's face. He wore a sou'wester and held a lantern aloft, seeming to peer out to sea. Engraved into the base were the names of all the town fishermen lost at sea—this was their monument.

The stone fisherman looked over all the missing, no matter where they were now. He was cut from granite, just like the blue rock cliffs above the town. Rose looked down at her blue fingertips; what if she turned blue all over, cold as stone? What would happen to her mother if she did?

"It's nearly the end of the day," her mother said. "I'll close up early."

Rose nodded. She watched as the oceanographer walked over to his office. He had a few words with Jessica, who was standing on the steps. Then he went inside. Rose's stomach flipped as Jessica came toward her. Their friendship had just changed; no matter what, once someone saw, everything was different.

"Are you okay?" Jessica asked.

"I'm fine," Rose said. "It was no big deal."

"You looked a little like a ghost—pure white."

"I'm better now."

"That's good," Jessica said.

"Would you like a ride home, Jessica?" Rose's mother asked.

Jessica hesitated, seeming to think about it. Rose felt her color rise—was their friendship over before it really started? Was Jessica embarrassed to be with her? Or did it have something to do with Jessica's secrets, the fact that her real name might not really be Jessica Taylor? Could she really be named after that singer, James Taylor? Maybe Jessica's mother liked love songs, like Rose.

"Well, I'm not really supposed to get into cars without asking my mother, but in this case I think it would be okay."

"We'll call your mother first—how's that?" Rose's mother asked.

And they did.

Chapter 3

Driving Jessica home, Lily was actually doing several things at once. Keeping her eye on the narrow road, keeping her eye on Rose, and trying to assess how upset Jessica was by what had happened. Lily glanced in the rearview mirror and smiled.

"Thank you for coming to get me," Lily said. "For thinking so fast."

"She didn't seem to be feeling too good," Jessica said.

"Well, she wasn't. But she's fine now."

"What happened?"

Lily glanced down at Rose. This was the moment Rose always dreaded. Because the town was so small, most people had known her for her whole life. They knew and loved her—and, the thing Rose disliked the most, compensated for her. Lily knew she could answer right now—say something vague and dismissive. Or she could take the direct approach and tell Jessica the truth. But she had learned over time to leave it to Rose. What Rose wanted her friend to know, she would tell.

"I had a spell," Rose said.

"You're under a spell?" Jessica asked, not understanding.

They drove past a few summer cottages and the old mill. The road was shadowed by steeply rising cliffs and tall spruce trees. Lily glanced down at her daughter—her wavy brown hair and gold-flecked green eyes. Lily had to hold herself back from explaining. She watched Rose formulate the words, knowing that once she said them, her friendship with Jessica would change, however slightly.

"Yes," Rose said. "An evil wizard put it on me."

Lily glanced down, taken by surprise.

"He turned your hands blue?"

"Yes. And sometimes makes me dizzy and weak. He attacked my heart."

"Rose . . ." Lily began.

"Is he real?" Jessica asked, sounding nervous. "Will he put a spell on me? It's Captain Hook, isn't it? I saw him standing there, just before you had to sit down!"

"No, it's not him. He's good," Rose said. "It's someone else. He lives far up the fjord, in a cave in the tallest cliffs, surrounded by straggly old pine trees. Sometimes he turns into a fish hawk. You hear him cawing in the early morning, gliding over the bay in search of sweet little things to eat."

"Rose Malone," Lily said. Her daughter looked up defiantly. She knew that Lily wasn't about to call her a liar in front of her friend; on the other hand, she had to know that Lily couldn't allow Jessica, newly moved to this remote and foreboding part of Canada, to think that there was an evil wizard attacking little girls. The road twisted up the crevasse behind the village, onto a flat stretch overlooking the bay's wide blue expanse.

"I live here," Jessica announced as they pulled up in front of a small white house.

"Jessica, there's not really an evil wizard," Lily said.

"There is," Rose insisted. "And he puts slivers in people's hearts so no one will ever love them. The heart is where love lives."

"Rose, everyone loves you," Lily said, smiling in spite of herself. "So you'd better make up a better story than that."

"Okay, then. He put a spell on my heart that makes all kinds of crazy things happen. He gave me a heart condition."

"But," Jessica said, frowning, "my grandmother has a heart condition—you're too young for that!"

"Even babies can have them. I did as soon as I was born."

"Will I get it?" Jessica asked, the frown deepening.

Now Lily knew she had to step in. "No, you won't," she said. "Rose was born with a heart defect—you can't catch it or anything. She's had all the best treatment, and she's doing great."

"I'm just not supposed to walk home from school," Rose said. "Or do things like that, till I have the last surgery. I'm having it this summer, and afterwards I'm going to be really fine. I'll be able to run and everything."

Just then the front door of her house opened, and a woman stepped onto the porch. She hung back, watching for Jessica to get out of the car. Lily waved. The woman seemed to hesitate—not sure whether to walk over and say hello or not. Lily saw her marshal herself—literally draw herself up taller—and she came toward the car.

Jessica opened the door to get out. Lily felt Rose's anxiety as she watched her friend go. This was the big moment, Lily knew. What would Jessica make of what had happened? Lily wished she could soothe her daughter, assure her that it didn't matter, that Jessica would like her no matter what.

"Thanks for giving Jess a ride home," the woman said.

"It's our pleasure," Lily said. "I'm Lily Malone, by the way—Rose's mom."

"I'm Marisa Taylor—Jessica's mom."

The women smiled, acknowledging that they knew there was much more to both their stories. Something mischievous flashed in Marisa's eyes, and Lily thought she saw a Nanouk Girl in the making. Jessica stood very close to her mother's side, staring through the car window at Rose.

"You like to garden," Lily said. "Your window boxes are beautiful." She gestured at them—pink, white, blue—geraniums, petunias, blue moon verbena, and cascading tendrils of ivy—stark against the white-washed cottage. Some old, thick-stemmed red roses, carefully pruned and tied to a trellis by the door, were just starting to bloom, tongues of fire in the afternoon sun.

"Thanks," Marisa said. "Yes, I do enjoy it."

"I like your roses," Rose said from the back seat.

"They're my favorite flower," Marisa said. "They have been, ever since I was a little girl. I love your name."

"Thank you." Rose smiled.

"I thought this would be a different growing season from what I'm used to. But seriously, my flowers are blooming as if we were in New England—or even farther south."

"You'll find that we're on an earlier schedule than the rest of Nova Scotia," Lily said. "The Annapolis Current runs just offshore, keeping us much warmer. It's amazing, but that's why your roses are already in bloom. We're at least three weeks ahead of Ingonish, and even Halifax."

"That explains it," Marisa said. Then, crouching down to look through the window, she added, "When Jessica called to say you'd be giving her a ride home, she said that something had happened to Rose. Is everything okay?"

"Rose has a bad heart—like Grandma," Jessica said. Her voice sounded thin, as if she'd been holding it in, and suddenly she started to cry.

"No, honey," Lily said. "What Rose has is different—she was born with heart defects. She's got the best doctors, and in July, right after her birthday, they'll be replacing an old VSD patch." Marisa nodded, as if she knew what Lily was talking about. Lily just kept talking: "We expect it to be her last surgery. Just wait—she'll be running races. . . ."

"Winning them," Rose said.

Jessica shuddered and cried harder. Marisa hugged her, and Lily looked on, feeling helpless. She could feel Rose's friendship dissolving right then and there.

"What happened to your grandma?" Rose asked.

"She . . . she . . ." Jessica said.

"She had a heart attack," Marisa said.

"Well, I won't have one," Rose said.

Once again Lily and Marisa's eyes met. The air was full of mothers and grandmothers and sisters who weren't there, yet somehow were. Lily felt the spirit of her own mother, coming to give her strength—she felt it all the time. Overhead, the tall pines rustled in the warm summer wind.

"You know we're counting on you," Lily said, glancing back at her daughter. "To help us celebrate Rose's birthday and give her a good send-off for her surgery. I hope you're both planning to come."

"It's a whale-watch cruise!" Rose said. "It's going to be my friends and the Nanouk Girls."

"The what?" Marisa asked.

"The Nanouk Girls of the Frozen North," Lily said. "After one winter here, you'll understand. We meet to needlepoint, eat, and gripe."

"Sounds divine," Marisa said.

"So you'll come on the cruise?"

"We're in," Marisa said. "Right, Jess?"

Jessica was still crying a little. She was an almost-nine-year-old who had seen a little too much hard truth about what can happen—to her father, to her new best friend. Lily felt a pang in her own heart. She'd been wanting to protect Rose from the hard truths as long as she'd been alive.

"It won't be the same without you," Rose said. "Please say you'll come, Jessica? Please? I swear, I'm almost normal!"

Almost normal. The words sliced Lily in half, and Marisa saw.

"We'll be there," Marisa said.

Jessica nodded, giving a real smile. She asked her mother if Rose and Lily could come in for a snack, but Marisa acted as if she hadn't heard. Instead she waved, walking Jessica toward the house. Rose pivoted in her seat as they pulled away, watching her friend and Marisa as long as possible, until Lily turned the corner beneath the granite cliffs, driving down the long, steep coast road toward home.

Marisa closed the door behind her, the palm of her hand slick, slipping on the brass knob. She wiped her hands on her jeans, walked into the kitchen to get Jessica her snack. "Can we invite them in?" Jess had asked. Lily had heard, had seen Marisa ignore the question. Staring at the sky, at the hawk flying overhead—an osprey, silver fish in its talons. Looking anywhere but into Lily's eyes. Mother to mother—the unspoken language of life. Lily had seen, and now she would wonder.

"Mom, we're really going to the party?" Jessica asked.

"Yes, you can go." Marisa heard her own voice speaking to Lily: the quick, enthusiastic *We're in.* So when she backed out, her regret would seem sincere.

"So I can pretend it's mine?"

"Honey—"

"I can't even tell my best friend that we have the same birthday!"

"Jess, you know why. People use last names and birthdays and social security numbers to search for other people."

"You mean Ted. Why don't you just say that, instead of pretending that everything is nice and normal? We're hiding from him, not *'people'*!"

Marisa took a deep breath. Jessica had been handling the move, and everything associated with it, so well. At first she had been so relieved to get away, she would have gone along with anything. She had taken to their new identities almost as if it were a game. With the help of Susan Cuccio at the Center, they had made up new names, birthdays, and family histories. Jessica had been so helpful with the history part, helping to weave in the real and beloved—her aunt, her first cat, their love of music—with the fictional.

But now, especially as her real birthday drew near, everything changed. Marisa had been fighting depression—finding it hard to stay the course, get up in the morning, do everything she had to do. She had been wavering, wondering whether they had done the right thing, coming up here. No wonder Jessica was upset and confused.

"You're letting me go to Rose's party, but I couldn't go to Paula's back home."

"That was different."

"Because *he's* not here?"

"Sweetheart . . ."

"Will he ever find us?"

"Let's not worry about Ted," Marisa said. "We've got plenty to do, just taking care of ourselves. Now—peanut butter and jelly, or oatmeal cookies?"

"Cookies and milk. I don't like it here that much, Mom. Except for Rose. She makes being in this cold, rocky place almost okay. Rose is the best, best friend I've ever had. Mom, is she really going to be okay?"

Marisa walked over to the refrigerator and opened the door, so Jessica couldn't see her face, or see her hands shaking. Mystification, it was called . . . not being straight with your own child, keeping them in the fog.

"Mom, is she?"

Marisa thought of what Lily had said—that Rose had been born with heart defects. That meant multiple. VSD, so that meant ventricular. Aortal as well? She still had her textbooks from nursing school—where were they? If she could put her hands on them, maybe she could learn more about what was happening with Rose. Pediatric cardiac care wasn't her specialty, but at least she could help Jessica understand.

"I want her to be okay," Jessica said, looking up as Marisa set down the milk and cookies.

"I know you do."

"Maybe we could use our secret savings, to pay for an operation and save her life. We have the money, right? Or one of our friends could do it for free?"

Marisa picked up the remote, turned on the TV. They had a satellite—up here, so far from civilization, it was the only game in town. Hundreds of channels, with endless choices. A person could grow old just clicking the remote. She found an Adam Sandler movie she thought Jessica would like and stopped there.

"Mom?"

"Jess, why are you saying that? Rose's mother is taking care of her."

"Okay. Fine. But you didn't see her down by the dock. She practically turned blue, and she couldn't breathe, and I didn't know what to do, and that horrible scary man with the fake hand had to help her!"

"But you did know what to do—you went to get her mother. You stayed calm."

"I did," Jessica agreed, munching her cookie in thoughtful agreement. Then she stopped and looked up. "Like I did when Ted hurt my puppy."

On the screen, Adam Sandler was being hilarious. All over the world, people were watching this movie and laughing. But not this mother and daughter. Marisa was too busy staring at Jessica, noticing the way she said "hurt"—when Ted had killed Tally, not just hurt her.

"I really don't mind that we're hiding. As long as he never finds us, and you never take him back. You know that, right?" Jessica asked.

"I know that," Marisa said.

Jessica nodded, accepting, good daughter that she was. She stared at the TV screen; Marisa felt a slide of guilt for parking her daughter in front of Adam Sandler, wanting to distract her from all the questions.

She went to the window and looked out, and as she did she remembered where her textbooks were: boxed up and stashed in the storage unit, along with almost everything else.

Through the trees, down the hill, she saw the wide blue sparkling bay embraced by craggy cliffs and granite headlands. The big white hotel with its long red roof lorded it over the small town—Lily's shop, the whale-watch boats. Marisa knew that although she'd let Jessica go on the birthday cruise, she herself would have to cancel. A woman's club might be a little too dangerous. She blinked into the bright early summer sun, and her eyes stung. In Boston, she knew this would be considered a house with a "million-dollar view." To Marisa, it just felt like somewhere far, far from home.

Because she didn't like feeling that way, and because she knew a way to feel closer to home, she went online. E-mails, her favorite message boards, and a secret chat room—better than cocktails in the afternoon for making everything nice and numb. Intimacy and friendship without the dangers of being found out. Instead though, bypassing her favorites, she went straight to the website for Johns Hopkins, the nursing school she had attended. She typed in her username and password, went straight to cardiac care, and started to read.

Chapter 4

Sharks, overfishing, and biodiversity," Gerard Lafarge said from the deck of the *Mar IV* as she came toward the pilings.

"Yeah, what about it?" Liam Neill replied, walking along the dock.

"We got a freaking genius in our midst."

"Something tells me you don't mean that in a good way," Liam said with a grin, using his right hand—his good hand—to catch the bow line Gerard threw, looping it around the cleat on the dock, then walking aft to do the same with the stern line.

"Seriously," Gerard said, jumping off his fishing boat to set the spring lines. He was grimy and unshaven from days at sea. The boat rocked in the gentle harbor swells. The smell of fish was strong, and flocks of seagulls swooped down, screaming. "You think articles like that are good for us? We make our living doing the stuff you write about. Mako brings big money at the market. Tastes like swordfish, only sweeter, and without the mercury. You're giving us a bad name."

"First of all, I'm impressed you saw the paper. I didn't know you read oceanographic journals." He might just as well have stopped with "I didn't know you *read*."

"Believe me, this one's making its way around the guys. Let's just say, you caught our attention."

"Second of all, mako sharks aren't endangered, so you're within your legal rights. But it's more a matter of thinking about the future. You overfish now, the species dwindles, and what'll your kids do?"

"You think I want my kids fishing? Shit, I don't want them working this hard, maybe buying it in a winter storm—I'm making all I can now, getting rich off the sea, to send the brats to McGill or Harvard, so they can stay on dry land and support me and Marguerite in our old age."

"Is that why you're going after dolphins now?"

The banter stopped, the look on Gerard's grizzled face turning ice cold. His glance slid to the deck, where his crew was icing the catch. Liam stared at the hacked-off dorsal fin lying in a pile of debris.

"What do you know, Neill?" Gerard barked. "The rest of your family does an honest day's work on the water—while you sit in judgment of us all. I heard what you said to your uncle. You want to stop him from whale-watching, just like you want to stop me from fishing."

"I don't want to stop anyone," Liam said. He continued out the dock, where he met his cousin Jude Neill. Jude had been hosing down the flat-bottom Zodiac, one of the smaller boats in the family's whale-watching fleet. He'd stopped, obviously to listen to Liam and Gerard.

"But you do," Jude said, smiling.

"I do—what?" Liam asked.

"Want to stop us from whale-watching."

"You going to start in on me too?" Liam asked.

"Someone's got to keep you in line," Jude said.

The cousins glared at each other, then broke into grins. Jude stood aside so Liam could climb aboard. Water from the hose splashed his boots. The day was sunny, but in the distance a dark wall of fog was approaching fast.

"See anything today?"

"Five fin whales, a few minkes, a whole lot of dolphins. The crowd was happy."

"That idiot Lafarge had a dolphin dorsal fin right there in the bottom of his boat. He didn't even try to hide it when I walked by."

"Look, I'm sure he didn't catch it on purpose. He long-lines, and there's no helping what you catch that way. What should he do, let the meat go to waste?"

"He shouldn't long-line."

"Truce, okay, cuz? I'm on your side with this one. All the tourists love dolphins—they're good for family business. So you're preaching to the converted. Just don't lecture me on the Marine Mammal Act, and on getting too close to the sweet, cuddly air-breathers. I got you and the patrol boats giving me grief on one side, and on the other I got my customers wanting to get the whales up close and personal on camera, pointing at my less conscientious competitors who practically let them pet the freaking things."

"Yeah, well . . ."

"Remember when you, me, and Connor used to go out, see how close we could get? Connor used to like to put his hand right over the blowhole. . . ."

"He'd say he could feel the warm air."

"No one could get close like Connor," Jude said.

"Nope. No one could," Liam said. The blue bay sparkled; as he squinted into the sun he thought he saw the back of a white whale, a beluga, surface about fifty yards out. Suddenly he remembered being twelve, when Jude was eleven and Connor was nine. Three boys with the whole summer ahead of them . . .

"The kid spoke their language. He spoke whale, that's just a fact. And when I—"

Liam interrupted him. "No human speaks whale. Look, the reason I came down here was to ask you about a charter."

"You want to charter a whale watch? *That's* a first," Jude said, trying to hide his hurt feelings with sarcasm. Liam just let it pass; he wanted to get off the dock, back to his dark office, away from any sightings of the white whale.

"Not me. A birthday charter—for Rose Malone's birthday party."

"Ah, yeah. This Saturday. Lily booked the big boat for the morning. Nine to eleven. Why? What about it?"

"Who's going to be captain?"

"Captain? I don't know. Let's see—sixteen giggling, screaming girls and their mothers? Whoever picks the short straw, I guess. Why?"

"I want you to do me a favor. I want you to captain."

Jude stared at him. One eyebrow dramatically raised, then lowered. He seemed to be waiting for the punch line. When none came, he said, "I never work Saturdays. It's the only single perk I get, owning the fleet, top of the food chain. You know?"

"I'm asking you a favor, Jude," Liam said. "It's important."

"Why?"

"Because you're the best, and because you never flinch, and because you know what to do in a crisis. Rose is going in for surgery soon. I don't think there's going to be a problem—"

"Her mother already told me there's nothing to worry about."

"Good. But still."

Jude squinted. "What are you trying to tell me? Is Rose Malone your secret love child? You did it with Lily? You and Miss Unapproachable 2005 got it on ten years ago and you're suddenly feeling protective?"

Liam shook his head, smiling. If it made Jude feel more like captaining the cruise, he'd let him think what he wanted. People had always speculated about Lily Malone, and because of his history with her, people always wondered.

"Will you do it?"

"Am I looking at liability here? The girl has a problem on board . . ."

"She won't, I'm sure. The surgery has been planned—it's routine, for her condition. Besides, if you're using the big boat, there's no faster way to get her to the heliport if it's necessary."

"Great. You're making me nervous. Maybe I should cancel."

"You won't. You're not going to ruin Rose's birthday."

"You're an arm-twister, you know that? Some cousin . . ."

Liam knew then that Jude would captain Rose's birthday party. He waved, walking back down the long dock,toward the town square and its statue of the fisherman—right where he had stood with Rose earlier. He felt a long shiver go down his spine.

The air was getting warmer, making you almost believe you could go swimming. These northern waters were still cold from the winter snows melting up north, filling the rivers, entering the Gulf. But on an early summer day like this, he traveled back in time. He was twelve, and Jude was eleven, and Connor was nine. He could almost believe they were all together. Liam could feel the way they all used to be, back when he still had both arms, back before Connor.

But he had trained himself not to think such thoughts—summer day or not—and he walked past the stone fisherman without even a sideways glance, up the stairs of his office, where he slammed the door shut behind him.

At home, Lily Malone sat on the porch, needlepointing while Rose knelt in the garden. She wore the half-glasses she'd recently started needing—bright pink rims to make the whole idea seem somehow festive instead of quite depressing. Peering over them, she kept one eye on her daughter while trying to be surreptitious about her project. Every year for her daughter's birthday, she had done a needlework square. Of course Rose knew she'd be getting one again this year, but it was part of the fun for Lily to hide it and for Rose to pretend to be surprised.

"Mom, look," Rose said. "The morning glories are coming up. And here—some zinnias. At least, I think that's what they are. The leaves are so tiny."

"Check your map," Lily suggested.

Rose pushed herself up and walked over to the garden shed. Lily watched how slowly she moved. She watched Rose's chest rise and fall, counting her breaths. She checked her color, which was pale, but not too pale—her lips weren't at all blue. Her balance seemed steady—she wasn't dizzy. Over the years, Lily had developed the ability to assess Rose's minute-to-minute health. She wasn't foolproof, but by tuning in to the small things, she felt she had a good sense of what was happening.

"Mom, they *are* the zinnias and morning glories we planted!" Rose said, emerging from the shed with the map they had drawn last month, after tilling the garden's hard earth, mixing it with potting soil, pressing in the tiny seeds.

"That's great, Rose!"

"I'm going to be a horti—how do you say it again?"

" 'Horticulturist,' " Lily said, smiling.

"Horticulturist," Rose repeated. "A plant scientist. A morning glory doctor!"

Lily glanced up. So much with Rose harkened back to medicine—because that was what she knew. Doctors, hospitals, tests, procedures, operations . . . Lily swallowed down the wish that her daughter could have an unfettered experience in the garden—without thinking about doctors.

"The morning glories are going to grow tall," Rose said, kneeling down again, brushing dirt away from their delicate stems, fragile green leaves. "They're going to climb up the trellis, all the way to the sky."

"With bright blue flowers," Lily said.

"I'm just so glad they're up already," Rose said.

"Already?"

Rose nodded. "So I don't have to worry about them, while we're gone. If I hadn't seen them, I might think the seeds hadn't worked. I'll be glad to picture them growing and blooming while I'm in the hospital."

"They grow like crazy," Lily said, smiling, hiding how fierce she felt at that moment. "They go wild all summer, right into September. They'll bloom, all right."

"Will I be home before September?"

"You will, sweetheart. You'll be in the hospital for one, maybe two weeks. You'll have plenty of summer left after we get back."

"Will it be my last surgery?"

"Yes," Lily said. She tried never to lie to Rose about her medical care; not because she wouldn't have done anything to protect her, shield her from the realities of being a cardiac patient, but because Rose always knew . . . she always knew when her mother was telling a lie, and that just made her worry more. But Lily was almost certain about this—the doctors had assured her that replacing the old patch should be *it*.

Rose crouched down, hands in the earth, pulling out weeds. She had an instinct, knowing what should stay, what should go. She had the innate ability to nurture a flower bed, just like her ancestors. Lily remembered childhood days in the garden, when her mother had told her that gardening was the same as prayer: being quiet, present, and appreciative of nature. The gardening gene was alive and well in Rose.

"How come Jessica's mother didn't want us to go inside, after we dropped her off?"

"Maybe she was busy."

"Jessie says her family has a mystery."

"All families do," Lily said, stitching slowly.

"Does Dr. Neill's?"

"Mmm," Lily said. One mystery was why he hadn't gotten married. Lily had watched him dating a little—a female ichthyologist from Halifax, a divorcée from Sydney. But Liam stayed unattached.

"I like him."

"Hmm."

"You don't, do you?"

"He's my landlord," Lily said. "I like him fine."

"But you don't act as if you like him. And he's our friend!"

"I'll try harder," she said, and her heart caught just slightly.

"I want him to come to my party."

Lily lifted her eyes over the rims of her fuchsia half-glasses. Rose was gazing back gravely—challenge in her green eyes.

"It's *my* party," Rose reminded her.

"I know, but we asked the Nanouk Girls too. We have that no-men rule, you know? We wrote up that charter, and we all signed it—you too, remember? Our gatherings are women only."

"Can't we make an exception? A birthday party exception?"

Lily's lips tightened. She really hated saying no to Rose. Her daughter was the least manipulative child on earth—when she wanted something, she came right out and asked for it. The unspoken words between them had to do with the upcoming surgery. Every request from Rose had a shimmer and a poignancy to it: what if Lily said no, and it was Rose's last request? She shook her head, reminding herself to be a mother—not a doomsday prophet.

"No, Rose. It wouldn't be fair to the other Nanouks. We can save him a slice of birthday cake. Okay?"

"Not okay," Rose said. She kept digging for a while. Then, leaving her pile of weeds on the grass, she walked up the porch stairs. Lily shielded her needlepoint so Rose wouldn't see, but she needn't have bothered. Her daughter walked straight by without even a glance, into the house, screen door banging behind her.

Lily took a deep breath. She thought of her no-lie policy and wondered whether Rose sensed that it had just gone flying out the proverbial window. Because her reasons for not wanting to invite Liam Neill to the party had nothing—or at least very little—to do with the Nanouk Girls' charter.

Nothing, in fact. Lily steadied her hands and just kept stitching. The wide needle slid in and out of the small white squares, one after another, as she tried not to think. There was so much not to think about: her daughter's surgery next week, whether she'd finish her needlepoint before the party, Liam Neill. The warm breeze blew, and the sun beat down on Rose's garden. Lily kept moving the needle, trying to finish the picture.

Rose went to her room. At the back of their one-story house, her window overlooked their yard, the heathery hillside, and the outer curve of the bay. Standing in her doorway, she took a deep breath. She began to move. She was walking, yes, using her feet, but in her mind, she was flying, held aloft by invisible wings, as hard and clear and indestructible as the cicada's wing she'd found in the garden last summer. Circling her room, she touched things—her maple bedpost; the bureau painted by her mother with fish, shells, whales, and dolphins; the books on her shelf; her collection of carved whales. Here she paused, making sure her fingertips brushed each one—whales carved from wood, soapstone, bone.

She felt the whales' power. They were mammals, just like her. They breathed air and raised their children. Now her wings turned into fins. Rose dived under the surface, swimming easily with the whales. She felt the water rush over her body as she swam deeper, deeper . . . she continued to touch everything in her room, all the precious things that reminded her of her life, of her mother.

By the time she reached the wall beside her bed, her eyes were full of salt water. She blinked the tears away, gazing at the eight framed birthday squares. Her mother had made her one for every year of her life. Rose stared at them now:

The first was a country cottage with a black door and pink shutters with four cutout hearts, a garden filled with lilies and roses.

The second was a white baby basket carried over the green countryside by a red-and-yellow hot-air balloon.

The third was a blue station wagon parked among snow-laden pine trees, with four golden-eyed owls hidden in the dark branches.

The fourth was a carousel with whales instead of horses.

The fifth was fish flying through the sky and birds swimming underwater.

The sixth was nighttime, with the spruce tree in their backyard decorated for Christmas, with hearts instead of bulbs, and real stars instead of lights.

The seventh was the same cottage as the first square, but shrunken down to the size of a doll's house . . . with a blue door instead of a black door . . . and with a hot-air balloon lifting it up, carrying it out to sea.

The eighth showed a group of girls and women, all wearing hats and heavy coats, warming their hands by a fire on the snowy, rocky shoreline while a white whale frolicked in the foreground; there were Rose and her mother, Cindy, Marlena, Nanny, and all the Nanouk Girls of the Frozen North. Rose recognized all the figures except two women off to the side . . . her mother had told her that they were her grandmother and great-grandmother.

The ninth . . . well, Rose knew that her mother was busy stitching the ninth one right now. Rose closed her eyes, wishing. . . . She knew how terribly much her mother loved her. Even though she was only almost nine, she knew that her mother sometimes hurt with loving her so much. Having such a fragile heart made Rose feel certain things more than normal. Her skin would tingle, as if a cool breeze were starting to blow, and she'd be filled with other people's dreams and words, as if their hearts were talking directly to hers.

Not everyone, but some. Nanny, for instance. Rose had always been able to read Nanny's mind. She could feel her joy and curiosity, her power and strength. And Rose's mother; Rose always knew when her mother was happy or sad, tired or, especially, worried—worried about Rose. Like now, waiting for her surgery, planning the trip to Boston— it was almost all her mother could think about, even with the birthday square to finish and the party to get ready for. But Rose wasn't tuned in to either of them, or even to Jessica, another kindred heart spirit.

Dr. Neill. She couldn't stop thinking of him. It was funny. At bad times, whenever she needed him, there he was. He had knelt with her down by the stone fisherman, holding her hand and letting her know she wasn't alone. Rose knew that if she had a father, that's what he would have done. He would have stayed with her and held her. He would take care of her.

Dr. Neill was so big. He had put his arm around her for a minute, when she was the most scared, when she felt the most unable to breathe. Rose closed her eyes and almost swooned. She wanted a father to hold and love her. All her friends had fathers—even Jessica, whose father was a stepfather; it didn't matter.

Rose felt her heart beating through her green T-shirt. She wished and wished for her heart to be whole again. She had a mother who loved her; if only she had a father too. All the birthday squares, all the parties, all the surgeries in the world couldn't do for her what that would do.

Why wouldn't her mother let Dr. Neill come to her party? Even if she didn't like him—and Rose wasn't dumb, she knew that her mother *did* like him, deep down—shouldn't Rose be allowed to invite him anyway? Even though the other kids were scared of his artificial arm, even though they called him Captain Hook, Rose loved him. She knew that if she had a father, he would be just like Dr. Neill.

He would love whales, dolphins, and even sharks. He would not give up, just because one part of his body didn't work right. And he would always stop, no matter what he was doing, to help a little girl having heart pains at the foot of the stone fisherman.

He would, he would . . .

Chapter 5

Secret Agent's desk was his flying machine. When he sat in his Aeron chair and hunkered down at his Dell laptop, he could be in Anywhere, USA. He could be on the wireless network, sailing on a cruise ship in the Caribbean or the Atlantic or the Indian Ocean for that matter. He could be in Paris, France. Or Akron, Ohio; Hartford, Connecticut; Phoenix, Arizona; or Walla Walla, Washington. He could be in Vancouver or Toronto. He could be at the South Pole. In reality, he was located in Boston's North End, above a café that smelled like espresso all day.

The apartment was small, but no one need know. It could be a penthouse on Park Avenue in Manhattan, a ranch in Montana, a beach house at the Jersey Shore with the Atlantic out one window and Barnegat Bay out another—or maybe a place near South Beach, not far from where that psycho had killed Gianni Versace a few years back. Or it could just be the house-next-door, where he was just a regular guy trying to bring home the bacon and keep everyone happy.

He was hungry. Before getting started, he grabbed a root beer and microwaved two beef burritos. Set the plate down on his desk, booted up, got ready to take off. Really hungry—ate one burrito in three bites. Waited for the machine to stop clicking, logged on. Where to go today? Where should the flying machine touch down this evening? It was Friday night. . . .

His favorite sites: scrolled down the list, looking. He had his ladies' sites, his playtime sites, his sports sites, his business sites. First and foremost in his mind was always the search: he was looking for someone, and he knew the kinds of Internet sites she liked to go. It was a full-time job, trying to find her. But he had other irons in the fire as well; might as well make some money while looking for his girl—the bitch formally known as his wife. Today, looking at the list, he focused on his "doing business" sites. The bank account was getting a little dry. One of his most fruitful and profitable Internet destinations had lately been SpiritTown.com. A fan site for the followers of the band Spirit.

The band was decent musically and popular enough to still be selling out stadiums and arenas twenty years after its first album. It could always be counted on to join all those group lovefests, raising money for good causes. Save the Rainforest, Free the Unjustly Accused, Women's Rights, Peace, all that bleeding-heart liberal stuff. His wife had loved Spirit. Little Miss Save-the-World . . .

Secret Agent trolled the SpiritTown message boards. The members liked to take their names from Spirit's song titles—so typical, and so easy for him to spot the soft touches. The names practically ensured that they'd give him the money he asked for—PeaceBabe,OneThinDime, Wish23, Love_or_die, LonesomeDaughter . . . His wife used to occasionally post here as "Aurora," but he had a feeling she'd changed her screen name after their breakup. He hadn't seen Aurora here in a long time. . . .

He took a glance at the list of recent topics—about half the threads were discussions of Spirit music, lyrics, shows, and bootlegs. The rest concerned politics and events of major interest to Spirit fans. This was sad—he actually chuckled as he prepared to start typing. These people were practically begging to be taken—they cared about everyone and everything. "Breast Cancer Awareness," "World Hunger," "Can We Help Kids Who Don't Have Enough?"

He had registered as a member of the site six months earlier, and during that time had posted six thousand times. He had established himself as a huge Spirit fan (not true), a collector of their CDs (not true), a left-leaning Democrat (totally not true), a divorced father of two (partly true). His log-on name, Secret Agent, was taken from one of Spirit's biggest hits, "Spy on You": "I look through your windows, I come through your door / I know why you're hiding, I know what it's for / You're afraid of the world, afraid of its pain / I'm your Secret Agent, I'll make you brave again. . . ."

He wolfed down his second burrito and got ready to make some money. He clicked the "New Topic" button and typed in the heading "Lost in the Hurricane." His name, Secret Agent, popped up. Then, in the body of the message, he started: "Hey everyone—did you read about that big storm, the first hurricane of the year? Hit South Florida pretty hard. My sister's family lost everything. Everything. Their roof blew off. Jake, my nephew, got hit with window glass—it's a nightmare."

Then he hit "Send." "Your message has been posted" appeared on his screen. He clicked "Return to Forum," then sat back to wait for replies.

Secret Agent was still hungry. He walked into the kitchen, threw two more burritos into the microwave. He predicted that by the time he got back to his desk, he'd have what he wanted. It was the dinner hour, prime time for all the losers—home from work, either single or not in the mood to talk to their loving husbands and wives—to log on and meet up with their friends.

The bell chimed, and he ate standing up at the counter. This way he could stare at his refrigerator door: pictures of his wife and Ellie covered every inch. Individual shots, the two of them, even some with him in the frame—rare, because he didn't like having his picture taken. He wiped the burrito grease from his lips and leaned forward to kiss his wife. The closeness made him mad—he started to feel the heat rise. How dare she leave him—how the hell dare she?

He rinsed his plate and cracked another root beer, cooling off a little. At least he didn't have to worry anymore about wiping out the cookies—the temporary Internet files stored in computers. His nosy wife had figured out how to check up on him. She'd get in there, snoop around, see what he'd been doing online for fun and work. . . . By the time he headed back to his desk, he had what he needed: five quick responses to Lost in the Hurricane. Secret Agent scrolled down, reading them quickly:

"Secret—that sucks!"

"Hey, man—is your nephew gonna be okay?"

"The roof blew off? Literally?"

"Where's the family going to stay? I read about that hurricane—it's super-bad. Lots of people evacuated, and the ones who didn't go got trapped. Is your nephew badly hurt?"

And then—paydirt:

"Secret Agent—what're friends for? Let's set up a fund on the board. I know everyone will want to help out. You've got a PayRight account—I know, cuz you sent me money for those boots last month. We'll send the contributions to you, you'll give it to your sister."

Secret Agent couldn't help smiling: what a kind bunch of people. His wife had very good taste in bands and message boards. She'd be proud of her online friends, to know they'd risen to this occasion. For that matter, she'd probably be proud of her husband—to think of him caring so much about the people harmed by the hurricane.

"Thanks, man," he typed. "My sister will be really thankful. You guys are great . . . let me check with her, to make sure. (She wouldn't want charity.) But I'll try to talk her into it—gotta think of my nephew's medical bills and all. . . ."

Even as he typed, more responses poured in:

"Any sister of Secret Agent is a sister of ours!"

"Your sister has one great brother, you know? I'll be the first—here's $100. Wish it could be more. . . ."

So do I, Secret Agent thought. He scanned the member names popping up on the message board. Looking for Aurora . . . Where are you? Where did you go? Do you think you can hide forever?

That would be his *real* payoff: finding what was his and bringing it home.

It was Friday evening, and Liam was working late. He spent too much time at the office, he knew. Right now, nearly nine P.M., the sky was still light—summer in the northern latitudes. His mind told him to keep working, but his body was telling him other things. He was hungry and tired, and he felt an old yearning that he'd thought was long dead.

He had piles of data to go through; sharks had been active in local waters this week. Liam logged onto the "Predator Report," a website originally designed to track near-shore sightings or attacks by sharks. Normally it dealt with seals, schools of bluefish and herring, the occasional dolphin or whale. But yesterday a man surfing the break just east of Halifax had reported a great white attacking his board.

Liam read the account—of course the board was yellow. Shark people referred to yellow surfboards as "yum-yums." Sharks would spot them from below, confusing their oblong shape and pale color with their favorite food—seals. Based on the fourteen-inch radius of the bloody bite mark, Liam figured the shark to be a juvenile great white. He read the account:

"I didn't see anything before the shark hit. He zoomed straight up and hit my board so hard, it sent me into space. I looked down from the air and saw a shark with his head out of the water, my board in his teeth. I landed on his back—smacked into his dorsal fin—at least eighteen inches high. I rolled off, and he turned and bumped me—right in the armpit. The impact tore my wetsuit, and I thought it was all over—but then the shark just went under and disappeared into the waves."

The words had a force all their own: Liam felt he was right there, seeing the shark break the surface, watching that huge dorsal fin rise out of the sea. He closed his eyes; he remembered the first and worst time he'd seen it in person, how the fin had looked like a black sail on the devil's boat. With his eyes shut, the water turned red in his mind . . . and when he opened them, he looked out at Cape Hawk harbor to see the darkness finally falling on the water, spreading over the still surface, making the blood disappear.

Liam took notes, writing down the guy's name and address. He checked his clock—maybe he'd call him, finish his report right now. But it was ten after nine on a Friday, and he decided against it. Not just out of courtesy, but also because he was sick of being the geek who worked all the time, sick of being someone so obsessed with sharks and shark attacks and people who survived predators and people who didn't.

He shut off his computer, stood, and stretched. Turned off the lights, locked the door, walked out of his office into old Tecumseh Neill's grand entry hall. The original chandelier gave off a soft, welcoming light. It bathed the wall hangings—most of them made by Lily, but a couple of paintings done by Rose. Liam stood quietly in the light, staring at the needlework. He felt as if this center hall was the warmest place he knew. *Home is where the heart is.* He read the words on Lily's sampler. How strange it was, to leave work to go home . . . yet to feel that this hallway—empty except for the few hangings—really *was* where the heart was.

As he stepped outside into the dim twilight, he headed toward his car. Strains of music, haunting and romantic, issued from the family inn. He hesitated, but the band was playing, calling him up there. The kitchen would be closing soon, but he knew he could get something to eat anyway. Besides, he could check up on his cousin, make sure everything was set for Rose's party tomorrow. . . .

He crossed the quiet street, followed the music up the stone steps to the walk that curved across the long, sloping lawn. White Adirondack chairs, arranged in pairs, faced the harbor; people sat in them, enjoying the sunset and the last light, watching the stars come out. An owl streaked across the sky, into the pine forest that rose behind the inn, that sheltered Lily's house above the town.

The inn seemed fairly full for a weekend this early in the summer. A placard advertised Boru, a Celtic band brought in from Prince Edward Island. Standing in the doorway, he listened to the guitar, fiddle, and pipes. His elderly aunt, Camille, swept by on her way into dinner. He faded back, not up for a third degree from the family grande dame.

"What brings you up here? I can't remember the last time I saw you out on a Friday night. . . ."

Liam wheeled around, came face-to-face with Jude's wife, Anne. While Jude oversaw the boats and whale-watch part of the family business, Anne managed the inn. She was equally excellent with people and with numbers, and she kept everything running well in the black. Liam knew their parents and grandparents would be proud. Camille had to grudgingly admit her talents. Camille had never been the same since her husband's death—on a trip to visit a shipbuilder in Ireland for their whale-watch fleet.

"Good band, Anne," he said.

"I've auditioned everyone from here to Quebec," she said. "So many good musicians out there, but there was something about these guys— I hear them play, and I want to fall in love."

Liam laughed. "You and Jude are coming up on your—what is it— twentieth anniversary?"

"And what's wrong with falling in love with my own husband?" she asked. Then, gently punching him in the arm, she added, "I understand that you are responsible for making him work tomorrow—this will be his first Saturday at the helm in I don't know how many years!"

"Well, I just thought someone really experienced should—"

"Captain the birthday cruise?" Anne teased. "You think the nine-year-old girls will mutiny? Or perhaps their mothers . . ."

Liam pictured Rose sitting in the town square, her head down, trying to get a good breath. His own heart squeezed as he remembered how cold her hand felt in his, the pleading in her eyes. "It's good for him to take the Saturday duty," Liam teased back. "Instead of getting too important for his own good."

"Well, he'd better find plenty of whales for the birthday girl," Anne said. "Or he'll have to answer to me."

"You?"

Anne nodded. "I'll be aboard. I'm a Nanouk Girl, you know."

"Lily's club, right?"

"Oh, we're just a bunch of friends. We all met through Lily and started a sewing circle. But we're all going aboard to celebrate Rose's birthday." At that, Anne's expression grew serious. "We're all worried that it could be—"

"Anne, no—it won't be," Liam said. He heard the echo of her unspoken words: *her last birthday.* Even with the doctors' optimism, laypeople were intimidated by Rose's condition.

"Lily has been so manic lately," Anne said. "Planning the party, making Rose's present, getting Rose ready for the surgery. I'm so glad you thought to ask Jude to captain. Honestly, if it weren't Lily, I wouldn't book the charter at all. The potential for liability, but that's not the main thing. It's just, well, you're a scientist, Liam. Not a doctor, a medical doctor, anyway. But you're a biologist—you must know—what are the chances Rose will survive? Not just this operation—but into adolescence, adulthood?"

"Like you said, I'm not a doctor," he said, his stomach flipping. "But Lily tells me Rose will be fine, so I believe her."

"I know it's serious," Anne said. "Lily tries to accent the positive, whenever possible. She's done such a good job of mainstreaming Rose. But even the name of her condition . . ."

"Tetralogy of Fallot," Liam said.

"It scares the heck out of me. Sounds like a monster."

"In a way, it is," he said. "Rose was born with a heart with four defects. From the Latin, *tetragonum*—quadrangle. Four."

"God," Anne said, shivering. "Lily is always so matter-of-fact about it. She talks about Rose so openly. Rose's illness is just a part of her life. She wants Rose to have all the fun and opportunities of any other nine-year-old."

"And she should."

"I worry about her, Liam. What would happen if . . . well, if something happened to Rose. I always remember your mother, after Connor . . .

"It's not the same," Liam said sharply.

"No, it's not. At least she still had your father, and you. Lily has no one."

Liam just stood there, listening to the band play. His arm began to tingle—not his right arm, his good limb, but his left, the one that wasn't there anymore. He felt the skin prickling—pins and needles, as if he had just lain on it for too long, as if the feeling were just starting to come back. The band slid into a sweet waltz, and people at the tables got up to dance.

"Lily," Anne began, but Liam interrupted. He turned to face his cousin-in-law, ice in his eyes.

"Lily won't have to face what my mother went through," he said. "I let Connor die, but I won't let Rose."

"Liam! It's not the same! You couldn't have saved Connor—no one could have. That shark really *was* a monster—and you were just a boy, hardly older than your brother."

"Sharks aren't monsters," Liam said. "They're just fish. My brother shouldn't have been in that water. None of us should. . . . Look—I have to go now. Have a good cruise tomorrow. Watch out for Rose, will you?"

"We all will," Anne said, her blue eyes troubled.

Liam turned to walk out. As he strode through the lobby—filled with weekenders in town to enjoy the scenery, the peace, the band—he sensed people giving him a wide berth. He was tall and dark, and he felt the scowl radiating out. People always noticed his prosthesis. He was different, *other.*

"Hook," some kids had called him in high school. "Scar," others had whispered, those who'd seen him with his shirt off in gym class, who'd seen the jagged tears. Reconstructive surgery wasn't what it was now, and the fourteen-inch bite radius—the shark had been a juvenile great white, just like the one he'd read about earlier that evening, attacking the surfer east of Halifax—looked like a crater in his flesh. The bite had been so deep, the serrated teeth had nicked three of his ribs.

The funny thing was, as he exited the lobby of the Cape Hawk Hotel, he realized that although he still felt different, it wasn't for the same old reason. It wasn't so much his arm or his scars anymore. They were part of him. No, he felt different because he was so alone. With all this family around him, all he could see were couples, families, here in Cape Hawk for the weekend. Spending time together . . .

When Anne had said Lily had no one, Liam had felt a stab in his heart. He felt that way himself.

And it was worse than anything.

 *Chapter 6*

The day was brilliant, clear and fine, perfect for the cruise. Rose woke up with the sun. She lay in her bed, watching orange rays come through the pines. They roused every bird in the forest, and suddenly the air was alive with song. She lay still, listening, wondering whether Nanny could hear the birds and know they were singing "Happy Birthday" to Rose. Would Nanny show up for her party? Almost nothing mattered to Rose more. Except for wishing that Dr. Neill would be allowed to join them . . .

As Rose began to sit up, she felt a tug in her chest. It took her breath away. She lay back down for a few minutes, on her side with knees drawn up, closing her eyes tight. Outside, the birds grew louder, as if more were arriving by the minute. They were migrating north after the long winter. Rose imagined how tired they must be, how fast their tiny hearts were beating.

Once Dr. Neill told her that pine siskins migrated all the way down to South America—birds no bigger than a pinecone! And he said that whales and dolphins migrated down to the Caribbean Sea. If they could do it—fly and swim all that way—then Rose could do it too. All she had to do was stay well enough to have her surgery. One more surgery, and she would be fine.

Sometimes thinking made her feel better—dreams of birds, or of Nanny, or of her birthday. Her best friend Jessica . . . she thought of Jess, joking that they had almost the same birthday. Only why didn't it feel like a joke? To Rose, it had seemed true—and how wonderful that would be, if it was. Very slowly she sat up again, swung her legs over the side of the bed. She looked down at her hand, gripping the mattress. Her condition had left her with slightly clubbed fingers—another way she was different. Today they didn't bother her—it was her birthday, she thought, getting out of bed. The spell had passed. Padding barefoot down the hall, she smelled fresh orange juice.

"Good morning, sweetheart," her mother said. "Happy birthday . . ."

"Thank you. I'm nine now," Rose said, smiling.

Her mother smiled back. She tried not to show that she was checking Rose for symptoms, and Rose, for her part, tried hard not to exhibit any. She knew she should tell her mother that she'd just had a blue spell, but she also knew that might make her mother cancel the party.

But she made it through the once-over, drank her orange juice and ate her cereal, took her vitamin and antibiotic—counting down to the surgery, preventing any possible heart infections that would delay things. Her mother was playing music on the CD player: one of Rose's favorites—"Aurora," by Spirit. It made her happy just to hear the song, and she knew her mother had put it on because she loved it so much.

"Should we save these for the boat?" her mother asked, standing there with several wrapped packages.

Rose rubbed her hands together and bounced in her seat. Her mother's smile widened, as if she were happy just to see Rose so excited. "Do we have to?" Rose asked.

Her mother shook her head. "Not at all, honey. It's your birthday—you can open them all right now."

So Rose did. Her mother had wrapped every package differently—with beautiful papers of pink roses and blue ribbons, of birds flying in formations shaped like hearts. Rose undid the bows, pulled off the paper, and found four new books, a telescope, a diary with a lock and key, and the new needlepoint square.

"Mama," she said, unrolling the canvas. It wasn't framed yet, like the others. Rose felt the square in her hands—the fine meshwork around the edges, the soft field of yarn creating a picture straight from her mother's heart—the latest in the story of Rose's life, to hang on her bedroom wall. "It's beautiful."

"Do you like it?" her mother asked, leaning over, arm across Rose's shoulders.

"I love it," Rose said, gazing at the images of Cape Hawk: the great sweeping bay backed by the tall cliffs and pines, the grand white hotel . . . and in the foreground, two girls—unmistakably Rose and Jessica—riding on the back of a white whale. "Me and my best friend," Rose said.

"Everyone needs a best friend, sweetheart," her mother said.

"Will she come today?"

"Jessica? Her mother said she would. Now, let's get ready. The boat leaves at nine sharp, and we don't want it to leave without the birthday girl."

Rose nodded. While her mother quickly did the dishes, she walked down the hall to her room, to change into her party clothes. She placed the canvas on her bed, staring down at the smiling faces—Rose and her two best friends: one old, one new. Closing her eyes, she stood by the window and wished, wished . . .

Her birthday had always brought many different wishes, most of them secret. In past years she had wished for her father to magically appear in her life, to love her, to want her, to want to be part of their family. She had wished for a grandmother to appear in the garden and make the flowers grow. She had wished for a healthy heart . . . not just so she could run and play, but also so her mother wouldn't have to be so scared, so worried about losing her.

But this year, Rose wished for just two things. They were so, so small—not so very much to ask, considering all the gigantic wishes she had made over the years. Two small, secret wishes . . .

At eight-thirty, Marisa and Jessica drove past the sign NEILL FAMILY WHALE-WATCH CRUISES and into the gravel parking lot. Marisa still hadn't completely stopped looking in her rearview mirror, checking to see that she wasn't being followed. She had chosen this location because it was so remote—the likelihood of Ted stumbling upon them—if he was searching at all—was so very small. But at the same time, she had a secret reason for coming here that would shock him if he ever figured it out.

Her husband's great-grandfather had been a whaler from Canada. And in one of his old photo albums, there had been a picture of the whaling ship—right here at this same dock, in winter—with the snowy cliffs of the fjord rising majestically behind the ice-coated spars. Marisa remembered staring at that picture, thinking it looked like a port at the end of the world. Beautiful, austere, and mysterious.

Now, parking the car, she backed into the spot—so she could see what was coming. She didn't like anyone coming up from behind her.

She had left a man so brutal, he had killed her daughter's puppy—just because she barked at night. Marisa had had to uproot her child, run away from their home, make up pretend birthdays to throw him off the track. She had learned to be careful, always.

Opening her purse, she pulled out a small box.

"Honey, I know we said we would stay completely true to our story, and our new lives, but I couldn't resist this. Happy birthday to you . . ."

"Mommy!" Jessica said. "It's for me? Can I open it?"

"Yes. Your real birthday is in just a few days. I thought we would use Rose's party for a secret celebration of our own."

Jessica pulled off the ribbon, tore the paper, and opened the little velvet box. The look in her eyes was worth every minute of trouble they'd been through: sheer and total happiness.

"It's Grammie's ring!"

"That's right, honey. Her nursing school ring . . ."

"She wore it when she was a Navy nurse, and a pediatric nurse, and a private nurse, right?"

"Yes. You know all the stories. She loved helping people so much, and that's what inspired me to become a nurse too. Maybe it will inspire you."

"So I can help Rose?"

Marisa nodded. She had been up late last night, reading as much as she could about pediatric cardiac care. She didn't know Rose's diagnosis, but from the symptoms she had exhibited and the fact she was scheduled for surgery, she knew that it was serious. Maybe having Marisa's mother's ring would give Jessica a feeling of some control, in the face of her friend's serious illness.

"Mommy, will we get seasick on the boat?"

"No. That's why I got you this bracelet," Marisa said, slipping the elastic circlet over Jess's thin wrist. "The little bead rests against your pulse, and it keeps you from feeling motion sick."

"What about you? Will you wear one?"

Marisa didn't reply, concentrating on getting the bracelet into position.

"Mom, you're coming, aren't you?"

"Honey, I have things to do at home."

"Like what? Sleeping?" The words snapped out before Jessica could call them back—Marisa saw the regret in her eyes.

"Don't say that," Marisa said, but Jess was right; since moving to Cape Hawk, Marisa had spent most of her time lying down. Depression did that to a person: sapped her strength, stole her hopes, made her feel like hiding in the darkness. And when she thought about the causes of her depression—the same reasons that had driven her to uproot herself and Jess, move hundreds of miles away—well, it made her feel so exhausted and helpless, sleep seemed all the more alluring.

"If you're not going, I'm not going," Jess said.

"Jess, it's not the same thing. Rose is your best friend, and she wants you at her party. You've got a nice gift for her, and you made her a beautiful card. Her mother has all her friends, and I don't know anyone . . . besides, I need to clean. You know I've let it get away from me. . . ."

Just then another car drove into the parking lot, horn tooting. It was Lily and Rose, with huge, bright smiles on their faces, hands waving, Rose bouncing in her seat with obvious joy. Marisa's heart skipped a beat, and she felt herself smile—a true smile, from inside. In that very same instant, tears popped into her eyes. She couldn't remember the last time anyone other than Jess had looked genuinely happy to see her.

Lily and Rose got out of their car and came over. Marisa rolled down her window.

"You don't have to wait in the car," Rose said. "We can go on the boat right now!" She grinned through the open window at Jess, who glanced at her mother.

"Please?" Jess whispered.

"You're coming, right?" Rose asked, now looking at Marisa.

"Oh, you have to," Lily said. "We made party favors for everyone—one has your name on it!"

"Mom?" Jessica asked.

Marisa felt the smile—not the one on her face, but the one inside—get bigger. Lily's eyes were bright and shining, staring into hers. Marisa had the strangest feeling—that Lily understood the hesitation she was feeling. For an instant, she wondered whether Lily could read her mind, know what was really going on; she'd been feeling so raw and transparent for so long.

"I can't," Marisa heard herself say, and suddenly tears began to flow as if someone had turned on a water faucet.

Lily reached into the open window and put her hand over Marisa's. Marisa felt electricity flowing right into her skin, and the look in Lily's eyes was sharp and understanding. At that moment, Jessica got out of the car and she and Rose backed away, to look into the souvenir shop windows.

"I'm only guessing," Lily said. "But I think I know."

"I never tell anyone," Marisa said.

"We need to talk," Lily said. "Not now, because of the party. But soon. Look, come on the boat with us. It's just women. Come, for Jessica's sake. She needs to see you strong, enjoying yourself."

"I just don't feel like seeing people. . . ."

Lily smiled. "Is that why you chose this place at the end of the world?"

"How did you guess?"

"I'll tell you another time . . . right now I have to get onboard the boat, for Rose. Will you come with us?"

Marisa's palms were sweating, but she felt herself nod. Funny, her years of working as a nurse had taught her plenty about dissociation—how people who'd been traumatized could go through the motions of life and barely notice what they were doing. As she gathered her purse, Jessica's present for Rose, and her car keys, she knew that she had been sleepwalking for most of the time they had been in Cape Hawk.

But as she locked the car, and felt Lily take her hand, squeeze it, she knew she was waking up. She wasn't sure she wanted to, but Lily's smile was so bright and real, she thought maybe she'd give it a try.

So together, two mothers and two daughters walked up the gangplank to the *Tecumseh II* and got down to the business of a birthday party.

At eight forty-five sharp, Liam sat in his office, watching Jude check the birthday party aboard the *Tecumseh II*. The dock parking lot filled up with cars, and girls and their mothers walked up the gangway, loaded with wrapped boxes, warm jackets and fleeces, and binoculars—Lily and Rose among them, climbing aboard with another woman and Jessica, the little girl who had come to find him when Rose needed help. Anne Neill ran down the long green hill from the inn, kissing Jude as she climbed on deck.

Liam's stomach jumped. Was it from thinking of the birthday party? Seeing Rose looking so happy? He held in his mind's eye the picture of her yesterday—crouching by the statue, such fear and exhaustion in her big green eyes.

He tried to look away from the whale boat, but found he couldn't. There was Anne standing with Jude, talking, seeming to cajole him, arm around his waist—Liam nearly smiled in spite of himself; his cousin's MO was to take weekends off, no matter what. Anne was just trying to smooth the fact that he was on duty on a Saturday. Liam could see the affection between them, and for some reason that gave his stomach another lurch.

Liam had spent the morning so far tracking various sharks, whales, and dolphins via transmitters attached during catch-and-release programs or ongoing tracking projects. He had lots more data to record, but now that it was nearly nine, he switched his program from the desk computer to his laptop. He could do the work later, from home. Grabbing his sweater and duffel bag, he shut the door behind him.

The crew cast off lines, Jude sounded a long blast from the wheelhouse, and as the *Tecumseh II* pulled away from the dock, the whale-watch cruise got under way. The whole party had gathered on the upper deck, facing seaward. All except Rose. Liam saw her standing in the aft section of the deck, smiling back—at him.

Liam gave her a big wave. He made his way down the pier, past the few fishing boats that hadn't left on the dawn tide. Gerard stood on deck, glaring as Liam walked past. They ignored each other—the battle lines had been drawn the minute Liam had spotted that dolphin fin, sliced off and lying among garbage in the bottom of Gerard's boat.

Climbing into his flat-bottomed Zodiac, Liam started up the Yamaha 150 and backed into the harbor. The *Tecumseh II* had a good head start, but Liam followed in its wake—a pale green swath of foam cutting a trail through the calm blue bay—just like kids in the fairy tale, tracking dropped bread crumbs. The thing was, he could find his way blindfolded. He knew that the whale boat was making for the feeding grounds—the best place to find whales.

Liam told himself he was on a research mission. He had positive transmission from at least seven migrating marine mammals, all scheduled to arrive in Cape Hawk waters sometime today. He had data coming in from a whale shark as well as a great white, not to mention the whales and dolphins that had already arrived from southern waters. He had himself practically convinced that his trip to the feeding grounds had nothing—or at least, very little—to do with Rose Malone's ninth birthday party.

The day was clear and beautiful. He told himself that he could follow the signal for MM122 (marine mammal 122, a nineteen-year-old Beluga whale) and greet her as she returned to her spawning grounds. MM122 was a local favorite, and summer wasn't summer until she arrived. Unlike other whales, she was coming from the north—she migrated in the opposite direction, loving and craving winters of ice and snow and northern lights. He knew by the beeps of her transmitter that she would appear on the scene today; whether it would happen during Rose's birthday cruise, he wasn't positive.

But *if* she showed up, and *if* he picked her up on his laptop, maybe he could radio Jude to send him in the right direction.

He pounded across the water, following the boat. Off in the distance were seven fine spouts—a pod of fin whales, reliably feeding on krill and small fry, detritus churned up by the flume coming down the fjord and upwelling caused by the wave action on the peninsula's west coast. As the *Tecumseh II* neared the whales, a great cry went up on deck—all the girls pointing, sighting the whales, laughing with excitement.

Liam pulled out his laptop, tapped in a password, pulled up the transmission screen. Okay, there it was—MM122. According to his data, she should be in the bay now—out by the headlands, swimming fast toward the feeding grounds. Liam flipped on his radio, called his cousin.

"T-Two, this is your Marine Bio Cuz—do you copy?"

"That's a roger. What are you doing out here?"

"Tracking belugas. If you steer due west one hundred meters, you should meet up with MM122 when she comes up for air."

"You're kidding me. You're deigning to share real-live scientific data with us money-grubbing whale watchers?"

"It's a one-shot deal. What are you waiting for? Change course now."

"You got it—and hey, thanks. I think."

Liam didn't even reply. As the big whale boat turned west, Liam gunned the engine, slicing over the *Tecumseh II*'s wake and around her starboard side in a big S. He drove alongside, guiding his cousin to the spot where MM122 was most likely to surface. One eye on the water ahead, one on his laptop, Liam slowed down. He heard the waves lapping the sides of his inflatable, as well as the disappointed voices of the girls and their mothers. They had seen the whales feeding—now about two hundred yards behind—and couldn't understand why the boat was turning away.

As the boats slapped over the small waves, Liam glanced up on deck. Rose and her mother were standing at the rail with several others. Lily had her arm around Rose's shoulders. She stared straight ahead—not back at the whales—as if she was ready for whatever would surface in her path. The morning sun hit her dark hair, making it look as sleek and glossy as a seal. Liam nearly couldn't look away, but he had to glance at his computer screen.

He saw that the depth of MM122 had changed; the whale was coming up for air.

"Rose," he called.

She looked down from the deck, shielding her eyes against the sun. She waved, seeming excited to see him. Lily looked down now, not even taking her arm off Rose's shoulders to wave or block the sun from her eyes. She just squinted hard, looking straight at Liam and sending a depth charge into his heart.

"Dead ahead," he said, letting go of the steering wheel to point with his good arm. Lily didn't ask questions, and if she had any doubts, they didn't show. For some reason she just trusted what he was saying to her—without even knowing why, and it was that fact more than anything that moved Liam to the core. He watched Lily shepherd Rose toward the bow, away from the other mothers and daughters. The *Tecumseh II* was fitted specially for observation, with a bow pulpit that extended ten feet over the open water. Lily held tight to the stainless steel rail and guided Rose straight out.

Liam gave Jude the signal, and he throttled back. The two boats waited, their engines idling in near silence. Liam's heart pounded with anticipation, scanning the open water. He imagined Jude doing the same thing. They had whale-watching in their blood; back when they were Rose's age, they would do this for fun, every day, every year, competing for who would see the whale first. Connor always won.

This time, Liam felt her before he saw her. Maybe it was the tension coming from Lily and Rose—he saw them gazing intently, their muscles tight, their eyes alert. Liam felt their energy—or was it that of the old whale, having made her mystical journey home, south from the frozen sea at the very top of the world, yet again?

What had she encountered along the way? What sharks had she dodged? What ice had she broken with her dorsal ridge, needing to breathe just as vitally as Liam himself? What fishing nets had she avoided? She was old now, and Liam had the passionate wish that he could understand her will to keep living, her desire to return again and again to this bay where she had been born. She was here—he felt it.

"Nanny!" Rose cried out.

And there she was: the white whale, the St. Lawrence beluga. She surfaced glinting brilliantly in the sun, white as ice, lifting her head as if to survey her surroundings. Four meters long, pure white, with no dorsal fin, but a thick dorsal ridge, running the length of her back. Her spout shot three feet in the air—hardly visible, compared to other whales. Liam heard her breathe once, twice. He wondered whether Rose and Lily could hear, all the way up on the big boat; he wished they were in his Zodiac; he wanted Rose to feel Nanny's great life force.

Just then he caught Lily's eye. Rose was still staring down at Nanny, reaching both her arms out, as if she could somehow embrace the old whale, take hold of her and go for a ride. But Lily stared at Liam. Her eyes were so big and round, wide with both wonder and something hidden, a shock of pain, he'd always thought, that she carried with her all the time. It was Rose, he thought . . . loving her girl so much. Living with all that worry.

"She's going to be fine," Liam said out loud, looking straight at her.

Lily cocked her head. Of course she couldn't hear over the low engine noise, or the excitement of everyone at Rose's party. He saw her mouth the word "What?"

The wind blew his hair into his eyes, and he had to let go of the wheel to brush it back. He didn't want to break eye contact with Lily. But in the instant he looked away, he heard Nanny take one deep breath and then sound. After up to ten breaths at the surface, she'd be down below for about fifteen minutes. Lily and Rose had turned away, inching down the bow pulpit, joining the others on deck.

Liam had done what he'd set out to do. He knew the party would go on without him. Revving his engine to return to the dock, he heard voices rising.

"Thank you, Dr. Neill!" Rose called. "For taking us to Nanny!"

"Happy birthday, Rose," he called back.

Lily didn't say anything, but she was staring at him again, those huge eyes so full of questions. He knew they had nothing to do with him, but he wanted to answer them anyway. He gazed back at her, letting certain realities shimmer between them. Rose had a big surgery ahead of her next week. This was her ninth birthday. Lily was as fierce as a mama bear, and she'd do anything to make sure her daughter stayed safe.

Liam and she were cut from the same cloth—he knew it. He had taken them to Nanny because it was Rose's heart's desire, and because he wanted Nanny's power to flow into her, take hold of her, fix her heart so she would live long. He was a scientist—he had gone to McGill University, and then to graduate school at the Marine Biological Lab in Woods Hole, Massachusetts. But he was also born by this northern bay and knew the force and magic that came from nature, from things unknown and unseen.

Just then another boat steamed away from the dock—it was Gerard Lafarge, coming closer to see what everyone was looking at. Liam's blood felt cold in his veins. He felt danger coming from the man—he knew that anyone who would do what he'd done to the dolphin would hurt other unprotected creatures. Liam kept the Zodiac between Lafarge's boat and Nanny; but even more so, between Lafarge and Lily and Rose. He saw Lafarge pick up his binoculars and train them on the white whale. Then he put them down and looked over at Lily—just stared at her for a long time.

Turning his boat around, Liam made a wide circle around the *Tecumseh II,* not unlike the way a male osprey will circle the nest, keeping an eye on things before flying off to fish. Liam's laptop was blinking with all the marine mammals returning from their long migration home, but for the moment Liam ignored them, driving his boat in wide, slow circles, just doing his job while his heart beat faster and faster.

 *Chapter 7*

They had come from all over, some driving a hundred miles, to gather together, to celebrate Rose Malone's ninth birthday. There were mothers and daughters, sisters, aunts, grandmothers, old friends, and new friends. Over the years, they had met in some pretty odd places—starting with In Stitches, Lily's needlework shop on the harbor, where their club had been born. They had met at the inn, people's homes, the visitors' lounge at the hospital, and, one summer evening, in a sunken garden. But this was the first time the Nanouk Girls of the Frozen North had ever met at a birthday party on a boat.

Rose sat right in the middle of the circle, Jessica by her side. The other young girls pushed in close, to watch her open her presents, and the older women stood back slightly, watching and talking. Lily felt her own heart beating, steady, steady. . . . She gazed at the daughter she loved so much and thought of every single birthday she'd ever had. They had streaked by, faster than a comet.

It touched Lily to see Rose surrounded by so much love. Every single person in the room cared about her and would be rooting for her when they went to Boston. The sound of Liam's engine came through the open windows; it kicked Lily's heartbeat up a beat, but she stayed focused on the girls and women inside the cabin: the Nanouks. Glancing around the circle, Lily knew every woman but Marisa so well. She knew all—or almost all—the thrills, joys, heartaches, sorrows that had made her friends the amazing women they were. This moment of celebration belied so much; life went on, it always would, but Lily knew how important it was to stop for moments like this.

Rose opened her packages—she got books, a watercolor set, modeling clay, a silver bracelet, a wallet, two CDs, and a sweatshirt with a beluga whale on the front. Lily could almost feel her daughter's delight. Sometimes it was as if they had one skin; was it because Rose had been sick for so long, or were all mothers wired into their children? But Lily just felt the joy pouring through her, straight from Rose.

Just then, the loudspeaker crackled, and Jude's voice filled the room: "Calling the birthday girl . . . you and your friends are wanted on deck. We have a few lessons for you, regarding *les baleines*. . . ."

"That means 'whales'!" Rose translated for Jessica.

But several of her friends were French Canadian, and Lily knew Jude had said it for them. She loved the Neill men's kindness, and she was grateful her daughter—who had never even known her father—could experience it.

As the girls went out on deck, Lily glanced at Marisa. Lily had started the Nanouk Girls out of a very personal, secret need; she recognized the exact same thing in Marisa.

"Fine party, Lil," Anne said, coming over to where Lily stood by the window.

"She's having a great time," Lily said, watching Rose laugh with her friends as Jude gathered them on deck.

"It didn't hurt that Nanny showed up."

"How did that happen? It was almost as if Jude and Liam got together and planned it."

"It wasn't Jude," Anne said.

"Well, Liam then. He's always tracking something on his computer. I walk past his office and see it blinking, hear it beeping. . . ."

"He spends too much time with sea creatures," Anne said. "And not enough with humans."

"I'd spend time with him," Marlena said, walking over with a glass of punch. "If I hadn't sworn off men forever."

"Oh, c'mon now," Anne said. "You don't mean that. Just because Arthur was a louse doesn't mean all men are."

"Hey, I know you're married to a great guy, but when my Barbara was just five, her father up and left, moved in with a whole other family, forgot all about us. So I don't know about all men, but I do know about one bad one. . . ."

Marisa stood off to the side, as if wondering whether she should join in. Lily smiled, drawing her closer, knowing that this was what Marisa had come for, whether she knew it or not.

"She missed her father so much," Marlena continued. "She'd work herself into a fever, crying every night. I'd read her a bedtime story, and any time there was a daddy in it, she'd be just inconsolable. She'd fall asleep and dream about her father, and then wake up crying so hard she couldn't get back to sleep. I had to keep her home from school a couple of days, because she was so tired."

"Do you think children can literally get sick from missing their fathers?" Cindy asked.

"Depends on the children," Jodie said.

"No, depends on the fathers," Marlena said. "When they don't care enough to be a part of the kids' lives . . ."

"Come on," Suzanne said, smiling. "You're not still that bitter, are you?"

"Trying not to be," Marlena said. "I'm working through it, as they say."

"Just don't let it eat you up, honey," Doreen said.

Lily listened with interest, but more for Marisa's sake than anything else. She had spent long hours with her own demons, many years ago. The Nanouk Girls had helped her exorcise them for good.

"I'd like it to eat him up," Marlena said. "Maybe a nice big shark. If Dr. Neill could find a white whale for Rosie, maybe he could find a nice big great white for Arthur."

"Don't joke about sharks with Liam," Anne said quietly. Even as she spoke, Lily turned slowly, to look out the window. She saw the Zodiac moving in wide, slow circles around the whale boat. Liam was tall and rangy, and at the wheel of his boat he hunched his shoulders. His hair was dark brown, but where it waved slightly, it glinted silver.

Lily stared out the window, watching Liam. There was another boat out there too. She squinted to see—Gerard Lafarge's. There was something in his manner—his cockiness, the entitled way he walked around—that Lily didn't like. Gerard was watching Nanny with binoculars, and the sight gave Lily a chill.

"No," Lily echoed. "Don't mention sharks in front of Liam—after what happened to him and his brother."

"And Jude," Anne said. "My husband was there too. They've never gotten over it, and I'm sure they never will."

"Some things are too terrible to get over," Marisa said.

Everyone turned and looked at her. Lily had introduced her when they first came aboard, and she knew they were all curious. But Marisa, as if she already regretted her words, was backing off, turning away. Lily glanced casually back at Gerard, and was relieved to see him turn around, driving the boat out to sea.

"Marisa, wait," Anne said. "Come talk with us."

"Yes—while the girls are on deck, tell us a little about yourself," Cindy said. "What brings you to Cape Hawk? Is your husband a fisherman? Or oceanographer?"

"I'm . . . um, I'm divorced," Marisa said. Lily's full attention was on her now, and she seemed very uncomfortable—not quite embarrassed, but more as if she were safeguarding a secret and didn't want to let any details out. Lily knew the dynamic so well.

"Only three things would bring a person way up here," Alison said. "Family in the area, an insane love of nature, or escape from a bad marriage."

From the way Marisa reddened, Lily thought Alison had guessed one of the reasons.

"When you said 'some things are too terrible to get over,' " Marlena said, "I thought—yep. Betrayal, beatings, and behaving like a four-year-old. The big three."

"I can't," Marisa began.

"The girls are outside," Anne said. "They won't hear."

Lily edged closer to Marisa. She wanted to explain—or at least to give her the sense—that the group wasn't about gossip. They didn't need to know the gory details of each other's lives.

"We're far from home, some of us," Lily said. "We've become each other's sisters."

"I have a sister," Marisa said, her eyes starting to glitter. "Who I haven't talked to in so long . . ."

"Do you miss her?" Lily asked.

"More than you can imagine."

"Why can't you call her?"

"Because he might have her phones tapped. He said he'd never—never—let us go."

"But you got away."

"We did," Marisa stammered. "But instead, we feel trapped."

"Because you're afraid?"

"That, and other things . . . we can't move freely. Can't be ourselves . . ."

"It passes," Lily said.

"I feel so lonely up here sometimes."

"You have us now," Cindy said. "We just met you, but we're your friends. We're glad you're here, Marisa."

Marisa tried to smile, but she couldn't quite. Sensing that it was all too much for her, Lily took her elbow. "Let's get some punch, okay?" she said, leading Marisa toward the buffet table.

It seemed so casual, two women pouring paper cups of pink punch, taking small plates of cut-up cheese and fruit. Jude's voice drifted in the open window, explaining to the girls about how baleen whales were filter feeders, eating four to five metric tons of krill a day, the weight of an adult elephant. The Nanouks were still talking, some of them embroidering or needlepointing as the stories poured out.

"When you said you were lonely," Lily said, "you meant for him, didn't you?"

"Him?" Marisa asked, looking shocked.

"Your husband. Or ex-husband—that's right, you said you were divorced. Is he Jessica's father?"

"He's her stepfather," Marisa said, the glass of pink punch halfway to her lips.

"You finally left him . . . it took so much courage. You're lonely for the dreams you had. The love you believed, right down till the last day, that was in him."

"How do you know?" Marisa whispered.

"I could be a fortune teller," Lily said quietly. "When it comes to this. Let me see. You loved him—more than you ever imagined possible. He swept you off your feet, right? He made you believe in love at first sight. You let him into your life. There were things, though."

"Things," Marisa said. Outside, on deck, Jude was saying that a blue whale's tongue weighed as much as a young elephant, its heart as much as a small car.

"The lies. How you never knew quite whether you could believe what he told you. And the way you were always wrong and he was always right. Scary things too."

"Yes," Marisa said. "Very scary . . ."

"You had doubts. You wondered sometimes, but you told yourself you were wrong. You loved him so much. Your poor wounded man . . ."

"How do you know he's wounded?"

"They all are," Lily said, smiling. "Terribly, terribly so. And it's always someone else's fault."

"It always is," Marisa said, starting to smile for the first time.

"Beginning with their parents. They always have the absolute worst childhoods. Straight out of Dickens, complete with utter poverty and someone who was horribly cruel and beat them black and blue. . . ."

"Which justifies them being cruel to us."

"Of course," Lily said.

"Do you think they actually have awful childhoods? Or is that just another lie?"

Lily took a slow, careful sip of punch. She closed her eyes and thought of all the very many times she had asked herself that same question, how many long-ago sleepless nights she had stared up at the moon and stars, asking them how such terrible things could be visited on human beings.

"I grieve for any child who is hit," she said. "Or hurt in any way. But you know, to grow up and use that as an excuse to hurt us—uh-uh. I don't buy it. So, in that way, whether it's true or not is beside the point."

"I never thought of it that way," Marisa said.

"Is that one of the things that makes you lonely for him?" Lily asked. "Remembering how you used to hold him and comfort him? Are you wondering how he's surviving without you?"

Marisa nodded, and the smile was gone. "I'm a nurse," she said. "He told me I was healing him."

"While he was destroying you?"

"He never actually hit me."

"No, neither did mine," Lily said. "There are worse ways to destroy a person. I'm glad you got away. It had to be bad, for you to have come so far away. Away from your friend. I think what you're actually missing is not him."

"But there's such a hole in my life," Marisa whispered, her voice so hoarse, it sounded like bark being torn from a tree.

"You miss love," Lily said. "You miss the dream. You miss the dream of love you thought you had with him. That's why I started the Nanouk Girls of the Frozen North."

"The Frozen North. Canada," Marisa said.

"Oh," Lily said. "Did you think the name refers to geography? It doesn't. It's here—" She touched her own heart. "The Frozen North is where we lived, loving them, for so long. You're free now, Marisa. Welcome to the thaw."

On deck, Rose believed she had never felt so happy. Her birthday party was a crazy wonderful success—all her friends were having the time of their lives. Captain Neill had showed them fin whales, humpbacks, minkes, one blue whale, and of course, Nanny. He had told them how Nanny and other belugas are born light brown, but molt every year, until turning white at age six.

He brought all the girls into the wheelhouse and let them take turns holding the wheel, reading the compass, watching the radar, and tuning in to Dr. Neill's reports on where Nanny and the other whales were.

"Would you like to talk on the radio, birthday girl?" Captain Neill asked.

"Me?" Jessica asked.

Rose laughed at her friend's joke, watching Jessica blush.

"I'm just kidding," Jessica said.

"You're a regular comedian," the captain said. "My wife runs the inn, and we could use you on Friday nights. We're always looking for a good act. What's your name?"

"Jessica Taylor."

"Ah. 'Jessica Taylor, the Birthday Girl,' " he said. "Not!"

All the girls laughed, as if he was the comedian. He was tall and ruddy, with dark brown hair like his cousin, Dr. Neill. He had lots of lines in his sun- and wind-weathered face, and a wide grin, as if he enjoyed joking and making people laugh. He drove the boat over the waves here at the mouth of the bay, with a sort of gentleness that Rose appreciated. Her chest hurt today. She felt breakable—as if the impact of going over the open water could crack her open, so everything inside would spill out. But somehow the salty air felt so fresh and cool going into her lungs, it soothed her into forgetting.

"What is your birthday, Jessica?" Allie asked. "Your real one, I mean."

"Today," Jessica said, laughing. "And tomorrow. Oh—and the next day too!"

"Come on, real birthday girl," the captain said over the giggling, tapping Rose on the shoulder. "Get on the radio and ask my cousin where the whales have gone."

"I don't know how," Rose said.

"You go like this—" the captain said, showing her how to lift the mouthpiece and push the button on the side. "Push to talk, and then say 'over,' and listen. All twelve-year-olds should know how to talk on the radio."

"But I'm only nine!" she said.

"You're kidding."

She shook her head.

He rolled his eyes and shook his head, as if he couldn't believe it. "Well, you had me fooled. I could have sworn you were twelve. You're such a big kid."

Rose liked the way he made a half-circle with one arm, for her to stand in. She also felt proud, listening to what he'd said about her age. She was so much smaller than her friends—with her heart condition, she had never really grown right. Some boys at school called her "midget" when she walked by. Captain Neill had just made her feel both normal and special at the same time. And now she was getting to use the radio.

"Dr. Neill," she said, pushing the button. "Over."

"Rose, is that you? Over."

"It's me. Thank you," she said.

Now, looking out the wheelhouse window as she held the mike, she saw him in the orange Zodiac, making wide circles.

"You saw Nanny on your birthday," he said. "How about that? She knew, and came back just in time."

"Do you think she really knew? Over."

"I do. I think she sensed that we wanted her here. Whales are very intelligent, Rose. Especially Nanny. She's been around a long time, and I think she knows the people who watch out for her."

The people who watch out for her . . . Rose heard him say those words, and she saw him in the Zodiac, and then turned to look at her mother in the main cabin, just through the wheelhouse door. The people who watch out for her . . .

"I want Nanny to watch out," Rose said in the lowest voice imaginable, without pushing the button, "for my mother."

"What's that you say, sweetheart?" the captain asked. "You've got to speak up—and don't forget to press that little button there. That's it. Talk into the mike—there you go."

"Thank you again, Dr. Neill," Rose said.

"Ask him where the whales are now," Captain Neill reminded her. "He's the expert."

"Where are the whales now?" Rose asked.

"Just east, a few hundred yards," Dr. Neill said. He was holding the mike in his good hand, so he pointed with his prosthesis. Rose followed with her eyes. She saw spouts, the vapor iridescent in the sunlight.

Behind her, Britney and Allie giggled and whispered; Rose felt a pang when she heard someone squeal, "Captain Hook!"

It felt like a punch in the chest.

She turned around, saw Britney imitating a person with a hook for a hand. Her hand bent sharply at the wrist, fingers extended and held tightly together, stiff as a paddle. Their eyes met, but instead of stopping, Britney waved with her claw-hand. That made Allie shriek with laughter. Rose felt Captain Neill's eyes on her and her friends, and her shoulders pulled together in front, with shame. She handed him the microphone, sure he wouldn't want her to use it anymore—not with friends who made fun of his cousin.

But the captain just patted her head, told her she was doing a great job. He was saying something about asking Liam where Nanny was, but just then Rose felt the leak get bigger. It was like a bicycle tire that has a tiny pinprick . . . the air just hisses out a little at a time, till the little hole becomes a tear, and then it starts to rush.

Rose swayed—bumping against the hard steel wheel, and then against the captain's arms. She heard Dr. Neill's engine idling—such a comforting sound, to know he was right there. She had to turn around, had to see Britney. Jessica stood between them.

"What's wrong, Rose?" Jessica asked.

Rose opened her mouth. She knew she didn't have much time.

"Rose—it's like what happened on the way home from school, right?" Jessica asked, but she didn't even wait for Rose to answer. Rose knew she was running for her mother.

"Britney," Rose said, staring into her friend's brown eyes. "Don't call him that . . . please? He's my friend. He wanted me to see Nanny for my birthday."

"I know, I'm sorry," Britney said, looking stricken—was it because of what Rose had said, or the fact that she was turning blue? Rose had seen that look in the eyes of so many of her friends when she started having a spell.

The dizziness flooded up, surrounding her like waves, pulling her under the sea. Her thoughts were crazy. She remembered her two wishes: one of them had come true. Nanny was back, and Rose had seen her. But her other wish—even greater, more urgent—came upon her now. She wanted it with such passion, she thought she would die of it, and she knew she might. Rose had never been intimidated by that thought—her heart was working so hard to keep her alive, but Rose knew it might not forever.

"I want my father to be," Rose mumbled, her legs giving out. "I want him to be, I want him to be . . ."

"What, sweetheart?" Captain Neill asked, grabbing her hard, lifting her up in his arms.

"I want my father to be a good man," Rose said. "A good daddy who loves me . . ."

And then she went away.

Chapter 8

The first Liam noticed that there was some kind of problem was when he saw that the *Tecumseh II* had stopped and was drifting. He had been heading east, following the undersea ridge—he could see it on the sonar, the geological phenomenon that created upwelling, attracting the whales with a rich food source. He had several screens going at once—sonar, radar, and tracking. There was MM122, dead ahead—right at the blue surface, glistening bright white in the sun. That's when Liam turned, to make sure Jude was steering in the right direction.

But Jude wasn't steering at all. The *Tecumseh II* was definitely not under command. Drifting slowly, sideways, miles from any land, but alarming nonetheless. Liam clicked on the radio. He made a quick call.

"Calling *Tecumseh II*—Jude, you there?"

The speaker was silent. One hundred yards away, the seventy-four-foot whale boat rode the current. Broadside to Liam, it reflected sunlight back at him. Squinting, he lifted the binoculars to his eyes and saw everyone on deck rushing to the wheelhouse. Without waiting for a reply, he pushed the throttle down and sped across the water.

Liam's heart was pounding faster the closer he got. He knew it was something bad, something terrible. From his own history, he knew that the worst cries for help were the silent ones. *Rose's birthday*, he thought. It was so sunny for her special day, her whale-watch cruise, and Nanny had come back. Weren't those signs? Didn't they count?

Then he thought of Connor. The warm water, the best swimming they'd had all summer . . . the amazing number of whales, all swimming so close to the harbor . . . the fact that Liam and Jude had counted twenty-five shooting stars the night before. How could something go wrong on the day after two boys had seen twenty-five shooting stars? Or on a little girl's ninth birthday?

Now he was close, circling the bigger boat in his Zodiac, calling on the radio again. "Pick up, Jude, someone, tell me what's going on. Tell me, someone. Who's with Lily and Rose? Is someone with them?" He wasn't getting an answer, and he wasn't waiting. He backtracked in a half-circle to the stern, and he looked up and wondered how he was going to climb aboard with one arm and no ladder.

Lily knew there was no time to blame herself, but that's the first thing she did: *You shouldn't have waited so long for the surgery, you should have overridden the surgeon's recommendations, you knew she was having more blue spells, you knew a whale-watch boat trip was risky. . . .*

Everything seemed to happen so fast.

Jude yelled her name, and she knew. She had been drinking pink punch with Marisa—festive bubbly punch, ginger ale mixed with raspberry juice, Rose's favorite birthday drink, dark pink like her favorite rambling roses—when she heard her name.

The look on Anne's face: *oh my God.*

Jude's voice—it was the panic in his voice that got them both. Lily dropped the punch. The glass tumbled from her hand, as if her bones had just turned to jelly, couldn't hold on for anything. But her legs worked. Her front covered with Rose's birthday punch, she ran through the main salon. The Nanouk Girls lined her way—she had the fleeting impression of mouths open. Spectators on the marathon route, cheering their friend to the finish line. Only this wasn't cheering.

Rose was in Jude's arms, against his chest. He was trying to lay her on the chart table, but she was so blue and delicate, he hesitated, as if he was afraid that the hard Plexiglas surface would bruise her or hurt her, as if he just didn't know what to do, where to go with her.

"Is she breathing?" Anne asked, because Lily couldn't. Lily was already with Rose, nearly crawling into Jude's arms herself, climbing aboard with her daughter, ear to her small mouth, the blue lips, darker than the rest of her skin. Lily prayed to feel the tiniest breath—just the small moist warmth of one breath. Her very skin was attuned to Rose's life—the hairs on her cheek were alive, alert for the exhalation.

"She's not," Lily heard herself say, her voice high and raw.

"What do we do?" Jude said.

"You're the captain, you know first aid," Anne said. "Calm down, Jude."

First aid? Lily thought. She nearly fell apart at the words. After all her baby had been through. First aid had been given before the end of her first week of life. And so many times since. Rose had fought and fought . . .

"She has a pulse," Jude said, frowning as he felt Rose's wrist.

"Okay, that's what we need to hear," Anne said.

In the background, from the main salon, Lily heard a ruckus. The girls were screaming, and one of them cried, "It's a pirate!"

The girls felt Rose's trauma, Lily knew—it was radiating through the party, and they all picked up on it, and suddenly everyone was sobbing. Lily clung to her daughter, grabbing her out of Jude's arms. If he didn't know first aid, well, Lily did, and she'd do it herself. She was already breathing into Rose's mouth, trying to remember how to count, one, two, one, no . . . Tasting the salt of her own tears, the sweetness of punch from Rose's lips, hearing the girls cry, and scream the name Captain Hook.

Oh, and that name made Lily start to cry herself. The first tears had been nothing, but now they turned into sobs. Liam was here, of course he was. She felt his good hand on her shoulder. Jude was explaining, talking fast and sharply, describing how Rose was steering the boat and then suddenly how she just collapsed. And Anne was shushing him, saying the details didn't matter but acting fast did.

Liam said, "Drive, Jude."

"But where?"

"Get us to Port Blaise."

"No!" Lily said. "That's too far! She won't make it. Take us to the dock, call the ambulance, we'll go to the medical center—Dr. Mead knows her, that's the best thing—"

"Port Blaise has a heliport, Lily. We can call the rescue helicopter right now."

"The Coast Guard," Anne said. "I'm calling right now."

Lily felt the push of the engines, throwing her off-balance as the *Tecumseh II* picked up speed. She was the "fast cat" in the Neill family fleet, and she was flying now, up on her plane, hydroplaning across the bay.

"But in the meantime," Lily tried to say. These people loved her and Rose, she had no doubt of that. But they hadn't spent nine years raising a child with cardiac defects. They didn't understand that *now* was what mattered—not getting to the heliport, flying to the medical center. Rose was still and cold. Lily wept with panic.

Liam's arm was prying them apart.

"No!" Lily shrieked.

"Come here," he said roughly. "Anne," he said, asking for help.

Now Anne was in on it—all the Nanouk Girls, pulling Lily away from Rose. Lily stretched like elastic—her hands wouldn't let go, her fingertips stuck to Rose's skin like the pads of a tree frog, suction cups holding tight with a death grip. She heard Marlena's voice, and Cindy's, Doreen's. . . .

"Come on, love," Marlena said. "She's in the best hands now—"

"She is, sweetheart," Anne said. "Let it happen."

And that made Lily look up and see—that Rose *was* in the best hands. . . .

Marisa had stepped forward. The pain in her eyes was gone. Her posture and attitude as a wounded bird, abused woman, had disappeared. She stood tall and confident, one hand resting gently on Rose's chest, the other sliding down her frail left arm, fingers finding the pulse. She nodded.

Beside Marisa, Liam fumbled with the first-aid bag, the emergency oxygen tank, using his one good hand to slide the green strap around Rose's head, the clear plastic mask over her mouth.

Held up by the Nanouk Girls, Lily almost felt the oxygen flowing directly into her own mouth and nose, into her bloodstream. Her lungs filled—the air was so clear and clean, and it was bringing life back to all the dead parts. Lily felt Marlena rubbing her back, Cindy holding her left hand, Anne clasping her right hand. The other girls were there, fanned out like a team, like Lily and Rose's team. Mothers and daughters; while Marisa treated Rose, Jessica stood glued to Lily's right leg. All the Nanouk Girls were here, silently watching. They were witnesses to this birthday, and this lifesaving. Lily shuddered with the terror that comes with a certain kind of joy, too primal to name.

"She's been through so much already," Lily cried.

"And she'll just keep going," Anne said, almost sternly.

"What if . . ."

No one even replied to the question Lily couldn't bring herself to ask. Instead they all just stood together as the boat went faster and faster. All these mothers and daughters, best friends in this cold climate, pulling together for Lily and Rose.

"May the sea cradle you, the angels protect you," Jessica whispered.

"What's that?" Allie asked.

"My father's Irish prayer," Jessica replied.

Marisa ministered to the patient, gently and with strength. Like a seasoned pediatric cardiac nurse, she turned her onto her side, helping her into the knees-to-chest position. Bending over, whispering in Rose's ear, counting the beats of her heart as she took her pulse, eyes on her watch.

Now she put her ear to Rose's chest, and when she stood up, she was frowning. She palpated Rose's side, spending time. Liam held the oxygen mask, adjusting the flow. Jude was talking on the SSB to the Coast Guard, but when he hit the big questions he couldn't answer, he handed the mike to Marisa, who said, "The patient is nine years old, female . . . Tetralogy of Fallot . . . scheduled for reparative surgery, but . . . yes . . . pulmonary stenosis . . . enlarged liver. Kidneys. The surgery was scheduled for Boston, but I don't think . . ."

Lily heard Marisa's words, but suddenly they were lost to her, a blur. Because Liam had turned—halfway around, to meet Lily's eyes with a great big smile, nodding, there at Rose, who had opened her eyes, her bright-green, alive, birthday-girl eyes. And Rose was looking around, and because Liam knew there was only one person Rose wanted to see, he stepped aside—still holding the mask—so Rose could look straight at her mother.

Chapter 9

Maeve Jameson sat in her garden, on the ancient wrought-iron bench, under the shade of the sea oaks. The smell of roses filled the salt air, and the warmth of summer lifted from the rocky earth. A soft breeze blew, rustling the leaves overhead. Her eyes were closed, and to anyone who might happen to pass by, she looked as if she were resting, at peace. That was far from the truth.

Down by the rocks, the tide was rising. She heard the waves splashing higher and higher. It was impossible to not think back, see that young girl playing in the water, swimming like a seal with her brown hair so sleek and smooth. She loved to dive, as deep as she could go, and come up with handfuls of shells and seaweed. Maeve had sat on this very bench, watching her dive and swim for hours on end.

When she heard the car door slam, she felt she could take a breath. She'd been waiting for this visit. It had to happen—it did every year. But this year, it felt different. Maeve's heart felt heavy, as if another layer of hope had been torn off.

"Top of the morning, Maeve," came the voice. She could barely open her eyes to look at him. But when she did, she smiled. Couldn't help herself. He still looked as young and handsome and eager as the young cop who had stood on her doorstep so many years ago. His dog, a black Lab, ran straight past Maeve, down to the water's edge.

"It's not morning," she said. "It's three in the afternoon."

"You going to start busting me before I even walk through your garden gates?"

"Darling, those garden gates were taken down years ago. Come on, enter the hallowed ground." She watched him walk past the wishing well—with its curved, wrought-iron arch, emblazoned with *Sea Garden*—the name Mara had given the house when she was just a little girl. Patrick stole a glance at the letters—spidery now, after all these years of salt air wearing away the iron.

"Hallowed ground," he said, standing before her.

"Sea Garden," she said. "Still waiting for the young maid to return."

"Maeve . . ."

"Darling—you're going to tell me to be realistic, aren't you? I can hear it in your tone. Nine years have passed. . . ."

"It does no good to hold out hope when we both know . . ."

"Both know what, dear? What do we actually know? That she lived here, that she disappeared, that her baby would be nine years old to-day—or yesterday, or tomorrow . . . I don't know her exact birthday."

"We don't know that she had a birthday," Patrick said. "It's most likely she didn't."

"Then why do you come to see me every year? Why do you keep asking questions, as if you still expect to find her?"

Patrick blushed, his freckled skin turning as red as sunburn. His blue eyes glinted in the sun. Sometimes Maeve thought he regretted telling her about aspects of his investigation, his sleepless nights, the way his marriage had broken up over his obsession with the case. Maeve had tried, as gently as possible, to impress upon him the crazi-ness—there was no other word for it—of trying, even though he was now retired, to solve the case of a missing woman he honestly, deep in his heart, believed to be dead.

Maeve just didn't find it credible.

"What does Angelo have to say about this?" she asked.

He let out a low whistle, shaking his head till the red hair fell right into his blue eyes. "Low blow, Maeve," he said.

"Didn't you tell me that Angelo was your friend, the one who tries to convince you you're chasing rainbows, still looking for my grand-daughter?"

"First of all, I'm not looking for her. The case is closed, and be-sides—I'm retired. Second of all, Angelo is an asshole."

"Really? I thought he was your best friend."

Patrick nodded. He was standing directly in front of Maeve, and she angled her position so his head would block the sun from shining in her eyes.

"Yeah, he is," he said. "But when it comes to solving cases, he doesn't know shit. Flora! Get away from that goddamned seaweed! You know she's going to have my car smelling like low tide, don't you?"

Maeve beamed. She didn't know why it tickled her so much, to have Patrick Murphy swear like this. Normally she didn't go in much for profanity. She supposed she liked it because it seemed to reflect the passion he felt for keeping the dream of Mara alive—in spite of what he was telling her out of one side of his mouth.

"Dogs love my rocks. Now, back to Angelo."

"He doesn't know squat about my cases."

"Well, he's not in law enforcement, is he? What would he know, when you get right down to it?"

"Not much," Patrick said. "What've you got there?"

"These?" she asked, holding up her hot-pink garden gloves. But he was shaking his head, pointing.

"That," he said.

"Oh," Maeve said. "I was just watering the roses."

"That's one old watering can," Patrick said. "Yellow. Kind of unusual."

"Hmm," Maeve said, pushing her dark glasses down from the top of her head, where they had been resting. She thought now would be a good time. The last thing she wanted was for this young man to see any eyes filling up with tears. She coughed, for good measure, kicking the yellow boots under the bench. Choosing her moments, Flora abandoned the tidal pools and sea wrack to come over for a pat. She nosed the boots while she was at it.

"What are those?" he asked, watching his dog lick the rubber boots.

"Enough," she said—to Patrick, not Flora.

"Maeve."

"Does the expression 'keep the home fires burning' mean nothing to you? What kind of sentimental Irishman are you, anyway?"

"A realistic one."

"Ah, yes. You gritty Irish cops would never understand anything like hoping a long-lost granddaughter and great-grandchild would come home again. You're too busy chasing after ghosts."

"She was wearing those boots and using that watering can the day she disappeared," he said, and he'd lost every speck of color from his face.

"She was."

"I should never have brought them back to you from the evidence room. Get rid of them, Maeve, for your own sake."

"Never."

"Maeve, we found flecks of blood on the toe. You want to live with those boots, and what happened to make Mara walk away from them?"

"Mara pricked her thumb on a thorn," Maeve said sharply. She couldn't stand to think about blood and Mara—or any hurt, any pain, any of the terrible scenarios imagined by the police at the time. She couldn't bear it. She set her jaw, letting Patrick know the subject was closed.

"Any word from what's-his-face?" Patrick asked.

"Mr. Wonderful," Maeve said.

"Why is it neither of us can stand to say his name?"

Maeve just gave Patrick her best deadpan gaze. Words couldn't express the depth of hatred she harbored for Edward Hunter; even thinking his name caused her stomach to tighten and her face to wizen. She let her left hand trail down beneath the seat, her fingers closing around the top of one of the yellow boots. It comforted her, to hold on to something Mara had once worn. Made Mara feel real and alive.

"He writes or calls on the big occasions. Holidays, her birthday . . ."

"What do you say to him?"

"I act, darling. I thank him and ask about his career, his 'family.' " She had to put the word—such a precious word at that, "family," in invisible quotation marks when using it in conjunction with Edward and his latest victims—he had had Mara declared dead, so that he could marry one of his brokerage clients. "I've learned to keep my enemy close. One never knows what he might reveal. He's living in . . ."

"Boston."

Maeve blinked with surprise. "No—he's been living in Weston, with his new wife."

"She left him last spring," Patrick said, enjoying giving her the news. "They had their house on the market, and as soon as it sold, she took off on him. Didn't get much of the money, from what I hear. Most of it was in escrow, but she just cut her losses, took her kid, and went away. He'll end up with all her money—what he hasn't already taken from her. Women do that with Edward. They give up everything they have to escape him."

Maeve had no retort to that. She just let her fingers trail around and around the rim of the boot. Oh, if only Mara would choose today as the day . . . to return from wherever she was hiding, just walk through the garden gate that Maeve had torn down so many years ago now . . . just walk in, carrying her baby.

The reality shocked her—the child wouldn't be a baby now, but a nine-year-old child.

"So much lost time," Maeve said. "When I think about the years I've spent without her. I raised her, you know."

"I know, Maeve. After her parents died in the ferry accident."

"In Ireland. Such a poetic place and poetic way to die. That's what I told myself at the time. But then I'd hold Mara, crying herself to sleep every night, and I realized—there's no poetic way to die."

"Nope."

"That's right. I'm talking to an old homicide cop, aren't I?"

"Major Crime Squad," he said.

"Did I ever tell you that you remind me of a darling old friend of mine, an Irish poet, Johnny Moore?"

"Every time I see you. I still can't figure out why."

"Because you write letters to a girl you believe to be dead," Maeve said. "That's why. Come on. Come inside, and I'll pour us some iced tea. Clara might stop by with some of her sugar cookies, if I tell her you're here."

"Sugar cookies," Patrick said, holding out his hand to pull Maeve up. As he did, his eyes fell upon the old bench. Made of wrought iron by the same person who'd done the wishing-well arch, it was weathering only slightly better—it was forged of thicker iron, and Maeve had been more fastidious, painting it every year with Rustoleum. She followed Patrick's gaze, looking at the bench.

There was room for four people to sit on it. The slatted seat sagged slightly in the middle; the arms and legs were ornate, decorated with Victorian curlicues. But it was the back that was the great work of art. There were four scenes depicted—of a boy and girl sitting beneath the same tree.

"Your four-seasons bench," he said. "Winter, spring, summer, and fall."

"Yes," Maeve said, lifting the yellow boots even as he took hold of the watering can, then linking her arm with his and walking down the narrow stone path that led to her front door. "My father had it made for my mother, by the same ironworker who made the *Sea Garden* arch. It symbolizes the passage of time."

The passage of time: since Mara's disappearance, since Patrick had started looking for her. Young people these days were always amazed by things that lasted. And she certainly included Patrick—who was probably about forty-five—in the category of "young." This was a throwaway society; Maeve and Clara said it to each other all the time. They were both dismayed by all the plastic wrapping everything came in. Not to mention the way rich young people would buy up lovely, gracious cottages, tear them down, and build the most unspeakable monstrosities. Even here in Hubbard's Point, the practice was rampant.

"Do you want to hear my theory?" Maeve asked.

"Of course," he said as she opened the front door and led him inside. The kitchen was cooled by shade and the sea breeze blowing through all the open windows.

"In the future, and not so far in the future, the properties that will be worth the most are cottages like this one. Lovely, small houses, built to nestle into the land. People with money are ruining everything— cutting down all the old trees, knocking down the small houses, and building their stupid showplaces."

"They think they're increasing the value of their real estate."

"Darling, I've heard about what's happened to the boatyard. I'm so sorry. But yes, it's the exact same phenomenon. After a while, when people tire of their big air-conditioned, fancy-hot-tubbed houses, they'll all yearn for places like this. That fit the shoreline so beautifully. I think of Mara coming home and not even recognizing the place, with all the ugly houses going up."

"She'd recognize the place," he said. "She'd know it anywhere."

"It was in her heart," Maeve said, opening the refrigerator, taking out the big pitcher of iced tea. Sprigs of mint from the garden floated on top, and she strained the tea into tall Kentucky Derby glasses. Then she poured a bowl of water for Flora, and the dog slurped thirstily.

"Tell me about her," Patrick said.

"You know everything there is to know about my granddaughter," Maeve said. "Probably as much as I do."

"No one knows as much as you, not when it comes to Mara," Patrick said. "Come on—tell me something I don't know about her."

Maeve frowned. What could, or should, she tell him? Leading him from the gray and yellow kitchen, past the old table with one end built into the wall, with the bright flowers and figures painted on the wood by Maeve herself long before such things were in decorating fashion— around the corner into the living room, with its sweeping views of Long Island Sound, Maeve's mind was racing with thoughts and memories.

Mara as a baby, as a three-year-old learning to swim, as a six-year-old constantly reading, as a teenager resisting the boys who fell in love with her as often as the east wind blew, as a successful needlework designer, as a young woman married to Edward Hunter.

"Which story should I tell you?" she asked. "From which part of her life?"

"Tell me the one that will help me find her," he said.

"Don't you think that if I could have, I already would have?" she asked, smiling sadly as he admitted—without coming right out and saying it—that he didn't really believe she was dead. Or didn't want to . . .

"I know I ask you this every time. But have you ever gotten anything that might be a sign from her?" he asked, trying a different tack. "A phone call, where the person hung up? Or a postcard without a signature? Or . . ."

"No."

"Anything odd, out of the ordinary, that gave you pause?"

"They undercharged me at the Shell station," she said.

Patrick rolled his eyes. Flora trotted over to lie panting at his feet. "Anything else? Along the lines of mistaken identity?"

"Mistaken identity?"

"Well, where something really unexpected occurred, and you thought there had to be some mistake. As if maybe it was meant for someone else."

"Well, last fall," Maeve said, her heart flipping as his words opened a door—an opportunity. She spoke slowly, to not betray emotions. "Late fall, I think. Just before the holidays."

"What was it?" Patrick asked.

"I got a phone call from the membership department at the Mystic Aquarium. The woman was so lovely and kind. She told me that she had been given my name by someone who thought I might be interested in joining, and wanted to offer me a membership."

From Patrick's expression, Maeve knew that this was not the sort of thing he'd been hoping for. But Maeve's pulse was racing—she felt a thread of electricity running up her spine, as if a ghost or angel had just flown into the room.

"Well, they know you live on the water," Patrick said. "They probably thought you'd like to go see the fish, or whatever they have there."

"Maybe," Maeve said. "I asked the woman who had given her my name, and she said the person wanted to be anonymous."

"Maybe she was just trying to sell you a membership."

"No. It was a gift. The person had bought it for me."

Now she had his attention. He raised his eyebrows, thinking. "A gift?"

"I thought it might have been Clara—she loves museums, and Mystic Seaport, and the aquarium. But it wasn't her. Then I thought it had to be one of my old students. I was always making them observe nature."

"Huh. Have you enjoyed the membership?"

"I've never gone," Maeve said. "Why go to an aquarium, when I have all this right out my window?" She gazed out at the blue Sound, waves pushing in from the east. The two granite islands, North and South Brother, lay half a mile offshore; she remembered the time Mara had wanted to swim to them, and Maeve had rowed alongside, to keep her safe.

"Right," Patrick said. "Why would you?"

Maeve stared at him.

They heard the kitchen door open—the screen door needed oil. She knew that it was Clara. She lived right next door, and she had probably spotted Patrick in the garden. Maeve could almost smell the sugar cookies.

"It's me," Clara called.

"We're in here," Maeve called back.

"But hey," Patrick said. "Humor me, will you? Do you have that woman's name? The one who called?"

"Somewhere, probably," Maeve said, sliding over on the sofa to make room for Clara. Flora stood at attention, tongue lolling out, and focused on the plate of cookies. Everyone said hello; Patrick stood to shake Clara's hand, and Maeve lifted her face to kiss her best friend. Of course she remembered the woman's name; she knew exactly where she had put the paper where she'd written it down.

"I brought some cookies, as this lovely dog can see," Clara said. "To go with Maeve's mint tea."

"I'm a lucky guy," Patrick said. "You behave yourself, Flora."

"It almost feels like a party," Clara said, slipping Flora a piece of cookie.

"A birthday party," Maeve said, feeling that electric shiver again as she went to get the name—it was on the membership materials that she had shoved into a middle shelf on her bookcase, right between *Islands in the Stream* and *Yeats's Collected Poems*.

Two of her favorite books.

Again, electricity zinged up her spine. She almost wondered whether a thunderstorm was on the way.

Chapter 10

The helicopter had so little room inside, Rose had to go without her mother. By the time the boat reached the dock at Port Blaise, and the helicopter landed to pick her up, Rose felt so much better. Not perfect, not even just okay, but no longer fainting and blue. She was awake, and she could hear, and she didn't like hearing that she had to fly alone to the hospital in Melbourne.

"Mommy," she said, lifting the oxygen mask so she could talk. "Come with me."

"There's no space, honey," her mother said, crouching right beside the gurney, where Rose lay flat, ready to be loaded onto the waiting helicopter. "But don't worry—I'll get in a car right now and drive down to Melbourne. I'll be there in an hour. Two at the most."

"Don't speed," Rose warned her.

"No," her mother said, and Rose was so relieved to see her smile.

"We'll take good care of her," the helicopter nurse said to her mother. They began to lift Rose, but her mother wouldn't let go of her hand. Jessica's mother, who had helped Rose on the boat, stood right there, waving at Rose. Rose's mother still clutched her hand. Finally, Dr. Neill stepped forward and gently put his good hand on Rose's mother's, pulling it away from Rose's.

"Let her get going," he said. "The sooner she does, the sooner you can see her in Melbourne." He was staring straight at Rose as he spoke; she saw the spark in his eyes, and it made her smile, even though she was a little scared of the roaring helicopter blades. Dr. Neill knew what Rose was thinking—she was positive of it.

"Don't be worried, Rose," her mother said. "These people will take care of you, and I'll be there as soon as I can."

Rose nodded and smiled wide. She held her lips in place, her teeth showing, so her mother would remember the smile. Then she gave her mother the thumbs-up she always gave when she was being wheeled into surgery. Her mother gave it back, with an equally brave grin on her face.

"Bye, Rosie! We love you, Rose!" called Jessica and her mother and all the Nanouk Girls. The oxygen mask was back over Rose's face, so she couldn't shout back. Dr. Neill was standing right by her mother, towering over her because he was so tall, and Rose had one fleeting impression of him as a mountain. Sturdy, steady, rock-fast. She liked thinking of him that way, and it brought the smile back to her face.

Things began to happen fast.

The EMTs made sure she was strapped in; the nurse hooked her up to the blood pressure cuff and began listening with her stethoscope. The pilot was talking on the radio. Now an EMT was on another radio, calling to the hospital. Rose had been through it all before. The ground crew slammed the helicopter door, and when she couldn't see her mother anymore, Rose closed her eyes.

Her mother had looked so worried, and Rose knew it was because she thought Rose was scared. But Rose wasn't. She had had a wonderful birthday, but now she was tired.

The fear her mother had seen in her eyes had actually been worry for her—her mother. Her mother always did so much. She worked so hard at the shop, and she tried to always make Rose happy and more healthy. As the helicopter began to lift—straight up, making Rose's heart drop, as if it could stay on the ground forever, with her mother and Dr. Neill and all the people she loved—Rose clenched her fists and thought of her mother.

She knew that as much as her own heart wanted to stay on the ground, her mother's heart was rising like the helicopter, flying right here with Rose. Rose could feel it, as if she held her mother's heart in her own hands. She worried about her mother's worry. When Rose thought about her illness, it wasn't herself that she felt bad for—it was her mother.

Jessica's mother had a healthy daughter; why couldn't Rose's? Rose thought back a few days, to when she had been teasing Jessica about the evil wizard that lived in the hills. Just thinking of him made the splinter in her heart hurt. It was ice, sharp as a needle.

She thought of the fairy tales her mother had read when she was little. Evil wizards put spells on people. But Rose didn't think that was what had happened. She thought that she must have done something bad. When she was a baby, or a very little girl. Her mother had never told her, but something to drive her father away forever. It left her with a broken heart, and an evil wizard instead of a father.

Her thoughts spun. She breathed in the oxygen, staring into the strange nurse's eyes. When she went through blue spells, she wasn't always sure what was real and what wasn't, what was a dream and what was awake.

There was no evil wizard—her mother had chided her for teasing Jessica. But, then, why did Rose feel that there was? Instead of a good father?

She forced herself to breathe, and to think of her mother. She wished that she would get well, so her mother wouldn't have to worry. They could do normal things together—running and playing, planning for next Christmas without wondering whether she would have to go back into the hospital, might need more surgery. Rose's condition made everything so up-in-the-air.

Just like flying in a helicopter.

This was real. It wasn't a dream. She wasn't being flown on devil wings to the mountain wizard's demon cave. She wasn't being kidnapped by anyone. Her father hadn't sent people to find her. No, no. She made herself stay awake and know where she was. The beat of the helicopter engine felt strong and comforting.

Real, real, she told herself. *Going to the hospital to get better. But still, up in the air.*

One minute she was at her birthday party, seeing Nanny, laughing with her friends, and the next she was in a helicopter, with a stranger listening to her heart and trying to smile, being flown to the hospital in Melbourne.

Up in the air. Rose was up in the air, but her heart was down on the ground, with her mother. It was all true, and all real.

Lily was numb, moving by rote. Anne and Marlena gathered up Rose's presents, boxed up the cake—and the candles, not yet lit and blown out—and promised to get them to Lily's house. Lily had only the vaguest sense of hearing Anne say she'd keep the cake in the inn's freezer till Rose came home.

She knew she should go home and pack a bag. From experience, she knew that trips to the hospital were usually longer than not, and once there she would need her toothbrush and the book she was reading and a few changes of clothes. But she couldn't take the time to drive all the way back home. She had to rent a car, right here in Port Blaise, and drive straight to the hospital.

"Would you like me to come with you?" Marisa asked.

"No, but you were wonderful on the boat. Thank you so much," Lily said.

They held hands, looking into each other's eyes. Lily saw something more awake than she had previously—as if by helping Rose, Marisa had connected with the deepest part of herself, long ignored in the heat of escape.

"I don't know much about Melbourne Hospital," Marisa said, "being so new here. But the chopper staff seemed really competent and attentive."

"They are, and the hospital's good. For palliative care, anyway," Lily said. "Rose has been there often. Marisa—I saw you listening to her belly. What did you hear?"

"Fluid," Marisa said hesitantly. "And Lily, her liver and kidneys felt enlarged."

Lily heard the information and stored it instantly in the part of her brain that wouldn't touch or talk to her heart—not, at least, while she was making the long drive from here to Melbourne. She couldn't let herself start crying now, or she might drive off the road, and that wouldn't do. Rose needed her too much.

She and Marisa hugged, and she felt surprised by how tight her new friend held on—as if she didn't want to let her go.

"What is it?" Lily asked.

"Just—thank you. For getting it."

"I get it because I've been there myself," Lily said softly. "The world is divided into two kinds of people. Those who have loved men like your husband and mine, and those who haven't. Ending a relationship is one thing. But recovering from a marriage to a sociopath is another. I'll see you when we get back, okay? I want to hear more of your story, and tell you mine."

"Thank you—give our love to Rose."

"I will," Lily said.

Lily was gearing up for the drive—she'd have to ask one of the Coast Guard guys for a ride to the mall, a few miles away, where she was 90 percent sure she had seen a car rental place—patting her pockets to make sure she had her house keys for when she got back, and checking her shoulder bag, over and over, just reassuring herself that she had it with her, hadn't left it on the boat. She knew she was in a familiar sort of shock—the one she entered every time Rose went to the hospital.

The Nanouk Girls had disembarked, trying to convince her to let them go with her. The *Tecumseh II* sat at the strange dock, with Jude and his crew on deck, gravely gazing up at the sky, where the helicopter was now no more than a dot.

"I have to get a car," Lily said to Anne.

"Liam's on it," she said. "He knows the Coast Guard commander, from sharing technology or some crap like that, and he's arranging for someone to take you to Hertz. Want me to drive with you?"

Lily shook her head. "I'll be fine." She just wanted to get on the road now. Every second was a second she wasn't with Rose.

The Nanouks huddled around her in one huge hug—as if they knew she didn't have time for individual goodbyes or kisses. But she felt the weight of her best friends and their daughters crushing against her, as if they could carry her themselves, on their shoulders, down to Melbourne.

"We love you, Lil."

"We'll be with you both."

"Call us, sweetheart."

"We'll send you anything you need."

"Let us know the minute you hear anything."

"I will," she promised, dry-eyed and resolute, fortified by their strength and love. Pulling away, she walked to the top of the dock. The Coast Guard station, white with its red roof, attached to the conical white brick lighthouse, stood nestled in short, wind-scrubbed pines at the top of a small hill.

Lily felt almost breathless, climbing the stairs. She had a long journey ahead of her—the drive would be the easy part. There was Liam, talking to the commander, in his white uniform. A younger Coast Guard member had been dispatched to get a car, and he was pulling it round, into the semicircular gravel drive.

Now Lily began to run—the car was here—all she had to do was jump in, and the young man would drive her to Hertz. She passed Liam, knowing she owed him thanks, but not able to take the time right now. Hand on the passenger door, she was dismayed to see the young Coast Guard man turn off the ignition and get out of the driver's side.

"No," she said, the panic rising. "Please—we have to go *now*. Get in, drive me, please—"

The young man looked sheepish, a little embarrassed. "Ma'am," he began.

"Now, oh, please—you're kind to drive me, but I'm late, I have to get to my daughter!"

"Get in, Lily," Liam said, opening the door for her.

"Oh, thank you, Liam," she said, all in a rush. Wow, she'd really owe him some thanks. "Tell them he has to take me right now, fast, okay?"

Liam didn't reply. He closed the door behind her. Now he was talking to the two Coast Guard men, just standing there—taking up the driver's time with who knows what. Lily watched the three of them talking, keys being handed off, words exchanged—for the love of *God*! She wanted to scream.

When Liam opened the driver's door, the look in her eyes was daggers and solid ice. Tears had formed—angry, furious, rageful tears—for the three men whose chatting meant she'd be that much later to the Hertz office, and for the fact Rose's birthday had been ruined, and for the fact that Rose's heart was giving out.

"Jesus, Liam," she said. "I've got to go!"

"I know, Lily," he said, climbing into the car, reaching across his body to close the door behind him with his good arm. Now he turned the key, starting the car.

"*You're* taking me to the car place?" she asked, not understanding.

"To the hospital," he said.

"But it's in Melbourne," she said, still not getting it, still envisioning the time it would take to rent a car, wondering why Liam didn't understand that she had one more step in the process of driving south to Rose.

"I know."

"Liam—"

"The commander is a friend of mine," Liam said. "This is his personal car—he's loaning it to us so I can drive you to the hospital."

Lily was too numb to argue, but it did begin to sink in as he pulled out onto the lighthouse road, accelerated as soon as he could, sped to the main highway that led south to Melbourne. The car was sporty, with four-wheel drive and roof racks, and the back seat was filled with buoys, nylon line encrusted with dried seaweed and mussel colonies, and an enormous flashlight.

"What will the commander do without his car?" Lily asked.

"He said he'll use the truck."

"Why are you doing this?" Lily asked.

"Because you need to get to Melbourne."

"I know, but I could have driven myself."

"You need to get to Melbourne fast. And honestly—I wasn't sure you were in any shape to drive."

"It's not your responsibility," Lily said.

Liam was quiet, pushing the pedal down. She cringed, hoping that she hadn't just sounded as ungrateful as she felt. Miles sped by—roadway lined with pines and oaks on one side, open water on the other. Even from shore, whale spouts were visible in the bay. Lily thought of Rose's face, the look in her green eyes when she had first spotted

Nanny. Lily squeezed her eyes shut to preserve the moment of amazement.

When she opened them again, she glanced across the seat at Liam.

"I'm sorry," she said.

"You're forgiven," he said. He looked intent on the road, as if he barely cared about conversation at all. His eyes were totally focused, dark gray-blue. Patches of sunlight came through boughs overhanging the road, flashes of light making his eyes look bright, then dark, then bright again.

"Seriously," she said. "I was wrong to say it. I didn't mean to be mean."

"Haven't we been down this road before?" he asked.

She knew he didn't mean the highway.

"Yes," she said. "And I've been sorry ever since."

He threw her a look across the seat.

"Not for the reasons you think," she said. "But because I don't like to be beholden to you. Or anyone."

"You're not beholden to me," he said. "In any way."

Lily stared out at the bay as they flew down the coast road. She knew he was telling her the truth. He had never expected anything from her—never, not once. But after what Lily had been through, before Rose was born, before arriving in Cape Hawk, she had lost the power to trust. She had once believed that people were good at heart, that they meant to help each other. That was how she had been raised.

But by the time she arrived in Cape Hawk, those beliefs had been shattered. It was Liam's misfortune, she thought, that he had been one of the first people she'd encountered after arriving in the small fishing village at the back-of-beyond on Nova Scotia's northernmost coastline.

She closed her eyes, went inward, back nine years. So pregnant she could hardly move. Just out to *there*—in a new place, in a house she was sure she couldn't afford, with a rattletrap car that needed a tune-up and four new tires after her long drive north, with not even enough money for an oil change. As she sat beside Liam in the commander's car now, she let her hands drift to her belly. She could remember carrying Rose as if it were yesterday.

"There's another reason, okay?" she asked, opening her eyes to look at him.

"Another reason for what?"

"That I've felt sorry ever since." She stopped herself, to think of how to phrase it. "Ever since we first met, and you did what you did."

"And why would that be? You feeling sorry?"

"It's just that I don't . . ." she said, no longer looking at him, but out the window instead—at the wide expanse of blue ocean, and the wheeling and circling white seabirds, and the occasional ripple that might or might not be the back of a whale. "I don't treat you very well. Not well enough, anyway."

"You treat me fine," he said.

"No," she said. "I know I don't."

They rode in silence for a few minutes. She was glad that he didn't try to contradict her. One thing she could count on about Liam was that he was very true to situations. He didn't sugarcoat things. He wouldn't try to make her feel better about something if it meant telling her a lie.

She glanced over at him. Why was she so tongue-tied today? What she wanted to say was, *I might treat you "fine," but it's not what you deserve. You've been nothing but wonderful since the day you met me, met us. Rose loves you.* She couldn't, and wouldn't, say such things.

So instead, she said, "Thanks for driving me, Liam."

And he didn't reply, but she saw him smile.

As he drove ever faster.

Chapter 11

The old brick hospital was on the crest of a hill overlooking Melbourne Harbor. The World War I memorial rose beside it, a single block of granite, quarried from Queensport. Liam and his brother had both been born here; so had most of their cousins. Liam remembered coming here to pick up Connor when he was three days old, the day they brought him home.

While waiting for his mother and the baby to be ready, his father had taken him to the reflecting pool, under the tall monument, and told him that his great-grandfather had fought in World War I. Liam still remembered holding his father's hand, listening to the story. His great-grandfather had been badly wounded in battle, and seen many soldiers killed.

The idea of his great-grandfather being so injured in a war made the three-year-old Liam cry—in spite of the happy fact that he had a new brother and his mother was coming home.

"Some things are worth fighting for," his father had told him, picking him up.

Liam remembered that now, parking the car and walking with Lily into the building. He had been here for many other reasons over the years. The first surgery on his arm had been done here; this was where they had brought Connor's body. He had also been here to visit Rose more than once. Both he and Lily were old hands at Melbourne General, so they bypassed the front desk and went straight up to the third-floor Pediatric ICU.

Lily seemed to be tightly wound, in control. He watched as she pushed the elevator button—purposeful yet calm. Doctors and visitors came on, pushing Lily and Liam to the back. She was just about five foot one. Maybe five one and a half in her sneakers. She wore jeans, a yellow T-shirt, and a dark blue Cape Hawk Elementary sweatshirt that zipped up the front and had a hood in back. Liam towered over her. He tried not to look down at her silky dark hair.

When the doors opened, she jostled through the crowd, with Liam right behind her. He registered people on the elevator looking at them with pity—getting off at Pediatric ICU. Lily didn't even notice. She went straight to the speaker box, mounted on the wall beside the locked ICU doors, and announced herself.

"I'm here to see my daughter, Rose Malone," she said.

"Someone will be right out to get you," the disembodied voice crackled.

The waiting room had one single window, facing the monument and reflecting pool. Several green chairs facing a television set, tuned to a talk show. Whatever was happening must have been hilarious, because the laugh track was deafening. Liam turned it down.

Lily remained standing right in front of the ICU doors, waiting for them to swing open.

"Why don't you sit down?" he asked.

"That's okay," she said, glancing over her shoulder. "Do you think she's up here yet? I just realized, they probably brought her in through the ER. Maybe we should have stopped there first."

"The nurse probably would have told you when you buzzed just now," Liam said. She was still looking at him—hadn't turned back to the door yet. Her eyes were somewhere between gray-green and gray-blue. Their color made him think of the great blue heron that lived in his pond. He watched the bird every morning, from the minute the sun rose. Lily's eyes were as still and grave and calm as the blue heron, and as beautiful, and he tried to smile with confident reassurance because they also looked so worried.

"You don't have to wait," she said. "I mean, I know you want to make sure she's okay. But after that. You have to get the commander's car back to him."

"I know," he said. "I do. But I'll wait for now. Just to see how she is."

"Okay. Right," Lily said. "Why aren't they coming to the door?"

"It's just been a minute."

"A minute's too long!"

It was the first sign that she wasn't as calm as she looked. Her voice rose, and she grimaced.

Liam went to the wall and pressed the buzzer.

"Yes?" came the voice.

"We're here to see Rose Malone."

"Yes, I know. Someone will be right—"

"Look," he said, using his shark researcher voice, the one that scared people, the one he used to get classified data out of Ottawa and Washington, and to get Harvard and Woods Hole to give him access to their mainframes. "We need someone right now. Rose's mother is out here, and Rose was airlifted out of her ninth birthday party, and her mother needs to see her *now*—okay?"

When he turned to Lily, he saw her chin wobbling, and her blue-heron eyes were creased with even more worry, and he just stood there instead of pulling her against his chest, the way he wanted to.

"They're coming," he said.

"Thank you."

Two seconds later the door opened. A tall, young nurse stood there with a clipboard. She smiled gently, as if completely unperturbed by Liam's shark voice.

"Mrs. Malone?" she asked.

"I have to see Rose," Lily said.

"Come with me," the nurse said.

Lily rushed past her, through the doors, which closed behind them. Liam stood in the green waiting room, his heart in his throat. He hadn't actually expected to go inside. That's what he told himself.

He went to stand by the window, gazing out at the monument. It was tall and narrow, elliptical, carved with deep grooves and topped with a peak. When he was three, it had seemed massive and austere. It still did. A monument to those who had served and those who had died. He could almost see himself and his father standing in its shadow; he could almost feel his three-year-old sorrow, for a great-grandfather he'd never known.

Two doctors stepped out of the elevator, both wearing white coats over green scrubs. They pressed the buzzer and were admitted to the ICU. Liam's stomach flipped, wondering whether they were here to see Rose, to talk to Lily.

When he turned back to the window, he noticed leaves on the trees, a bed of marigolds planted at the base of the monument. It was summertime. The monument's shadow was lengthening, like the day. He checked his watch—it was already seven o'clock—and as he did, he remembered another part of his great-grandfather's story, the part that involved the family left at home. The part about them waiting, about his great-grandmother not knowing whether he would ever come home again.

He thought of Lily inside the Pediatric ICU, waiting to learn what would come next for Rose. Sometimes waiting was the hardest thing of all.

The nurse, whose name was Bonnie McBeth, led Lily through the unit. There were infants and children hooked up to all kinds of machines, but Lily had eyes for no one but the girl in the second bed on the left: Rose.

The sight of her caught Lily's heart like a fishhook. Before she even saw her face, she knew it was Rose in that bed: the size of her body under the white honeycomb blanket, the funny way she always liked to hold on to the guardrail with her right hand. There were her small fingers now, holding the stainless steel rail. Lily came around the curtain and held that hand and leaned down to kiss Rose's face.

"Mommy," Rose said.

"Hi, sweetheart."

Her green eyes looked sharp at first as they looked Lily up and down, drinking her in, making sure she was really there. But then the lids flickered, up-down, and her eyes rolled back, and then focused again, and then closed. Lily knew then they were giving her morphine. She held Rose's hand a little tighter.

The machines clicked reassuringly. The IV was set. Lily examined Rose's arm, to make sure they hadn't bruised her inserting the needle. Her veins were sometimes thin and brittle, but since it had been a long time since her last IV, they were quite healthy. There were no bruises, no signs of false insertions. Lily had once gone nuts, truly insane, watching an IV technician stick Rose four times in a row without getting a vein.

While Rose slept and Lily held her hand, Bonnie McBeth stood close by. Lily glanced over at her. She had seen Bonnie on other visits, but she'd never been Rose's nurse before. Rose's main cardiologist was in Boston, so Melbourne was really only for emergencies—which, thankfully, Rose hadn't had many of recently.

"She's resting comfortably," Bonnie said in a low voice. "We gave her morphine to keep her calm. She was very agitated when she first arrived."

"Thank you," Lily said. "She had to fly by helicopter."

"That would agitate anyone," Bonnie said, smiling.

Lily nodded, still holding Rose's hand.

"Would you like to step over here, to the desk, where we can talk? I know she seems to be asleep, but . . ."

Lily hesitated. She didn't want to let go of Rose's hand. In fact, she couldn't. "It's okay," Lily said, but she was nearly whispering. "Rose is the captain of her own ship. She knows what's going on. You can tell me here."

Bonnie didn't really seem surprised. Mothers of cardiac peds patients were a tough bunch—but only half as tough as the patients themselves. Still, she pivoted away, and so did Lily, still holding Rose's hand.

"There's a note in her chart, that she's going to Boston for VSD surgery."

"Yes, she's scheduled for next week. The old patch is weakening."

"It is. We ran tests as soon as she arrived, of course. Her heart is enlarged, and her lungs are under pressure, which is why she's been cyanotic. She was able to tell us she's had some blue spells lately, and this is why."

Just then, two doctors walked over to say hello. Paul Colvin, whom Lily knew, and John Cyr, whom she didn't, explained that they were just doing rounds, and would Lily mind stepping outside the curtain.

"I'd like to stay," Lily said.

"I appreciate that," said Paul Colvin, the older doctor, a cardiac surgeon who had built a very respectable department here at Melbourne. "But we really need to ask you to step aside. Just for a few minutes." With silver hair and a steady stare, he might have intimidated a different mother. Lily shook her head, unable to let go of Rose's hand.

"Please, Doctor," she said. She didn't want to fight, and she didn't have to. He had encountered Lily before; he knew what he was up against, and let her stay.

The doctors listened with stethoscopes, checked machines, read the chart. Lily was glad it was just the two of them, and that Melbourne wasn't a teaching hospital. She thought back to when Rose was ten months old and they were in the Boston hospital, waiting for decisions to be made about surgery. Students were constantly stopping by to examine her—prodding and poking her, listening to her heart, surrounding her in their green scrubs—making her cry. Which made her turn blue.

It didn't take long for Lily—inexperienced though she was in the ways of hospital procedure—to complain to the cardiologist and put a stop to the student visits. She had learned right at the beginning how to be a mama bear, and she'd only gotten fiercer over the years.

Now, holding Rose's hand, she watched her daughter wake up, gaze at the two doctors working on her, and then look over at Lily for support. Lily squeezed her hand. Rose pressed back.

They were getting their fill of each other. The simple things. Just knowing the other was there; holding hands; smiling at each other; Rose drifting off, then waking up to see her mom at her side; Lily brushing her hair off her forehead. Soon it would be time for sleep, and Lily planned to sit in a chair beside Rose's bed.

When the doctors were done, Bonnie returned to Rose's bedside. She had the tray of medications, ready to administer. Lily felt better about leaving Rose for one minute with Bonnie than with the two doctors. While Bonnie measured out dosages, Lily walked to the desk with Drs. Colvin and Cyr.

"She's been having cyanotic episodes with increasing regularity," Dr. Colvin said, reading the chart. "She told us she had one today."

"Yes," Lily said. "It's the main reason she has surgery scheduled in Boston. To replace the patch for her VSD"—ventricular septal defect— "that they first put in when she was ten months old. Have you called her surgeon down there? Dr. Kenney?"

"Yes, as soon as she was admitted. He's aware of everything that's going on, but he's practicing in Baltimore now. He's recommending a surgeon in Boston, though, and he'd like you to call him later, after we've had a chance to finish testing her."

"What have you found so far?"

"Well, she's in congestive heart failure. She's got pulmonary edema with a substantial amount of swelling. We have her on Captopril and Lasix. I'd like to do a cardiac catheterization, to get a better idea of how her heart is functioning."

Lily was nodding—numb, in shock, on autopilot. When had she gotten used to hearing that Rose was in heart failure? It no longer punched her quite as viciously as it once had. She knew there was a finish line—the ER in Boston, where they would replace the patch and make her well again, almost good as new. If they could just get her stabilized here—and they would—Lily and Rose could keep to their plan, and the next surgery would be her last.

"When did she have the Blaylock-Taussig shunt?" Dr. Cyr asked.

"Ten months," Lily answered.

"In Boston," Dr. Colvin said.

Lily nodded, inching away, eager to get back to Rose.

"She's a fighter," Dr. Cyr said.

Those words made Lily's lips tighten, but she vowed not to explode. She had that geyser feeling—a buildup of pressure inside—that she was going to have to release somehow. Hearing about procedures sometimes had an extreme effect on her, as if the cells in her body remembered that first time Rose had had to kiss her goodbye as they wheeled her into surgery. That moment had nearly killed her, and it still did, every time she remembered it—or thought about what they had faced, and still had to face.

The doctors gave her a form to sign, which she did with a scrawl that would have done them proud. Sign fast, get back to Rose . . .

"Is that all?" she asked.

"Yes," Dr. Colvin said.

"I'd like to request that you stop the morphine," Lily said.

"She seemed rather upset when she arrived," Dr. Colvin said. "We need to keep her calm."

"Morphine makes her sick to her stomach. And she likes being more alert."

"Still, we don't want her agitated."

"I'm here with her now," Lily said. "I think that will do the trick."

The doctors both nodded, and Dr. Cyr shrugged. They didn't get it.

Lily didn't care whether they got it or not. As long as she and Rose did.

Chapter 12

Back in Cape Hawk, the party had broken up. The Nanouk Girls had loaded up their cars, driven home, fed their families, and were already on the phone or Internet, exchanging information. Plans were being made to box up Nanouk Girl care packages for both Lily and Rose—filled with yarn, canvas, books, CDs and DVDs, and photos taken at the birthday party, especially the many taken of Rose with Nanny frolicking in the background.

Anne Neill had placed Rose's birthday cake in the inn's freezer, as promised. She and Jude ate together in the dining room, amid all the hotel guests, barely able to talk or do more than pick at their food. Jude looked as if he had aged ten years since that morning.

"When Liam asked me to captain the cruise, I never expected this. Annie, have you ever seen Rose look so bad? So blue?"

"No, dear. I truly haven't."

"What does Lily say?"

"I haven't talked to her yet. Has Liam called you?"

"No, and he has his cell phone turned off. What did Lily say before the party?"

"Well, I knew that Rosie had been having some problems. But they seemed routine, given her condition, and they were going to get taken care of once and for all with the surgery she was scheduled to have in Boston."

"Is it worse than Lily thinks? You know we all love her, she's the greatest—and with such spirit, and positive attitude—but Annie . . . is she living in a dreamworld about Rose?"

"Jude, Lily once told me that she and Rose are just used to things that would scare other people. Being a cardiac patient means never knowing for sure, I guess."

"I think we should pray for them tonight," Jude said.

Anne smiled at him. She knew that he prayed for them every night already, as she did. He was her sea captain husband, straight from the wilds of maritime Canada, but he had a heart as big as the Gulf of St. Lawrence.

"All three of them," Jude continued.

"Three?"

"Yes, if you count Liam."

Anne nodded. How could they not count Liam? It was an unspoken fact that he was an intimate part of Lily's life. Probably Anne and Jude knew it better than Liam and Lily did. Probably Rose knew it better too. Never had two such guarded people come together, and with such frustrating results.

"You think they'll ever have a romance?" Jude asked. "Or is that like asking if there'll ever be palm trees in Cape Hawk?"

"I used to think palm trees were more likely," Anne said.

"Used to?"

Anne just shrugged. "Hope springs eternal."

"What do you hope for, my love?" Jude asked. He reached across the table, with its uneaten food, and covered her hand with his.

Anne whispered, "For my best friend to have a little more happiness than she's had so far in her life." When the waitress came over to clear, asking if there was something wrong with their meals, Anne was quite unable to speak.

Jude answered for both of them, saying no, everything was great, they were just still full from the birthday party. Anne thought of the uneaten birthday cake and had to reach for the starched napkin to dab her eyes. Jude took the opportunity to try Liam's cell again, but there was still no answer.

Anne looked across the table at her husband and wondered what was happening down in Melbourne.

Two days passed without any word. That night, Marisa and Jessica sat on the back porch. Cape Hawk was so far north, it stayed light hours past sunset in New England. The tips of the pine needles looked painted gold, and crickets chirped in the woods. They sat on the top step, their sides touching. Jessica hadn't smiled or said very much since Rose flew away in the helicopter.

After Rose's party, something in Marisa had given way, and she'd known that she had to be true to herself and her daughter, had to celebrate Jess's real birthday—just the two of them. What would be the harm in that? She—they—had been on guard for so long. Stopping at the grocery store earlier, Marisa had sent Jessica into the bookstore next door to pick out her summer reading choices, so Marisa could buy a cake. Now, while Jessica sat watching the stars just starting to come out in the darkening sky, Marisa went inside the kitchen.

When she came out, she was holding a cake burning with nine candles. "Happy birthday to you," she sang, and by the end of the song, Jessica was almost smiling.

"Mom, I thought we weren't having my real birthday this year."

"Well, we are. Go ahead, honey—blow out your candles. Make a wish!"

Jessica took a big breath, then blew. The nine candles went out in a rush. After today, Marisa felt extra grateful for her daughter's health, for the simple things like being able to blow out her candles. She began to cut two slices as Jessica slid the plates over.

"Know what I wished, Mom?"

"What, honey?"

"That Rose would come home soon."

"That's a good wish." Even as she said it, Marisa stopped herself. What would a bad wish be? She thought of Ted, how he would judge every single thing according to his own standards. Good wish, bad wish.

"Will she come home soon?"

"I don't know," Marisa said. "We're going to hope and pray that she does."

Jessica nodded, and together they dug into their slices of cake. Marisa felt a pang, remembering how her mother had always baked birthday cakes for her and her sister Sam. She had always made beautiful pink roses out of buttercream frosting, and written her name in pink script with a special pastry bag. What was Jessica missing, without extended family in her life?

Rose's party had felt exactly like a big family—Lily and Rose and all those strangers who by the end of the day had felt like sisters. Standing on the dock, watching Rose being loaded into the rescue copter, a woman Marisa had just met took her hand. They had all stood there, watching Rose take off in silence. Marisa and Doreen had held hands on one side, and Marisa and Jessica on the other side, and Jessica and Allie, and on down the line.

A gust of strength had entered Marisa at that moment, inspiring her to buy her daughter this birthday cake. She squeezed Jessica's shoulders and kissed the top of her head.

"It's expensive to go to the hospital, isn't it?" Jessica asked.

"Yes," Marisa said. Especially, she thought, when you're on the run and you don't have health care. She was sure Jessica was remembering falling right after they'd left Weston and having to get stitches. Marisa had had to pay with cash—health insurance was too easy to trace.

"Heart operations are a lot more expensive than stitches, right?"

"Quite a bit."

Jessica nodded. She ate her cake as the sun went down all the way, turning the forest purple, with shadows cast by the rising moon. A night bird called from the trees, long, throaty sounds that preceded the hunt.

"Mom," Jessica said, her mouth full. She chewed, swallowed, wiped her mouth. "I want to do something for Rose."

"I'm not sure she can have visitors," Marisa said, remembering the Pediatric ICU at Johns Hopkins, when she had done a rotation there, seeing all those sick children, knowing that Jessica wouldn't be allowed inside. "But I'm sure you could make her a card, and her mother would give it to her."

"I want to do more than a card."

"Like what?"

"I want to raise money for her. So she can have her operations and her mother won't have to worry or work so hard. Rose says she works all the time."

"Oh, Jess!"

"I want to make it so the hospital cures her. Makes her all well! Mom—why does Rose have to have heart defects? Why did she turn so blue?" Jessica asked, starting to sob. "I don't want her to die!"

Marisa pulled her onto her lap, rocking her and trying to soothe her. Jessica cried with unbridled grief—the way she had when her father died, and when she saw her puppy killed. Marisa's own eyes filled. She thought of all the sick children she had worked with, of the pain she had felt seeing them suffer. She had worked on learning detachment—it was taught in nursing school, but she had had to get extra help from groups and friends. It was the hardest thing she'd ever done, and it escaped her right now.

Holding Jessica, she wished she could soothe the anguish of losing her father, seeing Rose so sick, watching Ted kill Tally. Marisa knew that she would do anything to protect her daughter, keep her from the harshest realities of life. She thought back to the nursery, nine years ago today, when she had held her daughter in her arms, wrapped in a pink blanket. The baby had been so tiny; the blanket so soft. Yet Marisa's memory of the moment was ferocious—she felt love so enormous, she knew she would do anything to protect her baby.

She had once wondered whether she could ever love anyone enough to die for them. Jump into freezing water to save them, step in front of a wild animal, give up her life. Holding her baby, all doubt had been removed. Sitting on the back porch now, she remembered the feeling of love that had come over her, all the promises she had made to protect her tiny daughter from anything or anyone who ever tried to harm her.

Yet she couldn't protect Jessica from this: the terrible hurt she felt to see her best friend suffering.

"Mom?" Jessica asked now, wiping her eyes. "Will Rose die?"

"Her mother is doing everything she can to make sure she doesn't. She has excellent care."

"But you don't know?"

Marisa shook her head. She stared into Jessica's brown eyes, smoothed the hair from her high forehead, thinking of Jessica's father. His death had hit them both so hard, and she could hardly bear that Jessica had to go through the same kind of worry about Rose. "No, honey. We don't know."

"So many bad things happen," Jessica whispered. "Like when Ted kicked Tally downstairs, just because she was barking."

"Good things too, Jess. I want you to think about the good things."

"I have to help Rose," Jessica said, jumping up from the step as if she couldn't bear to waste even one minute.

"Honey—we can pray for her. Make her cards . . ."

Jessica shook her head. "That's not enough. I want to raise money, so Rose can be cured. I don't want her to die, like Daddy did, or Tally. I'm going to start now." She had been powerless to save her puppy, but she wasn't going to turn her back on her friend.

Marisa nodded. The screen door shut behind Jessica, leaving Marisa alone on the porch. Her thoughts were racing. Maybe it was the big event of her daughter's birthday here in hiding, or maybe it was the shock of seeing Rose taken to the hospital. She knew, from her rotation on psychiatric units, that old trauma could be triggered by the oddest things. From experience, after living with Ted, she knew how easily she went numb, shut down, wanted to pull the covers over her head. Those had been her old ways.

But something new was happening. She felt a ripple run through her body, like a river under her skin. She thought of Paul, Jessica's father, and suddenly shivered, feeling alive in the cool sea air. The bird called from the woods again, announcing itself to the night. As Marisa watched, it rose on wide, silent wings, beating high over the ground. She heard its wing beats as it flew up, and saw its yellow eyes: an owl.

For the months since April, when she and Jessica had left home, she had felt like a hunted creature. Change of name, change of home, change, even, of country. She had packed up her daughter and taken her away from every single thing that mattered to them. How many sleepless nights had she felt guilty for doing that to her daughter? Hugging her pillow every night, she had prayed for Paul to forgive her.

Tonight, it felt as if he had. Marisa felt her strength returning. Holding hands with the Nanouk Girls, seeing their love for Lily, and knowing that Lily understood, somehow, what Marisa and Jessica were going through—all those factors had changed Marisa today.

So when she saw that owl—with its hot gold eyes and killer talons—instead of feeling afraid, being reminded that she and Jessica were hunted by a man she still, crazily, wanted to understand—she felt thrilled and powerful. Ted had wormed his way into her life, pretending to help her invest the money Paul had left them. He had known Paul from business and golfing, and he had used that to win Marisa's trust. He had traded on Paul's friendship to work his way into Marisa and Jessica's life.

The problem was, Paul hadn't known Ted. Not really. Not like Marisa did. Life sometimes handed people strange, dangerous gifts. Ted had done terrible damage to the people Paul had loved most. She closed her eyes, listening for the owl, and she thought of herself and Jessica, Lily and Rose. She was beginning to see clearly now.

Jessica went into her bedroom and stared up at the crucifix. She made the sign of the cross. Then she went over to the statue of Mary—the one she loved the most, because she had several. This was Mary with her blue robe and crown of yellow stars, standing barefoot on a snake. Jessica stared down at the snake—which was very scary. Its mouth was unhinged and wide open, with yellow fangs and a pink throat. But Mary had killed it by stepping on it with her bare feet. Jessica had to check every time—that the snake was still dead. She kissed Mary's face.

Then she picked up *The Lion, the Witch, and the Wardrobe*. It was her and Rose's favorite book. She loved it for its magic, secrets, evil, and, especially, goodness. She thought probably Rose loved it for the same reasons, but in the way of newly nine-year-old girls, they had never talked about it.

Looking through the book—a hardcover edition her aunt Sam had bought her for Christmas two years ago—she found a picture of Aslan, the kind, wise lion. Jessica stared into his sad, knowing eyes and felt her heart tapping in her chest. She touched his picture and thought of Rose needing help and said, "Daddy."

In the book, Aslan let himself be attacked and killed, so the children and all the inhabitants of Narnia—the magical, secret world on the other side of the wardrobe door—could live free. When he rose from the stone table and came back to life, Jessica always felt chills and a little rush of tears—as if she couldn't believe that something so brave and true could happen.

Before Ted, Jessica had believed in brave and true. Her own father was like Aslan. He had died, and the last thing he said to Jessica was, "I'll be looking down from heaven, taking care of you and your mother. I'll never really be gone, sweetheart. I'll be looking over you. Call me when you need me." Jessica had held on to his hand as long as she could, till the doctor and her mother had pried her away. Then her mother had had some private time with him, and then he died.

Ted came along right after that. Well, maybe almost a year after that—but to Jessica, it had seemed fast. She could still smell her father in his closet, she knew that. She could stand in the dark, with her head in his suits, with her eyes closed, and bring him back. The smell of his sweat and cigarettes and just *him* was all around her. She would stand there and remember what he had told her: *I'll never really be gone. . . . I'll be looking over you and your mother. . . .*

And Jessica would breathe in his scent and know that he had spoken the truth. He was right there with her, protecting her. She liked the door to be partly closed, so no one would see her in the closet; it was her time alone with him. She would stand in a different spot each day. Although the closet was quite small, it seemed like a whole world—just like the wardrobe in the book.

Jessica would go through her father's pockets, one suit at a time. He had been a businessman who valued looking good. So he had seven suits and five sports coats, with lots of slacks. His pockets were like treasure to her. At first, before she had gone through them all, the things she found were thrilling and magical. A few coins, a business card, his tarnished silver Saint Christopher medal, a stray Rolaid, torn bits of foil from a pack of cigarettes, his mother's mass card.

After a time, some of the magic began to wear off. She would look in the left pocket of his glen plaid suit and know that she would find his money clip, matches, and appointment calendar. Or she would reach into the back pocket of his green golf pants and there would be a grass-stained tee and a short yellow pencil for keeping score. Standing on tiptoes to feel inside the breast pocket of his summer-weight blue blazer, she would find her kindergarten school picture and a pocket rosary.

Even without the excitement and anticipation of not knowing what she would find, spending time in her father's suits was the happiest Jessica felt during that time. She could smell her father's smell and know that he had been here, on this earth. That he wasn't just an angel or ghost looking down from heaven—but that he had walked and talked and saved her kindergarten picture and worn nice suits and sometimes forgotten to empty his pockets. Sometimes she'd stand there in the crush of wool blend and summer cotton and tell him about her day, and she would hear him talk back.

Once her mother opened the closet door while Jessica was in there. Jessica had held her breath, so her mother wouldn't see her there. Not because she'd thought her mother would be mad, but because she thought she might be sad—even at seven, Jessica had known how bad her mother would feel to see her there among her father's suits. But she needn't have worried; her mother had just stood there for a few minutes, and then she'd closed the door and walked away.

Maybe her mother liked to do the same thing, Jessica had thought—go back in time and remember how happy they had all once been, when he was still alive to wear all those beautiful suits. Maybe being near his suits made her mother able to hear his voice, just like Jessica did.

Then Ted had come.

Her father had known him from golf. Ted became his stockbroker, and he did a good job investing some of her family's money. Jessica remembered hearing her parents talking about Ted so often—"We couldn't do it without Ted," her father had said again and again about his business expansion. "He's a godsend," her mother had said. Oh, Ted had sounded like the family miracle. He had helped her father afford a new office for his title search company in downtown Boston—instead of out of the way, in Dorchester. The money had helped buy a new computer system, hire more people, and provide health insurance.

Jessica remembered wondering about Ted, before she met him. How did stocks work? Why would the family pick someone they barely knew and give him their money to grow? It had seemed almost unbelievably wonderful and benevolent. Could someone's job really be to oversee a family's savings and help them earn more? She asked her father once, and he told her, "He's a smart man, honey. He went to the best schools to learn business, and he only chooses stocks that he thinks will make money."

"But he's nice, right?" she had asked, unable to conceive of Ted's role in their lives any other way.

Her father had laughed. "Yes, he's a great guy. Everyone likes Ted. He has a lot of friends, and he's the vice president of the Rotary Club in the town where he lives."

Jessica didn't know what the Rotary Club was, but she thought it sounded very exciting. Her father's words made sense to Jessica. Ted had to be a great guy. Money was hard to come by—her parents worried about things like their mortgage, and car bills, building the business, and a college education for her when the time came. If they trusted Ted with their savings, then Jessica trusted him too. Her father once said that he was "as generous as they come," because of his volunteer work with poor kids.

Now, staring at the lion's sad face in *The Lion, the Witch, and the Wardrobe,* Jessica took a deep breath. She wished Aslan could come out of the book and talk to her. She wished her father would come down from heaven and tell her what to do. If Ted was "as generous as they come," Jessica wasn't sure she should try to raise money for Rose. She didn't want to be anything like Ted.

The problem was, she knew her father couldn't talk to her anymore. Not since that day, right after Ted had moved in. Jessica had come home from school and gone to the closet—not because she was upset or anything about Ted. Maybe just a little upset—but mainly, she just wanted to talk to her father the way she always did. It was spring, and she had caught a fly ball in baseball.

She had the baseball with her. Her mother and Ted were in the kitchen. She could have showed it to them, but instead she ran by, up the stairs, to her father's closet. And she opened the door, and—

All his suits were gone.

Instead, Ted's clothes were in there. Suits and jackets and pants and coats and his robe. Even now, remembering that moment, Jessica felt her chest cave in. She touched her heart and sat down on the bed. Staring at Aslan's face, she sobbed silently. *Mary, Jesus, God . . .* Seeing Rose turn blue and fly away to the hospital had brought it all back. People she loved going away. Her father, Rose . . . Her father had never really gone away, not until the day Ted and her mother threw his suits out.

"Tell me what to do," she whispered now, getting onto her knees.

Outside, the owls were hunting and calling. She had heard them every night since the snow melted. Sometimes she listened extra hard—as if she might be able to understand what they were saying. She stared at the picture in her favorite book, and listened for the owls, and she was sort of praying, but she was really asking her father.

If ever there was a day for him to come back to her, it was now: her real birthday.

Ted had chased him away. And because of Ted, she now had a pretend name, a pretend birthday, and a pretend story. Only her father knew who she really was. Only he could handle her huge requests. Her mother had once been able to, but those days had ended. Her mother was just a ghost now—a skinny, scared, scarred ghost left behind by Ted. She and Jessica were just bones spit out by the wild animal they had let into their lives.

Ted had often seemed so angry. Then he had killed her puppy, Tally. Jessica had thought he wanted to kill her and her mother too. He wasn't generous at all. Her father hadn't been wrong about much, but he had been wrong about that. That was Jessica's first request tonight:

"Daddy, don't be mad, but you were wrong. Ted wasn't generous. He came to hurt us; that's all he wanted. He took everything we had. Well, almost."

An owl called out in the woods, and Jessica smiled—her father answering her.

"Help me to help Rose—please, Dad? I don't want her to go to heaven yet. Help me, Dad. I want to keep her with me. I want her to live." She pictured her father standing in heaven with Saint Agatha and Saint Agnes and Joan of Arc.

And the owl screeched again, and a branch crashed to the ground, and Jessica knew: she had her inspiration. When the sun came up, she would go into the woods. And she would come out with secret treasure, to earn money for Rose.

Chapter 13

Getting Rose stabilized enough to travel to Boston was the goal, so that was all Lily could think of. Liam had gotten them two rooms at the Holiday Inn on the harbor, just down the hill from the hospital. She told him he should go back home, and he said he would as soon as Rose was out of the ICU. Meanwhile, he had arranged with his friend to keep the car indefinitely. And he could do his monitoring work on his laptop.

Lily shrugged. She didn't know what he was hanging around for. She barely even saw him, and because he wasn't a relative, he wasn't allowed into the unit to see Rose. She knew she should be appreciative of his support, but honestly—she was so exhausted and ragged by the time she got to her room each night, she barely had the energy to order soup from room service and eat it in front of the TV.

The first four mornings, she found him in the hotel lobby, waiting to drive her up the hill to Melbourne General. The weather was cool and foggy, with morning mist hovering over the water and town. They took the five-minute ride in silence, with Lily staring over the silver-coated harbor, thinking of questions for Rose's medical team.

On the fifth morning, the fog had lifted, and the sun shone brightly. When Lily entered the hotel lobby, Liam rose to greet her. She held up her hand.

"Look, this is silly," she said. "It's nice out. No more fog. I'm going to walk up to the hospital, and I think you should go back to Cape Hawk."

"It is a nice morning for a walk," he agreed.

"I'm glad you see it my way."

"Good. I'll walk you," he said.

"No! Liam," she said. "You have work to do, back home. The commander needs his car back. Rose is improving."

"She's still in the ICU," he said.

"I think they might release her to a regular pediatric floor today," Lily said. "She's so much better—the fluid around her heart is almost gone, and her lungs are nearly back to normal size."

"The Lasix is working," he said.

"Yes," Lily said, a little surprised by the fact he knew the name of Rose's diuretic, or even that she was taking one. She hardly ever talked details with anyone not a doctor.

"So, they might move her to the floor today?" he asked.

"Yes," Lily said.

"Good," he said. He nodded, smiling. Lily thought she could see the relief in his eyes—his self-imposed burden, whatever it was, had been lifted, and he could go back to the sharks and whales of Cape Hawk. They grinned at each other easily, among the hustle and bustle of the busy hotel lobby. He touched her arm as they walked out into the sunlight.

"Okay then," she said. "Thank you—for everything. Will you thank Anne for sending me that bag of my clothes? Tell her the laundry delivery guy was a brilliant idea—he delivered it when he brought the tablecloths to the hotel."

"Maybe you should just call her yourself," Liam said.

Huh? Lily thought. Was it really too much trouble for him to give his sister-in-law Lily's message? "No problem," she said. "I just thought you'd probably see her at the inn."

"I will, when I get there. But not today . . ."

"But you're heading home."

Liam shook his head. "No," he said. "Not till Rose is okay."

"Liam!"

"Don't even argue with me, Lily," he said. "Like it or not, I'm staying. Come on—if you don't want a ride, I'll walk you up to the hospital. Let's go—I know you want to catch the doctors on their morning rounds."

Lily opened her mouth to speak, but instead she just started walking up the steep hill that led to Melbourne General. Liam walked silently by her side. Even in the city, there was no doubt that they were in Nova Scotia. The scent of pine filled the air, and the sound of ship traffic—bells, horns, engines—wafted up from the harbor. Seagulls cried overhead. She thought back nine years, to her first days in Nova Scotia. Liam had been with her then too.

"Why are you doing this?" she asked.

"You know why," he said.

"It doesn't make sense. Not after all this time."

"It does to me."

"Look—I know what you said. I think your words are engraved on my heart. I'll be forever grateful. But that was a long time ago."

"Do you think time invalidates promises?" Liam asked.

And Lily had no answer for that. At least, not one she felt like saying out loud. The truth was, she did think time—and other things—invalidated promises. The world was full of evidence supporting just that: broken marriages, broken vows, changes of mind, changes of heart. It was easier to break promises than keep them, that was for sure.

The hill became so steep, her calves began to ache. They passed people walking down the hill, to work. The city park crowned this crest, and they entered between two stone gates. Traffic flowed into Melbourne through the park, coming from points north. As they walked along, they passed a long row of cars. For years now, Lily had been free of the habit of scanning—looking at every face and license plate while trying to keep her own face hidden. She almost wished she'd be seen sometimes—during certain sleepless nights, she actually longed, ached, for a final confrontation.

They walked briskly along a lane that led through the park's rose gardens. The air smelled sweetly of flowers and freshly tended earth. Lily thought of her own garden, which was inspired by the roses of her childhood. Rose loved digging, planting, pruning—and sometimes, when Rose was sick, unable to do more than lie in a hospital bed, Lily took comfort in thinking of rosebushes—how they had to stay dormant all winter, in order to bloom in summer. Rose would bloom again too.

Suddenly she realized that Liam wasn't walking beside her anymore. She stopped, turned, saw him standing still. Her first instinct was to be impatient—she literally didn't have time to stop and smell the roses. The doctors were making their rounds now, and she needed to catch them.

"What are you doing?" she asked, walking back.

But Liam didn't reply. He was just standing there, gazing over the roses and through the pine trees, to a pond in the woods. Lily tried to follow his gaze. She saw that the pond was ringed with tall, green marsh grass. The water was dark and appeared greenish-brown in the shadows of tall pines and oaks. At the other end of the pond was the World War I monument. In fact, Lily realized that its reflecting pool must be fed by this wilder, more rustic body of water.

"Liam, what are you looking at?" she asked.

"There," he said, pointing. "You have to look carefully. She's hiding in the shadows."

It was a blue heron, standing on the very edge of the pond. The bird was tall and almost unimaginably still—it might have been a statue. The morning sun shone through the trees and grass, silhouetting the long legs, long curved neck, sharp bill. The heron's posture was perfect and vigilant—as if waiting for something more important than anything in the world.

"She's so camouflaged," he said. "She wants to make sure no one sees her till she's ready."

"Why do you say 'she'?" Lily asked.

"I don't know," Liam said, looking her straight in the eye.

"It could be a male."

"I guess it could."

"Liam, there are plenty of herons back home. What's so special about this one?"

He gazed down at her. He had dark blue eyes with lines around them that made him look tired and worried. Yet the eyes themselves were bright as a young boy's, especially in this morning light. Lily blinked and frowned.

"She's in the middle of a city park," he said. "Don't you think that's amazing?"

"A city park in Nova Scotia," she said, "is not the same as a city park somewhere else. But you're a scientist," she continued, and shrugged. "I guess it's your job to catalogue natural phenomena."

"When you put it that way," he said, staring at her even more intently, "I suppose you're right."

"Come on," she said impatiently. "Can we hurry up, please?"

"Natural phenomenon," he said under his breath.

Lily felt a breeze swirl up the hill from the harbor. It came across the pond, through the trees, making the boughs and grasses rustle; it ruffled Lily's hair, and although it was warm, it made her shiver. The heron didn't stir, and neither did Liam. He was still staring at Lily, and he wouldn't look away.

"Come on," she said again. "I'm late."

"I know," he said.

And something about the way he said those words, "I know," made her shiver again. And she began to run, the rest of the way through the park, to the front steps of Melbourne General Hospital. She joined the flood of health care workers—doctors, nurses, aides, therapists—streaming through the double doors. There weren't many patients' parents in this flood—it was much too early for visiting hours.

The security guard noticed Lily, without an ID badge, and he signaled her to stop. She had wasted too much time already, so she just waved at him and jumped into the next elevator. Out of the corner of her eye, she caught sight of Liam—stopping to be grilled by the guard.

Oddly, as the doors closed, Lily felt a pang.

She was crushed in with twenty other people, and Liam wasn't one of them. He had walked her all the way up the steep hill, shown her the heron, accepted her slightly insulting comment about his cataloguing of natural phenomena. The funny thing was, she felt that he was the one making an inside joke. She didn't get it.

And she didn't get why she felt so sorry that she'd gotten on the elevator without him. He had come all this way with her. He was trying so hard to keep that stupid promise she'd never wanted him to make in the first place. Maybe this would give him the hint: he was off the hook. As far as she was concerned, she'd never wanted him on it.

So why did she feel so bad about the fact that he was no longer at her side? She shook the feeling and stepped off on Rose's floor, the Pediatric ICU.

Chapter 14

"Excuse me," the security guard said. "But may I see your ID?"

"ID?" Liam asked, watching the elevator doors close behind Lily.

"Your work badge, for here at the hospital."

"Oh," Liam said. "I don't work here."

"Well, sir, visiting hours don't begin until eleven. It's only eight forty-five now. Doctors have to make their rounds."

"I'm here to see someone in the Pediatric ICU," Liam said. "I think the visiting hours are more flexible up there."

"Yes, they are, sir. Family member?"

"Well, no. Close family friend."

"Sir, only family members are allowed in that unit. We have very strict rules about that. Very strict."

Liam nodded. He knew better than to argue with a security guard—he did. But he had to get up there, had to be with Lily and Rose. He nodded toward the elevator. "I'm with that woman, who just took that last car."

"The small dark-haired woman who ignored me? Shrugged me off?" the guard asked, raising his eyebrows.

"Uh, maybe."

"That one. That one ignores me every morning. It's like I'm not even here. That's right, I've seen you with her before. I took notice of you, on account of—" He stopped himself.

"My arm," Liam said. "Don't worry about it."

"Well, I caught you this morning. One of you, anyway."

Yeah, the one of us that's not a natural phenomenon, Liam thought, picturing Lily weaving through the crowded lobby like a waterspout. High velocity, with the speed of a tornado and even more force. Touching down just long enough to gain more strength from the water's surface, then whirling on her way to Rose.

"You're welcome to wait in the lobby for your friend," the guard said sternly. "But I can't allow you up on the unit without a special pass."

"How would I get one?"

"From a doctor. As well as permission from a parent of the patient. It's best you just wait here."

"Right," Liam said. "Thanks."

But instead, he walked back outside. He crossed the street, went over to the reflecting pool, looked up at the monument. He touched it with his good hand, thought of how strange it was that a big piece of stone would outlast so many of the people he loved: his parents, Connor. Now he gazed down the length of the pool, to the pond at the far end. He peered into the shadows, looking for the heron.

If she was there, she was too well hidden for him to see.

Lily hadn't wanted to pause long enough to look. Forces of nature were like that. They were too busy fulfilling their purpose. Hurricanes, waterspouts, heat waves, Lily Malone. Nothing was going to keep her from Rose for two seconds—not even the poetry of a blue heron, the same color as Lily's own eyes, in this city park.

Liam walked slowly along the west side of the long reflecting pool. He stayed in the shade—not because the sun was so hot, but because he wanted to stay hidden. He, his brother, and Jude had prided themselves on being able to sneak up on wildlife. They could swim silently into a pod of fin whales and not even disturb them. Connor had once swum up to a beluga and touched her dorsal ridge. And they had tracked a pair of snowy owls one winter solstice, crawling to within fifteen feet of them.

He had his cell phone on vibrate, and checked it to be sure: he hoped Lily would at least call him if there was some change.

The idea of Lily as a force of nature was not new to him. In fact, it had inspired their entire unbalanced, undefined, and completely confusing relationship. He thought back nine years, to the first time he'd ever seen her.

She had driven into town in a rusty old Volvo, with holes in the floor and the hood literally held down by baling wire. She had cut her hair very short, she wore glasses, then, that she hadn't really needed. Since his family basically ran Cape Hawk, her first encounter had been with Camille, his aunt, the family grande dame and owner of Neill Real Estate. Lily had been looking for a place to live. It had seemed odd enough to Camille—a pretty, young, and, oh yes, extremely pregnant woman, obviously American, looking for a house in Cape Hawk—to discuss at the family Friday night dinner. Although she was clearly trying to hide her pregnancy with bulky clothes, it was obvious to everyone.

"Cheap," Camille reported. "She actually said that was her main requirement."

"Where's her husband?" Jude, Camille's son, had asked.

"He's a fisherman," Camille said. "Gone for weeks at a time."

"What boat?"

"That's precisely what I asked. She was vague, to say the least. Do you think he's a drug smuggler?"

"Probably runs the maritime heroin trade," Liam said. He hadn't wanted to attend the dinner—he never did—but tonight his aunt had insisted. Sitting next to Anne, he felt her jab his side with her elbow. But she connected with his hard prothesis, so the whole table heard the crack.

"Don't be fresh, Liam," Camille said, giving her daughter-in-law an evil look. "As a matter of fact, this is why I wanted you to be here tonight."

"Because of my expertise with drug smugglers?"

"No. Because she is looking for something cheap, and I thought of that cabin on the back end of your property."

Liam's stomach churned. The building had started out as a shack—it had been his and Connor's fort, when they were kids. Two rooms that, over the years, his parents had turned into a fairly decent guest cottage.

"I thought you might rent it to her. But first, I thought you should meet her. If you get a bad feeling, or sense that there is indeed something suspicious about her and her husband—well then, we'll find something else. Do you know what I think?"

"No," Anne said. "Please, tell us, Camille."

"I think there is no husband. I think she's an unwed mother!"

"How vile," Anne said.

Now it was Liam's turn to jab her. But Camille took her seriously and nodded gravely. "Precisely. I think she may have moved to Canada to take advantage of our health system. The States' is so abysmal. I don't like the idea of supporting anything like fraud. . . ."

"But it's better than a drug dealer husband," Liam said.

"So true, my dear. Well then—I leave it to you. She is staying right here at the inn. Room 220. Will you take her to see the property?"

"Don't forget your revolver," Jude said. "Just in case."

"Don't you be fresh," his mother said, then hailed the waitress to clear their dessert plates.

As Liam prepared to go to room 220, Anne stopped him.

"It was nice to have you at dinner tonight. Jude was just saying, you've been such a stranger."

"It's hard to resist a Friday night with Camille," Liam grinned.

"I know. I find it's the centerpiece of my week," Anne said. "I think her whole problem comes from the fact that when she married Frederic, her name became Camille Neill. That's quite a handle. It sounds a little like something out of a comedy skit."

They chuckled, glancing around to make sure Camille's spies—her favorite waitstaff and chambermaids—weren't listening.

"Seriously," Anne said. "Where have you been? Have you fallen madly in love with that girl shark researcher who came up last summer?"

Liam shook his head. "No. She was just a colleague from Halifax."

"She was pretty. And she liked you, Liam. Jude and I both noticed."

"Hmm," Liam said.

"Well, at least you're not growling at me, the way you usually do when I try to ask about your love life. I wish you had more of one. You're my favorite in-law."

"Same to you," he said. "Now, I'd better go do my duty."

"Oh, right. Vetting the mysterious unwed drug dealer."

Liam had gone down the hall, not knowing what to expect, just wanting to get the whole thing over with. The hotel was big, rambling, with two long wings. Room 220 was all the way at the end of one, on the second floor. It was on the side of the hotel that faced the employees' parking lot, instead of looking out at Cape Hawk bay.

He knocked—no answer. So he tried again. He checked his watch—it was eight-thirty. Could she already be asleep? There wasn't much to do after dinner in Cape Hawk. Perhaps she had taken a walk. He leaned closer to the door. Small sounds were coming from inside.

Holding his breath, he listened. At first he thought it was the TV. A high thin voice came through the door. It sounded unnatural for a human—more like the keening of a seabird. Or the singing of a whale, picked up on hydrophones. But the sound did something to Liam's heart that made him realize that the source was very human after all, that it was the woman crying.

Liam had heard crying like that only once before: his mother, the day Connor died. He raised his hand to knock again, but stopped himself. The stranger's grief was too terrible and private to disturb. So he backed away, deciding to return the next morning.

He didn't have to.

Camille left him a message at his office: *"Never mind about the rental. She has found lodging elsewhere."*

Liam felt relieved. Whatever had been going on inside that room was too much for him. He had spent the night wondering what was wrong—and he warned himself that he couldn't get involved. Not that that would be so hard; not getting involved was what Liam did best. Just ask the Halifax shark researcher Anne had mentioned. Julie Grant. She still sent him letters—or did, until the last one, where she'd said, "Call me when you realize that people are better to spend time with than sharks. I thought we had a chance, but now I know I'm wrong. Goodbye."

Liam had learned that it was easier on the heart to stay distant from people—even, or especially, the ones he cared most about. After Connor's death, his mother had disappeared. Not in body, but in spirit. She had gotten quieter, lonelier, more distant, until it was just her and the bottle. No matter how hard Liam had tried to bring her back to life, remind her she still had a son, she wouldn't listen. When he had gone for surgeries on his arm, his father had dropped him off. His mother couldn't even bear to visit the hospital where Connor had been pronounced dead.

Now, walking the length of the reflecting pool, Liam looked over his shoulder at that same hospital. Lily and Rose were in there now. Lily's way of being a mother was so different, outwardly at least, from his mother's. Inwardly, he suspected they were exactly the same. Two women who loved their ailing children so much, it controlled every aspect of their lives.

The heron was right there—where he had seen her with Lily. Walking quietly in the shadows, Liam took a few steps closer. The heron didn't move. She held her elegant pose, blue neck craned, yellow bill pointed downward. The pond seemed as still as glass, but the heron saw movement and in one swift shot lunged, stabbed, came up with a silver fish.

Liam watched her swallow; when she was finished, she resumed her pose. He felt the surge and amazement of watching nature at work—much the way he felt watching Lily the natural phenomenon.

He figured the security guard had to take a break at some point, and in any case, regular visiting hours would soon commence.

So he turned and headed back toward the hospital, to keep the promise Lily had never even wanted him to make, wished he wouldn't keep, just because he really didn't feel he had a choice.

Rose had defied plenty of odds in her day, and today was no exception. By the time her mother arrived, she had already been moved onto a pediatric surgical floor. She was breathing well, and she'd lost five pounds of fluid, and her heart and lungs and all her organs were going back to normal size. So why was it so hard for her to even smile? Even a little smile seemed almost impossible.

"What's wrong, honey?" her mother asked, standing beside her bed.

"Nothing."

"Are you sure? You look upset."

Rose tried to make her lips turn up. It wasn't a real smile—it didn't come from inside. But she didn't want her mother to be worried. The doctors and therapists were always telling her that her feelings were *fine,* and that she should *honor* them, even when the feelings were unwanted: unhappy, sad, angry, hurt, things like that. But the one thing Rose couldn't bear was seeing her mother with those worry lines in her forehead—so she faked a smile.

"Mom," she said. "Did you see Dr. Colvin?"

"Yes. He told me you're making great improvements. And I know he talked to Dr. Garibaldi in Boston, to discuss how soon you can go there."

"I don't want to go to Boston, Mom."

"But, honey—"

Rose clenched her fists. The tips of her fingers were numb; they were always numb because her heart didn't pump enough blood fast enough. She had funny-looking little fingertips, almost like tiny paddles. She tried to keep the pretend smile on her face, but inside, she was melting.

"It's summer," she said. "Jessica's first summer in Cape Hawk. I've already been to the hospital now. I knew I had to go, and I had it planned, but now this is it. This is my hospital time. I want to have fun, Mom. Fun with Jessica."

"I know, sweetheart. And you will. That's what the surgery is for—to replace the patch, so you'll be able to have all the fun in the world."

Rose just stared. She wanted to believe her mother. She had been in so many hospital beds over the years. She remembered a time when she was five, and she'd had a valve replacement, and developed endocarditis—a bacterial infection that attacks people with heart problems. She spent months in the hospital, taking in antibiotics through her veins, which practically ruined her kidneys and liver and made her hair dry out. She had looked like a straw doll.

"Jessica will make a different best friend," she said.

"No, she won't."

"How do you know?"

"Because who could be a better best friend than you?"

"Someone who isn't in the hospital."

"Honey, why are you so down?"

Rose took some deep breaths, but it was getting harder to keep the smile on her face. How could she not be down? Her birthday party had been so wonderful, magical—and then Rose's heart had given out. The drugs were stabilizing her now, but she felt groggy all the time. And instead of getting to spend the summer in Cape Hawk, now she was going to have to go to another hospital—the big one in Boston. Jessica would probably just forget about her.

"That was a pretty stupid question, right?" her mother asked.

"No," Rose said. "It wasn't stupid. I'm sorry."

"Rose, never be sorry. You've been through so much, and we just keep asking you to go through more and more. No wonder you're—"

Her mother's voice was shaking, and she sounded so down herself that Rose thought she was going to start to cry. But just then, looking over her mother's shoulder, she saw something framed in the doorway that brought a true smile to her face—the first one she'd had all day.

Dr. Neill stood in the doorway, holding a huge bunch of balloons. Every bright color, just like a rainbow.

"Dr. Neill!" she said.

"Hi, Rose," he said, walking straight over to her, bending down to stroke her forehead. "How's my girl?"

"I'm glad you're here," she said, almost unable to believe her eyes. Why hadn't her mother mentioned it?

"Of course I'm here. You're a wonder, Rose. I thought you were still in the ICU, but when I asked at the desk, they told me you were here."

"You've been at the hospital since I got here?" Rose asked.

He nodded. Rose gave her mother a surprised look, and her mother just stood there trying to appear innocent.

"What about Nanny, and all the other whales and sharks? Aren't you supposed to be keeping watch over them?"

"Nanny told me this was more important."

"Whales don't talk!"

"Well, Nanny and I speak a certain language," he said. "It's hard to explain, to people who don't speak it. . . ."

Rose reached out. She touched his prothesis with one of her clubbed fingers. She felt a spark inside.

"I think I speak it too."

"So do I," he said.

"I'm feeling left out," her mother said. "Herons, whales. Could someone speak human to me?" Rose heard her, but this moment was completely between her and Dr. Neill. She knew that he understood being in the hospital, fearing that she might never get better, that she'd always be different. She held up her index finger. He stared at it, the way it broadened at the tip. She saw him look at the IV needle in the back of her hand. She even saw him look at the catheter that ran from her to the bag beside the bed, and she didn't feel embarrassed. She wanted him to pick her up, as if he were her father.

"I'm not happy today," she said.

"No," he said.

"I'm scared."

He nodded. He crouched down by the side of her bed and looked into her eyes. The balloons bobbed over his head. He tried to tie the strings to her bed rails, but he couldn't with one hand. Rose helped him out. Their fingers touched, and she smiled. She was still scared, but having him there made her feel like smiling anyway.

"You brought me balloons," she said.

"Yes, I did."

"I thought balloons were bad. Because if you let go of the string, they might float out over the ocean, and fall, and the sea turtles will think they're jellyfish, and eat them, and die."

"You're right, Rose. You make a very good oceanographer. That's why I knew it was safe to give the balloons to you."

"Because I care about the sea turtles?"

"Yes," he said, holding her hand. "Because of that."

Rose closed her eyes and felt her pulse beating fast and light. She thought of how everything had to be protected, in different ways. Her mother had to be protected from worry; the sea turtles had to be protected from balloons; Rose had to be protected from being so scared of what would happen next.

What did Dr. Neill have to be protected from? She didn't know. But she knew that there had to be something, and she squeezed his hand to let him know that she was there.

Chapter 15

The hot weather arrived in Cape Hawk, making it seem more like the summers Jessica knew. Every morning, haze clung to the cliffs and pines before burning off. Sunlight beat down, the breeze stopped blowing. Jessica wore shorts over her bathing suit, but instead of going to the swim cove, she was hard at work.

She held the burlap bag in one hand, picked up fallen pine needles with the other. This was messy work—her fingers were sticky with pitch, but she just pressed onward. Bent at the waist, she made her way through her backyard, covering every inch. She ignored fallen leaves or twigs, concentrating only on long needles fallen from white pines.

Sometimes she'd pass under a hemlock or spruce—trees with short needles. Those were fine too, as long as they were pine. She found many pinecones—tiny ones that looked like doll-size beehive ovens. The hemlock cones were perfect and compact, with their petals drawn in tight like rosebuds. When she found them, she slipped them into a different bag, slung over her shoulder. White-pine cones were longer, with their tips frosted with silvery pitch. She ignored those.

As she scoured her backyard and the lower fringe of the hilly woods behind her house, she thought of Rose. What was she doing now? Was she getting better? Last night one of the Nanouks had called her mother, and she'd heard them talking. The report had been the same: *Rose is holding her own*, which didn't sound bad but definitely didn't sound all that good, either. Then, afterwards, Jessica had watched her mother go online, to the Johns Hopkins site, and do some researchy thing with a worried crease in her brow.

Jess tried to tell herself that what the grownups thought didn't matter. She was working for Rose. Her back ached and fingers itched, but she didn't care. Back in Boston she had gone to Catholic school, and the nuns had told them about Saint Agnes and Saint Agatha, as well as

Joan of Arc: all young girls, martyrs, who had suffered for the Lord. Tales of hair shirts and beds of nails and being beheaded. Jessica had thought it sounded pretty lame at first. Especially hair shirts. She couldn't quite imagine such a thing; was it like a fur coat, only a shirt?

But then she had started thinking: maybe martyrdom could be a way to go—not beheading, but the other things. A lot of the problems those old saints had had involved demons. One Irish nun that kind of scared her, Sister Ignatius, had loved to tell them stories about the devil. "Lucifer is incarnate on this earth," she would say in her squeaky Wicklow accent. "He exists as surely as you or I. We encounter him on a daily basis and must fight to banish him from our lives!" Jessica believed Sister, and she began to think—if she was willing to suffer, or sacrifice something, maybe she could drive Ted out of the house.

For the first week, she tried giving up cinnamon Pop-Tarts. But Ted stayed and showed no signs of budging. Jessica began doing other things: sacrificing pudding at school lunch. Wearing shoes she had outgrown, that hurt her toes. Kneeling on the bare wood floor until not only her knees ached, but also her hips and spine. She didn't have a bed of nails, but she tried sleeping in the bathtub one night.

Her mother found her and thought she had been sleepwalking. She took Jessica back to bed very quickly—before Ted saw. Ted didn't like anything unusual. He would have somehow made Jessica sleeping in the bathtub seem like a slap in his face. He might have yelled, or he might just have gone silent—with those cold, evil eyes. Jessica could almost hear him hissing, "Why are you trying to hurt me this way?"

So with the bathtub off-limits and no bed of nails, Jessica had just changed her sheets—from the soft pink ones with white lambs imprinted on the fabric to the hard scratchy ones that her mother had bought by accident, on sale at Max-Mart. They didn't feel at all good on her skin. She also scratched her legs with pins. It used to give her fierce pleasure to see little dots of blood on the cheap sheets. Her mother just thought she'd been at her mosquito bites.

Jessica would never know whether her martyrdom actually worked—it didn't drive Ted from their house. It didn't save Tally. That was the night her mother decided they'd had enough: when Ted kicked the little dog and killed her, her mother packed them up in the dark of night, bundled them into the car, and drove them away.

Now, picking up more pine needles, she paused in front of a flat rock where she had seen a garter snake sunning itself last week. The serpent had opened its pink mouth and hissed at her, and even though it was very small, its presence had reminded Jessica of Ted, and shaken her.

Jessica wished the snake would come now. She would step on it, barefoot, and kill it like Mary. She wanted to drive the serpents and demons and evil wizards and Teds out, so that Rose could get well. It was the only way. She walked slowly through the pine woods, picking up more pine needles—her hand hot and sticky, her back aching—and she saw a flash of blue in the trees.

At first she thought it was Mary, leading her deeper into the woods, but then she looked up in the branches of a spruce and saw that it was just a blue jay. A bright, beautiful crested jay. Not Mary at all.

When Jessica had filled three large sacks, Marisa knew it was time to take her to town. They drove down to the harbor, parked in front of In Stitches. Marisa was glad to see that the door was ajar, the shop was open. For a moment she felt excited—to think that Lily might be back, working. But when she and Jessica went inside, she saw that it was Marlena behind the counter, with Cindy restocking shelves.

"Hi, girls," Marlena called. "How are you?"

"We're fine," Marisa said. "Have you heard from Lily?"

"Anne did. She came down with coffee and muffins for us, and said that Rose is improving quickly. She's lost almost all the extra fluid, and they're talking about flying her down to Boston in a few days."

"That's a good sign," Marisa said.

"You're a nurse?" Cindy asked. "Anne was telling us. A woman of medicine in our ranks!"

"Yes, I am," Marisa said, and it felt good to think of the Nanouk Girls talking about her, including her "in their ranks."

"What do you think it all means—all these complications?" Marlena asked. "Poor Rosie, having to go through so much."

"Tetralogy of Fallot is very complicated," she said, "but it's treatable, especially when the patient is young."

"I've known Lily since the year Rose was born," Marlena said. "There hasn't been a stretch I can remember when she wasn't taking her to some different hospital or specialist."

"Boston, Melbourne, once out to Cincinnati," Cindy said.

"Cincinnati has the best pediatric heart center in the country," Marisa said.

"I remember that what they did there had to do with 'transposition of the great vessels.' My father was a boat captain, and I thought it had to do with shipping. But it means that both Rose's main arteries were on the left side of her heart, instead of on either side," Marlena said.

"That's right. Her aorta was misplaced," Cindy said.

"What's her aorta?" Jessica asked, standing there with one of the sacks of pine needles.

"It's the large artery that pumps blood from the heart's left ventricle and sends it out into the body," Marisa explained.

"And the hospital lost it?" Jessica asked.

"No, honey," Cindy said. "It happened at birth. Before birth, in the womb. No one knows why, but it was on the wrong side of her heart."

"You mean, God did that to her?" Jessica asked, sounding outraged.

Marisa felt an aura, almost as if she was going to have a migraine. Only it wasn't that—it was Jessica about to go into a full-blown religious tirade. She watched her daughter's face turn red with outrage, and it reminded her of when Jessica would react against Ted, against his control and anger. Instead of getting mad at her, or even Ted, Jessica would get furious at God.

"Well, I wouldn't say he did it *to* her," Marlena said. "It's more like in his infinite wisdom and design, he thought it made sense at the time. We don't understand why."

"What kind of wisdom and design gives a misplaced artery to a baby?" Jess asked.

"Jessica," Marisa said warningly.

"I'm serious. It doesn't make any sense."

"The Lord isn't supposed to make sense," Marlena said, a little nervously. Marisa could see that she was rethinking the two newest Nanouks.

"That's right," Cindy said. "It's one big mystery. One big freaking mystery. Marlena, you might as well say he did it to her," Cindy said. "You sound all confused, and to tell you the truth, I've been confused myself. Who can understand why this happened? To think of our Rosie suffering . . ."

"It does pain me," Marlena replied. "From the time she was a tiny blue baby . . ."

"Probably it's not the Lord who did it," Jessica said. "Probably it was the devil."

"Jess, stop," Marisa said, feeling the blood drain out of her face. When Jessica got going on God, the devil, and Ted, anything could happen.

"The Lord doesn't hurt people," Jessica said. "I refuse to believe that."

Marisa stared at her. She thought of all the sickness she'd seen in her day. The injuries, illnesses, diseases, acts of violence. Although she had raised Jessica in the Church, she had been on a long, slow decline in belief herself. It had reached its final depths during the end of her time with Ted. "I do believe, help my unbelief," had once been her prayer. Now she just believed in science.

"God moves in mysterious ways," Marlena said. "But I'm with Jessica on this. I don't think God wants Rose or any of us to suffer. I'm going to bring this up the next time the Nanouks are all in one place. I think we should put it in our charter."

"Good idea," Cindy said, laughing. "We, the Nanouk Girls of the Frozen North, hereby decree that the Lord is off the hook when it comes to pain and suffering."

"I wouldn't go that far," Marlena said defensively. "I just don't think he does it on purpose."

"What's that lovely aroma?" Cindy asked, raising her eyebrow and changing the subject. "It smells like the North Woods in here."

"Pine needles," Jessica said.

"What are they for?"

"Well, to raise money for Rose's medical care."

"Heaven knows Lily could use help with it," Marlena said, "but how will pine needles help?"

"I want to make Cape Hawk pine pillows and sell them."

Marisa stood back, watching Jessica explain herself. This had been all her idea, coming down to In Stitches, buying the materials from Lily's shop—they had known the Nanouk Girls were keeping it open, taking turns covering different days.

"Where will you sell them, dear?"

"To the tourists who go on the whale boats."

"Pine pillows," Cindy said.

Jessica nodded. "They'll smell just like Cape Hawk. All the things that make it so special here—the woods, pine, birds, whales . . . I thought I could embroider little pictures of Nanny, or the owls that live in the forest behind my house, or the hawks that live on the rock ledges—right into the fabric, along with the words 'Cape Hawk,' or maybe even 'Get Well Soon, Rose.' "

"Do you do a lot of embroidery, dear?" Marlena asked.

"I've never done it before," Jessica said proudly, chin jutting out. Clearly she didn't see this as a setback—just another feat to master. Marisa watched Marlena and Cindy for their reactions. They both kept straight faces. What they didn't know was how determined Jessica could be, or how huge her heart was.

"It might take you a while to learn," Cindy said.

"And then even longer to actually embroider the fabric. And then put the pillows together," Marlena said.

Marisa's eyes filled up. She saw Jessica clutching her big sack of sticky pine needles, her fingers black with tar. Marisa foresaw hours of diligent embroidery ahead for her darling daughter. Jessica stood perfectly straight, undeterred by Marlena and Cindy's reservations. Her love for Rose was too strong for that. Suddenly Marisa had a memory—after Paul died, she had opened his closet, looking for something—she couldn't even remember what.

She'd seen a bulge in the center of his suits. And there, down below, were Jessica's thin legs. She was just standing there among her father's suits. She'd loved her father so much, and that was the only way she could think to be with him. Marisa knew that the pillow project was very much like that—a way to stay close to Rose.

"I'll help her learn," Marisa said.

"Thank you, Mom," Jessica said.

"So will I," Marlena said. "In fact, I give needlework lessons at the high school. I'll teach you for free, sweetheart."

"I'll go you one better," Cindy said. "I'll embroider the pillows myself! And I bet the other Nanouks will too. I'll call Anne and Doreen, you call Suzanne and Alison."

"Fine, and in that case, maybe Jessica and I can concentrate on making the pillow squares—cutting them out, sewing them together."

"And stuffing them with pine needles when they're done!" Jessica said. "And, of course, selling them—"

"I'll bet Anne will let us put some up at the inn's gift shop."

"We'll have to get them by Camille."

"Who's Camille?" Marisa asked.

"Oooh, Camille Neill," Cindy said. "She's the matriarch of the family. Mother, grandmother, great-grandmother of four generations of Neills. Think Catherine the Great meets the Wicked Witch of the West, with a soupçon of Lauren Bacall in the Fancy Feast commercials. She is the official owner of the inn and the whale boats."

"Imposing," Marisa said.

"Yes. And she's none too crazy about Lily."

"How could someone not be crazy about Lily?" Marisa asked.

"Well, it dates back to the year she first got here. And it has something to do with Liam."

"Captain Hook?" Jessica asked.

"The kids call him that, but he's really very dear. He's down in Melbourne with Lily and Rose right now."

"Really?" Marisa asked. "Are they—"

"An item? No one really knows," Cindy said. "There has been much speculation. Normally they act as if they can't stand the sight of each other."

"But whenever Rose has a problem, Liam is right there to help," Marlena said.

"We're gossiping," Cindy said. "It's beneath us, as Nanouk Girls."

"It's not gossip," Marlena scoffed. "It's concern. We love Lily and want her to be happy."

"With Liam Neill?" Marisa asked.

"I think we've said enough," Cindy said somberly. "Let's get cracking on the pillows. Unbleached muslin or canvas, Jessica? This is your project. We're just your assistants."

"I just hope the Fancy Feast lady lets us sell them at the inn and on the boats," Jessica said.

"Now is a time for prayer," Marlena said. "Because that's what it will take to soften the heart of Camille Neill."

Chapter 16

Taking Exit 90 off I-95, Patrick Murphy turned into the most crowded parking lot he'd ever seen. There were cars from every state, tour buses, motor homes, and not a parking spot to be found within walking distance of the Mystic Aquarium. He finally parked on the other side of the little shopping village, after beating a lady in a minivan out for the spot.

Ten minutes later, he was standing in line with a hundred other people, waiting to get in. Sandwiched between a family of five from Hartford and a honeymooning couple from Philadelphia, he eavesdropped to pass the time. Solving crimes was still his favorite pastime, and he liked to figure out as much as he could about every person he encountered, without them knowing he was listening.

After a few minutes, the mom of five had to take the youngest to the bathroom, and the dad of five took the opportunity to whip out his cell phone and call someone he addressed as "sweet baby." Behind him, he heard the young husband tell his new bride that the stocks her father had given them for a wedding present had gone up the night before, and he thought they should consider buying instead of renting their house.

Both instances affirmed his long-held belief that the only thing necessary to good police work was a deep curiosity about human nature and behavior. But then he got inside the aquarium—the super-cool air-conditioning very welcome after standing in the blistering heat—and was faced with the humbling reason for his mission here.

He asked directions to the membership office, thinking that over nine years later, he was still hot on the trail of the coldest case he'd ever had. All that deep curiosity about human nature had gotten him exactly nothing when it came to finding out what had happened to Mara

Jameson. He might as well just spend the rest of his life praying Hail Marys for a big fat clue to drop right in his lap.

Throngs of kids were racing around, giving him a headache. It was a beautiful sunny day outside. What were kids doing in here? When he was young, his parents would have handed him a bat and a ball, or a fishing rod, and told him to go out in the sunshine and not to come back till dinnertime. But as he followed the crowd, he found himself being mesmerized by the glowing tanks, the schools of fish, the eel weaving in and out of its green reef—he began to relax.

Patrick spoke the language of fish. He looked at these and thought of how great it would be to be in a boat on the open water, with all these fish swimming below. Sandra had never understood that. She had thought fishing was nothing more than sitting on deck with a beer and a pole. She hadn't understood that it was clouds in the sky, the water changing colors, schools of fish breaking the surface. It was one big mystery, but a beautiful mystery—not like the kinds that tore at Patrick's heart every day.

Not like Mara Jameson.

So the aquarium tanks gave him some insight into what went on below the surface, and when he'd had enough, he drifted out into the corridor, looking for the administrative offices. A receptionist asked if she could help him, and he said he hoped so, he needed to see someone in membership. A few minutes later, a pretty blond woman came out.

"Hello, I'm Viola de la Penne," she said. "I'm associate director of membership."

"Hi," he said. "I'm Patrick Murphy." He paused. This was where he wanted to whip out his old badge and show her that he was official. Instead, he said, "I'm a retired state police detective."

"Oh, and with all your free time you want to join the aquarium—or maybe even volunteer!" she said. The twinkle in her blue eyes let him think she was kidding. At least, he hoped so. He seriously hoped he looked too tough and seasoned to be giving seal tours to the kiddies.

"If only there was time for such things," he said, cracking a three-cornered smile.

"You mean, crimes still need to be solved, speeders still need to be stopped, stuff like that?"

"You got it, ma'am," he said.

"I'm only forty-two," she said. "Does that put me in the 'ma'am' category?"

"To retired cops, I'm afraid so."

"Hmm. That's a sobering thought. What can I do for you, Retired Officer Murphy?"

He grinned at her giving it back to him.

"I am here about a membership," he said. "You're right about that. Only, it's not for me. It was a gift to a friend of mine."

"What's the name?"

"Maeve Jameson."

"Was there a problem with the category of membership? Would she like to upgrade?"

"There's no problem. It's just that it was anonymous. Whoever gave it to her wanted to keep it secret. I was wondering whether you could help me figure it out. Maeve really wants to say thank you. That's just how she is."

"I can understand that. I obviously have to balance the wishes of the donor, but I don't think there's any harm in taking a look."

Patrick followed her into her office, which was filled with family photographs—a man on the deck of a sailboat, and a beautiful dark-haired daughter. Viola sat at her computer, looking through files. Patrick tried to lean around, to see her screen, but he couldn't do it discreetly enough, so he quit trying.

"Ah, here we go," Viola said.

"Do you have a name?"

"Actually I don't, which makes it easier for me to say no to you. There's a note here saying that the gift was to be completely anonymous—just as you said."

"There must be some record of who made the gift, right? Even if you can't tell me?"

Viola shook her head, peering at the screen. "No. All I have is a note to myself, that the giver wanted to be sure we still had beluga whales here. Somehow that was important—I don't suppose there's any harm in telling you that."

"Beluga? Isn't that caviar?"

"Retired Detective, it's also a type of whale, one of the few that can live in captivity. We've had beluga whales here at the acquarium for many, many years. People who are adults now still remember the thrill of seeing a whale for the first time—right here in our tanks. There's a show, starring Snowblind and Snowflake, beginning in just about fifteen minutes. Perhaps you'd like to go. . . ."

"Snowblind and Snowflake?"

"Yes. Belugas are white whales."

"Huh."

Patrick considered. Maybe Maeve loved whales, loved belugas in particular. Or maybe she had taken Mara to watch whales when she was little. Or maybe one of her ex-students wanted to give her a gift. Or maybe it was just a mistake, the gift had been from her insurance agent or greengrocer or freaking car repairman.

"How'd the person pay? Got a credit card number on file?"

"The payment was in cash. I have a note to myself, that the exchange rate was a little off. The payment was over—too much—once I calculated the rate."

"What rate?"

"The exchange rate—Canadian to U.S.," Viola said. "The currency was Canadian."

"Did you save the envelope?"

Viola shook her head, smiling. "Sorry. I didn't know we were going to be investigated for processing a gift."

Patrick smiled back. He thought for a minute she was flirting with him. But she had on a wedding ring, and there were those family pictures everywhere. He was so out of practice, he didn't know the difference between friendly banter and flirting. As Sandra had told him often enough, he was hopeless—in many areas.

"Look," Viola said. "Just to make it up to you, I'm going to comp you for the dolphin show."

"Dolphins?"

"Well, Snowflake and Snowblind make an appearance. That way, you can see the belugas for yourself, and hopefully report back to Mrs. Jameson that they're worth coming to see."

Patrick thanked her, shook her hand, and accepted the ticket. Who had sent Maeve the membership, and what did beluga whales have to do with anything?

He made his way up to the marine theater and took his seat among a crowd of people from Brooklyn. They were part of a bus tour, and by listening to the women beside him, he realized that the tour included the Seaport, the aquarium, and dinner and a show at the casino. One woman was divorced, and the other was a widow. The widow was saying her grandchildren loved dolphin shows.

Patrick squinted at the pool. He thought of Maeve, how much she missed her granddaughter, how she had never known the great-grandchild Mara had been carrying. What was he even doing here? Most of the time, he was 95 percent sure that Edward Hunter had killed her, that he had hidden her body where it would never be found. But that other 5 percent was powerful enough to send Patrick following crazy leads, even to the marine theater.

Some marine biologist took his place up on a platform and began his spiel about bottlenose dolphins and Atlantic dolphins, and then some dolphins—Patrick didn't really notice which kind—came out and began leaping into the air like circus animals doing tricks. Blowing the horn, catching the rings, bumping the beach ball.

He remembered going to Sea World with Sandra. She had worn white shorts and a blue halter, and she'd had a sunburn. Patrick had spread sunscreen on her shoulders and wanted to forget about the dolphin show and go back to the hotel. Now, he forced himself to stay in the moment. Sugar, one of the dolphins, landed with a huge splash, and half the audience got soaked.

Then the dolphins went away, and the ringmaster guy made his voice very serious. Patrick thought it was sad that he was a scientist who spent his time making dolphins do tricks. It made Patrick feel depressed somehow. And then the water's surface broke, and this big white creature stuck its head up.

Patrick was shocked—it was huge. A whale, a real whale, right here in a tank in Mystic, Connecticut. "This is Snowflake, our oldest beluga whale," the ringmaster said. "Her sister, Snowblind, is on vacation today, and won't be performing. The sisters come from northern waters, up in Maritime Canada, and we . . ."

Some kids in the crowd sounded disappointed. Patrick found himself standing up, pushing past the women from Brooklyn, casting one last look back at the white whale. Her eyes looked bright and solemn. Patrick felt them following him out the door, watching him go. It was the oddest sensation, being watched by a whale.

The scientist had said the belugas came from Canada. Viola had said the membership money came from Canada. Patrick wondered—was there anything Canadian in Mara Jameson's file? He had to get back to the boat to dig up his old notes and find out.

Maeve wasn't feeling very well. The heat had closed in on Hubbard's Point, making everything—including the roses and her—wilt. She was standing in the backyard, filling the yellow watering can from the hose, when she heard a car door close. It was probably Clara's son stopping by with his kids to take a swim, she thought. She leaned against the weathered shingle house, splashing her feet with the hose.

The spigot was attached to a corner of the house, right next to a small cement circle. Mara had always loved to create pictures out of odd materials: she would sew little quilts, make small pillows, embroider wall hangings, needlepoint bookmarks. But this was really her pride and joy: Maeve had helped her mix up cement, they had poured it into a one-foot-diameter circle, and Mara had pressed shells, sea glass, and a large sand dollar into the wet concrete. It was still beautiful.

"Hello, Maeve," came the low, familiar voice that she had heard only on the phone these last many years.

Maeve jumped. It was Edward—holding a small glossy blue bag. She saw that he was still tall, broad-shouldered, confident. He wore a white shirt over pressed khakis. No belt, no socks. Polished brown loafers. Rolex watch—the same one Mara had bought him with some of her inheritance. The sight of that watch made her stomach turn, and she had to literally hold on to the side of the house. She raised her eyes to his—they were the same, cold black fire. Icy yet scorching at the same time—the damnedest eyes she'd ever seen. And dark hair combed back, and a tan—a golf tan, or maybe this year it was a tennis tan, or maybe he'd bought a yacht and now it was a yachting tan.

"Edward. What brings you here?" she asked with enough coolness to keep him from kissing her cheek.

"I was in the neighborhood on business," he said.

"Really. Hubbard's Point?" She glanced around—beach, rocks, salt water, roses, wishing well. "Not much business here."

"Not Hubbard's Point, exactly. Black Hall, Silver Bay, and Hawthorne. I have clients in all three towns."

"Aren't you successful. Three of the most affluent towns on the Connecticut shoreline. You've always known where to find new prospects." She felt the words burning on her tongue. During the investigation, she had been quoted as saying he was a predator and Mara had been nothing more than a mark to him.

"Yes, I am successful," he said, staring at her, unable to keep himself from taking her on. Everything to Edward was a challenge. Maeve knew that she could push his buttons and have him slobbering with rage in ten seconds flat. Instead, she counted to ten and smiled.

"Your mother must be very proud," she said. "That you made something of yourself."

His jaw rippled. My, but he was transparent. Maeve could almost see the wheels turning. Should he put her through the plate glass window, or just continue his Ivy League act? Maeve would refrain from pointing out that it *was*, in fact, an act. That Mara had discovered his lies about Harvard and Columbia Business School. Sadly, in his profession of stock brokerage, they didn't matter. Too bad they couldn't disbar him or revoke privileges or something.

"She *is* proud," he said.

"Of course she is. And so must your new wife be." Maeve thought of what Patrick had told her about the marriage falling apart. Edward flinched.

"How have you been?" he asked, not taking the bait.

Maeve smiled gently and didn't reply.

He waited for a few seconds. When he realized that she wasn't going to answer, he nodded briskly, as if he hadn't really asked the question. They stood there, facing off. Did he really have the nerve to show his face here? The last place on earth Mara had been seen alive? Maeve found her attention drifting across the yard, to the only flat section big enough to hold a tent.

It had actually straddled the property line between her and Clara's houses. For Mara and Edward's wedding, eleven years ago this month, they had put up a pretty yellow-and-white-striped tent in that very spot. There had been tables with pale yellow tablecloths, white wooden chairs, vases of roses and wildflowers picked from Maeve and Clara's gardens, and a string quartet.

Everyone from Hubbard's Point had attended. All of Mara's child-hood friends: Bay McCabe, Tara O'Toole, Dana and Lily Underhill, and all the other now grown-up Point kids. Maeve had invited people from school—other retired teachers, as well as some still at Black Hall High, her old principal—and her roommate from Connecticut College, who had flown out from Chicago, and some of her son and daughter-in-law's friends. Aida Von Lichen, Johnny Moore's sister, had come, and his daughter Stevie—from whom Mara had once taken art lessons—had read a love poem of Johnny's.

Edward's side of the aisle had been less populated. That should have been a red flag, she knew now. But at the time, it had been just another reason to feel sorry for him. His sister hadn't been able to get time off; his mother had come down with pneumonia; his father had spent the airfare Edward had sent him on booze. It was all so sad; so Mara had worked overtime, extra hard, to make sure every one of her and Maeve's friends gave him extra love and attention.

Those thoughts were crackling in Maeve's mind as she stared at Edward now. Her fingers literally twitched—she wanted that badly to rip his eyes out. She had never known that she was capable of true, passionate, unadulterated hatred until after Mara disappeared. Eight and a half months pregnant, her darling, beloved Mara had just fallen off the face of the earth. . . .

"Let's forget the pleasantries, shall we?" she asked now. "What brings you here?"

"I found some things of Mara's I thought you should have," he said, now clutching the bag to his chest. "The police had them for a while, but they returned them to me. They've been in my trunk, waiting for a chance to bring them to you."

"I don't want them," she said.

His eyes widened with surprise. Maeve's lips trembled. She half-turned away, began to train the hose on the roots of the rosebushes climbing up the side of the house. They were thick, hardy bushes of white and yellow roses—and they were in full, delicious bloom right now. She couldn't bring herself to look up, to where the roses were most lush. The trellis stopped just short of a bedroom window—Mara's childhood bedroom, and the one they had decided would be the nursery when the baby visited.

"I'm sure you do want them," he pressed.

"Hmm," she said, feigning indifference. Her hands shook, she wanted so badly to look inside that bag. But Maeve had learned something about Edward, through Mara. She remembered one of Mara's visits, early in her pregnancy. Some of the truth about Edward had started leaking out—and Mara was fighting awareness with every inch of her body. She wanted to stay in the denial of a "happy" marriage, part of a couple expecting a much-wanted—by Mara, at least—child.

"I don't get it, Granny," she said. "As soon as I let him know I'm happy about something, or excited, it's as if he wants to take it away from me. Like last night. He's told me all spring that he wanted to take me to dinner at the Hawthorne Inn. But at first I was sick, and then I was so tired, and I've had lots of work—so last night was the first time I really wanted to go. We were all dressed and ready—out the door—when he changed his mind. He just looked at me and said he didn't feel like it. That now *he* was too tired to go."

"Maybe he was," Maeve had said. She kicked herself now, but back then, she had tried to help Mara give him the benefit of the doubt.

"No," Mara had said, starting to cry. "He left me home, and went to hit golf balls at One Hundred Acres."

Maeve remembered Mara's tears. She stared at the spray coming from the hose and thought of all the tears Mara must have cried—that she didn't let her grandmother see. She could almost feel Edward twitching with frustration.

"These are things of Mara's," he repeated. "I thought you'd want—"

"Leave them by the door," she said.

"You're her grandmother," he said. "I thought you'd care—"

Maeve glared down at the roots of the rosebushes. A cool breeze blew off Long Island Sound. Did Edward remember the times he and Mara had gone sailing? The times they had rinsed off in this exact spot, using this exact hose? Maeve heard a screen door slam, and not thirty seconds later, a breathless Clara appeared.

"Hello, Edward."

"Hi, Mrs. Littlefield. Wow, you look great. I haven't seen you in so long!"

"It has been a long time," Clara said, her tone slightly more friendly than Maeve wanted it to be.

"I came to give these things of Mara's to Maeve, but it seems she doesn't want them."

"I'll take them," Clara said, and the instant Maeve heard the bag passed from Edward's hand to Clara's, she felt something relax inside— as if the wire holding her stiff and brittle had been cut, and she was suddenly a rag doll.

"It's been a long time," Edward said. "I thought by now there'd be water under the bridge. Every June and July, just past the time of year Mara disappeared, I miss her so much. I swear, I've never gotten over it. I just thought that we could maybe talk—"

"Nine years," Maeve said. "Three weeks, six days . . ."

"But if we could just talk—"

"I don't think that's such a good idea," Clara said. "Why don't you leave now, Edward?"

"I'm staying at the Hawthorne Inn," he said. "For the next three days. I live near Boston now, but I have business in the area . . . in case you change your mind, Maeve."

"Thank you for dropping Mara's things off," Clara said as coolly as she—the warmest person in the world—was able. Just then a noise clanked—the hot-water heater under the cottage, trying to restart itself. Odd, Maeve thought—she hadn't been running the hot water.

"What's that sound?" Edward asked.

"None of your concern," she said.

"Better get it looked at," he said, but Maeve ignored him. She looked away until she heard Edward's car start up. Then she did look—it was a big black Mercedes with low-number Massachusetts plates. She watched him put on dark aviator glasses, check his face in the mirror. He backed out into the dead-end turnaround, drove away.

"He still looks at himself in the mirror every chance he gets," Clara said. "I remember you saying you didn't trust him, the very first time Mara brought him home, because he couldn't take his eyes off himself."

"She loved him."

"And you accepted that. Why wouldn't you take the bag from him?"

Maeve wiped tears from her eyes. "Because I was afraid that if he knew how badly I wanted it, he'd change his mind."

"But he'd brought it all this way—to give you."

"You don't know Edward the way I do," Maeve said. "No one does."

"He's always seemed so charming," Clara confessed. "And vulnerable. Even today . . . In spite of what we know about him."

Maeve nodded. Her stomach flipped. Edward's charm and friendly manner had gotten him far in this world. He still fooled people like Clara. Only Patrick Murphy had really seen through him. Even with a murder accusation hanging over his head, Edward had been able to get clients. People had short memories, especially when dealing with charmers like Edward.

"Let's go inside," Maeve said. She heard that clanking again—the hot-water heater making noise. She'd have to remember to call the plumber to come look at it. "I can hardly stand to wait another second. Clara, hold my hand."

"Are you okay?"

"I just have to see what's in that bag," Maeve said, feeling as if she might faint, her eyes glittering with tears as she realized she was about to see and touch items that had once belonged to Mara.

Chapter 17

L iam had driven home to Cape Hawk, to give the commander his car back, check the mail, make a few changes to a program he had running along the beaches east of Halifax—where the great white attack had been last month—and pick up clothes and other things for Lily.

He stopped at the inn to see Anne, who had been to Lily's house. She took the laundry bag of old clothes from Liam, handed him back a bag of clean ones. They stood by the front desk, and Anne wanted to know everything. There was a Ceili band playing that night, and their Celtic music filled the lobby.

"Rose has been doing better and better, every day," he said. "She'll be moving to Boston tomorrow. The doctors say she's ready."

"Thank God," Anne said. "How is Lily holding up?"

"She's fine," Liam said, holding the truth inside. His eyes must have told more than his words, because Anne came around the counter to give him a hug.

"You give her this from me," she said, holding him hard.

He nodded, thinking that would be the day. He'd have to get through about six inches of body armor as well as a Kevlar force field before that happened. The hide of a bull shark was less rugged than Lily's. But he told Anne he would deliver her good wishes. Just then he happened to notice the display set up at the front desk.

"What's that?" he asked, pointing to the placard saying "Help Our Rose Grow." There were pictures of Rose—in her school class, at her birthday party, and standing with Lily.

"Oh!" Anne said. "I almost forgot. Rose's best friend, Jessica Taylor, came up with it three days ago, and the Nanouks immediately got on board. We're selling these pine pillows, raising money for Rose. You know—pine is such a Nova Scotia thing, the visitors love it. The girls have been staying up all night to make them."

Liam picked one up—it had a picture of Nanny embroidered in green thread, with the words "Bring Rose Home" underneath. It smelled unmistakably of pine. Anne showed him the cash box, with twenty dollars inside. "We've sold four already. People checking out of the hotel have been snapping them up."

"I'll take one," he said.

"We'll give it to you," she said. "You're doing plenty for the cause."

"Let me pay," he said. "I want to."

Almost reluctantly, she took his money. She handed him change, along with a small bag. Looking inside, he saw jewelry made of tiny pinecones spray-painted gold. Several pairs of earrings, a couple of necklaces, and a ring.

"Jessica made them for the nurses," Anne said. "She wanted to be sure they treat Rose right."

"She's a good best friend," Liam said, feeling proud of Rose for instilling that sort of love and loyalty. He wasn't surprised. She'd been special since the day she'd been born.

Just then Camille came around the corner. She had had a small stroke last year, and she walked with a cane. But her expression was just as dour, and her white hair was tinted just as blue as ever. Liam knew that she hadn't had a happy life—ever since her husband had drowned in Ireland.

"Liam, dear," she said, coming over to kiss him. "Where have you been?"

"In Melbourne," he said.

"Melbourne? Courting someone new in town?" she smiled.

"No," he said, and gestured at the poster emblazoned with Rose's picture. "I'm down there with Lily and Rose."

Camille's smile dissolved. "You know, I've never felt the front desk is quite the place to raise money. Our guests pay quite enough to stay here, without guilting them into giving to our local charities."

"It's Rose," Liam said, staring her down. "Not a local charity."

She laughed nervously. He was very tall, and he had just used his shark researcher voice on his own aunt, but she was so imposing on her own, he didn't feel bad.

"Dear. You'd almost think she was *your* daughter, the way you act. If I didn't know for sure that her mother was pregnant on arrival, I might have my suspicions."

"Pregnant on arrival," Anne said dryly. "POA."

"She's not my daughter," Liam said quietly.

"But you care about her. It's touching, it really is. Only you know—I'm going out on a limb to say this, and I'm sure I'll get my head bitten off—as the stand-in for your dear parents, and the last of their generation alive, I have to state the facts as I see them. It just seems to me that this attention you pay to the Malones has kept you from meeting women of your station. Intelligent, educated women who would be just dying to marry such a fine young man!"

"Women of my station?" he asked, feeling—as he often did when talking to his aunt—as if he had wandered into a Victorian novel. He also knew, complicated woman that she was, that she had contributed money to the trust he had established for Rose years ago, once her problems had become obvious.

"Yes. I'm sure you know what I mean. You have a *doctorate*."

"Look," Liam said, shaking his head, "I've got to head back to Melbourne. Thank Jessica for trying to raise money."

Anne's eyes twinkled. "We all know who takes care of Rose."

"Sssh," Liam said.

"The pine pillows can stay," Camille interjected. "They're charming, in a rustic way. No one will say that Camille Neill is so hard-hearted as to banish the pine pillows!"

"Thank you, Camille," Anne said, winking behind her back at Liam. "Ever the humanitarian."

"She's right, Aunt Camille," he said, giving her a hug.

"Let's not get carried away," Camille said, resting her head against his shoulder before limping off.

" 'Women of your station,' " Anne said, smiling. "Sounds like the strangest combination between Jane Austen and *Debbie Does Dallas*."

Liam chuckled, trying to gather everything together with his good arm. Anne helped load him up, but suddenly she stopped, reaching up to pat his cheek.

"You're a really good man, Liam Neill. Right up there with your cousin Jude."

"Thanks," he said.

"My friend Lily is a hard case, but don't give up on her."

"It's not like that between us," Liam said. "I just care about Rose."

"Uh-huh," Anne said. "Just remember what I say—don't give up. She needs you, Liam. She always has."

Liam shook his head, trying to hide how her words made him feel. He was very good at that—shoving his emotions out of sight—so he scowled and hoisted the bag over his shoulder.

"She has," Anne said, giving him one last pat on the cheek. "Ever since she arrived in town POA. Give her my love, will you?"

"Sure," Liam said, somehow unable to laugh, even though the twinkle in Anne's eye was asking him to. He started to stick the pine pillow in the bag.

Anne glanced down, pointed at the embroidered image. "You know, no one has seen Nanny since Rose's birthday," she said. "Jude says the whale boats are all watching for her, but she's just not there."

"Really? Once she comes for the summer, she usually stays till the snow falls."

"I know. Jude says it's strange."

They said goodbye, and Liam left. He walked out of the inn, through the parking lot to his truck, having dropped his friend's car off at the Coast Guard dock and hitched a ride from the lighthouse keeper. Climbing in, heading south on the rocky road, he looked out at the bay. He saw the black backs of several fin whales, on their way to the feeding grounds. Glossy black cresting the surface, disappearing underneath.

He had his laptop beside him, and he pulled over to the roadside to tap in data. The screen began blinking with dots of green and purple. Lots of sharks in the Halifax area—more than usual. The purple dots, indicating great whites, were especially thick down there. Liam typed in "MM122," waiting for Nanny's green dot to start blinking on the LED, but it didn't.

Liam typed it in again—still no sign. Could her transmitter have failed? The battery pack was a few months old; he had been planning to replace it, if Jude could get him close enough this summer. His stomach fell, thinking of predators. Sharks were everywhere in this bay—he didn't even need the purple dots to tell him that. Suddenly he remembered how avidly Gerard Lafarge had watched Nanny with binoculars the day of Rose's party. Predators came in all species. He felt sick to think of it.

He dialed Jude's cell number.

"Hey, where the hell have you been?" Jude asked, answering instantly upon seeing Liam's number on caller ID.

"At the hospital."

"How are they?"

"Strong as ever. Listen—Anne tells me none of the boats have seen Nanny."

"That's right," he said. "She's disappeared."

"You know what? I saw Lafarge watching her. He hates me, and he knows how I feel about belugas, her in particular."

"More like he knows how you feel about Rose, and he saw Rose and her friends going crazy for Nanny that day of her party. That scum of the earth."

"Do you think . . ."

"Fuck. I wouldn't put anything past him. I'll ask around. Some of his crew hang out at the inn bar. Maybe I can get something out of them."

Liam thanked his cousin and hung up. He had to get on the road, get down to Melbourne. He kept his laptop on, and he keyed "MM122" to beep if it showed up. Every mile seemed longer and longer as the computer stayed silent.

Losing Nanny—he couldn't even think of it. Thoughts of Connor filled his head, but even more so, of Rose. How could he tell Rose, if something had happened to Nanny?

He couldn't. That was one thing even the rough, tough shark researcher wasn't brave enough to do.

Lily sat beside Rose as she slept. Sunlight streamed through the window. She hadn't been outside all day; it was easy to forget what summer was like. She had pulled out her needlework—she always stitched in the hospital; it was one of the reasons she finished so many things—and was finding comfort in pulling and pushing the needle in and out of the canvas, just repeating the motion over and over, just like breathing, or the beating of a heart. After a few minutes, she closed her eyes, and the images that filled her mind were from summers long ago—those of her childhood.

A garden full of red roses, orange day lilies, honeysuckle, their sweet fragrance mingled with the tang of salt air . . . So different from the salt air of rocky Cape Hawk, the scent of her childhood sea mist mingled with the tide lines of a sandy beach and the sweet decay of marsh flats. Not that there weren't rocks . . . there were. Long granite ledges sloping down to the water, in front of the cottage, the place she had called home for as long as she could remember. And the woman who loved her, had raised her—

Lily opened her eyes. Don't think of that, she told herself. It was too hard, too painful. Staring at Rose, all hooked up with wires and machines, she knew that if she started remembering that other time of her life, she would not be able to get through this next part. She would cave in. Her hands began to move, soothing her as she started stitching again.

She had made the decisions she had out of love. People's lives had been at stake: it was nothing less than that. Lily had grown up reading Nancy Drew mysteries. She had heard stories about people who disappeared, assumed other identities. There was so much loss—the sacrifice of family, relationships, endless love between the generations. But look at what was saved—people's actual lives. There was evil in the world, and Lily had encountered it. No one would have believed her, because his mask was so effective. He was so good at hiding who he really was.

She thought of Scott Peterson, the case that had so recently dominated the news, of how even Laci's family had supported him at first. Lily believed that even Laci didn't know she was going to be murdered until she looked up and saw her husband with his hands around her neck. How could Lily make everyone understand that she would have done anything, anything, to protect herself and Rose from becoming like Laci and her baby, Conner?

Shaking those feelings away, she gazed down at her half-finished canvas and thought of Liam, wondered where he was, why he hadn't gotten back yet. He was picking up all the stuff she'd need for Boston—she couldn't leave without it. She told herself that's all it was; she wasn't missing him, didn't need his or anyone's support. The Nanouk Girls were there for her, and Liam had certainly pitched in more than his share. But other than that, it was just Lily and Rose, the way it had always been.

With Rose fast asleep, Lily put her needlework down and reached over to touch her chest. Light fingertips, wanting to feel the heartbeat. She remembered when Rose was just a few days old. The birth had gone so smoothly; Lily had had her at home. All had been fine. She was overjoyed, relieved that they were safe, but so sad to know her grandmother couldn't meet the baby, not yet, and she didn't know when she would.

Rose's first bath . . .

Lily had filled the sink, tested the water with her elbow, just as her grandmother had told her in the early months of her pregnancy, when everything was a lesson, when the idea of having a baby was so incredible and new. It was as if her grandmother were right there with her, telling her she was doing a good job.

Holding Rose, regarding her with total love, she had touched her tiny chest. What was that feeling beneath her fingertips? Not just the reassuring thump, thump of the heart, but more like a trembling, like the purring of a cat. But the timing felt different; while cats purr along with their breath, this sensation seemed to follow each heartbeat. Rose gazed up at Lily, immersed in the warm water, seeming to love her first bath, so Lily tried to dismiss it. But it bothered her, and she kept checking.

Rose's first blue spell didn't occur till a few days later.

Liam had come back—as he had every day since Rose's birth. Lily had felt shy with him, knowing what he'd seen and heard that night, but she secretly welcomed his visits.

The days were long, so it was still light when he arrived after his day's work on the research vessel. He was administering shark studies down on the surfing beaches east of Halifax, but he'd rush back to Cape Hawk to check on Rose and Lily.

The sun was setting behind the pines, and the cottage was filled with long shadows and golden light. Lily was too content to turn on a lamp; she rocked Rose, breastfeeding her in the dim light. When Liam's truck rattled down the stony drive, she wrapped Rose in a blanket and waited for his footsteps on the porch.

Liam came in, bearing groceries. Lily felt uncomfortable—he refused to take money for them, and she really wasn't sure what he wanted from her. After she had moved out of the inn, they had met in town—when he saw her, a pregnant stranger, he'd realized instantly she was the woman he'd heard crying in the inn room. He told her that she had left some of her books there, and asked if he could bring them to her new place. It had been a complete accident that he'd stopped by to drop them off the night Rose was born—and discovered her in labor.

He never really left after that. He came by every day. He told Lily she could have the lease on the store beside his office, for any kind of shop she wanted. And he brought food and diapers—told her she could start paying him after she got her feet on the ground.

While Lily was putting away the groceries, she handed Rose to Liam to hold. It seemed like the least she could do—he cared about this baby he'd helped bring into the world. But when she glanced over, saw him holding her against his chest with his one arm, her eyes had filled with tears. That kind of tenderness should be reserved for a baby's father—but Rose's father would never know her, never see her, never even learn of her existence if Lily had anything to do with it.

"Lily?" Liam called.

His voice was calm, but there was something that made Lily drop the bag on the floor and walk right over.

"What's wrong?" she asked.

Rose's expression was anxious; she was breathing at twice her normal rate. The shadows falling through the window, from the pines, had masked it at first—the room was violet, slate, purple—but when Lily flipped on the lamp, and the room was light, she saw that Rose was blue.

"What should I do?" Lily asked, panicked.

"Stay calm," Liam said. "She's breathing . . . she's not choking or anything. Let's call the pediatrician."

Lily's hands were shaking, so he found the number of the doctor in Port Blaise—recommended by Anne. Lily had taken Rose in for her checkup, and everything had been fine. But now, on the phone, Dr. Durance was asking questions that made Lily worry.

"Is Rose anxious? Has she been fussing? Does she feed eagerly? Does she sweat during or after feeding? Skin is bluish?"

"Yes," Lily answered to all the questions, denial falling away, everything suddenly pointing back to that strange feeling under her fingertips. Yes, yes, yes . . . She told the doctor about that sensation, and he said, "Sounds like a heart murmur."

Were heart murmurs serious? No, they weren't—were they? Lily remembered a girl from school who had one. She had used it to get excused from gym—that was all. Didn't kids outgrow them? She asked Dr. Durance, and he said, "Usually."

They called, and were told to bring Rose in. That was the first time Liam insisted on going along—and Lily was too worried to decline. He drove, and Lily held Rose in her lap.

Dr. Durance did a standard exam, found a heart murmur, and immediately referred Rose for further tests at the regional medical center. There, they did a Doppler echocardiogram. Several views were obtained: Rose's heart was observed beating in her tiny chest, the thickness of the heart wall was measured, and the valves were counted.

Lily knew the test was similar to the many ultrasounds she had had during her pregnancy, home in New England. She knew the doctor would hold a transducer against Rose's chest wall, and Lily hoped he would remember to warm it. She knew that high-frequency sound waves sent into the chest would return with images of the heart and other structures.

Now, nine years later, she kept her hand on Rose's chest while her daughter slept. She thought of how intrigued Rose had become with ultrasound—she loved to collect the pictures the doctors printed out for her, and she had done a school project on how ultrasound works the same way bats see in the dark—through sound waves bouncing off objects. At night in Cape Hawk, when Lily and Rose heard bats screeching through the woods, they felt comforted by the tiny creatures, instead of scared.

Still touching Rose, Lily thought of how those first ultrasounds had led to the diagnosis of Tetralogy of Fallot: four complex heart defects. She learned that Rose's bluish skin tone was due to cyanosis—reduced blood flow to the lungs. It was called Blue Baby Syndrome. But that was just a symptom—the Tetralogy of Fallot was the cause. It sounded like a monster to her, and was one: a four-headed creature, brutally danger- ous, fatal if ignored. It required open-heart surgery, so Lily had flown her infant daughter to Boston, one of the best heart centers in the country. And Liam had paid.

"I can't accept," Lily had said, panicked.

"You will," Liam had said. "It's not for you. It's for Rose."

And he had surprised her, showing up at the hospital just before Rose went under sedation. "I have to see my girl," he said.

Lily tried to hold it together. *My girl . . .* That's what Rose's father should be saying; emotions seething just below the surface began to pour out. Lily had to run out of the room, sobbing.

"What's wrong, what did I say?" Liam asked, coming to find her.

"You're not her father," she sobbed. "What do you care, why are you here?"

"Of course I care, Lily. I helped deliver her."

"It never should have happened," Lily wept, standing in a corner of the hospital corridor, people rushing by without paying any atten- tion—it was the pediatric cardiac care unit, and mothers losing it were a common sight.

"What never should have? My being there?"

Lily sobbed, thinking she might break apart. When she went into la- bor, the night Rose was born, Liam had been like an angel sent by God. Lily was all alone, in the rocky wilds of the northernmost part of Nova Scotia, on the run from a man who wanted to kill her, the father of her baby. She was lying on the kitchen floor, wracked by hard labor, screaming out loud because she knew she was safe enough—for no one to hear her.

And Liam had walked in, dropped the books he'd been carrying on the floor, come to her, crouched by her side—a total stranger, at her greatest hour of need.

"What does it mean, that I felt safer having my baby alone than ask- ing anyone for help?" she said.

"You had no one to trust," he said.

"I didn't know anyone; I didn't know whether he might have been looking for me, asking around. . . . I was afraid someone would tell him."

"You were all alone, Lily."

Lily had looked up into his eyes—no one but Liam knew how alone she really was. He knew, because he was too.

She couldn't tell him about the dreams she had about him—beauti- ful dreams of a one-armed man leaning over her with tears rolling down his cheeks, holding her, supporting her as she gave birth on her kitchen floor, as he caught Rose as she came out, nestling her and handing her to Lily with his good hand.

Since leaving her husband just weeks earlier, Lily had had dreams of monsters. Frightening, shape-shifting monsters that wanted to eat her alive. Lily had married a handsome, charming man. He could sell anybody anything. His smile was perfect—his teeth so white and straight. But in her dreams, he used those perfect teeth to bite her flesh, drain her blood—just as he'd drained her bank accounts in real life.

He had broken Lily's heart. She thought of all the lies he'd told her. All the ways he had made her feel their problems were all her fault. She was too demanding, possessive, questioning, he had told her. Any time she suspected him of cheating on her, or being somewhere other than where he said he was, he turned it on her. By the time she found out the truth, her heart was shattered.

In Lily's dreams, her handsome husband was grotesque, and the shark-ravaged Liam was gentle, beautiful. Life painted such pictures of confusion.

That day in the hospital, Lily had cried in the corner, feeling Liam's breath warm on the back of her neck.

"Don't cry, Lily," he whispered. "The doctors here are the best. She's in good hands. . . ."

"I think I brought her heart condition on," she whispered.

"How? That's not possible."

"You don't know," she said, pacing. "I was so anxious, all the time I was with him, Rose's father. I felt such tightness in my chest—I used to think I was having a heart attack. I was afraid, and I felt turned inside out. The baby was inside me all that time, being affected."

"By your emotions? No."

"I should have left him sooner," Lily cried.

"Lily—I don't know what happened, why you left. I wish you would tell me."

"I can't," she said, upset she'd said as much as she had. Her husband had always been so careful to do everything in secret. He had never hit her—not once. He'd never left even one bruise. She had never called the police—because the things he did weren't illegal. They were murderous, but not illegal. No one would believe Lily, that her husband was a killer.

"You can," Liam pressed. "I'll do anything I can to help you. . . . You already got away from him. I'll help make sure he never hurts you again."

"You don't understand," Lily said. "The law isn't on my side. If you're not a victim of domestic violence, you don't understand. He was a predator."

"I believe you."

"And do you also believe that Rose is here because of what happened to us before she was born? Because it's true. We both have broken hearts."

"If you say so," Liam said solemnly, touching her face. "I do believe you."

"Thank you."

"Then listen to me, Lily. Whatever he did to you, I want you to know this. You and Rose can count on me—forever. No matter what you need, I'll give it to you."

"I can't—"

"If you can't for yourself, do it for Rose," he said. "I'm a biologist, not a doctor. But I know this—the two of you were imprinted on my heart the minute I helped bring Rose into this world. I never thought I'd say this, Lily—I've never been married, never been engaged, never been a father. I'm none of those things to you and Rose, but I'm yours for life. It's just the way it is."

"Liam—"

"It's just the way it is," he repeated, his blue eyes serious and steady. "Like it or not."

And then the doctor had called them in. It was time for Rose to be wheeled away for open-heart surgery. Standing there as they took her daughter away, Lily thought her own heart would explode—but Liam held her hand. He held it the whole time Rose was in surgery. The team performed a double bypass on her baby daughter, using the Blaylock-Taussig shunt.

When the doctors emerged, Lily let go of Liam's hand. What he had said was nice—very noble. But Rose had survived the surgery, and now Liam could go back to his own life and they'd continue on with theirs. The surgeons explained to her and Liam that the procedure was merely palliative, until Rose grew big enough for more-extensive surgery.

"More?" Lily asked, feeling her knees go weak.

"Ms. Malone, Tetralogy of Fallot means that there are four different defects. Rose will need extensive, complex open-heart surgery to re-construct her heart. A hard road lies ahead. But Rose is amazing—strong, a fighter." They kept talking, but Lily stopped listening. She just shut down, unable to take it all in.

"We can't go through all this," Lily said to Liam, sobbing again when the doctors left.

"Yes, you can. You have to."

"I can't," she cried. "I can't watch her suffer!"

"Lily, my mother couldn't stand to see me suffer after we lost my brother. I had a lot of surgeries too. But she just . . . went away. I needed her, just like Rose needs you. I promised you, and I'll never break it—I'm going to help you. Anytime you need to be strong, call me and I'll help. The doctor is right: Rose *is* a fighter. You'll see. She's a miracle girl."

"A miracle girl," Lily murmured, grasping the phrase, looking up with red, swollen eyes.

"She is," Liam said. "I knew it from the minute she was born."

"How?" Lily asked.

"Well," he said. "I'll tell you sometime."

Now, nine years later, they were all still on that same hard road. Lily sat by Rose's bed. The balloons Liam had brought were still tied to the rail. They had fizzled out some, but Rose refused to let them be taken away. Lily looked at her watch—Liam still wasn't back. She tried to needlepoint again, but her heart wasn't in it—she couldn't concentrate on the canvas.

She constantly told him she didn't want him there, but the truth was, when he wasn't, she felt empty. During the nine years since leaving Rose's father, she had become very strong and sure of herself. She had done a lot of research on domestic violence, realized the danger she'd been in. She had dealt with her guilt over staying as long as she had, and her grief over having to leave behind everything she'd left. She was a fighter, like Rose.

But at moments like this, she realized how much Liam's promise had meant to her. Being so strong and tough, she didn't want to rely on anyone else. Liam was in a category all his own—he wasn't "anyone else." She told herself that the promise was for Rose. Rose loved him—that was for sure.

So, on Rose's account, Lily stood up from her chair and went to the window. The World War I monument shimmered in the reflecting pool. A few doctors and hospital visitors had pulled park chairs into the shade and were reading beneath the trees. Lily pressed her forehead against the glass, trying to see the heron. She couldn't—the bird wasn't visible from here.

And neither was Liam. Maybe he had finally gotten tired of strong-arming her into letting him keep his promise. She could hardly blame him.

The thing was, she realized she'd never gotten him to tell her why he'd first called Rose "the miracle girl." Maybe she hadn't wanted to hear, was afraid to believe. But knowing the difficult surgery that lay ahead for Rose, the one that might finally fix her heart, Lily thought that now would be a really good time for her to hear that story. She found herself hoping Liam would come back soon.

Chapter 18

Liam pulled into the hospital parking lot just before eight—he wanted a chance to see Rose before visiting hours ended, and he was elated by what he had just seen on his computer screen—MM122 blinking away, safe and alive, but in a spot so completely unexpected, he had failed to plug the GPS coordinates into the program—because it had been too unlikely.

Walking into the lobby, climbing into the elevator, he was struck by the juxtaposition—from the wild, fresh air of Cape Hawk to the hermetically sealed atmosphere of the hospital. When would Rose be well enough to stay out of places like this? Liam's excitement over finding Nanny disappeared, replaced by a physical aching for Rose's confinement—the nine-year-old girl he loved, having to spend so many summer days imprisoned in here, in her body.

But by the time he got to the floor, he'd calmed himself down, set the expression on his face. He paused at the door to her room.

Lily had pulled the chair next to the bed, and was needlepointing while Rose read. Liam saw the way Lily's dark hair fell across her face, sharply angled and neatly cut, a raven's wing. It blocked her vision, but Rose looked up from the book, over her mother's head, and saw Liam standing there. He put on his biggest smile for Rose.

"You're here," Rose said.

"Wild horses couldn't keep me away."

"Are there wild horses in Nova Scotia?"

He looked deep in thought. "Wild eagles, I should have said."

"Or wild whales."

Lily smiled, but she seemed to be looking everywhere but at Liam. He couldn't quite figure it out—usually she had no problem just gazing at him head-on, with that inscrutable look in her eyes. There was most often a challenge in Lily's gaze—her chin tilted slightly up, as if saying "Bring it on." But right now, she looked almost fragile, as if the fight had gone out of her, her hands trembling as they held the canvas.

He wanted to ask, but he knew he had to wait until they were out of earshot. So instead, he unpacked the bag Anne had sent.

"Anne wanted me to give you these things," he said. "Your friend Jessica made this pillow—"

"My best friend!"

"Well, that's obviously how she feels too."

"It's Nanny," Rose said, touching the embroidered whale. "It smells like home."

"Filled with Cape Hawk pine needles," Liam said.

"Why does it say 'Bring Rose Home'?" she asked.

"She misses you," Lily said as she gave Rose a secret look of pleasure and triumph.

"She does," Liam said. "The Nanouk Girls are helping her make more of these, and they're selling them at the inn, to raise money to get you well as soon as possible. Nanny wants it too. Rose, she's telling you in as strong a way as possible."

"I want to get well," Rose said with a tiny voice.

"You will," Lily said. "You are getting well. It's happening right now, every minute."

"Jessica also made these," Liam said. "For you to give the nurses."

He watched Lily and Rose look through the plastic bag of pinecone jewelry, and suddenly Lily excused herself, dropped her needlework, and walked out into the hallway. Liam wanted to follow her, but Rose was watching her mother anxiously, so he stayed.

"Why did she go out?" Rose asked.

"Maybe she went to get the nurses," he said.

"We're going to Boston tomorrow," Rose said.

"I know."

"Did you see Jessica? I thought maybe she wanted a new best friend. I wouldn't blame her—I'm not there anymore."

"You'll be home soon," Liam said. "And it seems to me that she has only one best friend—you. That's why she wants to 'bring Rose home.'"

"She and Nanny are waiting for me?"

"Rose," Liam began, not even knowing how to tell her. It seemed so scientifically impossible—he hesitated to mention it, until he was able to tell for sure.

"Are you coming to Boston with us?" Rose asked, interrupting his thoughts.

"I wouldn't miss it," he said.

"Sometimes I wonder . . ." she said, stopping herself. Liam didn't push, or try to urge the words out of her. He just waited. She cleared her throat. He saw all the tubes and wires going in and out of her body, listened to the machines whirring and clicking around her. He wanted to pick her up and hold her, tell her that everything would be all right. But Rose knew too much for such platitudes. Her nine-year-old eyes were wiser than those of most of the professors he'd had in college.

"What do you wonder, Rose?"

"I wonder what Mom would do without me. I'm all she has."

Liam saw her reaching across the bed to hold his hand. He started to squeeze her fingers, but she reached past his good hand and held his prosthesis instead. Her tiny hand, tinged blue, with those clubbed fingers, grasping his big, fake, clunky hand. The gesture touched and shocked him, and he had to fight from showing it. Rose stared into his eyes.

"Maybe I'm not all she has," Rose said.

Liam felt his pulse racing. She wouldn't look away.

"Maybe not, Rose," he said.

They gazed at each other for a long time, and Liam felt himself making a new promise, too deep for words.

By the time Lily walked back into the room, everything was clear. Outside, the sun had set, and the footlights had come up on the tall monument. Liam saw it glowing out the window. He thought back many years, to the day his brother was born. He thought of how much love there was in the world, of how impossible it seems that it will ever be taken away.

Gazing down at Rose Malone, watching her mother brush her hair and get her ready for bed, her last night in this hospital, he realized something he'd never known before: it had to do with Connor, and his parents, and Lily, and Rose, and Liam himself. He had never realized it before, but now he knew he'd never forget it. He had to tell Lily, and he had to tell her tonight. And he had something to show her, that not even he could believe.

After Rose gave the nurses their pinecone earrings, and the doctor came for one last visit, and the night nurse gave Rose her sedative, and Rose fell asleep, Lily gathered up her things. She kept looking around the room, thinking she'd forgotten something. But she had her bag, her needlepointing stuff, her hotel key, the pine pillow Liam had brought. Liam waited at the door, watching her—with anticipation, but as if he wanted to give her all the time in the world.

They walked outside, and the night air felt so hot compared to the air-conditioned hospital chill. Lily felt nervous and keyed up about tomorrow, but also exhausted. She headed for his truck, when she felt him grab her arm.

"What?" she asked.

"Come with me," he said.

Lily gave him a puzzled look, but he didn't explain. He led her in the opposite direction, toward the city park. Kids were hanging out at the band shell, laughing and playing music on a radio. Liam steered her around the public garden, straight to the reflecting pool. The monument, lit by bright halogen lamps, rose into the hazy sky. Lily saw its image shimmering in the long pool of water, and she felt a pang of homesickness for the sea.

"I miss . . ." she began.

"What do you miss, Lily?"

"Salt water," she said.

"It's right down the hill," he said. "Melbourne Harbor . . ."

"I know," she said. "But I miss Cape Hawk. And even more than that, I miss my home."

"I thought Cape Hawk was your home."

"Before Cape Hawk," Lily said. Her throat was tight, memories flooding in of warm sand, silver-green marshes, and a beloved rose garden tended by a woman she had loved her whole life. What did it mean? Lily usually held herself together so well, especially gearing up for one of Rose's procedures. But right now, she felt as if she might die of old sorrow and longing.

"The night Rose was born," Liam said, "you were crying for home."

"I knew I'd never see it again," she said.

"And you cried out 'I need you, I need you . . .' "

Lily nodded, staring up at the granite column. He was waiting for an explanation, but Lily couldn't trust herself to give it. She felt as if an earthquake was just starting deep inside. She needed to contain it— hold back the emotions, try to keep the plates from shifting. She felt the waves beginning, rising, and she didn't want to test their power.

"Who did you need, Lily?"

"I want to tell you, Liam," she said. "But I can't."

"Don't you know you're safe? I'd protect you from anything."

"You can't protect me from my own heart. It breaks when I think of her—I can't talk about her."

He was so silent for so long; crickets sang in the bushes, and animals rustled in the woods. Lily's heart ached—for love so deeply buried, she had almost forgotten it was there. She saw flashes of an old smile she knew so well, blue eyes, silver hair, gnarled fingers closed around the wooden handle of a garden trowel.

"I wish I could introduce you to her," she said, letting her gaze move upward, to Liam's deeply set blue eyes. "She's someone who was very important to me—the most important person, until Rose. Liam, I don't seem very grateful to you, I know. But that's changed this time. I know what you've done for me, for Rose. Thank you for staying with us. The waiting has been so hard . . . I'm so scared, Liam."

"About the surgery?"

Lily nodded, hugging herself. The crickets sounded so loud. She looked up, saw bats circling the monument in the orange light. Her heart split, to think of Rose's school report, the one she had done on echocardiograms and the sonar of bats.

"I've never been like this before. Rose is just—well, you know. Everyone says she's 'such a fighter,' and she is. She is! She's had this condition since she was born. You were there—you know. We've just lived with it, never questioned it. I've followed her lead, and she's always been so brave. But this time—Liam, the waiting is so much harder. What if something terrible happens? Or what if the surgery doesn't work?"

"It will work," Liam said, standing very close. She couldn't stop looking into his eyes—he sounded so sure.

"I just can't stand waiting," she whispered.

"You told me you had someone you wished I could meet," he said. "It's the same with me," he said. "I wish I could introduce you to my family."

"I know Jude," she said, puzzled at the change of subject. "And Anne, and all the other Neills. Camille—"

Liam shook his head. "Others, who aren't here anymore. It's why I wanted to walk you over here, to the monument. I stood here with my father the day my brother was born."

"Connor," she said. The little boy who had been killed by a shark . . .

"Yes," he said. "The day he was born, my father and I were standing out here. I was just three, and I was really worried about my mother. She was in the hospital, and I didn't understand. My father pointed up at the monument, and he told me a family story. My great-grandfather had fought in the war."

"Your father's grandfather?"

"Yes. Tecumseh Neill—the son of the sea captain that founded Cape Hawk, the one we named the boats after. He was over in France, and letters were very scarce. Even his father, the fearsome whale captain, was terrified that his son would never come home."

"What happened?"

"My father told me that his grandfather had been wounded on the battlefront and was last seen lying in a muddy trench. His squadron had retreated—and when they got back to camp, he was gone. The word came that he was missing in action. The whole family waited for word, but thought he must have been killed. Time went past—weeks and then months."

"How awful," Lily said.

"Everyone gave up hope except his sweetheart—my great-grand-mother," Liam said. "She just knew."

Lily nodded eagerly—she understood that. The connection that was there, even when you couldn't see the other person. She had never lost it, for the woman in the garden that she loved so much. It glimmered, alive in her now. And she had it for Rose, always.

"She knew that he was alive?" Lily asked.

"Yes. She was positive. But every day that went by without word was like torture. She knew he was there, but she couldn't get to him. She knew that he needed her—just as she needed him."

"Your father told you, because you needed your mother," Lily said.

"I did. And I believed, in that three-year-old-boy way, that she needed me."

"I'm sure she did," Lily said, thinking of Rose at three, of the hospitalization here, and of how every second without her had been excruciating and almost impossible to bear. "What happened to your great-grandfather?"

"He had been badly injured behind enemy lines. He was taken to a field hospital, and it took months for the word to get out. At first, it was just a rumor. Just a hint, that maybe he was alive after all. My great-grandmother didn't care about the rumors—because she had something better. She knew for sure—in her heart—that he was coming home. And he did, Lily. He spent time as a prisoner of war, but eventually he came home to her."

"She knew."

"Yes, she did. All that time."

"She waited for him."

"It's what I want to say to you right now, Lily Malone," Liam said. "People say Rose is a fighter, and she is. Just like my great-grandfather. But as much as anyone, my great-grandmother is the hero of the story."

"She never gave up on him."

"No, she didn't. Some things are worth fighting for, Lily. And some things are worth waiting for."

Lily stared up at him, the monument silhouetted behind his head, her heart pounding in her chest. He was talking about his great-grandmother, so in love with her husband, their connection so mysterious it didn't need letters or telephone calls or spoken words. And he was talking about three-year-old Liam Neill, waiting for his brother to be born—so he could meet him for the first time, and see his mother again. And he was talking about Rose, just about to have the final, and most important, surgery of her life, replacing the old VSD patch once and for all. But he hovered over Lily, his face just inches away, and she knew—he was talking about something else too.

"You told me once," she whispered. "That Rose was a miracle girl. You told me you'd tell me what that means. Will you tell me now?"

He nodded. He put his arms around her—both arms, and the left one felt just as tender as his right. She had the feeling her legs were dissolving; she leaned into him, hoping her heart wouldn't fly out of her chest.

"The night I helped deliver Rose," he said, "and watched you give birth . . . she brought me back to life."

Lily couldn't speak. She thought back, remembered the crashing pain—she had been traumatized by what had driven her to Cape Hawk, so much so that she was in hiding like a wild animal in a cave, not even daring to go to the hospital—for fear that her husband would be looking, or that the news accounts would cause doctors and nurses to recognize her, to call the police.

Liam had been the only person she dared trust—and only by necessity. Because he was *there*.

"Brought you back to life?" she asked finally.

He nodded, brushed the hair from her eyes, and caressed the side of her face.

"The shark that killed my brother," he said, "killed my whole family as well."

"He took your arm," Lily said.

"He took my heart," Liam said. "And you and Rose gave it back to me."

"You hardly knew us—"

"I know," Liam said. "I guess that's what made it a miracle. A stranger I'd never even met—you. In a cabin, in the middle of the woods. Giving birth to this beautiful, tiny little girl. And trusting me enough to bring her into the world."

"I did trust you," Lily whispered. And she knew that—given what she was running from—that in itself was a miracle.

"There's something else I want to show you tonight," Liam said. "If you wouldn't mind taking a ride with me."

"Anywhere," she whispered.

The passenger seat of his truck was cluttered, so when Lily climbed in, she had to push his laptop aside. He drove through the park, through the stone gates, and down the hill toward town. Melbourne Harbor twinkled with lights—the business district and hotels, restaurants and houses. Liam drove past the citadel—the old battlements that had once guarded the harbor, dating back to when the land was known to the French as Acadia.

They headed southwest, along the south shore. Lily felt the tug of home—whenever she was in a vehicle pointing toward New England, it overcame her. She wedged herself lower in the seat, feeling the sea breeze through the open windows. She felt a special tingle tonight, almost as if her grandmother was calling her name.

The sky was filled with stars. They swung low on the horizon. The rock scree slanted down to the Atlantic, and the constellations seemed to spring straight out of the ocean.

They rounded a bend, came upon the lighthouse at the outer edge of Melbourne Harbor. Its beam flashed across the sky. Liam turned left, taking an unpaved road out to the farthest reaches of the lighthouse's promontory. Now he reached across for his laptop; he balanced it on his knee, turned it on. Lily saw the screen light up with green and purple dots of light.

"What are they?" she asked.

"Sharks and whales," he said.

"How can you see them?" she asked, fascinated.

"I run a catch-and-release program," he said. "To research migratory and predatory patterns."

Predatory. The word had old associations, and made Lily shiver.

"Which ones are sharks?" she asked.

"The purple ones," he said.

"Where are they?"

"This screen represents this coastline right here," he said. "See the darkest section? That is the landmass—southern Nova Scotia, from Melbourne to Halifax."

"I never really noticed before how Nova Scotia is shaped like a lobster," Lily said, staring at the computer screen and the island's silhouette against the lighter, slate-colored sea—filled, alarmingly, with purple dots.

She glanced up at Liam's face. He looked so content and gentle—how was it possible, considering that the sea was filled with sharks just like the one that had killed Connor?

"Why do you do it?" she asked. "Dedicate your life to studying something so evil?"

"Sharks?"

"Yes."

"They're not evil, Lily. They're dangerous, though. There's a difference."

"What is it?" she asked, thinking of another predator.

"Sharks don't kill to inflict pain or suffering. They kill to eat. It's just their instinct—the way they stay alive. I had to learn that about them, so I could stop hating them."

Lily thought of her broken heart, and Rose's. She knew that a human shark had caused the hurt and stress that had nearly ripped her apart, driven her from her home, caused Rose to be born with four heart defects. "How can you stop hating something that did such damage?"

"You have to," Liam said. "Or it will kill you too."

Lily stared at the purple lights on the screen. Then she looked out the truck window. They were facing south. A few hundred miles away, straight across the water, was Boston; beyond that was her old home. She wondered how many sharks were swimming between her and the place she loved so much.

"I know about hatred," she said.

"I know you do," Liam said. "It's one of the reasons I wanted to bring you here tonight."

"How do you know? Does it show?"

He paused, staring out at the dark sea. The lighthouse swung its beam across the smooth water, illuminating it in four-second flashes. Then he turned to her. "It does show," he said. "You let some of your friends in—Anne, the Nanouk Girls. But you've kept yourself and Rose hidden from everyone else."

"You should talk," Lily said, smiling.

"I know—that's why I recognize it in you. I've got this computer program, to help me learn about the thing I hated most."

"I've done my best to study him," Lily said. "But he's not like a shark—he inflicts hurt on purpose. I know a little about the dynamic."

"You can get lost in it," Liam said, turning the computer screen to face Lily. "If you're not careful, all you see are the purple lights. You forget to look for the green ones."

"The green ones?"

"Whales," he said. "The most gentle animals in the ocean."

Lily studied the screen. "There aren't many whales on here," she said. "Look at all those purple lights—and only three green ones."

"Whales are harder to tag," he said. "We don't like to crowd them."

"So you're saying there might be lots of undercover whales?" She smiled.

"Yes," he said. "Along with one very visible one." He tapped the screen with his finger. "This one right here." He hit a few keys, and the whale's ID showed up in a window. Lily read out loud.

"MM122," she said.

"That whale was in Cape Hawk just a week ago," he said. "She disappeared for a few days, but that was only because I had narrowed the program to track her in familiar waters—the area I always expect to find her in the summer months."

"The whale swam down to the southern shore?" Lily asked, feeling a shiver run down her spine. She knew but didn't know.

"Specifically, to Melbourne," Liam said. "The waters closest to Melbourne."

"Is that surprising? Unusual?"

"Very."

"Why?"

"She's a beluga," Liam said. "Belugas rarely travel south of Cape Hawk. They are northern whales."

"But why would this one be here?" Lily whispered. Liam lowered the laptop and reached across the console between them. He held her hand. She felt a new shiver go down the backs of her legs. Liam held her hand only rarely. His palm and fingertips were rough, from all the work he did on boats. Lily felt a chill, and she was afraid he had taken her hand because he was about to tell her something that was going to scare her.

"To be near Rose, I think," he said.

"What do you mean?"

"It's Nanny," he said.

Lily stared at the blinking green light marked "MM122." Then she lifted her eyes to look out at the endless black sea. The lighthouse beam spread across the water, highlighting whitecaps of small waves. Liam took a pair of binoculars from his door pocket. He scanned the surface, then stopped.

"It's too dark to see," he said, "but she's there."

"She can't possibly be here because of Rose," Lily said.

"Why not?" Liam asked. "Why isn't it possible?"

"Because she's a whale—she can't feel emotion. She can't know how much Rose needs her and loves her."

"Why can't she?" Liam whispered, touching Lily's face. His hand was warm, and she leaned into it.

"Could it be like a bat, sending out signals, just like in Rose's report?

Or like sound waves, in her echocardiograms?" Lily asked. "Could Nanny feel how much Rose loves her? No . . ."

Liam didn't reply—at least not with words. He pulled Lily tenderly close, leaning across the console, to kiss her. His mouth was hot, and she melted into him. Waves beat against the rocky shore, wearing it down, smoothing the edges. Lily heard the waves, and she felt the earthquake. It trembled inside her chest, and she reached up to caress Liam's cheek.

Lily heard her own question, reverberating in her ears. And she knew—yes, Nanny could feel Rose's love. Lily had been frozen solid for so long, she had forgotten that love came in waves—mysterious, long-reaching, never-ending waves. If you waited long enough, they eventually touched the distant shore. The waves never gave up.

She reached up both arms, put them around Liam's neck, and kissed him with nine years' worth of passion. He wrapped his good arm around her waist. Outside the truck, the sea splashed against the granite. One wave flew up, and the fine spray misted their faces. Lily tasted salt water, blinked it away.

"What does it mean?" she asked.

"Whatever we want it to, Lily Malone," he said.

The lighthouse beam clicked on again, lighting up the bay. She stared up at Liam, and she knew—if she turned her head right that instant, that very second, she would see Nanny. She would see the white whale, the mystical beluga who had followed Rose south. But Lily couldn't look away. She was lost in Liam's eyes, which were filled with mystery and miracles of their own.

Chapter 19

Patrick Murphy sat in the main salon of the *Probable Cause*, Flora at his feet, looking up whales online. Specifically, beluga whales. It was all very strange, all the websites devoted to marine mammals. There were boat tours on the east coast, west coast, Mexico, and Canada. But very few places boasted the presence of the elusive white beluga.

Angelo sat up on deck, smoking a cigar, listening to the Yankees.

"Hey. Bases are loaded. Will you get up here?"

"In a minute."

"You invite me over for beer and baseball, and you ignore me. What've you got down there? A sweetheart in a chat room?"

"I'm doing police work."

"You're freaking retired."

"Shut up for a minute, will you?" Patrick asked, making a list of places that ran tours to see beluga whales. He was drinking Coke, because he had sworn off beer and stronger things eight years earlier, but he was getting a caffeine buzz. Or maybe it was just the thrill of knowing he was close to something.

"You tell me 'shut up'? I'm your best friend, I brought nachos, and you tell me 'shut up'?"

"You're right—I'm sorry. I'm looking up beluga whales."

"Beluga? Like the caviar?"

"That's what I thought, but no. They're white whales."

"Like Moby Dick?"

"Huh. Maybe. I'll have to ask Maeve. She was a teacher—she'll know."

"Fuck—is this about Mara Jameson? Tell me it's not. Whatever else you're doing down there, tell me you're not wasting another night of your life on the case that went nowhere, is going nowhere, and will always go nowhere."

"I can't tell you that," Patrick said. He had a list, and started studying it: beluga whales could be viewed during summer months at several places in Canada's Gulf of St. Lawrence—Newfoundland, New Brunswick, Nova Scotia, and even Quebec Province. Whale-watch tours were offered by companies leaving from Tadoussac, St. John, Gaspé, Cape Hawk, and Chéticamp.

"Martinez just homered," Angelo called down. "Grand slam. You missed it."

"Hang on. I'll be right up," Patrick said, trying to find the names of all the tour operators. What was he going to do—call each one and ask them if they'd ever had a passenger on any of their whale-watch boats that looked like Mara Jameson?

"Yankees are up 6–1."

"Go Yanks," Patrick said, typing "Mara Jameson, beluga whales," into the search engine. Nothing. He tried "Mara Jameson, Tadoussac," then "Mara Jameson, St. John," and so on. Police work was still often a thankless job. Only, now he wasn't getting paid for it.

His cell phone didn't work in the cabin, so he climbed up on deck. Angelo gave him a reproachful glance, reminding him of how Sandra used to look at him, back when he was ruining their marriage by dogging the Jameson case every minute of the day.

"Hang on," Patrick said, walking up to the bow for privacy.

"The nachos are getting cold!" Angelo called. "And my beer's getting warm!"

Patrick put one hand over his ear to block out all the boatyard noise—including his friend's voice—and dialed Maeve's number.

"Hello?" she answered.

"Maeve," he said. "I've got to ask you something. Did Mara ever say much to you about whales?"

"Whales?"

"Beluga whales, white ones, like the kind they have at Mystic Aquarium?"

She was silent, thinking. "Not that I can remember," she said.

"Huh."

"Ask her about Moby Dick," Angelo called from up front.

"Will you shut up a minute?" Patrick called back.

"Shut—?" Maeve began, shocked.

"Not you, Maeve," Patrick said hurriedly. "Did she, Mara, ever mention places up north? Spots she wanted to visit, maybe? In Canada, is what I'm getting at."

"Canada?" Maeve asked, sounding interested.

"Specifically, places on the Gulf of St. Lawrence?"

"How funny you should ask," Maeve said. "Because Edward stopped by with a bag of Mara's things—"

"Edward Hunter? He stopped by to see *you*?"

"Mmm," Maeve said, coughing. It went on for a moment, until she composed herself.

"And he gave you a bag of Mara's things?"

"Yes. That's what I'm trying to tell you. I didn't think much of it," she said. "But there was something very odd, having to do with Canada. Nothing to do with whales, though . . ."

"What was it?"

"Just something to do with her parents' deaths. It surprised me."

"Can you stay right where you are, Maeve? I want to see it."

"Where would I go?" she said, chuckling.

"I'll be right over," he said, watching Angelo smack his head with frustration and stuff his face with the last nachos.

Maeve and Clara were sitting in the living room, playing setback and listening to the Red Sox game on WTIC. The cards were very old, somewhat waterlogged, from so many years in the salt air. Maeve wondered how many games of setback she and Clara had played, dating all the way back to their girlhoods. Candles blazed inside tall hurricane lamps so that they wouldn't be blown out by the sea breeze. The windows were open, and the smell of salt and honeysuckle filled the room. Maeve felt a bit dizzy, feverish, as if she were coming down with something.

"What time will he be here?" Clara asked.

"Well, he said he'd be right over. As long as it takes to drive from Silver Bay."

"Twenty minutes, at the most. Now that he's retired, I wonder whether he ever misses using lights and sirens."

"I wonder," Maeve said, swallowing hard. She had a touch of indigestion. Perhaps she had eaten something that didn't agree with her. Or maybe it was just a little stress—waiting for Patrick, after the excitement she'd heard in his voice. Reaching for her old needleworked eyeglass case, she tapped her bifocals out and put them on.

"Do you have Mara's things all ready to show him?" Clara asked.

Maeve gave her a deadpan look: *What do you think?*

"Well, excuse me! I just wonder what he'll find that no one else has found before. It seems like a wasted trip."

Maeve's mouth dropped open, shocked at her best friend's words. "How can you say that?"

"I just . . . I just don't want you getting your hopes up."

Maeve closed her eyes. She wrapped her Irish linen shawl more tightly around her shoulders. Her stomach was bothering her, and it wasn't helping her mood. Clara, of all people, should know that her hopes would stay up until she had one breath of life left in her body. She hoped she was doing the right thing. She shivered; it had been chilly the last two nights, and she had turned on the heat. Getting old was no fun, she thought.

"So much time has passed," she murmured.

"Exactly," Clara said, taking it the wrong way. "That's what I'm concerned about. That so much time has passed, yet still you keep the home fires burning. My darling, what if this is just another false lead?"

Maeve nodded, seeming to agree. She had hoped never to see Edward Hunter again for as long as she ever lived. But he had given her a great gift, bringing the bag over. And Patrick Murphy—dedicated police detective, superior investigator that he was—had followed every clue, more diligently than any grandmother could ever hope or expect. He had never stopped looking for Mara, never for one day.

"He's here," Clara said, spotting Patrick's headlights.

Maeve rose, walked through the kitchen to the front door. Moths swirled around the outside lights, and the yellow watering can stood illuminated by the rose arbor. Opening the screen door, she let Patrick inside.

"Hi, Maeve. Thanks for letting me come over so late."

"Hello, Patrick. Clara and I are just having some tea, playing cards."

"Sorry to intrude. Hi, Clara," he said.

Clara had already poured him a cup of tea, and now handed it to him as he entered the living room. Maeve felt herself weave slightly. She steadied herself without the others seeing. On nights like this, when the summer stars rose out of Long Island Sound and an unexpected visitor came to the door, Maeve never quite got over wishing it was Mara. She saw Patrick waiting expectantly, and went to get the bag.

"This is it?" he asked.

She handed him the glossy bag and nodded.

"He brought it down last week!" Clara said. "The nerve of him, showing up in Maeve's garden."

"Edward Hunter has never lacked nerve," Patrick said. "May I look?"

"Certainly," Maeve said. She cleared off the card table, and Patrick spread the bag's contents on the surface. She had already gone through everything piece by piece, as had the police before her. She suspected that Patrick himself had already seen everything.

"Yep," he said. "Her phone book, her car keys, her silver pen, a little leather sewing kit . . . we've seen all this before. He gave it back to you—why?"

"I think he wanted to see me," Maeve said. "For another reason. This was just his excuse."

"What other reason?"

"To see whether I hate him or not. Edward could never stand to be hated. That is his entire reason for living—to be liked by everyone on earth. Even if it is just to get over on them."

"But he's such a slimy salesman," Clara said. "I never saw it myself, at the time. But now I do. And I can't understand why darling Mara fell in love with him."

"She fell in love with him because she thought she could help him," Maeve said. "She had the biggest heart in the world, and Edward has a very sad hard-luck story."

"But that was so long ago," Clara said, not getting it. "When he was a child. What does that have to do with Mara? Or the kind of man Edward became, for that matter?"

Patrick seemed not to be listening as he went through the rest of the items in the bag: a book of poetry by Yeats, one by Johnny Moore, and a collection of newspaper clippings about Mara's parents' deaths.

"It shouldn't have anything to do with it," Patrick said. "But guys like Edward use their childhoods as their bread and butter. It's currency, and they use it to gain sympathy."

"Mara's only mistake," Maeve said, "was in finally seeing through it."

"You think that's why Edward came back to see you? To see if you see through him?"

"I'm sure of it. He was bragging about his success as a broker. It's subtle—he taunts me. Knows that I'm onto him, but can't do anything about it."

"Where's the part about Canada?" Patrick said. "I don't see it."

"In this article," Maeve said, separating one yellowed clipping from the rest. Feeling queasy, she watched Patrick read.

Mara's parents had been killed in a famous ferry accident in Ireland. As a teenager, she had written to several local Irish papers and asked them to send her the clippings. Maeve's pulse quickened as she watched Patrick's face. She wondered what he would make of the mention—how would he put it together with the other clues?

" 'Residents of Ard na Mara,' " Patrick read. "What's Ard na Mara?"

"The town in the west of Ireland where her parents were killed."

"What does it mean?"

"In Gaelic, *Ard* means 'peak,' and *Mara* means 'sea.' "

"I never knew Mara was named for the sea!" Clara said.

Maeve nodded. "And for that town. It's where her mother was born. Keep reading, Patrick."

" 'Residents of Ard na Mara have set up a memorial for the victims of the ferry disaster. A brass plaque containing the names of each person aboard the fated vessel will be mounted on a slab of granite, donated by a family from Nova Scotia, Canada. Frederic Neill had come to Ard na Mara to meet with Aran Shipbuilders, to commission the third and largest vessel in his family's tour boat fleet. Camille Neill, his widow, was reached at her innkeeping office in Cape Hawk, Nova Scotia. "The family wishes to keep Frederic's memory alive," she said of the monument. She had no further comment.' "

"Wasn't that a lovely thing to do?" Clara asked.

"I wonder whether the family tour boat fleet includes whale-watching boats," Patrick said, staring into Maeve's eyes.

Her hands were shaking, so she held them quietly in her lap.

"What do you think, Maeve?" he asked.

"I really haven't any idea."

"Cape Hawk," he said. "That's one of the places people can go to see beluga whales."

Clara smiled. "Well, they have belugas right at the aquarium in Mystic. And Maeve, you have a membership!"

"Yes, you do," Patrick said. "Don't you?"

"Mmm," Maeve said, holding her shawl tighter. It wasn't a cold night by any means—the fireflies were dancing in the side yard, and the air smelled of summer flowers. But she felt something like an arctic chill blow through the open window. Perhaps her stomachache wasn't indigestion at all, but the beginning of the flu. She had had a terrible case last winter. It had nearly landed her in the hospital. Maybe she'd put the heat on again tonight.

"You look pale, Maeve," Patrick said.

"It's just the candlelight," she said.

"So, that's why it was so hard to read the stories," Patrick said, but he didn't smile. He seemed fixed on his plans, whatever they were. Maeve was sure he was just being polite, sipping his tea. She wished he'd hurry up, get started on the next phase of his investigation. Or did she? Her stomach churned at the thought. There had been so much hurt, danger, disappointment.

"Did you find the articles helpful?" Clara asked.

"I don't know yet," Patrick said. "There's at least a coincidence. . . ."

"What would that be?" Maeve asked.

"The mention of Cape Hawk in the story about the ferry memorial, and the fact that it came up in my research earlier tonight."

"Regarding whales," Maeve said.

"Isn't that an odd coincidence?" Patrick asked.

"I don't believe in coincidences, myself," Maeve said. Patrick was staring at her. She held his gaze for a few seconds, then saw his eyes flicker down to her eyeglass case. It was old and well worn, some of the needlepoint stitches worn off after so many years. He stared at it for a moment, as if trying to decipher the word and discern the shape. Could he make out the tail?

"You're saying you think there's a connection?" he asked, steering himself back to the matter at hand.

"No."

"You sure?"

"Quite."

She took off her bifocals and put them back into the case. Her hands were shaking, and she felt a sheen of sweat on her brow.

"You know, dear," Maeve said. "I'm not feeling well. I have quite a case of indigestion, and I might be coming down with a summer flu. I'm chilled to the bone. Why don't you take the articles with you?"

"I'll do that, Maeve," he said, not looking away.

And Maeve shivered—not because the room had gotten any colder, but because for the first time, Patrick Murphy had looked at her as if she were the enemy. And he had every reason to.

Chapter 20

Marisa's fingers ached from pushing the needle in and out, embroidering the words "Bring Rose Home" on pillow after pillow. Lily's shop was quiet, except for the Spirit CD playing on the stereo. Marisa had put in *Aurora*, and Jessica kept playing the title song over and over. The sounds of boats and seagulls drifted in from the harbor. As she sewed, Marisa's mind wandered back to her childhood, when she had sat at her mother's knee, learning how to mend her clothes.

"That's it, sweetheart," her mother had said, praising her for the worst, biggest stitches anyone had ever made. "You're really getting the hang of it!"

Marisa had loved all the time she'd spent with her mother. Sewing, cooking, gardening—it didn't matter. Even driving—her mother had let Marisa sit behind the wheel of her bright orange Volvo, driving it in and out of their cul-de-sac, when Marisa was only twelve years old. She'd been the envy of all her friends.

Her mother had taught Marisa and her sister how to drive a stick shift, how to prune roses just below the new growth, how to look for three- and five-leaf sets on old rosebushes, how to transplant orange day lilies, how to take ivy cuttings, where to look for wild blackberries, how they should never approach swans—because swans, although beautiful and graceful, were very aggressive, and would attack humans.

She had taught Marisa to protect herself from swans, but not from sweet-talking men. Not from Ted. Glancing up, Marisa looked at Jessica across the shop. It was their turn, among all the Nanouks, to work in Lily's store. They wanted to keep it open—keep Lily's business going strong—so that when Lily and Rose returned from the hospital, they wouldn't have to worry about an income.

Lily had told Anne, who was serving as the In Stitches bookkeeper until Lily's return, that she should pay everyone a salary for their work. Many of the Nanouks refused—donating their proceeds straight back into the "Bring Rose Home" account—but Marisa didn't have that luxury.

Their exodus had been a financial hardship. As carefully as she had planned the escape, she hadn't counted on such difficulties. She had followed instructions from a couple of different domestic violence websites: stayed as even-tempered as possible, so Ted wouldn't suspect her intentions, hidden money in a fake frozen orange juice can in the freezer, started emptying accounts, taken proceeds from the house sale.

He had charmed her into putting his name on so many of her investments, including her main account at the brokerage where he worked—United Bankers' Trust. All of her first husband's pension had been there, as well as her inheritance from her father. Ted had made such a show of caring, of wanting to help her invest wisely—"so you will never have to worry."

"You" meaning Marisa and Jessica. How benevolent he had sounded—when, in fact, he had been using them the whole time. The longer Marisa stayed away, the more she was beginning to see. Was it possible that just a few months ago—right after leaving him—she had had some doubts, had actually felt some longing for him? Had been missing the feeling of his arms around her shoulders?

He had been like Dr. Jekyll and Mr. Hyde. He could be so funny and sweet, but his mood could change in a flash—just like a storm whipping up on a summer day. His moods had kept both her and Jessica so off-balance.

Now, listening to Spirit sing "Lonesome Daughter," Marisa looked over at Jessica and wondered how long they would have to keep up the charade. Knowing that Lily was down in Boston, in New England, made Marisa homesick. She missed her sister Sam and the music they had played together. What had she been thinking, hauling her daughter way up here, to this far-north outpost? "White Dawn" came on, haunting and powerful.

"Mom?" Jessica asked.

"Yes, honey?"

"When is Rose coming back?"

"After she has surgery, it should take about two weeks before they let her leave the hospital."

"I want to talk to her."

"I know. You will, soon."

"She'll be happy to get home, won't she?"

Marisa nodded, looking over with curiosity. It seemed funny to hear Jessica refer to this place as "home."

"We're so lucky to have such a cool place to live," Jessica said. "With so many whales and hawks and owls, and friends. I never thought I'd be a member of a secret society."

"The Nanouk Girls?"

Jessica nodded. "They didn't even know us, but they took us right in and let us be members. And now look at us, raising all this money for Rose."

Marisa swallowed hard. Hearing her daughter sound so happy and grateful was worth almost everything—all the pain that had led up to her decision to do this, to drop out and abandon everything at home, even their real names and identities. It reminded her a little bit of the Internet—message boards, where everyone took on a phony name and tried on different personas. Discouraging, to say the least. Yet she did it too. Marisa had logged in her share of time chatting online, at times when she couldn't sleep or didn't want to feel.

Footsteps sounded on the porch, and then the bell above the door rang. Marisa looked up to see Anne, Marlena, Cindy, and two of Cindy's daughters walking in with sandwiches from the inn.

"Lunchtime," Anne announced.

"I'm almost finished with another pillow!" Jessica announced to Allie.

"We made two last night," Allie said.

"They're selling out, as fast as we can put them at the inn desk," Anne said as everyone pitched in. Thermoses of iced tea and lemonade, plastic cups, slices of lemon and orange, turkey sandwiches, chocolate chip cookies, paper plates, napkins, all came out. Marisa cleared off the counter; women friends amazed her. Although they hadn't known each other for very long, they had bonded completely over concern for Rose Malone.

Marisa watched Jessica, carefully passing out paper plates. Her heart swelled, thinking of how it was Jessica who had made this happen. While Marisa hid inside, afraid to trust anyone or show her real self, her daughter had reached out to Rose—and beyond that, to Lily and the Nanouks.

Now, looking around the circle, Marisa desperately wanted to tell them all the truth. It killed her, to hold so much back from these women who had given her—and continued to give her—so much. She thought back to nursing school, when she had first realized how generous and healing women were by nature. She thought of Sam. The Nanouk Girls of the Frozen North were further proof.

"I have to tell you all something," she said out loud, her mouth dry. They looked at her, smiling, ready for anything.

"Jessica and I . . ."

Anne paused, thermos poised over the empty glasses.

"We're not who we seem to be," she whispered.

"Mommy?" Jessica asked—and there was warning, even panic, in her eyes.

"What do you mean?" Cindy asked.

"We're on the run . . ."

"You told us," Marlena said. "On the boat, the day of Rose's birthday party. We understand, honey. You're escaping a bad marriage. It happens."

"But we're using false names."

"Mommy!"

The women stared at her. Marisa was shaking, thinking that they would feel so betrayed, they'd just walk out the front door. They wouldn't speak to her again; they'd kick her and Jess out of the Nanouks. Anne's eyes were bruised, as if she was terribly hurt. Marlena's eyes widened, and Cindy hung her head. Cindy's two daughters just stared at Jessica, and Jessica turned bright red.

Suddenly Anne stood up, came around the circle, put her arms around Marisa. She hugged her so hard, Marisa felt it in every bone in her body.

"I'm so sorry," Anne said. "For whatever you went through that made it necessary for you to do that."

"We know something about it," Cindy said. "Because one of our other members had to do it too."

Anne and Marlena nodded, exchanging glances with Cindy. Marisa knew, without them telling her, that they were talking about Lily.

"Did you ever go to a safe house?" Cindy asked. "Were you able to get a restraining order against him?"

"You don't have to tell us," Marlena said gently.

"Yes, I did try," Marisa said. "But the kinds of things he did were too subtle. The judge, when I went to court begging for an order of protection, told me that if Ted hadn't literally tried to kill me within the last twenty-four hours, he wouldn't issue one."

"Fucking idiot," Marlena said. "It's just what Lily told us. The courts don't understand domestic violence."

"You can say that again," Cindy said.

"How can it happen to such strong women?" Marisa asked, not understanding, thinking of Lily, with her clear eyes, with the fortitude she had to get through Rose's illness. "How did we attract them?"

"First of all, you can't blame yourself. That's what we told Lily," Marlena said. "You were both vulnerable. You'd lost your husband, and Lily had never really gotten over losing her parents. Her husband saw that she made good money—from her needlework design business—and he went after it."

"Mine did the same," Marisa said. "He came after my first husband's pension."

"The point is, you're both wonderful. We all have different sorts of issues and problems—that's life. Thank God we came together—to keep each other safe and warm. We have a lot to talk about, and a lot of strength and spirit to offer each other."

"It's not all about escaping rotten husbands," Cindy said. "In fact, they are completely beside the point. It's about being friends and having fun."

"We have plenty of other things in common," Anne said. "Beyond our problems and worries."

Marisa smiled, remembering how Lily had said, "Welcome to the thaw."

"See?" Marlena asked. "We don't care what your real names are. We love you for who you are inside."

"Sometimes I don't even know who that is," Marisa whispered. "I feel as if I left her someplace far away. . . ."

"Well, we know who you are," Anne said. "Someone loving, kind, caring, and open. A woman who'd give up her summer afternoons to look after Lily's store, and make pine pillows to raise money for Rose."

"Thank you," Marisa said.

"The pine pillows were my idea," Jessica reminded everyone, and they all laughed.

"That's right, they were," Cindy said.

"I still want to tell you our real names," Marisa said. "I trust you all, so much. And he—Ted—lives hundreds of miles away. He has no idea where we are—none at all. Cape Hawk is a mystery to him. He'd never suspect that we'd come here."

"He wouldn't," Jessica said, her eyes brightening at the idea of revealing the truth.

"Well," Anne said. "We can promise you that nothing you say will leave this room. We won't even tell the other Nanouks, unless and until you say it's okay."

"I believe you," Marisa said.

"So do I," Jessica said, smiling.

"Okay then," Cindy said.

"Who are you really?" Marlena asked, with a big grin.

And Marisa told them their real names.

The Florida disaster, Hurricane Catherina, had brought out the best in people—especially in Spirit fans. Secret Agent had filled his coffers the last few weeks, with contributions sent in by all his friends on the SpiritTown message board. He had woven a story that just kept getting better and better. His sister and her husband had lost everything—everything. The 150-mile-per-hour winds had blown the roof off their house in Homestead and destroyed everything inside. His poor little nephew Jake had needed stitches from all his cuts caused by flying glass. Now he needed plastic surgery.

Secret Agent started a new topic: "Jake Update." Then he typed in his message: "Hey you guys. Here's the latest on my nephew, Jake. Thanks to all of you, my sister was able to take him to the best plastic surgeon in Miami. And you *know* they've got great plastic surgeons in Miami. (We know all about face-lifts and boob jobs.) Anyway, now they're talking about a few operations."

He paused, wondering how far he could go with this. He had learned, over time, to set the hook and then be patient—let the people on the board reach into their hearts and pocketbooks and offer. He rarely had to actually ask. Rereading his writing, he deleted the part about face-lifts and boob jobs—it struck a wrong chord. Then he hit "Send."

Didn't have to wait too long, either. It was late night, past midnight, and there were plenty of Spirit fans camped out by their computers, chatting with each other.

"So sorry, man. That family's been through too much," came the reply from Spiritfan1955.

"What kind of surgery? How extensive?" came the question from SpiritGirl—who posted a signature picture that showed she was hot, blonde, and, interestingly enough, surgically enhanced.

"Pretty extensive," Secret Agent typed back. "His face is very scarred. He's only 13, so he's pretty devastated." Here came the bait: "The worst part is, my sister has used nearly all the money you folks have been so great to send—trying to fix up the house. It's a disaster."

Now he waited again. He was itching to get out of here. He had a porn site open at the same time, and he was really dying to get back to his hot, horny, barely legal honeys. But he couldn't resist making a little money tonight—not that he needed the funds. He had plenty from the bitch. But Secret Agent's theory was, if people wanted to give it, well then, it was his job to take it. He stared at his "Jake Update" heading, and opened the single new reply.

"Like you said: it's a disaster. That means it's a disaster area, and your sister is getting money from the government."

Whoa! Who the fuck was this? Secret Agent looked at the signature: White Dawn. Had to be a woman—no guy would sign on with a name like that. On the other hand, it was the title of a Spirit song, and these Spirit fans—men or women—were freakily obsessed. Then Secret Agent noticed the number positioned right next to the screen name: 1. It was this person's first post on the message board.

"Nice first post, White Dawn," Spiritfan1955 wrote back sarcastically. "You don't know the whole story."

"Exactly," wrote PeaceBabe. "Welcome to the board, White Dawn. Secret Agent's sister and her family were affected by Hurricane Catherina, and we've been pitching in to help. Disaster aid goes only so far— and it takes a long time to sort out the bureaucracy. We've just given the family a little boost."

That was Secret Agent's cue. He typed: "Thanks everyone. I'm sure White Dawn didn't mean any harm. It's just, we're like a family here, White Dawn. These guys have been a lifeline to my sister." Should he remind everyone about little Jake and his cut face, the reason for starting this topic in the first place? Money for young Jake's reconstructive surgery? People, get ready, there's a train a-comin' . . . He'd give it a couple of minutes. But he didn't have to: *bingo*.

"Hey White Dawn," Spiritfan1955 wrote. "Here's how the Spirit-Town board works. This thread started out with a story about Jake. Thirteen y/o boy, needs plastic surgery? I'm in—Secret Agent, PM me your PayRight info, and I'll make a contribution."

Secret Agent didn't waste a second: he sent Spiritfan-1955 a private message, containing his account information, along with the requisite "thanks, man."

"I'm in," wrote PeaceBabe. "I have a thirteen-year-old daughter."

"Dude, so sorry about Jake," wrote OneThinDime. "I'll help out as much as I can. My wife was in a car accident last year, and I know how bad it can be. Plastic surgery isn't cheap, and those bills mount up. She went through a lot—we all did. We listened to the box set *Spirit Days and Spirit Nights* for about a month straight—got us through. My prayers are with you."

"Thank you," Secret Agent wrote back. "I'm humbled by your generosity. Truly. And I think I'll get my sister that box set—great idea. Her spirits are very low right now, needless to say."

"We're with you, man," Spiritguy1974 wrote.

"Totally with you," LastCall25 chimed in.

The PayRight account was filling up—a good night's work, Secret Agent thought, just getting ready to say good night to his fabulous friends, his SpiritTown family. He had been slipping back and forth between websites, tuned in to a webcam focused on the nether regions of some horny housewife in the Badlands somewhere—but now the time had come to give Ms. Housewife his full attention.

Just then, White Dawn's screen name appeared in the "Jake Update" thread. Secret Agent chuckled. Another convert to the world of give-me-your-money. He'd had just about enough of this, and was really ready to click onto his porno screen. He'd just see what White Dawn had to offer, so he scrolled down to her post.

"Beware."

Secret Agent's blood turned ice cold. He couldn't believe it. Just one word there on the SpiritTown screen, for all to see: Beware. White Dawn's second post—warning the world. Secret Agent felt as if he had a new enemy—as if he had just turned over a rock and found a rattlesnake coiled and ready to attack him.

He couldn't believe his eyes. Another post had popped up, and he read it:

"Hurricane Catherina didn't hit Homestead. It tracked north, dude. You can do a better job conning people if you first check out the storm track on the NOAA website."

"You fucking bitch!" he yelled. But he didn't even know whether it was a man or woman—he knew nothing about White Dawn at all. He looked for the profile and found none. He was going to find out—that was for sure. He would learn this person's identity and make White Dawn sorry for shaming him on the board.

"Fuck you!" he said out loud, totally losing his erection.

Chapter 21

Boston was filled with kids. Lily saw them everywhere: with their families, with groups, on camp outings. Heading to the Public Gardens, the science museum, the Freedom Trail, Faneuil Hall, the aquarium. Kids having fun, too excited to walk slowly or in single file. They tried to outrun the rain. They tried to outshout the city noises. They tried to have more fun today than they'd had yesterday.

Lily hoped they would all succeed. Even more, she hoped that Rose would one day be able to join them. She turned away from the wide plate-glass window overlooking the playground on the banks of the Charles River. Then she sat in one of the orange chairs of the hospital waiting room, Liam by her side, while Rose was being prepped for surgery.

She glanced over at him. She felt she was in a dream, where everything was both normal and bizarre at the same time. Here she was, sitting with Liam Neill, as if they were a longtime couple. They were waiting for Rose to have open-heart surgery. Two nights ago he had kissed her.

That was the part that made life feel like a dream. Lily couldn't understand how she could be feeling so secretly happy and tender while her daughter was in the fight of her life. Liam touched the back of her hand, and Lily turned liquid inside. He asked if she would like a cup of tea, and she was so befuddled, she couldn't quite stop looking at his eyes.

But there had been no chance to talk about what had happened—or even to repeat it. Since getting to Boston, every minute had been focused on being with Rose and talking to the doctors. Lily knew that was for the best: she didn't want to be distracted. Rose was her full-time job, and more: she was Lily's life. And Lily didn't want to jeopardize anything by messing up her priorities.

At least, that's what she told herself about the fact that Liam hadn't kissed her again.

"Are you okay?" Liam asked now, sitting in the waiting room.

"I'm fine. Are you?"

"Yes," he said. But the way he said it, "yes," with his blue eyes glowing and fixed on Lily's—well, it confused her, made her blush.

"Um, good," she said.

"Something has changed," he said. "And you don't have to be afraid of it, Lily."

"About Rose? About her tests?"

Rose had had another echo test; she was so tired now from the cumulative effect of not getting enough oxygen, she slept while the technician rubbed cold jelly on her chest. She seemed oblivious to the loud sound made by the Doppler. But the test had revealed no surprises—Rose had been stabilized by her time in Melbourne, and she was now ready for surgery.

"No," Liam said, smiling. "Not about Rose."

"She's all I can think about right now, Liam."

"I know. We're almost there," he said.

"We've been here so many times before," Lily said—and as she looked up into Liam's weathered face, she felt her stomach flip. They had both said "we," and the word was apt. Liam had been with her and Rose every time. Why had Lily never let that sink in before?

"This time is different," Liam said.

"How do you know?" Lily asked.

Liam reached for her hand. She shivered, wanting him to hold her—she felt like a tornado of emotion. She wanted him to hold her together, keep her from flying apart. She felt her skin tingling—and the length of her spine, and the backs of her legs—all from some fantastic longing that confused and shocked her and seemed like the worst timing possible. All he had done was hold her hand.

"This time is different," he said, "because the procedure is straightforward. All they're doing is replacing an old patch. The hole in her heart hasn't torn or grown or widened. The only problem is the patch, and this surgery will be definitive."

"She's not getting worse," Lily said.

"No. She's not. Her symptoms are all related to the patch, and to the stenosis."

"I can't take it," she whispered.

"Yes, you can," he said, giving her hand a firm shake. "Just think it through, Lily. You know it's going to go well."

She watched Liam, who was watching the door through which the doctors would walk—to tell them Rose was ready. Her mind clicked through everything she knew about Rose, a laundry list of what would happen today. Although Tetralogy of Fallot included four defects, only two were of supreme importance today. Pulmonary stenosis—the outflow passage, where Rose's right ventricle and pulmonary artery connected, was narrow and blocked; and the large ventricular septal defect—the patch had become brittle, allowing blood to freely mix between the two ventricles.

Rose's severe stenosis meant that less blood reached the lungs with each heartbeat, causing her to turn blue. Her surgery today would involve removing the thickened muscle beneath the pulmonary valve and replacing the old worn-out patch with some brand-new felt Gortex. It all sounded so simple—yet Lily felt that she herself might not survive another minute of stress.

Now the doctors came out, wheeling Rose alongside. Prepped for surgery—groggy, hair held back by a paper cap, hooked up to monitors and an IV—she managed to lift her head slightly, searching for Lily. Only, the person she called for was Liam.

"Dr. Neill," she said.

"I'm here, Rose."

"Remember what I said."

"I do remember. I never forget."

Lily saw the looks pass between them, and felt that mysterious stomach drop—not knowing what they meant, but realizing it was important.

"Did you find her again? Nanny?"

"Yes," Liam said, crouching down, face-to-face with Rose. "I did. It's so unbelievable, but you know where she is?"

Rose shook her head, eyes rolling back as she tried to stay awake. Lily touched Liam's back—partly for support, and partly because they were all together in this.

"Tell Rose, Lily—"

"Honey," Lily said, hardly able to believe it herself. "Nanny is swimming south from Nova Scotia. While all the other whales are migrating north, we think she's coming to Boston, to find you—"

"Will she be okay?" Rose asked, looking worried.

Lily nodded. "Yes." The moment shimmered between them. "Nanny will be fine," she said. "And so will you, my darling girl."

"You will," Liam said.

"It's time to go now," Dr. Garibaldi said. "When you see Rose again, she'll be as good as new. She's told me all about this Nanny character—and she'll be back in Nova Scotia before the week's out, and by August, she'll be swimming with all the whales she wants. We're going to put on the best, strongest patch in the world, and this will be Miss Rose Malone's last surgery for a long, long time. Now come on—let's go."

Lily and Liam bent down to kiss Rose, and that was that—they wheeled her away. Lily's own heart nearly gave out, watching her go into the elevator. She felt Liam's arm come around her, she let him lead her to the chairs in the waiting room. There was a television on—there was always a television on—and a pile of magazines, and that morning's papers. But Lily just put her head in her hands and tried to hold herself together.

"You heard the doctor," Liam said. "He sounded so positive—he said Rose will be home by the end of the week. Lily—that's six days."

"I know," she said.

"Six days, Lily. We'll be back in Cape Hawk. Rose can have her summer."

Lily let him hold her. There were times when she couldn't talk, couldn't even really think. There were aspects to life nine years ago that were so traumatic, she had developed a fight-or-flight response. Her body would flood with adrenaline, and she would go totally numb. She was right there, right now.

Rose's father had created so much terror back then. He had been so angry about the pregnancy—and his behavior had gotten so much worse. Lily, not getting it, had tried every way possible to reassure him that she would love him as much—or even more—after the baby was born. But he was unmoved by her promises.

"Promises," she said now.

"Which promises?" Liam asked.

Lily was almost in a trance—her baby was about to be hooked up to the heart-lung machine. The idea was so terrifying, all Lily's old trauma was being reactivated. She started to tremble, and couldn't stop.

"I made promises to Rose's father," she said to Liam now. "I promised that we would stay together, that I would love him as much or more after the baby was born. I promised that she wouldn't take up all my time—that I'd still have plenty of time for him. More, I said. Because I was going to stop work and stay home . . ."

"Lily, what are you thinking of him for?" Liam asked. "You know he doesn't deserve your words or thoughts."

That's right, Lily thought. She had told Liam about him that very first night—when she was nearly crazed with pain—both physical, from giving birth, and emotional, from having run for her life from Rose's father. She gulped back a sob.

"And he doesn't deserve your tears," Liam said, leaning over to kiss her forehead, her cheek, the corner of her mouth.

"I used to drive myself mad," Lily said. "Wondering *why*."

"Why?"

"Why Rose? Why did she have to have these problems? We don't have heart disease in our family—the only person who ever had a heart attack was my great-grandfather, and he was ninety-one. I ate a healthy diet during pregnancy—gave up caffeine. I'd given up wine even before I got pregnant. . . . I didn't smoke. I exercised, but not too much. Why?"

"I don't know, Lily," Liam said, kissing her hands, looking into her eyes.

"The doctors didn't know either. They say Tetralogy of Fallot isn't hereditary. It just happens—and it's random. There's no knowing who gets it."

"Lily, don't do this—"

"It should be so simple—it is for other children. Air and blood meet in the lungs, and then the heart pumps the blood through the body. Why can't it work for Rose? It's so simple. . . ."

"But it does work for Rose," Liam said gently. "She's had some challenges, that's true. But I believe the doctors. They say that this will be her last surgery for a long time."

"A long, *long* time," Lily corrected.

"Right. A long, long time. And we're going to hold them to that."

We. That word again.

"There are mysteries about Rose, it's true," Liam said. "We don't know why. We might never know why. But there are other whys we might never know either. Such as why I went to your house that night, the night Rose was born. Why I had to take the books back to you that exact night. And why, once I walked through that door, I never wanted to walk out again."

"Liam," she whispered, remembering the promises he'd made that night, and for the first time, wanting him to keep them.

"Why," he began, but stopped himself. His lips moved against her skin, and she felt rather than heard him say "Why I love you both so much." But then she realized that he had just kissed her neck—he hadn't said anything at all. Of course he hadn't—they were in the middle of the waiting room—with nurses and doctors and other parents walking in and out.

She held his hand tighter, listening to him—feeling herself materialize more in her own body, no longer numb and floating up in the air, a traumatized ghost.

"We love you too," she wanted to say, but didn't. She wanted to tell him that, because it was finally washing over her—the reality, that this man had been with her and Rose, right by their side, since the very first day. He was like Rose's father. Rose's real father was nothing to them—nothing at all. Liam was one reason why Rose felt so loved, one of the reasons why she thrived.

"You're right," she said. "There are a lot of whys."

"And they're not all bad," he said.

"I know," Lily said, just smiling. But she looked up at the clock and saw that it was ten o'clock—the time that surgery was going to start. Open-heart surgery never took long. Generally sixty minutes at the most. So much could happen during that single hour. A life and death could pass before a family's eyes. . . . *Oh God,* Lily prayed, closing her eyes. *Help her through this hour. . . .*

Liam opened his laptop, hoping Lily would take pleasure and comfort in watching the green light that represented MM122 tracking ever closer to Boston Harbor. But Lily seemed unable to watch anything but the clock and the door through which the doctors would emerge post-surgery.

It was ten-fifteen. Liam tried to hide his own nervousness. He had sat beside Lily through Rose's other open-heart surgeries. Because of Rose's aortic valve stenosis and her ventricular defect, the very wall of the heart had to be opened.

To keep the blood flowing to other vital organs, Rose had to be hooked up to a heart-lung machine. Liam had studied up on it, spoken to a friend from McGill who'd gone into cardiac surgery in Vancouver. He knew that Rose was under deep anesthesia. Dr. Garibaldi would have gone in through her breastbone.

Catheters were draining blood from the veins in the right side of her heart into the heart-lung machine—which, in a pumping rhythm, was passing the blood over a special oxygen-containing filter, sending the oxygenated blood back into Rose's body through a catheter in her aorta.

Her heart itself was now without blood—and the doctors were working fast. The operating room was very cold, so Rose's heart and brain would require less oxygen. Liam tried to imagine what was going on, but he—like Lily—was now watching the clock. Ten thirty-five.

"Her last operation took forty minutes," Lily said. "The doctor will be out anytime."

"Yep," Liam said. "Any minute now."

"They're just going to remove the blockage and replace the patch."

"Right," Liam said. "Dr. Garibaldi has done this exact surgery hundreds of times."

"But not on Rose," Lily said. "He's never operated on her before. It was Dr. Kenney before. And then he took that position in Baltimore, at Johns Hopkins. We could have gone to Johns Hopkins."

"Boston is fine, Lily. It's the best. Dr. Garibaldi is the best."

"But we could have gone to Baltimore. . . ."

"I know. But Boston is closer to home. You like this hospital, and Rose feels comfortable here."

"That's right," Lily said, staring at him earnestly, as if he were telling her something she'd never heard before. "You're right. That's why we chose Boston—because it's so good, and because Rose feels comfortable here."

Ten-forty.

"She's been under for forty minutes," Lily murmured. "I think that's as long as she's ever been on the machine before. I'm not sure, but I think so."

"It's not too long, Lily. The doctor will be out in a minute."

"It's just . . ." Lily said. "They have to make sure the blood and oxygen mix properly. I never understand how a machine can do that. But it's been done before—lots of times before. Rose has always been fine afterwards. Except that time she got the bacterial infection—"

"She won't get one this time," Liam said, reaching for Lily's hand. But she wouldn't let him hold it. As if remembering that terrible time when Rose had contracted a virulent staph infection—she had survived the surgery but nearly died from the infection—Lily jumped out of her seat and began to pace. She went to the window, rested her forehead against the glass.

Liam ached with helplessness, so he forced himself to focus on science. He turned up the brightness of his computer screen—it wasn't like sitting in the dark with Lily, in his truck by the lighthouse, with the night so black, and the screen showing every dot, with his arm around Lily, and her skin soft against his. It wasn't like that here.

He peered at the screen. There she was—Nanny, MM122—blinking off Gloucester. She had swum her amazing journey in one and a half days—from Melbourne, slanting across the Atlantic to the Gulf of Maine, passing Matinicus and Monhegan, Christmas Cove, Boothbay Harbor, Yarmouth, Portland, swinging past the Isle of Shoals, down the coast of Massachusetts.

Here she was, right on Boston's North Shore, speeding south. Liam wanted to call Lily over, to show her, but something in Lily's posture told him that she couldn't take hearing about Nanny just now. Liam's own stomach dropped a little.

MM122 was way out of her range, out of the normal geographic areas where beluga whales were found in July. What if Nanny did have some mystical connection to Rose? What if her coming here was some sort of harbinger—living in Cape Hawk, the whale could certainly say hello to Rose any time she wanted to. What if Nanny was coming to Boston to say goodbye?

Liam refused to think that. Gazing at Lily across the room, he pushed himself up. The clock now read ten fifty-five. Rose had been under for five minutes shy of an hour. Liam tried to think of the things he could say to Lily: maybe the doctors got started late, maybe the operating room wasn't ready, maybe . . .

This wasn't the time for speculation. Liam was an oceanographer, and he knew: it was a time for science. He walked across the big space to Lily—a distance that seemed interminable. He was reminded of the first time he saw his mother, after Connor had died, and after Liam had had what was left of his arm amputated. His mother had been looking out a window then. Liam had called her name, and she didn't turn around.

"Lily?" he said.

When she wheeled at the sound of his voice, he felt so much relief, he felt his eyes fill.

"What?" Lily asked.

"I wanted to tell you something," he said, blinking back the tears. He wanted to come up with something factual, scientific, indisputable, and wise. But the thing was, he really had nothing to say. All he could think of was Rose.

"You were talking about the mix before," he said. "Blood and oxygen."

"Yes . . ."

"I was thinking back to grad school," he said, struggling for something that would comfort her. "We learned a lot about that in a marine biology class. Whales are mammals, as you know, and our professor was teaching us about the cetacean circulatory system."

Lily nodded, listening. She seemed to notice that his brow was sweating—she reached up and brushed his damp hair back from his forehead. Her smile was very gentle, as if encouraging him to go on.

"In the earliest days of medicine," Liam said, "dating back to the sixth century B.C., on the Greek island of Ionia, doctors had the idea that when air and blood mingled in the lungs, the blood gained a 'vital essence.' But it took many centuries until they realized that the vital essence was—"

"Oxygen," Lily said, and Liam smiled, knowing she probably knew more about the process than most scientists.

"Right," he said. "I still remember reading William Harvey's famous treatise—I think it's from 1628—on blood flow and circulation. Of course, my class was on whales, not humans."

"Hearts are hearts," Lily whispered, watching the time click to eleven o'clock.

Liam watched the blood drain from her face. She began to tremble, and he knew she was losing it. He put his arm around her, tried to hold her tight. She was shaking so hard, grabbing his arm, burying her face in his chest.

"Where are the doctors?" she asked.

"They're coming," he said.

And before they could look up, they heard Dr. Garibaldi's voice. "Lily, Liam?" he asked.

"How's Rose?" Lily asked. She lurched toward the doctor. Liam looked around—as if it was possible Dr. Garibaldi could have rolled Rose out with him, into the waiting room. Then Liam looked at the doctor's pale, deep-set eyes, and he knew what he was about to say, before he even spoke.

"She's fine," the doctor said. "Went through the surgery with no problems whatever. We removed the obstruction and replaced the patch. Gortex, this time—it should last her the rest of her life. She's in recovery now, but she's already out of the anesthesia, and they'll be bringing her up here to the ICU in just a few minutes."

"Thank you," Liam said. "Thank you, Doctor."

Lily shook Dr. Garibaldi's hand, touched her own heart, and thanked him. After the doctor left, she turned to Liam.

"You thanked him even before I did," she said.

"Oh," he said, suddenly embarrassed. "I did. I'm sorry—I just—"

"No, it's good," she said, turning bright pink. "It's just . . . it's just something a father would do."

Liam stood straight, couldn't quite speak. If only Lily knew what was going on inside his chest, how he had felt about Rose since the instant he'd brought her into this world.

"I was thinking," Lily said. "About what you were saying just before the doctor came up. About the Greeks, and the vital essence."

"Oxygen," he said. As she herself had said. . . .

"I was thinking it must be something else too," she said, staring at the elevator doors, hearing the lift coming closer. The doctor had said that Rose would be up in just a few minutes, and Lily was ready. She turned her gaze from the elevator to Liam.

"What else?" he asked.

"Well," she said, stopping herself.

Liam wanted to tell her what he thought, but he couldn't say the word out loud: *Love.* The most vital essence of all.

And just then the door opened, and an orderly wheeled Rose out—there on the bed, attached to monitors, but with her eyes open. She was strapped down—the sight of those straps tore Liam's heart. They had to keep her from moving, at least overnight. She looked from Lily to Liam, and then back to Lily.

"Hi, sweetheart," Lily said.

"It hurts," Rose said.

"I know, honey. But it won't for long."

"It won't, Rose," Liam said, hardly able to bear seeing her in pain, knowing that the nurses would give her pain meds in a second, and knowing that she would heal fast from the surgery. "It won't hurt for long."

"Promise?" Rose whispered hoarsely.

"Yes," Liam said, touching her head—as his own father had done when he'd made a similar promise after Liam's arm surgery—knowing that that was just what a father would say and do.

Chapter 22

Rose was awake, opening her eyes as soon as they wheeled her out of the operating room. The medicine they gave her made her groggy, but she kept trying to tear the straps off her chest anyway. She wanted to move, run, hug her mother, go home.

She slept a lot.

Her mother and Dr. Neill took turns sitting by her bed. Sometimes they were there together, sitting so close they looked like one person. Their voices threaded in and out of her dreams, joining her waking and sleeping hours. When she cried, she wasn't sure who hugged her. Her chest hurt.

And then it didn't. The next day, when Rose woke up, the sun was shining, and her chest didn't hurt at all. Well, maybe a little—the nurse helped her sit up, and then she washed her, and then the doctor came to look at her stitches.

Her mother and Liam stood back while the nurses got her ready to take her first walk. She knew that it was less than a day since her surgery, but she was used to being the wonder girl when it came to getting out of bed fast. She knew that walking and pooping were the big events. They were like getting an A+ on a book report or math test. Once you had them, you were on your way home.

Or at least out of ICU, to the normal floor.

"How's the pain, Rose?" the nurse asked.

"Not so bad. Mom, did you tell Jessica I'm coming home in a week?"

"Yes, honey."

"Dr. Neill, what's wrong?" She looked up, and he had a funny look on his face—as if he was frozen between wanting to stand back and trying to catch her. The nurse gave him a teacherly smile, as if he had a lot to learn.

"Children heal much faster than adults from open-heart surgery," the nurse said. "They experience much less pain in the chest wall. We're going to get Rose up and walking, so we can move her down to the pediatric floor."

"Okay," Dr. Neill said, holding his arms out, the way Rose remembered him doing when she was really tiny, learning to walk. The sight of him doing that made her laugh, which made her chest hurt. "Rose? What?" he asked.

"I can do it," she told him. "Watch."

"Ready when you are, honey," her mother said.

All the adults stood close by her side, and Rose inched to the edge of the bed. She reached her toes down to the floor, in her fuzzy slippers. The ground felt so solid. Rose hadn't wanted to tell her mother, but it had felt tippy for a long while, almost like the deck of the *Tecumseh II* at her birthday party. A boat, tilting fore and aft, sideways, all around. Rose had felt dizzy, and she knew it was because she hadn't been getting enough oxygen.

But that had changed. Already, just half a day after her operation, she felt ten, a hundred, a thousand times better than she had. She breathed in—and she actually felt her lungs expand and her strength return.

"I feel *good*," she said.

Everyone smiled, and her mother held out her hand.

"Walk with me?" her mother asked.

Rose nodded, but she didn't move her feet. She just kept waiting, staring up.

"Rose?" Dr. Neill asked.

She just reached out her hand, waiting for him to take it. He slid his fingers into hers, and then Rose was ready. She, her mother, and Dr. Neill took their first steps together. Through the ICU, around the nurses' station. She realized that in all the ICUs she had been in before, Dr. Neill had been there too.

Only family were allowed in ICU. Rose grinned, keeping her head down, afraid to let everyone know how happy that made her feel. Because she didn't know what it meant, and over the last nine years she had learned that she needed to take care of her heart, keep it from getting broken. But he squeezed her hand, and she decided to allow herself to hope.

Lily and Liam had started going down to Boston Harbor after leaving the hospital. They would cut through Faneuil Hall and end up on Long Wharf. People enjoying the summer night strolled by, but for Lily and

Liam it was much more urgent: they were both sustained by the sea, and they needed to see it and feel the salt air of home.

Liam brought binoculars so they could scan the blue water, searching for Nanny. But she never came close enough to the shore, seeming to stay out beyond the harbor islands, just hovering in the area.

That night, when they'd had their fill of sea breezes, they walked back toward the hotel. Lily stared down at the cobblestones, tension building inside. There was so much she wanted to say to him, but she felt shy and tongue-tied, as if all the words were bound in thick rope. He hadn't taken her hand once tonight—not once on their whole walk.

"Life is funny," he said as they walked along.

"In what way?"

"You can think you know what's best, what's right for you, and then all of a sudden something happens and turns your plans upside down."

"What do you mean?" she asked. Was he thinking of his summer? He had given up so much of it to be with Lily and Rose; perhaps he was starting to resent the time, and the loss of research time.

"Just, bad things happen, but they sometimes turn out to be . . . good."

She tilted her head, curious about what he meant, but he just walked in silence. The space between them seemed so great, but Lily was afraid to close it; he seemed to need some distance.

"I was thinking of the shark," he said after a few minutes.

"Nothing good came of the shark, I know," she said. "You lost Connor, and a part of yourself. Liam, you don't have to pretend anything about that is okay." He didn't reply.

She glanced over. His brown hair was wavy, with strands of silver in the streetlights. His blue eyes looked sad. They got to the Charles River Hotel, just behind the hospital, and went to the elevator. As it clicked up to their floors, Lily wished she knew what to say. She was on the fourteenth floor, and Liam was on the sixteenth. When the door opened at 14, he looked at her.

"Good night," she said.

"Good night, Lily," he said.

She walked to her room, feeling upset and churned up. Not just because he hadn't touched her at all, not once, on their walk—but because he had looked so troubled, and made that comment about the shark, and she hadn't comforted him.

Lily felt torment inside. She paced her hotel room. She had been so hurt by her husband, her trust had been shattered. She had sacrificed everything leaving him. She had swallowed an iceberg. It had frozen her, cell by cell, until she was brittle and hard; she had learned, over time, how to guard herself—be tough, never let any man get close to her. The Nanouks had been her only friends. But Liam . . .

Over these last weeks, she had felt herself melting.

"Welcome to the thaw," she had said to Marisa, at Rose's birthday party. What Marisa couldn't know was that Lily had never really believed those words for herself. She had thought she was too glacial, too long frozen, too trapped by winter, to ever really experience anything like internal springtime.

She thought of Liam—the look in his eyes when he'd mentioned the shark. After all he'd done for her these years—and, especially, this summer—why couldn't she have reached up, put her arms around him? Why couldn't she have told him she was there to listen if he felt like talking?

Lily was shaking inside. She grabbed her key and left the room. Not wanting to wait for the elevator, she took the stairs. With every step, she felt more and more afraid. What if she was making a mistake? She hadn't reached out to a man in so long—she had stopped believing that she ever would again. Liam's kindness, the way Rose adored him, Lily's own growing feelings for him all seemed insignificant in the face of her old, terrible, very real fears. But she pushed through them and just kept going.

She found his room, 1625. Took a deep breath and knocked.

Liam opened the door. He stood there, surprise in his blue eyes. He was wearing jeans and a blue oxford shirt. His left sleeve hung there, empty. Lily had never seen him that way before. She gasped.

"I'm sorry," he said, glancing down, patting his empty sleeve as if he could will his arm to appear there. "I should have—"

"No—don't be sorry," she said. "I'm the one—I'm sorry, Liam."

"If it makes you uncomfortable, I can put my prosthesis back on."

Lily smiled and shook her head. "Uncomfortable? No. Liam, you just spent two days sitting in the ICU with Rose. You saw her stitches, her incision. . . . I'm not uncomfortable with anything like that."

"Most people are."

"I'm not most people," she said.

They walked over to the small table with two chairs, right by the window. The room lights were dim, so they could see the river, dancing with city lights. It was such a different water view than the one they loved in Cape Hawk. But it was still water, and Lily felt things starting to flow.

"When you said that about the shark," she said, "I wanted to hear more."

"Really? It was nothing—just some philosophizing."

"So, philosophize," she said, leaning back in her chair.

"I guess, what I was thinking was, sometimes it seems that my life ended with that shark," he said. "Other times, it seems it began."

"How?"

"You don't know how close I was to Connor," he said. "We were inseparable. Even though he was three years younger, there was no one I'd rather hang around with. He was so funny. He'd swim up to whales while they were sleeping, and climb up on their backs. We used to dare him all the time."

"Is that what he was doing that day?"

"Yes," he said. "He was trying to get close to this one beluga. The whale was there, feeding on krill and herring. We didn't see the shark, until it was pulling Connor down."

"You saw?"

Liam nodded. "I did. Connor reached out both arms for me. I swam as fast as I could—I was pulling him, trying to get him away from the shark. And then he just . . . wasn't there anymore. I was there in my brother's blood, diving and diving for him. And the shark got me too."

Lily was silent, listening.

"He just—he grabbed my arm. It didn't hurt—I couldn't feel his teeth or anything. Later I learned they're so sharp, like razors, they just slice through skin and bone. It felt more like the most violent tug I'd ever felt. All I could think of was Connor—I tried to beat the shark with my other arm, pounding him, gouging his eyes. I dug my fingers into his eye socket—and that's what got him to let go."

Lily was so clenched, she felt like a closed fist. She knew what it was like to fight for her life. Liam's description of the teeth going in—so sharp and smooth, you almost don't know you're being eaten alive. She thought of the last day, pregnant with Rose, when her husband had knocked her to the ground—and pretended it was an accident.

"You got away," she whispered.

"I did," he said. "I was swimming on pure adrenaline—still diving for Connor, even though my arm was gone. I don't think I even knew. Jude was screaming—he had climbed up on the shore. He got someone's attention, and a boat came over. They had to haul me out—everyone was surprised I survived. The shark had severed an artery—I was bleeding out, right there in the spot where Connor went down."

"Oh, Liam." She jumped up, unable to withstand what he was telling her. Liam stood beside her; she was shaking so hard, she backed into the desk. Liam reached out to steady her—he surprised her, looking so calm. Beyond him, in the corner of the room, his artificial arm leaned against the wall.

"How do you do it?" she asked. "How do you go on, having lived through that?"

"How do you, Lily Malone?" he asked. "You encountered a shark too."

"Sometimes I wonder," she said.

"Good comes from bad," he said. "That's how. You got Rose out of it."

"That's true," she said. "But what about you?"

"Here I am with you," he said.

"That's . . ." she began.

"Something brought us together," he said. "To me, that's the good that came from bad."

Lily stood on tiptoes to reach up and slide her arms around his neck. She caressed the back of his head, looking into his eyes. She felt so much emotion, all of it just swirling around. She wanted to comfort him, but even more, she wanted to kiss him.

Liam took care of it. He held her tight, she tipped her head, and they kissed. It was so long and tender, as if the feelings had been building up forever, just like the last one. His touch was gentle, but so strong. Lily had come up to comfort him, but he was bringing tears to her eyes. She grabbed him, holding on, and with one arm he picked her up and carried her to the bed.

"I wanted to tell you," she said, lying beside him, eye to eye. "I think you're wonderful. You've been wonderful to me and Rose, and I'm sorry I didn't ask you before, when you—"

He put his finger to her lips.

"You don't have to be sorry for anything," he said.

And then it seemed that words were beside the point. They had nine years to make up for. Lily lay back, her hand on Liam's chest. He rolled over, on top of her, hiked up on his elbow, kissing her cheek, lips, the whole length of her neck, making her squirm and ache. She kept that arm between them, hand on his chest, and they both knew she was ready to push him away—she was always ready to push someone away.

It was now or never—she was sweating for his kisses, she needed them, but she was ready to fight. Tension coiled in her spine like a spring. Liam's eyes were bluer than any sea. They looked at her with such openness, all the while he was kissing her, slowly, one kiss at a time, and she felt the fight just go out of her.

She must have sighed, and Liam took it as a sign. He lay on his left side and, with his right arm, reached around her, stroking her back as he kissed her long and hard. His tongue was so hot, and she bit it—just lightly, but the unexpectedness of it just sent them both over the edge.

Their clothes came off. Lily wasn't sure who unbuttoned or un-zipped what—but their shirts, and his pants, and then her pants, and all that underwear, all got thrown on the floor, and then they were on the bed again. The only light came from the small table lamp, warm and dim. Lily had never seen Liam with his shirt off. She wanted to look but was afraid.

Liam lay on his back, staring up at her. She let her eyes travel from his strong, broad chest to his left shoulder. It looked powerful, and extended down to his upper arm, which ended about six inches below the shoulder bone.

She saw his left side—it looked raw and scraped, crisscrossed with scars and old stitches. His arm looked healed, but his side was a reminder of the shark's ravages, of old surgery. Lily leaned over and gently kissed the side of his body.

They held each other, kissing. Liam ran his fingers the length of her torso, making her arch her back. He kissed her harder, and she got lost in the moment. She lifted her hips, wanting him inside her more than she'd ever wanted anything.

His kiss held her steady, but his touch made her lose her mind. Lily shivered, and felt everything about his body: the curve of his spine, the narrowness of his hips, his broad shoulders, his strong legs. He held her and rocked her, even when she cried out, letting go of everything old and cold and frozen, and even when she trembled and cried again, afterwards, because she hadn't realized that she could still feel and still love.

They fell asleep together, holding each other tight. Lily woke up a few times, but she didn't want to move—she never wanted to let go of Liam. Lying beside him, she felt reckless joy. He had shifted in his sleep; his right arm grazed her chest. They embraced, as if it was the most normal and familiar thing in the world. As if they had loved each other for years, and had been just waiting for the perfect time for their lives together to start.

Lily held on, feeling her eyes flicker as sleep overtook her again, wanting to stay awake just a minute more, knowing she was with Liam, knowing Rose was safe.

From the time Rose moved down to the pediatric floor, her healing really did begin to seem miraculous. Lily's own heart soared—because of Rose's fast recovery, and because of Liam.

Rose was unhooked from all the tubes, wires, and machines within twenty-four hours of the surgery, and by the time she reached her new room, she was moving unrestricted. She wanted to take lots of walks so that the doctors would let her out soon. Lily had never seen Rose so eager to leave. And Lily had never felt so eager about life—as if she had finally found the magical key that other people had, the one that made every day worth living.

Usually after surgery Rose was a bit hesitant, very protective—keeping her left hand at her shoulder, hunching her back to protect the heart area. Lily understood such maneuvers very well. But this time, Lily watched her trying to walk free, to stand up straight, remembering many of the exercises she had been taught after other procedures—because she really disliked going to physical therapy. Lily had never been sure why—of all the hard things Rose went through, why did something so ostensibly benign seem so threatening?

Now that the surgery was over, Liam returned home to catch up on work. His leaving had been wrenching for both him and Lily—she had felt herself cave in, just knowing he was going. But he called every morning and every night, and on the third day, as if the distance was too great, he drove back down—and Lily was overjoyed.

So was Rose. She was blooming like her namesake flower, getting pinker and more healthy by the minute. Lily stood back, watching her and Liam laugh and talk, watching Liam show Rose his laptop with Nanny's light blinking just outside Boston Harbor.

"Why is she there?" Rose asked—although she had asked it before, she liked to hear the answer again and again.

"We have no way of knowing," Liam said, glancing at Lily. "But we think it's because she wants to be near you."

"But she doesn't even know me!"

"I think she knows you," Liam said.

"But I'm a girl and she's a whale. We've never talked or played or swum together. Mommy made me all those needlepoint pictures of her, and I have them hanging on my wall, but she doesn't *know* me."

"I want to tell you a story about that," Liam said. "About how Nanny just might know you. It's about a sea hawk and a black cat."

"But—" Rose began.

Rose's green eyes were wide, and she had a big smile on her face. But just then the physical therapist stopped by, to let Rose know what to expect when she went home. She showed her how to keep her left hand down, keep her spine straight, and checked with Lily to make sure they had the name of a PT office near Cape Hawk. Lily assured her they did.

When the therapist left, Rose was clearly drooping. She glanced over at Liam, as if waiting for him to cheer her up with the tale of the fish hawk and black cat.

Lily wanted to hear too. She had thought Liam would jump right in, tell Rose the story to take her mind off the fact that the physical therapist had just outlined a fairly arduous program. And although the program didn't seem bad—and even seemed *fun*—to Lily, clearly it was upsetting Rose. But Liam looked unsettled, disturbed himself.

"It's not fun, is it, Rose?" he asked.

She cocked her head, as if to ask what he meant. But she must have read something in his eyes—a kindred spirit who knew how she felt. Because she just shook her head, and then bowed it so low, her chin drooped to her chest. When she looked up, her face was wet with tears.

"I remember how hard it was," Liam said.

"What do you mean?" Rose asked. "You've had PT too?"

"Yes," Liam said. "About six months' worth at first—and then another year."

"For your arm?"

Liam nodded. "I had to learn how to do everything all over again. And how not to do things."

"Like what?"

"Well, when I first lost my arm, I thought it was still there. I would wake up at night and reach for a glass of water with my left arm. Only it wouldn't be there. So I'd get all confused and upset. If I felt it, it had to be real, right? But it wasn't. So I got . . . kind of angry."

"I get that way," Rose said in a low voice.

"I'll bet you do," he said.

"What else happened?"

"Well, I began to do everything with my right arm. Things my left arm used to do. So I'd always be reaching across my body. That ended up hurting my right shoulder. And also my left shoulder—because even though I no longer had a left arm, I still had muscles in my shoulder that were starting to shrink and contract—I had to make sure to use them."

"I reach across my body," Rose said. "Only it's with my left arm. I do it because I don't want anyone to bump my heart."

"That makes sense to me," Liam said.

"I know, but then it twists me all up and ruins my posture! But I don't even care about my posture!" Rose said.

"I didn't care about mine, either, Rose," Liam said. "I just cared about doing twice as much with one arm. But you want to have good posture, you know? Even if you think you don't. You want to have a healthy spine, right? Let's see—we have to make a list of things to do. 'Protect heart, protect spine—' Anything else?"

"Use both arms!" Rose said, and giggled.

"Oh, yes. How could we forget?" Liam asked, pretending to write on a pretend pad. Seeing him hold the pad with his prosthesis, writing with his real hand, captivated Rose. Lily saw her staring intently, and she felt a spill of gratitude inside. Looking at Liam, her own heart melted a little more, and she just faded back, watching the two of them.

"What was it like?" Rose asked quietly after a moment.

"When I got my prosthesis? Well, that was the reason I had to go back to PT for a year. To learn how to use it right."

"And the whole time, you must have been so sad," Rose said.

"I was," Liam said, looking up. "How did you know?"

"Because I'm sad sometimes," she said. "Because I lost someone too. You lost your brother, but Mommy and I lost someone."

"Rose?" Lily asked, having no idea what she meant.

"My father," Rose said. "I've never had a father. The one that was there didn't want me."

"Rose, it wasn't you," Lily said. She had purposely never discussed him with her. "You weren't the reason he's not in our lives!"

"No matter what the reason, that's what she feels," Liam said, holding Rose's hand—and for the first time in a long time, Lily felt impatient with him. He was supposed to go along with Lily on this—reassure Rose that nothing she did had driven her father away!

"It is," Rose whispered. "It's why my heart doesn't work right."

"I felt the same way," Liam said. "I was with my brother when he died. I was his older brother, Rose. And I thought—if only I had protected him more. Swum faster, rescued him—it should have been me, not him." Lily steeled herself, remembering what he had told her the other night.

"And you thought the reason the shark took your arm was because you were bad?" Rose asked.

"Yes," Liam said. "For a long time I thought that."

"Just like me. Thinking I must have been bad, to have no father with me."

"Sweetheart—" Lily began, and stopped, searching for the right words.

"But you know it's not true," Liam said, stepping in. "You know that, don't you, Rose? You're the most wonderful girl there is. Sometimes things just happen. You were born with heart defects—but it wasn't because of who you are, the kind of girl you are. If that were true, you would have the healthiest, most beautiful heart in the world."

"And the shark didn't bite your arm because you're bad, right?"

"Right," Liam said, looking up at Lily. "I finally figured out that that wasn't true."

"When did you figure that out?"

"The night you were born, Rose."

"Really?" Rose asked.

Liam nodded. "Really."

Glad for something to do with her hands, Lily continued her needlepoint, watching them. She had heard Liam's story their last night in Melbourne, but she watched Rose's eyes widen as she took it in. What a gift for Liam to give a fatherless girl, Lily thought. Rose thinking herself so bad, she drove her father away—yet here was Liam, telling her the opposite, that she had given him back a sense of worth the night she came into the world.

Sitting back, Lily just kept needlepointing. She let her fatherless daughter and this daughterless man continue their conversation, and she tried to imagine what would happen next.

Anne Neill stood in the garden between the inn and the parking lot, clipping flowers to put on the dining room tables. She wore a wide straw hat and carried a flat basket, which she was filling with freshly cut zinnias, snapdragons, larkspur, and cosmos. She was well aware that Camille was stationed on a porch rocker, watching every move; these gardens were showpieces because of Camille's many years creating and tending them. As impatient as Anne sometimes felt with her mother-in-law, she never had any doubt about whose domain the flowers were.

Glancing up, she saw a hotel guest heading down the brick path. He had unruly red hair, glinting in the sun—it was curly and wild hair, the kind that must have driven his mother crazy when he was a kid. Anne smiled as he approached.

"Whew," he said, before she had a chance to speak. "I drove all night, and thought I'd never get here."

"Hello," she said. "Welcome."

"Thanks," he said. "So—this is the Cape Hawk Inn?"

"Yes, it is."

"Huh," he said, swiveling his head to look around. A slice of the harbor was visible between the trees. "So, that's where all the whale boats are?" he asked.

"Yes," she said. "Did you book a whale-watch package? Because I'll be happy to go inside with you and schedule you on a cruise." She slipped off her garden gloves, aware of Camille watching every move—at least Camille had stopped, after all these years, suspecting Anne of flirting with every unattached male guest. Her own marital tragedy had colored the way she looked at everyone else's marriage—including

Anne's very happy one to Jude. Anne hitched the basket over her arm and began to walk with him up the front steps.

"Um, I didn't book a package," he said. "In fact, I don't have a reservation."

Anne grimaced. "Oh dear," she said. "We're completely booked."

"Really?" he asked, his blue eyes sharp with surprise. "You're so far away from civilization, I didn't think I'd have a problem."

"Well, many people come here for that exact reason," she said. "Especially during the summer. If you'd come in December, you could have had the place to yourself. I'm so sorry."

He sighed, leaning against the doorjamb and looking around the lobby. Because the day was so clear and fine, hardly anyone was around. An older couple sat on the sofa, gazing out at the blue bay. Chambermaids crisscrossed the wide space, on their way to clean rooms. The huge fireplaces at either end of the lobby were swept clean, stacked with fresh wood. Bouquets of flowers graced nearly every table.

"Would you like to have lunch in our dining room?" Anne said. "That might be a good idea, if you really drove all night."

"I did," he said, but he didn't look a bit tired. He had fire in his eyes, as if resting or eating was the last thing on his mind.

"Well, if you came up for whale-watching, I might be able to get you onto the afternoon boat. I actually have quite a bit of pull—my husband is the captain."

The man chuckled, his freckled face creasing into a wonderful smile. Anne found herself checking his left hand—wedding ring alert for her Nanouk friends. Not married, she noticed.

"Do you see any beluga whales around here?" he asked.

"Absolutely," she said.

"The same belugas that sometimes wind up in aquariums? Like the one in Mystic, Connecticut?"

"Yes," Anne said. "Although we think they belong in the wild."

"Right," the man said.

"I might be able to help you find a different place to stay," Anne said. "Some locals take boarders—and there's a motel a few miles up the road that might have a vacancy. It has a good view too."

"I might not stay," he said. "I've just come for some information." He seemed to be studying her face—as if trying to see if he knew her, or maybe she just reminded him of someone. "Are you from here? Cape Hawk, I mean? Have you lived here long?"

"My whole life," she said.

"So you know the people who come and go, I imagine."

"Yes," she said cautiously. "I married into the Neill family, which owns the inn and whale-watch boats. We sort of keep an eye on things."

"The Neill family?" he asked, reaching into his pocket, patting it madly, searching for something. "Are you related to Camille Neill?"

"Yes," Anne said. She glanced out the screen door, but Camille had left her porch rocking chair—probably to lie down for her nap.

"Holy shit," the man said.

"Excuse me?"

"I'd like to talk to her," he said. "If she's still here. Is she still . . . alive?"

"Very much so," Anne said, chuckling. "I think she's just resting right now. I can check on that, if you'll wait for just a minute,"

Anne straightened out the display of "Bring Rose Home" pillows and began to lift the phone, when the man took a picture out of his pocket. He cleared his throat and showed Anne a badge.

"I'm Detective Patrick Murphy," he said. "Actually, retired detective, from the Connecticut State Police. Major Crime Squad. I've just recently gotten a lead on an old case, and it's led me here—to Cape Hawk. I'm looking for a woman who disappeared nine years ago. Mara Jameson, from Black Hall, Connecticut. She was pregnant at the time, so she would have a nine-year-old child. I'm going to show you her picture—"

Anne took the photo from his hand, and her heart stopped. There was her friend, eyes bright and shining, beaming for the camera as if she were the happiest woman on earth.

"Where did you get this?" she asked.

"You know her?" Patrick Murphy asked.

"I didn't say that," Anne said. She tried to keep anything from showing on her face. She swallowed hard, buying time. The picture itself might have been taken just yesterday—not nine years ago. Her fellow Nanouk Girl had hardly changed at all. . . .

Just then, she happened to look out the window and saw Marisa and Jessica Taylor walking up the hill from the harbor. Jessica was laden down with a big bag—obviously more pine pillows. Anne tried to catch Marisa's eye, to steer her around back—but she couldn't. Marisa was beaming—all those dark fears she'd arrived with seemed to have evaporated during the last weeks.

Very casually, Anne came around the desk, took the retired detective by the arm, and led him back onto the garden porch—opposite the entrance Marisa was about to use. Her heart was racing. She knew she had to check with her fellow Nanouk before deciding to tell the detective anything.

"I can help you," she said. "You say you want to talk to Camille? Well, that can definitely be arranged."

"But the picture," he pressed. "Have you seen Mara Jameson?"

"She looked a little familiar at first," Anne said. "But I really don't think I've seen her."

"I could have sworn . . ." the retired cop said, suddenly crestfallen. He looked pale, every freckle standing out.

Anne patted his arm. She had to get him out of here—now—to a place where he couldn't ask any questions that mattered.

"Look," she said. "You're tired—you've driven all this way. I know just the perfect spot for you to go and rest and wait for me to get hold of Camille." As she talked, she started walking him to the car. Not a moment too soon—because there was Camille, not napping at all, but right back on the porch, settling into her rocking chair with a cup of tea, this time with the old suspicion back in her eyes as she watched Anne walking this stranger to his car.

"Maybe I'll try your restaurant," he said. "For lunch."

"Of course," Anne said, cursing inwardly. "But why don't you drop your bag at the guesthouse first? It's absolutely lovely—just up the road, half a mile. It's called Rose Gables. It's run by a friend of mine, Marlena Talbot, and I know she would love to have you. Perhaps you can show her the picture—she might have seen this Mara Jameson."

Jessica opened the inn door and yelled out, "Hi, Anne! We brought more pillows for Rose!"

"Lovely, dear," Anne called back, flashing a smile at the detective, heart tumbling as she prayed he wouldn't turn around to see the nine-year-old girl standing there. He didn't. "Pillows," she said. "I really must go attend to the pillows. But you go to Marlena's and check in, and we'll see you back here for lunch in a short time. I'll round up Camille for you."

"Hey, thanks," Patrick Murphy said, stifling a yawn. "That drive really did me in. I drove straight through—it's a long way from the Connecticut shoreline."

"Yes, no wonder you're tired. By the way," Anne said, hoping she sounded cool. "What did this Mara Jameson do?"

"She disappeared," Patrick said. "At the very least, she married the wrong guy, and he beat her up. At the very worst, he killed her. But lately something happened, to make me think she might have come up here, to hide out."

"Hide out? Is she in trouble?"

"No. Hide out from her husband. She was afraid for her life."

"The poor woman," Anne murmured. Then she gave Patrick directions to Marlena's, pointed him on the way, and ran back into the inn. Camille tried to call her over as she rushed by, but Anne didn't even stop or say a word. She just tore into the lobby.

Jessica and Marisa had piled the pine pillows behind the front desk. Anne's pulse was speeding as she picked up the phone, looking left and right for Marisa. Where had she gone? Anne had to find her. But first, she dialed Marlena's number and prayed she would be home.

"Hello?" Marlena said.

"Thank God you're there!" Anne said. "I've just sent a guest over, to stay at your house."

"A guest? What are you talking about? I don't take guests!"

"You do now. It's a Nanouk imperative—it's for the sisterhood. Listen, Mar, you have to give him a room, and then force him to stay for lunch. I don't care what you give him, but don't let him come back to the inn until I tell you it's okay."

"Who is he?"

"A retired cop. Working on an old case—a missing-persons case, Marlena. He's going to show you a picture, and just try not to drop your teeth when you look at it. Just tell him she looks vaguely familiar—keep him interested enough talking to you, so he doesn't come back here till I've had the chance to talk to our girl. Marisa, where are you? She was just here, two seconds ago—"

"How should I keep him occupied? Should I bed him?"

"If you have to."

"Mata Hari used to do that for the cause," Marlena said. And then she gasped, and through the phone wire came the sound of a car door slamming. "He's here," she said. "And he's a redhead. *Very* cute—although I was only joking about bedding him. I think."

"Just give him something good for lunch," Anne said, trying to get her breath. "Remember now—for the Nanouks."

"For the Nanouks," Marlena said, and hung up.

Chapter 23

When the time came for Rose to be discharged from the hospital, all the nurses lined up, wearing the gold-and-silver-painted hemlock pinecone earrings Jessica had made for them, her second batch, after Melbourne. They all wished Rose a good summer, telling her they would miss her, but not to hurry back too soon.

Rose thanked them all for everything, and so did Liam and Lily, and they climbed into the taxi for the airport. Rose kept wanting to reach up with her left hand—trying to keep her heart safe—but Dr. Neill kept gently touching her hand to remind her not to. She thought of his arm, knew that if he had gotten used to something so foreign to his body, she could get used to new habits too.

On the way to the airport, she couldn't help noticing that her mother and Dr. Neill kept looking at each other. Rose had seen Anne and Jude doing that before. It made her happy, but at the same time, scared. What if Dr. Neill was just being nice because Rose had been so sick? What if now that she was getting well, he went back to hiding out in his boat and office and house on the hill, far from everyone, including Rose?

And what if Rose's mother got busy at her shop again, frowning at everyone except Rose and the Nanouk Girls of the Frozen North? Sometimes Rose wanted to remind her mother that the club was supposed to be for escaping the Frozen North—*not* for building up icebergs, snow walls, and igloos as a fortress all around them.

So this new way of looking at each other—Rose's mother and Dr. Neill—was making her very nervous. Suddenly, she remembered something.

"Is Nanny going home too?" she asked.

"I don't know," Dr. Neill said. "It will be really interesting to observe, after you head back to Cape Hawk."

"Have you checked her on the computer today?" Rose asked.

"No, not yet," he said. "We can do that now. . . ."

As he was opening his computer case, trying not to jostle Rose, Rose held her breath. She didn't know why, but she felt scared and worried. What if Dr. Neill couldn't locate Nanny on the screen? What if she didn't return home? Rose thought of all the dangers in Boston Harbor—all those ships with their big propellers.

"Hmm," Dr. Neill said after a minute.

"What's wrong?" Rose asked, feeling cold inside.

"I don't see her," he said.

"Liam?" her mother asked.

He was silent a few more seconds, tapping keys. Rose gazed at the screen, and she saw all the purple lights. Suddenly she felt terrified, as if she knew for sure that Nanny had been eaten by a shark.

"Maybe expand the field?" her mother asked, leaning over Rose, as if she cared just as much as Rose did about Nanny—and *no one* cared as much as Rose did about Nanny.

"That's it," he said, sounding excited at first. "There she is—" He touched her green dot with his finger. "But . . .   she's going in the wrong direction."

"What do you mean?" Rose asked, still unable to make sense of all the blinking lights, the curvy shape of the shoreline.

"She's going south," Liam said. "She's already far from Boston—see? She's rounded Cape Cod, and she's swimming toward Martha's Vineyard."

"But belugas need cold water," Rose said, remembering from her birthday cruise. "They live in the Arctic, and never go past Cape Hawk in the summer!"

"It's very rare," Liam said.

"I thought she came to Boston for me," Rose said, her eyes filling. Suddenly her heart ached—but not her real heart, the one that was just operated on, but the other heart, the one inside, the one no one could ever really see.

"She did," Liam said. "I'm so sure of it, Rose, I'd bet anything."

"Then why is she going the other way, away from home? Away from us?"

"I don't know," he said, hugging her. "Maybe she's confused. Sometimes a change in temperature can cause disorientation. We'll watch her for the rest of the day—I'll bet she turns herself around."

"She has to," Rose said, hot tears running down her cheeks. "If she gets lost because she came to find me, I don't know what I'll do."

"Honey," her mother said. "Haven't we convinced you to stop blaming yourself about such big things? Please, Rose—"

"I think it's time," Dr. Neill said, "to tell you that story."

"The story," she said out loud. When her mother looked confused, she said, "The sea hawk and the black cat! You were going to tell me that story," she said. "Two days ago, when the PT lady walked in."

"Yes, you were," her mother said, remembering.

"It was after you asked me how such different creatures can be friends. A little girl and a white whale. Or a sea hawk and a black cat."

"Tell us," Rose said.

"In the world of biology," he said. "Some animals are compatible, and others are natural enemies. Others might just be neutral—living in close proximity, with basic respect. Which, in the animal world, means that they don't eat or attack each other."

"Easier said than done," her mother murmured, staring out the window.

"Well, there was this sea hawk. He was an old guy, with tattered old feathers, and a fishhook caught in his left wing. He had once flown into a school of herring, and one of the fishermen accidentally caught him. The line was so taut and hard, and the tug broke the hawk's wing.

"All the young hawks used to laugh at him. They ignored him, didn't make him a part of their crowd. So he flew away, all by himself, up to the low, dark cliffs—you know, the ones at the top of the fjord, where the trees grow so thick, the light hardly ever shines.

"He was a pretty good sea hawk, though. He figured out how to fish, even with his broken wing. He let things heal—his bones and tendons, his feathers. And he'd sit on the banks of the fjord, and his timing got so good, he could just grab silver herring and salmon out of the water without even having to spread his wings.

"None of the other hawks ever went up there. The fjord was terrible and beautiful, but it was his alone. He had no competition for the fish that swam by. Until one day he noticed a black cat, sitting on the opposite bank.

"She was so glossy—at first he thought she was a seal. Her fur was black and smooth, and she had green eyes brighter than any star. But they weren't happy eyes. They were eyes that had seen danger—cruelty and brutality and starvation. She was a skinny cat, but she caught enough fish to feed an army of cats.

"So one day, the sea hawk watched her. Sea hawks have good eyes, even when they have broken wings. He saw her stalk through the brush, carrying a huge fish. When foxes and badgers tried to take it from her, she would fight them off. No animal was going to get her fish—and the sea hawk discovered why."

"Why?" Rose asked. The cab went into the tunnel beneath Boston Harbor.

"Because she had a kitten. This tiny, skinny black kitten with green eyes just as bright as her mother's." Dr. Neill looked across Rose's head at her mother, and Rose could see him swallow before continuing his story. "The sea hawk wasn't used to seeing any other animal fish his stretch of the fjord. He had gotten used to his independence, and to being on his own.

"But something about her made him glad she was there. He began to look forward to seeing her fish the water, on the other side. He found himself feeling lonely on the days she didn't show up. And when her kitten got big enough and began coming to the water to fish, well, it made him very happy."

"The kitten fished?"

"Yes. Because the mother taught her so well."

"Is this a story about animals who think they shouldn't be friends being friends?" Rose asked.

"Yes," he said. "Like you and Nanny."

"It's not about me and Nanny," Rose said, looking at Dr. Neill very hard.

"No?"

Rose shook her head.

"I think it is, Rose," her mother said.

"No," she said stubbornly. "The hawk had a broken wing, right?"

"Right," Dr. Neill said.

"Did the kitten have funny, flattened paws?" Rose asked, holding up her hands, wiggling her clubbed fingers.

"As a matter of fact, she did."

Rose nodded. She glanced up at her mother.

"Black cat," Rose said, reaching up to touch her mother's glossy black hair. Then she turned to Dr. Neill and touched his prosthesis. She didn't even bother to say, "Broken wing."

Instead, as the cab pulled up at Logan Airport, Rose just sighed. Dr. Neill had told a nice story, but it wasn't going to turn Nanny around. Rose felt so glad to be feeling better—that the operation was a success, and she was on her way home to spend the summer. But what did it matter, if Nanny was lost, swimming south? Couldn't everything work out, just for once?

Gone were the days of his youth, Patrick thought. All-night police work, when his mind stayed alert, and his body stayed strong, and his vision was sharp and didn't miss a thing. He remembered twenty-four-hour stakeouts, and long-distance chases, and investigations that meant visiting jurisdictions in twelve states and Canada. But last night's run—from Silver Bay, up I-95 to the Maine Turnpike, and straight on to Cape Hawk—forget it. He was only forty-six, but he felt like an old man.

After "checking in" to Marlena Talbot's "guesthouse"—Patrick was pretty sure that paying guests weren't a regular thing here—he followed Marlena upstairs to a very nice bedroom, thanked her, and lay down for a quick nap.

Three hours later, after sleeping through lunch and most of the afternoon, Patrick found himself in Marlena's dining room. He rubbed his eyes, reached for the glass of Coke she'd poured, sipped and looked around. Driving all night had completely done him in, and now he felt jet-lagged, paying the price.

"Seriously," he said. "I can just head down to the inn for dinner."

"I wouldn't hear of it!" she said. "It's part of the charm of my establishment—you get a home-cooked meal. Can the inn provide that? I think not!"

"Your establishment," he said, taking a bigger slug of Coke, looking around. Never had he seen a homier place. She had knickknacks everywhere—personal things, like clay paperweights obviously made by children or grandchildren, needlepoint covers on every chair seat, samplers on the wall, and a pile of square pillows that all smelled of pine and said "Bring Rose Home."

"Yes," she said. "My establishment. It's not easy, working in the shadow of the Cape Hawk Inn. With all their central booking equipment and the whale-watch boats, it's not easy to compete with them. All I have is my home cooking to attract my share of the tourist dollar."

"I'm sure," he said, checking his watch. Why hadn't that woman from the inn called about Camille Neill?

Marlena was in the kitchen, bustling around. Patrick pulled out the newspaper article and Mara's picture. Marlena gazed at it, stone-faced. She read the story, took in the dark hair, the bright smile, the fact that she'd been pregnant when she went missing. No, she said: she couldn't recall seeing her here in Cape Hawk.

"Look," Patrick said, "I'm sure your cooking is delicious, but I'd better get over to the inn. It's dinnertime there, and I have to ask some questions. I hope Camille Neill hasn't left—"

"Left? She never leaves. She owns the place, and runs it with an iron glove. Please don't go, Detective Murphy. What will Camille think, if you tell her you were staying at Rose Gables and I didn't feed you? Speaking of Rose Gables, would you like to know how my house got its name? Did you notice those white roses growing over the trellis as you came in? Well, I planted and trained them. Now, I know that this is a modest, humble little abode. . ."

"Marlena," he said.

"Not at all grand, not what you would expect of a house called Rose Gables, but it was the first home of my own. The very first place I ever bought on my own. And I did it, after the divorce."

"That's a good story, but—"

"And I got so much support from all my friends, my darling friends the Nanouks."

"The what?" he asked, wondering why that name sounded so familiar.

Marlena opened and closed the oven door. He heard the air escaping as she opened a bag of chips. The lid of a jar was unscrewed. A moment later, she entered the dining room bearing a tray. On it was an embroidered cloth, a vase holding a single white rose, and a plate covered by a second embroidered cloth.

Whipping off the cloth, Marlena said, "Voilà!"

Patrick stared down at his dinner: a grilled cheese sandwich, pickles, and some barbecue potato chips.

"Wow," he said. Was she kidding? For the first time, he wondered whether he had wandered into the Nova Scotia version of the Bates Motel. Or maybe she was like the crazy lady in *Misery*. The sandwich looked good, so he ate it—quickly. Maybe she really was proud of her grilled cheese sandwiches . . . but he thought the protestations about her food versus the inn's were a little odd.

"Very good," he said. "Thank you. Okay, I'm going to head over to the inn now—"

"Would you like to listen to the baseball game?" she asked, sounding manic and a little desperate. "Or would you like me to play the recorder? I like it very much—I played it as a child and have been practicing ever since my divorce. Oh—or I could show you my needlework! I know most men don't care about—"

Before he could stop her, she had whipped out a bag of sewing, or something. He looked at the mesh, the yarn, the whatever. Marlena's needlework reminded him of something, but he didn't know what. Even less, he wasn't sure why he opened his mouth and said, "What did you say earlier? The Nanouks? What are they?"

"A tribe of ancient warrior women," she said, her face ashen. "From right here in Nova Scotia. They dressed in the aurora borealis, seaweed, and mother-of-pearl, and they hunted the cliffs and bays, and they survived every ice age that came their way."

"And they've helped you recover from your divorce?" he asked, staring at her needlework, suddenly getting a very clear picture as the music played.

"Yes," she said defiantly.

"You're lying to me, aren't you, Marlena?"

"I am not lying. They helped me."

"You know Mara Jameson, don't you?" he asked.

Marlena Talbot didn't reply, but her reddening face and the angry tears in her eyes told him all he needed to know. Patrick Murphy grabbed the picture and his car keys, and he stalked out of Rose Gables.

When he got to his car, he grabbed for his cell phone. There was one person he had to call—to tell her how close he was to tracking down Mara. Someone who had known where she was all along—he was now sure of it. Hearing the word "Nanouk" made it all so clear. He dialed the number he knew by heart, ready to rip into her—but she didn't pick up, and he got the machine instead.

"Hello," said the woman's voice. "I'm not here right now, but if you'll leave your name and number, I'll call you back as soon as I can."

From the very first time he'd heard it, Patrick had told Maeve she should change her message. She should have a man's voice on the machine—or at least say "we" instead of "*I'm* not here right now." But just try getting Maeve to do anything.

"Maeve," he said. "It's Patrick Murphy. There's something I have to say to you. I'll call you later. But—I may have good news soon," he said. And he hung up, thinking that, of course, Maeve already knew that.

Chapter 24

Secret Agent had been checking every day, trying to beat back the tide of trouble caused by White Dawn. The whole message board was filled with threads titled "Secret Agent Stole My Money!" or things like that. Ever since White Dawn's post about checking the NOAA weather map, the whole SpiritTown message board had realized that Secret Agent's sister lived many miles south of the storm track and that her house couldn't possibly have been destroyed—or even badly damaged. And everyone wanted their money back.

Many thoughts ran through Secret Agent's mind. How could he have missed checking the path of Hurricane Catherina? He thought of all the people who were homeless, injured, just waiting for aid from the disaster relief fund. Why couldn't he have gotten better information?

The bitch had shamed him in the eyes of the message board. Whoever she was, she was as bad as his wife. Always blowing the whistle on him, spoiling his projects. No matter how hard he tried, it had never been good enough for her. Just like White Dawn—ruining his plans. And his reputation. He had carefully constructed the whole thing, and White Dawn had brought it down like a house of cards.

What if Secret Agent had really had a sister—and what if she had really lost her house in a severe hurricane? All it took was one vindictive bitch to take the candy cane away. Take the goodwill away. Take the money right out of homeless people's hands. All that money Secret Agent had collected—what if he had really sent it to his sister? These were the kinds of issues a vindictive bitch had no idea about.

White Dawn.

He signed onto the board, clicked onto her profile. What he saw gave him a start. Before, when he had looked, she had nothing listed there. Now he saw that she had filled in a name:

"Patty Nanouk." Patricia—that was his wife's real name. Could it really be her? Out there in cyberspace, bringing him down? And what did "Nanouk" mean?

He scrolled a few lines down, to the place where it said "occupation." Then he read what she—White Dawn, Patty Nanouk, whoever she was—had written:

"Crusader for justice against psychopathic con men."

It was her. It really was. How often had she called him a psychopath? And how often had he tried to soothe her, telling her that yes—he was one, it was true. But that was just because of his terrible, abusive childhood. No one had ever, ever loved him as she did, no one else was capable of healing him as she was.

He was getting therapy, he had told her. He was going to workshops. There was help available—he was trying to get better. Didn't she understand that? Was she willing to just walk away—throw it all away? Destroy him in the process? Because if she did, then she was no better than he was. In fact, she was worse.

He couldn't help who he was. Depression was an accepted illness, and so was what he had. He wanted to love her, and he was trying—but being a psychopath was hard. When they said he had no conscience or empathy, well, that just wasn't true. He did have empathy. He felt things. Deep in his soul, he felt the pain of being an abused child, and of what that made him. It kept him from all the pleasure he should have as an adult—as a husband or father. He grieved for himself!

How could they say he had no empathy?

Well, fuck White Dawn, Patty Nanouk, and his wife. He wondered whether they were all the same person. Honestly, he didn't really care. He had porn open at the same time, and he was in an incest survivor's chat room with a girl he'd met online last night, and he was totally over what had happened at SpiritTown.

Over it. There were plenty of other message boards out there, plenty of other bleeding hearts with too much money and a need to give it away—and Secret Agent had a PayRight account.

No more "Secret Agent" for him. That name was toast. From now on, at least until he found an interesting prospect that required a more creative handle, he'd just go by "Edward."

Patrick finally made it back to the Cape Hawk Inn, just as the sun was setting over the harbor. The last of the whale boats was steaming back to the dock, leaving a wake of silver out behind. The big lightbulb going on about Maeve had thrown him into a dark sadness—he had thought they trusted each other.

He felt a tug to walk down to the water, get aboard a boat. He didn't like having ground beneath his feet for too long—he needed the feel of a deck, and the waves rocking. He hoped that Flora was okay without him, guarding the *Probable Cause* along with Angelo. More than anything, he hoped he would have this case solved for good by the end of the night.

Pushing those thoughts from his mind, he again climbed the porch steps to the inn. Inside, the lobby was lively. Strains of Celtic music wafted down the hall from the bar. People dressed for dinner walked in and out of the formal dining room. Waiters served drinks by the lobby fireplace, which was crackling with a fire. Even though it was July, the northern air had a slight chill.

The minute he stepped through the door, he noticed a semicircle of women looking over at him. The woman who had first greeted him—and sent him to Rose Gables—stood out front, and he made his way across the room to her. The women behind her were not smiling.

"Well, well," he said. "If it isn't the lady who told me there was no room at the inn. I really have to thank you—sending me along to Casa de Grilled Cheese. That was a clever diversion."

"Marlena sends her apologies. I really caught her up short. She's quite an excellent cook, but I didn't give her enough notice. I'm sorry."

He ignored the apology. "Is there really a Camille Neill?"

"There is. I'm her daughter-in-law, Anne Neill."

"So, that part's true."

"Yes. I'm sorry to say, though, that she really is asleep right now. She'll be up tomorrow morning. You can ask her anything you want then."

"Why are you stonewalling me," he asked, "when it's obvious that you know Mara Jameson?"

"How is it obvious?" Anne asked. She was tall and elegant, and she had a lot of practice dealing with people. Working at an inn, she probably had to handle lots of drunks and jerks. But Patrick's patience was pretty thin right now.

"Lady," Patrick said, trying to stay polite, "it's obvious because your eyes practically jumped out of your face when you saw her picture. And because you sent me on a wild-goose chase to poor Marlena's house—what the hell do you know about me? What if I were a serial killer? I'm a total stranger, and you sent me to your friend's house to take a freaking nap. Oh—and because she told me about the Nanouks."

"Excuse me?" Anne asked, and it was echoed by several of the women standing behind her, glaring at Patrick with daggers.

"The Nanouks. She said the Nanouks got her through her divorce, and then I knew."

"And just what do you think you know?" one of the other women asked.

"She told me they're a tribe of warrior women," he said. "Some ancient crew of women who wear the dawn and sunset or something like that."

"Ancient," one of the other women said, chuckling.

"The aurora borealis, not the dawn and sunset," someone else corrected.

"*We're* the Nanouks," Anne explained. "We're a club of friends."

"Friends?" he said, gazing across their heads at a poster advertising whale-watch cruises—with the outline of a whale's tail flaring out of the sea.

"Yes," she said. "We support each other."

Patrick frowned, puzzled. If that was true . . . he put it all together with the embroidered glasses case that he had seen at Maeve's. Just a small thing, always on her side table, with her stack of books—the eyeglass case had a cream background, with the word "Nanouk" done in block letters, in several different shades of blue yarn. And the very faint outline of a whale's tail, the stitches wearing out.

"If that's true," he said, "then I believe that Mara Jameson is a member of your club."

"We don't know any Mara Jameson," Anne said as Patrick began to pass her picture around the group.

"You may not know her by that name," he said. "But she's here, I know it. And she has a nine-year-old daughter."

Marisa and Jessica sat in Anne's office, off the lobby, watching everything through the glass door. Anne had warned Marisa about the detective's visit. She had intercepted Marisa and Jess earlier, when they had arrived with the latest batch of pine pillows. Because of the confusion—having a retired police officer here, looking for a woman who had disappeared nine years earlier—Anne had called a meeting of the Nanouks, to decide what to do.

Some of the women, having been victims of domestic violence, had had bad run-ins with the police and courts. The legal system didn't understand the problem. They would look at a handsome, well-spoken man like Ted, and at a shrieking, dissembling woman like Marisa, and more often than not, they would believe the man.

Once Marisa went to court to ask for a restraining order against him—but since she didn't have any physical evidence of beatings, and since his threats were over ten hours old, the judge had refused to grant an order. Marisa had left, trembling. How could she explain that she was in so much shock, she could hardly remember the details of what he had said, the terror of having him hold her by the hair and tell her that if she ever tried to run away from him, he'd track her down and make her daughter suffer?

Marisa knew that some of the Nanouks—older, wiser, and more recovered than Marisa—had had similar experiences with the police. Anne knew it too, and hadn't wanted to make any decisions without consulting with everyone. And Marisa had certainly needed her friends' advice, regarding the best tack to take.

"If you tell him, maybe Ted will go to jail," Jessica said, peeking out the window.

"Or maybe he won't," Marisa said.

"He killed Tally."

"I know, honey."

"And he said he'd hurt us."

"Exactly. That's why I want to be careful. Telling on Ted isn't necessarily safe."

"You mean people might not believe us?"

"Yes," Marisa said. But she couldn't look Jessica straight in the eye as she said it. She no longer felt sure about that. Back when she had first run away, she had been so afraid—a quivering wreck of her former self. But she had had the guts to pack up her daughter, take her to safety. Over the last month, she had made friends with these great women, and they had believed her—every single one of them. Making Marisa finally able to believe in herself.

"What would be so bad, telling?" Jessica asked. "We've already told the Nanouks our real names. We could go right out there and tell the policeman. And he could arrest Ted."

"Hmm."

"We could see our friends, back home. Aunt Sam . . . I wouldn't want to leave Cape Hawk for good—I'd miss Rose too much. But Mommy—don't you want to be able to go home again? If we want to?"

"Yes," Marisa said quietly, missing her old life so much she ached.

"So do I. Let's go out there, Mommy."

"Are you sure? Are we doing the right thing?"

Her daughter looked at her, long and hard. She tilted her head, touched Marisa's cheek. Her eyes were pleading with her, and Marisa could read the message even before Jessica said it out loud.

"You're the mother," she said. "You have to decide."

And Marisa knew she was right. She kissed the top of her daughter's head, took a deep breath, and because she was the mother, opened the office door.

The flight had been long, and the drive from the airport had taken forever, but to Lily's amazement, Rose was wide awake and feeling strong. The windows of Liam's truck were down, and cool, fresh Cape Hawk salt air blew through the cab. Lily had her arm around Rose's shoulders, and she breathed in the spruce and pine.

"Smells like my pillows," Rose said.

"It does," Lily said.

"Jess's card said they're selling them at the inn," Rose said. "Next to a picture of you and me."

"Wow," Lily said. "That's so nice."

"It's true," Liam said. "It's a big display, right in the lobby."

"Can we see it?" Rose asked. "On our way home?"

"Oh, sweetheart—it's so late. We have to get you to bed."

"But I'm excited," Rose said. "I want to see. And besides, don't you want to see Anne? And maybe some of the other Nanouks? And show them I'm okay?"

Lily's lips tightened. She had been longing so deeply to see her own most beloved relative—missing her so much during this last difficult time with Rose. Having Liam with her had been wonderful, but she had a primal need to connect with her grandmother, the closest person she had to a mother. Or in her place, the Nanouk Girls of the Frozen North.

Even if only one of them was at the inn—and she was sure that at least Anne would be there—she would so deeply love a hug, and the chance to celebrate with the friends who had been so supportive of her and Rose. She glanced over at Liam, concentrating on the road. It was as if her grandmother had tapped her shoulder, telling her to pull over.

"Would you mind if we stopped there?" she asked. "You must want to get home."

"Lily," he said, "if you and Rose want to go there, I'm going with you."

"So we can?" Rose asked, as the truck crossed the bridge over the fjord, and the lights of Cape Hawk—nestled in the valley between two formidable rock cliffs—came into view.

"We can," Lily said.

Anne was a nervous wreck. A total, complete basket case. Duplicity had never been her strong suit—she could barely even handle telling a white lie to Camille, telling her she looked pretty when in fact she looked very cranky and mean. But she had started lying almost from the minute Detective Murphy had arrived—and she hadn't stopped yet.

Getting poor Marlena to pretend she was running a bed-and-breakfast—and then practically mortifying her by getting her to serve a cheese sandwich with all the fanfare of a cordon bleu chef! God, the Nanouks would be teasing her about that forever.

Having the presence of mind to whisk Marisa aside, tell her to hide Jessica—and keep her hidden, until the coast was clear, and they were sure Murphy had departed—where had that come from? Anne was on top of her game, that was for sure—thinking fast, making sure *all* her friends were protected.

She had called in the Nanouks for reinforcements, and of course everyone who could get away had come—Cindy, Doreen, Alison, Suzanne, Kathy, Paula, Claire, and even Marlena, just behind Patrick Murphy. They all gathered around him, passing the very familiar photo—God, she had been so young, smiling and innocent—around the circle. Everyone had been coached to say the same thing: "She looks familiar."

A comment about her hair, her smile, her beautiful shining eyes. She had been so sweet, pregnant with the girl that they all loved so much. Just knowing that—and what she had run from—brought tears to Anne's eyes. She wiped them away, but they just kept coming.

"Mother in heaven," said Cindy, under her breath.

Anne looked up, and here came Camille, limping down the hall that led to the family's private quarters. Anne lurched, to try to stop her, but she knew she would look too obvious and forced herself to hold back.

"Good evening," Camille said, giving Anne a strange look. "Aren't you working tonight?"

"Genny is covering in the dining room," Anne said.

"I noticed this gentleman arriving earlier," Camille said, approaching Patrick. "Talking to you in the garden. Where ever is Jude? Still out on the boat?"

"Yes," Anne said.

"Hi, Camille," Marlena said from across the circle. She was trying to be helpful, but in that instant, Anne knew they were sunk.

"Camille Neill?" Patrick asked.

"Yes. And who might you be?"

"I am Patrick Murphy. Are you the same Camille Neill as mentioned in this article?"

Camille put on her reading glasses and looked at the yellowed newspaper clipping. She gasped, looking up at Patrick. "This is from the Ard na Mara paper—about Frederic's memorial. What are you doing with it? Did you know Frederic?"

"No, ma'am," he said. "I'm investigating the disappearance, nine years ago, of Mara Jameson." He took the photo back from Cindy, handed it to Camille. "Do you recognize her?"

Anne felt her pulse beating in her throat. It was just a matter of time now—before Camille blurted out the truth, and Patrick knew where to look. She glanced over at the office door—and froze. There were Marisa and Jessica, letting themselves out of the office, walking this way.

Camille cleared her throat, slid a glance at Anne. She shook her head. "No," she said firmly. "I don't recognize her."

But it was too late. Anne couldn't believe her eyes. She stared at Marisa, seeing steel in her posture she'd never seen before. Jessica skipped ahead, flinging herself into the circle, right in front of Patrick Murphy. And he turned—his long, lanky body just wheeling around, as if he had noticed the nine-year-old girl and wanted to see her mother—just as the front door of the inn opened.

Liam, Lily, and Rose stood there.

Everyone started shouting, shrieking, laughing, and crying. Every last Nanouk rushed across the lobby, arms open wide, to greet Lily and Rose. Marisa and Jessica were first in line, and the four of them hugged and kissed, and wept, jumbled in a pack by the other Nanouk Girls, all wanting to get close.

Anne held Camille's hand, walking a little behind the others, alongside Patrick Murphy. Camille squeezed Anne's hand, and Anne squeezed back.

"I've always felt bad, you know, Anne, dear," Camille whispered. "I've tried to help Rose in my own way, financially." She lifted her chin. "Even if I'm not a Nanouk."

Anne whirled to look at her mother-in-law with amazement, and to whisper back, "After what you just did, you're in, Camille."

The women were all clustered together, Liam off to the side, and as Anne got closer, she saw that everyone was hovering around Rose. They didn't want to get too close, to crush her—but they wanted to touch her, caress her, let her know how grateful they were that their girl had come home safely. The reunion was for everyone and Rose, and for Lily too. Anne watched as Marisa gave Lily a huge hug, then whispered something in her ear.

The room was buzzing so loudly—with everyone's laughter, tears, and talk, and with the Celtic music from down the hall, and from

Anne's heartbeat thudding in her ears—she wondered whether anyone would hear him.

"Mara," Patrick Murphy called sharply.

And both Marisa and Lily looked up.

Chapter 25

"Yes?" Lily said.

The whole lobby went silent. Rose clung to her hand, looking up at the strange man approaching.

"I'm Marisa," Marisa said.

"I said *Mara*," the man said. Walking through the crowd, he stared at Lily as if he knew her. Not only that, but his eyes were filled with a mixture of victory and disbelief, as if he had come here to get her, but couldn't quite believe that his quest was over.

"Lily—don't say anything," Anne said, stepping forward. "Don't say one word. Liam, will you get Jude?"

But Liam just pressed closer to Lily; she felt his arm come around her shoulder. She had the vaguest of impressions of her friends not knowing whether to smile about Lily and Liam, or be afraid of what was happening.

"I have this picture," the man said, handing it to Lily. "And this news clipping."

She stared at them. They were artifacts from such a different time and place, but they made her eyes swim with tears. Not so much for the photo, or the content of the news story, but for seeing the date written in that fine handwriting on the upper right-hand corner.

"I'm Patrick Murphy," he said. "I'd say 'Detective Patrick Murphy,' but I'm actually retired. Your case was my swan song to a long career. Too bad I didn't manage to solve it."

Lily sensed Liam relax, just slightly. Until the man spoke, she realized that Liam might have taken him for the shark, her husband. Still staring at the handwriting, Lily wasn't quite ready to speak yet.

"Touché to your friends here," Patrick Murphy said dryly. "They all recognized you in the picture—how could they not? You haven't changed one bit. But they stayed cool, acted as if they'd never seen you.

Of course, I only got here this afternoon. I'd have worn them down with my relentless questioning."

Someone, probably Marlena, snorted.

"I know about the Nanouks," he said.

"Is there a crime in belonging to a club?" Anne asked.

"No crime," he said. "No crime in that at all. The only crime that's been committed was long ago. And it was by someone who never answered for it."

Lily cringed. Was there some statute against running away? She knew there had been a huge investigation—many hours of police work, costing lots of money. Lily wondered what sort of penalties there were for disappearing.

"She didn't do anything wrong," Cindy growled. "I'll kick your ass for saying so, even if you are a retired policeman. You don't know what she went through—"

"Cindy," Anne said evenly.

"The only crime was committed by the man who beat you up," Patrick said. He took a step closer. "Beat up his pregnant wife. That's right—after you disappeared, we treated your house as a crime scene, and we went over every inch with luminol. You should have seen the blood light up like a lightning storm. Everywhere in the kitchen. He must have hurt you, Mara. He must have."

"He did," Lily said. "But he never hit me."

"But the blood—"

"He sometimes knocked me down when he passed by," she said. "And he'd tell me it was because I was pregnant and clumsy, and he didn't have enough room. I hit my head, split it open. He said it was an accident." She paused, an old life coming back. "And I believed him for the longest time . . ."

"But not that night?"

"No," she said. "There was something different that night. His rage—" She stopped herself, looking down at Rose. "Excuse me, but I can't talk to you right now. I have to get my daughter to bed."

"She's beautiful," the red-haired cop said. For some reason, his eyes were glittering.

"Of course she is," Marlena said. "She looks just like Lily."

"I was going to say," Patrick Murphy said, "that she looks just like Maeve."

"Granny!" Lily gasped.

"She misses you, Mara. Whatever reasons you had for leaving, she must believe in them mighty hard. Because I never saw such love, and

I know that willingly letting you go had to be the hugest sacrifice any grandmother could ever make."

"She had nothing to do with it," Lily said, trembling, not wanting her grandmother to be in trouble.

"Be that as it may," the cop said. "She uses that Nanouk eyeglass case you made for her every day. And she finally got around to putting me onto the aquarium membership. You gave it to her—what was that, so she could visit with the beluga whales and imagine seeing you?"

"She told you?"

The cop nodded. "And she gave me that clipping—" He pointed to the one Lily held in her hand, the one about the ferry accident in Ard na Mara. "You know what I think?"

"What?" Lily asked, wrapping her arms around Rose, holding Liam's hand, knowing that she had to get out of there—out of the inn, away from the cop, away from all this talk about her grandmother. It was all too much—first Rose's surgery, then being with Liam, now this . . .

"That she needed me to find you. She sent me here, Mara."

"She wouldn't do that," Lily said. "She didn't even know where I went."

"Maybe not," he said. "But she knew I'd find you. I think she's done without you long enough. Something's changed, and she needs you to come home. Think about it, Mara."

"Mommy?" Rose asked, sounding distressed and tired. Jessica stood beside her, as if standing guard. Allie, Cindy's daughter, was just a few feet away, looking equally fierce.

"My name is Lily," she said. "Mara fell off the face of the earth. Do you understand? I want it to stay that way. Right now, I have to get my daughter home."

"As long as you know I have some more questions for you."

Lily nodded, but didn't say another word. She just let Liam bundle both her and Rose out of the inn, into his truck, and they left the lights of Cape Hawk behind as they drove into the dark, secret cliffs and pines that Lily had for so long—and still—called home.

But just to be in the presence of a man who had recently seen her grandmother—that sent such a fierce tremble through Lily's body, she had to hold tight to Rose, just to keep herself together.

Marisa leaned on the desk, watching Jessica follow Rose out to the porch, to wave goodbye. As she did, all the Nanouks began buzzing.

"Did you know?"

"I knew that she had run away from something."

"Did you know what she was running from?"

"I guessed. She had such a hunted look, the minute she arrived in Cape Hawk."

"She stumbled the first time she said her name," Cindy said. "Alison and I talked about it right away. We figured 'Lily' was an alias. But it was so obvious she wanted to keep her identity secret, it was just an unspoken thing."

"We wouldn't have dreamed of questioning her about that," Doreen agreed.

"But you didn't even talk about it among yourselves?" Marisa asked.

Anne shook her head. "Not really. I didn't figure it out for a long time. She had her hair cut very short when she first got here—almost like a boy. She wore a pair of tortoiseshell glasses at first. She tried to hide her pregnancy with big shirts. But after a time, her hair grew in, and the glasses went. I guess she started feeling safer."

"She eventually began to talk about her abusive marriage," Cindy said to Marisa. "That's how she began to heal. Opening up to us. We didn't care about the details of where she was from. Where she came from didn't matter. We just cared about helping her realize she didn't deserve the way he'd treated her."

"I knew who she was," Marlena said quietly. "I have a satellite dish, so I got local news from the States. Her story had such power over me—even before she got here. A husband everyone liked, handsome and popular, a beautiful young wife, five feet tall and pregnant out to there, with the biggest smile you've ever seen."

"Why?" Marisa asked.

"Because I had to know—were they the perfect couple? Or was he her murderer? Had he pulled off the perfect crime?"

"Those are good questions," Detective Murphy said, overhearing the conversation and walking over. "Very good questions."

"Were you the officer in charge?" Marisa asked.

"I was," he said. He had bright red hair with a little white around the temples, a freckled face, and a great grin—it surprised Marisa to see him using it. He didn't seem mad at all, and she had expected he would—having been fooled for so long.

"What did you think? Did you think the husband killed her?"

"I was sure of it," he said.

"Why?" Marisa asked. He was looking past everyone in the crowd, directly at her—as if they were all alone in the lobby.

"Because he's a bad guy."

"But how do you know that? Since you just found out that Mara—

Lily—is alive, he obviously didn't kill her; so, how do you know he's a bad guy?"

Patrick Murphy just stared at her, as if trying to read her story in her eyes. If only he could, she thought—he'd think her husband was a bad guy too.

"Because I saw the blood in their kitchen."

"But she said he never hit her."

Patrick shrugged. "I saw the blood," he said. "It got there somehow. There was a lot of it, as if she had lain there bleeding for some time. He knocked her down, and if he made it seem accidental—so she would think she was crazy—then he's even worse. I interviewed a lot of people that first year. . . . Mara Jameson tried to protect her husband, weave a story about a happy marriage. But it wasn't happy. And he wasn't a good person."

"Is he—still out there?"

Patrick nodded. "Yes," he said.

Just then Anne began lugging things out from inside her office: the basket of pine pillows for Rose, and the easel holding the placard with Lily and Rose's pictures on it. She and Marlena set everything up by the desk again. Anne had taken everything down when Patrick had started asking questions, because she knew he'd recognize Lily's picture.

Marisa saw Patrick glance at the front desk, piled high with CDs, posters, and photographs of the Celtic bands competing in Cape Hawk's upcoming Ceili Festival. A small smile touched his lips.

"What?" Marisa asked.

"Just that," Patrick said, gesturing at the pile of CDs. "A world with music like that can't be all bad."

"I played the fiddle when I was young," Marisa said, staring at the picture of one band, but remembering another: four young women wearing white dresses, holding guitars and fiddles, under the banner *Fallen Angels*. "I put myself through nursing school playing at Irish bars on Friday nights."

"Maybe you'll find the music again," he said.

"Mommy," Jessica said, coming over. "Allie asked if I can sleep over."

"It's fine with me," Cindy said.

Shaken by the conversation, Marisa thanked Patrick Murphy, then walked over to Cindy and Allie to discuss details. Jessica would be welcome to borrow a nightgown—and Cindy would have her home tomorrow by noon. Marisa said yes; she was glad Allie had asked Jessica to spend the night—she wanted to be alone. To think, and to investigate something just a little further.

She kissed her daughter good night, said goodbye to her friends, and shook Patrick Murphy's hand. He held on for a fraction of a second too long; Marisa looked up into his eyes, blue eyes shadowed with worry, and she saw a question. He was asking her something she couldn't begin to answer: she could almost hear the words coming out of his mouth, *Is everything okay?*

He wasn't a cop anymore—he was retired. And this wasn't—had never been—his jurisdiction, anyway. Marisa opened her mouth, wishing she could ask him a question of her own. But it seemed too presumptuous. It wasn't his problem. And besides, Marisa had never been one to ask for help.

"Don't forget that music," he called after her.

So she walked out to her car, got in, and drove past the stone gates of the inn's parking lot. Starlight sparkled on the onyx bay. Through her open windows, she heard the night birds calling. She thought of their golden eyes, watching her as she drove home. They were like sentries, keeping watch, protecting her from harm. The pine woods closed in around the road, branches interlocking overhead.

Jessica was settling in to Cape Hawk. Marisa thought of all the good that had happened since they'd arrived here. Love for Rose had driven Jessica into such a frenzy, making the pine pillows and pinecone earrings. Marisa felt so proud to have raised a child capable of such industry, and for such a generous reason.

She turned on her car stereo. When she heard Spirit's "Aurora"—Jessica's favorite—playing, she quickly changed the CD. Another good thing ruined. Marisa drove along, reflecting on how many good things in her life had been spoiled by a person she had loved so much. In spite of Patrick's words about music, right now the notes filled her with pain.

Since Jessica wasn't in the car, Marisa felt freer to let the emotions come—they had been living inside, deep in her heart and bones. They had wakened her at night, shaking her like little earthquakes. Now she began to cry, softly at first, and then she wailed. The cliffs rose high, and the trees muffled her sobs, and she just drove along, letting it all out.

Seeing Lily with Liam and Rose, having her real name and story out in the open—Marisa longed for that. She missed her mother. There were so many things she had given up, running away from Ted. But right now, it all coalesced into one sweet wish: to see her mother.

She parked behind the house, opened the car door, and just sat there for a minute. The smell of the woods and sea, spicy with pine and wild berries, salt and verbena, was like summer wine—heady, intoxicating.

Marisa breathed it in, knowing that she had come here for a reason. Meeting Lily and the Nanouks had made her stronger.

Was she strong enough for what she had to do next? She wasn't sure.

But she shut the car door behind her, senses alert for anyone who might be hiding in the bushes—no matter how far she went from Boston and Ted, she was still on high vigilance—and walked into her house, alone.

Once the truth was out, and she realized her friend was in no trouble or danger, Anne managed to find a room for Patrick at the inn. He told her there were no hard feelings, and he told Marlena he'd be sorry to miss whatever she would have made him for breakfast. A Celtic band was playing—the music beautiful and haunting, just the way Patrick liked it.

"Why don't you come in and listen for a while?" Anne asked. "You can help me and Jude practice judging the band. We're getting set for this summer's Ceili Festival—with a big competition for the best band. How about joining us?"

Patrick hesitated, but shook his head. He was too keyed up to sit still. Instead, he went to his room, at the far end of the first floor, and threw his bag on the bed. A shower really seemed like the thing to do, so he stood under the spray for a long time—until his nerve endings started returning to normal. He couldn't get over the fact that he had found Mara—or Lily—he wasn't sure what to call her now.

When he got out, he wrapped a towel around his waist and tried Maeve again. Once again, he got the machine. He had to hold himself back from blurting out any number of messages: "Guess what, Maeve—I found your granddaughter. Too bad I was the only one who actually thought she was lost!" Or, "Hi, Maeve—Mara is alive and well. Thanks for keeping it a big secret—at least I got my salary paid while I looked for her."

He hung up, threw the phone on the bed. It was hard to feel elated—which he did actually feel—while feeling bitter—which he also actually felt. It was a mixed blessing, to say the least.

Who could he call? Sandra—he could call her, tell her the crime was now officially solved and, by the way, wasn't a crime at all. Could he please come home now? He could just hear her laughing at him. A crime that wasn't even a crime had wrecked their marriage. The great detective had really been on top of his game, all the way.

He could call Angelo. Angelo, boat- and dog-sitting for the *Probable Cause* and Flora, would be sitting up on deck, listening to the Yanks, watching the moon rise over Silver Bay, and enjoying the company of a great, loyal, and loving dog. Angelo might not be the kind of friend to say "I told you so," but then again, he might. Patrick just didn't feel he could risk it. He was feeling, in the words of the marriage counselor he'd gone to for a few sessions with Sandra, the sessions during which she'd broken to him her plans to leave him, "fragile."

"Fuck fragile," he said out loud, and started pulling on his pants and shirt. So what if he had blown his marriage and screwed up his career, so what if he was a washed-up retiree who even got fooled—let's face it, the side trip to Rose Gables was just icing on the cake—by a club of menopausal and premenopausal psychos?

Patrick Murphy was going to take a walk down to the dock. There would be men and fishing boats there. Probably some of them would have beer. Patrick had been sober for eight years now, but tonight might be a good time to go off the wagon. He could almost feel the liquid relief of alcohol burning down his throat, spreading like hot wire through his body.

One hand on the doorknob, the phone rang.

Not his cell—so it couldn't be Maeve calling back. No, it was the house phone. He picked up, and a woman's voice spoke.

"Detective Murphy?"

"Not officially," he said wryly. "I'm retired."

"Well, then, *retired* Detective Murphy?"

"Yes?"

"This is Marisa Taylor. I met you earlier tonight."

"Right—the fiddle player. You have a daughter. Is it a joke among all of you—that I saw your nine-year-old and thought she had to be Mara's?"

She didn't reply. Then, "No. It's not."

Patrick didn't speak for a minute, and in the silence, something clicked in his brain. This wasn't about him. Mara hadn't hidden to thwart him. He heard in Marisa's voice the same fear that he knew had driven Mara to leave home. His stomach tightened.

"What is it, Marisa?" he asked.

"There's something I'd like to show you. I know this isn't your job, but I'd really like to ask you about it. Would you come over?"

"Yes, I will," he said.

She gave him the directions—involving driving over a chain bridge, taking a left at the chasm, going past the sawmill—landmarks appropriate to the kind of place a woman would come to hide in. Patrick had been on a roller coaster since getting to Cape Hawk, and it showed no signs of stopping.

He buttoned his shirt, strapped on his ankle holster, and tried Maeve once more—if she didn't answer tomorrow, he'd start to worry. Then he was out the door. Whatever Marisa was calling for, Patrick felt glad to be solving crimes again.

The road seemed like something out of a fantasy saga—it wound high into the rocky cliffs and was lined with tall trees that formed a crazily primeval forest. Patrick saw a family of moose staring out from the side of the road. A little further along, a black bear lumbered across. Owls called, and something swooped in for a kill, and the screams were terrible and then stopped.

Patrick actually found it comforting. Having worked the Major Crime Squad for so many years, he knew that people were capable of much worse cruelty than the vilest predator in nature. He could understand why a battered woman would find this environment so soothing. It was far from civilization—better known in America as "suburbia"— where everyone dresses nice, talks nice, and acts upstanding. Patrick had seen what went on behind the closed doors of some of those "nice" houses, including Mara Jameson's.

He turned into Marisa's driveway, saw her standing in the doorway. Her body was silhouetted from behind, and her loose cotton blouse rippled in the summer breeze. Patrick reminded himself she had called him as a cop.

"Hi," she said as he approached.

"Hi," he said.

"I feel funny, for calling you," she said, hugging herself, seeming very nervous as she looked up at him.

"Why?" he asked. She had beautiful eyes, brown velvet, soft and intelligent. She stared up at him.

"Because I once asked for a restraining order. I wasn't believed, and my request was denied."

"I'm sorry about that," he said carefully. He'd never want to bash his fellow law-enforcement officials. But he knew about some domestic violence complaints—especially upscale people, with successful, well-spoken husbands. By the time the woman was ready to ask for help, she often felt and sounded crazy—because he had driven her there, and because she had protected him for so long.

"My daughter's not here tonight," Marisa said. "I thought maybe I could talk to you a little. And run something by you."

"Sure," Patrick said. She was tall and slender, and she moved with grace and hesitation—as if she had been unsure of herself for a long time. Patrick saw her glancing back at him, as if assessing his thoughts and moves.

They walked through the living room, and she gave him an apologetic glance. "My computer is in the bedroom," she said.

"That's fine," he said, knowing she needed reassurance that he didn't have the wrong idea.

Nodding, she led him across the room to the desk. Her computer was a workhorse. The keyboard looked ancient, and the monitor was enormous. A worn Johns Hopkins sticker was stuck to the side of the monitor.

"You went there for college?" he asked.

"Nursing school," she said. "I've had this computer since then. When I left home, in April, it was one of the only things I took. It was so important to me, so I could have the Internet and e-mail—a way to stay in touch with some people I loved. My mother . . ."

"Why did you leave home?"

"The same reason as Lily. Mara."

"I'm sorry," Patrick said.

"Thank you," she said, looking over, as if she knew he meant it. Should he tell her that she shouldn't feel bad or ashamed, that it wasn't her fault? Did she know that already? Did she know that men like that often targeted women in the healing professions? But then, Patrick didn't like statistics. That particular statistic left out people like Lily—if that's what she wanted to call herself, that's how he'd try to think of her. He gazed at Marisa, sitting down at her computer, her thin shoulders drawn up toward her ears, and wondered how long she'd been carrying this kind of stress.

"Do you go online?" she asked. "Are you used to the Internet?"

"I'm retired." He smiled. "It's one of the ways I make the days go by. Fishing, the Yankees, and research online."

"I do that too," she said. "Research. Like, when I found out Rose had Tetralogy of Fallot, I spent days on the nursing school website."

"Tetralogy of what?"

"Fallot," Marisa said. "It's a complex heart defect."

Patrick nodded and felt a tug inside. He pictured Lily and her daughter standing there at the inn door—and then he remembered Anne putting back the signboard—looking just like one of those small-town fundraisers you saw at diners and dry cleaners everywhere, where some child in the community needed medical help. Something new for Maeve to deal with—her granddaughter had heart problems. That made Patrick think of Maeve again, but right now he was focused on Marisa.

"Anyway," Marisa said. "There's a band I like—Spirit."

"Everyone likes Spirit," Patrick said, and he hummed a few bars of "Lonesome Daughter."

"Not bad," Marisa said, giving him a real smile for the first time since he'd arrived.

"Do you play their music on your fiddle?"

"Every so often. But that's not what this is about. . . ."

"What, then?"

Glancing toward the computer, her smile faded. "Well, there's a Spirit fan website. It's embarrassing to admit, but I go there some-times—and have, for a few years. Spirit fans tend to be, well, kind of like the band itself. Smart, playful, but with social consciences. My kind of people."

Smart, playful, social conscience: Patrick checked them off, nodding. Well, maybe not so smart. He found himself wanting to be the kind of person this woman with the brown velvet eyes would like.

"Besides which, there's a fair amount of trading of CDs and live concert recordings not available anywhere else. I mean, well—I know you're a police officer, so this isn't anything I do, but it is sometimes done on the board—bootlegs."

Patrick nodded, trying not to look too stern.

"Well, recently I was reading the posts on the board, and I realized that someone has been committing fraud."

"Fraud? How?"

"By pretending his sister lost her home in a hurricane. He told everyone that Hurricane Catherina swept through, wrecking her house and injuring her son very badly. Spirit fans, well, they came out in droves. He calls himself Secret Agent. I've printed out a few of his posts—" She handed them to Patrick and he began to read through them.

He saw the setup instantly—bait and hook. He shook his head. Years ago he had worked with the FBI on a case of Internet fraud. Chat rooms and message boards were prime opportunities for con men and predators. They were the perfect places for the Dr. Jekylls of the world—no one could look through the screen and see that the person they were chatting with was really Mr. Hyde.

"You can see that many people responded. At one point, Secret Agent kept a running tally of what people had sent. Right here, it's up to seven thousand dollars. Just like one of those fundraiser signs that looks like a thermometer—'Help us meet our goal.' In this case, he wanted to get to ten thousand."

"Look at all the people who wrote in," Patrick said, amazed at the goodwill and innocence of strangers. He thought back to the FBI case he'd worked on—he and Joe Holmes, an agent who had married a local Hubbard's Point woman, Tara O'Toole, had run down a couple who had gotten retirees to invest their life savings in penny stocks. The couple had lived in a huge house overlooking Silver Bay. The retirees had lost everything.

"We're a trusting bunch," Marisa said.

"Spirit fans?"

"People in general," she said. "I trusted this man myself."

"You sent in money for his sister?"

She shook her head, and angry tears appeared in her eyes. "I married him," she said.

"Secret Agent is your husband?" he asked.

"My ex-husband," she corrected. "I think so. I know he used to troll message boards—I used to go on his computer sometimes, to find out if he was having an affair. There's something about the style of his posts here—earnest, funny—that makes me think it's Ted."

"Why would he choose the Spirit board?"

"He knows I'm a fan. I think maybe he was hoping to find me online. 'Secret Agent' is the title of the only Spirit song he really likes. The thing is, I never posted here until very recently—so he couldn't find me."

"That's good," Patrick said. "That's good."

"Here are my only posts," she said. "My screen name is White Dawn."

Patrick read the first, about how the sister would be getting money from the government if she was in a disaster area. Then he read the second, "Beware," and smiled. Then he read the third: "Hurricane Catherina didn't hit Homestead. It tracked north, dude. You can do a better job conning people if you first check out the storm track on the NOAA website."

"You wrote that?" he asked, grinning.

"Yep."

"Whoa," he said, reading the flurry of angry replies from the board. "And a shitstorm ensued."

"Yes, it did. Did he commit fraud? Can you catch him for it?"

"Well," Patrick said, remembering back to the FBI investigation. "Whenever you go online, you leave a trail. There's always a signature left at the website, of your IP number—which is really like a fingerprint." He took out his cell phone—to see whether he still had Joe Holmes programmed in. "I think it's a good possibility we can nail him," he said.

"Who are you going to call?" she asked.

"FBI," he said. "But first, do you mind if I try someone else? Just to update her on a different case?"

"Lily's grandmother?" Mara asked, smiling. "Go ahead."

Patrick hit redial, and the number rang, but again there was no answer. His stomach knotted—it was now ten at night, and Maeve should definitely be there. Before gathering his thoughts on her whereabouts, he needed to stay focused on this Secret Agent guy. Scrolling through his stored phone numbers, he found Joe Holmes's. Just before dialing, he glanced over at Marisa. "What's your ex-husband's real name?" he asked.

"Ted," she said. "Ted Hunter."

Patrick nearly dropped the phone. "What did you say?"

"Ted Hunter."

"As in—" It couldn't be possible. "What's his whole name? The one on his driver's license."

"Edward Hunter," she said.

And then Patrick had to sit down.

Chapter 26

L iam had a family now. That was how it felt to him, taking care of
Lily and Rose. After the situation at the inn, he had felt them too
vulnerable to go back to their own house, so he had brought them up
the hill, to his home. Lily seemed relieved, as if she'd been on the run,
making decisions for so long, and tonight she just needed a rest.

Determined to give that to her, Liam drove through the stone posts
at the bottom of his property and then up a long, curving drive. He
lived in a spruce forest, in a large stone house that had once belonged
to a quarry owner. Because the house wasn't visible from the road, he
knew that the local kids had turned it into a mythological mansion—
where Captain Hook lived. He glanced over at Rose and hoped she
wouldn't be scared. But she was half-asleep, just smiling to be back in
Cape Hawk.

Liam carried her, and together the three of them walked in his front
door. Liam's heart was pounding with excitement and nervousness and
pride. To have Rose and Lily here meant everything to him.

"It's been a long time," Lily said, smiling wearily.

"Do you remember the first time you came here?" he asked.

"When Rose was about three weeks old," she said. "She had a fever,
and there'd been a bad storm, and the phones were out, and a big oak
was blocking my road, so I couldn't get out. I hiked up here, to ask you
to help."

"Did he help?" Rose asked.

"He always helped," Lily said softly.

Liam smiled gratefully. He turned on lights, hoping his bachelor
style wouldn't turn them away. He had stacks of oceanographic journals everywhere, alongside piles of shark books, photos of shark attacks
on marine mammals, tapes and videos of eyewitness accounts of shark
attacks on humans. He had solid oak furniture and a bunch of red pil-

lows, a big Tabriz rug Camille had given him from the family collection, a lot of bookcases without space for even one more book, and a TV in the corner, as if by afterthought.

"It's cozy here," Rose said.

"Do you think so?" he asked, crouching down beside her. "I'm glad."

"I don't understand why we came here," she said. "Instead of our regular house."

Liam exchanged a look with Lily, wanting her to answer.

"Is it because of that man at the inn?" Rose pressed.

"Yes, honey," Lily said. "He's someone . . . who knows a person I knew long ago. It's not important tonight. The only thing we have to do is get you to bed."

Liam carried Rose upstairs, to one of the spare bedrooms. Lily checked out the hallway and saw a second empty bedroom next door. Liam pulled out clean sheets from the linen closet in the hall, put them on the twin bed. Rose seemed to be studying him more carefully than usual. Every time he glanced over, he saw her gazing at him with complete intensity. Lily set Rose's medication out on the bureau and went to get a glass of water.

"What is it, Rose?" he asked.

"This is what I wished for," she said. "On my birthday."

"Coming here?" he asked.

But Rose was either too tired to talk, or she had decided she'd said enough. Lily returned with the water, and they went through the long process of giving Rose all her medication. Then Liam and Lily tucked her into bed, and Lily told her she'd be sleeping in the spare room just next door.

"Where will Dr. Neill be?" Rose asked.

"My room's downstairs. But I'll hear you if either of you needs anything."

"Thank you," Rose said, putting her arms around his neck to kiss him good night. Having this child in his house, knowing what she had just gone through, moved Liam to the core.

After Rose was settled, he and Lily went back downstairs. He put a kettle on the stove and turned to look at her. She stood there, leaning on his kitchen counter. Her sable hair gleamed in the lamplight. He went to her, tilted her face up, kissed her the way he'd been wanting to kiss her all day.

They were hungry for each other—in a way Liam had never experienced before. It was as if they were separate from real life, completely swept up in whatever was happening between them. But the reality was so deep and great, Liam knew he had to pull away.

"Are you okay?" he asked.

"I think so. I'm just not sure which end is up. Rose's surgery went so miraculously well, and then to come home to—my past."

"How did he find you?" Liam asked.

Lily blinked and smiled, looking down at her feet. Liam had expected her to be upset, even frantic, but she didn't seem that way at all. "My grandmother," she said.

"She knew?"

Lily nodded. "She didn't know where I was going, but I couldn't just run away without telling her. I could never do that to her. You don't know her, Liam, but she is the smartest, most amazing woman in the world. She raised me to be so strong. I thought I could go through anything."

Liam listened and watched, seeing sparks in the blue eyes he loved so much.

"But I couldn't. Not Edward—not when I was about to have a baby. I knew he'd never let me get away, and there was no way I was ever going to subject my daughter to him."

"You knew the baby was a girl," Liam said. "I remember that, the night she was born. You held out your arms and said, 'Give her to me,' even before I told you."

"Yes, I knew. I'd had a lot of ultrasounds. He used to knock me down—I told you. And pretend it was my fault, try to convince me I was the clumsiest person. A cow, he called me."

"I'll kill him," Liam said, and he meant it. He felt hatred and rage boiling inside—something he'd never felt before. Even for the shark—when he was young, before he'd understood shark behavior and predation, even then he'd never felt this level of cold burning hatred.

"I couldn't let him be part of Rose's life," Lily said. "If I'd waited till after she was born, there would have been custody issues. Not that he wanted her—he didn't. He made it really clear. But I just knew—he would have used her to get to me. He would have tortured us both, and I don't use that word by mistake. Edward lived to cause pain."

"What kind of person would do that?"

"One without conscience or empathy," Lily said quietly. "And there's more too. Edward is a killer."

"What do you mean?"

"I'll tell you sometime," she said. "Not tonight, but soon."

"And your grandmother knew it?"

Lily nodded. "Most of it. Enough so she wanted to help me get away."

"Did she help you find Cape Hawk? As a place to run to?"

"No," Lily said. "I found it on my own. It turns out that I have a connection with Camille, and that she has a connection with Edward."

"My aunt? Camille Neill?"

"Yes," Lily said. "My parents died in the same ferry disaster as her husband, Frederic. I used to keep all the clippings about it, and once I came upon something about how Camille donated the memorial stone. I felt so grateful to her for that."

"She'd be happy to know that," Liam said.

Lily smiled. "I'm glad. I know she's scarred, just as I am. Losing someone that way is terrible. It makes you vulnerable . . . I think it made me an easier mark for Edward. I was an orphan—it didn't matter that I was thirty years old. I was still needy."

"How is Edward connected to Camille?" Liam asked, confused.

"He had this old framed photograph hanging on the wall. It showed an old whaling ship at the dock in winter. So beautiful, haunting—all the spars and shrouds covered in ice. He would tell people that his great-grandfather was a whaling captain. It was just a lie, like his story about going to Harvard, but he told it so often, I think he almost believed it himself."

"What was the ship's name?" Liam asked.

"The *Pinnacle*," Lily said, her eyes shining.

"My great-great-grandfather's ship," he said quietly. "The first Tecumseh Neill."

"I know," Lily said. "I used to stare at the picture and feel as if the ice in my heart was right there in the photo. My frozen veins—all the cold I felt inside from living with Edward. All he cared about the picture was using it to convince people he came from a sea captain background. But I felt haunted by the scenery. The cliffs, the frozen fjord, and the depth of winter, were so austere. They matched how extreme I felt inside."

"How did you find where the picture had been taken?"

"The provenance was very easy to track. It was an original taken by a well-known photographer. Sepia-toned, silver gelatin print, fairly valuable. The gallery stamp was on the back, and I called to ask. You see, it had once been owned by Camille."

"She has a fairly substantial collection of local maritime art," Liam said, amazed by the coincidence.

"I remember seeing the receipt and being shocked, because that was the woman who had donated the ferry memorial. And I remember thinking she had an odd name. Camille Neill. I never thought I'd meet her."

"So that's why you came here?" Liam asked. "Those two reasons?"

"Partly," she said. "I liked the connection with my parents, and I thought I'd never seen anyplace as beautiful as Cape Hawk. I felt a tiny, secret revenge, coming to a place Edward actually looked at every day—the picture he used to support the lies he told about his illustrious ancestor. He would tell people it was Newfoundland, because he had no idea."

"Good one, Lily," Liam said, hugging her.

"And also because it was so very far away."

"From Edward."

Lily nodded. "Which was wonderful. But also terrible, because it was so far from my grandmother. She wanted me to run far and disappear—she gave me money and helped me cover my tracks, lied to the police, I'm sure."

"Patrick Murphy," Liam said. When everyone else was busy greeting Rose and rallying round Lily, Liam had noticed the cop's eyes—happy, to see the woman he called Mara, but also something else. Sad, betrayed. Liam had felt for him.

"Yes," Lily said. "Do you think it's true, what he said? That my grandmother wanted him to find me?"

"I thought she knew where you were. Why didn't she just call?"

"She didn't know where I ran to. We decided that was the only way to really protect me and Rose. I sent her small, secret things. The clipping, a glasses case—making her an honorary Nanouk—a membership to a local aquarium. I thought that if Nanny brought such happiness to me and Rose, then maybe her relatives could somehow connect us with Maeve."

"Why don't you call your grandmother?" Liam asked, reacting to Lily's mention of Nanny, but not wanting to show how worried he felt about her whereabouts and the tracking data—she continued swimming south, and when he'd last checked, seemed to be feeding in the waters off Block Island.

"I would," Lily said. "But I'm still not sure we're safe. If Edward finds out I'm alive, he'll come after Rose for sure. And I may just have given him grounds for custody—by disappearing. Liam, what if he tries to get Rose?"

"I meant what I said before," Liam said steadily, more seriously than he'd ever said anything in his life. He knew for certain that if Edward Hunter—or anyone else—ever tried to harm Lily or Rose, he would kill them without looking back. After what the man had done to Lily, he would almost welcome the chance.

Lily leaned into him, standing on tiptoes to rise up and kiss him. Liam felt a rush of heat inside, flooding every part of his body. He had kept his feelings for Lily and Rose secret for so long—because he'd known that she was too closed off, that her defenses were too impenetrable. Maybe he knew that his had been as well.

But now, kissing in his kitchen while Rose slept upstairs, Liam felt all the walls breaking apart. They were inside each other's fortresses, together and standing strong. She held him tight with both her arms, and Liam held her right back—with everything he had, his entire heart. He wanted to touch every part of her, every inch of her skin, right now. This is how people know they're alive, he thought. Making each other feel joy, because what else is life for? Both he and Lily had missed out on so much for so long. But not tonight—and not ever again, he thought, kissing the woman he loved.

Joe Holmes was fast asleep at home in Hubbard's Point. The windows were open, and the breeze cooled his bare back. It carried scents of beach grass, tidal flats, and his wife Tara's garden. Joe had been working the night shift on a white-collar-crime case, listening in on a wiretap on a banker in Stamford. So when his cell phone rang, he slept right through it. Then it rang again, and he cursed the caller. Then the house phone rang, and Tara shook his shoulder.

"Honey," she said. "It's Patrick Murphy. That retired Statie? Worked on Mara's case?"

"Rrrrungh," Joe said, taking the phone. "Holmes," he said.

"Hey, Joe. It's Patrick Murphy. Sorry to wake you up, but I have something big."

"Is it information on a dickhead banker in Stamford, I hope?"

"No. It's on Edward Hunter."

"Mara Jameson's husband?"

"Yes."

"You have new information? About Mara?"

"Yes," Patrick said. "And I'll get to that, but first—you know about Internet fraud. Do you know anything about people who run cons on message boards? Get people to donate to phony charities?"

"Yeah. Hard to prove, hard to prosecute. Generally because the con artists are so slippery. They run the con, then disappear. They change screen names so fast, and if someone doesn't think to check out their IP address before they fade away, then it's almost impossible."

"What if someone managed to save printouts of the entire scam?"

Joe was awake now, hiked up on his elbow. He had to wake up in an hour anyway—he could already smell Tara brewing the coffee.

"I'd say we could look into it," he said. "If it's not too late, if the guy hasn't bolted, we might be able to nail down his IP link and then trace him to an actual street address in real time. You want to tell me what this has to do with Mara?"

"Just this for now, Joe—the guy might be Edward Hunter."

"I'd love to nail that fucking arrogant jerk," Joe said.

"You and me both," Patrick said. Joe heard him breathing hard, probably excited about the possibility of finally taking Edward to task for something—even if they couldn't get him on Mara's disappearance. Joe yawned, blinking his eyes.

"It's such a shame about Maeve," he said.

"Maeve?"

"Yeah," Joe said. "Tara said she saw the ambulance up there two days ago. Clara Littlefield told her Maeve had some sort of attack, got taken to Shoreline General. I hope she pulls through—I know she'd love to see the heat go up on Edward. That slimeball."

"Thanks, Joe," Patrick said.

"No problem," Joe said. "Listen—"

But Patrick had disconnected. The line was dead. Joe just stared at the phone, shook his head. People had said Patrick wasn't the same— that he'd gotten too emotionally involved in the Jameson case. Joe knew better than to throw stones—people were human, even cops. He had a lot of respect for Pat Murphy, and he had felt very sorry to hear his marriage had fallen apart. Joe knew he never wanted that to happen—he had too much to lose with Tara.

Waking up fully, he smelled the coffee. Then got out of his bed, still naked, and went to kiss his wife.

It took some doing, but Patrick managed to convince Marisa to tell him where Lily lived. She was so elated by the fact that he had called his FBI friend and learned that there might be a possibility of getting Ted. And then she was so confused by the fact that Patrick seemed to be saying that "Edward Hunter"—Ted's legal name—was also the name of the man Lily had been married to.

"It's not possible," she said.

"Why?" he asked. "He just cast a wide net."

"But for Lily and me both to end up here, in the same place, so far away from our homes—"

"I'll bet that once you and Lily start talking, you'll realize that something sparked you to choose Cape Hawk. A very similar reason."

"For me, it was partly spite," Marisa said, remembering the photo of Ted's great-grandfather's whaling vessel, so majestic with its spars coated in ice, with the Cape Hawk cliffs rising in the background. "I will confess that with pride. To get back at him, just a little, for all the humiliation he put me through."

"I bet Mara—Lily—has something like that in her story too. Deep down, she chose this location as a big fuck-you to the bastard who chased her from her home. Excuse my language."

"I understand," Marisa said. "It's very late. We're tired. Listen—I know that something's happened to Lily's grandmother, and she needs to know. But she's just been through the wringer with Rose. Her daughter had open-heart surgery a week ago, and I just can't let you disturb them tonight. Come back here tomorrow morning, and I'll take you to them. I promise."

Patrick Murphy stood at her door. He looked down, as if trying to decide whether to trust her or not. Marisa knew that he had reasons to be suspicious. Women like Marisa and Lily had to become very smart and shrewd and wily about protecting themselves. They had learned, with their abusers, to pretend everything was fine—while secretly forming escape plans in their own minds.

To let him know that she was true to her word, Marisa reached for his hand. The corners of his eyes were deeply lined, and his palm felt callused. He held on tight; Marisa could feel him wanting to anchor himself, to know that he was in a safe port. She gazed back at him with gravity, without smiling at all.

"I want you to believe me," she said. "So I'm going to tell you something. Just so you trust me. And then I want you to forget it. Okay?"

"Okay," he said. His voice sounded ragged, as if he was an old, finished fighter.

"My real name is Patricia."

"Patricia," he said.

"And my daughter's real name is Grace."

"Patricia and Grace," he said.

"But you can never call us by those names," she said. "Ever."

"They're pretty names," he said.

"They're the names we had when we were with Ted," she said. "And no matter what happens, we are no longer those people. We're Marisa and Jessica now, forever. Okay?"

"Okay," he said. She squeezed his hand, and she saw light behind his tired eyes.

"Till tomorrow morning," she said. "Come back at nine, and I'll take you to see Lily."

"Till then," he said. And as he walked out to his car, Marisa watched his back and hoped he knew that he didn't have to worry. He could go to sleep knowing she wasn't going to run away on him.

Chapter 27

Waking up in Liam's house, at first Lily didn't know where she was. The sun shining through the trees, and the wide blue bay out his window, seemed almost like a dream. She had hardly slept all night—walking into Rose's room several times, to make sure she was breathing regularly and sleeping well. Midway through the night, she had felt Liam lie down beside her, on the twin bed in his spare room.

The rusty old springs creaking under his weight, he had curled up against her back. The night was warm, even up here where the wind blew steadily off the Gulf of St. Lawrence. Liam's steady heartbeat and his breath on the back of her neck finally soothed her into a fitful sleep. Troubled dreams came and went, but when the sun finally rose, she sat straight up and said, "Granny."

"Lily," Liam whispered.

She looked around, trying to get her bearings. The stone walls, the leaded windows, the dark green trim—this wasn't Hubbard's Point. The fog cleared from her brain, and she realized she had dreamed of the beach. Of walking into her grandmother's rose garden with sand on her feet, of her grandmother rinsing them off with the watering can. She could almost see the little circle of shells and a sand dollar embedded in the cement.

"Lie down a little longer," Liam urged. "You hardly got any rest at all. You might have a long day ahead of you."

Somehow Lily knew he meant answering the police officer's questions, and getting Rose reacclimated to life outside the hospital, but Lily just thought of her grandmother and felt a warm breeze blow through the window. She swore it smelled of Hubbard's Point roses. Climbing out of bed, Lily checked Rose again. Her sense of vigilance was on very high alert.

She cuddled back into Liam's embrace, trying to close her eyes and settle down. Her body was so tense, her spine arched. Liam stroked her shoulder, rubbed her back. Just knowing that he was there made it safe enough for her to let the thoughts come. The dream had shaken her. Lately she'd been feeling her grandmother's presence. Starting with that night before they went down to Boston, it was almost as if Maeve had been calling to her; she'd heard her voice in the summer air.

The pull to southern New England had been strong. But Lily had been so focused on Rose getting well, she had pushed it from her mind. But the dream was so powerful tonight, Lily couldn't ignore her feelings any longer. She stared into the darkness, thinking about everything.

Her greatest fears had always been regarding Edward, and what he would do to her, her grandmother, and, now, Rose. Nine years on this rocky, austere Canadian coast had toughened Lily some—but so had being a mother. Giving birth to Rose had changed Lily and the world. From the very instant Liam had placed Rose into Lily's arms, she had turned into a mother tiger. She would fight to the death to protect her baby.

Lying with Liam now, Lily thought about what to do. She saw it as a quest: nothing less than life and death, with her and Rose's freedom as the prize. If she was brave and true, followed her heart, she would win their freedom. They could go wherever and whenever they wanted, and they would never have to worry about Edward again.

All that had come before had brought them to this point. What if Lily just faced Edward down? No more hiding, no more missing Maeve. She could finally go home, and introduce Rose to her great-grandmother.

"Why can't you sleep?" Liam asked after a few more minutes.

"I'm thinking," she said. "Of my old home."

"You're leaving, aren't you?"

"Liam," she whispered.

He didn't reply, but just held her tighter. Lily didn't know what to do, so she didn't know what to say. She linked her fingers with his, leaned down to kiss the back of his hand.

She never did get back to sleep. When she heard Rose stirring, she got up and walked into the next room so Rose would see her when she wakened. Rose struggled to sit up—she had gotten stiff during the night. Her left hand instinctively rested at her neck, protecting her heart. Lily helped her out of bed, eased her feet into her slippers.

They went downstairs, where Liam was in the kitchen, making coffee and pouring orange juice.

"Good morning, Rose," he said. "How did you sleep?"

"It was the best sleep I ever had," she said, smiling.

They sat at the round oak table, and then Lily saw what it had been too dark to see last night: pictures on the wall and refrigerator. Rose's school pictures in frames on the wall, a couple of her old drawings—from kindergarten and first grade—on the refrigerator. Lily had only vague memories of Rose insisting that they cross the hallway to Liam's office, to give them to him.

"You saved them?" Rose asked.

"Of course," he said. "Did you think I wouldn't?"

"Yes," she said. "I thought you wouldn't."

Liam chuckled, although when Lily saw him logging on to his laptop, she knew he was checking on Nanny. She glanced at Rose, to see whether she had picked up on it, but Rose was busily looking down her nightgown to see her stitches.

"How do they look?" Lily asked.

"Good," Rose said.

Lily leaned over to check—everything looked as if it was healing fine, the edges of the long incision drawn perfectly together, no clear fluid, no sign of yellow fluid or infection of any kind.

"You're right," Lily said. "Good."

They poured bowls of cereal, and then Liam came over to eat with them. Whatever he had seen onscreen was a mystery, because he didn't mention it. Lily's heart sank—she had the feeling that meant that Nanny was wandering even farther south. If only joy could follow joy. If only people could have everything, everyone they loved—all at the same time.

She thought of the singular love she had felt just twenty-four hours ago—when they were still in Boston, when her entire world was made up of newly found love and a newly healthy daughter. She had made peace long ago with her decision to leave Hubbard's Point, leave that life behind. But now, a day later, her world had been rocked by the hint of her grandmother needing her.

Lily stared out Liam's kitchen window, at the wide, amazing, blue Gulf of St. Lawrence. When she turned from the window, she caught Liam watching her. His eyes were sad, as if he could read her mind.

But because Rose was right there, no words were possible. They all just ate breakfast—or, in the case of Lily and Liam, didn't eat, but just pushed their cereal around with their spoons.

A knock sounded at the door, and Liam went to answer. Lily took a deep breath. Even before he returned, she knew that Patrick Murphy would be with him. And he was; but Lily was surprised to see Marisa there too. The looks on their faces told Lily that she needed to move Rose into a room where she wouldn't hear.

She settled Rose on the sun porch—with a book and her bag of needlepoint. Rose had started doing a project at the end of school, and this was the first she'd felt well enough to continue. Kissing Rose on the top of her head, Lily returned to the kitchen. The expression in Patrick Murphy's eyes made her feel she was about to be arrested.

"What is it?" she asked. "Are you going to put me in handcuffs?"

"He wouldn't do that to you or me," Marisa said. "We've done nothing wrong. But Edward has."

"Edward?" Lily asked, feeling electricity racing down her neck.

"Ted," Marisa said.

"Ted—that's your husband."

Ted, Edward, she thought, suddenly seeing the dull hurt in Marisa's eyes. Don't let this be happening. "No," Lily said.

"What made you come to Cape Hawk?" Patrick asked.

"It's a long story," Lily said. "I think you already know most of it. You have the news article about the ferry memorial stone. The other part has to do with a lie my husband used to tell—to get people to think he was descended from a ship captain."

"The whaling ship," Marisa said. "With ice on the rigging. And the cliffs of the fjord in the background."

"Tell me this isn't happening," Lily said, feeling the blood drain from her face. "You were married to Edward Hunter?"

Marisa nodded.

"Didn't you know he was under suspicion for killing his wife?" Lily whispered.

"No," Marisa said. "I had no idea until last night. You've been missing for nine years. I must have missed the story when it all started, because I was pregnant with Jessica—she was born the week after Rose, but it was a difficult pregnancy, and I had to go into the hospital. I vaguely remember hearing about a pregnant woman missing in Connecticut—but Lily, I couldn't bear to hear about the case. I was just about to have my baby, and I couldn't stand to think about what you might have gone through."

"Jessica and Rose have almost the same birthday."

"I know. Exactly. When I think of it now," Marisa said, holding Lily's hands, "I wonder whether that was part of the allure. Ted, Edward, knew my husband from the golf club. He'd done some stock transactions for us—he had all our family information, including birthdays. My husband liked him. So when Paul died, I just continued using Ted.

He managed the inheritance funds—and when I remember that first meeting, he commented on Jessica's birthday."

"He did?"

Marisa nodded. "He told me that someone he had cared about deeply had had a baby at that time—and it was very sacred for him."

"Sacred!" Lily exploded.

"That's what he said."

"He scammed you," Lily gasped, grabbing her, hugging her and feeling them both shaking so hard, the two wives of Edward Hunter. "Just the way he scammed me."

"We almost had him too," Marisa said. "Patrick called his friend in the FBI, and we were right on Ted's trail—with another scam, on the Internet. But the agent called Patrick this morning to say he'd erased his account, and the message board doesn't archive old messages."

"It's true," Patrick said. "We'll have to get him another way. But never mind that for now. Mara, Lily—"

"Lily," she said. "Please, Mara is from another time and place. I can't think of her now."

"You might have to," he said. "There's no good way to tell you this."

"What is it?" Liam asked, stepping closer to Lily, putting his arm around her for support.

"It's your grandmother," Patrick said. "I spoke with Clara Littlefield this morning, and Maeve had a seizure at home three days ago. The ambulance took her to Shoreline General, and she's in a coma."

"Oh, Granny," Lily said, tears flooding. "It can't be true!"

"I'm sorry," Patrick said.

Lily leaned against Liam's chest, weeping. If only she had listened to her heart on that trip to Boston. Something was telling her to go home, go to Hubbard's Point. She had dismissed it, thinking it was just her old homesickness, kicked by being in New England. But it had been Maeve, calling her. They had always been so connected; how could Lily have thought she would go on forever, just waiting for the time when Lily felt safe enough to return?

"Why did I wait so long?" Lily wept. "She needed me, and I wasn't there."

"You had to think of Rose," Liam said, kissing her hair. "You had good reason to stay hidden."

"Maeve loves you," Patrick said. "She must have felt good, knowing she helped you get away. She wouldn't have wanted you to walk into harm's way."

"Patrick told me that she always carries the needlepoint case you made her," Marisa said.

"I made her an honorary Nanouk," Lily said, sniffling.

"The Nanouks will be with you," Marisa said. "Wherever you go, whatever you do. You know that—"

"I do," Lily said, touching her cheek. "And the same is true of you. They saved my life when I first got here."

"And you've saved mine," Marisa said.

"What are you going to do?" Patrick asked.

"I could go there," Lily said. "And Edward wouldn't necessarily have to know."

"Or he could find out," Patrick said. "And we could help you fight him."

"He'd find out about Rose," Lily whispered, her blood running cold. She knew that if she returned to Connecticut, she would have to face hard truths about the man she had left. He was the father of her daughter. She had been afraid of him for so long, but suddenly she knew that some emotions were bigger than fear.

"Maeve needs you," Patrick said.

"You have to go to her," Liam said.

"Oh God," Lily whispered. She held his hand and looked deeply into his eyes. They were as grave and sad as she felt. Now that Rose's heart was mending, she felt hers was breaking. What if her grandmother was very sick? Lily would stay and take care of her. There was so much she wanted to make up to Maeve: all the lost years, the birthdays and holidays she had missed. Maeve had never even met Rose. As wonderful a grandmother as she had been to Lily, she'd be all that to Rose. Edward had deprived them all of each other for too long.

"Liam," she said, looking into his eyes. How could she leave him now, just as they had found each other? "I can't go away from you."

"Nanny's leading you there," he said. "You know that, don't you?"

"What do you mean?"

He held her hand, leading her to the computer, showed her MM122's latest position: swimming in Long Island Sound, right off the tip of Hubbard's Point. Lily could barely take in the information—evidence of another miracle. How could she doubt it?

"She's leading you back home," Liam said.

"Home is here," she said.

"Lily," Liam said. "I know you're scared. But look—look at what's happening. Do you know how amazing it is that a beluga whale would make her way down the eastern seaboard, all the way south to Hubbard's Point?"

"Is it possible?" Lily asked, her throat so tight.

"It's happening," he said. "That is evidence that goes beyond possible—straight to reality."

Lily closed her eyes. When she opened them again, she saw a picture hanging above Liam's desk: Tecumseh Neill, the family patriarch, standing with his whaling vessel, the *Pinnacle*. Beside it, the copy of a letter he had written to his wife, waiting at home in Cape Hawk:

"I have been in pursuit of a single whale," he wrote in fine, elegant script. "She sings by night, when there's not a sound to answer her but the wind in the rigging. When she breached at first light, she was the color of blood—a sight to strike fear into every heart and yet make every man aboard gaze upon her with awe and reverence—that such a creature could exist! I will follow her, my darling, but I made a promise to return home to you, and that I shall do. . . ."

"Liam," Lily said, turning to look into his eyes. "Would you come to Connecticut with us? You made that promise to Rose. . . ."

"I made it to you too," he said.

"Then is that a yes?" Lily asked. Her heart was beating in her throat. Her pulse, the rhythm of life. Blood, oxygen, and that other vital essence mixing together in her body. Her Rose, reading on the sun porch. Liam took her hand.

Behind him, the windows were wide open. From up here on the hill, you could see forever—or just about. Way out into the Gulf of St. Lawrence, Lily could see whales playing. They breached, shooting straight out of the icy blue water like silver missiles, landing with exuberant, sky-high splashes. The day was brilliant.

Summer
of
Roses

TO ROSEMARY GOETTSCHE,

Willoughby Moon, the most beautiful rose of all

"In which Christopher Robin and Pooh
come to an enchanted place . . .

I
And all your friends
Sends—
I mean all your friend
Send—
*(Very awkward this, it keeps
going wrong)*
Well, anyhow, we send
Our love
END."

—CHAPTER X,
from *The House at Pooh Corner*,
by A. A. Milne

Acknowledgments

This is the Summer of Roses, but it is also the summer of wonderful publishers. Gratitude beyond words to everyone at Bantam, for all their kindness, patience, generosity, and vision: Irwyn Applebaum, Nita Taublib, Tracy Devine, Betsy Hulsebosch, Carolyn Schwartz, Cynthia Lasky, Barb Burg, Susan Corcoran, Gina Wachtel, Melissa Lord, Kerri Buckley, Kenneth Wohlrob, Jennifer Campaniolo, Igor Aronov, Mandy Lau, and Janet Rutledge.

Thank you to Deborah Dwyer and to Bantam's production staff, who work miracles: Anna Forgione, Kathleen Baldonado, Tracy Heydweiller, Virginia Norey, Christine Tanigawa, and Susan Hood.

Much admiration and affection to Jim Plumeri.

Boundless love and thanks to my agent, Andrea Cirillo, and everyone at the Jane Rotrosen Agency: Jane Berkey, Don Cleary, Meg Ruley, Peggy Gordijn, Annelise Robey, Maggie Kelly, Hilary Demby, Christina Hogrebe, and Chris Ruen.

Epic gratitude to Ron Bernstein, who is nothing less than amazing.

In celebration of the Whale Trail sculpture event of southeastern Connecticut, with thanks to Diana Atwood Johnson and to Suzanne Mylar of K & M Productions. Amelia Onorato, my brilliant niece, is the artist for my beluga whale (for the Old Lyme–Phoebe Griffin Noyes Library), and I'm very proud of her work. Love and thanks also to Maureen and Olivier Onorato for all the support and celestial navigation.

Much love and thanks also to Rosemary's wonderful family— her husband, Roger Goettsche, and their brilliant daughters, Kate, Molly, and Emily.

Thank you, Lyn Gammill Walker, with much love and appreciation for such wonderful connection and insight.

Gratitude to SEA, the Sea Education Association of Woods Hole, Massachusetts, for that first voyage to see the whales, so long ago.

Thank you to E. J. McAdams, the poet of New York City nature.

Many thanks to Subhankar Banerjee for his brilliant, sensitive photographs of the Arctic National Wildlife Refuge.

Thank you to the staff at the Cape Hatteras National Seashore, the dolphins of Rodanthe, and protectors of the environment everywhere.

Unending awe to William Twigg Crawford, Paul James, and J.M., for their wealth of knowledge about sharks.

Much gratitude to Susan Caruso, Mary Lou Cuccio, Ellie and Bud Ford, and the women at Domestic Violence Valley Shore Services.

Love and thanks to Sarah Walker, who is by far the most hilarious person in New York City.

Much appreciation to Carolyn Schwartz, for everything in Charleston, and to everyone at *Family Circle* magazine and the *Family Circle* Cup, for a wonderful event.

Thank you and love to the dauntless and inspiring Sam Whitney and Sadie Whitney-Havlicak.

With much love to Diana Atwood Johnson and John S. Johnson.

Love forever to Marta Curro and Mary Perrin.

Thank you to some wonderful musicians and artists, my friends: Mark Lonergan, Dore Dedrick, the Atwaters, Maura Fogarty, and Fletcher Buckley.

Much gratitude to Dr. Matthew Goulet.

I am grateful beyond words to Dr. Susan Robertson. Her support, vision, clarity, and insight have sustained me throughout the writing of this novel, and many others.

My wedding was like a dream. It was almost everything a wedding should be, and when I think of it, even now, I see it unfolding like the kind of beautiful story that always has a happy ending.

I got married in my grandmother's garden, by the sea, on a brilliant early July morning at Hubbard's Point. The daylilies were in bloom. That's what I remember, almost as much as the roses: orange, cream, lemon, golden daylilies on tall green stalks, tossed by the summer breeze, trumpeting exultation up to the wild blue sky. But the roses were my grandmother's specialty, her pride and joy, and that year, for my wedding, they were all blooming.

Scarlet Dublin Bay roses climbed the trellis beside the front door of the weathered-shingle cottage, while Garnet-and-Golds and pale pink New Dawns meandered up the stone chimney. The beds by the iron bench bloomed with red, yellow, peach, and pink classic English varieties, while those along the stone wall, by the old wishing well and the steps up to the road, were low shrubs of white and cream roses. A six-foot hedge of *Rosa rugosa*—white and pink beach roses—lined the seawall, along with deep blue delphiniums and hydrangeas.

It was a perfect setting for a perfect wedding—something that most people, including me, never imagined would happen. I guess I thought I wasn't the marrying kind. Let's just say that I was a little on the guarded side. I had lost my parents very young. As a child I had been in love with our family. I know how dramatic that sounds, but it's true. We were so happy, and my parents had loved each other with wild, reckless, ends-of-the-earth abandon. I had watched them together, and taken it in, and decided, even at four, that nothing less would ever do for me. When they were killed in a ferry accident during a trip to Ireland, although I wasn't there, but home in Connecticut with my grandmother, I think I died with them.

So my wedding—and everything that had led up to it—the miracle of meeting Edward Hunter, and falling so madly in love with him, and being swept off my feet in a way I'd never expected or believed could happen—was a resurrection of sorts. A rising from the dead, of a little girl who went down to the bottom of the Irish Sea with her parents, twenty-seven years earlier.

Edward. He seemed to love me with everything he had, not wanting to let me out of his sight. His expression, his embrace, his presence— all had the intensity of a hurricane lamp turned up high. And when he poured that light on me, I was transfixed.

He was just over five-eight, but since I'm just under five-two, I had to stand on tiptoes to kiss him. A rugby player at Harvard, he was broad-shouldered and muscular. His red Saab bore three stickers: Harvard University, Columbia Business School, and a bumper sticker that said *Rugby Players Eat Their Dead.* The joke was, Edward was so gentle, I couldn't even imagine him playing such a rough sport.

When I go back to our wedding day, I see his red car parked in the road up at the top of the stone steps, behind the rose-and-ivy-covered wishing well. I can see the graceful arch curving over the well—with *Sea Garden,* the name of my grandmother's cottage, forged in wrought iron back when my great-grandfather was still alive—the black letters rusting away in the salt air even back then, twelve years ago. I remember the moment so well: standing there in my grandmother's yard, knowing that soon I would drive away with Edward in that red car— that I would be his wife, and we would be off on our honeymoon.

Can I say now, for certain, that I looked at that iron arch and saw the corroding letters as a reminder that even that which is most beautiful, intended to endure forever, can be corrupted or destroyed? No, I can't. But I do remember that the sight of it gave me my first cold feeling of the day.

My grandmother and Clara Littlefield—her next-door neighbor and best friend from childhood—had gone all out to make my wedding a dream come true. The yellow-and-white-striped tent stood in the side yard between their houses, on the very tip of Hubbard's Point, jutting proudly into Long Island Sound. Tables with long golden-cream tablecloths were scattered around, all decorated with flowers from the garden. A string quartet from the Hartt School of Music, in Hartford, played Vivaldi. My friends were in their summer best—bright sundresses, straw hats, blue blazers.

Granny stood before me, looking into my eyes. We were the same height, and we laughed, because we were both so happy. I wore a white wedding gown; she wore a pale yellow chiffon dress. My veil blew in the sea breeze; my bouquet was white roses, off-white lace hydrangeas, and ivy from the wishing well. Granny wore a yellow straw hat with a band of blue flowers.

"I wish Edward's family had been able to come," she said as we stood by the wishing well, ready to begin the procession.

"I know," I said. "He's trying to make the best of it."

"Well," she said. "Things happen . . . you'll see them soon, I'm sure. One thing I know, Mara—your parents are with you today."

"Granny, don't get me started."

"I won't," my grandmother said, wriggling her shoulders with resolve. "We're staying strong as I walk you down the aisle, or I'm not Maeve Jameson."

"My parents would be proud of you," I said, because I knew she was thinking of them every bit as much as I was trying not to—and I gave her a big smile, just to prove I wasn't going to cry.

"Of us both," she said, linking arms with me as the quartet started playing Bach.

So much time has passed, but certain memories are still clear and sharp. The pressure of Granny's hand on mine, holding steady, as we walked across the grass; my beach friends Bay and Tara beaming at me; the smell of roses and salt air; Edward's short dark hair, his golden tan set off by a pale blue shirt and wheat linen blazer; his wide-eyed gaze.

I remember thinking his eyes looked like a little boy's. Hazel eyes. He had been so helpful all morning—taking charge of where the tables went, which direction the quartet should face. It was sort of odd, having a man "in charge," here on this point of land filled with strong women. Granny and I had exchanged an amused glance—letting him do his thing. But here he was, standing at our makeshift altar in the side yard, looking for all the world like a lost little boy as I approached him. But then I caught that blank stare—blank, yet somehow charged—and it made me hesitate, holding tight to my grandmother's hand.

Yes, I remember that stare, the look in his hazel eyes. It was fear— standing there under the striped tent, watching me approach, my betrothed was afraid of something. The years have gone by and told me all I need to know about his fear—but let's go back to my wedding day and pretend we don't have all this knowledge. Back then, in quick succession, I thought one thing and felt another. No—that's backwards. I felt first, thought second.

I felt cold—the same chilly primal shiver I'd experienced looking up at his car, seeing that salt-pitted, rusty metal arch. But I chased the unwanted, ugly chill with this thought: *Edward—hey, honey, Edward!*

Don't be afraid . . . please don't worry that it's too soon, or my grand-mother doubts you. I love you. . . . I love you.

I love you.

Words I had said so rarely up until that time—but since meeting Edward, I had used almost constantly. The old Mara Jameson had been too closed off and guarded to let them slip off her tongue; but the new Mara Jameson couldn't say them enough.

This was my home, my side yard, my family and friends—Edward was far from everything comfortable and familiar to him. His family hadn't been able to make it. These thoughts were flying through my mind as my grandmother passed my hand into his with the whispered words "Take care of her, Edward." Edward nodded, but the expression in his eyes didn't ease.

Memo to self and brides everywhere: if you're standing in front of a justice of the peace, about to get married, and all you can think about is why your husband-to-be looks very uncomfortable, it's a red flag worth paying attention to.

The ceremony occurred. That's how I think of it now: words and music. What did they all mean? It's hard to say, harder still to not be cynical. The ceremony disguised one basic truth: marriage is a con-tract. Let's put romance aside. First and foremost, marriage is a legal, binding contract, where two people are joined in partnership, their as-sets merged, their fates legally entwined through powers vested by no less than the state.

When I think back to the look in Edward's eyes, I believe that he was afraid that I might not follow through on the deal, might not sign on the dotted line. What would have happened if I hadn't? If I had listened to that tiny voice inside, if I had felt the cold chill and known that it meant something worth paying attention to?

But I didn't listen. I pushed my feelings aside and pulled other things out of the summer air: love, hope, faith, resolve. I held Edward's hand. "I do," I said. "I do," he said. He kissed the bride. People cheered, and when I looked out at my friends, I saw more than one of them cry-ing and grinning at the same time. They were so very happy for me.

We stood there, husband and wife. Our brilliant summer wedding day, blue sky and sparkles on the calm water, Bach giving way to Mozart and the sound of leaves fluttering in the breeze—everything was so beautiful, so spectacular, it had to be a harbinger of a joyful life to come.

I turned to look at him. It's true, my own eyes were moist, and my voice was thin with wild and rising emotion. "Edward," I said, trailing off into all the hopes and dreams and possibilities of our future together. He stared at me—the fear gone from his eyes, replaced by something else. It was the first time I saw—well, you'll hear about what I saw as my story goes on. All I can say is, I felt the earth—the thin layer of grass on granite ledge—tilt beneath my feet.

He touched the flowers in my bouquet and said, "You're so delicate, Mara. Like a white rose. And white roses bruise so easily. Is that what your grandmother meant when she said I should take care of you?"

His words took my breath away. Don't they imply great tenderness? Show true depth of caring, of understanding? Of course they do. He could be so tender. I'll never deny that. But do you also see, as I do now, that his words implied a threat?

It was as if he'd been focused on Granny's gentle direction—just an offhand comment was how I'd taken it, a rather protective grandmother giving away the bride. Had Edward even heard the ceremony? Had he even *been* there? His hazel eyes flashed black as he mentioned Granny's words.

Just recently, I dreamed of a woman who lived under veils. Black, gray, white, silver, slate, dark blue—layers of veils covering her face. Take one off, there's another underneath. The woman lived in darkness, even when the sun was shining. She existed under cover. She could barely see out, and others could not see in. The question was: who put those veils on her? Did she do it to herself? In the dream, she took them off one by one—and at the very bottom, the very last, or first, was a white wedding veil. In my life, I had them torn from me. I wanted to keep them on—you have no idea how much I needed those veils.

Women learn how to hide the worst. We love the best, and show it to all who want to see. Our accomplishments, our careers, our awards, our homes, our gardens, our happy marriages, our beautiful children. We learn, by tacit agreement, to look away from—and hide—the hurt, the blight, the dark, the monster in the closet, the darkness in our new husband's eyes.

But in some lives, there comes a time when the monster comes out of the closet and won't go back in. That happened to me. He began to show himself. My grandmother was the first to see. Only the wisest people can observe a woman in such a relationship and not sit in judgment. Judgment is easy: it is black and white, as brutal as a gavel strike. It keeps a person from having to ask the hard questions: what can I do to help? Could that be me?

My grandmother didn't judge. She tried to understand—and if anyone could understand, it would be her, the woman who had raised me in her rose-covered cottage by Long Island Sound. A woman patient enough to coax red, pink, peach, yellow, and white roses from the stony Connecticut soil, to ease her brokenhearted orphan granddaughter back into life, could sit still long enough to see through the lies, see past the veils—and instead of judging, try to help, really help.

People said, "How could you have stayed with him so long?" The true answer, of course, is that I had the veils. But the answer I gave was "I loved him." In its way, that answer was true too. My grandmother understood that.

It wasn't real love. I didn't know that for a long time. Real love is a boomerang—it comes back to you. With Edward, love was a sinkhole. It nearly consumed me, taking every single thing I had, and then some—until I, and everything surrounding me, collapsed.

I have Liam now, so I have learned the difference. And I have my daughter, Rose. The day Rose was born, nine years ago, I was on the run. I had left my home, my grandmother, my beloved Connecticut shoreline, where I had always lived, to escape Edward and try to save something of my life. The Connecticut motto is *Qui Transtulit Sustinet*—"He who transplants sustains."

Leave it to the founding fathers to say "he." Perhaps they knew that "she"—or at least "me"—"who transplants shatters." I left home, pregnant with Rose, and I fell apart. But Rose coaxed the love right from my bones. I built myself back, with the help of Rose and Liam. And, although she wasn't right there in person, my grandmother. She was with me, in my heart, guiding me, every single day while I lived in hiding, in another country, far from home.

You see, my grandmother let me go. She made the ultimate sacrifice for me—gave me and Rose, her great-granddaughter, the chance and means to get away from Edward. She was a one-woman underground railway for one emotionally battered woman. And it cost her so dearly, I don't know whether she will survive.

My name is Lily Malone now. It was my on-the-run name, and it has stuck. I have decided to keep it forever. *Lily* for the orange and yellow daylilies growing along the stone wall of my grandmother's sea garden, waving on long, slender green stalks in the salt breeze. *Malone* for the song she used to sing me when I was little:

> *In Dublin's fair city, where girls are so pretty,*
> *I once laid my eyes on sweet Molly Malone.*
> *She wheeled her wheelbarrow through streets*
> > *broad and narrow,*
> *Singing "cockles and mussels alive, alive-oh."*

Those lyrics are so sweet, and because my grandmother sang them to me when I was little and couldn't sleep, they seemed full of life and romance and the promise of unexpected love. I took the name Malone to honor my grandmother's lullaby, but also for a darker reason. The name helps me stay on guard—reminds me that someone once laid eyes on me too. And like Molly Malone, I was a hardworking woman; he liked that about me. He liked it very much.

I would like to explain my chosen name to my grandmother. I would like to see her again. To introduce her to Liam—and, especially, to Rose.

More than anything, I've come back from my nine-year exile to try to save my grandmother, as she once saved me. I am remembering all this for her. I want to recapture every detail, so I can appreciate exactly what she did for me—for the woman I was, and the woman I have become.

This story is a prayer for her, Maeve Jameson.

It begins twelve years ago, three years before I left Hubbard's Point for the most remote place I could find—back when I was Mara. Back when I was a rose that bruised so easily.

Chapter 1

How does a person reenter a life she left nine years earlier? Knowing that there had been a relentless search for her, that her picture had been plastered on the front pages of every newspaper in Connecticut and beyond? Understanding that every local police department remained on the lookout for her? Realizing that all but one of her friends and family have given her up for dead?

The answer is, she walks right in the front door.

That's what Lily Malone did in the very-early-morning hours of August ninth. Just past one A.M., Liam Neill parked his truck in the turnaround at Hubbard's Point, lifted Rose—sleeping, after the long drive from Nova Scotia—and followed Lily down the stone steps.

Lily glanced at the arch over the wishing well—there was the house name, *Sea Garden,* its letters just a little more rusty, a bit more filigreed from the salt air, than they had been nine years earlier. The sight gave her a pang so deep, she gasped out loud. Lily was really home. A breeze blew off Long Island Sound—salt water, just like the Gulf of St. Lawrence in Maritime Canada, where she had lived and hidden these last nine years. But this night breeze was warm, gentle, filled with scents of marsh grass and sandy beaches—instead of the fjord's arctic cliffs and cold, clear water flowing straight off the pack ice.

"Oh my," she said out loud, alive with the thrill of finally coming home. The roses greeted her—their perfume filled the air, and if the ones growing up the trellis beside the front door were slightly less well tended than they'd been nine years ago, they were still profuse and extravagant. Lily reached up, through the thorns, to feel underneath the shingle just beside the dark porch light, and there it was—the key her grandmother had always kept hidden there, guarded by the roses' foliage and thorns. "She didn't move it," she whispered.

"Of course she didn't," Liam said in her ear, standing behind her with Rose. "She never stopped hoping you'd come back."

"Maeve is coming home too," Lily said, opening the squeaky screen door, holding it open with her shoulder, fumbling with the key in the rusty old door lock. "Right? Tell me she's going to be okay—"

"She will be, Lily," Liam said.

Lily felt the key turn. Nine years later, the door made the same bump as it opened, one of the hinges hanging just slightly. Stepping into the kitchen . . . smelling beach-house dampness encroaching from the absence of its owner. Yet someone—Clara, obviously—had opened a few windows. Lily walked through the first floor as if she were a ghost, haunting her most beloved, familiar place on earth.

Lily began to smile. "It's all the same," she whispered. The moon had risen out of the Sound, casting a gleaming white light on the calm water, its pale light flooding the room. Lily saw the familiar slipcovers, braided rugs, pillows she had needlepointed for her grandmother. She ran her fingers over her old shell collection, books in the bookcase, moonstones gathered at low tide on Little Beach.

She had to see everything, yet she couldn't turn on a lamp yet. If she turned on a light, it would mean she was committed to this. "This" meaning that she was really here, that her exile was over, that she had returned to the land of the living. Neighbors would see the light and come over. People would know that she was back.

Edward would find out.

"Where does Rose sleep?" Liam asked.

"In my room," Lily whispered. She led him up the narrow stairs. The second floor had four small bedrooms—beach-cottage in size and feel. Lily's heart was racing as she entered her old room. Under the eaves on the north side, it had funny ceiling angles, a twin bed, and her old Betsy McCall paper dolls right there on the bureau. Pulling down the covers, she choked up to see the sheets—imprinted with tiny bouquets of blue roses—and a pink summer-weight blanket. She bent down to smell the bedding—it was fresh.

"My grandmother knew we were coming," she said. "Somehow, before she went to the hospital, she made up the bed for Rose."

Together they tucked Rose in. The little girl stirred, opening her eyes, glancing around the unfamiliar room in dream-state wonder. "Are we here?" she asked.

"Yes, honey. You'll see it all tomorrow morning. Good night."

"Night," Rose murmured as her eyes fluttered shut.

Lily and Liam went back downstairs. Moonlight was dazzling on the water in front of the house. Lily had watched countless moonrises from this room, through the wide, curtainless windows overlooking the rocks and sea. Everything seemed so open compared to the pine-shrouded cabin she'd lived in at Cape Hawk, Nova Scotia—she had hidden in a boreal forest, with hawks and owls as sentries.

Liam had been one of the first people she'd met, arriving in the distant, unfamiliar town—disguised by cropping her long dark hair, dyeing it light brown, wearing the old horn-rimmed spectacles her grandmother had given her. He had been her friend and savior, even though she had rejected him every step of the way. She had to, to protect herself and her unborn baby.

Lily's first weeks in Nova Scotia had been a dark fairy tale, complete with cabin deep in the North Woods, a bounty on her head in the form of a reward posted by Edward, and the benevolent presence of the fierce and kindly Liam—there for Rose's birth, delivering the baby on the kitchen floor, and swearing to protect forever this mother and child. And there had been plenty of protecting for him to do: born with complex heart defects, Rose had just completed her last round of surgery earlier that summer.

Brokenhearted baby, brokenhearted mother, Lily thought, gazing out at the moon on the Sound. Her arm was around Liam, and his around her. Gulls called from across the water, from their rookery on the rock islands half a mile offshore. Lily felt the sound in her heart, and thought of the annual Ceili Festival, just about to start in Cape Hawk, the Irish music as haunting as the gulls' cries.

She looked up at Liam—tall and lean, his blue eyes shadowed with his own private sorrows. Ravaged by the shark that killed his brother, Liam had one arm—and the childhood nickname, "Captain Hook," that had made him both a laughingstock and a tragic figure in his small town. Liam would have none of that—he blazed his way through university and graduate school, becoming a respected oceanographer and ichthyologist—studying great whites, the species that had torn apart his family and his own body.

Lily wasn't exactly sure what had brought them together. And she wasn't even sure she cared. They had found each other in that far-northern town. She had run so far from home, and found something like a replacement family. Anne, Marisa, Marlena . . . her friends and needlepointing club, the Nanouk Girls of the Frozen North, were like her sisters. And Liam. He had been present at Rose's birth, and he'd never gone away. Those nine years in Cape Hawk had strengthened Lily more than anything she could have imagined.

Her grandmother's illness had called her back to Hubbard's Point. Patrick Murphy, the lead detective on the case of Lily's disappearance, had finally found her in Cape Hawk. The minute she heard of Maeve's illness, everything else fell away. Lily knew what she had to do.

She came home.

"I'm really here," she said, leaning against Liam.

"Are you ready for tomorrow?" he asked.

"I have to be," she said. "My grandmother needs me."

"I know," he said. His voice was low and calm. He touched her hair, and her skin tingled. They were still very new. Was it possible that just a few weeks ago they had kissed for the first time? After a whole lifetime of loving Rose, they were really together.

"I don't want Rose to ever know him," Lily said, and she didn't even have to say his name.

"Let me take her away," Liam said. "I'll hide her. Only you'll know where we are."

Lily's heart skipped, a stone scaling over the water's surface. What if he really could? What if she could hide Rose from Edward forever?

"Living in Canada," she said, "I've felt so powerful. I had complete control over her safety. Now that we're back in the States, what if he comes after her? He'll see her as a way to get to me. And me as a way to get to *her*."

She leaned back against his strong chest, as his one arm came around her from behind. They rocked against each other, staring at the moon's silver path across the water.

"I think you should go see your grandmother," he said. "But you should let me take Rose somewhere safe."

"We could ask Patrick for help," Lily said.

"We could," Liam said. "But I have an old friend at the University of Rhode Island. Graduate school of oceanography. He has a place near Scarborough Beach, on Narragansett Bay. He'd let us stay with him. It's not that far away."

"Rose has never been away from me," Lily said, feeling her heart tighten. "Except for going to the hospital."

"You'd be doing it for her," Liam said. "To keep her away from Edward, until you know what to expect."

"She'd love being with you," Lily murmured. Rose loved Liam with everything she had. For her ninth birthday, barely a month ago, she had wished for two things: to see Nanny, the legendary white whale of Cape Hawk, and to have a real father like Liam. "How much should I tell Rose?"

"However much you think she can handle."

How could Lily begin to know what that was? Rose had just come through open-heart surgery. She was healing from what was supposed to be the final operation necessary to correct the last of the multiple heart defects—Tetralogy of Fallot—she'd been born with.

"I don't know," she said. "She'll have so many questions."

"It's going to work out, Lily," Liam said.

"You've made big promises to me before," Lily said, smiling. None bigger than the fact that he would always be there, never desert Rose— the heart-stricken baby he had brought into this world.

"And they've come true, right?"

"So far," she said, turning to tilt her head back, kissing him long and hard, feeling her blood tingle as it moved through her body. Every touch of Liam's was a promise, with the energy of magic. Outside, the waves hit the rocks, and leaves rustled in the breeze. Lily shivered, wanting more of everything.

"So the answer is yes?" Liam asked.

Lily closed her eyes, unable to speak. Everything had been happening so fast—from hearing about Maeve, to deciding to come out of hiding, to driving down from Nova Scotia.

"You don't have to decide right now," he said. "You need some sleep, Lily. You'll know what to do in the morning."

"Once the sun comes up," Lily said, "Clara will see your truck. She'll come over to investigate. If she sees you and Rose, there'll be no keeping it secret. Not that she means any harm—in fact, I can't wait to see her."

"I know," Liam said. "You're thinking it would be unfair to ask her to go along with something she might not understand. Let's go to bed—we have until dawn to decide."

"In just a few hours," Lily said.

Holding hands, they went upstairs again. Lily still hadn't turned on a light. She still hadn't let herself take that extra step. It didn't matter— she knew every inch of this house in the dark. Every draft, every creaky board, every piece of furniture. Her grandmother hadn't changed anything since Lily had left.

Yet here in this cottage she knew better than any place on earth, Lily waited for the answers. She couldn't help the joy she felt—she loved the warm breeze, the smell of her grandmother's roses. She led Liam into the largest bedroom—the one her grandmother had always saved for guests—in the front of the house, where dormer windows jutted out over the sloping roof, facing the moonlit bay. Lily cranked open the casement windows as wide as they could go.

A gust of air fluttered the sheer white curtains and cooled Lily's hot

skin. The sound of waves, rhythmically splashing the rocks down below, came through the windows. Lily went to check on Rose. She bent
down, watched her daughter's chest rise and fall. Rose's breaths were
like the waves—steady, sure, one after the other. Lily knew that Rose
would be in good hands with Liam, but the idea of letting her beautiful girl out of her sight was almost impossible to bear.

"Lily," Liam whispered, in the doorway behind her, his hand on her
shoulder. "Come to bed."

Lily shook her head. She couldn't move. How could something so
peaceful fill her with such fear? Rose was sleeping in Lily's own childhood bed; the summer breeze carried scents of honeysuckle and
hundreds of red, pink, and white roses. The old words came back to
her: *White roses bruise so easily.* Staring down at her daughter, she
calmed herself with the hard-won certainty that Edward wasn't even
aware that Rose existed.

As far as Edward knew, Lily was dead. She had died—everyone
believed—nine years ago, when she was eight and a half months
pregnant. Lily felt a rush, and she shuddered. It was as if she had just
been granted a free pass by the gods. Edward didn't know about
Rose. . . .

"I want you to do it," she said without turning around, not taking
her eyes off her daughter's face, long brown lashes resting on delicate
cheekbones, mouth ever-so-slightly open. Her left arm was bent at the
elbow, fingertips on her neck, protecting the scar where she'd had
open-heart surgery. "I want you to take her."

"I'll take care of her," Liam whispered.

Lily nodded. "I know you will. You always have."

She knelt by Rose's bed, staring at her for a long minute—until Rose
sighed and turned. Not wanting to wake her up, Lily kissed her sleeping daughter's head, and followed Liam into the bedroom. She knew
that nothing in the world could make her send Rose away, force her to
take this action, except for one thing: a need to see her grandmother,
the woman who had raised her, and make sure she got well.

Nothing else could do it.

Pulling down the white chenille bedspread, curling up beside Liam,
she closed her eyes. The sound of the waves merged with the rise
and fall of Liam's chest. She counted the waves, felt his heartbeats. Outside the open window, the gulls on their island rookeries cried and
cried.

Lily just stared at the moon, hanging outside the window, as she listened to the cries of the gulls, Liam's breath on her neck. She pulled his

arm even tighter around her, and she prayed that she was doing the right thing.

Dawn came up like thunder, and Liam Neill knew there wasn't much time. He knew he had to get Rose away, and yet he didn't know how to leave. He wanted to stay with Lily.

Lily made coffee and oatmeal, and then she got Rose washed and dressed. The sky went from deep purple to cerulean blue as the sun crowned the eastern horizon. Liam had heard so much about Hubbard's Point—it was almost mythical to him, the place where Lily had grown up, where her beloved Maeve had raised prizewinning roses and nurtured a strong, beautiful granddaughter. Liam stepped out on the side porch, drinking coffee and staring at the granite ledges sloping down to Long Island Sound. The cottage sat almost at the tip of a promontory—the Point of Hubbard's Point, as Lily had told him and Rose on the drive down from Cape Hawk.

Liam looked across the side yard toward a similar cottage—built of weather-silvered shingles, with turquoise shutters and door, white window boxes filled with red geraniums—and saw someone peering out a window.

He faded back, close to the house, then disappeared inside. Finding Lily and Rose in the kitchen, talking at the table, he tapped Lily's shoulder.

"Someone just saw me," he said. "Looking over from next door."

"That's Clara," Lily said. "She always gets up with the sun, in time for the *Hartford Courant.*"

"We'd better go," Liam said.

"But I don't get it," Rose said, her brow wrinkled. "I thought we just got here."

Lily took a deep breath. Liam knew what this was doing to her—he touched her glossy dark hair, stroking it for support. She looked Rose in the eyes.

"Honey," she said. "You and Liam are going to stay somewhere else for a few days. It won't be far away from here—not too far, anyway—and I'll know where you are every minute."

"Why aren't you coming?" Rose asked.

"I have to see about my grandmother."

"Your granny?"

Lily nodded. "Yes. You know she's sick—"

"That's why we came here, from Cape Hawk."

Lily stared at Rose, as if trying to decide how much to say. Liam kept watch out the side window, knowing that they didn't have much time.

"It is why we came," Lily said. "But long ago, there was a reason why I left here. I have to . . . take care of all that, before you come back to stay."

"Mommy," Rose said, her voice breaking with panic.

"Rose, it won't take very long."

"I want you to come with us."

"I will come find you," Lily said. "Very soon, Rose—as soon as I straighten everything out. It won't be long—I promise you. And in the meantime, you'll be with Liam."

Rose hesitated. She still looked worried, but she glanced up at Liam for reassurance. He smiled down at her and squeezed her hand. She raised her arms, and he lifted her up. He leaned close to Lily—their eyes met and locked.

"Take good care of her," Lily said.

"I will. As if she were my own," Liam said, leaning forward, so Lily could embrace Rose and Liam could hold them both at the same time. Their bags were in the truck. Lily had his cell phone number and he had left her all the additional information he could—addresses and telephone numbers for John Stanley's home and lab, a hand-drawn map of how to find his house in Narragansett.

"Bye, sweetheart," Lily said, her voice thin and her eyes moist.

"Bye, Mommy."

"I'll call you," Liam promised.

Lily waved him away. He glanced across the yard—the grass deep green, wet with dew—and saw the curtains fall again. Holding Rose, he walked up the sidewalk and stone steps, past the rose-covered well.

"What's that?" Rose asked.

"A wishing well," Liam said as he opened the truck door, buckled Rose into her seat. He strode around to the driver's side and started the engine.

"In my great-grandmother's yard?" Rose asked, sounding surprised.

"Yes," Liam said, putting the truck in reverse just as he saw the door to the house next door open and a gray-haired woman start hurrying down her sidewalk.

"I wish," Rose whispered. "I wish . . ."

Liam's pulse was racing as he backed into the cul-de-sac. The Sound spread out on both sides of the Point, blue water surrounding the land. Graceful cottages perched on rock ledges, gardens spilling over with beach roses and wildflowers. He couldn't take his eyes off Lily. She stood in the front yard, arms crossed tightly across her chest, hardly able to move.

"Who's that lady?" Rose asked, watching the white-haired woman stop in her tracks. Then the woman shrieked, and started running toward Lily.

"It's Clara," Liam said, although he had never met her himself. "You'll meet her someday."

"I hope so," Rose said, her voice thick. "She looks so happy to see Mommy."

"She sure does," Liam said. And then, with Lily holding out her arms to embrace her grandmother's oldest friend, he shifted into gear and headed for Rhode Island.

Chapter 2

"It can't be true! I must be seeing things!" Clara Littlefield said, stopping two feet from Lily, just long enough to make sure she wasn't staring at an apparition.

"It's me, Clara," Lily said. "I've come home."

"Oh, darling," Clara said, breaking down as she pulled Lily close in a hug. Lily held her tight, feeling like a child. This woman had been the closest thing Lily had had to an aunt—Clara and Maeve had been as close as sisters.

"Clara, tell me about Granny."

"I hardly know where to begin. I have a thousand questions—what happened to you? Where have you been? How did you get here?"

"A friend dropped me off. I'll tell you the rest, but first I have to go see her."

"She's at Shoreline General."

"I know. Will you take me to her? I couldn't find the keys to her car."

"I have her purse at my house. I brought it back from the hospital, that first day. Of course I'll take you."

Lily took a deep breath. She'd made it over the first hurdle. She ran into the cottage, grabbed her bag, locked the door behind her. She stuck her cell phone in the pocket of her cotton pants—it was her lifeline to Rose and Liam. Then she and Clara climbed into Clara's blue Chrysler.

Driving through Hubbard's Point for the first time in daylight, Lily noticed how much had stayed the same—and how much had changed. Most cottages had retained their charming, nestled-into-the-rustic-landscape feel. But others . . .

"What happened there?" Lily asked as they passed the Langtrys' old property.

"Oh, dear. It's happening more and more. People buy a beach

cottage and try to turn it into a showplace—frosted glass and all. How they manage to make a Hubbard's Point cottage look like a Meriden funeral home, I'll never know."

"I can just imagine what Granny says about it," Lily said.

"She says, 'They're embracing their nouveau richeness,'" Clara said. "Oh, I miss talking with her. No one makes me laugh like Maeve."

Makes. Lily heard the present tense and took hope.

"What do the doctors say?" Lily asked.

"They're confused. She's had some sort of what they're calling a 'neurological event.' Even that would give Maeve a chuckle. An *event.* She'd say they're making it sound like a lunar eclipse."

"But what sort of neurological event?" Lily asked, feeling frozen.

"That's what we don't know yet. They're running tests."

"Clara—Shoreline General? It's not exactly Yale–New Haven. . . ."

"Honey, it was an emergency, to get your grandmother seen to. You were born there, so was your father. Your grandfather died there—"

"Not exactly a testament—"

"Your grandmother is being treated very well. I didn't know what to do. You know, after all these years, she still has you down as her 'in case of emergency' person."

Lily took that in, the reality reverberating like an earthquake through her bones.

"It's as if she knew," Clara said, turning onto Shore Road. "That you were coming back."

"Hmm."

"Mara? Did she?"

"I'm not Mara anymore," Lily said. "I'm Lily now. Lily Malone."

"Lily. That will take some getting used to," Clara said. "Lily, Mara, this is very confusing. Can you tell me where you've been?"

"I ran away, Clara. From Edward."

"We thought he killed you."

"I know."

"It was a terrible thing to put your grandmother through," Clara said, sounding reproachful for the first time.

"There's a lot to the story that you don't know," Lily said, wondering how Clara would feel when she found out that Maeve had known exactly what Lily had done—and kept it from her best friend.

"Well, I'd like to know," Clara said. "And so would your grandmother, I'm sure. The stress built up in her, Mar—I mean, Lily. And everything changed after Edward showed up."

"What do you mean?"

Clara nodded. "Earlier this summer. Out of the clear blue, he just stopped by at Maeve's one day. He had a bag of things that had belonged to you—he wanted to give them to her."

"Just an excuse to upset her," Lily said.

"Well, he succeeded," Clara said. "She was so agitated. You see, she thought he had killed you . . ." she began again, glancing over at Lily.

Lily looked out the window. *No she didn't,* she wanted to say.

"I'm not blaming you," Clara said, her face growing flushed, her eyes red. "Please don't take it that way. Even before Edward upset her so— her grief has been unimaginable. Every summer day, she would wish you could be here, at the Point, enjoying it. She would imagine how old your baby would be. . . ."

Lily didn't reply.

"Your baby, Lily. What happened . . . ?"

"I lost the baby. A boy. Please don't ask me about it, Clara."

"No—I'm so sorry, dear."

Lily nodded, but said no more. Every word had to steer Clara, and anyone she might tell, away from the truth. Glancing over, Lily saw how she had aged: her hair was all white now, instead of just silver streaking the chestnut brown. Her face was wrinkled, and so were her hands on the steering wheel. Lily's stomach clenched, realizing how many years she had missed in Clara's life. In Maeve's. What would she find at the hospital?

Clara drove the back way, along the Shore Road, instead of taking the highway. Lily soaked in all the sights—old stores, new houses, fewer woods, a sense of the shoreline changing, becoming more suburban and homogenized. She felt a sharp, sudden longing for her far-northern refuge.

They approached the hospital, between Sachem and Seaside avenues, turning into the large parking lot. The day was early, before official visiting hours, so there weren't many cars.

"Is she in the ICU?" Lily asked.

"She's on a medical floor," Clara said. "I'll come up with you."

Lily felt a burning need to see her grandmother alone, but she held back the words. She couldn't hurt Clara. They walked in through the main doors, into the elevator, and went to the fifth floor. Lily's heart pounded as they walked down the long, sterile corridor.

"In here," Clara said. It was a private room. Sun slanted through the tall windows, rising over the Thames River. Lily blinked at the brightness. She heard the sounds of a monitor beeping. A yellow curtain was pulled partway around the bed. White blankets were pulled up, and Lily saw the shape of feet and legs underneath.

"Granny," Lily breathed, coming around the curtain.

"Maeve, darling," Clara said. "It's Mara. Mara has come home to see you. Darling, can you hear me? She's home . . ." Her voice broke, and she had to step away.

Lily stood by the bed. Her grandmother was right there, right there. She lay on her back, her long white hair spread behind her on the pillow. Her eyes were ever-so-slightly open—Lily saw their clear blue color as they flicked back and forth. Bending over, Lily took her hand. She pressed her lips to her grandmother's forehead.

The smell of sickness was in the air. It was perhaps that, almost more than anything, that brought hot, quick tears to Lily's eyes. Her grandmother had never smelled sick. She had always been followed by scents of roses, salt water, lemonade, orange tea, ginger cookies, and L'Air du Temps.

"Granny," Lily whispered, her lips still touching her grandmother's skin. "I came back. I had to see you. Please wake up. Please wake up."

"I thought," Clara said quietly, "that hearing your voice might get through to her. Oh, dear, she has to know you're alive. I can't bear this happening to her, with her not knowing."

Lily stroked her grandmother's hand. She knelt down so that her face was very close to Maeve's. She gazed at the familiar profile, lying there on the pillow. After her parents' deaths, she had been afraid to close her eyes and go to sleep. It was as if she couldn't bear knowing that she would have to wake up to a new day, knowing they wouldn't be there.

The last nine years had been like that. Every morning had been so hard to face—knowing that she had run away from someone just as close, just as dear, as her parents. Having to raise her daughter Rose never to know Maeve—depriving Rose of all the love that Maeve would have for them both—had been the hardest choice Lily had ever had to make.

"Did I do this?" Lily whispered, stroking her hair. "Did you just get too tired of waiting for us to come back?"

"Hello, Doctor," she heard Clara say.

"Hi, Mrs. Littlefield. The nurses told me that you were here with someone—"

"She's a relative," Clara said. "Maeve's next of kin."

"I'm Dr. Kirkland," he said.

"I'm Lily Malone, her granddaughter," Lily said, turning, rising. She saw the doctor standing in the doorway—he was tall, young, blond hair pushed back, wire-rimmed glasses. A nurse stood behind him, and at Lily's words, her mouth dropped open.

"It's you! But that's not the name . . ." the nurse said, her words trailing off. The shock registered in her eyes—she had just seen a ghost. Lily was returning from the dead, moment by moment.

"It's not the name she was born with," Clara said, always polite and trying to be helpful. "But it's the one she goes by now."

"I need to know about my grandmother," Lily said steadily, standing up, walking toward the door, then out into the hall with the doctor. "What's wrong with her?"

"The short answer is, we don't know," the doctor said.

"What tests have you done?"

"CT scan, EEG, EKG, blood panels . . ."

"Clara said you're calling it a neurological event. Did she have a stroke?" Lily asked. She was already preparing to call Rose's cardiologist in Boston. He was a specialist, preeminent in his field. They would transfer Maeve immediately—she would get the best cardiac care in the world, reverse the damage done, bring her back to consciousness.

"It's the first thing we thought of," Dr. Kirkland said. "She was brought here in a comatose state. But her EKG was normal. And almost immediately, she began having convulsions."

Lily struggled to maintain her composure. She couldn't bear thinking of her grandmother having seizures.

"A brain tumor seemed possible. I'm her primary-care physician, so I called in a neurologist. Dr. Mead. I'm sure you'll meet her."

"You said 'seemed possible.' It's not a brain tumor?"

He shook his head. "No. It seems not to be."

"Then—what?"

"We did blood tests that showed, well . . ."

"Showed what?"

"This is odd. Her blood carboxyhemoglobin was very elevated. That's what we normally see during very cold winters, in people whose furnaces have been malfunctioning. Or in cars that are left running, with the heaters—"

"Carbon monoxide poisoning?" Lily asked. Living so long in such a cold climate, she had known to have the heating unit checked, install a detector, crack windows when the car was idling, to be ever vigilant about the odorless gas. But this was summer.

"Yes, but Ms. Jameson—er, Malone—we're really not sure. There is no obvious explanation, but the blood levels do seem to indicate—"

"I know what happened," she said.

The doctor just stood there looking intrigued, at least as much about her identity and sudden reappearance as about her theory of her grandmother's case. The first nurse had obviously told others, because a cluster of people stood down the hall, out of earshot, but looking on.

"Edward did it," Lily said steadily.

"What do you mean?"

"My husband," Lily said. "He tried to kill her."

"Kill?" the doctor asked, densely, forehead wrinkled as he tried to understand.

"My grandmother," Lily said, eyes filling with tears as she wished that Maeve had run away with her nine years ago, that they had gone to Cape Hawk together, that they had both run as far from Edward Hunter as they could.

Chapter 3

The days were long in Cape Hawk, Nova Scotia, with bright northern light lingering until well past nine at night, when fireflies would flash in the pines, and owls would begin their long hunts down from their mountain nests. A heat wave had settled over the area, and every morning dawned clear and golden, the bay's flat, calm surface unbroken by anything but whales coming up for air.

The whale-watching fleet would begin its daily trips at eight-thirty in the morning. Tourists flocked to the wharf, to board the Neill family boats. Many of them had spent the night at the Cape Hawk Inn, owned by the same family. Jude Neill captained the vessels, his wife Anne operated the inn, and his cousin Liam was the town's resident oceanographer.

Honeybees buzzed in the roses, but the real buzz took place in the hotel—where preparations for the monthlong Ceili Festival were fast and furious. Marisa Taylor walked along the harbor path, hearing strains of all the different Irish bands—fiddles, tin whistles, guitars, and accordions filling the air. She stared at the ferry coming across the strait, laden with vans full of musicians and their instruments.

When she got to the wharf, she reached for the brass key ring and unlocked the door to In Stitches, Lily's needlework shop. Marisa and all of Lily's friends had been taking turns keeping the shop open while she saw to things back home in Connecticut. The walls and baskets featured Lily's needlepoint canvases—of summer gardens spilling over with roses, lilies, delphinium, and larkspur; of Cape Hawk's blue harbor, bright with whale-watching boats; of Nanny, the famous and beloved pure white beluga whale, native to these waters; scenes of mothers, daughters, friends, and sisters.

Sisters, Marisa thought as the music drifted down from the hotel, through the shop's open door. Turning on the shop computer, Marisa instantly checked her own e-mail—although she had checked at home just thirty minutes ago, before leaving her kitchen. Still nothing.

Jessica, her nine-year-old daughter, came running down the dock, waving madly. She had come down to the harbor early, to look for starfish at low tide. Her jeans were rolled up, and her sneakers squeaked as they slapped the wharf slats.

"Did she write back yet?" Jessica asked, flying through the door.

"Whoa, wet feet!" Marisa called. "It's not our shop, remember?"

"I know," Jessica said, kicking off her sneakers. "Did she write back?"

"Not yet," Marisa said, watching her daughter's face fall.

"This is a sad summer so far," Jessica said. "Aunt Sam's not writing back to you, and my best friend went away."

"Not forever," Marisa reminded her. But when Lily left for Connecticut, she took her daughter Rose with her—leaving both Marisa and Jessica without best friends until they got back to Cape Hawk.

"It seems funny, to hear Irish music without you and Aunt Sam playing it," Jessica said.

"Seems that way to me too."

"Do you think she's coming?"

"I don't know," Marisa said. She didn't want Jessica to get her hopes up.

"You'd win the ceili contest," Jessica said. "Your band was good enough to put you both through nursing school."

"We got by," Marisa said. And they had. She remembered what the *Baltimore Sun* had said about their last performance together, at the Molly Maguire Pub just off the Johns Hopkins campus: "Fallen Angels play with holy ardor, sexy and thrilling, and somehow make traditional Irish music—as well as their original material—surprising and new. If you want a different kind of religious experience, head down to the Molly Maguire Pub to check out these fiddle-playing sisters."

"Did you send her the website?" Jessica asked.

"I did," Marisa said.

"Well," Jessica said, "maybe it's just because she hasn't seen your e-mail yet. We're so far apart, and Aunt Sam is in South America—right?"

"Peru," Marisa said.

"Well, that's why she hasn't written," Jessica said, sounding uncertain. "She's just busy. She's such a good nurse, like you were. I'm sure she's just caring for lots of sick people. She'll write or call us as soon as she gets back to Baltimore. We're just so far apart, that's all."

"I'm sure you're right, honey," Marisa said. She tried to smile, but Jess's words hit her like a lightning bolt: *We're just so far apart.* Jess was right, and it had nothing to do with miles. Her sister had ignored all

Marisa's recent attempts to reach out. The breach between them seemed so deep now, and passing time only made it more so. Marisa had hoped the ceili contest would pique Sam's interest, so she would come north and they could talk.

"What if she's lost?" Jessica asked.

"Lost?"

"In Peru," Jessica said, looking worried. "What if something happened to her?"

"Oh, Jess—Sam travels all the time. I'm sure she's fine."

"But what if she isn't? Maybe you should ask that detective to help us find her," Jessica said.

"Hmm," Marisa said.

"The one who came up here, searching for Lily. Patrick. He was nice."

"He was," Marisa said. "He's also very far away."

"There's such a thing as planes, Mom," Jessica said.

"I know," Marisa said, hugging Jessica. Maybe Patrick *could* help. Marisa could call him—it would have nothing to do with his blue eyes, or the time they had spent together when he was up in Cape Hawk.

She could just ask him how a detective would go about finding someone who wasn't answering her e-mail. Someone who had once been Marisa's fellow nurse, music partner, and best friend. A sister who seemed to have fallen off the face of the earth . . .

Anne knelt in the inn's garden, transplanting Shasta daisies and gazing down the hill at Lily's shop. While Lily, Liam, and Rose took care of business down south, Anne had set up a schedule for the Nanouk Girls to keep In Stitches running smoothly. The needlework shop had long been a gathering place for the women of the area, so Anne knew it wasn't really much trouble for them to keep it open till Lily got back.

Right now she spotted Marisa and Jessica standing in the doorway—looking across the water, like those women of old, watching for their men to come sailing over the horizon on whaling ships.

"What are you doing, hiding out here in the garden?" Jude asked, coming down the walkway from the inn, a coffee mug in each hand, a hammer stuck in his waistband. "When the whole place is going crazy in there?"

"You're a fine one to talk, about to get on board and go out in the bay all day. Thank you, love," she said, accepting a mug from her husband.

"Well, we have to find moments of peace while we can get them. Camille is in there, dealing with one band who forgot to book enough rooms, and another who wants to switch places on the roster with yet another, who lost its accordion player in Halifax. . . ."

"Oh yes. Had his nose broken in a fight with the mandolin player—apparently they were fighting over their new singer, a lassie from Dublin. I've heard all about it. That's why I'm out here. Shasta daisies are so much easier to take at nine A.M. than musicians."

"You've got the right idea, Annie," Jude said. "Flowers for you, whales for me—leave the craziness aside for a little while. At least till you go back inside. The music's nice to hear, though, isn't it?"

"It is," Anne said, listening as the uilleann pipes began to play, twining and weaving into a haunting rendition of "Minstrel Boy."

"Ah, that song . . ." Jude said.

"It's beautiful," Anne said.

"They played it at Connor's funeral," Jude said. "I'll never forget it."

"So long ago. You were only eleven."

"Aye."

Anne sipped her coffee, staring out over the placid bay. It was hard to believe that such a brutal attack could have occurred right out there, within sight of shore. The shark had taken Liam's arm and Connor's life—but it had taken something from Jude too. Anne had been in his class at school—one year behind his cousin Liam—and she remembered that when Jude came back after the funeral, his eyes were hollow and his shoulders were hunched, as if guarding his heart.

"C'mon," he said. "Wipe the dirt off your hands and help me out."

"Doing what?"

"The grandstand, my love. Camille says it's too rickety, and she wants me to tighten it up."

They took their coffees over to the gazebo, beside which had been erected a four-tier viewing stand. It was brought out of storage every year for the Gaelic music competition—and every year, Aunt Camille worried that the whole thing would give way, sending Cape Hawk's local dignitaries toppling down the hill.

Jude gave the wooden stand a good shake; although it seemed completely solid to Anne, he pulled some nails from his jeans pocket, began driving them in with the hammer. The sound effectively blocked out "Minstrel Boy"—which, Anne realized, may have been the whole point.

Anne climbed to the top tier, four rows up. A nail was sticking up from the bench—she gestured to Jude, and he handed up the hammer. She whacked the nail in, then made her way down the bench, making sure there weren't any more like it. The breeze was fresh, full of music and excitement—she had the feeling that this year's festival was going to bring something completely unexpected to the town.

"What do you think Liam is doing right now?" Jude asked.

"I think he's helping Lily, so she and Rose can get back home here."

"Did you ever think he'd find someone?"

"I know we all had our doubts," Anne said. "But then Lily came along."

"It's not sealed yet," Jude said. "She might still see the light—ask herself what she's doing with a one-armed shark researcher."

Anne looked down the hill, taking in the beautiful view. Life had a way of healing even the worst injuries. She gazed across the sparkling blue bay, ringed by rock ledges and tall pines. She had been in love with Jude since first grade, even before the shark attack—and she loved him still. She wanted to tell him that one-armed shark researchers didn't have the lock on being difficult, but she just held her tongue and hammered in another nail.

"Finally that song is finished," Jude said.

"So it is," Anne said.

"You're in charge of the festival and contest. Maybe you can make it a requirement that the bands leave 'Minstrel Boy' out of their repertoires next year."

"Hmm," Anne said, smiling out over the water again, as if she was giving his idea due consideration. She wasn't. She hoped every band would play it—this year and all years. When she heard it, she knew that Connor was close—and she suspected that Jude knew it too. It was what she loved about Irish music—especially the fiddles that played it. Fiddlers caught spirits and dreams whirling through the air, pulled them down to earth, where mere mortals could hear and see them. They brought the dead to life, and brought magic down from the sky, and made dreams more real than logic.

Down the hill, Marisa was back in the shop doorway, scanning the incoming ferry. Anne knew she was hoping for signs of her long-lost sister. Anne was saving a special spot on the festival bill for Fallen Angels, the fiddle-playing sisters. She knew that there were many ways of being lost, many ways of finding a way back to each other. She thought of Lily, down in Connecticut with Rose and Liam, a miracle story if ever there was one. She thought of Patrick, the cute cop who had so clearly taken a shine to Marisa. Her skin tingled as the piper hit his high note, as a salt wind blew off the bay. Cape Hawk was a magical place, and the music made it more so.

Even for residents who were hundreds of miles away . . .

Lily, sitting at her grandmother's bedside, felt like the girl who cried wolf. What did she really know? What proof did she have? What evidence had she had nine years ago? Seeing the doctor's blank expression reminded her of that day in the Berkshires, when she had been so hysterical—and the other hikers had, at first, just stared at her with disbelief.

She tried to shrug off that terrible memory, concentrating on her grandmother lying so still. The doctor had stepped back to talk to Clara; Lily could hear their voices whispering, then fade as they walked down the hall together. She could only imagine what they were saying, what everyone was thinking.

The room was suddenly quiet—it was just Lily and Maeve. Lily had been dreaming of this moment for so long. She clasped her grandmother's hand and felt like a little girl. Holding this hand . . . walking to the school bus . . . to swimming lessons . . . to the post office . . . to Foley's store for penny candy . . .

"Well, if it's not the prodigal granddaughter," a deep voice growled.

Lily blinked, looking over her shoulder.

Patrick Murphy stood in the doorway. He pulled the door partway closed behind him, then came closer, staring down at Maeve. His curly red hair glinted in the sun. The expression in his bright blue eyes was grave, as if it were his own grandmother lying in the bed.

"You should hear what they're saying out in the hall," he said.

"Did they tell you that Edward did this?" she asked.

"We'll get to that in a minute," Patrick said. "Cops are on the way. You make an accusation like that, it's going to bring the heat."

"You're a cop," she said. "I want you to investigate it."

"I'm off the force, as you already know. Finished, *finito*, done. You did me in, Mara. Looking for you—well, for your body, actually—nearly an entire decade. I was positive Edward Hunter had murdered you. We found lime in his trunk. You know about lime? Makes things dissolve quickly. Yep, I thought he'd poured it on your bones."

Lily tried to hold back a shiver.

"I saw that," he said.

"He did this to my grandmother, Patrick. Did you know he came to see her recently? Clara told me."

"Yep, I know all about it. By the way, I think they're sending Clara down for a cardiac workup. You nearly gave her a heart attack."

"Don't joke about that," Lily warned, thinking of Rose and her long rounds of heart surgery.

"They're saying you're back from the dead. Much speculation is swirling out there—and it's not just Clara and the nurses, either. Nope. We've got doctors in on the guessing game—I'm serious. They're all gathered round the nurses' station. Let's see. You were kidnapped nine years ago. Your husband did it. No, wait—a cult did it. Satanists. Or—now, get this: you staged your own disappearance."

Lily ignored Patrick, but she felt herself trembling as she kept hold of her grandmother's hand.

"Never mind what they think," she said. "Edward put Maeve here, Patrick! He poisoned her."

"The doctors told me you think that."

"Then pay attention to that, and never mind about what happened nine years ago."

"Maybe you really don't know what you're in for," he said. "You're a phenomenon. Can you grasp the amount of interest there was in your disappearance?"

"No," she said. "And I don't care. It's my life—no one else's."

"Mara," he said. Catching her dirty look, he shook his head. "Lily. Sorry. I've thought of you as Mara Jameson for nine years. I retired in semi-disgrace over not being able to find you, and my wife accused me of being obsessed with you and divorced me, so I think you kind of owe me a little kindness, okay?"

"You did find me," she said. "That's why I'm here now."

"Took me nine years to find you," he said. "And your grandmother practically had to draw me a goddamn road map to get there." His eyes moved from Lily to Maeve. "Jesus, Maeve. I wish you'd wake up, so I could yell at you. Keeping it a secret all this time."

"She did what she had to do. We both did."

Patrick shook his head. "It must have killed her, to not know Rose."

Lily jolted at Rose's name. "Listen to me, Patrick," she said. "Edward doesn't know about her."

"Hiding Rose in Canada was one thing. But now you're back here—at home, in the United States. A kid is going to stand out, you know?"

"She's somewhere safe—help us keep it that way."

"Us?"

"Liam and me. Please, Patrick."

"The cops are going to want to interview you," he said. "And me—because I found you."

"I know that," Lily said. "And I'm going to tell them the truth—about everything except Rose. I can't let Edward get to her."

"I'm trying to figure out why you're doing this," he said, peering at her, his blue eyes flashing in the sunlight streaming through the windows. "I'd really like to know the whole story. Did he beat you? Kick you? Were you battered?"

She paused, stared at him, wondered what he was capable of understanding. "Not in the way most people think of 'battered,'" she said, her heart racing.

"So, what did you do? The guy tried to kill you, you say now. What did you do about it? Did you call the cops?"

"No," Lily said.

"Why not?"

"Because I knew they wouldn't believe me. I didn't have any evidence, not really. Edward could be so charming, so persuasive. And I wasn't going to let him even lay eyes on my baby while I tried to convince them."

"You should have called the cops," he said stubbornly.

"I told my grandmother," she said. "Because I knew she'd believe me."

"And did she?"

"You know she did."

"So, you told Maeve—"

"And then I started making my plans to leave. *We* started, that is. Maeve and I."

"Christ," he said, staring down at Lily's grandmother lying motionless in the hospital bed. Lily saw a lot going on behind his eyes—thoughts and memories of the investigation, maybe. Ways Maeve had lied to protect Lily, to help her get away and stay hidden. "Why didn't Maeve go with you?"

"She had to stay behind, to throw Edward off."

"By lying to the police?"

"If that's what it took."

"And that's what you're about to do now?" Patrick asked as the sound of radios came from the hall, along with heavy footsteps. The police were here. Lily felt chills racing up her spine, desperate feelings of near-panic as she wondered what Patrick would say to them.

"If that's what it takes to protect Rose," she said.

"Jesus Christ, Lily."

"You don't know the whole story yet, Patrick. Please—don't give us away. Don't give her away. She's just gotten her life back—you have no idea what she's been through, so many surgeries to save her life—"

"I know," Patrick said. A knock sounded on the door. Patrick moved to answer it, but Lily grabbed his arm.

"Please, Patrick."

"Tell me this, Lily. Where is she? I have to know she's okay."

"She's with Liam Neill—that's all I can tell you. But she's with him. He's taking care of her, until I can be there. You know Liam from Cape Hawk—you and Marisa found us at his house. You must know what Rose means to him. Please, Patrick."

She saw something flicker in his eyes, as if he was making up his mind. Just then the door swung open, and a man and woman peered in.

"Hey, Murphy," the woman said to Patrick. "What're you doing here?"

"Ah, I just stopped by to see my friend Maeve. Come on in," Patrick said. "Let me make a few introductions."

Lily stepped back, leaning against her grandmother's bed, reaching behind to touch her grandmother's hand. They were together in this. She and Maeve, protecting Rose. Lily felt strong enough to face whatever would come—but she needed her grandmother's presence to give her courage.

"Detectives Christine Dunne and Lance Sheridan, meet Lily Malone."

"We were told this was Mara Jameson."

"*Was* being the operative word," Patrick said. He glanced at Lily. "You're gonna get really sick of this Mara business, aren't you?"

"Yep," she said.

"Well, I'll let you explain," Patrick said, looking stoic as he stepped back.

He hadn't mentioned Rose. That was all Lily cared about. She gave him a grateful but guarded glance, and turned to face the two detectives. They both looked suspicious but curious; the woman was about thirty-five, with short blond hair and wide green eyes. Lily turned slightly, facing her directly.

"I told the doctor," Lily said, "that I think someone tried to kill my grandmother."

"That's why we're here," Detective Dunne said.

"One reason, anyway," Patrick said. Then, when the two detectives shot him a glance, he shrugged. "Call it what it is. You came to solve my case. As of this minute, it's officially on the books—you've found Mara Jameson. Congratulations."

The male detective, Lance Sheridan, smiled and nodded. But Christine Dunne never took her eyes off Lily, and Lily didn't look away. Lily felt that she was being studied and read, that all her answers would be filtered through the impressions Detective Dunne was filing away right now.

"Where have you been?" Detective Sheridan asked.

Chapter 4

Patrick Murphy faded back against the white hospital wall and listened to the two detectives put Lily through her paces. She ran through the story, or some version of the story, the one that Patrick already knew.

Nine years ago, pregnant with Edward Hunter's child, she escaped from him. She had lived with domestic violence. She couldn't stand the idea of bringing a child into that home—she refused. No, she didn't "stage" a disappearance—she just disappeared. Did anyone help her? No. Where did she go? Not prepared to answer that question. Where is the baby? He was born dead.

"He?" Patrick couldn't help himself.

"Yes." Lily was still and solemn. He gazed over at her, watching her stare back unblinking. The pulse throbbing in her throat was the only giveaway. She had pale skin, so striking against her jet black hair, cut sharply at shoulder length. Her cornflower blue eyes were pained and vulnerable as she made her case to the detectives about the carbon monoxide.

He almost snorted. Lily Malone was about as vulnerable as a ninja sword dancer. This woman was strength personified. Patrick's pride was still smarting from the way she'd outfoxed him every step of the way. He had to hand it to her.

Lily glanced over at him once or twice. He didn't say a word. The detectives were asking her again about the baby. Lily's voice shook as she told them it was too painful to talk about. Her distress was real—Patrick knew she was probably thinking about Rose, calling up to mind any one of her many surgeries, or the fact that she was somewhere hidden now. Her movements were small, careful. He watched the way she held her hands, gestured as she spoke.

Chasing her to Canada, he had met Marisa. Life had a funny way of unfolding.

"Now, if you'll all excuse me," Lily finally said, "I'd like to be alone with my grandmother."

Officers Dunne and Sheridan thanked her and said they'd be by Maeve's house later to look around. They headed for the door. Patrick hesitated. He thought maybe Lily would want to have a private word with him. But it was as if he were just a part of the unwelcome investigating team—she had turned her back on the three of them, ministering to her grandmother. Her profile was so delicate, bent over Maeve, smoothing the hair back from her forehead.

Patrick backed out of the room, came face-to-face with the other two. Down the hall, the crowd remained around the nurses' station. When police showed up at the hospital, word got around. And in this case—considering the fact that Mara Jameson had just reappeared—word was spreading like wildfire.

"What's going on?" Chris Dunne asked.

"What are you talking about?" Patrick replied.

"There's something between you—it's obvious."

"Between us?"

"You and Mara. Lily. Whatever the hell she calls herself. You two were exchanging looks as if you've known each other for years."

"I have known her for years," Patrick said. "I know her better than she knows herself. Her birthday, her blood type, her favorite dessert—it's blueberry pie, in case you're wondering—her favorite movies, the reason she likes needlepointing so much, and oh—the difference between needlepointing and cross-stitch. That's significant, when it comes to understanding the inner workings of her mind. You know why?"

"Shit, Murphy," Chris said.

"I'll tell you why," he continued as if she hadn't spoken. "Because her mother did needlepoint, see? Her mother was Irish. We're big storytellers, us micks, and if we can't get you to listen with your ears, we'll tell you stories any way we can. Young Lily was quite the genius with a needle and canvas when she was little, and her grandmother told me she used to get all her grief and pain out by stitching away."

"Maeve Jameson told you that?"

"Yep. During one of our many interviews."

"Do you believe her about the dead baby boy?"

Patrick thought of Rose—smiling, arms around Lily's neck, freckles across her cheeks, her brown braids, her big green eyes.

"Mmm," he said. "Why wouldn't I?"

"Well, the tabloids are gonna have a field day," Lance said. "Can you imagine, once they find out Mara Jameson has come back from the grave? The only thing that would make them happier would be if she had a tousle-haired little moppet with her—that and a nice custody tug-of-war with the father."

"The Sociopath Also Known As Edward Hunter," Christine Dunne said.

Patrick looked over at her, obviously with more than a little curiosity at her tone, because Chris blushed slightly.

"It's pretty clear, isn't it? The guy must have been some piece of work, to send Mara/Lily underground all this time."

"Maybe she's lying about that," Lance said.

"I believe her," Chris said.

Patrick let himself smile, just a little. He liked Christine Dunne better already.

Rose Malone sat on the rocks, staring at the water. In some ways, this was her favorite place to be. Right near salt water, with spray misting her face and a thick ribbon of silver fish swimming by, close enough for her to watch. Narragansett Bay wasn't as cold and clear as Cape Hawk Harbor, an inlet off the Gulf of St. Lawrence, but still—bending close, Rose could see lots of marine life under the surface.

"Dr. Neill, come look," she said.

"What have you got there?" he asked.

"Rock crabs," she said, pointing at the dark green crabs scuttling along the bottom. "And minnows. Why are there so many of them?"

"I'm not sure," he said. "They might be staying close to the shore to avoid bigger fish farther out."

Up in Cape Hawk, Dr. Neill was known far and wide as the person who knew more about sharks and whales than anyone in Canada. Maybe more than anyone in the world. Rose glanced at his face. Tan, with lines around his blue eyes, staring out at the water.

"What are you looking for?" Rose asked. "Nanny?"

"How'd you guess?"

"Because I was looking for her too," Rose said.

Nanny was the beluga—the white whale—who had swum down here to New England, far from her home in the Gulf of St. Lawrence, at the same time Rose's mother had found out about her grandmother. It seemed so magical to Rose, that the whale she had grown up loving would end up on this faraway coastline at the same time Rose and her mother did, almost as if she was following them—or leading them.

"Will you check on your computer?" Rose asked, scrambling up the rocks to look over his shoulder. Dr. Neill had a laptop programmed to follow the tracking devices on many sharks and whales and other marine species he and his friends had tagged. Rose loved to watch the lights blink—green for whales, purple for sharks. But right now, she could barely even see the lights.

She leaned against Dr. Neill's side. He hit some computer keys, but he mainly just seemed to be watching for Nanny the old-fashioned way—staring at the water's surface. A few seagulls flew low over the waves.

"I miss Mommy," Rose said suddenly.

"I miss her too, Rose."

"Is she coming soon?"

"She's looking after her grandmother right now. I'm sure she'll call us as soon as she makes sure everything is okay."

Rose nodded. If a person was sick, there was no one better in the world for looking after them than Rose's mother. Rose had been born with four defects in her heart. She had been a blue baby—her skin had actually turned indigo, her mother had told her—from not getting enough oxygen. It was why she hadn't grown as much as other kids her age, and why her fingertips were spatulate, clubbed.

Rose looked down at Dr. Neill's arm. Not his real one, but his prosthesis. It fit in his sleeve, but his fake hand was odd and clublike compared to a normal hand. The kids in Cape Hawk had whispered things their parents had told them—that when Dr. Neill was a boy, right after the shark had attacked him and his brother, killing Connor and ripping his arm off, he had had a hook.

The kids had called him Captain Hook, and the name had stuck. Rose couldn't bear to think of people teasing him. Rose loved him. Her mother had told her the story of how Dr. Neill had been her first friend in Cape Hawk. He had stopped by her cabin one day. Rose loved to picture this: the house deep in the woods, with no one around, and Dr. Neill heard noises coming from inside, and that was because Rose was being born. He had brought Rose into the world. . . .

"Why do you look so worried?" she asked, watching him gaze out over the water.

"I'm not worried," he said. "I'm just wondering about those menhaden—minnows."

"Do they have something to do with Nanny?"

"They could," he said, typing something into his computer, bringing up a whole new screen. It showed some graphs of currents and water temperatures. Rose watched him type in "Narragansett, Rhode Island,"

and the screen changed yet again. Outside, the seagulls screeched and started diving. Rose heard some kids shout, and she saw them pointing at the water.

Dr. Neill grabbed her hand instantly. The kids were yelling, pointing at the surf. Dr. Neill gave her a look, and then he and Rose hurried across the yard.

Two boys had run all the way to the end of the rock breakwater that stuck out from the narrow, pebbly beach. They were calling to their friend, who was tearing along the seawall with a fishing rod in one hand and a net in the other.

"What are you fishing for?" Dr. Neill asked the young boy.

"Fins, man!" he called over his shoulder.

"Fins? Does he mean sharks?" Rose asked, worried.

"Yes," Dr. Neill said gently.

"Look!" the boy said, gesturing with his fishing pole.

And suddenly Rose saw what they were pointing at: huge black triangles zigzagging around the blue cove.

"Will they get Nanny?" she asked.

"She's not here, honey," he said, staring at the water. "We couldn't locate her on the computer, remember?"

Dr. Neill looked into her eyes then, smiled to reassure her. He put his good arm around Rose's shoulders, and then they both looked back at the sharks swimming in the bay. Seeing them made her miss her mother even more. She knew that only something bad could keep them apart, something as bad as sharks, and she bit her lip to hold in the tears and threw both her arms around Dr. Neill's neck.

Chapter 5

As the day went on, the needlework shop got really busy. Jessica sat at the desk while her mother helped people choose yarn and pick out canvases to take home for souvenirs. The music festival was lots of fun for many reasons, and it was certainly really good for business. Cape Hawk was filling up with musicians and the tourists who had come to hear them, and everyone seemed to be stopping by to see what the shop had for sale.

Jessica was quiet, like a cat. She listened for clues to what was going on between her mother and aunt. They were sparse and few, and Jessica hoarded them when they came. Here was one right now.

"Oh, you're from Washington?" Jessica heard her mother ask a woman with a guitar case over her shoulder. "Do you play at the Golden Harp?"

"Yes, do you know it?" the woman asked.

"I used to play there, ages ago. My sister and I were at school in Baltimore, and we'd head into Georgetown on some weekends."

Jessica's ears perked up—and she looked over at her mother's face for extra clues. She saw one right away, the bruised look in her eyes that came from thinking back to that happy time in nursing school.

"All those lawyers and congresspeople," the woman said, laughing. "Looking for their lost Irishness and lost poetry."

"Their lost souls," Jessica's mother said quietly. "That's what my sister used to say."

"Well, we give 'em back their souls, don't we?" the woman asked. "That's why they come to hear us play. That's what ceili music is all about. Giving people back their hearts and souls. Aren't you lucky, living here in such a beautiful place? Does the music just pour out of you?"

Jessica watched her mother tallying up the woman's purchases, pretending to concentrate on the numbers so she wouldn't have to answer.

"Are you performing at the festival?" the woman asked, after another moment.

"Well, if my sister gets here in time. But she's out of the country right now."

"Tell her to hurry back for the Ceili Festival!" the woman said, gathering up her things.

"I will," her mother said.

Jessica's heart fell like a stone. Looking over at her mother again, she saw the bright sheen of tears in her eyes. It pierced Jessica to know how much her mother wanted Aunt Sam to hurry back. Sitting by the big display of needlepoint yarn, Jessica ducked her head, to hide her own eyes.

"Honey?" her mother asked, after the woman had gone. "You're being so quiet."

"The lady asked if the music poured out of you."

"I know."

"It used to," Jessica said.

"The music never leaves," her mother said. "Once you have it, you can't lose it."

Jessica's stomach ached. She wanted to believe that that was true. When she was younger, and so sad because her father had died, her aunt would come up from Baltimore to visit. She and her mother would talk softly, and their voices alone were music to Jessica. Later, after supper, they would take out their fiddles, and they would start to play. They had been doing it since they were girls, as young as Jessica. She would listen to the music—incredible, beautiful enough to destroy the pain of missing her father.

"Then why—" Jessica started to ask now.

"Why what, Jess?"

"Why do you never play it?" Jessica asked.

"I guess I need Sam for that."

Jessica nodded. She clasped her hands tight, so her mother wouldn't see the waves of emotion passing through her. Having taken recorder lessons in school, she had been secretly practicing—so her mother would have someone to play with in case Aunt Sam really didn't come back.

Just then, another musician walked in, and Jessica thought her mother seemed relieved to stop talking about everything.

"Mom, can I e-mail Rose?" Jessica asked.

"Sure, honey," her mother said. The new customer was friendly, and Jessica's mother asked about her guitar. The woman seemed happy to show her, so she opened the case. Jessica's mother seemed lost in the workmanship of the woman's Gibson guitar—Emmylou Harris edition.

"I went straight to the factory in Memphis to get it," the woman said, playing a few notes.

Jessica concentrated on the computer screen. No new e-mails. She tapped out a quick hello to her best friend, Rose: "I miss you. The summer music festival is starting, and my aunt will be here soon. . . ." She has to be, Jessica thought, hitting "Send."

Glancing up at her mother, she furtively went into the "Old Mail" folder. There were her aunt's e-mails. Her mother always saved them, as if they were precious, personal notes, instead of group e-mails sent out to a huge number of people. Jessica read one from last month— "Hola from Peru":

> Hola everyone,
> Made it to Peru safely! I'm in Iquitos, along the Amazonia—it's hot and humid and raining and colorful and poor and lively. . . .
> Set up clinic in a school yesterday—there were hundreds lined up when we arrived—gave out lots of anti-parasite medication, as the malnourishment is overwhelming. We have a pediatric surgeon and podiatrist, a dental team that has already pulled hundreds of teeth—and we have 2 more docs coming today—what we need is a dermatologist. . . .
> I'm running the OBGYN clinic. Saw about 20 patients—lots of pregnant teens, half a dozen healthy women with normal pregnancies, one gal who looked as if she had some kind of hepatitis, a woman with a pelvic mass (with no money for referral), many worried well who just wanted TLC. Let's see what today brings.
> It's invigorating to be in this world, for it sure expands mine.
> Adios for now,
> Sam

And then she read another, "Peru Update," written nearly two weeks ago—almost immediately after the reminder e-mail Jessica's mother had sent, telling Aunt Sam that the Ceili Festival was fast approaching, that she really hoped they could reunite onstage and let their music soften each other's heart.

> Hola,
> It's 7:30 a.m., I'm gearing up for another day in the jungle slums—We had an incredible day yesterday in our clinic—a school amidst shacks on stilts. Though this group has always had great

experiences in this area—there was a little too much action yester-day . . . a stabbing and robbery by 8:30—we had to triage the stabbing—that was a first. So now we get police escorts every-where.

I have 2 awesome med students as my translators—and we must have seen 40 people yesterday. Many worried well who needed TLC and vitamins and parasite meds. Some hypertension, lots of cataracts, lots of dermatology issues, 2 women with severe rheumatoid arthritis, every woman has back pain and headache. That is understandable, as many of them have birthed 6–10 ba-bies at home alone, work in a market every day, and have noth-ing . . . These women are amazing— One woman yesterday had 7 kids—6 of whom have died related to accidents and infec-tions . . . also saw many relatively healthy pregnant women—though they are 14–17 year olds—2 high risk, history of toxemia and were delivered at 27 weeks . . . women seem to go through menopause in their early 40´s—with money these women can get good care . . . we have a great team, the pod guys have repaired club feet, the dentists have pulled hundreds of teeth, and peds surg have had many cases . . .

Anyway, my team is leaving now so I must run—we head up the river to work in a few small villages tomorrow. And then I'm heading home . . .

Life is good, more later,

Sam

Heading home, her aunt had written. What did that mean? Jessica read the e-mails over and over, looking for clues. Could her aunt really just return home to Baltimore without coming here to the ceili? Here to see her family? Jessica couldn't believe that was possible. Not the aunt she loved . . .

But as she stared at the screen, one clue was just too powerful to un-derstand, and it made her stomach hurt even worse than before. The e-mail was to every single person her aunt knew. Jessica's mother's name was just part of a long list at the top of the page. It was as if Aunt Sam couldn't quite strike her from her life, but didn't care enough to write her something personal.

Closing her eyes, Jessica fought back the tears. They were coming hard and fast—not because she thought her aunt didn't care, but because she thought maybe her aunt cared too much. The hurt had been too bad for her to ignore. Jessica knew, because she had felt it too.

Glancing over at her mother, still admiring the woman's guitar, Jessica knew that her mother had been wrong about one thing. Sometimes the music *did* leave. Maybe it still lived somewhere, locked deep inside, but what did that matter, if you couldn't hear it play?

Jessica looked up, above her mother's head, out the open door of the shop. She looked past the inn, where the ceili was under way. Past the cliffs of Cape Hawk, up into the bright summer blue sky. She wished she could send a song through the air. Notes of music that had wings, just like tiny birds, flying south over the earth, asking Aunt Sam to come back to her family.

For the next two and a half days, Lily's life ceased to be her own. She yearned to be with Liam and Rose, but settled for the crackling, fuzzy connection of cell phone calls. Rose described the big house and wide blue bay, the excitement of something happening along the shore—lots more fish than usual, making Liam think it had something to do with why Nanny had come so far south.

Her old beach friends, Tara O'Toole and Bay McCabe, rode their bikes up the hill, leaned them against the old stone wall of the road's turnaround, running into the yard.

"You're back!" Bay cried. "It's true, it's true. . . ."

"Oh my God," Tara said, holding her, rocking her childhood friend back and forth, as if she needed to hold her to know she was really here. Lily held on tight, taking her friends' love right into her bones.

There were so many questions, so much catching up to do. It wasn't just that a few years had passed—Lily's life had changed entirely. She was Lily now, not Mara. The women had been children together, and now they had children of their own. The subject of Rose shimmered in Lily's mind and heart as she listened to Bay and Tara talk about their own kids.

"Maybe you underestimate what it was like when you disappeared," Bay said. She pointed at the yellow boots and watering can in the corner of Maeve's kitchen. "Those were on every news show in the state. You seemed to disappear into thin air."

"In a way, I did," Lily said.

"Tara and I were part of the search party that went out looking for you. Hundreds of volunteers—almost everyone from Hubbard's Point joined in, combing the beach and woods, Little Beach and the marsh and the Indian Grave. Then people from Black Hall came, and beyond."

"We wondered," Tara said, "whether you'd just decided to walk away."

"Oh, Tara . . ."

"Who could have blamed you?" Bay asked, holding her hand. "You never wanted to talk about it back then, but we knew . . ."

Lily just stared at her two friends, across all the years that had separated them.

"You were an expectant mother, about to have his baby," Tara said fiercely. "You must have been frantic to escape. Oh, Mara . . . Lily . . . I understand. I'm glad you got away. Your poor baby."

Lily's heart seized with the words. She flushed, afraid her friends would look at her and see evidence of Rose all over her. Couldn't they see the truth written in Lily's eyes? Looking back and forth, she could hardly breathe. Was it safe? Did she dare? Keeping Rose a secret had seemed the only way, but she *couldn't* keep it from these two good women, her first best friends. They were mothers themselves, wonderful and loving and kind. Taking a deep breath, she decided.

"You have to promise not to tell, not a soul, not anyone," she said.

"Promise what?" Tara asked.

Bay's eyes gleamed, and Lily could tell that she already suspected. "Lily?"

"I have a daughter," Lily said quietly.

"Oh, Lily," Bay said. "That's wonderful."

"I can't wait for you to meet her, but she's in Rhode Island," Lily said. "Where Edward won't find her."

"That's good," Tara said. "You're so right to keep her from him. What's her name?"

"Rose," Lily said.

Bay nodded, smiling. "That's beautiful."

"It was for Granny. Granny and her garden. I missed her so much."

"Does she know?" Tara asked.

Lily nodded. "Right after Rose was born, I called her at my great-uncle's in Providence. I couldn't call her at home, because I wasn't sure whether the phones were tapped or not. It was his seventieth birthday—a party that had been planned for months. I knew Granny would be there—he was her only brother."

"Maeve must have felt such mixed emotions," Bay said. "Knowing she had a great-granddaughter . . ."

"But being unable to meet her or know her," Lily said. "I often wonder how she held it together, right after I left. It must have been so hard."

"For all of us," Bay said, squeezing her hand, gazing into her eyes as if she still couldn't quite believe Lily was really here. "We couldn't believe it, couldn't bear it."

"We had a candlelight vigil," Tara continued. "Down on the board-walk. There were so many people, they filled the beach. It was such a warm night, so beautiful—we had all been searching for you, for days. Everyone was exhausted, losing hope."

"I'm so sorry," Lily said.

"Maeve spoke," Tara said. "At the vigil. I know it's crazy, but I wished you could be there—so you could know how much everyone loved you."

"We all had candles," Bay said. "We waited for Maeve, and I can remember her coming down the path behind the yellow cottage, wear-ing a long dress. It looked so familiar—and it wasn't until she came across the footbridge that I realized when I'd seen it before. She'd worn it to your wedding."

"Yellow chiffon," Lily said, picturing it.

"Her eyes were so red," Bay went on. "She'd been crying all day, it was obvious. Clara was with her—standing by her side. All your old friends, us beach kids, gathered around her. I was standing so close to her, Mar—I mean, Lily. She was just sobbing silently, as if her heart had just washed out to sea. I thought her tears would fill the creek."

"I'm so sorry I put her through that," Lily whispered. She pictured her grandmother weeping—not because she feared Lily was dead, but that she believed she would never see her again.

"Someone gave the signal—I'm not sure who. But suddenly one candle was lit, and then the flame passed to another, and on and on. Af-ter a few minutes, the entire beach was lit up by candlelight down be-low—and all the stars coming out above."

"She stood up on one of the white benches on the boardwalk," Tara said. "Bay and I stood right by her, to make sure she didn't fall. We thought she was going to beg everyone to keep looking for you, not give up—but she didn't. Instead, she just took this deep breath and stared over the crowd."

"Everything got so hushed," Bay said. "You couldn't hear a thing ex-cept the waves hitting the beach. Everyone was just waiting to hear what she would say."

"I still remember it," Tara said. "She said, 'You're all here because you love her so much, just as I do. My granddaughter is good, and sweet. She deserved only to be loved, not . . .'" And then she just broke down. Bay and I helped her walk back across the beach to the footbridge, and home."

"Edward must be going crazy, now that he knows you're back," Bay said. "You know he had you declared dead? And the marriage annulled for good measure?"

"I think he's the reason I'm back," Lily said quietly.

"What do you mean?"

"I think he did something to Maeve."

"Why now?" Tara asked.

"Edward is patient," Lily said. "His specialty is waiting. I think he's been waiting to punish Maeve all this time—and not just for speaking out about him. Her worst sin, to Edward, was in knowing about him—seeing through his act. Maeve was the first who did."

"We're going to make sure he doesn't hurt you," Tara said. "We'll take turns staying with you, or standing watch over you. He's not going to hurt you again."

"I'm sure Danny and Joe will want to help, too," Bay said of their husbands.

"You don't have to do this," Lily said, but inside she felt relieved.

"He's left a lot of wreckage," Tara said, her eyes dark and flashing.

Lily nodded. "Yes, he has. When I was in Cape Hawk, I met someone who knows him as well as I do. His next wife. The woman he was with after me."

"You've met her?" Tara asked. "You're kidding. How?"

"Ironically, Edward gave us a road map to each other," Lily said. "Without even knowing. She called him Ted, but everything else was the same. We connected right away."

"I'm glad you weren't all alone," Bay said. "That you had a friend."

"Cape Hawk is wonderful," Lily said. "I missed you both so much, and I dreamed of Hubbard's Point. But there are so many strong, wise women up there, and Marisa and I were really lucky to find them."

Her throat caught as she gazed out the side window, at the pink roses brushing the screen, and the wide blue Sound beyond. Seagulls wheeled and cried, and something silver splashed at the surface. Lily thought of the whales of Cape Hawk, and the miracle of Nanny swimming so far south this summer. She remembered Rose's ninth birthday party, on one of Liam's family's whale-watch boats, just weeks earlier.

There had been so much love present that day. Rose had been surrounded by all her friends and Lily by all of hers. The Nanouks had gathered together, mothers and daughters, to celebrate Rose's birthday before her big surgery. Marisa had confided things she had never before told anyone. Lily had hugged her close, reassuring her that life got better.

Lily thought of Marisa now. They had both gotten away from the same dangerous man. Lily wondered whether Marisa would stay in touch with Patrick. There had been an obvious spark between them.

Lily had thought she was too scarred to love again, but Liam had helped her to know that it wasn't true. She wished that for Marisa too.

A car backfired in the turnaround, and Lily jumped. The scent of roses filled the air. She had told Marisa that life got better, but what if it didn't? Lily wondered where Edward was now, whether he was watching, when he planned to reenter her life. As if sensing her unease, Bay took her hand.

"Everything will be fine," she said.

"Edward is a patient man," Lily whispered again.

"Then we'll wait him out," Tara said.

Lily heard the kitchen clock ticking, and hoped that her friends would be with her when he finally came.

Chapter 6

The fiddle case was all the way at the back of the hall closet, behind a pile of suitcases and winter boots. Digging it out, Marisa dislodged a box of mittens from the overhead shelf, bumped her head trying to avoid it. But finally she held the case in her hands, dusting the pebbled leather off with a red and white mitten.

Her hands were shaking slightly. Unlatching the top, she opened it up, looked in at her instrument. She'd had it a long time, and there were scratches to prove it. The fine, varnished cherrywood was nicked in places, and there was a small chip halfway up the neck. Lifting it out, Marisa rubbed the surface with her palm.

Oh, it felt so beautiful. She plucked the strings, began to tune by ear.

She had started missing her violin yesterday, when the woman in the shop had let her look at her guitar. All summer she had been fighting the urge, especially with Jessica asking her if the music had left. . . .

Living with Ted, Marisa had stopped playing. Not all at once. At first he had pretended to like hearing her, and he'd request specific songs when she'd practice. After a while, the opposite would happen; she would start playing, and he would tell her he needed to concentrate, or he had a headache, or he couldn't think through the music. Once he had said "through the noise," and that had shut her down.

Her love for fiddle music went back a long way before that, before him. She had started playing in fourth grade. She loved the tension of the strings under her fingers, teasing music out of them with the bow. Running through scales, she went straight into "O'er the Hills"—her and Sam's signature song.

Playing it pulled tears straight into her eyes. There had been so many hurt feelings between them these last few years. The thing about a breach between two people who loved each other was that the longer it went on, the harder it was to go back and undo it.

The music came back now. So easily, it was as if she'd never stopped. She played her childhood songs, the ones she and Sam had learned together when they were in fourth and third grades, respectively—"Mary Had a Little Lamb," "London Bridge Is Falling Down," "Twinkle Twinkle Little Star," "Row Row Row Your Boat." She could almost believe Sam was with her now, urging her on.

As Marisa began to play a few notes of Mozart's Violin Concerto No. 3, she remembered how much awe she used to feel for her little sister as she'd fly through new pieces as if she'd written them. Even before they began to play violin, Sam had proven herself to be gifted with music. She sang before she could even talk. The two girls had shared a room, and Sam would sing herself to sleep every night—"Me, me, me, me . . ." she'd sing, always right on pitch, right in tune.

Marisa would sing harmony. She couldn't wait for Sam to learn to talk—and as soon as she did, the girls sang rounds, played musical games, wrote songs for their parents and each other. Sam sang like an angel, and she played like one too. At the age of four, she could pick out songs on the piano. Marisa taught her everything she knew, and before long, Sam was teaching her back.

The two sisters would sit on the back porch, practicing songs in the light of the moon, and sometimes it seemed they could continue all night, just to be together. Marisa remembered how their bows would move in unison, playing the tunes, and how she would feel so lucky to have a sister who loved doing the same thing.

"We can do this together for our whole lives," Marisa had said when she was nine, still called Patty.

"What do you mean?" Sam had asked.

"No one else will know all the same songs . . . we'll play these forever, the two of us, until we're old."

"What if we move apart from each other?"

"We won't."

"But sometimes sisters do," Sam pressed.

"Well then," she said, "we have to make a pact. If we do ever live apart, we'll always come back together every summer and play."

"Do you promise?" Sam asked.

"I do," she said. And they shook on it, right there under the rising moon.

For a long time, the promise never came up. They were so close, there wasn't a summer—or any other season—that they were apart. Marisa's first year of nursing school was the hardest, because Sam was still a senior in high school. But as soon as she could, Sam enrolled in Johns Hopkins just like her older sister.

Tuition was expensive, so at the end of every school week they would pack up their equipment and go to Irish bars, to play music and earn money to pay for their education. Their shows took them to places with names like Molly Maguire Pub, Blarney Stone, Galway Bay, Moran's Ale House. The crowd would be full of young people with bright eyes and open hearts, who would sing and stomp to the music, who would toast the sisters.

Their band was called Fallen Angels, because they both thought it was more realistic and fun to be sinners than saints. The truth was, Marisa thought Sam was a real angel. She was so bright and kind, always there for everyone. She gave so much to her patients, she needed those weekend shows just to play her heart out, purify all the pain she'd absorbed trying to help everyone. More often than not, it was just the two of them, with others sitting in as the spirit moved them.

Once, after they had both graduated and were working in a Baltimore clinic, they took a vacation to Paris, spent one afternoon drinking wine in a café along the Seine, near the Pont de l'Alma. A man had taken the table next to them. He was solid and tan, with a short dark ponytail and wraparound sunglasses, a black leather vest revealing bare arms so strong they were like iron. It was Bono.

The sisters fell in love with him on the spot. They bought him a drink. Then he bought them one. They started talking. It was all so Irish: words, heart, soul, and lots of wine. Bono smoked. Sam lit up, just because she had to keep him company. He was completely enamored of her desire to become a world health nurse.

They drank toasts to the poor, the rich, Ireland, America, Dublin, Baltimore, Elvis, music, poetry, sex, rock, and fallen angels everywhere.

"Here's to the Virgin Mary," Bono said, clinking glasses with the sisters. "May she bring us world peace and sold-out stadium shows."

"*Her* middle name is Mary," Sam said, pointing at her sister.

"That's the name you should go by," Bono said. "Mary. Or some version of it. Maureen, Muire, Maura, Marisa . . ."

"That's what I'm going to call you from now on," Sam said, eyes gleaming. "*Marisa*. No more Patty—" Years later, fleeing her life, abandoning her past, Marisa had made the name her own.

At the end of the night, Bono shook their hands. He smelled of cigarettes, sweat, leather, and St. Emilion. The pads of his fingertips felt hard and scarred, the stigmata of his guitar strings.

"I never want to forget this," Sam said, smiling into the ghostly gold light shimmering above the Seine and all Paris as he walked away into the night. The moment had seemed magical, almost as if they had conjured it.

"You sounded like you're really going to do it," Marisa had said. "Become a world health nurse."

"You know I want to," Sam said, hugging her. "But I'd miss you too much to go away for too long."

As it turned out, Marisa had been the first to leave. They both had jobs in Baltimore, and soon Sam began to travel with a world health organization—not full-time, but once or twice a year. But they kept playing music together in Baltimore, and until Marisa got married and moved to Boston, they shared an old row house just a few blocks from the harbor.

Now, holding her violin, Marisa thought of how easy their long-ago promise had been to keep—they would always get together to play, at least once every summer. Sam had loved Marisa's first husband, and she had been over the moon to become an aunt. Marisa knew that her daughter had made them closer than ever. It had seemed a bond that could never be broken, no matter what came along.

"That's pretty, Mom," Jessica said, coming in from the garden now. "What is it?"

"Mozart," Marisa said.

"That doesn't sound like fiddle music."

"It's not. It's violin music."

Jessica smiled. She looked so happy to hear her mother playing, Marisa felt a twinge in her heart.

"How do you know the difference?"

"Jess," Marisa said, "I think you know."

Jessica nodded, and her eyes filled with tears—because her aunt had been the one to teach her.

"They're the same instrument," Marisa said. "But it depends on how it's played."

"The violin speaks to the mind, and the fiddle speaks to the heart," Jessica said, but Marisa swore she could hear Sam's voice. Her sister had loved to quote Miss Tilly Lonergan, an old fiddle player from Baltimore.

"A violin has 'strings,' and a fiddle has 'strangs,'" Jessica said. "A violin is played sitting down, and a fiddle is played standing up." The differences usually made Jessica smile, but right now she had tears running down her face.

"Oh, honey . . ."

"Mom," she said, "why won't Aunt Sam come see us?"

"She's mad at me," Marisa said.

Marisa reached for her, and Jessica sobbed against her chest. Trying to console her, trying to help her, Marisa almost wished she had left her fiddle in the closet.

"She's not upset with you," Marisa said. "You can't think that."

"But I'm not enough to make her forget what happened," Jessica wept. "Or she would be here now."

Marisa's heart skipped several beats. Being angry at Marisa was one thing, but hurting Jessica was something else. She whispered that everything would get better, that Sam would probably call or write as soon as she got back to the States. But inside, she was shaking. Somehow she had to tell Sam what this was doing to Jess.

Easing away, Jessica picked up the violin and bow, handed them to her mother. Marisa saw the plea in her eyes, and remembered how comforted Jess had always been by their music—Marisa and Sam's—especially after her father had died.

"What would you like to hear, honey?" she asked.

"'O'er the Hills,'" Jessica said.

Somehow, Marisa had known that's what it would be. She drew the bow over the strings, began the sweet, sentimental tune. Jessica's eyes were closed. She looked so young and innocent. For a moment, Marisa saw the echo of her sister in her daughter's face.

What if something had happened? What if Sam had had an accident in Peru? Maybe Marisa was just grasping at straws, but she couldn't believe, any more than Jessica, that Sam would turn against them forever.

She thought of Patrick Murphy. He had seemed so stalwart, so steady, when he'd come up to Cape Hawk last month. She knew that he had spent many years trying to track down Lily. Maybe Marisa could call him, ask him to check on Sam and make sure she was okay. Could he do that?

Still playing the song, glancing down at Jessica, she knew she had to try.

Returning from visiting Maeve at the hospital, Patrick sat on the deck of his boat, *Probable Cause,* watching terns dive for minnows in the cove. The baitfish had been thick this week, and it was very unusual to see them in these numbers this far up the river. They swam in the estuary, but Patrick's dock was nearly seven miles inland. The water was brackish here, but right now it was a haven for fish and seabirds. Looking over the rail, Patrick saw a bluefish come to the surface, snapping at everything that moved. His phone rang and he didn't even check caller ID—he was too engrossed in the fishing ballet.

"Hello," he said.

"Patrick?" came the voice.

He knew it instantly. Patrick had a cop's instinct for identifying characteristics, and Marisa Taylor's voice had imprinted itself in his inner data bank.

"Marisa?"

She laughed, a quick, nervous ripple that made his skin tingle. "Yes, it's me. I'm surprised you knew—"

"I'm a detective, ma'am," he said. "It's my job to know."

"Ahh," she said, chuckling softly.

"How is life in Cape Hawk?" he asked.

"It's . . . well . . . it's fine."

Patrick listened, watching gulls circle overhead, waiting for her to continue, wondering why she sounded so hesitant.

"You must miss your friends," he said. "Lily and Rose. And Liam."

"Lily called me, and I do miss her—more than you can imagine." She paused. "It seems I'm missing everyone right now."

Patrick's heart jumped. Was she talking about him? He had promised himself to play it cool the next time he talked to her or saw her—meeting her at Cape Hawk had done something to his insides that hadn't been done since . . . well, since Sandra. He'd gotten all turned inside out. He was glad she couldn't see him right now—he felt his face turning bright red.

"Missing everyone?" he managed to ask.

"Yes," she said. "Well, one person in particular. My sister."

Okay, he told himself. That made more sense. He cleared his throat. She was calling him in his professional capacity. "Is she actually missing?" he asked.

"Well, I wouldn't say that," she said. "I hope not, anyway. She's a nurse, and her work takes her all over the world. Last I heard, she was in Peru. The thing is, I invited her up here for the Ceili Festival, and—"

"Whoa, stop a minute. The what?"

"The Ceili Festival."

"That's right, that's right," Patrick said. "Keep in mind, you're talking to a Murphy. The word 'ceili' makes my heart beat a little faster. It's in the genes. So, you're saying your sister is invited, but she hasn't replied?"

"Pretty much."

"That doesn't sound like angelic behavior to me. Even a fallen angel."

"You remembered," Marisa said, thinking about how Patrick's encouragement in Cape Hawk had fired her desire to play again.

Patrick's eyes narrowed as he stared at the birds wheeling over the smooth blue water. "That wasn't a band a good Irishman would forget hearing about. I'm still hoping to hear you play one of these days." He had the Chieftains on the CD player, and he turned it up. "So, go on. Your sister hasn't replied to your invitation. Have you been in close touch, in general?"

"Well . . ." Marisa said, trailing off.

"Not so close?"

"We were, always. But then I married Ted . . ."

"Edward Hunter strikes again," Patrick said. He thought of Lily and Maeve, the years of separation between them. Such wonderful women, taken in by such a creep.

"What happened?" he asked.

"I ask myself that all the time. It wasn't any one thing. She just couldn't stand to see me losing myself. She's such a strong woman, the way I used to be. We became nurses because we wanted to help the sickest of the sick and the poorest of the poor." Her voice closed down, and she trailed off.

Patrick held the receiver, wishing he could comfort her. He'd seen the haunted look in her eyes up at Cape Hawk, and he recognized it from other women he'd seen.

"Abuse takes a lot out of a person," he said. "You should forgive yourself."

"I just wish Sam would forgive me," she said softly.

"You might have pushed her away," he said. "That's what seems to happen."

"I did," she said. "That's the hardest thing to live with. Jessica loves Sam so much—and the longer it goes on without hearing from her, the more it seems as if we never will."

"Are you worried about her?"

When she didn't respond, he went in another direction. "You say your sister is in Peru?"

"Yes. In the mountains, traveling around to poor villages."

"Do you know the name of the group she's with?"

"It's based in Baltimore, out of Johns Hopkins—Global Care."

Patrick wrote it down. "You're sure she's still in Peru?"

"Positive. She sent out a group e-mail recently, and she mentioned going to another area."

"What's her name—as it appears on her passport?"

"Samantha Joan Mahon."

"Would you like me to call some people I know? International law enforcement types? They could track her down."

"Seriously?"

"Yes."

Marisa was silent for a long time, wrestling with her own loneliness and Jessica's, but thinking hard about what Sam would want. "I don't think she'd like that much," she finally said. "I know that permits can be hard to get, visiting certain regions of the countries she visits. I wouldn't want to cause any problems for them. I guess it's better that I just wait to hear from her on her own."

"I understand. Has she been up to Cape Hawk?"

"No," Marisa said. "But I know she'd love it here. Especially now, with the music festival. Jessica's going to have a lemonade stand tomorrow, right by the gazebo. I can just imagine how Sam would love to see that. The old Sam, anyway."

Patrick held the phone, filled with sudden longing. He heard the love in her voice and knew he'd do just about anything he could to help. They were connected by something Patrick couldn't put into words.

Marisa broke the silence. "I want to thank you for offering that, Patrick."

"You don't have to thank me."

"I'm going to play you something. Our favorite song," she said. "Mine and Sam's." And then he heard her lay down the receiver, and a bow being drawn across strings, and then the most beautiful notes he'd ever heard issued through the telephone.

Patrick Murphy closed his eyes, feeling his boat rock beneath him. His world had felt so unstable, ever since his divorce. He had been feeling as if the earth's axis had slipped, set him on a course for falling off its surface. But right now, even with waves from a passing tug making his boat toss in the wake, he felt as if he was getting ground under his feet.

The music filled his ears and his heart. He wanted it never to end. He wanted the music to play all night. Marisa's playing was beautiful, and evoked the hills and the cliffs and the whales and the rocks of Cape Hawk. It made Patrick want to start his engines and steam north, through the Cape Cod Canal, straight across the wide water to Nova Scotia.

He contained his feelings, told himself that she was just playing him a song, not inviting him to visit. He listened to her play, his tense muscles relaxing as the music filled his body and spirit.

He swore he heard her heart pouring through the wire—nothing less than all that passion he'd heard earlier, coming straight at him. He couldn't believe it, but he felt something just like hope. Hope in what—it didn't even matter. He just listened to Marisa's music with his eyes closed and knew he'd do whatever it took to bring her sister back to her.

Chapter 7

A summer night at Hubbard's Point—the closest thing to heaven most people would ever find on earth. Waves splashed the shore, crickets rasped in the thick, tangled honeysuckle vines, and the spice of roses, wild thyme, and sassafras wafted through the salt air. Stars blazed overhead, and fireflies flitted through the yards.

Lily sat on the back porch, huddled in a blanket and listening to the waves. Her nerves crackled, and every sound made her jump. Lights on the Point had gone off one by one. She'd heard a whippoorwill calling across the swamp, and another answering. Even nature seemed ominous, as if danger lurked in every shadow. She almost wished Edward would appear, because she couldn't stand the tension of waiting and wondering what his first move would be.

Now, staring across the water, she wondered whether Rose was asleep yet. They had spoken by phone a few hours earlier, and Rose told her Liam had read her a bedtime story, but she didn't want to go to bed.

Lily felt the same way. She saw a meteor shoot across the sky and held her breath. She wanted to reach for Rose—for Liam—but they weren't there. They were in Rhode Island, and Lily had been apart from them for three days now.

How could any of this have happened? Was everything in life like a meteor—blazing, sudden, out of her control? Or was there some pattern, some sense, to where she found herself tonight? It all seemed to hinge on Edward . . . and she found herself spinning back in time, to memories she had tried to put aside, to the day she met him, back when she was Mara.

What if she had been a starving artist, instead of a rising young designer? No one would suspect that there was a lot of money in designing canvases for upscale needlework shops, but there was. And Edward had seen his opportunity.

Two weeks before Christmas 1993, Mara Jameson flew out of Providence's T.F. Green Airport for Washington, D.C. Larkspur and Ivy, a shop in Georgetown and one of her best customers, had invited her down for a tea, to meet their clients and her fans. Because it was snowing, because it was almost Christmas, because she had been working late every night, and because her grandmother told her to treat herself, she had used her airline miles for a business-class seat and booked a room at the Hay-Adams.

The flight was bumpy, but Mara wasn't scared. Whenever she had a rough flight, she would think of her father. He had flown during World War II—had been a hero for the twenty-five bombing runs he had made across the English Channel to Germany. She thought of all the bad weather he had encountered, all the attacks he had survived. After so much terror in the air, he had died on what should have been a peaceful cruise—a ferry excursion across a wide inlet, with Mara's mother on a trip to Ireland, when Mara was just four.

She had grown up believing that you can't predict your fate; you don't see death coming. You just do your best, staying as open to life's possibilities as you can. Worrying about rough flights was a waste of time.

On the final approach to National Airport, Mara realized that everyone on the plane was holding their breath; everyone but her. She turned toward the window and stared out. She felt an old ache in her chest—a hollowness that rang and echoed, as if she were a bell. The vibrations ran through her bones and nerves as the plane jostled against the headwinds. The person next to her was praying.

The plane shook, as if it might break apart. One person cried out sharply. Mara just watched the snow outside. Her eyes filled with tears; she wished she were afraid of dying. But she wasn't, and she hadn't been since the day her parents died. Sometimes she wished she had been with them on that ferry, instead of home in Connecticut with her grandmother.

She had built a life on work, needlepoint, and her grandmother. She was thirty-one years old, and she had never really been in love. Why fall in love, when it could all end on a summer day, on a peaceful ferry crossing in Ireland? When they finally touched down, bouncing hard on the tarmac, the other passengers cheered. Mara just gathered her things.

The business-class passengers were let off first. Mara noticed the other passengers waiting; a young man wearing a tweed sports coat stood at the front of the coach cabin, seeming to watch her as she gathered her things. Thinking she was holding everyone up, she gave him a quick smile and hurried off the plane.

The flight attendants and captain stood at the plane door, obviously shaken by the rough flight. She thanked them as she passed. The captain said, "Hope you'll fly with us again." "I will!" Mara said. She walked a little taller—shaken not so much by the flight as by her own emotional turmoil. Maybe she could make a New Year's resolution to try to open her heart a little.

Still troubled, she went to the taxi line. Standing at the curb, she noticed the man in the tweed jacket hurrying over. He had a stocky build; his shoulders looked very strong, straining the fabric. It was snowing, and she wondered whether he was cold without a topcoat. His briefcase looked a bit battered, as if he had had it since high school. His hair was brown and wavy, cut very short. She glimpsed the Harvard tag on his luggage, and that made her look away—a little too much advertising that he was an Ivy Leaguer, she thought.

A cab stopped, and Mara put her hand on the door to get in at the same time as the man. His eyes looked dark, charged—and for a minute she thought he was going to fight her for the cab. His energy frightened her, and she stepped back.

"It's all yours," she said.

"Want to share it?" he asked, seeming to regroup quickly.

"No. That's okay."

"Come on. Where are you going?" Suddenly the darkness in his eyes was replaced by one of the brightest smiles she'd ever seen. He looked sweet, charming, and insouciant—as if he was about to ask her to join some mad adventure in the nation's capital. In spite of her initial aversion to him, his smile was undeniably cute, and the tone of his voice was totally flirtatious.

Mara just smiled politely and ran for the next cab, telling the driver, "Hay-Adams, please," and climbing in as quickly as possible to get away from the man, who stood at the curb with a smitten look in his hazel eyes and—adorably—his hand over his heart.

She got to the wonderful hotel across Lafayette Park from the White House. Her grandparents had stayed here long ago, and Mara felt the blessing of her grandmother as she checked in at the grand lobby desk, rode upstairs in a burnished mahogany elevator, and entered a beautiful yellow room overlooking snow falling on the park and White House. She had just opened her suitcase—to unpack her dress and her latest needlepoint canvas designs—when she heard a knock at the door.

Peeking through the peephole, she saw someone standing with a big bouquet of red tulips. *Granny must have sent them,* she thought. Grabbing her bag for a tip for the porter, she threw open the door.

"It's you," she said, recognizing the young man from the cab stand.

"You needed tulips," he said. "It's snowing out and you're beautiful, and all I could think was, I have to give that girl some red tulips."

"But how did you know where I'd be?"

"Fate led me here," he said.

She raised her eyebrows. The door was half open, and she was inside, and he was out in the hall. Her heart was pounding, and her mouth was dry. She felt scared, but also thrilled. Men didn't do things like this. Maybe they did in Paris, or Rome, or incredibly romantic places halfway around the world. But men flying from Providence to Washington didn't.

"Fate didn't know where I was staying," she said.

"A plane, a snowstorm, some tulips, I, and thou," he said, grinning wickedly, poetically.

"Hmm," she said.

She looked up and down the hallway. They were completely alone. If he had bad intentions, wouldn't he have already pushed his way in? As if reading her mind, he took half a step backward, away from her.

"Regardless of how fate brought us together," he said. "I know one thing. The tulips are for you. And you alone." Again, that grin. "I'll just take myself off to my room and dream about you."

"Your room? You're staying in the hotel?"

He nodded. "Okay—now you know my secret. I pulled up, walked in, and saw you just getting into the elevator. I thought—wow. We really *should* have shared that cab. Two coincidences in a row—same plane, same cab, same hotel. Whoa, that's three."

"So you jumped into the next elevator and guessed my floor?"

"Nope." Hazel eyes twinkling. "I bribed the bellman. I'm sorry. It's forward of me, I know. I ran to the florist, picked out the prettiest flowers I could find, and got back as soon as I could. Honestly, I didn't want to miss a minute of time with you."

She chuckled. He really was funny—and very handsome. He had sharp features that reminded her of a young Cary Grant, with bright eyes and a strong jaw and that quick, fun-loving smile. Lily felt herself smiling in his presence—after just five minutes. People were always telling her she was too serious, and she knew she was.

"Let me take you to dinner," he said.

"We don't even know each other's names," she said.

"I'm Edward Hunter," he said.

"I'm Mara Jameson," she said.

"Okay—now we know each other's names!"

She laughed. He handed her the tulips; she brought them up to her nose so she could smell them. Tulips in December—how extravagant, she thought.

"Please, Mara?" he asked. "I've come all this way. Don't send me away without letting me take you to dinner."

"All this way?"

His smile lit up his eyes, and he stepped so close, she could feel his warm breath on her forehead. Mara had come to Washington for work—she was very focused and ambitious, trying to get her business off the ground. She felt hesitant, afraid to say yes, but he was smiling at her with such bright eyes.

"Don't break my heart, Mara Jameson," he said, cupping the side of her face.

"I don't know you well enough to break your heart," she said hoarsely, mesmerized by his green eyes.

"Don't you be too sure of that," he said. "I've never bought red tulips in the snow for anyone in my entire life."

And then he kissed her.

She had literally kissed a stranger within minutes of meeting him. She had trusted his words, his smile, his warm eyes, the flowers he had bought her. How much had those tulips cost, after all? Ten dollars? Fifteen? When she thought back now, she wondered whether she had sold her entire life for the price of that single bouquet of out-of-season flowers.

Had he actually had a room at the hotel, or just followed her? She didn't know and doubted she ever would. She did know that she had been wearing an elegant black cashmere coat, her grandfather's thick gold watch chain as a necklace, a pair of emerald earrings—an outfit that she thought her Georgetown clients would appreciate. She had looked like a New England girl with money. He had heard her, she was positive, tell the driver of that cab her destination—one of the finest hotels in Washington.

Sitting on Maeve's porch, she pulled the blanket around her tighter. She stared across the bay, at the moon's path on the water. Her guarded heart—so easily softened by Edward's charm—had hardened as if frozen. The moon sparkled silver, breaking into a million pieces on the water. Lily had shut down after Edward—almost completely. There had been no quick romances, no sweeping her off her feet.

Her love for Liam had grown slowly. With every year of Rose's life, it had gotten truer and deeper. Lily hadn't even let herself feel or believe it. Very gently, he had melted her heart. Too quick a thaw might have destroyed her—Liam let her come around in her own time.

Three days without him and Rose was too much. It was after midnight, but she threw off the blanket and traded her nightgown for jeans and a sweatshirt. She fumbled for her grandmother's house and car keys, locked the door, and hurried up the stone steps.

The Point was deserted. All her neighbors had gone to bed. Her protectors—Bay and Tara—had been by earlier, and there had been no sign of Edward. Checking her pocket for the map and directions Liam had given her, she drove out Eight Mile River Road to I-95.

She had the car windows down, and she turned on the radio. Bonnie Raitt came on, and Lily sang along. The miles sped by, with warm air blowing through the car. Lily glanced in the rearview mirror. A car had pulled out of Hubbard's Point just behind her, and it was still there. Her stomach clenched—what if she was making a mistake, leading some reporter, or even worse, Edward—straight to Rose?

By the time she got to New London, the car was gone. A stream of trucks passed her, just normal traffic on this stretch of turnpike. Lily reached for her cell phone. Maybe she should let Liam know she was on her way. But it was so late—after midnight. Let him get some sleep—she'd wake him up soon enough.

She was so excited about the idea of seeing the people she loved, she didn't notice the car following her, three or four vehicles behind, about half a mile back. If she had seen it, she wouldn't have known whether it was friend or foe.

She hadn't given her protectors an itinerary.

And they hadn't given her one, either.

Liam had been tossing and turning for hours when he heard the footsteps on the porch. He hiked himself up on his elbow, glanced at the door of the small guesthouse the Stanleys were letting him stay in with Rose. He had turned off the outside light, but he saw a moonlit silhouette pass the window, and he knew—more than even recognizing her, he felt her coming toward him.

He pulled open the door, and Lily stood there on the whitewashed porch, her dark hair blowing in the cool breeze. Without any words they reached for each other and hugged, rocking, in the darkness. Now that she was here, he was home. It didn't matter that they were in a house they'd never been before. Home was where Lily was. He felt her hands on his back, sliding up under his T-shirt, and he kissed the top of her head.

They were new at this. Liam had been in love with her most of the nine years they had known each other, but they had both been so careful, being polite, appropriate, and guarded. That had all ended at the beginning of this summer—on the way to Boston, for Rose to have her last lifesaving operation. Liam had known—there was more than one life that needed to be saved. He and Lily couldn't live without each other. He had felt it for a long time, but he knew it more deeply with every passing day.

"I couldn't stay away from you and Rose," she said.

"We couldn't stand not being with you," he said.

She tipped her head back, so that he could kiss her, and she tasted sweet and salty. When he closed the door, she pushed back the curtain, looking into the darkness. Her eyes looked worried.

"What's wrong?" he asked.

"I'm sure I'm just being overly careful, but I thought a car was following me when I left the beach."

"I'll go out and check," he said, but she caught his wrist and kissed him again. He wanted to carry her to his bed right then. But he looked down at her and smiled and took her hand as he led her through the small house to the yellow bedroom where Rose slept.

"My Rosie." Lily smiled.

"She misses you, but she's fine."

He watched Lily crouch, then kneel beside the bed. She kissed Rose's face, peeked down at her scar to make sure it was healing well, gently eased her daughter's left hand down from its protective spot across her collarbone. Rose slept through these ministrations, sighing contentedly as if she sensed her mother's presence through her dreams.

They walked into the living room, and Lily seemed to take in the old wicker furniture with faded chintz cushions, the marine charts of Narragansett Bay and Block Island Sound, the brass telescope pointed at the bay, and the bookshelves full of oceanographic journals and reference books. Then, as if she'd absorbed as much as she needed to know about the place that sheltered her daughter, she threw herself against Liam's chest.

He held her with his one arm. He kissed her, felt her skin moist against his. She reached up to touch his face, and he felt her fingertips light on his skin. He thought maybe she'd want to talk—he started to turn on a lamp, but she stopped him, finger on his lips.

They walked into the bedroom. Liam felt protective of Lily, and wanted to be strong—he knew how hard it had to be for her, worried about her grandmother, separated from Rose. But inside, he was shaking with excitement. Being with her made him feel seventeen.

The way she leaned against him, her breath hot on his neck, her pelvis pressing into his thighs. Her kisses were urgent, as if she couldn't wait. His heart was banging in his chest, and he tried to stay calm enough to remember to breathe. Her hands were at the buttons of his shirt, undoing them, sliding in and caressing his skin.

They had so much to say to each other, and they did it with their bodies. Words weren't enough for how he felt about Lily. They had lived a lifetime together—Rose's lifetime. Their shared dream had been to keep her alive, to give her a wonderful life. Liam's own heart was strong because of his love of Lily and Rose—he could and would do anything for them, to protect them.

That's what he wanted to tell Lily, and it's what he did tell her—with his lips, his tongue, his fingers, every bit of his body and soul. They were together tonight, and Liam knew that deep down they would never really be apart again.

"I don't want to leave," she whispered, lying under the sheets with him as the sky began to turn from black to deep blue with dawn's approach.

"I don't want you to," he said, kissing her hair as she lay on his shoulder.

"He hasn't called or showed up," Lily said. "I was sure he would, the minute the news got out."

"There's been a lot of news," Liam said. "I've kept the TV off, so Rose wouldn't see. But the Stanleys told me your return has been in the papers and on lots of programs. Are you sure that wasn't him, in the car?"

"I don't know. I've just gotten so jumpy," she said. "I know that he's waiting for the right moment, and I keep expecting him around every corner."

"I know we want to keep Rose away from him," Liam said. "But I think I should be with you—to keep you safe."

"Taking care of Rose is the best thing you can do for me," Lily said. "I wish we were all home in Cape Hawk again."

"Maybe we should go back home for a few days," he said. "You, me, and Rose. We could listen to some ceili bands—it would be good for us."

"Sssh," she said, kissing him hard. "You're tempting me, but I've got to see about Granny."

"I know," he said.

He took her hand, leading her across the room. His desk was piled high with books and journals from John Stanley's personal library. Liam had been amazed to find old editions of *Copeia*, the prestigious nineteenth-century ichthyologic journal, dedicated to the study and conservation of sharks. He'd been looking for theories to explain the phenomenon he'd been observing along the shore these past few days—the massing of baitfish in such unusual volume.

Lily drifted toward the open door. Liam followed her outside. The stars were white and brilliant in the dark blue sky. The night seemed to reflect the ocean, spreading out from the rocks all the way to the far horizon. The constellations made a canopy overhead, arching straight out of the sea. They illuminated the salt spray, fine and bright as snow.

"What's that?" Lily asked, pointing offshore, at iridescence streaking through the water.

"Bioluminescence," Liam said. "Marine creatures that produce light."

"It looks like the northern lights, underwater," she said.

"It's unusual, that's for sure," Liam said.

"Could it be Nanny?" Lily asked, sounding excited. "Maybe she really has followed us down from Nova Scotia!"

Looking at the white streaks, Liam could understand why Lily would think they were made by their favorite beluga whale, come all the way from Cape Hawk. Although Nanny hadn't shown up on his computer tracking screen, he was pretty sure the source of light was a marine mammal or another large sea creature.

As they approached the seawall, the roaring of distant waves grew stronger. The inshore waters were turbulent, and silhouetted in the breaking waves were filmy white jellyfish and hordes of silver menhaden, swimming parallel to the shore.

"It's so loud," Lily said, staring out at the water.

"It's a phenomenon called Ghost Hills," Liam told her.

"What is that?"

"There's a reef between here and Block Island. Normally, oceanographic activity there is fairly predictable. I've just been reading some old journals, and it seems that when the conditions are right—usually midway through hurricane season, like now—the winds and tides can conspire to send huge waves, 'Ghost Hills,' over the reef."

"It sounds more like galloping horses," Lily said, standing still, listening.

"I know. The waves can be sixty feet high—rogue waves. The surfers love them—they get towed out to the reef by motorboats or Jet Skis. The problem is, when Ghost Hills come, so do the sharks."

Lily hugged him. She knew about Liam and sharks. They stood close to the seawall, and felt the salt spray mist their faces. The beach smelled like fish, from the influx of bait. This was the food chain at work: Ghost Hills changed the whole marine environment. They pulled southern organisms in from the Gulf Stream and attracted northern species from the Labrador Current.

"Is this why Nanny came south?" Lily asked.

"I think so," Liam said. "Partly, at least. The rogue waves create a food source for large marine animals that wouldn't normally be there."

"Rose thinks Nanny followed us—that she was looking out for us."

"That can also be true—I'm sure it is," Liam said, smiling at Lily, wishing she would never leave.

"I just hope she's safe," Lily said, gazing out over the flashing, churning sea. In the distance, a large trawler made a long, slow turn, coming from the northeast. Silhouetted by the stars and the glowing waves, its familiar profile made Liam stare more closely.

"It's late," Lily said. "I want to go see Rose for a little while, but then I should be getting back to Hubbard's Point."

"I don't want you to go," Liam said, turning away from the dark boat, kissing her as star followed star through the night sky, as if holding her could make everything right, keep them safe and together. Then they both walked into the small house, to sit with Rose for as long as they could before Lily had to leave again.

Liam wished he could keep her from going back to the place where she'd been so afraid. Not even the dark waters where his brother had been killed had made him feel as powerless.

Patrick held himself back from calling his contacts in Baltimore. Marisa had asked him not to try tracking her sister. He told himself to stay out of it. As much as he wanted to take action, she had been very clear.

Instead, he began to have dreams of the North. They were filled with dark pines growing on craggy cliffs, mirror-smooth bottomless bays, ice blue skies, golden-eyed bobcats in the woods, broadtail hawks on the wing, and Marisa.

And now, for the third night in a row, he was dreaming of her again: they held hands in the snow and went swimming in a frozen cove, through a hole in the ice. The water was hot, and they held each other, kissing. . . .

Patrick moaned and woke himself up. He had thrashed the covers off his bunk. His chest and legs were soaking wet, his heart beating out of his chest. Swinging his legs out, he sat at the edge of his bunk, his head in his hands. Flora, his big black Lab, lay on her dog bed, watching him with huge eyes.

"Do you know what dreams mean?" he asked her.

She just thumped her tail.

The night was warm and still. He grabbed a bottle of water, headed up on deck. The air was cooler up here. He sat in the cockpit in his boxer shorts, letting the breeze evaporate the sweat from his body. The dream was so vivid, even now—he looked around, almost surprised to be in this protected Connecticut boatyard instead of lost in the northern wilds with Marisa.

He drank water, leaning his head back to look up at the sky. The stars were so bold, pinpoints of fire in the black night. Patrick grounded himself by finding the North Star. There it was, Polaris. He wondered whether he could follow it straight to Marisa. All he would have to do was cast off his lines—his boat was seaworthy enough to make the trip.

Sighing, he went back down to his bunk and waited for sleep to come again. His grandmother used to tell him stories about an angel who flew over the world at night, spreading her white wings to protect everyone, hold everyone together, bring the lost ones home. She'd point at the Milky Way, tell him it was the angel's shadow. Patrick hoped that she could bring Sam and Marisa together again.

"That's bullshit," he said out loud when he woke up the next morning. Maybe angels worked for grandmothers, but cops knew that the only way to get something done was to make it happen.

Picking up the phone, he got the number for Johns Hopkins, asked to be connected to Global Care.

"Hi," he said to the woman who answered the phone. "My name is Patrick Murphy."

"Yes?"

"I'm calling in regard to a nurse who is with your group in Peru. I need to get hold of her."

"Is this a family emergency?"

"No, no it's not," he said, frowning. He paused. This person didn't sound as if she'd be impressed by the phrase "retired detective." But he thought of Marisa and Jessica, and knew he had to go for it. "Listen, I'm a detective with the Connecticut State Police."

"Oh—what happened?"

"The woman I'm looking for is not in any trouble," he said quickly, mindful of what Marisa had said about Sam's work. "I'm trying to contact her because—"

"Sir," she said, cutting him off, "we are very protective of our health care workers, and I'm unable to give out any information about their whereabouts. If you'd like to send a letter to this office, I'll see if I can forward it on—"

"Thank you," Patrick growled. "That won't be necessary."

Flora needed to go for her morning walk. He let her off the boat, watched her prowl the woods around the boatyard's perimeter. That gave Patrick a chance to think. He could try calling Peru directly, try to get through to someone at the Global Care group. Or he could dial an old friend in the Baltimore PD, call in some old favors.

He didn't know the number by heart, had to look it up—but there it was in his old address book, written in years before. Patrick dialed, looking forward to hearing his pal's voice. Instead, he got Detective James Hanley's voicemail.

"Hey, Jim," he said. "It's Pat Murphy. A blast from the past, right? Listen, I'm trying to get some information on the whereabouts of a Baltimore woman, Samantha Mahon. . . ."

Patrick left him a long message about Global Care, Sam being somewhere in the wilds of Peru, her sister getting worried. Then he hung up, wondering how long it would take Jim to get back to him.

He hoped it was soon. Because he knew how badly Marisa wanted to find her sister, and if it took too long, Patrick just might have to fly down to South America to bring her back himself.

Chapter 8

On her way back to Hubbard's Point from Rhode Island, Lily felt recharged and energized. Holding Liam had triggered even more desire, and seeing Rose had unleashed a hurricane of love—just like Ghost Hills, pounding the reef. When dawn broke, Rose woke up to find her mother sitting there, and Lily could still hear her cry of joy.

She drove under the train trestle that marked the entrance to Hubbard's Point and saw early-morning walkers out for their daily constitutional. There were the strollers, out to enjoy the gardens and scenery, and the power-walkers, out for exercise. They walked in groups, talking and laughing, or alone, just listening to the music of the waves and leaves rustling in the wind.

Driving around the bend and up the first hill, she saw Bay and Tara. Tara was pushing a stroller, with baby Joey inside, and she and Bay were winded and sweating and gave huge waves. Lily waved back, her heart lifting. Seeing Liam and Rose had done a lot to chase last night's demons away.

When she pulled up to the house, she came face-to-face with a man she didn't know. Tall, dark-haired, wearing a navy blue FBI T-shirt, he was sitting in the shade on Maeve's iron four-seasons garden bench.

"I'm Joe Holmes," he said, rising to shake her hand. "Tara's husband."

"I'm Lily Malone," she said.

"Nice to meet you," he said, smiling. "I've heard so much about you. Sorry about the intrusion—"

She shook her head. "No, I'm grateful. It's such a lot to ask you all to do this. In fact, maybe—"

"Don't try to talk us out of it," he said sternly. "You know Tara. Or—maybe you've forgotten. But trying to argue with her is like trying to convince a hurricane it should to go east when it wants to go west."

"I remember," Lily said.

"Besides, just from a professional standpoint," he said, "we'd like to get something right in your case. Protect you now, you know? You really pulled it off. Someday I'd like to interview you, to ask you how you did it. Hid for nine whole years."

"Can I ask you a question?" she asked quietly, remembering the headlights in her rearview mirror. "Did you follow me last night?"

"No," Joe said. "When I got up here, your car was gone. Tara figured you'd stayed at the hospital."

"I went to Rhode Island, to see my daughter. But I thought someone was following me for a while. . . ."

"Edward, you think?"

"God, I hope not," she said.

"He's bad news," Joe said. "I'll see what I can find out about where he was last night. Look—you just go about your business, do what you have to do. We'll watch your house."

"I saw Tara and Joey," she said. "Your family has better things to do than stand watch over me."

"Better things to do than help a friend?" He shook his head. "I'm with Tara on that. Nothing's more important, Lily."

The summer day was warm. The grass tickled Rose's bare feet. She played outside while Dr. Neill did his work. A swing hung from a tall branch of one of the trees in the front yard, so she walked over to it and climbed on. The breeze ruffled the leaves overhead. A bird flew into the neat green hedge. Rose's mother had been there for breakfast, and Rose felt empty now, because she was gone again.

From the swing, Rose could look up and down the street. The family next door had older children; she had watched them climb into a blue station wagon and go driving off. Seeing kids made her miss Jessica. She glanced at the house. Dr. Neill was right there in the window. She waved, and he waved back, and that made her feel better.

Swinging back and forth, she watched a car drive down the street. It passed the house and kept going. She kept swinging, and after a few minutes, the car came back, driving slowly now. When it got to the driveway, it came to a complete stop, but didn't turn in.

Maybe the man driving was lost, Rose thought. She glanced at the window; Dr. Neill was still there, looking down at his desk. Although the car was parked in the street, not the driveway, the man got out and stepped into the yard. He was much shorter than Dr. Neill, but heavier.

He had short, sort of frizzy brown hair. At first, Rose felt alarmed, but then he smiled.

He looked so friendly and nice. Rose didn't move. She wasn't scared, but her mother had told her not to talk to strangers. Shade from the tall tree dappled his face, making it hard to see anything but his smile.

"Do you live here?" he asked.

Rose shook her head.

"Are you just visiting?" he asked, just a few feet away now. She could see his eyes now—bright but dead, like green marbles.

She nodded and stayed very still, glancing at the window. Dr. Neill was there, watching the man come closer. Suddenly he was on his feet.

"With your parents?"

The door opened. Dr. Neill started toward her, and something about the look on his face made her know she should run to him. She did, her heart galloping. When she turned around, the man was walking back to his car.

"You have such pretty green eyes," the man called. "And brown hair. I like your braids."

"Just a minute," Dr. Neill said, starting across the yard. "I want to talk to you."

The man didn't answer. He just kept staring at Rose as he climbed into his car. Slamming the door behind him hard, he began to pull away. The whole time, he just kept watching Rose. Then his car disappeared from sight.

"Who was that?" she asked Dr. Neill.

"Someone we have to be careful of," he said. "I won't let you outside alone again, okay?"

"Okay," she said.

He looked down into her eyes. Rose blinked, staring. She didn't know what had just happened, but she knew it made her heart beat too fast. The man had stared. He had smiled, as if he was nice. But his eyes had frightened her, flashing and hollow. They had reminded her of a hungry animal, and she shivered.

Dr. Neill hugged her, and then he led her inside.

※

Liam sat at his computer, surrounded by early editions of *Copeia*, trying to shake off the disturbance he felt. He had no question about the visitor they'd just had. Edward had followed Lily last night, and he'd come back this morning to see the place in daylight. If only Liam hadn't let Rose go out by herself. If only he had told her to stay in the backyard, out of sight of the street.

He called Lily right away.

"What did he say? What did he do?" she asked.

"He didn't say much," Liam said. "He asked if she was visiting with her parents. Then he just stood there, staring at her."

"Oh no," Lily said. "He knows now—what are we going to do?"

"I think Rose and I should come to Hubbard's Point now," Liam said. "Why stay away if he already knows?"

"But what if it wasn't him? What if it was someone else, just a neighbor passing by, or—"

"Lily," Liam said gently.

"I don't know what to do," she said. "It seemed like such a good idea, for you to keep Rose away from here. Maybe that's still best—he doesn't know she's his. He has no idea."

"He mentioned her green eyes and brown hair," Liam said.

"Like his."

"Yes," Liam said.

"Oh God. I have to think . . ."

"Okay," he said. "But don't think too long. I want us all to be together."

After he hung up, Liam turned to see Rose sitting in a chair by the window, sunlight turning her brown hair shiny as copper. She had asked him for help braiding it that morning after Lily had left, and he had tried—tricky, with one arm. Now he saw it tumbling free to her shoulders—she had unbraided it after Edward's comment.

Hearing a knock at the front door, Liam's stomach clenched. He almost wished it would be Edward, so he could do battle. Rushing through the airy living room, he found his old friend John Stanley standing there—tan in a white polo shirt and faded Breton red shorts, wearing wire-rimmed spectacles and a Panama hat. John's grin evaporated at the look in Liam's eyes.

"Whoa," John said. "It's just me."

"We had an unwelcome visitor this morning," Liam said. He leaned around John, looked up and down the street. "Come on in."

"He found you?" John asked, frowning. Of course, Liam had told him all about the reason he and Rose needed to stay there. "Look, I have just the thing to take your mind off that. Have you noticed all the activity out there?" He pointed at the water.

"Hard to miss it," Liam said as he gazed at the cove churning and turning white with froth, fish in a feeding frenzy.

"Come take a boat ride. I'll show you something unreal."

"I have Rose with me. . . ."

"My kids used to love coming on oceanographic projects. We'll make her part of the team."

Liam nodded. Getting Rose away for the day would be the best possible thing to do. "Let me ask her," he said.

He hurried out, into the living room. Rose was curled up in a chair. She had a book open on her lap, but her gaze was troubled. Liam could see that Edward's visit had disturbed her. "Rose," Liam said, "my friend wants to take us for a boat ride. Would you like that?"

"I want Mommy," she said.

Liam went to sit beside her. "I know," he said. "We're going to be with her really soon. But we can't today, so I thought maybe this would be the next best thing."

"I didn't like that man," she said.

"I know," he said.

"If we're on a boat ride, he can't come back and try to talk to me again, right?"

"Right," Liam said.

"Okay," Rose said, nodding.

Liam grabbed his laptop, cell phone, and binoculars, and stuffed them into his satchel. He put on his sunglasses and cap, then grabbed a snack and some juice for Rose. Leading John into the living room, he stood next to Rose.

"Rose, this is Dr. Stanley, whose house we're staying in."

"Thank you," Rose said politely.

"It's nice to meet you, Rose. Do you like boats?"

A smile began on her lips, spread to her green eyes. Her face brightened, and she nodded. "Yes," she said. "I love them."

"Do you like science?" John asked. "Oceanography?"

"Yes," she said, her smile growing.

"Good," he said. "Because we have an oceanographic mystery going on right here, and it's pretty much up to us to solve it."

Liam rippled with excitement—the mystery of Ghost Hills. Generations of oceanographers had observed the phenomenon, pondered its cause. He gave Rose sunscreen to spread on her arms and legs, double-checked his bag to make sure he had everything. Then the three of them set off across John's yard.

A sturdy, thirty-foot stone breakwater jutted out from the beach. Liam could see that it kept the beachhead from eroding, pulling in crescents of sand and smooth sea-washed pebbles from the waves. Two boats were docked alongside—*Respite*, a J-24 racing sloop, and *Blue Heron*, a thirty-six-foot down east lobster boat overhauled and refitted for oceanography work.

Rose was an old hand, from all her years aboard Liam's family's whale-watching fleet up in Cape Hawk. She jumped aboard *Blue Heron,* standing back while John started up the engine and Liam walked along the breakwater, scanning once more for any sign of Edward, then casting off lines before leaping on board.

The water was calm as John steered south along the shore of the west passage of Narragansett Bay. The boat moved slowly, engines quiet, creating a lazy white wake rippling out behind. Two flocks of sandpipers flew low over the waves, just ahead of the big blue boat. Rose pointed, looking up to make sure Liam saw. He nodded and smiled, but his attention was fixed on larger birds—gulls and terns, swooping and diving along the beach.

"Birds working," Liam said, rummaging for his binoculars, lifting them to his eyes as he watched the shorebirds feasting on tiny silver fish—minnows, menhaden. All around them splashed fins and tails of larger fish.

"Yep," John said.

"What's running? Blues, stripers?"

"Everything," John said, and Liam gave him a look—he had already surmised the same thing. But John just continued steering the boat. They passed Narragansett Town Beach and Scarborough Beach, where surfers sat on their boards, staring out toward the open sea—toward the roar of Ghost Hills—while waiting for something worth riding amid the comparatively gentle swells. A pair of osprey fished along the shallows, wings gleaming white in the sun.

As they rounded Point Judith, the smell of fish became stronger. Liam wasn't surprised—this was home to the Galilee fishing fleet. Big diesel trawlers passed in and out of the breachway, to and from the Harbor of Refuge. These boats fished Georges Bank, the edge of the continental shelf, for haddock, cod, hake, whiting, flounder, and lobster, and they were every bit as hardy as the fleet out of Cape Hawk, Nova Scotia.

Liam had smelled lots of old bait and discarded fish in his day—but this was different. It was alive, and smelled of the sea, deep and blue and mysterious. It made the hair on the back of his neck stand on end. He looked at John, saw him frowning as he drove the boat. Instinctively Liam reached for Rose, drew her closer as they faced forward and the boat sliced through the water.

"Where are we going?" Rose asked.

"Not much farther," John said.

Liam glanced down the coast—Lily was just about twenty miles west of here. He wondered what she was doing right now, and he wondered whether the sudden, atavistic fear he felt welling up from inside had anything to do with Lily and what she was going through.

"This is it," John said, pulling back on the throttle, slowing the engine to a dull hum.

"Where are we?" Rose asked.

"That's the Point Judith Lighthouse," John said, pointing at the fifty-foot tower. Built of brownstone, the lower half whitewashed, it was crowned by a Fresnel lens that glinted in the brilliant sunlight.

"And seven miles out there is Block Island," Liam said.

"Six-point-four," John said. "From the tip of Point Jude to the north tip of Block. I remember, from when I got my pilot's license. Three-point-two miles to glide if I lost an engine. Three minutes of gliding is one afternoon of swimming. But I wouldn't want to swim in this water right now. Can you hear it?"

Rose frowned. With the engine down so low, the sound of small waves hitting the hull became more insistent. Only it wasn't waves at all: the sound was rapid and hard, almost like hundreds of hands clapping. Below, and more insistent, was a growing roar.

"What's that?" Rose asked, hurrying to the side. She gripped the rail, with Liam standing right beside her. They looked down into the blue water and saw silver everywhere. Silver tails, fins, scales. Thousands, hundreds of thousands, of small fish, right at the surface of the sea.

"Fish feeding," he said.

"We don't expect to see anything like this until September, if then," John said. "It's a rare year with this kind of activity."

The boat flushed ten, twenty herring gulls, black-backed gulls, laughing gulls, roseate terns—all rising in a screeching, cawing white cloud of wings. Liam looked over the side, saw the silver ribbon of fish extending in all directions. John drove out toward Block Island, across the Sound. The silver fish swam in a stream, a river of small fish weaving out to sea. And the oceangoing birds followed them in—more gulls and terns than Liam could believe.

"Is that—?" he asked, pointing up.

"A northern gannet," John said. "Spends most of its life at sea."

"Yet it's here in Block Island Sound?"

John's lips tightened. Liam knew that he had to be thinking the same thing—if these quantities of bait could pull in a northern gannet flying above the surface, what species of fish might there be swimming beneath? Liam thought of Nanny—whose whereabouts had been unknown these last days—and shivered.

A flotilla of motorboats—Boston Whalers, Grady-Whites, Aquasports—and Jet Skis towing surfers on surfboards passed by. Liam's at-

tention was captured by another boat—a dark green trawler with a familiar low profile. Raising the binocs to his eyes, he felt his blood run
cold. The ship was *Mar IV,* with its home port of Cape Hawk emblazoned in gold on the transom. There was its captain, Gerard Lafarge,
standing at the bridge.

"A friend of yours?" John asked.

"Hardly," Liam said. "He's a fisherman I know from home. We've
had a few run-ins, with him catching dolphins and selling them as
tuna."

"We'll turn him in," John said, reaching for the radio transmitter. "If
he's Canadian, he's not supposed to be fishing in Rhode Island."

"He's not fishing," Liam said, staring through the glasses. Lafarge
was standing still, gazing at the waves. His outriggers were pulled in;
the nets were rolled tight, the trawl doors up and inactive.

"So what's he doing here?" John said.

"That's what I'd like to know," Liam said as *Mar IV* steamed toward
the action with the rest of the boats.

Just ahead, the giants were rising to life: Ghost Hills. Liam felt the
water temperature rise—these ocean waves were straight off the Gulf
Stream, brilliant cerulean blue, clear as sunshine. They rose fifty feet
into the air, wild and thunderous, sliding over the reef, enormous and
unbroken, then exploding into white foam.

"What are they?" Rose asked, sounding amazed.

"The biggest waves we've ever seen," Liam said, his arm around her.

"In the middle of the sea? I thought waves only broke on the beach,"
she said.

"They're breaking on an undersea reef," John said. "It only happens
once or twice a century—when the wind and currents and tides are
right."

Liam pulled his laptop out of the case, booted up, and waited for the
predator program to load. He tapped in some coordinates, watching
weather data flash across the screen. A tropical storm had swung east
of Hatteras, north to Nova Scotia; a rare vacuum effect had been created, sending a whirl of monster rogue waves back in its wake.

"What we're seeing here is extremely rare on the East Coast," John
said as a surfer made the drop and rode one wild wave to the screams
and cheers of onlookers. "This sort of thing is seen on Maui's north
coast in Hawaii, a notorious surf-towing spot—"

"It's called Jaws," Liam said. "For obvious reasons."

"Exactly," John said. "Just like Mavericks—a giant wave spot off Half
Moon Bay, just north of San Francisco. Shark infested as well . . ."

"Just like Ghost Hills," Liam said. He had finally logged into the predator program and was looking at the incredible number of purple dots blinking in the immediate area.

"Green dots for whales, purple for sharks?" Rose asked, frowning.

"Yes," Liam said, giving her a reassuring hug.

"So, one of those green dots could be Nanny?"

"She's not here," Liam said, scanning the screen for MM122, Nanny's tag number.

"I'm glad," Rose said. "Because look at all those sharks."

It was true; Liam marked down the identities of all previously tagged sharks, swimming just below the surface: makos, tigers, two bulls, and, circling far beneath the others, two great whites. Some surfers dared the rip, oblivious to what was beneath their boards. Liam felt an adrenaline rush, as if he were riding a monster wave himself.

He thought of the car cruising so slowly down their street. With all the sharks down below in the tumultuous sea, he knew there were human predators much worse. They were just as hungry, just as vicious. Liam put his arm around Rose, held her close. There were fins all around the boat, but he stared past them, straight toward the road that meandered past their borrowed house, all the way back to Lily.

Chapter 9

Lily knew that something big had happened as soon as she stepped off the elevator on Shoreline General's fifth floor. Several doctors were huddled outside Maeve's room. They looked up fast, and her heart started thudding.

"Ms. Malone!" Dr. Mead said. "We were just trying to call you."

"What is it?" she asked, steadying herself against the wall.

"Good news," she said. "Your grandmother has been responsive today."

"She's out of the coma?"

"Not completely," Dr. Mead said with a touch of hesitation in her smile. "But she opened her eyes, looked around, and responded with marked improvement to some neuro tests."

"Did she say anything?"

"She said 'Mara,'" Dr. Mead said, smiling for real now.

"I have to see her," Lily said.

"Of course you do," Dr. Mead said, and she and the other doctors stepped aside for Lily to enter the room.

Maeve was having a white dream. She had had them her whole life, from the time she was very young and struggling to wake up from a very sound sleep. White dreams usually came on nights before exciting, wonderful days. For example, Maeve had had a white dream the night before she went to the statewide spelling bee in fourth grade, and won on the word "pyrometallurgical." She had had one the night before she won a tennis match her senior year at Black Hall High School. And very early in the morning of the day she married her husband.

White dreams were harbingers of great joy. They came in different forms—they might take place amid light-infused cumulus clouds, or in the sea foam of gentle waves off the west coast of Corsica, or in the softest white feathers of a dove's wings—but the feeling they imparted was always the same. They filled the dreamer with the most exquisite sensations of life—every particle of existence that filled a person's soul with love and light and wonder, and made getting up in the morning worth doing.

Today's white dream took place in a garden. Maeve stood on a path surrounded by white roses. She felt the weight of her clippers in one hand, and she heard the reassuring slap, slap of the waves on the rocks down front. It was her own garden, and she was pruning the White Dawns, climbing the trellis by the stone chimney. The air was brilliant and clear, softened with salt. Her hair was white, and so was that of the woman working beside her. Clara, of course.

They didn't even have to speak. They were a team. Oh, they had had their fights over the years. They didn't see eye to eye about everything, that was for sure. But in white dreams, all strife is secondary to love.

"Mara," Maeve said, clipping back some thorns and briars.

"That means 'sea,'" Clara said. "In Gaelic."

"Ard na Mara," Maeve said, "is where my son and his wife died in Ireland."

"But you sound so happy!"

"I am," Maeve said. "I'll see him soon."

"You can't leave now," Clara said cheerily. "Your granddaughter is here."

"Mara," Maeve said, and heard herself say, her voice echoing in her ears, as if she were half awake, as if the white dream were coming to an end, as if real life were calling her down from the bliss of it all. "Mara, Mara . . ."

"Granny," came the voice, and it wasn't Clara's. "Granny, I'm here!"

"Sweetheart," Maeve said. Someone squeezed her hand. Oh, it felt so wonderful and real. She would know that touch anywhere! It was the hand she had held on walks to school and the beach, the hand she had held at doctors' visits and dentist appointments, the hand she had held at the funerals of her son and daughter-in-law.

"Can you hear me?" the voice asked. It wasn't Clara—this wasn't a dream. Maeve blinked—oh, it couldn't be. . . .

"Mara?" she asked.

"It's me, Granny!" she said, sounding so happy and excited. Maeve blinked her eyes, trying to focus and register. She coughed, and the chemical taste—that sweet syrupy air she had drunk down like a potion—came back, filled her senses, made her dizzy all over again. She couldn't quite do it, not now, not yet . . . soon, she thought. Don't leave, don't go away, just give me five more minutes. . . .

"Wake up, Granny." Mara's low voice. "Please, wake up. I want to see you, want to tell you about Rose. She's nine, Granny. She's so beautiful."

"Rose," Maeve murmured, back in the garden, the scent of flowers so heavy, pulling her back to sleep, away from the beautiful voice, Mara's voice. She struggled to open her eyes, look at the face of the person sitting there; oh, if only she could lift her eyelids, they were so heavy, and the smell was overpowering. . . . What had Mara told her he'd said once, so long ago: *White roses bruise so easily.* . . .

"Granny!" Mara said, her voice rising. "Stay with me, wake up! I need you, Granny!"

White roses bruise so easily. . . .

The white dream dissolved into darkness, and Maeve knew—she had to warn Mara. She had to wake up, do whatever it took, warn her darling granddaughter that the danger was back, and that she had to do whatever she could to protect herself and her child.

But sleep was too strong to fight, and it bound her up and took Maeve deeper, back to where no one could reach her for now.

Lily's first instinct was despair, but Dr. Mead, the neurologist, tried to assure her that it was common for coma patients to go in and out of consciousness for a while before coming fully awake. Holding on to her words was very hard—her hopes had been so far up when she'd seen her grandmother's soft blue eyes—for the first time in nine whole years—and heard that familiar voice she thought she'd never hear again whisper her name.

Shaken, she decided to go down to the cafeteria for a cup of tea. She waited in line, aware of people whispering as she passed. Choosing the tea, filling a cup with boiling water, she tried to keep her hands from trembling and spilling the water. She found an empty table at the far end of the room, with windows overlooking the parking lot.

"Hello, Lily."

Her name was new, but the voice was old. She felt a trickle of fear run like an ice cube down her back. Her breath stopped cold—just like Rose's when she was a baby, unable to get air into her lungs. One word—her new name—and she felt the old familiar terror.

"Edward," she said.

"Well," he said, towering over her. He looked pale, older. He had lost his boyish sparkle. There were lines around his eyes and mouth. Or maybe it was just the moment—Edward had always been able to transform and morph, almost before her very eyes.

She held on to her Styrofoam cup. It was filled with boiling water. She held it in her hands, fingers wrapped around it, letting herself actually feel it. She thought maybe she was going into shock, and holding on to the hot cup was grounding her. She could throw it at him, she thought. Right now, and escape.

"My wife," he said. "I never thought I would see my wife again."

"What do you want?" she asked without looking up at him.

"What do I want?" he asked. "Hmm. That's a good question. I'd like to know what happened. Why you ran away from me. What did I do that was so terrible?"

"We're alone here, Edward," she said. "You know and I know the truth. Let's not pretend otherwise. We were both there."

"You humiliated me," he said. "No, worse than that . . . 'humiliated' doesn't really start to cover—you let me think that you were dead. And you let me be investigated for your murder."

She wanted to block her ears; she knew she had to stop him before he got going. Yet she couldn't help feeling curious, fascinated by his presence—just like staring at a shark's fin circling the boat on a summer day, or a copperhead sunning itself on a shady stretch of road, there was something irresistible about the most dangerous creatures. Almost as if normal people couldn't quite fathom sharing their existence with something so pretty and deadly and right there in the open.

"Edward," she said, "What are you doing here?"

"The newspapers said you came home because your grandmother was in the hospital. I've come to visit her. We've stayed in touch, you know, Maeve and I."

Lily wanted to jump up and scratch his eyes out. Her pulse shot up, her breathing went crazy, but she held on to her cup to keep herself steady. She could almost hear her grandmother's voice telling her to stay calm, not give him the satisfaction of seeing her true feelings.

"Did Maeve tell you I visited?" he asked pleasantly.

Lily stared into her cup. Why hadn't he mentioned Rose? Maybe Liam was wrong. Maybe the person in Rhode Island hadn't been Edward after all. If Edward knew about Rose, why wasn't he asking about her?

He chuckled slightly. "Of course she didn't," he said. "Maeve didn't know you were alive. You kept her in the dark, just like the rest of the world. So much for the close Jameson family."

"You put her here," she said.

He smiled, sending a chill down her spine.

"Guess who I saw this morning?" he asked.

Lily's mouth was dry. She sipped again, thinking *Don't react, don't blush, don't give him any clue that Rose exists.* Edward was the most instinctive person she had ever met. He had eyes in the back of his head and nerve endings that never quit.

"A girl with green eyes," he said.

She felt the blood coursing through her body, a rush that made her feel dizzy. She stared at him, and with the eye contact, his face turned cold and hard.

"You know what's the most unforgivable? The cruelest thing anyone has ever done to me?" he asked. "It was when you pretended to love me, and then just treated me like dirt. You don't know what's coming, Lily. Just like I didn't know that you were going to walk out on me."

Lily was shaking. Across the room, Patrick Murphy was coming through the door. He saw them and crossed the room in two seconds flat. At six-three, he towered over Edward. The tension between them was tight and ugly, but it gave Lily the first chance she'd had to actually study her onetime husband.

At five-eight, he was as muscular as ever. He was tan, and he wore chinos and a blue polo shirt with a New York Yacht Club insignia and the Rolex watch she'd given him while they were still together. His brown hair was longer, still wiry, gray at the temples. His hazel eyes were still bright and piercing, but there were bags and pouches underneath—he looked as if he'd done some drinking. He probably hung around with a swanky boating crowd, she thought. She thought of the lies he had told her about his sea captain great-grandfather.

"Well," Patrick said. "Look who's here. How's life treating you, Edward?"

"Fine," he replied in an absolutely clipped tone. He stared Patrick straight in the eye for no more than two seconds, then looked everywhere but at him.

"Doing a lot of golfing these days with all that free time? Sailing, maybe? Got yourself a big boat?"

"Big enough," Edward said. Then he smiled, as if he'd just thought up the best joke in the world. "Bigger than yours."

"Huh," Patrick said, glaring. "What are you doing here?"

"As I told Lily," he said, "I'm visiting Maeve."

"No you're not," Patrick said. "There's a police investigation."

"But you're off the police force," Edward said, smiling—with a hint of the old charm, the rippling delight he could bring to a statement. "I guess spending most of a decade trying to nail an innocent man for a murder that never happened didn't do wonders for your career."

"Stay away from Maeve and her family," Patrick said, staring steadily into Edward's eyes.

"Really? Do you plan to stop me?"

"Absolutely," Patrick said, smiling now. "They found your prints on Maeve's hot-water heater. You're going to have to answer some questions."

"I adjusted her thermostat," Edward said, glaring. "I'm happy to admit that. Her granddaughter wasn't there to help her, so I did!"

"My grandmother would never take your help," Lily said. "No matter what she needed, she would never ask you. You're lying."

Suddenly Edward's face turned bright red, the way it always did whenever she had challenged him. His lips thinned, and his hazel eyes turned black with rage. She saw the hate building in him, coming from that secret pool deep inside, and she felt a quick rush of fear.

"You think I'm lying? Why don't you ask Maeve?" Edward asked, stepping forward.

Lily felt as if he'd punched her in the stomach. He knew Maeve was in a coma.

"Come on, Lily. Let's go upstairs and see Maeve," Patrick said, taking her arm.

Lily nodded, still watching Edward. As she backed away, he tracked her with his eyes.

"Stay away, Edward," Patrick said. "There's an investigation going on."

"I think I *will* stay away," Edward said, staring at Lily. "I have something better to do. Someone better to visit."

Lily wanted to spring at him, but suddenly he turned and walked away fast. Lily made a small sound—something between fear and frustration—and Patrick looked down at her.

"What was that all about?" Patrick asked.

"He saw Rose today," Lily said. "This morning. He followed me to Rhode Island last night. I thought I saw a car, but then it seemed to disappear. I was so excited about seeing Rose and Liam, I just wasn't paying enough attention." She raised her hands to her head, twisted them into her hair. "After all these years I led him straight to her."

"How do you know he saw her?"

"Someone stopped to talk to Rose, out in the yard. Liam told me he thought it was Edward—and Edward just told me he'd seen 'a girl with green eyes.'"

"Playing a game with you," Patrick said, eyes narrowing.

"What's he going to do?" Lily asked.

Patrick shrugged. "I don't like this, that's for sure. It haunted me for years, wondering what he did to you. And now, knowing Marisa, I see it even more. There's something in that man that made two women like you run as far as they could."

"Is what you said true? About his fingerprints?" Lily asked.

Patrick shook his head. "Nah. But his reaction was interesting, wasn't it? The point is, the police don't want him anywhere near Maeve. I'll call them." He looked down at Lily. "You know what I noticed? He called you Lily so easily."

She nodded, her pulse still racing.

"He knew you as Mara. It's harder for me to get used to your new name, and I wasn't married to you."

"I know," she said, staring into Patrick's bright blue eyes. "You see, he wouldn't have any problem with that. A changed name. Everything is interchangeable to him. Names, people, wives. Me, Marisa. Nothing is real to him, none of it matters. Not even Rose."

"No, I suppose not. He's left a lot of wreckage in his wake," Patrick said. "He got right in there, took what he wanted. Cops learn all about the statistics, all about emotional abuse, and how women who are more educated, or make more money than their husbands, are more likely to suffer it. But meeting you and Marisa . . . really woke me up."

"Emotional abuse," she said, an earthquake sending shock waves through her bones. The phrase—language—seemed so subtle, so polite, so *nothing,* compared to the reality of living through it.

"He took everything he could from you," Patrick said. "Got his hooks into you—heart, soul, and pocketbook."

"I know," Lily said. "I could never figure out where his paychecks were going. One night I dreamed he had a double life."

"Maeve had us check out that possibility," Patrick said wryly.

"Really?" Lily asked, remembering the desperate conversations she had had with her grandmother.

"Those trips he took," Patrick said.

Lily nodded. Hawthorne was an affluent town, and Edward had told her he had to cultivate business by visiting clients at their other houses. Some of them wintered in Naples or Palm Beach; the Ocean Reef Club in Key Largo; Aspen or Taos. Some had summer places in Edgartown, Sag Harbor, or Nantucket. "Edward was always flying off," she said.

"We never found much evidence of business he actually did in those places," Patrick said.

Lily glanced up, her heart kicking over.

"What?" he asked.

She looked away, wondering whether to tell him or not, remembering her state of mind back then.

"Go ahead," he said. "I want to hear."

"Once I was cleaning out the garage," she said. "I found an old pair of golf shoes. Really old, and mildewed, ones he never wore. He kept his good ones in a closet in the apartment. I started to throw them away, and something rattled inside. It was an earring."

"Not one of yours?" Patrick asked.

She shook her head, slowly, spinning back, as if in a dream.

"No. I held it in my hand. . . . It wasn't valuable or anything. Just cheap silver metal, with rhinestones."

"Did you ask him about it?"

"Yes. He said he had no idea where it came from. But his eyes—" She shuddered. "His eyes turned black, as if he had a monster inside. He was furious that I'd found the earring."

"What did you do?"

"I threw out the old shoe, and the earring." She dug her nails into her palms, so Patrick couldn't see. She had been so scared, at such a deep level. She had never let the thoughts come into shape until she got away from Edward, until she'd run away to Nova Scotia.

"Did you ever find another earring?"

"Yes. In the toe of the same golf shoes. He must have dug them out of the garbage after I threw them out. I came across them in the back of the closet, on his side with all his old sneakers. There were three mismatched earrings in there. The original one with rhinestones, and two others. All pierced, dangling. Only one of them was made of real gold. The others were costume jewelry."

"Did you think he was having affairs?" Patrick asked. "When he went away on those trips?"

Lily shook her head, tears flooding her eyes. "No," she said. "I thought he was killing women."

Patrick's silence was deafening, but his eyes were so kind. After a minute, he handed her his handkerchief.

"I'm so sorry," he said, "for how scared you have been."

Lily buried her face in her hands.

"He's very careful and methodical," Patrick said. "We looked into every trip he took, every city he visited. He had an explanation for everything."

"Everything?"

Patrick paused. "There was nothing we could nail him for, Lily. Let's just say he has a nasty history."

"Patrick, what if he comes after Rose?" Lily asked.

Patrick glanced over, surprise in his blue eyes. "What do you mean?" he asked.

"I mean, what if he decides he wants her in his life? What if he decides to try for custody?"

Patrick blinked slowly. His gaze was gentle, but he seemed to be looking at Lily as if he thought she were kidding, or half mad.

"It's not 'if,' Lily," he said softly. "It's 'when.' You know that, don't you?"

Chapter 10

Probable Cause rocked in the wake of a passing cabin cruiser, causing Patrick to bump against the chart table. He glared at the cruiser's transom, tempted to untie the lines and go charging after it and tell the captain to slow down. The truth was, he'd been feeling pent up for days.

Seeing Edward at the hospital had just made things worse—knowing what Lily had experienced and was still going through, and realizing that Marisa was still in exile so far north, far from her home and worried about her sister. He really wished he'd been able to nail that creep on something, years ago. He hated the fact that Lily and her family were in limbo, waiting for the other shoe to drop.

His cell phone rang, and he answered.

"Hello?" he said.

"Patrick Murphy, was I surprised to hear from you!"

"Jim Hanley?"

"You bet. How are you?"

"I'm great, Jim. Retired now."

"Catching fish instead of bad guys?" Jim asked, laughing.

"That's about the extent of it," Patrick said. "How about you?"

"Oh, working a fraud case," Jim said, and they talked shop for a while. They'd met eight years ago when Jim had apprehended a Connecticut robbery suspect. Patrick had been the lead detective, and Jim had done his best to get the suspect sent back to New London with as little fanfare as possible. The two of them had worked well together.

"Sorry it took me so long to get back to you on your message," Jim said finally, "but I wanted to check things out. To be honest, I thought I'd gotten it wrong the first time—your message said Samantha Mahon was still in Peru—"

"That's right. Traveling with Global Care, from the university . . ."

"I called over there, they wouldn't talk to me," Jim said. "So I looked Samantha up in the phone book, took a ride over to her house. She lives in a two-family house, not far from the hospital."

"What do you mean—she was there?"

"That's right. Just came from seeing her today. She got back from Peru a week ago."

Patrick's stomach fell. That was before he'd talked to Marisa—her sister had returned home and not even told her. He thought of Marisa and Jessica checking e-mail, feeling excited about the possibility of Sam heading up to Cape Hawk when she returned to the States, and here she'd been back a week already.

"What did she say to you?" he asked.

"Not much," Jim said. "I pretty much had to tell her the truth, to explain why Baltimore PD cared about her whereabouts."

"Yeah? What'd you tell her?"

"That her sister was worried enough about her to send the cops. I told her she should give her sister a call."

"How did she react?"

"She said something strange," Jim said, pausing.

"What?"

"She said that her sister was lost. And then she closed the door in my face."

"Wow," Patrick said. "That's cold."

"Yeah. Family feuds are weird things. That's what it sounded like to me. You want her address and number, or do you just want to give it a rest?"

"Why don't you give it to me?" Patrick said, writing it down. "And while you're at it, why don't you keep tomorrow night free? We can go to some crab place on the harbor, and you can tell me about your fraud case."

"You've got a hankering for crabs?" Jim asked.

"I've got a friend who misses her sister," Patrick said. "And she isn't lost at all. See you tomorrow."

Lily sat at her grandmother's bedside. The air-conditioning hummed, the monitors beeped, and the lights were dim. The nurse had asked her to leave, telling her visiting hours were over, but something in Lily's face had made the nurse leave the room, gently closing the door behind her.

Holding Maeve's hand, Lily tried to will her awake. She needed her so much. She needed help in knowing what to do. One man had done so much harm to Lily and this woman she loved like a mother. And now he was setting his sights on Rose.

"Granny," Lily said, "please wake up. I need you."

Maeve stirred, her mouth twitching. Lily could almost believe she was listening, trying to come out of her deep sleep. What had Edward done to her?

Seeing Edward again had left her feeling frayed and raw. In spite of Patrick's assurance that he would not bother her here, that police were keeping an eye on him, she jumped at footsteps in the hallway, and when shadows fell across the door to Maeve's room.

He was so good at convincing people that he was good and kind, she could imagine him talking his way past the nurses. At one time, he had made her feel so safe. The way he had held her at night, stroking her hair, wanting to hear about her family, her upbringing, her terrible sadness at losing her parents.

She remembered lying in his bed in the apartment he rented in Hawthorne, the week after they'd returned from Washington, right after Christmas. He had listened, holding her. She'd talked about painting and needlepointing canvases with pictures that told stories.

Images of the shoreline—the Connecticut Impressionists at their easels by the banks of the Lieutenant River; children playing on the beach at Hubbard's Point; sailboats frostbiting in Hawthorne Harbor.

"I just love telling stories, and doing the work," she'd said. "Especially, I love the people I meet."

"I hope they pay you what you're worth," he'd said.

He'd drawn her out, getting her to admit she earned a good living, printing her canvases and selling them to fine gift shops up and down the East Coast, from Bar Harbor to Palm Beach.

He was a stockbroker at Connecticut–Wall Street Associates. Although he had worked at several places after graduating from Harvard, this firm was the best, he said. He had wealthy clients who treated him like a friend—or even a son.

"I coach Little League too," he said. "And basketball. Trying to give kids some of the . . ." He paused, kissing her forehead in a thoughtful way. "Let's just say, some of the advantages I never had."

"But you went to Harvard," she said.

He laughed. "On a baseball and rugby scholarship," he said. "My parents couldn't have afforded it otherwise. Believe me, the only college my parents ever saw was the one where my mother mopped floors. My father's institution of higher learning was Somers Prison."

"I'm so sorry," she said, shocked.

"Well, it taught me where I didn't want to go in life," he said, kissing her head again. "And my father's chaplain was a great guy—he used to sort of mentor me while my father was 'unavailable.' Showed me that service is the only way to go in life—helping others, you find your own way."

"That's such a wonderful attitude," Mara said.

"My life hasn't been easy," Edward said, rolling over so he could look straight into her eyes. She remembered the sweetness in his gaze, the all-consuming love she felt flowing from him into her. "I was beaten when I was young, Mara. I won't tell you the details—I want to spare you them."

"Edward!"

"I would never, ever hurt a soul," he said, stroking her cheek so tenderly, as if she was the most precious person in the world to him. "That's what my childhood taught me. To show love, and be gentle."

"You *are* gentle," she'd said.

He nodded. "I want to be even more so," he said. "Help show me how?"

"I don't have to," she said, so touched by his openness and honesty. She had always kept her own pain locked deep inside, but now she told him about her parents' drowning.

"We've both been through a lot," he'd said, his mouth pressed into her neck. She felt his cheeks, moist against her skin, and she sensed him trying to keep from breaking down. "I've never met anyone who understands me the way you do. It's as if we were meant to be together."

His words made her wonder. Was this what love was like? Letting your guard down and maybe beginning to have faith that the world was not such a bad place after all?

"I love you," he had said.

And the words were out before Mara could even think about holding them back—"I love you too." The first time she had ever said them to a man.

"I want to be with you forever," he said.

Mara felt a shiver—between thrill and fear—down her spine. Wasn't he moving a little too fast?

He had a photograph on his apartment wall—a beautiful old sepia-toned photo, of a whaling ship covered with ice. Tall cliffs rose behind it, everything glittering in ice. The ship's name, *The Pinnacle*, was lettered on the transom. Mara stared at the picture—this image of endless, brutal winter, and wondered whether two people could keep each other warm and happy in life.

"My great-grandfather's whaling ship," he said, following her gaze.

"Really?"

He nodded, gazing at the picture, as if it were a window into another, better world. "He was the captain—I'm named after him. Back in the early nineteenth century, our family was very wealthy, respected by everyone. Edward Hunter was an adventurer and an explorer. On some maps, it shows that there are straits near Tierra del Fuego named after him."

"That's incredible," she said.

"I let him be my guide sometimes," he said. "When I'm feeling overwhelmed, I just think of him at the helm, steering through terrible ice in the Arctic. I don't know what happened to our family. We were so respected—and then we crashed somehow. I actually feel sorry for my parents. But my North Star is him—Captain Edward Hunter."

"That's how I feel about my grandmother."

"Take me to meet her," he said.

She held him, trying to get her pulse to slow down. Granny had been saying the same thing. She'd been so thrilled to know that Mara had met someone—and relieved to know that he lived locally, in Hawthorne, just up the Connecticut River Valley from Black Hall, instead of far away.

"I'm not good enough for her, right?" he asked, pulling back.

"Of course you are."

"Because I'm a stockbroker and I went to Harvard, and because my great-grandfather was a sea captain?"

She laughed, kissing his lips. "No," she said. "Because you're a good person."

His reaction rocked her—his eyes filled, as if no one had ever said that to him before. He held her so tight, she could hardly breathe.

"You believe in me," he said. "That means everything to me."

"I'm glad," she said, feeling overwhelmed and unsure.

"I want us to be together forever," he murmured. "Till we go into the ground together."

The phrase had chilled her. Yet she'd ignored her own inner sense of alarm, telling herself it meant that he loved her, that his feelings for her went beyond anything she had yet known.

There were so many ways she had sold herself out. Ignoring small things, telling herself they didn't matter, even that first day when she'd seen the cold fury in his eyes at the airport taxi stand.

Now, staring at her grandmother sleeping in her hospital bed, Lily thought of how quickly everything had happened, and how often she had pushed away big and small warning signs. Like how often he left his jobs, how the intervals between them grew longer and longer. How, after a while, it seemed easier to just put his name on her accounts than to keep giving him money to pay the bills.

Like his comment at their wedding: *White roses bruise so easily.*

Patrick had mentioned Edward's nasty history. Lily knew about his pattern of violence toward women all too well. On their wedding night, Edward told her about an old girlfriend, Judy Houghton. They hadn't exactly lived together, but he stayed with her most nights. She'd had a big old Victorian house in Haddam, inherited from her great-aunt. Judy had gone out one night, to the Hawthorne Inn. When she came home, Edward said he smelled another man on her. She got angry at him for accusing her, and he punched her.

"Oh my God," Mara said, covering her mouth with her hand.

"Her jaw was broken. Her mother called the police on me. It was between me and Judy, but her mother was always getting involved. She didn't understand, Mara. She never understood any of it, but she was always sticking her nose in. It was her interfering that broke us up."

"But Edward—" Mara hardly knew where to start. Why had Edward never even mentioned Judy until now? And why would he tell her this story on their wedding night?

"I would never do that to you," he said, soothing her, brushing her hair back from her eyes. "Please don't worry, or be scared. You're nothing like Judy."

"Edward—no matter what she did, she didn't deserve to be punched!"

His eyes had flickered—she saw just a hint of the blackness she'd spotted at their first meeting. "She cheated on me," he said.

"But still. If a man ever hit me, ever laid one hand on me—I would leave him," she said. "In one second flat."

Edward had gazed at her, long and slow. She felt almost like a fly being eyed by a lizard trying to decide whether to eat her or not. But then the spell broke. He smiled. Thinking of his smiles now, she saw that he had a repertoire—should he pull out the flashy boyish grin, or the slow seductive melting lip twist? This was somewhere in between— détente. A peace accord.

The line in the sand had been drawn.

Edward had let her know that he had fists, and would use them if provoked. She had let Edward know that if he used them on her, she would be out the door.

Important information for both sides. Unfortunately for Mara, she had just put Edward on notice. Otherwise, she might have saved herself a lot of trouble. He might just have gotten mad one day and hit her—and Mara would have been out of there before he'd had the chance to do worse. As it was, she'd let him know he had to find sub-tler ways to break her spirit.

Gazing at Maeve now, in her hospital bed, Lily felt a lump in her throat. She had been married to Mr. Hyde. Dr. Jekyll had just been one of his masks. It had taken Lily years to figure out that Edward was chip-ping away at her—so slowly, she barely noticed. He'd found ways to buy time, keep her on the string, throw her little bits of hope so she'd stay another day, week, month, year. How had she ever stayed stupid for so long?

Lily knew that Liam was taking care, keeping watch over Rose. Patrick's words, *It's not "if," it's "when,"* rang in her ears. She had brought the people she loved into the same danger that she had known so long ago. And she didn't know what she could do to protect them. Especially Rose, her Rose.

Chapter 11

Driving down to Baltimore, Patrick kept the windows open and let the wind keep him cool. He had left Flora at the boatyard with Angelo, his friend and sometime dog sitter, because he wasn't sure how long his investigation would take, and he didn't want to leave her shut up in the car. But he missed her company, so when his cell phone rang, he was happy to hear Liam's voice.

"Any more signs of Edward?" Patrick asked.

"Not since that one time," Liam said. "I haven't let Rose out of my sight."

"Good," Patrick said.

"I want to be with Lily in Hubbard's Point," Liam said. "But she thinks that keeping Rose away is somehow safer."

"She might be right," Patrick said. "Edward can't be in two places at once. I think the reason he was at the hospital that day is that he's nervous about Maeve coming out of the coma. She's making progress, and he has to be afraid she'll talk."

"Is there any evidence he was involved?"

"One partial fingerprint on the hot-water heater. It will be interesting to hear what Maeve has to say about what was going on right before she collapsed."

"Do you think she'll wake up, Patrick?"

Patrick drove in silence for a few seconds. He pictured Maeve's bright, determined eyes, thought of the way she protected Lily's secret so selflessly these last nine years. "Don't count her out," he said quietly.

"I hope you're right," Liam said. "For Lily's sake."

"I know. They were very close; this has to be incredibly hard on her. Especially having to worry now about what Edward plans to do about Rose. I think you should stay where you are for now. Just keep a close watch on her. Don't let him near her."

"Don't worry," Liam said sharply. "He'd better not try. Besides, we've spent most of our time on the water, in a friend's boat. In fact, that's one reason I'm calling."

"What is it?"

"There's a guy from Cape Hawk," Liam said. "Gerard Lafarge. He's a fisherman with a bad reputation for netting dolphins and whales. There's an oceanographic anomaly going on here in Rhode Island— big ocean waves pulling in lots of unusual species, lots of activity. . . ."

"Not just in Rhode Island," Patrick said, thinking of how he'd seen thousands of small fish break the water's surface of his normally quiet cove.

"Lafarge isn't fishing, and there's no law against him cruising the area," Liam said. "But he's here for a reason, and I want to know what it is."

"Have you called up to Cape Hawk?" Patrick asked.

"Yes—I've asked my cousin, but he doesn't know anything."

As the Baltimore skyline rose into view, Patrick signaled to get off the highway. He glanced down at the seat beside him, trying to read the address Jim had offered up. "Look," he said. "There's a chance I'll be heading up to Cape Hawk myself in just a few days. If I do get up there, I'll see what I can find out."

"I'd really appreciate that," Liam said. "Are you going to the ceili?"

"If things work out," Patrick said, following Jim's directions, "I'll be delivering one of the musicians."

Liam thanked him, and they said goodbye.

Once Patrick got off I-95, he began to smell the salt water. He thought about how Marisa had basically followed the Atlantic coastline her whole life. From Newport down here to Baltimore, then north again, through Boston, and up to Cape Hawk. Patrick was the same way, feeling most alive when he was breathing salt air. It spurred him on now as he wound his way through the narrow streets.

He found the address Jim Hanley had given him, drove around the block until he found a parking space. The neighborhood was behind the hospital, and he heard a siren in the distance, getting closer. The frame houses were two-family, neatly kept, with small yards and front porches. Kids played on the sidewalk, and older people sat on the stoops. Patrick walked up the front sidewalk of 64 Fish Street, up the steps, and knocked on the door.

Waiting a few minutes, he felt his heart pounding, just the way it always had when he was on a case and the stakes were very high. He tried to peer through a crack in the curtains at the door window. They were lace, pretty. Although many other houses on the street had gardens or window boxes, this one didn't. He figured that if Sam traveled a lot, she didn't have time to tend flowers.

When she didn't come to the door, he went back to his car. Jim had said six at the Crab Claw, and Patrick was a little early. He drove around the city a little, heading toward the hospital. This was where Marisa had gotten her start as a nurse, he knew. He looked up at the big brick building, wondering how many people she had helped in there.

Maybe Sam was back at work, here in the city. He wondered what had happened between the two sisters, what he was doing here—this was really none of his business. But he couldn't forget the look in Marisa's eyes, when he'd been up in Cape Hawk, and the sound of her voice, singing that song to him over the telephone line, and he just kept driving.

The Crab Claw sat right on the Inner Harbor. Patrick parked and walked down the cobblestone streets, into the raucous bar. He scanned the scene, saw Jim sitting with another man at a table on the deck. Making his way through the crowd, he saw who it was—Jack O'Brien, the assistant district attorney who had helped him with his case several years ago.

"Hey, Patrick, great to see you," Jim said.

"You too," Patrick said, shaking hands. "And, Jack—how are you?"

"Fine, Pat," Jack said. "Jim told me you were in town, so I thought I'd join in. It's been a long time. What's this I hear about you retiring?"

"The time had come," Patrick said, grinning. "Too much police work, not enough life." They caught up on the case they had shared, Patrick telling them that the suspect they'd caught was still in Somers, doing fifteen years for bank robbery. They asked him about Mara Jameson, and he filled them in on how she had returned as if from the dead. The waiter came and took their order, and Patrick sipped his Coke, watching boats in the harbor.

"So, you're retired," Jim said, "but you're still doing police work."

"Not really," Patrick said. "I'm just looking for a friend's sister."

"Yeah, Jim tells me you're looking for one of the Mahon girls," Jack said. "The Fallen Angels."

"You know them?"

"I did. And I remember their music even now—fifteen years later. They played in a pub just around the corner from the courthouse. Half the cops and lawyers were in love with them. Sam went out with a friend of mine for a little while, right after Patty first moved away."

Patrick did his best to interview his old friend as subtly as possible. Sam Mahon had stayed on staff at Johns Hopkins after graduation, heading up a team of nurses that would travel to South America, Africa, and the Far East as they were needed and funding would allow.

"She missed her sister a lot," Jack said. "I remember that so well. They'd been inseparable. Sam had come to Johns Hopkins because her big sister was already here. They were really close. So when Patty got married and moved to Boston, Sam had a tough time."

"She didn't play music after that?" Patrick asked.

"Not unless her sister came back to visit. They had a few reunion shows. Everyone loved them."

"What happened?" Patrick asked.

"I don't know. Patty's first husband died, and she married someone else—too soon, maybe. He was a jerk, I think. Sam didn't like him, didn't like what he was doing to her sister."

"Did he beat her?" Jim asked.

Patrick sipped his Coke. Cops always asked that—"Did he beat her?" As if the only damage could be done with fists. "No," Patrick said.

"That's right, you know her," Jack said.

"Yes," Patrick said. "She's the reason I'm here. She misses her sister. There's a music festival up in Nova Scotia, and she's trying to get Sam to come up and play with her."

"That's something I'd like to hear," Jack said. "I'm married now, two kids, happy and settled down. But there was something about hearing those two sing that made men turn stupid and go crazy. . . ." He slid a tape across the table to Patrick.

"What's this?"

"It's a bootleg tape of a Saint Paddy's Day show they did at the Blarney Stone, many years ago now. I've had it since then, but my wife doesn't like me to play it. She thinks the sisters sound too sexy for her husband to be listening to. Why don't you take it?"

"Thanks," Patrick said, slipping it into his shirt pocket.

As seagulls cried overhead, the waiter delivered their dinners. Platters of hard-shell crabs, baskets of french fries, and coleslaw. The three men cracked the crabs with mallets, talking about their lives, families, and cases. When they'd finished, Patrick thanked them for everything, said he hoped he'd see them sooner the next time.

He drove back to 64 Fish Street, listening to the tape Jack had given him. Beautiful, haunting notes played on a pair of fiddles . . . and then the sisters' voices singing "Cliffs of Dooneen."

God, his knees went weak. The breeze blew in his hair through the car's open window. Marisa's voice sang harmony with her sister's. It trembled with emotion, and he felt she was with him now, whispering the sweet, romantic lyrics right into his ear. The recording quality was pretty bad—someone must have taped it right there in the crowded bar. The sound of glasses clinking and people talking came through, but nothing could block that strain of pure longing in her voice.

She might well be singing about Cape Hawk—the cliffs, the mountains, the foam. He could almost see her standing in her cottage door, feel her in his arms. How would she feel if he was able to convince Sam to come? He wanted to do that for her. . . .

Finding a parking spot a block away, he popped the tape out and stuck it in his pocket for luck. Then he walked up the steps to Sam's house again. This time there were lights on inside. When he knocked, he heard footsteps.

After a few seconds, a woman opened the door. Her hair was soft, golden red, much lighter than Marisa's. But Patrick would have known her anywhere; the family resemblance was in the eyes—kind, curious, and full of good humor.

"Hello," she said.

"Hi," he said. "I'm Patrick Murphy."

"A good Irish name." She smiled.

"You're Samantha Mahon?" he asked.

"Yep, that's me. What can I do for you?"

"I was hoping you could play me some Celtic music," he said.

She laughed, but looked a little skeptical. "Time was, maybe I would have, but not now. Do I know you from somewhere?"

"You don't know me," he said.

"Then—" she said.

"I'm a friend of your sister's," he said.

"Is she okay? Is Gracie?" The question flew out, almost before she could think.

"They're fine," he said. "Although I think of Gracie as Jessica."

Her smile went away. She studied him, her green eyes narrowing. Her jaw was clenched, and she had one hand on the door, ready to close it.

"Why are you here?" she asked.

"Because she wants you to come up to Nova Scotia—Cape Hawk," he said. "She thinks you're still in Peru, and she's sitting by her computer waiting for you to send her an e-mail from the back of beyond."

"That's between me and my sister," she said, emotion rising in her face. "You'd better go now."

"Please, Sam."

Her hand was firmly on the door, and she'd pulled it nearly closed. She was behind it, and he couldn't see her face. He heard her breathing, high and rapid. He could almost feel her trying to decide.

"Are you her boyfriend?" she asked.

Patrick felt surprised by the pointed question. "No," he said. "Just a friend."

She hesitated, but for some reason, that tipped the balance. She opened the door, and he walked in.

The living room was small, with a sofa and two chairs. She gestured for him to sit in one of the chairs, and she took the other. He watched her perch on the edge, as if she hadn't really committed to sitting yet. He gazed around the room, decorated with bright blankets and banners, obviously from her travels. A violin case lay on top of the bookshelf.

There were framed photos on one wall, and he scanned them and saw several of Marisa. Patrick took a deep breath and looked Sam in the eye.

"You and your sister used to live here together?" he asked, remembering what Jack had said.

"Yes. This was her apartment first." She pointed at a small mahogany table, some brass candlesticks, a crystal owl. "That was our grandmother's silver chest. The candlesticks and owl were Patty's—she bought them when she first moved in, to make her apartment feel grown-up and cozy. I moved to Baltimore to be with her. I became a nurse because of her."

"You were inspired by your big sister."

"Yes."

"She misses you, Sam."

Sam looked down at her feet; Patrick watched her composing herself and realized how much she resembled Marisa: the shape of her face, oval with high cheekbones and pale, freckled skin. Green eyes, a wide, expressive mouth. But where Marisa's hair was dark, reddish brown, Sam's was bright copper.

"I know you mean well," Sam said. "But you really don't understand."

"Can you tell me?"

She tilted her head, opened her mouth. For a second he thought she was going to tell him it was none of his business. But she didn't.

"How can I explain it," she began, "to someone who didn't know her before, who didn't know what she used to be like? She was like a one-woman high-wire act. You should have seen her—working the ER by day, bringing down the house by night. She was so talented—this'll sound weird, if you're not in the field, but she could get an IV line in a vein and the patient wouldn't even feel it. She could comfort the littlest kids, make them smile even while the doc was stitching them up. She loved everyone she treated, and they loved her."

Patrick listened. He pictured Marisa's smile, and he could believe it.

"She helped found Horizon House, right around the corner from the hospital. It's health care for low-income women and kids. People who can't afford the kind of help they need." Sam looked down, seeming to study her shoes for a long time. When she looked up, her eyes were glittering. "I was so proud of her for that," she said.

"Is that why you do the kind of work you do?" he asked.

"Someone has to," she said, letting the rest of the sentence hang in the air.

"Because Marisa doesn't?" he asked.

She let out something between a snort and a laugh. "'Marisa,'" she said. "That nickname used to make us smile. Bono gave it to her in Paris, one drunken night."

"But that's not why she uses it now," Patrick said.

"No, it's not," Sam said. "It's her alias. Want to know the biggest irony? A lot of what Horizon House does is geared toward helping abused women. My sister knew all about the dynamic, and it happened to her anyway."

"Is that what you can't forgive her for?" Patrick asked. The question sounded harsh, even to his ears, and Sam looked as if she'd been slapped.

"You don't know anything," she said. "You don't know my sister and me, the way we used to be." Her face was bright red, her eyes pooling with tears.

"Then tell me," he said. "Please?"

"We were so close," Sam said, her face still flushed. "We'd tell each other everything. If I needed her, she'd be on the next train. When Paul—her first husband—died, I took a month's leave, to go up and stay with her and Gracie. They needed me—and I needed them. I loved Paul as if he were my brother." She held in a sob, turning her head.

Patrick sat still, watching her walk over to the wall of pictures, taking down and handing him one of Marisa as a bride, Sam as her maid of honor. The man with Marisa had to be Paul—tall, blond, full of life and joy. Then Sam handed him another—of Sam and her sister holding a baby between them.

"My niece," she said, wiping her eyes. "I loved her as if she were my own. I'm her godmother, and no one ever took that role more seriously."

"I'm sure that's true," Patrick said, watching her stare at the picture.

"After Paul died, my sister was so vulnerable. She was really almost out of her mind—I know, because I was there. Everything was too much for her. That's why I had to stay for a month. She had this investment advisor—"

"Edward Hunter," Patrick said.

Sam looked up, shocked. "We called him Ted. You know him?"

"Yes. I was a detective, and he was a suspect in one of my cases."

"Then I don't need to tell you."

"Nope. You don't."

"He was a user. I held back from telling her what I thought—because she seemed so happy. He was there—right time, right place. She told me he was helping her pick up the pieces. Instead, she shattered into a million more."

"She wouldn't listen to you?"

"She wouldn't even *talk* to me."

Patrick watched the fire return to her green eyes. They flashed with anger as she stared down at the picture of her sister and niece. "He took her away from me," Sam said. "First she stopped calling me. Then she began dodging my calls. Grace would phone me, tell me that her mother was in bed crying. I'd say put her on, but Patty wouldn't take my call. When I'd finally get through to her, she'd say everything was great—she was fine, Ted was wonderful, they were all so happy. I wanted to throw up."

"You must have been really worried."

"Worried and frustrated. Angry. I actually considered going up and getting Gracie out of there. I am her godmother, after all."

"Maybe that wouldn't have been such a bad idea."

"After a while, my sister wouldn't let me near her. She was so busy protecting Ted. It was a nightmare."

"I'm sure it was for her too," Patrick said.

Sam gave him a long, hard look. "She made her choices."

"That coming from you?" he asked.

"What do you mean?"

"A world health nurse," he said. "Who cares about the well-being of women. What about your sister?"

"The sister I knew and adored disappeared. She doesn't exist anymore."

"How do you know?" Patrick asked. "You haven't seen her in a long time."

"I can't stand to see her," Sam said. "It's too hard, seeing a woman who's afraid of her own shadow. And teaching her daughter to be afraid of hers."

"That's what trauma will do to people," Patrick said. "That's why they need their loved ones around, to help them get better. I hear that music is a really good way to get through to the other side."

Sam shook her head. Patrick recognized the stubbornness of a fellow redhead.

"The Cape Hawk ceili is supposed to be great. There's a fierce competition, and your sister wants to enter. Is that how a woman afraid of her own shadow would act?"

"I'm not going," Sam said.

Patrick took a deep breath. He could see that she was dug in to her position, and he knew better than to argue. Standing up, taking one last look at the picture of her sister, he looked up at her again.

"Got a tape deck?" he asked.

"Why?"

He just tilted his head, and she shrugged. He reached into his pocket, handed her the tape. She pushed PLAY, and suddenly the room was filled with music and fallen angels:

> You may travel far,
> Far from your own native home,
> Far away o'er the mountains,
> Far away o'er the foam,
> But of all the fine places I've ever been,
> Oh, there's none can compare
> With the cliffs of Dooneen.

Patrick watched tears spill from her eyes, and he felt them in his own. He wondered if she was remembering the night she and her sister had sung those words. He knew she was hearing the harmony between them, and he saw her eyes slide to the photo, and then to her fiddle.

Clearing his throat, Patrick handed her his card.

"If you change your mind," he said, "I'm driving up in a few days."

"Thank you," she said, taking the card, placing it on the table. She didn't smile, and she didn't even glance at it.

Patrick wanted to ask her for the tape back, but she didn't offer. He figured she needed it more. They said goodbye, and as Patrick walked down the steps, he could almost feel her eyes on the back of his head. Behind him, the music rose into the night, and Patrick could still hear it, even as he drove away.

Chapter 12

Right after Lily got home that evening, she took a swim. The salt water washed over her, cooling her skin and easing her mind. In the bay, she felt connected to Liam and Rose. She bobbed in the small waves, imagining that they must have come from the east, from the Atlantic. They must have passed Rhode Island.

Small fish bumped her legs, but she didn't even flinch. Maybe they were part of the Ghost Hills phenomenon. Maybe they were harbingers of Nanny—Lily closed her eyes and thought that if only she could see Rose's beloved beluga, everything would be fine. She needed something as magical as Nanny to make her believe that all would be well.

She climbed out and toweled off, then sat on the porch steps. Hearing voices, she felt her heart skip. She knew that Edward would return—it was just a matter of time. But glancing through the trellis, she saw Bay and Tara coming down the steps, through the rose garden. They were dressed in shorts and sneakers, and they carried tennis rackets.

"Time to test that backhand," Tara called. "Do you still have your racket?"

"It's nearly dark out," Lily said.

"One of the big changes since you left Hubbard's Point," Bay said, "is lights at the tennis courts."

"Come on," Tara said. "No excuses. Let's go play."

Lily stared at the water. She felt so ragged tonight, after keeping vigil for Maeve, who just wouldn't wake up; she missed her child so badly, her bones ached. And she missed Liam, her only true love, with every breath in her body. She couldn't leave the house again.

"I can't," she said.

"Lily, if there's any change with Maeve," Tara said, "the hospital will call your cell phone. So will Liam, if Rose needs you."

If Rose needs you . . . Lily knew that Rose needed her all the time, just as Lily needed Rose. What was she doing, apart from the people she loved?

"We don't have to play long," Bay said. "Just half an hour."

"We'll wear you out, so you'll sleep better," Tara said, tugging her arm.

"Okay," Lily said slowly. "Let me get dressed and find my racket." And she did.

The three women hurried down the road with their tennis rackets. Darkness settled on Hubbard's Point, and roses, honeysuckle, and pine scented the salt air. The breeze felt fresh, with a tiny chill to remind them that August was almost over, and September would soon be upon them. Stars twinkled through the branches overhead, and lights had started to come on in the cottages.

With every step, Lily felt younger. Walking the roads of Hubbard's Point, she was a child again. These were her best friends. Her grandmother loved her, and would be watching over her forever. Nothing bad could ever happen.

When they got to the tennis courts, they found them empty. They were old asphalt courts, nothing fancy. Because they were built at the far end of the sandy beach parking lot, they were constantly flooding. The tar would crack, and the beach crew would have to patch it. Tara walked over to a wooden box mounted on a tall pole. She opened the door and flipped a switch. Light flooded down, illuminating the courts.

"Let there be light," Tara said.

"I can't believe the beach sprang for lights," Lily said. "So much has changed from the days when we used to play in the dark. We couldn't even see the ball, but we'd be having too much fun to quit."

"So much has stayed the same, too," Bay said, giving her a quick hug. "We still have fun."

Lily pretended to tie her laces. She didn't want Bay to see her face. Having fun seemed very distant.

"Are we going to play Canadian doubles?" Tara asked. "You and I against Bay?"

"Sure," Lily said. "Whatever you want."

"That's what I want," Tara said, hugging her too, handing her a ball.

Lily jogged to the baseline. The light cast long shadows on the gray court. The lines had been freshly painted, and they gleamed white. Bay bounced the ball on the other side of the net. Somewhere across the swamp, a screech owl cried, a descending trill.

"Are you ready?" Bay asked. "Here it comes."

"Whack the hell out of it," Tara said. "Let the ball have it."

Bay hit, and the ball bounced, and Lily swung her racket. She connected, and the ball sailed back. Bay hit, now to Tara. *Thwack,* the ball returned. Lily's heart pounded. She crouched, ready for her turn.

Tennis came back to her in ten seconds or less. She hadn't played in over nine years, since before Rose was born. How many times had she and her friends played on this very court, hitting the ball until their arms were so tired they couldn't move? Lily had loved the game. She had played in the beach Labor Day tournament nearly every year. She had played in high school, been the number three singles player at Black Hall High.

Thwack, thwack.

She had been in discussions with a New York publisher about launching her own needlepoint magazine, and she had planned a tennis issue. A way to bring women readers, athletes, and needlepointers together. It would have been for spring, April or May. She had envisioned a racket and yellow ball. There would have been interviews with top women players inside. A story about women friends who'd grown up playing tennis together.

Thwack.

Lily stood on the baseline. The ball came, and she hit it hard. It returned, and she hit it harder. Her legs burned. Bay put the ball nearly in the alley, and Lily got to it, hit a backhand. It fired over the net like a bullet. She gritted her teeth, hitting the next and the next. Bay gave her a lob, she put it away. The ball came back, and Lily sent it to the far corner. Bay returned fire, and Lily stuck her racket out.

Tara had stepped off the court. It belonged to Lily now. She smashed every shot she could. She had power in her arm, and it flowed into her racket. *Whack the hell out of it,* Tara had said, and that's what Lily was doing.

She was whacking the hell out of everything Edward had done to her, taken from her. Every hit was for Rose and Maeve. For Liam. For every dream Lily had ever had. For the life that still beat in her body, in spite of everything he had done to quash it. Lily thought of her magazine that never was, of the years she had missed with her friends, of the fact that Liam and Rose were miles away.

"Go for it, Lily," she heard Tara say now.

Hitting the tennis ball, Lily felt sobs welling up from deep inside. The night was silent, except for the owl's call, the sound of the ball bouncing and hitting their rackets, and the breath tearing from Lily's chest as she fought her way back, trying to become that Hubbard's Point girl of long ago, who used to have so much fun.

Driving back from Baltimore, Patrick was all torn up about what had happened. He had failed on his mission. He felt more dejected with every mile he traveled. He knew he should call Marisa, let her know that at least Sam was safe at home, but he just didn't have the heart. When he got to the Black Hall exit, he turned off the highway and headed down the shore road. Picking up Flora at the boatyard, he drove toward Hubbard's Point—he'd check on Lily for Liam, buy some time before he broke the news.

But when he got to Maeve's place and knocked, no one was home. The car was in the turnaround, a light was on in the kitchen, but Lily didn't answer. Patrick's heart thudded—she had disappeared from here once before. He thought of the thumbprint on the hot-water heater and walked around the house, to try to get into the basement.

Maeve's house was almost like a ship; it sat right on the rock ledge, jutting out into Long Island Sound. Although it was dark, the sky was filled with stars, and the almost-full moon had started to rise in the east. Heading through the rose garden, he saw the damnedest thing. Staring at the dark water, he saw it again: a flash of white.

It rose up from the deep, crested the surface. In the moonlight, it looked shiny and hard, almost like a huge, glistening piece of driftwood. A massive tree trunk, stripped of its bark, polished by months in the waves. But as Patrick leaned closer, he saw that it had eyes. Large, liquid dark eyes that blinked at him.

"Holy shit," Patrick said, jumping back.

Flora started to growl. She ran down to the seawall, just above the tidal pools, pacing back and forth. The sea creature didn't move. Unperturbed by one large Labrador retriever, it just rested on the surface of the water twenty yards out, gazing straight at Patrick.

Flora barked. She dug in her front paws, pointing at the leviathan, barking and howling. Patrick was a fisherman; he often took *Probable Cause* out to the Race, to go after stripers. He had once hooked a prizewinning bluefish that weighed in at close to forty pounds. This monster put anything Patrick had ever caught to shame. It had to be four meters long. And he knew, from having been to Mystic Aquarium and having visited Nova Scotia, that it was a beluga whale.

Beluga whales were native to Cape Hawk. While there a month ago, when he first found Lily and Rose, he had heard the whole story about Nanny. Supposedly she had swum down to Boston while Rose had her heart surgery. Could this be the same damn whale, here in the waters of Hubbard's Point? Was this part of the oceanographic anomaly Liam had spoken about?

Wherever it had come from, it didn't seem in a big hurry to leave. Patrick's heart was beating like a snare drum, so fast he could hardly breathe. Flora, on the other hand, seemed to have made her peace with the whale. She lay on the seawall, panting. The whale rose to the surface, eyes on Patrick.

As Patrick followed the whale, he felt his heart start to calm down. In fact, he felt an ease spread through his body that he hadn't felt in a long time. There was something very beautiful about the animal; its eyes looked almost human, as if there was a soul deep inside. It gave him a sense of peace, and he suddenly knew what he had to do.

Almost without thinking, Patrick reached for his cell phone. He dialed a number that he had rarely called before, but that he had somehow committed to memory.

"Hello?" she said.

"Marisa," he said. "It's Patrick."

"Hi, Patrick," she said.

"I had to call you, Marisa," he said. "I took a drive today."

"Really?" she asked. "Where did you go?"

"Baltimore," he said.

"Oh!" she said, sounding excited. "Where I used to live with Sam. She'll be back there soon, unless she comes straight up here, to the ceili."

"Marisa, I went to see Sam," he said.

"But she's in Peru," Marisa said.

Patrick stared out at the whale. Her dark, sweet eyes gazed out from the gentle waves. He wished he could somehow soften what he had to say. He held the phone with both hands, just as he would have held Marisa's hand.

"She's home," he said.

Marisa was silent for a few long moments. "No," she said.

"I'm sorry," he said. "She got home last week."

"Why didn't she call me?" Marisa whispered.

Patrick heard the shock in her voice. He pictured Sam's face, the emotion in her eyes as she'd talked about how her sister had changed. He couldn't bring himself to tell Marisa. He couldn't stand to think of her being so hurt. "I think she's been pretty busy," he said. "The traveling and all . . ."

"What about Gracie?" Marisa asked, slipping up for the first time since Patrick had met her. "Jessica . . ."

"She told me she's her godmother."

"The only person I would ever trust with my daughter," Marisa said, her voice low and lost.

"I know she loves her," Patrick said. "Loves you both."

"Did she say that?"

"She didn't have to," he said. "Her house is full of you. Pictures everywhere. Your brass candlesticks and crystal owl."

"I thought . . ." Marisa said, then paused for a long minute. "I thought she might have gotten rid of them. I think she wants to forget about me—about me and Jess."

"How can she?" Patrick asked, wishing he could hold her. "No one could forget you, Marisa."

He waited for a few seconds, hearing his words sink in. Did she know how much he thought of her? He wanted to tell her that he wanted to listen to her sing all day and night; that he dreamed about her . . . and that he had wanted so badly to bring her sister back to her.

"It was so kind of you to try . . . you didn't have to do that, go see her," she said. "It means a lot to me. Even if . . ."

"Don't give up hope," Patrick said. "Give her a chance to think things over. She's a redhead, remember? We're stubborn as hell."

She laughed a little, and he felt a smile come to his lips, the happiest he'd felt in days. "What do you think I'm looking at?" he asked.

"I can't imagine."

"A white whale," he said. "Right here, off the coast of Connecticut. Not twenty yards away from where I'm sitting."

"Is it Nanny?" Marisa asked, sounding shocked and thrilled.

"I think so," Patrick said. "But why would she be here?"

"Well, probably because of Rose."

"Because of Rose . . ." Patrick repeated. He watched the whale watching him. It was the oddest sensation, as if she actually knew him. Her eyes blinked in the liquid light. They were dark and eloquent, as if the whale somehow knew what Patrick didn't.

"Yes," Marisa said. "What other explanation could there be?"

"I wonder what Liam would say," Patrick said. "He seems to think there's some kind of oceanographic mystery going on around here."

"Well, I agree with him there. Love is always a mystery," Marisa said.

"Love?" Patrick asked, his heart beating harder.

"Why shouldn't it be love? Whales are mammals. They make connections and feel bonds, just the way we do."

Patrick couldn't quite speak, listening to her gentle voice.

"I'm a nurse," she said. "I've studied anatomy. There are plenty of physical similarities. Why not emotional ones?"

Patrick frowned. He had seen the kind of connections humans made. He'd been at many crime scenes where husbands had killed wives, wives had killed husbands, parents had killed children. He had seen every possible permutation of hurt and evil known to mankind. His divorce had left him bitter and afraid to believe in love, yet talking to Marisa filled him with the strangest feeling of peace.

"You don't believe me," she said.

"I want to . . ." he said, trailing off.

"Is she still there?" Marisa asked.

"The whale? Yes," he said, peering into the dark water. There she was, just resting on the surface. The waves and incoming tide would move her toward shore, and she would circle around, just so she could stay facing him. The rising moon cast a silver net all around her, but she was unfettered and free, and just rode the waves.

"Patrick?" Marisa asked after a few seconds.

"I'm here," he said. He stared out over the water. A few fine clouds had blown in, covering the bright moon with gossamer folds. He was afraid the whale might be too hard to see, with the light slightly dimmed, but she was still there.

"Thank you for today," Marisa said. "For going to see Sam."

"You're welcome."

"I just wish . . ." Marisa said.

"What?"

"I just wish you were both coming here," she said. "You and Sam. To the ceili." Then, as if she couldn't speak anymore, she said goodbye quickly, and hung up the phone.

Patrick sat on the porch steps, trying to catch his breath. She had just said she wished he were coming . . . Sam, but him too. He bowed his head, staring at the phone. He hadn't wanted the call to end; he wasn't ready for the connection to be broken.

He took a deep breath. He took a picture of Nanny with his cell phone and sent it to Marisa. He hoped that she would like seeing the whale, that it would remind her that wonderful, unlikely things could happen.

Then he stood up and moved to Maeve's wicker rocker, watching the whale swim in the moon's silver path. He had Marisa's voice in his ear, and he felt it in his pounding heart. He thought of Liam, too far away. Talking to Marisa had made certain things clear to him, so he sent Liam a picture too, along with a quick message. Just then, he heard a puff of air, saw the whale arch her gleaming back and disappear into the black sea.

Patrick sat back, wondering what had just happened.

Chapter 13

As night fell, Liam worked at his desk, collating reports from oceanographers in the field. Rose was out on the screen porch, reading *The Lion, the Witch, and the Wardrobe*. It was her favorite book, reminding her of her best friend, Jessica, and she never got tired of it. Liam knew that the familiar story probably comforted her, and it made him feel good to think of how often Lily had probably read it to her.

His laptop was open, the screen filled with a picture of Nanny sent to him by Patrick Murphy. The picture was a silver blur, with one clear dark eye. Patrick's message read:

> Look who dropped by to see the Malone girls. Too bad only one of them is here. Why don't you pack up Rose and bring her home? It's a mistake to stay apart from the people you love—take it from one who knows. Lily really needs you.

Liam stared and stared. All day he'd been amassing data on the Ghost Hills phenomenon—cataloguing all the tagged sharks and whales he and John had been able to identify—but right now he had another project under way.

More than anything, he wanted to take Patrick's suggestion. He couldn't sleep, because all he could think of was Lily. She had been right here, in this house, in his bed. When he lay down on the sheet where she had been, he felt on fire. The pillow smelled like her. Every day the scent faded a little more.

Was Patrick right? Should Liam and Rose return to Hubbard's Point? He needed Lily as much as Patrick said she needed him. But he had to really think this over—he didn't want to underestimate Edward. And Patrick didn't know Lily the way Liam did.

Liam had been there when Lily had given birth to Rose. He had showed up at her cabin in the woods, far down a logging road from anything close to civilization. She had run nearly a thousand miles to get away from her husband, and she was so scared of being found, she would rather give birth in the middle of nowhere than risk going to a hospital.

Liam had boiled water and gotten towels, just like in the movies. Lily was lying on her kitchen floor, bathed in sweat and tears. Liam was little more than a stranger, but he was all she'd had. He remembered how she'd squeezed his hand with every contraction, crying with anguish.

Somehow he'd known that her pain was deeper even than childbirth. She howled, and he heard echoes of terror. He knew he'd never seen a person more alone, and he knew that someone had scared her half to death. She was without a husband, without family, and even before Liam knew her whole story, he knew that he would love her forever.

It didn't matter to him that she had been married before, that she'd never gotten divorced. He didn't care. Liam knew that there were ways of being connected that went beyond ceremonies and licenses. He loved Lily with every part of himself. She owned his heart, and so did Rose. No matter what happened, they were his life.

So time didn't really matter to Liam. His desire for Lily had no bounds. He knew he'd sell his soul to be with her for ten minutes. But that would be as true tomorrow or next year or in twenty years as it was now. She made his skin tingle, and his heart pound, just to think of her.

As much as he wanted to take Patrick up on his idea, Liam knew they had to be very careful. The person who had scared her half to death had been her husband, her baby's father. He had had Lily declared dead, so he could collect on her insurance and cash in her stocks and bonds. Patrick had filled Liam in on all the details.

Lily had existed merely as a food source to Edward Hunter. Liam understood the dynamic very well. Although he studied whales, they were collateral to his main academic focus.

Sharks.

Liam's brother Connor had been killed by the same great white shark that had taken Liam's arm. Liam knew that sharks ate to live. They patrolled the oceans, always in search of prey. They didn't attack out of any sense of hate. They were emotionless in their quest for food.

Liam knew that Edward Hunter was like a shark. He had targeted Lily because she was a good prospect. He had probably thought he'd live off her for the rest of his life. But unlike sharks, human predators possessed great capacities for rage when thwarted. Liam knew that when she walked out on him, Edward had been viciously angry—and people were still paying for it.

Liam had been quietly researching, and he believed that Edward Hunter was a very specific type of personality. He looked and acted like other people. He knew just what to say and do to get people to trust him. He "groomed" people—Lily, Marisa—even before he'd made his move: listened to them talk, figured out what moved and motivated them, and then appeared to give them what they most wanted.

As Dr. Robert Hare stated on page one of *Without Conscience,* "Everybody has met these people, been deceived and manipulated by them, and forced to live with or repair the damage they have wrought. These often charming—but always deadly—individuals have a clinical name: *psychopaths.* Their hallmark is a stunning lack of conscience; their game is self-gratification at the other person's expense. Many spend time in prison, but many do not. All take far more than they give."

If Liam couldn't literally be with the woman he loved, protecting her with his presence, he would do what he did best—study and learn. Maybe he would find something that would be helpful to her in dealing with Edward. He sat hunched over the books, itching to rip the guy apart.

He knew one thing: he had never felt this way about a shark.

Picking up the phone, he called Lily. The phone barely rang, and then she answered it.

"I want to bring Rose home to you," Liam said without preamble. "We're letting this idiot dictate our lives."

Lily was silent. Liam felt her, a million miles away, lost in her old life. He wanted to reel her back, remind her of what they had, show her how much he loved her, how strong they would be together. Strong enough to face anything.

The rumble of monster waves came through the open window, shook the cottage. Ghost Hills were alive tonight. They pounded the beach, and he felt the rhythm in his body.

"Lily?" he asked.

"I want that," Lily said, her voice so quiet, it was nearly drowned out by the roar of the waves ten miles out at sea. "But I'm afraid for Rose. I have to think, Liam."

"And I have to see you, Lily," he said.

When she hung up, all he could hear was the sound of his own heart. It was pounding, like the carrying echoes of Ghost Hills crashing on the reef. It swamped him and pushed him under, made it impossible to breathe. Liam shut down the computer, walked through the small house, and stood at the open porch door.

Stars flashed overhead. He hoped that Lily could see them. The constellations rose out of the sea, as if living creatures glowing with bioluminescence had flown into the sky. The stars told stories of myth and love. The sea was full of Ghost Hills and white whales. Didn't Lily know what a miracle it all was? He hoped that Nanny was watching over her—because Liam couldn't be there to do it.

Marisa had never seen a Cape Hawk evening like this. The normally sleepy streets were bustling with people, some carrying instrument cases, some running to make their performance times. People picnicked on the lawn of the inn, and down along the wharf. The Nanouk Girls had all come into town to listen to the night's ceili offerings, and Marisa tried to enjoy it all.

They spread their blankets in a row beside the stone fisherman in the village square. Marlena had brought grapes, bread, and cheese, Cindy had brought wine for the grownups and lemonade for the kids, Alison had made a big salad, Anne had raided the inn's kitchen and supplied lobster rolls for everyone. Marisa and Jessica had made Toll House cookies for dessert.

While the others talked, Marisa sat back and watched the musicians. There were so many women, from all over. She wondered how many of them were sisters, traveling all this way to Nova Scotia together. She looked for family resemblances, saw them everywhere. She felt happy for all these women, and she felt a terrible hollow hurt inside, for Sam.

Anne Neill saw Marisa sitting outside the circle, and she edged over. She had big blue eyes, chestnut brown hair pulled back in a French twist. She wore a peach cable knit sweater over lime green slacks— Marisa thought her bright clothes reflected her spirit. Anne was an innkeeper in every sense of the word, and her hospitality showed even when she wasn't at the inn's desk.

"How are you?" Anne said.

"I'm fine," Marisa said, trying to smile. "You've done a wonderful job with the ceili."

"Thank you," Anne said. "It's the most fun part of the year, but it does keep me busy. It's nice to sit down and listen to the music for a while."

Marisa nodded. "I've been to so many. In Newport, and on the Eastern Shore of Maryland, lots in Boston . . ."

"Always with your sister?" Anne asked.

Marisa nodded. She didn't want to cry, so she swallowed hard and looked away.

"We're holding a space on the bill for the two of you," Anne said.

"I don't think," Marisa began, "we'll be needing it."

Anne didn't say anything, but her blue eyes were so warm and kind, her smile so steadying, Marisa felt her heart crack. She heard the women on stage playing "*Taibreamh.*" It was sweet and traditional, and meant "Dreams" in Gaelic, and had always been Sam's favorite lullaby. Tears popped into Marisa's eyes and spilled over, and she thought she might break in two.

"Where's your sister now?" Anne asked gently.

"In Baltimore," Marisa said. "I'd thought she was in Peru. But she came home last week."

"And didn't tell you," Anne said.

Marisa shook her head, picturing Patrick going to the little house on Fish Street, talking to Sam. "A friend of mine found her," she said.

"Are you and Sam very close?" Anne asked.

"We were."

"Sisters," Anne said. "You grow up knowing everything about each other, living in the same house, sharing the same secrets, having the same feelings."

"That was Sam and I," Marisa said, suddenly knowing that Anne had to have a sister. "We were exactly like that."

"When we were young, my sister Emily and I were so close, we did everything together. You and Sam played fiddle, Emily and I did step dancing."

"At ceilis?" Marisa asked.

Anne nodded. "Until she went to college. And then took a job in Toronto, and then moved to Vancouver. It was never the same after that. I felt so abandoned. How could someone I'd spent every free moment with, loved more than anyone—my best friend in the world— just leave me that way?"

"But she wasn't leaving you," Marisa said, remembering how she had left Sam at home first, going to school in Baltimore. And how she had then left her in Baltimore, to marry Paul and live outside Boston. "She was just living her life."

"I know that now," Anne said. "But back then . . ." She shook her head.

"I think it's different for me and Sam," Marisa said. "She always celebrated my choices, no matter what. We'd miss each other, but we always found a way to be together. This time, though . . . I let myself be treated badly by someone, and I wouldn't let Sam help me."

"Are you the oldest?" Anne asked.

"Yes."

Anne's smile was loving and wise. "Younger sisters," she said. "Always want their older sisters to be smarter than they are. They want them to know more than they know. They want them to show the way."

"Are you the youngest?" Marisa asked.

Anne nodded. "Yes, I am."

"And you and Emily . . . ?"

"We're closer than ever. It took me a while, but I came around. She was patient, right there waiting for me. I think sometimes sisters have to rebel against each other, just the way teenagers do with their parents. It doesn't mean they don't love each other. Sometimes you just have to go apart, to come back together."

Marisa nodded, wishing it could be true.

"Who's the friend?" Anne asked.

"Excuse me?"

"The friend who went to Baltimore to find Sam," Anne said. "Who was that?"

"Patrick Murphy," Marisa said.

"The detective who came—?"

Marisa nodded. "Yes," she said. "The one who came here to find Lily."

"Maybe," Anne said, "you should invite him to the ceili."

"I mentioned it to him," Marisa said. "But he won't come. I don't . . . I don't even really want him to. I'm not ready." She thought of Ted, of the damage between her and Sam, of Jessica. "I don't think I'll ever be ready again."

"You know," Anne said gently, "I heard Lily say the same thing. But there was Liam. . . . Life had hurt them both. Lily's marriage to Edward—and Liam's brother being killed by that shark, Liam losing his arm. His family fell apart after that. They were both so closed off, but somehow they helped each other to live again. You and Patrick—"

"No," Marisa said. "It's different. We hardly know each other."

Anne tilted her head. "I think people look for each other. That's what ceili music is all about—so full of heart and love. We're all out at sea in our storm-tossed boats, getting washed clean of life's pain, making space for love to come in."

Just then, Jude hailed Anne from the steps of the inn. She gave him a wave, then looked Marisa in the eyes. "I'm not giving up on Sam," she said. "I'm saving you that spot in the program."

"But—" Marisa began.

Anne shook her head, her smile wide. Giving Marisa a hug, she went back to work. "If she comes, we'll be ready for her," she called back over her shoulder.

Telling her friends she was taking a walk, Marisa headed down toward the harbor. The water shimmered, blue and silver under starlight. She looked out at the fishing fleet, tugging at their moorings in the flood tide. Gazing south, she imagined Patrick on his boat in Connecticut, Sam in her apartment in Baltimore. It seemed so easy to imagine them both coming to Cape Hawk, yet impossible at the same time.

She pulled out a paper and pen and wrote the words "storm tossed." She knew they were the beginning of a song. She even thought she knew who it was for.

Chapter 14

Maeve had been dreaming of her granddaughter, the two of them working in the garden, tending the roses. The sea air was so fresh and clean, the fragrance of roses so sweet. She heard her own voice in her ears, calling for someone to come. Blinking, her eyes blurred as a man approached. Was it Patrick? An angel down from heaven? Or someone else? Maeve wiped her eyes, and she saw.

Edward Hunter stood over Maeve's bed. He stared down at her with cold eyes. Maeve felt her mouth drop open. Sweat sprang out on her brow, and waves of nausea passed through her. She never felt afraid, or at least never let people see her fear. But she couldn't help it now. She must have been making sounds, because he leaned down, put his ear near her mouth.

"You're babbling," she heard him say. "You're not making any sense at all. That's why you're in here. Because you're losing it. You're an old lady, and no one cares about you. Even your precious granddaughter can't be bothered with you."

Maeve felt like shrieking, but instead she just closed her eyes. She heard his voice and knew his cruelty. It reassured her in some small way. She wasn't crazy, wasn't crazy at all. Edward was being Edward. It was one thing she had always been able to count on.

She went deep inside. His voice continued, but she no longer heard it. She saw his vicious face, but then honeysuckle and roses emerged from the darkness to crowd him out.

The roses were beautiful. They grew in a tangle, deep in the garden. The sound of the waves was a lulling shush, shush, shush against the sun-kissed rocks The wishing well was cool and deep. Maeve dropped a penny down, as she had so many times over the years. She made a wish. Her eyes closed, she waited for the wish to come true.

"I want my granddaughter," she wished silently. "Mara, Mara . . ."

Rose felt better every day since her last surgery, except for one thing. She missed her mother. She didn't think there were any four words in the world worse than "I miss my mother." Although she didn't say them out loud very often, because she didn't want to upset Dr. Neill, the words were inside her, more with every breath, and embroidered on her heart.

The beautiful summer days just seemed sad and strange, here in the salty old beach house by Narragansett Bay. Dr. Neill had appointed her official whale watcher, and when they weren't out in the boat with Dr. Stanley, Rose spent a lot of time by the wide window, the brass telescope trained on the water's surface.

She'd seen fish jumping, their backs silver and blue, some of them marked with dark stripes, their tails and fins delicate as hammered metal. She'd watched seagulls flying overhead with crabs hanging out of their yellow bills. And Rose had even seen a sea turtle paddling by.

But no whales at all. No Nanny.

"Can I see her picture again?" Rose asked, going over to stand by Dr. Neill at his desk. He had lots of books and papers spread out. There were pictures of blue, tiger, mako, basking, Greenland, great white sharks; marine mammals, including humpbacks, minkes, blue, fin, sperm, and beluga whales, Atlantic bottlenose dolphins, harbor and harp seals. The documents reassured Rose because they reminded her of his office in Cape Hawk. He pushed some of them aside so she could lean closer to see Nanny's picture on his laptop screen.

"There she is," Dr. Neill said.

"Who took the picture again?"

"Patrick Murphy."

"The man who came to Nova Scotia to tell Mommy her grandmother was sick?"

"Yes."

"He took Nanny's picture in Hubbard's Point, in front of Mom's grandmother's house?"

"Yes."

Rose raised her eyebrows and wiggled them. Didn't Dr. Neill know how ridiculous it seemed? She and he were in this house where they didn't really know anyone, and the person they loved most, Rose's mother, was in Hubbard's Point. Even Nanny was there. He sat at his computer, entering information about all the different species they had seen out at the reef.

"Dr. Neill," she said.

"You know, Rose," he said, "I've been thinking. You should call me Liam. Don't you think?"

She shook her head. He had tried telling her this before. But she didn't want to. It didn't suit the way she felt about him. "Liam" was a name for her mother to call him. It was a grown-up name. Rose wouldn't feel right calling him that. Besides . . . she swallowed, thinking about the name she wanted to use for him. It made her blush to think about, and she felt the blood making her face hot.

"No?" he asked.

"Nope," she said stubbornly. "Dr. Neill's fine. So, Dr. Neill, why don't we go there?"

"Well, because your mother has to take care of some things," he said. "And she thought it would be better for you to be here while she does them."

"We could help her," Rose said.

"I know," he said. "I agree with you, and I'm working on it." Rose leaned comfortably against his side. She rested her head on his shoulder, not because she was tired, but just because she wanted to. They just stayed like that for a few minutes, looking at Nanny's picture on the screen, and Rose imagined how happy they could be if they could all be together.

"When will things be . . ." She searched for the word. She was thinking that so much happened in life. She had had heart defects, and Dr. Neill only had one arm, and her mother's grandmother was in the hospital, and they were in different places. "When will things be right?" she asked finally.

"I think they are now," Dr. Neill said.

Rose frowned. She knew what he was thinking. Her mother had always told her to be grateful, to count her blessings. Even when Rose couldn't breathe right or play with her friends, even when she had to stay in the ICU because her heart had too much fluid, even during those hardest times, her mother would press her lips to Rose's ear and whisper, "We are so lucky, because we love each other."

"You think things are right, now?" Rose asked. "But how can you say that? When we're here, and Mommy and Nanny are at Hubbard's Point?"

Dr. Neill turned away from his computer screen to look her straight in the eye. She knew how important his work was, how much he had been learning about those big waves and strange fish. She knew that he had seen a fishing boat from Cape Hawk, and that he was worried about it. But right now, he was giving Rose every bit of his attention.

"Rose," he said, "I know that none of it makes sense."

"Even to you?" she asked.

"Yes," he said.

"Because you miss her too?"

"More than I've ever missed anyone or anything."

"But I thought you liked working here—going out to Ghost Hills on Dr. Stanley's boat. . . ."

"That's my job," Dr. Neill said, smiling. "You and your mother are my life."

Rose nodded. She knew that it was true; she had felt it for a long time, maybe since the day she was born. He was like her father, in every important way. When other kids talked about their dads, Rose knew deep down, somehow, that she had a father somewhere in the world. But she'd never cared, or asked about him, because Dr. Neill was enough for her.

Just then, Dr. Neill raised his eyes, looked over her head. Rose saw his expression change, and she felt a little thrill—as if a mysterious wind had just started to blow, as if the weather had just changed in some wonderful way.

"Rose," Dr. Neill said, glancing down at her, his eyes shining, "I think that things just started to make sense."

And Rose looked, and she saw what he meant—a blue car pulling into the driveway, beside the tall boxwood hedge.

"Mommy!" Rose shouted, as she flew out the front door and went tearing barefoot across the manicured lawn, straight into the arms of her mother.

Chapter 15

It didn't take long to pack up and get on the road for Hubbard's Point. Liam had been ready ever since the night before. He had pretty much made up his mind the minute he read Patrick's message. When an idea was right, it was right; the important thing was that Lily felt good about it too.

"What changed?" he asked, driving along Route 1, holding hands with Lily across the seat.

"I came to my senses," Lily said. "Everything was happening so fast, I hardly had time to think."

"He can't do anything to us," Liam said.

"Who can't?" Rose asked from the back seat.

"Rosie, Rosie," Lily said, turning half around, sidestepping the question. "Wait till you see who's waiting for you at Hubbard's Point."

"Nanny!" Rose said. "Dr. Neill has her picture on his laptop!"

"Patrick took it," Liam said, glancing at Lily. Spotting a service station up ahead, he turned in. The gas gauge was down below a quarter full.

The three of them got out of the car. While the attendant filled the tank, Rose wanted to go into the store. Liam and Lily followed her, arms around each other. The shop was odd and quirky, a wood frame building that looked as if it had once been a house. Several boats were parked out front on trailers, some with For Sale signs.

The building's front porch had benches and rockers, racks of local papers, and a bulletin board covered with business cards, notices, and pictures of boats for sale. Another board was filled with pictures of fishermen holding up prize catches—ten-foot makos, fifty-two-inch stripers, a fourteen-foot blue shark.

Inside, the wide floorboards creaked under their feet. A soda fountain ran along the right-hand wall, and the front of the store was filled with bushel baskets of local produce. Lily grabbed a cart and loaded it with fresh tomatoes, basil, corn, and squash. Rose ran toward the back of the shop, and suddenly squealed.

"What is it?" Liam asked as he and Lily hurried back.

"Look!" Rose said, pointing.

A faded red curtain divided the store in half. Rose had peeked behind; looking over her head, Liam saw that the room was filled with shark jaws hanging on every inch of wall space. A rack of jars leaned precariously against a table—they contained tiny sharks in formaldehyde. Their eyes were clouded, their snouts sharp, their shark shapes unmistakable. A pile of ragged hacked-off shark and dolphin fins lay on the rickety blue table. Everything had a price tag. After a quick look, Lily hurried Rose back into the grocery area.

"Can I help you?" a man asked, coming through a door at the back of the room. He had a dark five-o'clock shadow, salt-damp hair, and a T-shirt that said "Captain Nick's Sportfish Charters."

"Are you Captain Nick?" Liam asked.

"You got it," he said. "Interested in a charter? There's plenty to go after right now, twenty-foot great whites up from the Bahamas and even bigger white whales down from Nova Scotia."

"Belugas are an endangered species," Liam said.

The man laughed. "Oh, I know," he said. "We're not going to hook them—just see them. I have to admit, I get a little carried away. There's never been a summer like this one—pure fishing madness, thanks to some gigantic waves rolling in from out at sea. You should've seen what we bagged yesterday—purple back, pink sides, and bright red fins, five or six feet long, swimming zigzag like a sea snake. Had to be straight up from the tropics."

"An opah," Liam said.

"Whatever it's called, it was something else. Check it out on the board in front—got a whole gallery of my customers' catches out there."

"I'm actually interested in your catches here," Liam said, getting ready to blast Captain Nick for the baby sharks and boiled jaws and ruined fins. But just then Lily called his name, and he backed away. It was just as well. His emotions were running so high from seeing Lily again, he wasn't quite in command of himself.

She stood on the porch, right in front of the board Captain Nick had just mentioned. While Rose rocked happily in one of the wooden porch chairs, Lily pointed at a blurry photo.

"Is that who I think it is?" she asked.

Liam focused on the board. There was the photograph Nick had mentioned—a six-foot opah, brilliant colors sparkling. His eyes swept over the gallery of trophy fish—marlin, sharks, swordfish, and tuna. The pictures had been taken dockside, with the fishermen standing proudly by the hanging scales. Lily was pointing at a photo of a fifteen-foot Atlantic bottlenose dolphin, hanging upside down, caught in a net.

"Don't get bent out of shape or anything," Captain Nick said, coming up behind them. "That fish isn't dead."

"It's not a fish," Liam said. "It's a mammal."

"Who caught it?" Lily asked, her voice trembling.

"Oh, never mind who caught it," Captain Nick said. "The important thing is, it's still alive. We kept it alive, according to any regulation you want to name."

"Why do you want to catch dolphins?" Lily asked, glaring at him.

"With all due respect," he said, "that's not your business."

"Come on, Lily," Liam said, putting his arm around her, gathering Rose, heading toward the car. He was shaking inside, but he didn't want to show it. Lily had been through enough and now they were bringing Rose home. Liam would call John later—Jude and Patrick too. Something was going on, and he needed help to figure it out.

He took one last glance back at the bulletin board. The camera must have moved, because it was impossible to read the name of the boat just behind the netted dolphin. But Liam would know the boat anywhere, because he recognized the grinning skipper.

The ship was the *Mar IV.*

"Did you see that?" Lily whispered.

"Gerard Lafarge," Liam said.

And in spite of what Captain Nick had said, the dolphin was dead.

Getting out of the car at Hubbard's Point, Liam knew they were home. The three of them stood there holding each other for the longest time. He couldn't let go of Lily, and she couldn't let go of him. Her eyes were as blue as the summer bay. He kissed her, hardly able to believe they were together again.

They broke apart, and Liam saw people coming from around the house. Lily had asked her friends to be there. She grabbed his arm, making introductions: Bay McCabe and Dan Connolly and Tara O'Toole and Joe Holmes, two of Lily's oldest childhood friends and their husbands and children. Liam shook hands with everyone. He couldn't quite get over how normal it all seemed, after the long days and nights of their enforced separation, and then the shock of that strange roadside shop.

Watching Lily introduce Rose to her friends, Liam's heart pounded. Her slim fingers protectively on Rose's shoulder, the pride and joy in her eyes—her friends' eyes welled up, gazing down at Rose, then up at Lily. Liam knew what a momentous day this was for all of them, and he stood back smiling.

"Bay and I have known your mom forever," Tara said, crouching down. "We were all best friends when we were your age."

"What did you do together?" Rose asked.

Tara had a wonderful, wicked smile that filled her eyes with mischief. "We rowed boats out to Gull Island, and went to the Indian Grave, dug for treasure at Little Beach, collected sea glass and moonstones, made necklaces out of jingle shells, played tennis till the middle of the night, went to movies on the beach, left notes for each other in the drawers at Foley's Store. . . ."

"Sounds fun," Rose said. "A lot like what I do with Jessica."

"Your best friend?"

Rose nodded. "At Cape Hawk."

"Well, that's the kind of stuff we'll all do at Hubbard's Point," Tara said. "I think you're really going to like it here."

"We're just so happy to meet you, Rose," Bay said. "We love your mother, and we already love you."

Rose blushed, and smiled shyly.

Liam watched her, feeling as proud as any father. She had her mother's kindness and curiosity. Her natural desire to learn pushed her to try new things and read books beyond her school level; two days ago, Liam had found her on her knees by the bookcase, pulling out old copies of *Cetacean Journal,* looking for articles about belugas.

"They're toothed whales," she'd announced to Liam. "They eat a diet of crustaceans, cephalopods, and sea worms. Crustaceans—that's crabs and lobsters! No wonder Nanny likes it down south here. I've seen so many seagulls flying by with crabs in their bills."

"Yes." Liam had smiled, overflowing with pride. "You'll be quite an oceanographer, Rose Malone. You proved it on the boat at Ghost Hills."

"Like you," she'd said, beaming.

Evening breezes blew off the Sound, salty and warm. The sun began to set, casting gold light on the waves and long ledges of glacial moraine. Tara and Bay had brought over pizza, keeping it warm in the oven. Lily steamed corn and sliced tomatoes. Bay and Dan's kids—Eliza, Annie, Billy, and Pegeen—gathered with Tara and Joe's little boy, Joe Jr., around Rose, obviously thrilled to welcome the latest addition to a long line of Hubbard's Point children.

Liam sat beside Lily on the porch swing, his arm around her shoulders. With the kids around, the talk was very general—summer weather, tennis plans, back to school, the latest on Maeve. Liam opened his laptop, logged onto his whale program, felt a wave of relief to see the familiar green light.

"Where's Nanny?" Rose asked, scanning the bay.

"She's out there," Liam said. He pointed at his screen, at her light registering in a spot just about two hundred yards offshore.

"Maybe she's looking for crabs to eat," Rose said. "Beluga whales eat crustaceans."

"We could go crabbing down front," Billy suggested.

Lily set them up with strings and sinkers, and Annie and Eliza led all the younger kids down on the rocks. The sound of rocks clicking as they broke open mussels for bait chimed through the air. The minute the coast was clear, all the adults started talking.

"I can't believe you're all here now," Bay said to Lily and Liam.

"I can't believe it took you so long!" Tara said.

"It's so great to meet you after hearing so much about you," Dan said.

"Liam, it's official, you're now a Hubbard's Pointer," Tara said.

"Thanks for the great welcome," Liam said. And then, directing the question at Tara's husband Joe—Lily had told him Joe was in the FBI— "Are we making a mistake? Coming back here with Rose right out in the open for Edward to see?"

"That's a tough question to answer," Joe said. "It depends."

"On what?" Lily asked.

"It's probably more of a mistake to give him the power he's been getting, having you hide out all this time, Lily. That makes him feel like a big shot. For a narcissist like Hunter, he gets off on any reaction he can get out of you. If he makes you swoon, he likes that. If he makes you cry, he likes that too."

"Did Edward know Lily was still alive?" Liam asked.

"He knows he didn't kill her," Joe said. "So I suspect that, yes, he knew she was alive."

"Was he looking for me? Us?" Lily asked, gazing down at Rose, crouched by the tidal pool.

"He may have been," Joe said. "I suspect he was keeping a low profile. He was under investigation, and even though he knew he hadn't killed you, he had other things to hide. During a murder investigation like that, he had to behave himself. There were areas of his life he wouldn't want us looking at."

"Like what?" Liam asked.

Joe shrugged. "He's a con man. The fact that he does most of it legally—through stockbrokering and marriage—doesn't minimize the fact that he tricks people into giving him their money."

"And their hearts," Lily said.

Hearing her say that was like a punch in Liam's stomach. Lily had given this man her love, her heart. He looked over, saw the worry and hurt in her eyes, wished he could erase every bit of pain. She had told him some of the details about her life with Edward; he knew she had buried some of it so deep, she hoped never to think of it again. Her nine years in Cape Hawk had been a time of healing; the fact that she was ready for this confrontation said a lot about her strength and the passage of time.

"We were at your wedding," Tara said. "And we watched you go farther and farther away from us. The longer you were married to him, the more you hid out from us."

"We were very isolated," Lily said. "He didn't even like *me* to be with my friends." She shivered, wrapping her arms around herself.

Liam moved closer, wishing he could keep her warm. But he knew that the chill she felt had nothing to do with the evening air, the sea breeze. It came from deep inside, from memories of living with a man who had crushed her dreams and sent her fleeing from everything she loved.

A demon had come out. Lily had brought him out for all to see. Talking about him a little bit at a time, she was exposing him for what he was. Liam felt shaken by the group's emotion as they talked about the old days and truths about Lily's life with Edward that they had suspected but never really known.

Lily stood up abruptly, craning her neck, checking on Rose playing on the rocks. The summer night was warm and peaceful. The children laughed and talked, splashing in the shallow tidal pool halfway down the rock ledge. Although the sun was down now, the rising moon spread white light on the Sound, the granite, and the rock pool. Bay called for Annie and Eliza to bring Joey up to the porch.

Liam expected Lily to call Rose, but she didn't. She leaned over the porch rail, watching her daughter crouch by the pool's edge. The dark surface rippled with moonlight. Rose seemed mesmerized by the life she could still see in the dim light, the deep green seaweed, silver-blue periwinkles, purple mussels, and speckled crabs. Liam remembered his own young fascination with the sea, and he whispered in Lily's ear, "Our marine biologist in the making."

"Yes," Lily whispered back, her eyes shining.

Liam hugged her, loving how happy she was here. She took it all in: her daughter, the moon, her great friends, her grandmother's house.

Lily could never be kept down for long. Her spirit was too naturally buoyant.

Just then, Rose sprang to her feet. She jumped up and down, pointing out to sea. "Nanny!" she cried.

Liam had seen a lot of whales in his life. He had grown up on the northwest coast of Nova Scotia, where whales were a way of life. But he never remembered feeling such excitement and joy at the sight of a whale as he felt right now—spotting Marine Mammal 122, the St. Lawrence beluga also known as Nanny, right here in the water in front of the house.

"Do you see her?" Rose called.

"We do," all Lily's friends called back, stunned and delighted by the rare sight.

Liam took Lily's hand. They ran down the steps, down the grassy hill, to the seawall. They jumped down, climbed across the rocks to be with Rose. Just offshore, the beluga gazed at them with her dark eyes, the most expressive of any whale's. Liam felt as if his heart were on display for the whale, and anyone who might look, to examine.

"It's really her," Rose breathed.

"It really is," Lily said.

"Everything is going to be fine now," Rose said.

"We're together," Lily said. "That's what matters."

They heard the phone ringing inside the house and Lily ran to answer it. Liam heard her shriek of joy.

He jumped up to grab her as she flew back down the bank and leapt into his arms.

"It's Granny!" she cried. "She's awake!"

Chapter 16

Maeve wanted a drink of water. She was so parched. It had been like being lost in a desert, with nothing but heat rising from the endless brown sand. Waking up was like stumbling into an oasis.

"May I please have some water?" she asked one of the doctors, hovering above her with a light shining in her eyes. She realized that they were the first words she'd spoken in some time. The image of the desert was still with her, and her mind flickered with mirages of Mara.

"Sure thing, in just a minute. Can you tell me your name?"

"Maeve Jameson," she said.

"Do you know how old you are?"

"I'm eighty-three years old."

"Very good," he said. Now he took her pulse, holding her hand for a maddeningly long time. Didn't he know what it was like to be terribly thirsty? And to boot, Maeve had an awful, chemical taste in her throat.

"Do you know where you are?"

She pursed her lips. He had her there. Last she remembered, she'd been at the Point. She had been in the garden, clipping roses. Clara had been there, and someone else. But then the wind had picked up, and the rain had started, turning into one of those blustery nor'easters when there was really nothing much to do but stay inside, warm and dry, while the storm battered the coast. She remembered pulling on a shawl because she was chilly. She'd gone to pick out a good book to read by the fire, but then she'd noticed how dusty the shelves were, and she'd started to dust. . . .

She looked around now. White walls, fluorescent lights, sterile environment. She decided to take a stab in the dark. "The hospital?" she ventured.

"Yes," he said. "One more question. Do you know why you're here?"

She couldn't help herself; she nearly began to cry. Suddenly she remembered the dreams she had had of Mara. It was as if Mara had been right here, beside her. Holding her hand, whispering in her ear, giving her a sponge bath. Maeve thought Clara had been here too. But that was probably real. Of course Clara would come.

The dreams of Mara, though . . . such sweet dreams of love. Their special bond, as close as can be, all the secrets they'd shared through life, all the gardens they had planted, the years when Maeve had watched Mara growing up. The most beautiful feelings Maeve could remember having, right here in this hospital bed, dreaming of her granddaughter. But that's all they were—dreams.

"Young man," she said, and her throat was so dry she sounded raspy and horrible, like a witch in the movies. "You're treating me as if I'm crazy." She felt a terrible wave of fear. She probably was out of her mind. In and out of dreams, such longed-for reality, trying to pull Mara out of thin air. Had Maeve gone round the bend without knowing it? She could think of almost nothing worse.

"No. I'm sorry if it seems I've been vague. I'm giving you what's called a mental status test. You see, you've been in a coma."

"A coma!" Maeve blurted out the word, somewhat marveling at the thought. How dramatic and rather glamorous. It was certainly better than losing one's mind.

"We've been worried about you. It's been over two weeks now."

"My goodness," Maeve said. She felt a combination of elation, to know she was out of the coma, and weakness, to know she'd been in one at all. Those dreams of Mara made a little more sense now. Perhaps she had gone "into the tunnel." She'd been walking toward the light, into the love she had felt for her granddaughter. It had kept her going all these years, worried and missing her.

She felt herself shrink into the bedclothes now. "What happened to me? Was I in a car wreck?" She asked the question, but didn't remember anything about a car. No squeal of brakes, no swerving to avoid an animal, nothing.

"No, Mrs. Jameson. You had carbon monoxide poisoning."

The taste in her mouth, she thought. She tried to lick her lips, but her tongue was too dry. This young doctor was being very thorough; she watched him now, consulting with another doctor, a woman, and two nurses. They were huddled at the end of her bed, talking earnestly, glancing at the door. They sounded excited. Maeve figured it wasn't every day that someone came out of a coma in their hospital.

She cleared her throat.

"Water . . ." she asked.

"Mrs. Jameson," the other doctor, a woman with curly dark hair and a soft smile, said. "I'm Dr. Mead. I have some good news for you. It's very good news, but I just want to make sure you're ready for it."

"I'm always ready for good news," Maeve said, accepting the plastic cup with the straw, sipping thirstily.

"It's about your granddaughter," Dr. Mead said. Suddenly the doctor's smile grew radiant, and she glanced at the door.

Maeve handed the doctor her glass. Oh, it was better than any water, better than any well or spring or river, better than every drop of rain that had ever fallen upon any garden. It couldn't be true, but it was. It had to be a dream, but it wasn't. Maeve sat up tall and held out her arms.

"Mara!" she gasped.

There were more doctors standing at the door to the room, trying to hold her back, but Mara would have none of it. She had a man and a child at her side, and together they broke through the hospital personnel, and Maeve heard Mara start to sob before she was even halfway across the room.

"Granny!" she cried.

"Oh, my darling!"

"I'm home, Granny," Mara said, flinging herself into Maeve's arms, holding on to her so tight, with those hands Maeve knew and loved so well. Maeve held Mara as if she were still her baby granddaughter, with all the love she had always had, every minute of the time she had been gone, holding on and knowing that she would never let her go again.

Lily sat on the edge of Maeve's bed, with her arm around Rose. She had introduced her grandmother to Liam, but this was one of the greatest moments in her life, bringing Maeve and Rose face-to-face, a meeting she had imagined for nine long years. And it was exactly as Lily had known it would be: Maeve acted as if she'd known Rose since the day she was born, and Rose was quiet and shy, but immensely curious, and unable to stop smiling at her great-grandmother.

"You turned nine years old this summer," Maeve said smiling.

"Yes. On June twenty-seventh," Rose said. "How did you know?"

"I've kept track of you," Maeve said. "Every second."

"Even though we weren't together?" Rose asked.

"Yes. Even though."

Lily loved the way her grandmother was taking Rose in. Gazing at her sun-lightened brown braids, her green-gold eyes, her pink mouth. Rose was very small for her age, because of her heart defects, but Maeve would never mention it, just love her all the more.

"I have a scar," Rose said.

"You do?"

Rose nodded. She glanced at Lily, to see if it was okay to show her. Lily's throat tightened. Rose's heart condition had always been such a big part of who Rose was, and Lily was touched to see Rose wanting her great-grandmother to know it all right away.

Lily helped Rose pull her shirt down below her collarbone, so Maeve could see the newest scar, from the latest operation.

"Rose had open-heart surgery early this summer," Lily said. "But she's fine now."

"That's so good to hear," Maeve said. She didn't frown or look worried. She just smiled calmly at Rose, as if she knew that some people have open-heart surgery and go into comas, but that life just flows on. "Does the scar hurt?"

"It itches," Rose said.

"Ahh," Maeve said, as if she understood. She held Rose's hand, shaking it gently.

"I love your name. Rose."

"Thank you. We're both named after flowers. Me and Mommy."

"Your mother is named after a flower?" Maeve asked, looking up, meeting Lily's eyes.

"Lily," she said. "That's the name I've used since I left. I took it, to remind me of your garden. All those daylilies, so bright in the sun."

"My garden missed you," Maeve said, eyes glittering.

"I missed it, and you, so much. I needlepointed so many canvases of Sea Garden. The wishing well, the cottage, the roses growing up the door, the four-seasons bench."

"It's a beautiful place," Liam said.

"Thank you," Maeve said, smiling and squinting at him, as if trying to be friendly while still taking his measure. "Have you known my granddaughter long?"

"Since a few days before your great-granddaughter was born."

Maeve blinked, taking that in. She seemed to be resting in the knowledge that she was really awake, her family was really with her. She suddenly looked so old and tired, as if the weight of the last nine years had just caught up with her. Lily watched the way she held Liam's gaze. She felt safe with him, Lily could see.

"You've known them a long time," Maeve said.

"Known and loved them," Liam said, smiling.

"Granny," Lily said, "we don't want to tire you out. You need lots of rest."

"Darling, I feel I could dance right now," Maeve said. Lily knew what she meant—she felt the same way. But her grandmother looked frail, her cheeks sunken and pale. The nurses seemed to be edging into the room, giving the signal that it was time to go.

Lily held her grandmother's hand. It seemed almost impossible to leave, even though she knew she could come back in the morning. Being apart for so long made their time together seem rare, precious, and fragile. If Lily let go, who could guarantee that she would ever have a moment like this again? She felt her hand start to tremble, and her grandmother felt it too.

"It will be all right, darling," her grandmother said.

"How do you know?" Lily asked.

"I just know. Please tell her, Liam."

"She's right, Lily," he said, putting his hand on her shoulder.

"There's a prayer," her grandmother said. "By Julian of Norwich. She was a wonderful saint, a mystic. All my favorite saints are mystics, because they have so much faith. They can see the most impossible things, because they see with the eyes of the heart. I prayed Julian's prayer every day, while you were away. It goes, 'All will be well, and all will be well, and all manner of things will be well.'"

"I like that prayer," Rose said.

"So do I," Liam said.

"It's a very good one," Maeve said. "Will you try it, darling?"

"I'll try," Lily said doubtfully. She still couldn't let go of Maeve's hand.

"When can I go home?" Maeve asked the only doctor still remaining, making notes on her chart.

"We'll have to see," he said. "We'll send you down to neuro tomorrow for some tests, and we'll know better after that."

"Don't worry, Granny," Lily said, kissing her. "We'll get you home as soon as possible. Your house is waiting for you."

"I can't wait," Maeve said. Then, smiling at Liam: "Take care of her till I get back there, okay?"

"You can count on it," he said.

Lily hugged her grandmother, then held her face between her hands, looking into her soft blue eyes. It had seemed an eternity since she'd been able to do that, and she felt that tears were imminent again.

Maeve kissed them all, long and hard. When they started to leave the room, they walked backwards, waving. Maeve blew them kisses.

"Goodbye, darlings," she said. "Goodbye, Lily and Liam and Rose."

Lily smiled, turning away as the tears really began to flow. Her grandmother had just called her Lily. Mara was gone forever.

It was past ten o'clock at night. Across the Gold Star Bridge, on the other side of the Thames River, they went to Rosie's, an old silver diner, with turquoise leatherette booths. Rose was thrilled to go to a place with her name, and about getting to order blueberry pancakes late at night.

Lily sat beside Rose, and she and Liam held hands across the table. They talked about Maeve, and Rose asked what she should call her, should it be Granny? Lily said they'd better ask Maeve.

"I like the name Maeve," Rose said.

"Maeve was a warrior queen in Irish legend," Lily said. "She was from the Connaught, in the west of Ireland."

"Named for a queen, wow," Rose said.

"A warrior queen, no less," Liam said, nodding his head to Lily. "Granddaughter of Maeve."

"Do I seem as if I have the blood of a warrior queen?" she asked.

"Totally, Mommy," Rose said. "The way you boss people around in hospitals, when they're not paying attention to me."

"I've done that," Lily agreed.

The waitress came over with their blueberry pancakes. She knocked over Liam's water glass, and a small amount spilled on his lap. He cleaned it up quickly, smiling, and Lily felt a small, quiet, unexpected sense of safety. A memory arose: Edward going into a rage because a waiter spilled his water. The evening had been turned upside down over that one small thing. He had stopped speaking, eaten in silence, slammed the money down on the table without leaving a tip.

That had been crazy, Lily thought now, watching Liam and Rose happily eat their pancakes. Lily took a deep breath, feeling how safe and normal her life had become.

"I could call her Maeve," Rose said between bites.

"Your great-grandmother?" Lily asked.

"Yes," Rose said. "I like the name a lot. I'm glad she's named after Queen Maeve. I want to call her that."

"But I thought you didn't like to call adults by their first names," Liam said.

"I didn't say that," Rose said, frowning.

Lily sipped her milk, wondering what conversation she had missed.

"Well, when I asked if you wanted to call me Liam."

Rose instantly turned bright red.

"What is it, honey?" Lily asked. "Do you think it's too impolite for you to stop calling him Dr. Neill and start calling him Liam? Is it because he's our friend instead of a relative, like Granny?"

"It's not because of that," Rose said, her voice falling to a whisper as she dropped her fork on her plate. Her eyes got big, and tears pooled on the bottom rims. "It's just that I want to call him something else."

"What do you want to call him?" Lily asked.

Liam already knew. Lily could tell, because she felt him squeeze her hand.

"Daddy," Rose said.

Chapter 17

Patrick Murphy went to the hospital as soon as he heard. When he first got there, Maeve was not in her room. They had taken her down for some tests, and then she had physical therapy. So he sat in the chair by the side of the bed where she had lain so long, waiting for her to return.

He thought of Marisa and Sam, the nursing sisters. He thought of how many people they had helped, and it stung him to think he'd been unable to bring them back together. As Patrick stared at Maeve's hospital bed, he knew that these were all casualties of the same man; he blamed Edward Hunter for all of it.

On the Major Crime Squad, he had investigated many comas. Blunt-force trauma, poisoning, falls from high places, the gamut. He had observed coma patients go through stages. When they got to the place of drawing inward, trying to move into a fetal position, Patrick had seen very few of them come back. So, waiting for Maeve, he knew that her waking up was a miracle. But he didn't know what she had lost, whether she'd still be the same Maeve he knew.

When he heard the wheels coming down the corridor, he jumped up. He expected to see her on a gurney. Honestly, he expected to see a shrunken old woman who had aged a lot, who had lost ground. When he saw her in a wheelchair, sitting up, her white hair neatly brushed and her blue eyes sharp and bright, he felt himself start to grin.

"Well, if you're not a sight for sore eyes," he said, grinning wider.

"Patrick Murphy," she said, smiling just as much.

He bent down to peck her cheek, but she put her arms around his neck and gave him a long hug. Good thing too. He buried his face in her shoulder for a few seconds, so she wouldn't see tears in his eyes.

"What was that for?" he asked when she stopped.

"You found her," Maeve said.

"Mara?"

"Her name is Lily now," Maeve said.

Patrick chuckled. "Maeve, Maeve, Maeve," he said. "You sure do get with the program faster than any other eighty-three-year-old I know."

"Well, she doesn't want to live in the past," Maeve said. "Who can blame her? Have you met Rose?"

"I sure have. Your great-granddaughter."

"She's beautiful. I can't wait to get home to Hubbard's Point, so I can watch her swimming and crabbing on the rocks. And Liam? You've met him?"

Patrick nodded. "He's a good guy. I checked him out, of course. No priors, never been married, lots of publications and awards in his field, ichthyology. That's the study of—"

"Fish—sharks. I know, dear. Is that what happened to his arm?"

"Yes, as a matter of fact," Patrick said. "How would you know that?"

Maeve stared past his head, at clouds going by the window. The expression on her face was beatific, like Saint Theresa or the Mona Lisa. Patrick had seen that gaze a million times during the years he was investigating the case. It jostled him slightly now. She was a wise woman. The aide asked if she wanted to get into bed, but Maeve just shook her head. She wanted to stay sitting up, in the chair.

"I guess I know because of something in his eyes," Maeve said. "He's a very handsome man. He loves Lily—that's obvious to anyone who looks at him. But there is sorrow in his eyes. I think he is very reserved, except with Lily and Rose. He has the look of someone who has been terribly wounded."

"You can tell all that just by looking in his eyes?" Patrick asked. "Jeez, Maeve. You should have been the detective, not me."

"Oh, teachers have to be detectives," she said, peering at him. "Don't think I don't see the same thing in you."

"The same?"

"My darling, tough detective. Wounded by life and love and this investigation."

"Maeve, let's leave it at 'tough,' okay?"

She sighed. "I had a boy in my class once, thirty years ago now. Peter Liffey—he came to school with his arm in a sling one day. All we were told was that he had a broken arm."

Patrick listened, seeing infinite compassion in Maeve's eyes.

"His schoolwork suffered. I had him come after school, for extra help. Little by little, I began to find out about him. Small things he'd let drop. Like, his mother had a black eye. His father got mad when Peter forgot to take out the trash. Or when Peter asked too many questions. You get the idea."

"Domestic violence back in the day," Patrick said. "Back when guys could beat their wives and kids behind closed doors, and the cops would look the other way. It used to be called 'family business.'"

"Yes."

"What happened to Peter? Did you turn him around? Or did he go the way of his father? Is he somewhere beating his own wife right now?"

"He turned around," Maeve said. "He went to college, and then to medical school. We stayed in touch the entire time. He became a psychiatrist, and he has written many papers and books on the subject of family violence. He studies the very thing that hurt him the most in his young life."

"That's why you guessed the ichthyologist had been attacked by a shark?"

"Yes. Liam has the same haunted look as Peter. Some people have to understand the things that scare them most."

Patrick grabbed a chair and pulled it over right next to her wheelchair and sat down. "Maeve, I have to ask you something. Do you remember Edward stopping by the cottage?"

She frowned, gazing out the window. "Yes. Clara and I were out in the garden. He said he was in the area on business."

"Did you ask him to check your furnace?"

Maeve snorted. "Of course not. Why?"

"Lily has made some allegations. And we're taking them very seriously."

"What are they?"

"She thinks Edward messed around with the heating system, poisoned you. Maybe he suspected she was alive. And he knew the only way to get to her was through you."

"She would come home if she thought I needed her," Maeve said, her eyes open wide.

"We think maybe he did something to your furnace, under the house. There's access from outside, through the door above the seawall. It's possible he blocked the outflow, or stuffed something into the ventilation ducts. We've checked, and there was a partial fingerprint, but no signs of tampering. We suspect that he did something to cause carbon dioxide to build up. You couldn't smell it, you couldn't see it."

"It's summertime; I wouldn't even have thought of carbon monoxide," Maeve said. "But I'm old, and I get cold. I'm always chilly, even when other people are warm. I turn the heat up on cool nights. Or I light a fire."

"Edward might have taken advantage of that. Did anything seem different? Anything you can think of? Anything at all, Maeve. It would help. . . ."

"I can't remember," Maeve murmured, and Patrick could see that he had upset her. She was suddenly paler than before, slumping slightly in her chair. He held her hand. It was cold.

The hospital's air-conditioning was humming. He didn't see a thermostat to turn it down. But he got up and pulled the white cotton blanket off Maeve's bed. He tucked it around her shoulders, down over her knees. Then he sat down beside her and held her hand again. After all the time they'd spent together, Patrick loved her almost as much as his own grandmother.

"At least two good things have come of all this," Maeve said. "Lily had Rose. And she met Liam."

Patrick nodded, and he caught Maeve looking at him with a worried gaze.

Maeve dabbed at her eyes with a tissue, smiling slightly. "I once hoped you and my granddaughter would fall in love. After your marriage broke up, and during all the years you were looking for Lily and I could tell how much you cared . . . I wondered. You were so fascinated by her. . . ."

Patrick folded his arms over his chest, staring out the window.

"Oh, I used to dream that you'd find her," Maeve said. "And love her and the baby. I'm so happy that she's found Liam, of course. But what about you? How do you feel about it?"

Patrick stared at the clouds for a minute, then looked down at Maeve.

"I've met someone," he said.

"Patrick!" she said, her eyes shining.

He shook his head. "She's wonderful, but she's far away. And not just in miles—she's been through too much. She's—well, she's been very hurt. You're not going to believe this, Maeve. She was Edward's wife, after Lily."

"The one from outside Boston? Patty, wasn't it? With a daughter who'd be about Rose's age . . . Grace?"

Patrick nodded, feeling a tingle run down his spine. "She ran away from him too, up to Nova Scotia—Cape Hawk—just like Lily . . . because of a picture Edward had, an old photograph of a whaling ship in the Cape Hawk harbor. She goes by the name Marisa Taylor now. Her daughter is Jessica."

"And you . . ."

"I met her, when I went up to find Lily. She's beautiful. Plays music, and used to have a band with her sister. They're estranged now—because of what happened with Edward. He kept Marisa from seeing her sister, and a lot of damage was done. I tried to help, to convince her sister to forgive her, go up to Cape Hawk and reunite. But she wouldn't listen."

Maeve stared at him with such light in her blue eyes. "Oh, Patrick," she said. "You've done so much to pick up the pieces of lives shattered by that man. Lily's, mine. And now these other women . . . what about you?"

"What do you mean?"

"Your marriage, dear. I know you're 'tough,' as you said earlier. But I also know how that wounded you. Why don't you go up to see Marisa? Even if she can't reunite with her sister just yet, she would be a lucky person indeed to have a friend like you."

"I don't know, Maeve."

"Darling, if there's one thing this experience has taught me, it's that life is so short, and so precious. I feel so sorry that the sisters are losing time, and the chance to be together. Don't you lose it too. Go to Cape Hawk."

Patrick looked at her as if he were her grandson and she was the wisest woman on earth.

"Please, Patrick," she said, her eyes gleaming. "Don't let Edward Hunter take one more thing from any of us. Take back your life, and give Marisa back hers. Don't give up."

He couldn't speak, but he nodded. Maeve squeezed his hand, pulled him closer for a hug. Maeve had said *Don't give up.* Patrick let the words play in his mind, and he knew he had to try once more—if that didn't work, then so be it. Either way, he had a trip to make, and it was time he got started.

Of course it had to happen. Liam and Lily both knew it was just a matter of time. Still, when the confrontation came, it was both worse and less eventful than Liam would have expected.

Lily was in the kitchen, making dinner. She had been at the hospital for most of the afternoon, and Liam and Rose had gone to the fish store to get lobsters. They'd stopped at the vegetable stand for corn, picked up a blueberry pie from a bakery in Black Hall, some fresh peach ice cream from Paradise Ice Cream. Liam enjoyed getting to know the area where Lily had grown up, and Rose seemed to love driving around and doing errands with him.

"Are there lobsters here in the Sound?" Rose asked as they walked down the rocks to fill the big pot with seawater.

"Definitely," Liam said. "This is a perfect habitat for them, with all the rock ledges to hide in."

"And there are lobsters up in Cape Hawk?"

"Yes. A lot of the fishing boats down in the harbor actually go out for lobsters. It's a big part of the fleet's catch."

"Could we catch them ourselves here?" Rose asked, helping Liam hold the pot steady so the water would flow in. When they had enough, they righted it, and then picked tufts of rockweed. Liam's family had always steamed lobsters with seaweed, and Lily wanted to try it. Rose had bare feet; she navigated the rocks with no trouble. The air was chilly, so she wore a sweatshirt. The sleeves were pushed up, and the legs of her jeans were rolled up to her knees. Liam loved watching her be a kid, so carefree on a summer night.

"We could," he said. "All we'd need is a boat and some pots."

"Can we get a boat?" Rose asked, her eyes sparkling with excitement.

"If your mom says so."

They gathered some mussels to cook with the lobsters. Liam couldn't help telling Rose the Latin names for everything—*Homarus americanus* for lobster, *Mytilus edulis* for blue mussels—for her future career in oceanography. They scanned the waves for Nanny, although it was still a little early for her to appear. She wasn't there, so they scrambled up the rocks to the yard.

As they rounded the corner of the house, Liam saw him. He recognized his stocky, muscular build, his intense smile, those gleaming green eyes from his brief appearance in Rhode Island.

Liam held the heavy pot, filled with water, in the crook of his arm. He wanted to grab for Rose, to pull her back, but he was not dexterous with his prosthesis, and he didn't move fast enough. She walked straight into Edward's path. Liam felt as if he saw a Mack truck bearing down on her, when it was just a man getting out of his Jaguar.

"Rose," he said quietly.

She seemed transfixed by the man coming down the stairs to stand beside the wishing well.

Edward crouched down, smiling at her. He had eyes only for Rose. Liam put down the pot, grasped Rose's hand, and pulled her toward him. It was instinctive, one-two-three, like pulling her away from a snake. She looked up at him with surprise. Liam's heart was racing, and he didn't want to take his eyes off Edward, but he registered Rose's shock at Liam's rudeness.

"Go inside," he told her. Liam knew he sounded sharp, but he couldn't stop to think. He pushed Rose toward the door, then stood between her and Edward.

"My daughter," Edward said, meeting Liam's eyes. "That's my daughter, isn't it? My kid. She looks like me. I'd know her anywhere."

"You have no place here," Liam said.

"Oh, really? Her mother and I got married in that side yard, right there. Who are you?"

"Liam Neill," he said, rising up, towering over Edward Hunter, standing between him and the house, just wishing Edward would make a move to get by him.

"That's my baby," Edward said. "And I have every right to her. Get out of my way."

"You're not welcome here," Liam said. His voice was deep and held violence. He had become an ichthyologist because a shark had killed his brother, and right now, facing Edward Hunter, he felt primal hatred surging up for the predators of all species.

"Liam." The door slammed as Lily came out to stand beside him. Liam glared at Edward. He wanted the fight to be between them, but he respected Lily too much to keep her out of it. This was her battle, all hers. But Edward had to know that if he faced Lily, he was facing Liam too.

"Mara, you're a liar," Edward said. "You put me through hell, do you know that? I was investigated for *murder*. Do you know what that was like? It was a nightmare. You lied about our baby. That is my daughter. She has my face, my eyes. She's like looking in the mirror! She's mine."

"She's not *yours*," Lily said. "She doesn't belong to you or anyone. She is her own person, beautiful and true, and she has nothing to do with you."

"She has my blood!"

"How dare you come here?" Lily asked, sounding calm. "After what you did to me? Your act might work for new people, who don't know you. But not here, not with me. I see who you are."

"You're crazy. I was a wonderful husband. Ask anyone. You had no right to take my child away. She's mine! I'm going to have her, I swear to you. I'm going to get what's mine!"

"Did you hear Lily?" Liam asked. "She just told you the child doesn't belong to you. Can you grasp that concept? You don't own people. Lily doesn't want anything to do with you. Leave now."

"One-armed wonder," Edward said, smirking.

It's funny, Liam thought. That was the moment he knew. He had seen Edward's glittering hazel eyes, he had heard his possessiveness about what was "his," he had seen the arrogance and aggression in showing up here. But it was in that small comment, that throwaway cruelty, that Liam saw the man for exactly who he was.

"Don't you dare!" Lily shouted, her outward calm dissolving. "Liam is the most wonderful man in the world. He loves my daughter! *Our* daughter," Lily said, gazing up at Liam with sheer panic, making his heart pound, because he knew she wanted it to be true, that she finally accepted the way Liam had felt all along—that he had always loved Rose as if she were his own.

"What?" Edward asked. "She's *his* daughter?"

Lily was shaking too hard to answer. Liam held her, rocking her in the front yard as the sun set, its orange rays making all the roses look as if they were on fire.

"I don't believe you," Edward shouted. "She looks like me. She's the right age. I swear to God, I'm going to take her from you. I swear you'll be sorry for this."

Liam tried to shield Lily with his body. He felt her quivering against him, her body trembling with sobs.

Edward's words, *I'm going to take her from you,* rang in Liam's ears. He wanted to take two steps and kill Edward with his bare hands. But he had to take care of Lily right now. He turned his back on the monster and led the woman he loved into her grandmother's house.

Rose was standing inside the kitchen door, her expression pure shock. She had never seen her mother like this. Liam doubted she had ever heard her mother raise her voice. He could see Edward through the kitchen door window, standing right by the wishing well, laughing.

"Why is that man laughing?" Rose asked. "While Mommy's crying?"

"Rose," Lily said, falling to her knees and pulling Rose into her arms.

"Mommy, what's wrong?" Rose asked, her words muffled by Lily's shoulder—Lily was holding her so hard.

Liam had to get them away from the door. He shepherded them into the living room, sat beside them on the sofa. He held Lily while she cried, and Rose just looked up at him with confusion in her eyes. Edward was wrong. Rose looked nothing like him. Yes, her eyes were green, but they were warm, deep, crackling with lively intelligence. Looking into the eyes of Edward Hunter, Liam had had the cold sensation of a reptile, primitive and undeveloped.

"Tell me what's wrong," Rose repeated. "That's the man from Rhode Island. Who is he?"

"His name is Edward Hunter," Liam said.

"He's my real father," Rose said. It wasn't a question.

"I'm so sorry to put you through this," Lily said. "I don't think of him as your father. He doesn't know you at all. I took you away from him before you were born. I've only wanted good for you, my sweetheart."

"I didn't like him in Rhode Island, and I don't like him now," Rose said. "The way he smiled at me." She shivered. "Even before he started yelling. It wasn't a real smile."

Liam nodded at her, struck by her perception. No falling for Edward's glib charm—not Rose. The sun went all the way down, and the room grew dark. No one moved for a long time. They had no appetite anymore.

When the moon began to rise, Liam stood up and went into the kitchen. Edward had left. His Jaguar was gone. Rose stood at Liam's side, gazing out into the shadows. The moon cast a cold, blue light on all the rocks and roses. The beauty of Hubbard's Point suddenly seemed sinister.

Liam asked Rose if she wanted her lobster, but she didn't. She asked if they could let them go, on the rocks. Liam got the plastic bag out of the refrigerator, and he heard the lobsters scratching inside. The sound made him feel sick. Holding hands, he and Rose walked down to the water. Nanny was there, swimming in a circle of moonlight.

"We've fed her crabs," Rose said, "but I don't want to feed her the lobsters."

"I know," Liam said.

He took the rubber bands off their claws. Showing Rose how to hold them by the carapace so she wouldn't get pinched, he helped her to set them free in the tidal pool. They had plenty of life force, instantly swimming to safety, to hide in crevices under the seaweed.

They stood looking at Nanny for a long time. Liam knew Lily was in the window, up above. His mind was racing, thinking of what she had said to Edward. Rose waved at Nanny, and then it was time to go to bed.

Liam lingered in the hallway, looking at them. Lily sat on the edge of Rose's bed, reading from *A Wrinkle in Time,* one of her own favorite childhood books. Liam didn't want to let them out of his sight. He wanted to give Lily this time alone with Rose, and he wanted to get his words straight.

When Lily came out, she looked drained and tired. He took her hand, led her back downstairs. They went onto the porch, where they could see both Nanny and the tidal pool, both bathed in moonlight.

"Rose wanted to let those lobsters go," Lily said.

"She did," Liam said. "Do you know why?"

Lily shook her head.

"I think it was a completely gentle instinct. She had seen someone being controlling and cruel, and even though she didn't completely understand, she wanted to express herself by doing something kind."

"She is kind," Lily said, her eyes quickly filling with tears. "She's nothing like him."

"I know," Liam said. He held her hand, stroking it, trying to soothe her. "Lily, I heard what you said to him."

"The whole Point heard," Lily said.

"No. I mean, I heard what you said about me. About Rose being ours."

Lily's tears spilled over. "Do you think he'll believe that? Will it keep him from coming after her? I should never have come back here. In spite of how I feel about Maeve . . ."

"Lily," Liam said, holding her, making her look him in the eye. "She *is* ours."

She shook her head. "But she's not . . . if he forced her to have a blood test . . ."

"In every way that matters," Liam said, "she's our daughter. I was with you when she was born. I helped her come into the world, and I put her on your stomach for you to hold. I felt like a father that day, Lily. And I've never stopped feeling like one ever since. Rose's father."

"You've been there for her," Lily whispered.

"I've tried," he said. "All I've ever cared about was being there for you and Rose."

"You promised us you'd look after us," she cried. "Liam, I tried to push you away for so long. I didn't trust you, didn't trust the world. But I've never forgotten that promise, or that you were there at the beginning. Yours were the very first eyes Rose ever looked into."

There were stars burning in the sky, so bright they couldn't even be dimmed by the white moonlight, and he felt they were shining for Lily and Rose now. "You're my family," he said, kissing her hand. "You and Rose."

"You're ours," she whispered.

"That's what you were getting at, when you said to Edward that Rose is our daughter. I knew that was what you meant. No matter what the obstacles, we've been a family since that first day."

"You've been with us at the hospitals. You've paid Rose's hospital bills," she said. "I never thank you enough for that, because, in so many ways, it's been the least of what you do. You look over us, Liam. Even when I haven't let you be close, you've stayed right there. I've always known that all I'd ever have to do is call you. And you'd come."

"Even more than you know," he said.

"I used to think she was born with heart defects because I let *my* heart be broken," Lily said.

"I've always known you had a broken heart," Liam said. "And I've wanted more than anything for you to let me try to help you heal it."

"You have," she whispered.

Liam's own heart was pounding, a feeling of giant waves in his chest. He pulled Lily closer, kissed her. Stars flashed in the sky, in his eyes. Her body was so hot, as if she had a fever. When they stopped, he still held her tight, their gazes locked.

"Lily, I want to marry you," he said.

"Oh, Liam—"

"I always have. Don't you know that, Lily?"

"We've loved each other for so long," she whispered. "Even before I knew it."

"Do you know it now?"

"I do," she said.

Her eyes were shining, and Liam swore he saw happiness for the first time that night. It gave him the hope he needed, reinforced the ineffable connection they had had for so long.

"Lily, I want us to get married right away. This weekend, as soon as we can get the license. I want to adopt Rose. So he can't come after her at all."

Lily led him down the porch steps, around the house, to the grassy strip between the cottage and the seawall. The grass was cool beneath his bare feet, and she pulled him down and slid on top of him, her body firm, hot, and glistening with sweat. Liam could hardly breathe, his mind on fire with everything.

She ran her hands down his body, sliding them up under his shirt, untucking the tails from the waistband of his jeans. He felt her undo the button, start to tug the zipper down. Her mouth was on his, open and ravenous. He held her with his one good arm, letting her work her way down his face, his neck, kissing his collarbone.

Liam's thoughts flew out of his head. They had spent too much time operating with their minds—every step of the way had had to be negotiated, navigated, calculated. Lily had been on the run, and that had been her prison: so far from home, trapped by the need to stay hidden. He felt her breaking free, and he was right there with her.

They made love with their bodies, and maybe for the first time ever, they weren't thinking at all. Liam just felt their bare skin on the cool grass, Lily's body hot from running and his aching for her touch. A chilly breeze blew off the water, signaling that August's end was coming.

He held her afterward, their heartbeats slowing to something close to normal. Seagulls cried out on Gull Island. He remembered when their sound had made Lily break down, with all her worry and fear bottled up over Maeve and what Edward might try to do. Right now she lay flat on her back, staring up at the sky, holding out her arms as if she could catch all the stars.

"Liam," she said.

"Lily," he said back.

"How many stars are there?"

"More than anyone can count."

"That's not a very scientific answer," she said, laughing.

"Well, there are about one hundred billion stars in our galaxy."

She smiled, as if satisfied. What's the scientific name of Nanny?"

"*Delphinapterus leucas,*" he said, raising himself up to watch Nanny swimming close to the shore. "Rose already knows that."

"What does that translate to?"

"*Delphinapterus,* without fins, *leucas,* white. Why?"

"You're an oceanographer. Can oceanographers predict what the weather will be in September?" she asked.

"I don't know," he said, his pulse kicking over. "Why?"

"Liam," she said. "Maeve is home, Rose is well. You and I—it's just so wonderful. I never thought we'd have all this. I was just thinking . . . why should we wait? September is almost here."

"Lily," he said, pulling her close. Her eyes were bright blue, even in the dark.

"I love you, Liam," she whispered, their gazes locking. "I want you. *Yes,* Liam."

"Yes?"

"I want to marry you. A September wedding . . ."

He stared into her eyes so deeply, and he saw the smile come to her lips. His own heart was pounding. He thought of everything he knew about what Lily had been through, and he pictured Ghost Hills, monster waves crashing over the reef. They were sixty feet tall, capable of killing anyone in their path. He knew that Lily had nearly been swept under once; Liam was going to make sure it never happened again.

Chapter 18

The late afternoon held golden light, spilling it down the rock cliffs, into the fjord, across the calm bay. Fiddles and tin whistles played, inviting the town to dance, calling everyone from their houses for the last days of the ceili. Marisa and Jessica sat by the stone fisherman, listening to the music.

"Mommy, why don't you play?" Jessica asked.

"I can't play without Sam," Marisa said.

"You wrote your new song and everything. . . ."

It was true. Inspired by Anne's phrase, and by knowing Patrick Murphy, Marisa had written a new song, "Storm Tossed"—it was ready to play, but she knew that it would have to wait until she had her partner and fellow Fallen Angel, her sister Sam, with her again.

A group of young girls, Irish dancers, ran along the wharf in their green dresses; a van from Prince Edward Island rumbled down the cobbled street, band members jammed in, singing at the top of their lungs. A quartet from Yarmouth sat on stage, two fiddle players racing through "Maureen's Reel," the tin whistle and accordion players tapping their feet for percussion.

Marisa lifted her head for every car that drove through town. She watched as the ferry slid across the strait, its white wheelhouse glinting in the butterscotch light. A single whale arched its back, a glossy black island that disappeared in the ferry's wake. Night would fall soon, and another day would be over. Another chance to play gone . . . Marisa tried to concentrate on the band playing. They were very good, but Marisa knew that she and Sam could beat them.

Jessica went down to the water's edge to watch for the whales to reappear. They always did—after diving, fishing down below in the plankton-rich waters flowing in from the Gulf of St. Lawrence, whales always resurfaced to take a breath. Marisa had learned that it was something to count on.

She had lost faith over her years with Ted—there hadn't been much to count on, including herself. Her music had stopped, and even Sam had given up on her. After years of always meeting at the Blarney Stone for Saint Patrick's Day—no matter where in the world Sam was working, she would travel back to Baltimore, and Marisa would take the train down from Boston, and they would take the stage and set the bar on fire with their fiddles.

Marisa had gotten lost in a bad relationship—the kind of thing she'd never thought could happen to a woman like her. She was strong, tough, and brave. She'd managed to run a clinic for low-income families in Baltimore. She had opened another in South Boston—and kept working even while taking care of her first husband, Paul, after he was diagnosed with lymphoma. If only she had stayed strong after his death—instead of falling for the stockbroker Paul had trusted with their investments, the man who had trashed her, driven her apart from her sister, and killed her daughter's puppy before she finally found the courage to get herself and Jessica away from him.

"Mom, look!" Jessica said, pointing as the whale surfaced. A spout of fine mist shot up, gold in the last light of day. Marisa smiled, to let Jessica know that she saw. But as she gazed across the bay, something on the ferry caught her attention.

The vessel was midway across the passage, the narrow strait leading between the fjord's high, granite cliffs. Its deck was filled with cars and trucks, more people coming to Cape Hawk for the ceili. Some of the drivers and passengers had left their vehicles, to stand along the ferry's railing, to breathe the clear sea air and catch their first notes of the Irish music. A pair of hawks circled overhead, and most of the people looked up to watch them disappear into the thick pine forest.

All except one person—who had caught sight of Marisa, and was standing at the rail, grinning and waving. She gasped at the sight of him.

"Jess, come on!" Marisa called.

She grabbed her daughter's hand, and they ran along the wharf. The fiddles soared into "Geese in the Bog," and people in the grandstand and on blankets spread over the Cape Hawk Inn's wide green lawn began to clap in time. Marisa spotted Anne and Jude Neill, standing in the gazebo, leaning against the rail. Anne saw what was happening and called to Marisa.

The ferry's engines roared into reverse, and the water churned white around the dark red hull. One dockhand manned the controls, gears shifting as the metal plates creaked into place. Thick lines were thrown and tied. Car engines were started. Marisa held out her hands, as if she could touch the person standing at the rail.

People waiting in their cars began to toot their horns. Only one car remained unmanned, and it was Patrick's. He leaned against the rail right across from them, the setting sun making his red hair shine like copper, his blue eyes sparkle. His black Lab stood beside him, wagging her tail and seeming to grin with her red tongue hanging out.

"You came," Marisa said.

"I had to," he said.

"Had to?"

"I'm on a mission."

Marisa tilted her head, and Jessica reached out, as if she could touch the dog from across the narrow gap that separated them.

"My aunt goes on missions," Jessica said. "To places like Peru. That's where she is now."

"Jess," Marisa said, because she knew how wound up her daughter got on the topic of Sam, and she felt her disappointment that the ferry had delivered someone else.

Patrick's smile widened.

"She's coming," Jessica said stubbornly. "She's on her way—she has to be! She knows it's the ceili, and she knows we're waiting. She wouldn't miss the chance to play fiddle with you, and she wouldn't let me down!"

"Jessica," Marisa said, wondering why Patrick looked so happy; his blue eyes locked onto hers, and he wouldn't look away, his smile growing.

"I think you're right," Patrick said. "Your aunt wouldn't let you down."

"Patrick," Marisa said. He didn't know how much Jess loved Sam, how crushed she would be when Sam didn't come.

"You'd better get off the ferry," Jessica said, still holding out her hand toward the friendly dog. "Whatever your mission was, you're here now."

"My mission . . ." Patrick said, staring at Marisa.

"You beat Aunt Sam here," Jessica said.

"Not by much," a voice rang out from above.

Marisa raised her eyes. The wheelhouse was a tall rectangle, right in the middle of the deck. Wide windows looked in all directions, so the captain could see anything coming at him from any direction—whales, dolphins, fishing boats, seabirds. Maybe even fallen angels . . .

Because he seemed to have met one along the way, somewhere between the other shore and the Cape Hawk landing. The captain stood grinning, waving through the open window. Standing beside him was a tall, freckle-faced vision with bright green eyes and a halo of wild red hair, lifting her fiddle case high above her head in greeting, and her voice in song—sounding like anything but a fallen angel, sounding as if she had wings:

"I'm here!" she called.

"Aunt Sam!" Jessica cried back.

Once the ferry had docked, and Patrick had driven off and parked his car, he'd stood there quietly with his dog, watching the sisters and Jessica reunite. Marisa had been hugging Sam, pulling Jessica into the embrace. They cried, holding each other. Marisa looked into her sister's eyes, hardly able to believe she was here.

"You came," Marisa said. "Oh, Sam . . ."

"With a little help," Sam said, her eyes glinting as she looked at Patrick.

"Patrick. Thank you so much," Marisa said, turning to smile at him. Only then did he step forward, give Marisa a surprisingly shy glance and a quick hug. Marisa felt him in her arms, and her heart jumped. He kissed her lightly, and she reached up to touch his cheek.

"I'm so glad it worked out," he said, his blue eyes burning into hers.

"What happened?" Marisa asked.

"I called your sister," he said. "And she had already made up her mind. She was on her way—all she needed was a ride."

"You were on your way?" Marisa asked Sam.

Sam nodded, tears spilling down her cheeks. It had been over two years since Marisa had looked into her eyes. They were bright green, with fine lines radiating out at the corners. Marisa wanted to touch her face, wipe her tears away. She held back, trembling.

"I *was* on my way," Sam said, her voice throaty and low. "Patrick's visit . . . well, it helped me realize how much I needed to see you."

"We needed to see you too," Marisa said.

"We did, Aunt Sam," Jessica said.

"You've grown so much," Sam said, crouching down. "I can hardly believe it." She shook, sobbing. "I've missed two years of your life."

"I never stopped thinking of you," Jessica said, staring at her with wide eyes.

"Oh, honey." Sam wept. "I thought of you and your mother every day. No matter where I was or what I was doing."

"We love you, Sam," Marisa said.

"We do, Aunt Sam," Jessica said.

"It's time we'll never get back," Sam said, looking at them both. "Can you forgive me?"

Oh, what a question. Sam's eyes were so hopeful, beseeching. Marisa gazed into them and saw the little sister she had always loved, to whom she had read *The House at Pooh Corner*, and with whom she had studied biochemistry and epidemiology.

"Sam," Marisa whispered.

"I didn't know," Sam said, holding her hands, "that you had left him for good. You always went back. I just couldn't watch you do it anymore."

"I'm so sorry," Marisa said.

The sisters embraced. For Marisa, all the years melted away. Wherever in the world Sam had been, whether they had been speaking or not, they had never lost touch. They were sisters, connected forever.

"It's over now," Jessica said, "and we're all together."

Marisa looked up at Patrick, her gratitude so deep it was beyond words. This reunion had happened only because of him, yet he was standing apart. Their eyes locked; she wanted to reach out her hand, to invite him over, but she felt stunned with emotion. His eyes were filled with such a gentle expression, one she hadn't seen for so long—she shivered, because it reminded her of how Paul used to look at her.

"Patrick," she said again. "Thank you."

"You don't have to thank me," he said, his voice soft and gruff.

"How can I not?" she asked. "After what you've done for us?"

"You needed to find your sister," he said. "And she needed to find you."

"I know," Marisa said, wanting to say so much more.

"You should let Sam settle in," Patrick said, stepping back. Marisa opened her mouth to speak, but she faltered. Maybe he had just delivered Sam—and didn't plan on staying. Perhaps she had the wrong idea . . . but there was still that look in his blue eyes, reminding her of the only real love she had ever known, watching her as if he never wanted to look away.

"Aunt Sam, you brought your fiddle," Jessica said.

"I did," Sam said, glancing at Marisa. "We're going to clean up at the competition, knock those other bands right off the stage."

"Are we really going to play together?" Marisa asked, almost unable to believe it.

"I think we should, don't you?" Sam asked softly. "After Patrick went to all the trouble to get me here?"

"It's good to see you all together," Patrick said, his eyes still locked on hers. Her heart beat fast in her throat, and she swayed slightly.

"I love your dog," Jessica said as she crouched to hug and pet the black Lab.

"Flora, meet Jessica," Patrick said, finally turning away from Marisa. He stretched after his long drive, looking around, possibly looking for a way out of the family reunion. "I hope the inn takes dogs. I probably should have called first, to check." So he *was* planning to stay. Marisa smiled with relief.

"Anne and Jude are over at the ceili," Marisa said. "I'm sure they'll find a place for you and Flora. Let's go over and see. . . ."

"Yes, and check out who's playing," Sam said. Then she glanced back at the ferry. The captain, a man Marisa had often seen but never met, had just loaded up the next group of cars, preparing to cross back to the other side. He was lean and lanky, with short brown hair under a Greek fisherman's cap, and a sexy way of leaning over the controls. He smiled straight at Sam.

"You know him?" Marisa asked.

"That's T. J. McGuinn," Sam said, giving him a last wave as the horn sounded and the ferry pulled away, into the strait.

"You took a twenty-minute ferry ride and you got to know the captain? I've lived in town for months, and I didn't even know his name."

Sam smiled, her dimples showing, looking half-embarrassed as she shrugged. "T.J. and I hit it off—what can I say?"

"Can we please find Flora a hotel room?" Jessica asked. "And make sure there's a spot on the ceili schedule for Fallen Angels?"

"Sounds like a great plan," Patrick said, grinning at Marisa.

Then Sam linked arms with her and began to march toward the inn. Glancing over her shoulder, Marisa saw Patrick handing Jessica one end of Flora's red leash, showing her how to slip her hand through the loop.

"I had a puppy once," Jessica said.

"You did?" Patrick asked. "So, you like dogs?"

"I love them," Jessica said.

"Me too," Patrick said.

And Marisa was glad she was walking ahead, with Sam, because she wouldn't have wanted them to see the look in her eyes, realizing what it meant to Jessica to encounter a man who loved his dog.

Chapter 19

On the day Maeve finally came home from the hospital, Lily and Liam and Rose went to pick her up. The nurses pushed Maeve down to the lobby in a wheelchair, and Liam helped her into the car. All the way home, Maeve kept exclaiming about how wonderful everything was: the greenness of the marshes, the blue of the sky, the brightness of the day, the smell of salt in the air. She kept leaning forward to touch Lily on the shoulder, as if she couldn't quite believe they were together again. Then she'd pat Rose's hand, sitting next to her.

"I can't believe this," she said. "We're all together."

"I tried to call Patrick, to invite him to join us," Lily said. "But he's gone to Cape Hawk."

"Ah," Maeve said. "That's my dear boy."

As Liam pulled under the train trestle, into Hubbard's Point, Lily fell in love with the place all over again. Could a landscape actually be in a person's blood? The summer wind blew through the open car window, bringing the essence of roses and the sea, soothing her more than anything she'd ever known. Yet a strong longing for the wilds of Cape Hawk surged within her as well.

Clara was waiting by the wishing well. Rose had made a sign saying WELCOME HOME, MAEVE! Liam had hung it over the front door. When Clara came forward to embrace the friend she'd known and loved for the whole eighty-three years of their shared life, Maeve began openly weeping.

"I'm so sorry, my dearest," Maeve cried, gripping Clara's hands. "I wanted to tell you the truth, but I couldn't."

"You were desperate to protect our girl. I understand, darling. I do, and I'm so grateful you've come home safe. I don't think I'd be able to live without you!"

In honor of all the summer's blessings, Liam and Rose had caught lobsters. Liam had bought a rowboat with a small engine and three pots, set them just off the rocks with buoys marked with white and green stripes. That morning at dawn, while Nanny swam in the waves— her white back and dorsal ridge pink in the light of the rising sun— Liam and Rose had rowed out to haul their first catch.

Ten lobsters came up in the pots. Lily had watched from the porch as Liam showed Rose how to measure the carapace, and then how to throw back the undersize ones, and the egg-bearing female. All but three were keepers. Rose still seemed hesitant about eating lobsters, but she wanted to celebrate for Maeve's sake.

Maeve walked through her house, checking out everything. Rose stayed by her side, pointing out pictures she had drawn, flowers she had picked, asters she had pressed in the family Bible, just as Lily had done as a child. Maeve in turn had pointed out the doorway in the downstairs bedroom where she had measured Lily's growth every summer, the blue ribbons Lily had won in beach swim races, her first tennis trophy, and her very first needlepoint pillow—of a rose garden.

"See?" Maeve asked. "Your mother has always loved roses."

Rose beamed.

"Let's measure you," Maeve said, rummaging through her dresser drawer for a pencil.

"I'm short for my age," Rose said, standing against the door. Her head came up to where Lily's had been when she was six, three years younger. Lily, watching from the hall, felt a pang.

"That doesn't matter," Maeve said, making the pencil mark. "It's no use comparing yourself with others. Not just in height, but in life. It's how you grow inside—how you try and how you learn from your mistakes—that counts. That's all that matters, sweetheart."

"Thank you," Rose said, looking up at her great-grandmother with grave eyes. She turned to look at the mark and smiled.

"I used to imagine us doing this," Maeve said. "I've always saved a place for you on this door."

"Even though you didn't know me?"

"Oh, Rose. I've always known you," Maeve said, hugging her. "Right where it matters."

"Where?"

"In my heart," Maeve said.

Rose nodded. That was something she understood very well.

Liam called to say the lobsters were almost done. Lily put out corn, melted butter, and tossed the salad with tomatoes freshly picked from Clara's garden.

They sat around the kitchen table. Everyone joined hands, and Maeve said grace. Lily bowed her head. She could barely look up—all of them together at one table: Maeve, Liam, Rose, and Lily. This was a day she had so often thought would never come.

One morning while Maeve was resting and Liam and Rose were out in the boat, Lily took her coffee into the garden, to read on the iron bench. The weather was changing; the end of summer was near. A cool fog hung over the Point, softening the contours of rocks and rosebushes. The bell buoy tolled in the channel, and foghorns mourned in the distance.

"Hello, Mara."

Just like that, she thought, her hair standing on end: nine years away from him, and he just walked in as if he owned the place. Edward came out of the fog and stood before her. She glanced around for his car.

"I parked down at the beach and walked up," he said.

She stared at him without speaking. She was shaking, and she didn't want him to see. Nine years, and this was the first time they were completely alone together. He was stocky as ever, heavier than he used to be. There was gray in his brown hair. Only his eyes were the same. Bright hazel-gold, piercing in the fog.

"Why are you here?" she asked calmly. "We've asked you to leave us alone."

"'Us'?" he asked. "The only 'us' is you and me, Mara. You're my wife."

"You had the marriage annulled," she said, "and me declared dead."

"You wanted that, didn't you?" he asked, anger already starting to leak out, like steam. "Do you know what you put me through? Police grilling me as if I were a criminal. I was treated like a dog, taken in for questioning, hounded by the press."

Lily gazed beyond him, to the cottage. She didn't want to look at his eyes. His tone was quiet, but his eyes were burning with rage.

"You don't know what it was like, staring into camera after camera, knowing that the whole world wondered whether I had killed you, chopped up your body, and thrown it into the Sound."

Lily held back the shiver so he couldn't see. He sounded as if he had given the grisly scenario some careful thought. *Chopped up your body.* The words reverberated.

"The only reason you were upset about my disappearing," she said, "is that it made you look bad. Your feelings had nothing to do with me, or the baby. You didn't want the baby, Edward. You barely spoke to me the whole time I was pregnant, except to tell me how unhappy you were about our lives changing."

"You *did* make me look bad!" he said, as if she hadn't even mentioned the baby. But Lily stayed focused.

"You'd bump into me, hard, every chance you got. You spilled things on me. When I passed you, you tripped me. How many times did I fall when I was pregnant?"

"I can't help that you fell."

"You were too much of a coward to come out and hit me. But you made sure I felt your force. You beat me in every way but with your fists."

Again, the smug look touched his eyes and mouth. His lips twitched in a smile. Maybe he was remembering his old cruelties. Maybe it gave him pleasure to know that she had figured him out.

"You were clumsy, Mara. You always have been."

Lily's muscles rippled. She thought of herself on the tennis court, getting to the hard shots, putting the ball away. She thought of herself carrying Rose as a baby, a toddler, a small child—Rose in one arm, groceries or bags of yarn or rock salt for the icy walkway in Cape Hawk balanced in the other. She had never fallen, not once, in the years since she'd left him.

"It's over, Edward. I see you now."

"What does that mean?" he asked.

"It means that I get who you are. You can't hurt me the way you used to, because I understand the kind of person you are."

He took a step forward. They were very close, touching toe to toe. Lily felt his breath on her forehead. He was just a few inches taller than she was, but he seemed as aggressive as a giant. His skin gave off violence.

"I'm getting to you right now," he said, his teeth gritted, his face hot red.

"Leave," she said.

"You. Can't. Get. Away. With. What. You. Did," he said staccato, with his fists clenched. "You humiliated me."

"Edward, I was trying to save my own life," she said. "Do you remember the mountain? Think of that the next time you wonder why I ran away."

Their eyes met, and now Lily couldn't look away. Nine and a half years ago, she had seen him for exactly who he really was, and he knew it. Bringing it up now felt powerful, vindicating. But seeing the blood in his face, dark red and boiling, made her stomach drop.

"You didn't call the police that day," he said, eyes glinting, because he knew that her mistake in not calling for help had given him the upper hand.

"You were my husband," she said. "I tried to tell myself I was wrong." He stared, fists clenched.

"I was pregnant. I couldn't bear to face what I was actually married to."

"*What*? You say that as if I'm a *thing*," he said. "You treat me as if I'm a nothing, and you always have. That's the problem, Mara. You don't like men. You don't respect us. I feel sorry for what's-his-name. The one-armed wonder."

She started to back away. Edward was so ugly, in his words and heart. She just wanted to go inside, gather her family to her, remind herself of the light and goodness in her life.

"You should have told the police that day," he said. "You realize that, don't you?"

She didn't answer.

"It would have been your best chance." He smiled. "Found any earrings lately?"

Lily started to tremble, feeling wrenched inside, just like when she had lived with him, feeling twisted like a skein of yarn.

"There's no one to hear you. Don't worry—I checked before I let you see me. My daughter is out in the boat with your freak, and Maeve is napping on her bed. I looked in the window. Having her bedroom on the first floor really comes in handy."

"You leave her alone," Lily said, her voice rising.

"I don't waste my time with people like Maeve," he said. "She means *nothing* to me. Did she stand up for me after you walked out? No. She knew you were alive, and she let me suffer through all those police visits." He reached into his back pocket, took out a rolled-up piece of paper.

"See," he said, tapping the paper on the palm of one hand, "you really don't know. You don't *know* whether you were imagining what happened on the mountain. You've always had such a good imagination, Mara. You're so *creative*. Seeing things that aren't there, thinking I mean one thing when I'm saying another. You doubt yourself, don't you? Even now, you're asking yourself, 'Was I right? Or was I wrong?' Right?" He smiled, as if he'd just told a great joke.

Lily's heart was pounding. "I don't doubt myself, Edward, not now. And neither does your other wife. We both know what you did, who you are."

"What?" he asked.

"Patty," she said. "Grace's mother."

He looked shocked. "Where are they?"

"We all run away from you, Edward," she said. "She's a wonderful woman. I'm just sorry she had to go through what I did. You'll be happy to know that she's thriving—just as I did."

Lily had gone too far. She saw his expression change—from anger, to shock, and now white-hot fury. He smacked the rolled-up paper down on the arm of the bench. It flew into the low cedar growing just behind the bench as a windscreen.

"Read *that*, Mara," he said. "Then let's see you *thrive*. I hope you enjoy every minute of it."

Lily shook her head. She began to walk slowly toward the cottage.

"Pick it up!" he shouted. "Read it!"

She just ignored him. Her body was quaking from the inside out, but she made herself walk erect and steady, one foot in front of the other. She felt the glass doorknob, cool under her palm. Turned it, pushed the door open, quietly closed it behind her.

Edward stood in the yard, staring at the house. She saw him gazing straight through the kitchen window, shadowy in the fog. Lily's heart was in her throat. She backed away, so she was in the dark hallway, where he couldn't see her. He looked immobile, hands on his hips, as if he might stand there forever.

After a while, he walked over to retrieve the paper that was lodged in the cedar branches. He smoothed it, brushing away needles. Then he folded it. She watched him walk toward the front door, but her view was blocked by the rosebush growing up alongside. He seemed to pause for a minute, and then she heard the screen door screech open. Her heart was racing, and she looked wildly for the portable phone, ready to dial 911.

Then the screen door slammed, and she saw him walk past the wishing well, up the stone steps, and out of sight toward the beach. Lily went upstairs, to the bedroom overlooking the front yard and dead-end road for a better view. He was nowhere in sight. Maeve was still dozing, and Liam and Rose hadn't returned from their boat ride. Lily walked down the stairs, through the first floor, and into the kitchen.

Hands trembling, she opened the door. The paper was wedged in the crack. As she reached for it, she pricked her finger on a thorn; he had slid a white rose into the paper's fold. She let the rose fall to the floor. Blood from her finger smeared the paper as she spread it open.

It was a subpoena:

THE CONNECTICUT STATUTE
Sec. 46b-168. (Formerly Sec. 52-184).
Genetic tests when paternity is in dispute.
Assessment of costs.

(a) In any proceeding in which the question of paternity is at issue, the court or a family support magistrate, on motion of any party, may order genetic tests which shall mean deoxyribonucleic acid tests, to be performed by a hospital, accredited laboratory, qualified physician or other qualified person designated by the court, to determine whether or not the putative father or husband is the father of the child. The results of such tests, whether ordered under this section or required by the IV-D agency under section 46b-168a, shall be admissible in evidence to either establish definite exclusion of the putative father or husband or as evidence that he is the father of the child without the need for foundation testimony or other proof of authenticity or accuracy, unless objection is made in writing not later than twenty days prior to the hearing at which such results may be introduced in evidence.

Lily sank into a chair. She stared and stared at the paper. Patrick's words had just come true. The minutes passed, and she had no sense of time at all. She heard voices outside. Looking up, she saw Rose's face in the window. Happy, carefree, just back from her boat ride. She held up a hand in greeting, her eyes elated and full of joy.

Such pretty green eyes. Lily smiled through the window. She picked up the rose and the subpoena. Going to the door, she couldn't stop gazing at her happy daughter. Eyes are the window to the soul, she thought, smiling at Rose's. They revealed what a person had inside, and what Rose had was beautiful.

This can't be happening, Lily thought. She felt wild, overwhelmed, as if she'd just gotten off a dangerous flight. Her feet were on solid ground, but her body was still rattling, from all the fear and bumps. From the minute she had decided to return to Hubbard's Point, she had known in her heart that this day would come. That didn't lessen the impact of now confronting the reality of a no-holds-barred battle with Edward—with Rose, precious Rose, in the center of it all.

Opening the door, she felt her daughter charge into her arms.

"Do we have any old bread?" Rose asked. "The swans are swimming by, and I want to feed them."

"Sure," Lily said. She rummaged through the bread box.

"Want to come down on the rocks?" Rose asked. "And feed them with us?"

Lily started to say no. She had to call a lawyer, she had to research Connecticut law, she had to pack all their bags and get ready to go into hiding again, slip out of Hubbard's Point, Black Hall, Connecticut, the United States. Her veins were flooded with adrenaline, literally compelling her with fight-or-flight instincts. But Rose was staring up at her, eyes sparkling, chest rising and falling from the everyday exertion of being nine years old.

"Of course," Lily said. She grabbed the bread, and Rose's hand. Rose led her down the hill beside the cottage, past the cement medallion embedded with shells and a sand dollar that Lily had made when she was a young girl. Liam stood on the rocks. Rose scrambled down to him, bread in hand. The swans were swimming out of the silver mist, around the Point. Liam stared at Lily, and she knew that he knew something was wrong.

The swans glided up, graceful white birds with orange bills. They looked so lovely and serene. The babies they had had at the beginning of the summer had grown; their feathers were still dark, but getting whiter.

"Mom," Rose said. "Dr. Neill told me swans are like belugas. They're born dark, as a way of staying camouflaged from predators. Then they get lighter as they grow up, until they turn pure white when they're adults."

Lily nodded, unable to speak.

"Aren't they beautiful?" Rose asked. She held out her hand, and the mother swan got close enough to almost nip her fingers. Lily cried out as she lunged forward to grab Rose and hold her tight. They lost their balance slightly, and Lily scraped her bare foot on the barnacles.

"Mommy!" Rose said, alarmed.

"Be careful," Lily said, holding back tears as she gripped Rose. "I just don't want you to get hurt, honey."

"Okay, Mom. I'll be careful," Rose said looking surprised. "I'm fine."

"She's fine," Liam said, steadying them both.

Lily nodded, but he just didn't know. He didn't know that *none* of them was fine, that everything had changed. The fog seemed so soft, and it drained color from the landscape. The water was silver, the rocks were gray, the weathered cottage was silvery brown, the roses seemed bleached of life. Nothing felt familiar, nothing at all.

It was a different world.

Chapter 20

They had the subpoena out on the kitchen table, taking turns reading it. Only Lily couldn't pick it up again. She knew that no amount of staring at it would make it go away.

Clara had invited Rose over for a tea party, which was really just an excuse to get her out of the house while Lily, Liam, and Maeve tried to figure out what to do. Fog had settled on the landscape, contributing to the uneasy feeling inside.

"He's going to try to take her away from me," Lily said.

"That will never happen," Liam said.

"This is all my fault," Maeve said. "If only I hadn't gotten sick . . ."

"Oh, Granny," Lily said.

"You shouldn't have come home," Maeve said. "Darling, why don't you just leave? Just take Rose and go back to Canada. Hide her even deeper than before."

"We couldn't leave you," Liam said.

Lily felt stunned by how quickly a feeling of well-being could evaporate. Even knowing that Edward knew she was back, she'd been lulled into a sense of safety. Being home with her grandmother, reuniting with her friends, getting even closer to Liam and seeing how much he loved it here, saying yes to his proposal, all had given Lily a feeling of her own power.

But now Edward was going to enlist the courts to help him play his games. Lily remembered seeing him with children when they were married. Bay's kids were little, and they would often run up from the beach, to ask if they could play on the rocks. Sometimes Lily and Edward would be visiting from Hawthorne, and Lily had loved their visits.

She'd get bread for them to feed the swans, drop-lines so they could go crabbing, fishing poles so they could see what was biting. There were two girls and a boy, and Lily had imagined what it would be like when she and Edward had their family. How many children would they have? Would they love the beach and the sea, like Lily? Or the mountains and the woods, like Edward?

She had expected Edward to join in. Bay's kids were adorable, bright, and funny. They loved to joke and laugh, and they weren't the least bit squeamish about seaweed, crabs, or bait. But Edward would never even talk to them.

"Come on," Lily would say, tugging his hand. "Let's take them swimming. We can go out to the big rock."

"It's covered with bird shit," he would say, sitting on the porch, absorbed in his laptop. He barely even looked up, so he didn't see the looks of first exasperation and then resolve pass across Lily's face.

"Okay then," she said, patiently trying another angle. "Let's take them snorkeling. I saw some lobsters in the cove yesterday."

"I'm trying to get my resumé together," he'd snap. "Can't you see that?"

Lily didn't believe him. She knew that he was playing computer games, because she could see his screen reflected in the cottage window behind him. She thought of asking him why he never seemed to care about getting his resumé together except when the kids were over. He seemed completely unconcerned with finding a job he really liked, just coasting from brokerage firm to brokerage firm, never really getting entrenched anywhere, sometimes leaving even before his commission checks came in. Lily took a deep breath, determined to salvage the day. She grabbed his hand.

"Edward," she said.

He didn't reply.

"Please?"

"Go have fun with your little friends," he said.

"I will," she said. "I hope you'll play with our kids when we have them."

He just kept tapping on the keyboard, and she shook her head, feeling frustrated. The kids waited on the rocks, faces turned up toward the cottage. They had seen this same interaction before; Lily could see they weren't expecting much from Edward.

She was halfway down the small grassy hill to the seawall, when Edward said, "Hey." Lily turned back, shielding her eyes against the sun to look at him.

"You look good," he said, smiling. She was wearing a blue tank suit, and her body was thin and strong.

"Thank you," she said, wondering if this was supposed to be a peace offering. In case it was, she smiled.

"Women ruin their figures when they get pregnant," he said. His smile widened.

Lily had reddened, stopped in her tracks. Why did he have to say that, with the kids right there? Her eyes stung with hot, sudden tears. Down on the rocks, she went through the motions of tying on sinkers, baiting hooks, helping the children cast into the bay. She had felt numb, though. Edward's words could do that to her.

That night, in bed, he had seemed so avid, as if he wanted to make it up to her. Edward's ardor was really rare, so she fought to push her hurt aside, wrapping her arms around his neck, arching her back, trying to work up feelings of passion.

She had started feeling unconnected to her body. Her heart and soul seemed to be in a completely different place than her bones and skin. She ached to really be touched, in a way she could feel it. But his hand on her skin was rough, hurtful—harsh and abrasive, as if making her flinch was more the point than giving her pleasure.

Was this what marriage was like? Once the thrills and excitement of early courtship were over, was this what everyone did? She couldn't even remember the last time he had wanted to have sex with her. Usually he slept with a wall of pillows between them, flinching when she'd run a tentative hand down his spine.

Before they got married, he had told her he wanted to be a father. But after the wedding, she heard only how much he didn't want to be a parent, wanted her to keep her figure, wanted her all to himself.

But right now, here they were in their bed, having sex. There was no eye contact; he stared at the headboard, and Lily felt tears come to her eyes. The friction hurt. It was as if he had forgotten he was inside a woman, inside the softest place in her body. She gripped the rails of the headboard, bracing herself.

Lily's tears began to leak out because she used to think *Maybe tonight we'll make a baby, maybe I'll get to be a mother.* She cried because this felt like destruction, not creation.

Lily remembered that now, shivering at Maeve's table. She closed her eyes. She had a collection of worst moments in her life, and that was one of them—the night she had conceived Rose. She had wept inconsolably afterward.

Lily remembered driving over to Maeve's house the next day. She hadn't told her grandmother that she was upset. By then, she was practiced in the lie: smiling, laughing, acting as if everything was great. She was always "fine."

"How are you, darling?" *Fine.*

"Would you like some tea?" *Yes, that would be fine.*

"How was your weekend?" *Just fine, thank you.*

It was always worst after a fight. In fact, after one of the worst yelling matches—with Lily losing it totally, screaming so loudly she hurt her throat, and Edward looking at her with the smug victory he always seemed to feel when he made her that angry—she felt like she was about to collapse. He huffed into bed, covers pulled over his head. Her chest hurt, and she felt afraid.

She was young. Her family had no history of heart trouble. This was just stress, she told herself. She took her own pulse, but she was too upset to count her heartbeats.

Not wanting to overreact, she went into the bedroom. "Edward," she said.

He didn't reply.

"I think I might be having a heart attack."

He ignored her, as if she had just said she was tired, or cold, or had a stomachache. Lily's thinking was very skewed. She didn't want to dial 911. It would just call attention to their chaotic life and marriage. Neighbors had called the police a few weeks earlier, after they'd been yelling into the night. "Everything is okay, Officer," Edward had said. And Lily had done her part—smiling at the cops, both of whom she'd seen around their small town. "I'm fine," she said. "Everything is fine."

Domestic squabblers, she'd heard the neighbor woman whisper to a friend in the hall one day after that, while Lily stood on the other side of her apartment door, cringing with shame.

So, not wanting another siren to come to their apartment, she'd pulled on her coat and driven herself to the Shoreline Clinic. The closer she got, the worse she felt. The pain seemed hot, as if someone had stuck a piece of blazing coal right in the spot where her heart should be. She touched her sternum and felt pain radiating into her ribs. It felt as if someone had punched her, as if someone's knuckles had come slamming into her chest.

By the time she got inside the clinic, she could barely walk. Quivering, hand on her heart, she'd sat at the triage desk, silently weeping. She had been coming to this clinic since she was a baby. Her parents had brought her here for croup when she was a year old. She had come here at four, when she'd stepped on a rusty nail and needed a tetanus shot. She'd come here to get her blood test, the week before marrying Edward. They had her records—and they knew her by sight.

The desk nurse had bought needlework supplies from her. The ER attending had ordered several needlepoint pillows for her dining room chairs. They all knew Maeve, from years of living in the area. As she sat at the nurses' station, Lily thought she should have gone somewhere else. She should have driven to another clinic, where no one knew her, no one would recognize Edward and look at him with judgment the next time they saw him at the IGA.

"I think," Lily said, trying to get the words out, "I'm having a heart attack."

They were so kind. They took her right in—to a doctor she'd never met. She wanted to ask them to give her a woman doctor, but she didn't have the strength. She was afraid of a man laughing at her, thinking she was making something out of nothing. The doctor did an EKG. He sat beside her the whole time. He just gazed at her with kind eyes, and his presence was so restful and gentle, it made Lily cry all the more.

He listened to her heart. His touch, one hand on her shoulder, the other on the stethoscope as he moved it over her chest, was softer than her husband's. It told her that she mattered, she was worth caring about, her heart was worth listening to.

When he reached her sternum, he pressed it gently with two fingers. Lily nearly shrieked with pain. "There," he said. "That's where it hurts?"

"Yes," she sobbed.

And deeper inside, where he couldn't get to with his examining touch. She just sat there on the table, while the doctor read her tests, took her blood pressure, waited for her to stop crying. He asked her about stress. Shaking, she said she was under some. At work? He asked. "At home," she said, and they might have been the two hardest words she'd ever spoken. He nodded.

"I haven't found anything cardiac," he said when he had finished.

She waited, listening.

"That doesn't mean there's not something there. But I've found no evidence of a heart attack, or heart failure, anything like that."

"But my heart hurts so much."

He nodded, taking her so seriously. She remembered how much that meant to her, the way he was really believing her, not thinking she was crazy or overreacting. It made it possible for her to take a deep breath.

"I'm going to order a stress test," he said. "I'll recommend a cardiologist for you. But I don't think it will show anything wrong."

"Then what?" she asked.

He stared into her eyes. He was young, tall, thin, with big blue eyes and thinning blond hair. He wore a white coat. As he spoke, he took her hand, as if it were the most natural thing in the world.

"I think you have a broken heart," he said.

The words unleashed new tears. Lily sat there crying softly, just holding the hand of this doctor she'd never met. Deep down she knew he was right; she just never thought she'd hear a doctor say it. He gave her the name of a cardiologist, written on a sheet of notepaper. He also wrote down the name of someplace else he thought she should call: Shoreline Domestic Violence Services.

"He doesn't hit me," she whispered, shocked by seeing the words.

"Emotional and verbal abuse can be just as bad."

"But it's not domestic *violence.* Is it?"

"Ask your heart," the doctor said quietly. He patted her shoulder, then left the room.

Lily got dressed. She was shaking as she pulled on her clothes. The contact jelly from the EKG stuck to her bra and shirt. She wondered whether Edward would be up when she got home. Maybe he would be worried, shaken up by the fact that she had actually left.

Or maybe he wouldn't. Her mind was racing, and her heart still hurt. She was worried about what she would find at home, the kind of mood Edward would be in. Domestic violence? She shook her head. The doctor had been so nice, but he didn't understand after all. Edward never laid a hand on her. They fought; they had problems. His terrible childhood had left him with so much anger.

Lily had read about the cycle of violence. She knew that men who were beaten as children often beat their wives and kids. Edward had hit Judy, but he had resisted hitting Lily. Wasn't that a sign of his willingness to be different, to treat her well? Lily should have explained that to the doctor.

She had been too shy to tell him about their sex life, how painful it all was. Leaving the clinic, she had taken care of the paperwork on the way out. The doctor was busy with another patient, but he nodded to Lily as she passed by. She mustered a smile for him. *Look,* it seemed to say. *I'm fine now.*

She dropped the sheet of notepaper in the garbage on the way out, in the pail in the parking lot, but only when she was sure he wouldn't see. And then she drove home. Little did she know, she was already pregnant.

Now, so many years, so many miles later, she looked out the window, at her beautiful Rose playing in her grandmother's garden.

"We have to get a lawyer," Lily said.

The August day was cool and misty, the contours of every tree and cliff blurred, Cape Hawk's dark pines and black rock ravines painted soft gray by the weather. Only the inn's long red roof remained vivid, visible even across the water, pulling everyone to the ceili.

It was Marisa's day to work at In Stitches, so she and Sam had to practice right there in the shop, doors flung open to the foggy wharf and bay. The two sisters hadn't played together in a long time—over two years. Marisa, dark-haired and tall, sat on one stool, while Sam, redheaded and even taller, perched on another, running through scales on their fiddles.

They were so happy to be together again, and in some ways it was as comfortable as ever—Marisa had brought Sam coffee on the couch that morning, Sam had brushed and braided Jessica's hair—they all had that bone-level comfort that comes from being family. Practicing their music, Marisa wondered when they'd start to talk.

She gazed out the shop door, and she watched as Jessica took Flora for a walk across the inn's lawn. It was too damp for people to picnic on blankets, but nothing could keep them away from the ceili—some had set up folding chairs, others stood in clusters, and all were dressed for the weather in raincoats, slickers, and plastic sheets. Marisa knew that Patrick had told Jess that she could walk Flora anytime. She kept her eyes peeled for him, but he was nowhere to be seen.

"Want to take a break?" Sam asked after a few minutes.

Marisa nodded. "I was thinking the same thing."

They went into the back, poured glasses of iced tea from the small refrigerator Lily kept in the workroom. Clinking glasses, both sisters smiled.

"I'm so glad you're here," Marisa said. "I never thought you'd come."

"I almost didn't," Sam said.

"When Patrick told me you were back in Baltimore," Marisa said, "I was so shocked."

"I didn't mean to hurt you," Sam said.

Marisa felt so tight; they had been building to this for so long, after the years of Ted. Her chest ached, and she stared into her younger sister's eyes. She flooded with emotion, just as she had at their reunion. "My terrible marriage," she said.

Sam took her hands. "Ted," she said.

"I was so lonely," Marisa said. "It was after Paul had died, and you went back to Baltimore. He was there—he seemed to love me. And he seemed to love Jessica."

"I know," Sam said. "I was happy for you at first—I was. But I just watched you disappearing. You were losing yourself, and I was losing you."

"Sam," Marisa said. She swallowed, thinking of how she had always wanted her little sister to look up to her. She wanted to be a good example, wanted to show Sam the way. "I didn't know what to do. It's so hard to explain—"

"You don't have to," Sam said.

"But—"

"You ran those clinics. You treated so many battered women. I thought you would know—I never thought it would happen to you."

"I never did either. I thought I knew the signs—but he was so charming at first. He seemed to love me so much."

"Isn't that what all the women tell us?" Sam asked softly. "When we ask them what's going on?"

Marisa nodded, remembering the many hands she had held, the tired and confused and terrified faces she'd looked into.

"The worst part," she said, "was what he did to Jessica's puppy. I still can't believe I put her in a situation like that."

"I know," Sam said. "When you told me, I wanted to come kill him myself."

"That was the last thing I did tell you," Marisa said. "You seemed so disgusted with me. That's when I finally got out. How could I have let it go so far?"

"I just felt so helpless. You know what the worst part for me was? It was hearing you stop realizing how wonderful you are," Sam said.

"What?" Marisa asked, shocked.

Sam blinked hard, her green eyes glittering. "I just watched you giving in so much to him," she said. "You were such a star in nursing school. Who, in our whole class, would volunteer every spare minute she had, to vaccinate little kids in the worst sections of town? My sister."

Marisa listened, spellbound.

"Who would practice her fiddle every night, after her labs and homework were done, just so she could put on a fabulously terrific performance Friday and Saturday nights—to make sure the tip jar overflowed, so we could pay the next semester's tuition? My sister."

"Oh, Sam," Marisa said.

"You played like an angel, and I'm not talking *fallen*," Sam said. "You were never a fallen angel—that was me. I rode my big sister's coattails all through nursing school. I was the one with too many boyfriends, not enough A's."

"No, Sam," Marisa said. "You were always wonderful. You have the most compassionate heart I know. That's what makes you such a great nurse . . . and sister, and aunt."

"Well, I don't think the family compassion has ever been an issue,"

Sam said. "You had love to spare with him. You have a solid-gold heart, and he cashed in."

Marisa chuckled, wiping away tears as she reached for a pen. "That's a great line," she said. "I think we could sell it in Nashville. . . ."

"'She had a solid-gold heart,'" Sam sang, making up a tune on the fiddle as she went along.

"'And he cashed in,'" Marisa harmonized.

"'He was a solid-gold jerk,'" Sam continued.

"'With a heart of tin,'" Marisa sang.

Sam cracked up. They improvised the music, playing together as if they'd never stopped. The notes flew out of their fiddles, their rhythm was suddenly in sync, their toes tapped time, and Marisa knew that everything was going to be okay. The sisters had always worked out their lives in music. They had started off more than one show worried about exams, or a patient, or so many other things, and ended the night toasting and hugging and dancing with joy.

It had always been that way, and it was still. They ranged from their brand-new, just-written song straight into "Galway Lasses," and from there into "Geese in the Bog." Then for something sweeter, "Maud-abawn Chapel."

"I wrote a new song," Marisa said eventually.

"Really?"

"Yep. It's called 'Storm Tossed.'"

"A little autobiographical?" Sam asked, grinning.

"Slightly," Marisa said, glancing out the door again, looking for Patrick. "It's pretty easy—it's in G."

"Ooh," Sam said, after listening to the first few bars. "Pretty. Love that E minor."

"Heartstrings, right?" Marisa asked.

"Oh yeah."

Nursing was the sisters' way, every bit as much as music. *Heartstrings,* Sam had said, and Marisa knew that they were what counted. Playing fiddle with her sister, Marisa stared out the door as the Cape Hawk ferry crossed the water. She was concentrating on her rhythm, on keeping time with Sam, but she was also looking for the big red-headed Irishman who had brought them back together, who had tugged Marisa's heartstrings and inspired her song.

Chapter 21

The lawyer's name was Lindsey Grant Winship. She was a partner in a Hartford firm, with offices in Constitution Plaza. Tall windows overlooked the Old State House, redbrick and gold-domed, an austere reminder of Connecticut's colonial beginnings. Lily sat in her office with Liam, her heart hammering as if she had just finished a race—instead of being about to begin one.

Lindsey was about fifty, tall and lean, with softly streaked brown hair. She was warm and welcoming, instantly comforting and understanding and somehow maternal—yet her brown eyes were filled with the curiosity and enthusiasm of a young girl. Her office was filled with color: paintings by her daughter, wonderful abstract portraits and landscapes, touched with gold leaf. Photographs of her daughter, from babyhood up until the present, graduate school. And shells and rocks picked up from the many beaches Lindsey and her family had visited over a lifetime of vacations.

Lindsey listened carefully, filling a yellow legal pad with notes as Lily gave background on her marriage, escape, Rose's birth and life, up until the present.

"He delivered the subpoena himself, instead of having a process server do it. That was very aggressive of him," Lindsey said when Lily was finished.

"Edward was never lacking in aggression. He never hit me, though. . . ." Lily said.

"The sophisticated ones never do," Lindsey said. "They use threats to instill fear, just like Edward did when he told you about Judy. He made sure you understood the potential for future consequences—that if you stepped out of line, you might very well have been beaten, just like Judy. That's one way he tried to control you."

"What can I expect now?"

"He will try to use Family Court to attack you. Men like him use custody battles to destroy their mates, while also maintaining a connection with them. Lily, I'm sorry . . . but many women experience the most brutal abuse during this process."

"But won't the judge see through him?" Liam asked.

Lindsey grimaced. "He'll play a role—the part of someone unfairly accused. Not only will he not admit his behavior, he'll deny it. He'll highlight his volunteer work, presenting himself as kindhearted and caring. Just as he did with Lily, during the marriage."

"He kept me off balance for so long," Lily said. "I was so confused about what he was really like. He would tell me he was one way, but he would behave another. He'd tell me he loved me—but he acted as if he hated me. It took me over two years to realize that I had to pay attention to what he *did*—not what he *said*."

Lindsey nodded. "Edward is a textbook case. He's controlling, manipulative, feels fully entitled, and massively disrespectful. He really believed he owned you, Lily. Once you married him, you became his. His outrage over your escape, your seeing him for who he really is, will fuel him now."

"Fuel him?" Lily asked.

"Any attempt you make to stand up for your rights he'll take as an act of aggression against him. And Edward's propensity to see you as his personal property will no doubt extend to Rose," Lindsey said. "What was his reaction when you first told him you were pregnant?"

"When I told him," she said, "he threw a lamp against the door. He kicked a hole in the wall. I never saw him so violent. He said, 'Don't I have any say in this?' His eyes went blank, the way they always did when he raged."

"Lily," Liam said, taking her hand.

"Was that when you decided to leave him?" Lindsey asked.

"Almost," she said, not wanting to remember.

"What happened, Lily?"

Lily closed her eyes. "Once his anger passed, he put his arms around me, rocked me, told me that everything would be different. I thought, Maybe this will be the turning point. Maybe he'll finally 'get it.' He told me he had made a picnic for us."

She opened her eyes, watching Lindsey as she took notes.

"We got into the car, went for a drive. It was late fall, and most of the leaves were off the trees. But it was a beautiful, bright, sunny day. When Edward was good, he was really fun. He put in a CD, and he held my hand. I felt so turned around—I just wanted to believe that we could

make it work. I thought maybe a baby would make everything different."

Lindsey nodded.

"We drove north, up into Massachusetts. Edward had been born in
Springfield, and he said he always felt happiest, rejuvenated, when he
went to back to his home state. In spite of his bad childhood, his
favorite teacher and aunts lived up there. I thought maybe we were going to visit his family."

"But you weren't?"

Lily shook her head, remembering. "No," she said. "We drove into
the Berkshires. There was a little ski area, where he had learned how to
ski as a boy. The road was so pretty. It wound into the hills, through the
woods. Edward told me that he loved the forest—trees made him feel
closest to his roots. The sea belonged to me, but he loved getting lost in
the woods. We drove up the mountain trail . . ."

"Which ski area?"

"Mount Blantyre," Lily said. "There were just a few yellow leaves left
on the branches, but we climbed the mountain, into the darkest pines.
Suddenly we emerged—at this amazing overlook. We parked in a lot
filled with other cars. The day was quite warm. People had come to
hike."

"And you were pregnant?"

"Yes. But by then I wasn't sick anymore. I really wanted to stretch my
legs, get some air after the drive. He got the picnic basket out . . ."

Liam looked away, as if he couldn't bear to hear about a day with
Edward. Or perhaps he knew what was coming next.

"We headed up the trail," Lily said. "We passed a few people, everyone smiling and saying hi. Edward was telling me how when the baby
was born, he'd teach him or her how to ski. We'd come here every
weekend in the winter—and maybe even in the summer or fall, for
hikes. Hubbard's Point would be for summer, of course."

"Did you pass a lot of people?" Lindsey asked.

"At first," Lily said. "But they began thinning out." She breathed
steadily, remembering. "Everything was fine. I was getting hungry,
thinking we should stop soon. The trail wasn't steeply pitched. He had
chosen a long, lazy hike, and I remember feeling touched by his care.
Edward liked extreme hiking—almost rock climbing. That day we took
the easy route—but even so, there were some serious drop-offs. I remember feeling a little vertigo, but not too bad. I'm a New Englan-
der—good and hardy when it comes to the outdoors."

"Lily . . ." Liam said. He gazed at her; he could feel what she was
about to say.

"Suddenly Edward stopped. We were on a long straight stretch of trail, at the head of a rock face. It was such a simple thing he did . . . he looked left, then right—" Lily said. "And I knew."

Lindsey and Liam just stared at her.

The hair still stood up on the back of Lily's neck when she remembered. Edward had been looking to make sure no one would see him push her off. "The look on his face was all-business. His eyes were black, focused. He stepped toward me, grabbed my wrist."

Lily swallowed, cringed, reliving it as she so often had in her dreams, nightmares of Edward. The coldest, most fearful part was also the seemingly most innocent: when he had stopped, looked oh-so-casually back and forth.

"He tried to push you off the cliff?" Lindsey asked. "Tried to kill you?"

Lily nodded.

"He didn't want the baby," Liam said.

"Or me," Lily said.

"But he probably would have inherited everything you had," Lindsey said, tapping the financial documents Lily had brought.

"My instincts kicked in," Lily said. "I heard myself scream, and I started scrambling up the bank. He began tugging my arm, yelling at me. Almost immediately, someone came running—a young man, hiking alone. I was hysterical. I grabbed him and begged him to walk me down to the base lodge."

"What did Edward do?"

"He said I was just afraid of heights, making the whole thing up. The young hiker looked at me as if I was crazy. He believed Edward, I could see it! I was babbling. Some older couples came along; I'm not sure what they thought, but they helped me get down the mountain. Edward just stalked off. Lindsey, I know he wanted to kill me—do you believe me?"

"I do, Lily," Lindsey said.

In that moment, Lily knew in her soul that she could completely trust Lindsey Grant Winship. The lawyer's eyes were steady, her voice resolute.

"I wouldn't let him drive me home," Lily said. "I called my grandmother, and she came to get me."

"Good for you."

"I never went back to the apartment in Hawthorne," Lily said. "And on that ride home with my grandmother, I began to think of how I would get away. I had just seen how convincing he was. I was the crazy one—he was sane. That's what it would be like. He'd never let me get away. My grandmother and I began to plan."

"And then you ran away."

"To Cape Hawk," Lily said. She tried to compose herself. She stared out the window at the Old State House.

"He's not on the birth certificate," Liam said.

"That's why he's filed this motion to compel a DNA test," Lindsey said.

"Can we fight it?"

"Yes. We can stall, but he will win. The judge will force you to have Rose tested. You have to prepare yourself, Lily. Edward is going to present himself as the victim here—you took his child away for nine years. You'll see him in court as a hurt, sensitive man, trying to work things out for the good of Rose."

Lily's heart began to race—she could see him already, his puppy-dog eyes, his boyish grin, his false humility. She tried to imagine the way the judge would view him—as a wronged man.

"What does he want?" Liam asked.

"That's a very good question," Lindsey said. "Because what he says he wants and what he really wants are two different things. Lily, you'll need all your strength for this. Edward will probably claim to want full custody."

"Oh God!"

"He doesn't, of course."

Lily held on tight, stomach muscles rigid as she steeled herself to sit still and hear Lindsey out.

"He sees this as a game—the whole point is beating you. He's going to use the courts to attack you, and he's going to use Rose as a pawn. He doesn't want full custody. He probably doesn't even want shared custody. If the court grants him visitation, he will most likely not even keep to the schedule. He'll miss every date and appointment. There is one very serious weapon that we have in our arsenal."

"What's that?" Liam asked, because Lily was too sick to respond.

"Child support. If he is found to be Rose's father, we can ask the court to order that he pay child support."

"I wouldn't take his money if I were broke and penniless!" Lily said.

"Lily, I know," Lindsey said. "It's just the way this kind of litigation is played."

Played—was this some kind of game? Lily bowed her head—she was in a nightmare beyond imagining. She felt dizzy, completely overwhelmed.

"The court will appoint what's called a 'guardian ad litem,'" Lindsey said. "Someone designated by the court to look out for the child's best interests, during the pendency of the case."

Lily felt the world tilt. She was skidding off the earth, into space, into the void. A person designated to look after Rose's best interests? Someone other than Lily? She felt Liam take her hand.

"I can't believe this," Lily said. "I don't want Edward in her life at *all*!"

"I know," Lindsey said.

"Let's not even let it get that far. Fight the paternity test for as long as you can," Liam said. "No matter what it costs. If it takes everything we have, it will be worth it, to keep him away from Lily and Rose."

"The hearing is scheduled for next week," Lindsey said. "We're ordered to appear before Judge Porter, at Family Court in Silver Bay, and I plan to play Rose's medical history strong and hard."

"We'll be there," Liam said. "And we'll tell him exactly who Edward Hunter is."

Lindsey was gazing at Lily, as if assessing her strength, her capability for withstanding the prolonged court battle that lay ahead.

"I should have stayed hidden," Lily whispered. "Shouldn't I?"

Lindsey didn't reply.

Chapter 22

From the top deck of the *Redtail*—the Cape Hawk ferry—Patrick could see forever, or almost. A fine mist obscured only the very tops of the massive cliffs lining the great fjord, pine trees clinging to ledges, branches dotted with the white heads of adult male bald eagles; Cape Hawk harbor and bay, silver in the fog, sliced with the white wakes of fishing and whale-watch boats, rippled by the black backs of diving whales; the long, red-roofed inn, where Patrick and Flora were staying, nestled into the town; and the wharf, where Marisa was currently tending Lily's shop.

He leaned over the rail, as if he could hear the music over the ferry engine's roar as the vessel pulled away from the Cape Hawk wharf. He could still see the look in Marisa's eyes the moment she'd caught sight of her sister. Nothing had ever made him feel better than bringing Sam north. As he stared at the shop, he imagined telling Marisa how it had all come to pass.

On the other hand, maybe he should just head back to Connecticut. He'd find out what he could for Liam, then drive home. After what he and Sandra had gone through in the divorce, trusting wasn't easy. Maeve had called him on it, telling him to take this chance with Marisa. He stared toward the shop, and his heart raced just knowing that she was inside.

"Sorry it took me so long," the voice sounded behind him. "But I had to make sure my copilot was up from below."

"No problem," Patrick said, turning toward T. J. McGuinn, coming out of the *Redtail* wheelhouse.

"So, you're a friend of the Mahon sisters?" T.J. asked.

"Yes," Patrick said.

"I've noticed Marisa around town, and my buddy Liam Neill sees her friend Lily," T.J. said. "She keeps to herself. I'd never guess she and Sam are related."

"No?" Patrick asked. "Why not?"

T.J. laughed. "That Sam's a hot ticket. Yesterday, first time on the ferry, she walked straight up to the wheelhouse and asked to come inside. It's sort of against regulations . . ."

"Yeah, the Coast Guard tends to frown on flirting while operating a hundred-ton vessel," Patrick said, chuckling.

"Don't report me," T.J. said. "But anyway, I let her in. How do you say no to green eyes like that?"

"What did she want?"

"She asked me to show her the sights as we approached the town— she wanted an overview. I guess she spotted that—" He pointed at a sticker affixed to the wheelhouse window. Patrick peered more closely, saw that it was from the Peace Corps. "She told me she knew a kindred spirit when she saw one."

"Good line," Patrick said.

"Turns out it's more than a line. We've worked in some of the same places. I learned how to drive a ferry in South America, building a school for a village on the other side of a river from where she just helped set up a hospital. Anyway, I pointed out the main landmarks of town—the inn, the grandstand for the ceili, the docks, the whale boats. When people come to Cape Hawk, it's fairly predictable what they hope to see."

"Not much going on up here?"

"Nope. Just the way I like it," T.J. said. "The world's too crazy a place. I like the peace and quiet of Cape Hawk."

Patrick nodded. He looked back across the water, toward the wharf. T.J. was right—it looked very peaceful from out here. A sleepy little town right at the base of a seaside mountain. So why did Patrick feel anything but at peace? There was Jessica walking Flora—he saw them on the inn lawn. The shop door was open, but Marisa was still nowhere in sight.

"So, do you live in town?" he asked, narrowing his eyes at T.J.

"Yes—an apartment just above the ferry office, by the dock. Why?"

"I figured you might know some of the characters who hang around the waterfront."

T.J. laughed. "Most of them are Neills. That's the family that owns half the town. Anne's the innkeeper, Jude operates the whaleboats, and Liam runs an oceanographic program. He's away, though."

Patrick nodded knowingly, in his seasoned-cop way. "I know Liam," he said. "Actually, the person I'm interested in is Gerard Lafarge."

T.J.'s expression changed, his guard suddenly up.

"What about him?"

"I'll be straight with you. I'm investigating his whereabouts."

"What for? What do you want to know about a lowlife like him for? What's he done? And—for that matter—why are you asking me?"

Patrick had clearly lost some of his edge. During his years of following the Mara Jameson disappearance, none of his interrogation subjects would have asked more questions than he did.

"Look," Patrick said. "I'm just a retired cop, doing a favor for Liam."

"Oh," T.J. said, relaxing again. "For Liam, no problem. Liam's a great guy, a true conservationist. The opposite of the Lafarge bunch. Those guys think natural resources were put on earth just for their personal use. They're the most unethical fishermen I've ever seen—and making my living on the water, I've seen lots of fishing practices."

"Do you have any idea where Gerry might be right now?"

T.J. peered out, seeming to gaze over the flat, pewter bay. "Funny you should ask," he said. "I've heard things lately."

"Like what?"

"Someone said he was down south, fishing a reef in Rhode Island."

"That's pretty far to go, isn't it?"

"Not for Lafarge—not if there's money in it."

"What kind of money could there be there?"

"I don't know. I've heard about some monster waves, driven inshore by the tail end of a hurricane. They began breaking over the reef, bringing lots of unusual fish into the area."

"Yeah, Liam mentioned that," Patrick said. "But half the species are from up here—northern waters. Lots of sharks, I guess, plus a bunch of marine mammals that are off-limits to fishermen anyway."

"Lafarge doesn't care what comes up in his nets," T.J. said, shaking his head.

Just then the ferry began to slow her engines. They were pulling into the slip on the other side of the strait. T.J. excused himself, went into the wheelhouse to take the controls. Patrick drifted toward the back of the deck. He watched people getting into their cars.

The whole operation took about fifteen minutes—the deckhands directed cars and trucks off quickly, and then loaded up the Cape Hawk–bound vehicles. Patrick breathed in the sea air, feeling the ferry rise and fall with the easy onshore waves. He found himself staring across the narrow passage, eyes on the shop door. And he made up his mind. When he got back to Cape Hawk, he'd head right over and ask Marisa out to dinner. He couldn't leave without talking to her, taking the chance.

Just then, out of the corner of his eye, he noticed a white van driving onto the ferry. White vans were anything but uncommon, especially during the ceili—lots of bands were still arriving, and many of them needed vans and panel trucks to hold all the musicians and their instruments. Their vehicles had windows and passenger seats, and were decorated with the band names and illustrations of shamrocks, harps, guitars, maps of Ireland.

But this particular van, the one that had Patrick's attention, was quite different. It had no windows in the back, but it contained a refrigerator unit; Patrick saw the vents above, and the trail of water dripping on the ferry's metal deck below. Its logo, far from being Irish or musical, showed a lone dolphin: smiling, standing on its tail, balancing a beach ball on one flipper. Patrick reached into his pocket, pulled out the picture he had printed out from the police website. He checked it to be sure, and he felt that click he always felt when police work yielded something interesting.

Most interesting of all: Gerard Lafarge was in the driver's seat.

After such a short time of rehearsing with Sam, Marisa felt they were almost ready to play. They ran through all their old favorites, and by the end of the afternoon, Sam knew "Storm Tossed" by heart.

Marisa felt so tender toward her sister, so glad they were together again. She remembered starting the violin in fourth grade, coming home from her lessons and teaching her younger sister everything she had learned. The next year, when Sam was ready for music lessons, she had amazed the teacher by already knowing how to play vibrato— while the rest of her class was dutifully plucking, pizzicato, the notes to "Mary Had a Little Lamb."

After so long apart, it seemed amazing to have Sam here now. Marisa thought of what Anne had said, about sometimes sisters needing to separate for a while. Although she never would have believed it possible, it seemed they had come back stronger than ever. And she knew she had Patrick to thank for it.

"What did Patrick say to you?" Marisa asked now. "To make you want to come see me?"

"He said a lot," Sam said. "But what really got me was a tape of us playing."

"Us?"

"Fallen Angels," Sam said.

"How did he get it?"

"A friend of his in the Baltimore DA's office. An old fan of ours, apparently."

"And Patrick had it?" Marisa asked, gazing out at the harbor.

"Yes. He seemed to know it by heart, the way he cued it to the spot of you singing 'Cliffs of Dooneen.'"

Marisa shivered to think of Patrick listening to a tape of her singing.

"He said the two of you were just friends," Sam said.

"That's true," Marisa said.

Sam nodded, holding back a smile. "Okay," she said.

"What do you mean?"

"Just," Sam said, taking her older sister's hand, "maybe you've forgotten how to read your own hearts. Both of you."

"Both of us?"

"You and Patrick," Sam said softly. "He reminds me of Paul, you know, when you first met. He really went all out to get me here."

"He wanted us to be together," Marisa said.

"That wasn't for me," Sam said.

Marisa gazed out the door, feeling a tingle go down her spine.

"You haven't stopped watching for him," Sam said. "Not once, all day."

"I just want to thank him," Marisa said. "For bringing you back to me and Jessica."

"Here comes the ferry," Sam said, waving.

"Are you going to see T.J.?" Marisa asked.

"He said he might stop up at the inn for a drink later," Sam said. "I'll probably drop in too."

"Well, let's head up there now," Marisa said. "We'll talk to Anne and find out when we're playing."

The two sisters walked across the wharf, then up the long, grassy hill. Late-day sun had burned off the remaining mist, turning the afternoon bright and golden. Even the lawn was dry, so people had spread blankets and were starting to picnic. A twelve-member band from Dublin had taken the stage, and their music was lively and joyous. Jessica and her friend Allie were on the gazebo with Flora, who faced out to sea as if waiting for her master.

The sisters walked up the steps, across the broad porch, and into the inn's lobby. Anne stood at the front desk, making notations in the guest book. She looked up, smiling.

"Hi, Marisa. And let me guess—you must be Sam!"

"And you must be Anne."

"Welcome," Anne said. "We've all heard so much about you. We'd begun to think you'd gotten lost in the Andes."

"I almost did," Sam said, squeezing Marisa's hand.

Marisa and Anne exchanged a glance, and Marisa felt grateful to have such a good friend.

"Well, you made it in time for the ceili," Anne said. "We're waiting with bated breath—nobody's heard Marisa play yet, and we can't wait to hear the two of you together. How does Sunday night sound? It's the last night of the festival and we should have a great crowd."

"Great," Sam said.

The side door opened, and a bunch of men walked in. Marisa recognized them—the day shift of *Redtail*, the Cape Hawk ferry. They were just off duty, heading into the bar.

T. J. McGuinn was among them, his Greek fisherman's hat pulled down over one eye—a slow smile coming to his lips as he caught sight of Sam. "Hi," he said. "How are you?"

"I'm great," Sam said. "I'm with my sister."

"Could I buy you both a drink, to celebrate your reunion?" he asked.

"I think I'll wait for Patrick," Marisa said.

"Patrick? I talked to him on the ferry," T.J. said. "He came back with us and I saw him drive off, going up toward the cliffs."

Marisa's heart fell. She glanced at Sam, saw her look of concern. Sam had always been able to read Marisa's emotions, and she knew she could see how disappointed she felt.

"Are you sure you don't want to join us?" Sam asked.

"Yes," Marisa said, trying to smile. "Go ahead. Have fun."

Sam squeezed Marisa's hand. "See you later," she said, and headed into the bar with T.J.

"You bet," Marisa said.

Then Anne got busy, with people just off the ferry wanting to check in. Marisa wandered over to the door. She stood on the front porch, listening to the band from Dublin, watching Jessica and Allie playing fetch with Patrick's Flora.

Marisa sat on the top step, facing the band, the long lawn, and the bright blue bay spreading out between the two rocky headlands. The water was so calm . . . there was nothing storm-tossed about it. The song played in her head, though, and she thought of how funny it was to have written such a song for a man she hardly knew.

Chapter 23

By the time Patrick had finished following the white van, it was nearly eight o'clock. He returned to town and drove past In Stitches, afraid that Marisa had gone home, and sure enough—the shop was dark and locked for the night. He had missed his chance to ask her out for dinner. His truck window was down; hearing a familiar bark, he glanced up at the inn and saw Flora. She was playing ball with Jessica, so he parked and headed across the grass.

A band called the Seven Harps was playing some music that reminded him of the Chieftains and got his blood flowing. He paused to listen, and that's when he spied Marisa. She hadn't seen him yet—sitting on the top step of the inn, she was watching her daughter and gazing over the bay, seemingly lost in thought. Patrick hung back.

This was the moment he'd been waiting for. He'd come all the way from Connecticut to spend time with Marisa. She had been so friendly, encouraging him on the phone. So why did he feel so nervous?

Her dark hair was so pretty, the way it fell across her eyes. He took a deep breath. His heart was racing as he walked slowly up to the inn, sat down beside her. They didn't speak right away, but just looked at each other, smiling. Patrick couldn't quite believe that he was here, in this hidden little northern town, with this quiet, careful woman who had haunted him since he first saw her.

Without knowing he was going to do it, he reached over and brushed the hair behind her ear. He let his hand linger for just a minute, then dropped it to his side.

"Oh," she said, sounding surprised.

"Your eyes are too pretty to hide," he said.

"Thank you," she said.

"You probably thought I disappeared," he said.

"Well, a little," she said.

"I wanted to give you and your sister some time to reunite," he said.

"I appreciate that," she said. "But I was just starting to miss you."

He couldn't take his eyes off her, shocked by how happy her words made him. The evening was cool and clear, with every trace of mist gone from the air. Stars had started to come out, glowing in the deepening blue sky over the rippling bay.

"What have you been doing?" she asked.

"Detective work," he said.

"For Liam?" she asked.

"Yes," he said, and smiled. "I was on a stakeout." He'd been hot on the trail of Lafarge, and the only thing that could have pulled him away was the idea of seeing her—too late for dinner, just for a few minutes, sitting on the steps of the Cape Hawk Inn.

"I wouldn't want to hold you back from an investigation," she said.

He glanced over at her.

"In fact," she continued, "I was thinking you might like some help."

His smile widened. "Really?"

Marisa nodded. "I think my sister would sit for Jessica and Flora if you wanted me to keep you company. I can imagine that stakeouts can get really boring without someone to talk to."

"They can," he agreed.

"Then let me check with Sam," Marisa said. "And I'll be right back, okay?"

"Okay," Patrick said, hardly able to believe it as he watched her run into the inn, toward the pub. Sandra had hated when he had work to do; she had never wanted to hear about it, and she'd sure never wanted to tag along on a stakeout. Marisa probably wouldn't either, once she saw what it was like.

Flora ran over, with Jessica right behind her. Patrick petted his dog behind the ears, just the way she liked it, smiling at the little girl standing by her side.

"It sure is nice of you to take such good care of Flora," he said.

"She's wonderful," Jessica said. "She's the best dog I've ever met, except for one."

"One?"

Jessica nodded. "Tally," she said.

"Who's Tally?" Patrick asked.

But Jessica turned and threw the yellow tennis ball again, and Flora went bounding away. Jessica followed, tearing across the grass. A Frisbee game was in progress, but she and Flora ran around it, toward the gazebo. Patrick watched Flora snatch the ball, then gallop up the steps of the small, round structure right in the middle of the inn's lawn.

"Hi, Patrick," Sam said, coming out onto the porch.

"Hi, Sam."

"That's been their spot all day," Sam said, gazing at Jessica and Flora. "First with Jess's friend Allie, and then just the two of them."

Patrick looked at the way Jessica sat there, her arm looped around Flora's neck, whispering in her ear.

"She's been really nice, looking after my dog," Patrick said.

Sam glanced at him with surprise. "Don't you know?" she asked. "Your dog is looking after her." Something in her voice was so tender, almost sorrowful, Patrick wanted to ask her what she meant. But just then Marisa came out the inn door, with T. J. McGuinn behind her.

"Are you sure you don't mind?" Marisa asked.

"Hanging out with my niece?" Sam asked. "Never."

"I might keep you company for a few more minutes, if that's okay," T.J. said. "Then I'll head home—I've got the dawn ferry shift tomorrow."

Sam smiled and nodded, and Marisa gathered up her jacket and bag. She called to Jessica that she'd be back before too long, and Jessica waved to show she'd heard. Glancing up at Patrick, Marisa let him know she was ready.

The two of them crossed the lawn to Patrick's truck. With so many people spread out on the grass on blankets and lawn chairs to listen to the ceili, he felt eyes on them, and it gave him a feeling of pride to be seen with Marisa. The Irish music played, carried on the evening breeze. Patrick opened Marisa's door, then went around the truck to get in and start it up.

They drove along the wharf, and then turned onto a road that took them winding into the pine-dark Cape Hawk hills. From here, looking down at the bay, everything was shades of dark blue. Shadowed by the cliffs, the water blended into the land across the strait. The twilight sky was clear, deep blue, sprinkled with silver stars. They seemed to hang in the tree branches, sweeping low over the narrow road.

Patrick traced the route he had come earlier, following Gerard Lafarge in the white van. There weren't many houses on this stretch, only old unpaved logging roads that reached into the forest.

"Can you tell me what we're doing?" Marisa asked.

"Of course," he said. "Liam saw someone from Cape Hawk down at the Block Island reef last week. Canadian fishermen can't fish in U.S. waters, for one thing. But Liam said not only was the guy fishing, he was catching dolphins. I just happened to see the person in question driving off the Cape Hawk ferry today."

"So that's good news, right?" Marisa asked. "If he's here, he can't be in New England, bothering dolphins."

"Seems that way," Patrick said. "But from what Liam and T.J. say,

Gerard Lafarge is a slippery customer. He was driving a reefer truck, and I want to get a look inside."

"Gerard Lafarge?" Marisa asked, sounding surprised.

"Yes," Patrick said, turning right onto a gravel road that wound down into the valley, just alongside the fjord.

"But he doesn't live up here," she said. "I don't know him well, but I've seen him coming out of a house on the other side of town—behind the post office. His driveway is right next to the parking lot, and I often see him or his wife driving out when I go to get the mail."

Patrick narrowed his eyes. That was odd information. He'd watched Lafarge pull in behind a small red house, get out of his van, and be met by a woman. Patrick had assumed he was watching a poacher's home-coming—but maybe it was something more seedy. Maybe Lafarge had a girlfriend on this side of town.

The woods were so thick on this stretch of road, Patrick had to turn on his headlights. Darkness would hide his truck once they got to their destination, but having to use lights made him nervous. Residents wouldn't expect much traffic out here—there really wasn't anything but a handful of houses, a few logging roads, and a smokehouse or two.

"Do you know his wife?" Patrick asked.

"Not really. But I've seen her."

"Is she small, light-haired, athletic-looking?" he asked, picturing the woman he'd seen meet Lafarge at the door.

"No," Marisa said. "She's as tall as I am. Red-haired like Sam."

"Hmm," Patrick said.

When they got close to the red house, he doused the truck lights. Cruising past slowly, he saw that the van was still there, and that there were lights on in the house. The front curtains were drawn, and smoke wisped from the chimney. Blue light flickered from a TV in the room on the left. Patrick went a quarter mile farther, then turned into the un-marked road he'd spotted earlier. It snaked through the thick woods, stopping just beyond the clearing around the red house. From here, he and Marisa had a perfect view. He turned off the truck engine.

Branches interlocked overhead, and pine boughs formed a natural screen. Patrick couldn't have a chosen a better place from which to watch Lafarge. Or to sit with Marisa. Enclosed by the trees, they were completely alone. The realization made his heart pound in a way that had nothing to do with the stakeout itself.

"I love the smell of the woods," Marisa said.

"Me too," Patrick said. "Did you grow up in the country?"

"No, Newport, Rhode Island. Right on Spring Street, across from Trinity Church. It's like a small city."

"I know Newport," Patrick said. "Growing up on the Connecticut shoreline, we went there a lot on weekends. It was always fun—but I didn't sail, and my father wasn't rich, so I felt pretty out of place."

"I didn't sail, and my father wasn't rich either," Marisa said. Patrick took his eyes off the red house long enough to see her smile at him.

"Really?" Patrick asked. "I guess I thought all the girls down on Bannister's Wharf were sailors. I imagined them all going to private schools, having trust funds, things like that. And I was just a cop's son, about to become a cop myself."

"My father was a teacher," Marisa said. "And my mother was a nurse."

"Is that why you and Sam . . . ?"

"Yes," Marisa said. "We went to public school, where our father taught, and we used to hear our mother talking about the people she treated in the emergency room where she worked. She really cared about everyone—we could see she loved her work, loved making a difference. She saved a lot of lives over the years—car accidents, near drownings, little kids choking, or with high fevers . . . she really inspired both me and Sam."

"Who inspired the music?" Patrick asked.

Marisa laughed. "There were a lot of musical people in Newport. One family had ten kids, and they used to give concerts at our church. Everyone played an instrument. Sam and I wanted to be like that—so I took up violin in fourth grade, and she followed the next year."

"And you got good enough to put yourselves through nursing school," Patrick said.

Marisa nodded. "We loved doing it too. We'd be working so hard all week, we'd barely even have time to see each other. But when weekends came, we'd jump into our car and head for Georgetown, or one of about twenty bars in Baltimore, wherever we were booked to play. We'd hit the stage together, and even if we hadn't rehearsed once all week, we'd just play our fiddles and sing in harmony, as if we did it every single night."

"You two were something to hear, that's for sure," Patrick said softly. "I'm sure you still are."

"How do you know?" Marisa asked.

"I made Sam give this back to me," he said, reaching into his door pocket, sliding the cassette into the tape deck. He pushed PLAY, made sure the volume was low, and watched Marisa's face as the sweet sound of her and Sam singing "O'er the Hills" came lilting out of the speakers.

"Sam and I never made any recordings," Marisa said.

"It's a bootleg." Patrick smiled. "Rare and valuable."

"She told me this tape is what convinced her to come up here," Marisa said.

Patrick shook his head. "She might say that," he said. "But it wasn't."

"No?"

"No," he said. "It was you. The way she feels about you."

"How do you know?"

Patrick held the words inside. He listened to the beautiful music, smelled the pine forest, glanced across the front seat. Marisa was right here with him, singing softly along to her own voice on the tape. His skin tingled with the excitement of being so close to her. He hadn't felt anything like this in a long time. And he'd felt it from the moment he met her, when he was still on the trail he'd begun to follow all those years ago, searching so doggedly for Mara Jameson. Maybe he'd been looking for Marisa all along.

"I love your voice," he said quietly.

She shook her head. "Sam has the best voice," she said. "Wait till tomorrow, when you hear us sing at the ceili. When you hear her hitting those high notes . . ."

"I'm listening to *you* hit them," he said, reaching for her hand. "Right now."

Patrick looked into her eyes. Clear emerald green, sparkling in the starlight. He had never seen eyes like them, and he never wanted to look away. He put his arms around her, and kissed her.

They held each other for a long time, and then Marisa leaned her head against his chest. Patrick wondered whether she could hear his heart thumping. Her shoulder dug gently into his side, and he wished she would never move. After a long time, a few minutes, he remembered that they were supposed to be watching the red house. But he no longer cared.

A tree branch jostled, and a big gray bird flew out. Patrick barely felt startled; all he could think about was Marisa, pressed against his body. He held her more tightly, thinking she might have felt afraid. But she tilted her head up, smiling and looking him in the eyes.

"That was an owl," she said.

"It was?"

She nodded. "They sleep all day, and fly out at night, just after twilight. The woods around my house are filled with them."

Patrick had never thought of owls as being particularly romantic before, but suddenly they seemed wildly so. Everything seemed like a harbinger—the twilight owl flying out of the tree above them, straight up to the stars. The whales in the bay surging up from the depths, bringing mystery and magic to Patrick's tired old soul. Mostly, Marisa—her voice on the tape, and her in his arms—the most beautiful nature of all.

Reaching up, she caressed his face. He kissed her again, sliding deeper down the seat to hold her closer. Her skin was the softest thing he'd ever felt. He wanted the moment to go on forever, but after a minute, she pulled back a little.

"Can I ask you something?" she asked.

"Sure," he said.

"Why have you helped us so much? Why did you bring Sam up here?"

"Can't you tell?" he asked.

She gazed up at him, her green eyes huge, watching him as if she was in total suspense, waiting for him to tell her something that would shock her. He felt her hand on his forearm, and he wanted to raise it to his lips and kiss it. But he suddenly couldn't move. All he could do was stare into her eyes.

"I think so," she said. "But I have to ask you anyway. See, I have Jessica . . ."

"I know," he said. "Your daughter."

"Whatever I do," she said, "whatever I feel, I worry about what it will mean to her. I could never . . ."

Patrick waited, watching her get her thoughts together.

"Never put her in a position to be so hurt again."

"No," Patrick said. They didn't even have to say his name: Edward Hunter.

"I've been watching Jess with your dog. She loves Flora. Loves all dogs—so much. That's just how she is, full of love for everyone and everything. But Flora is the first dog she's really known, played with—in a long time."

"She mentioned she had a puppy," Patrick said.

Marisa nodded slowly.

"Can you tell me what happened?"

"Ted kicked her," Marisa said. "And my daughter saw. She watched as I tried to save her, but Tally died."

"I'm so sorry," Patrick said.

"See, I brought that pain into Jess's life. I know you're a wonderful man—I can tell. Anyone can tell. But because of Jess, I have to be careful. Do you understand?"

Patrick nodded. He wanted to tell her about his marriage. How he had believed in his vows, how he'd thought that being a husband was the most important thing he'd ever do. He wanted to explain to her that he'd made the worst mistake of his life—not paying enough attention to the person he'd held most dear in the world, how his police work had cost him his wife. But his throat was too tight to say all that.

"Marisa," he said.

"Jess loves your dog," she said.

"I'm glad," he said. "That's good."

"It is?" she asked, gazing up at him, waiting for what seemed like forever, before he could swallow, could get rid of the lump in his throat.

"It is," he said. He wanted to say, *because she's going to be spending a lot of time with her.* He'd been on his own for four years now, hadn't even come close to falling in love with someone else. But now, sitting with Marisa, he felt that changing.

They kissed again, and he felt her run her fingers down his forearm. He shivered in spite of the warm thawing right in the center of his chest, where his heart had been frozen for so long.

Outside the truck, the night burst into tiny red stars. They sparkled in the sky, coming out of the chimney. Marisa saw them and sat up straight, and Patrick suddenly remembered what they were actually doing here, parked in the woods.

"What's that?" she asked.

"They're burning something in the fireplace," he said, watching sparks fly into the night. "It's dry—maybe paper. I'm going to try to look through the curtains, see what they're doing."

He started to open the truck door, and Marisa did the same.

"I want to come with you," she said when he glanced across the seat.

Patrick wanted to tell her to stay here, where it was safe. But he saw the determination in her eyes, so he nodded. They closed the doors silently, began cautiously covering ground. Fallen pine needles formed a soft cushion under their feet, muffling their steps. The smell of wood smoke mingled with the fresh sea air and an unpleasant smell of dead fish.

When they got to the van parked in the driveway, Patrick gestured for Marisa to hang back. She nodded, edging into the van's shadow. He moved forward, closer to the red house. The yard was almost totally clear of trees and bushes, but the surrounding woods were so thick and tall, they blocked much light from moon or stars. Patrick reached the structure, crouched as he walked under the two front windows.

He could hear the TV blaring inside. One voice rose above it, and Patrick raised his head slowly, to look through the window. Although the dark green curtains were pulled tight, he could see through a crack underneath. The room was small and square, stuffed with furniture.

Two people sat on the couch—the woman Patrick had seen earlier, eyes glued to the TV, and Lafarge, talking on a telephone. He tried to listen, but the TV was so loud, it made the words unclear. Lafarge sud-

denly jumped up, phone to his ear, to stir the fire with a poker. Patrick
saw the logs crackle, and when he looked up, he saw another geyser of
sparks come out the chimney.

At least Lafarge had moved closer to the window, so Patrick was able
to hear a snatch of conversation: ". . . won't last much longer, since the
waves are already dying down . . . yes, of course I know that . . . last
chance before she comes back and becomes the star tourist attraction
again . . . why not, money for us?" Patrick heard him say three more
words: "get the white . . ." Then Lafarge went back to the couch, sat
down beside the woman, and continued talking into the phone.

Just then, Patrick heard a door hinge creak. He wheeled around, and
couldn't believe his eyes: Marisa had opened the van's door, and was
climbing inside. Running across the yard, he reached the van in time to
see her disappear between the two front seats, into the compartment in
back.

"What are you doing?" he whispered.

"Get the back doors open," she said, sounding frantic.

Patrick raced around back. He jiggled the door handle, found it
locked. Glancing at the house, he made sure no one was coming. He
paused for a second—entering someone's vehicle was against the law,
and he didn't have a warrant or probable cause or anything that would
give him the right to enter the van. But Marisa was in there, and she
needed his help, so he reached for the keys—still in the ignition—and
went around back to unlock the van door.

The odor nearly bowled him over. The back of the van had no
windows, so the darkness was almost total. He heard a faint barking—
almost like a puppy whimpering for its mother. Crawling in, he knocked
over a bucket of herring—dead and rotting, from the smell of it.

"I heard them crying," Marisa explained.

As Patrick's eyes got used to the darkness, he saw that she was
crouched over an animal crate, trying to tug it toward the open door.
Without seeing inside, Patrick grabbed the handle and pulled it free.

Standing in the yard, he looked in through the wire grate. Four
enormous eyes stared out at him out of two white faces, two black
noses, two thatches of whiskers catching the very faint light from a rising moon.

"What are they?" he asked.

"Seal pups," Marisa said.

Patrick stood, staring at their dark eyes in that soft white fur, and he
thought of Lafarge's words: *Get the white.* Baby seals, he thought. That's
what they're poaching now. He reached up to help Marisa out of the
van. She jumped down, then bent to look inside the cage.

"We have to get them out of here," she said.

"You're right," Patrick said. He had no idea why Lafarge had them, whether he had any sort of right or permit—but he remembered raiding a dog breeder once, where the conditions were unimaginably inhumane, and this scene was even worse. The seals lay on their sides, panting, their sides rising and falling in quick breaths.

If the cops came, Patrick would be arrested for stealing, but he didn't care. He carried the crate to his truck, placed it in the back. Marisa began to climb in over the side, and he grabbed her arm.

"You can't ride back here," he said. "Come in front with me—I'll drive slow, they'll be okay. Better than they were in the van . . ."

She shook her head, her eyes flashing with wild emotion. "I have to ride with them," she said.

Patrick started to argue with her, but he suddenly knew she was thinking of Tally. It wasn't her fault that Jessica's puppy had died, but Patrick knew the feeling of wanting to make up for the pain and mistakes of the past. So he kissed her and handed her his jacket to sit on, promising he'd drive as carefully as he could. She stuck a few papers in his hand, telling him she'd grabbed them out of the van.

Backing the truck out of the narrow road, he kept the lights off. He felt every rut, every root across the track, hoping Marisa and the baby seals weren't being jostled too badly. His adrenaline was surging as he thought of Lafarge's words and the squalor in which he'd kept the seals. He wondered about that dolphin in the picture Liam had seen, trying to figure out what was going on.

Once he hit the open road, he turned on the truck lights, including the one in the cab. The papers Marisa had handed him were scattered on the seat beside him, and he glanced down as he drove. One envelope bore the same logo as the one on the side of Lafarge's van—a smiling dolphin standing on its tail. The letterhead said "Sea Canyon Resort."

Patrick wanted to read the letter, but he knew he had to drive—and he knew he had to call Liam. His eye had caught the name of the addressee and suddenly one thing fell into place.

But Marisa was rapping on the window behind Patrick's head, telling him to hurry, the seals were dying. So he called to her to hold tight, and he drove out of the fjord's valley and down the other side of the mountain toward the village of Cape Hawk, as fast as he dared. And then his cell phone rang.

❧

It wasn't until after everyone went to bed and Liam had the cottage to himself that he made the phone call he'd been waiting to make all day.

His heart was heavy with worry over the look in Lily's eyes after their meeting with the lawyer. He took his cell phone out onto the porch and dialed Patrick's cell phone number.

"Hello?" came the deep voice.

"Hi, it's Liam," he said.

"You read my mind," Patrick said. "I was just about to call you."

"You sound as if you're driving," Liam said. "Are you in Cape Hawk?"

"Yes," Patrick said. "I'm in my truck, with Marisa in back trying to keep two seal pups alive. We took them out of Lafarge's van."

"Lafarge's van? What are you talking about? He has a black pickup truck. And besides, he's not in Nova Scotia—he's still here in the area."

"I know," Patrick said. "More on that in a minute. You're the oceanographer—where do I go for a seal emergency?"

"There's a wildlife rehab about ten miles east of Cape Hawk. Head out of town, take a right at the lighthouse, and it's on that road. I'll call my friend Jean Olivier—he runs it, and I'll make sure he's there waiting for you."

"Great," Patrick said. "I see the lighthouse from here."

"Tell me about this van."

"It seems to be owned by a place called Sea Canyon Resort—at least it has their logo stenciled on the side. There were letters inside, on their stationery, addressed to Gilbert Lafarge."

"Gerard's brother," Liam said. "So he's in this too. And I've heard about this resort. It's a big development near Digby."

"I heard him talking to someone on the phone," Patrick said. "Something about the waves dying down."

"Ghost Hills," Liam said. With the shock of Edward's appearance, and the court order for Rose's blood test, he had barely had time to register the fact that the oceanic phenomenon was dwindling faster every day. John had told him the pelagic species were getting back to normal, with the more rare visitors returning to their home waters.

"He said 'Get the white,'" Patrick said. "I guess he meant the seals—their fur is almost pure white, with these black spots on their backs. He said something after that, but the TV was too loud for me to hear."

Liam could barely listen or think about the Lafarge brothers, or even the white seal pups. He was too focused on Lily, and what would happen at court.

"How are you doing?" Patrick asked. "Why did you call, by the way?"

"It's about Rose," Liam said. "We're really worried. Lily's beside herself."

"Rose's heart?"

"No," Liam said. "Edward has gotten a court order. He's making Rose get a DNA test."

"We can't let him near Rose," Patrick said. "That's for sure."

"I know, but court's in two days. We need an eleventh-hour miracle."

"Like what?"

Liam had been thinking all night, and he had a plan. "Do you know where I thought we could start?" he asked.

"Talk to me," Patrick said.

And Liam did.

Patrick listened carefully, and then he offered his own ideas. He gave Liam the name he needed, and they agreed to get Joe Holmes involved too, so he could do the necessary tracking to find the witness they needed for court.

"I'll be there myself," Patrick said.

"Are you sure you'll be able to?" Liam said.

"I'll do my best. Marisa's playing in the music competition the night before, so it would mean getting a late start. But I'll drive all night, and get there when I can."

"Thank you," Liam said.

"Okay," Patrick said. "Let me go now—I don't want to miss the wildlife place."

"I'll call Jean," Liam said.

They said goodbye and hung up. Liam dialed his friend's number, caught him working in the office, and told him to expect visitors with two sick seal pups. *Get the white,* Patrick had quoted Gilbert Lafarge as saying.

The words shimmered in Liam's mind, troubling him like a disturbance under the water's surface. He couldn't quite make out the source of what was bothering him—he had too much to concentrate on, plotting what had to happen at the court hearing. So he just stared out at the calm cove, taking some deep breaths.

Looking around, he realized that he couldn't see Nanny. He peered into the darkness, listening for any sound she might make—her tail slapping the surface, an exhalation before diving—but there was nothing.

Get the white.

It couldn't be, could it? Liam's heart thudded, scanning the sea. He leaned against the porch rail, watching for a few minutes more. Feeling an undercurrent of worry, he decided to go upstairs and try to forget the white whale, try to forget the weeks ahead, try to forget everything except holding Lily.

Chapter 24

Sitting on the porch of the Cape Hawk Inn the next morning, Patrick made one very long phone call. It was to Joe Holmes, of the FBI's Connecticut Field Office—but since it was Sunday morning, Patrick caught him at home, in Hubbard's Point.

They talked for nearly an hour, covering everything Liam had mentioned last night. Patrick gave Joe the address he remembered from the Mara Jameson case file, and Joe told him he would take care of it. Almost as an aside, he also gave Joe the details he knew about Gilbert Lafarge, as well as the name of the Sea Canyon Resort.

"Oceanographic rescue work isn't exactly my area of expertise," Joe said. "But if it helps Liam, I'll do what I can."

"I figure there's someone you can call in Canada," Patrick said. "To see if they can stop what's going on. If you could have seen these two seals . . ."

"I'll do my best," Joe said. "But the main thing is to track down the witness for Lily, hope she's willing to cooperate."

"It's a long shot, and very last-minute. If it works, it'll be a home run for Lily," Patrick said. "And Liam came up with it. I wish I had."

"Me too," Joe said. "If it happens, that is."

"Big if," Patrick said, hanging up.

There was a time when Patrick would have needed to leave immediately, to return to Connecticut so he could be in the thick of the action that was brewing down there. He would have turned on his lights and sirens, gotten there by late tonight. But court wasn't until ten tomorrow morning, when he'd told Liam he'd be there. So for now, he just walked inside the inn, told Anne that he was reporting for duty.

"Are you sure?" she asked. "Because today is going to be the biggest day of the ceili. We're expecting a busload from Halifax—and with our very own Marisa on the bill, all the Nanouks will be arriving in droves."

"I'm positive," he said.

Anne gave him a hammer and a tool belt, and he joined the team of workmen out on the lawn. Throughout the monthlong music festival, the entries had been winnowed down to just a few finalists. Today the big bands, quartets, and duos would be competing for the grand prizes and bragging rights. Patrick and the others were adding another row of reviewing stands, to make room for all the judges and fans.

He lifted planks, hammered nails, carried two-by-fours on his shoulders. Working up a sweat, he pulled off his T-shirt and threw it on the grass. He'd volunteered for the project the day he'd checked into the inn, as his way of supporting Marisa and Sam. Although Fallen Angels hadn't entered any of the previous levels of competition, Camille Neill, the family matriarch and founder of the festival, had granted them special dispensation—because of Sam's work as an international nurse, and the fact that she'd traveled the longest distance to compete.

At about noon, he looked up to see Marisa, Sam, Jessica, and Flora coming across the lawn. He wiped his face and put his shirt back on, bending down to pet Flora as she came bounding ahead of the others, with Jessica running right behind.

"Did she behave herself last night?" he asked.

"Yes!" Jessica said. "She slept right at the end of my bed."

"And that was okay with your mom?" he asked.

"It was fine with me," Marisa said, smiling. They had shared a long, sweet kiss when he had finally gotten her home last night. He held back now, not sure of how she wanted to be in front of her sister and daughter, but he was thrilled when she came forward and stood on her toes to kiss his cheek.

"How are you today," he asked, "after the eventful time we had last night?"

"I'm great. I called Jean this morning, and he said the seals are going to be fine. They were dehydrated, but other than that, they're healthy. He's going to try to introduce them into a colony of harp seals as soon as they're ready."

"I'd like to lock that Lafarge guy in the back of a van without fresh water and feed him rotten herring," Sam said. "See how he likes it. T.J. told me he was on the first ferry this morning, looking apoplectic. I can just imagine what he must have thought when he opened the door this morning and found them missing."

"Maybe he thinks they escaped!" Jessica giggled.

"When actually they were rescued by your mother," Patrick said, wondering where Gilbert Lafarge was going in such a hurry. He hoped that Joe would be able to connect with his Canadian counterpart, to check in on the Sea Canyon Resort and figure out what the Lafarges were up to.

They all walked around the grandstand, the sisters and Jessica admiring the work Patrick and the others had done. Patrick linked his hand with Marisa's, and they strolled a few steps behind Sam and Jess. He thought of the conversations he'd had with Liam and Joe, and as he looked her in the eye, he knew he had to tell her.

"There's something you have to know," he said.

"What?" she asked, glancing up.

"Lily's facing a court fight this week. Edward is forcing Rose to take a DNA test."

"Paternity?"

Patrick nodded, and he saw her face fall.

"She can't let him win," Marisa said.

Patrick saw how determined she looked, how bright her green eyes were. She was a different woman from when he'd met her, just weeks earlier, when he'd first come up to Cape Hawk in search of Mara Jameson. As he felt the cool breeze blowing off the bay, swirling in from the Gulf of St. Lawrence, he knew that he was a different man too.

"What can we do?" Marisa asked.

"I'm going to go down there, after the ceili," he said, looking straight into her eyes. "To be there when they face him in court."

"I don't want Ted to hurt Rose," Jessica said, holding on to Flora.

"I've been worried about seals," Marisa said. "When it's my friend that really needs my help."

Patrick nodded, and waited for her to say more. He could see the thoughts just behind her eyes; he knew that she'd want to head to Connecticut, to help Lily, but he knew she had made a life for herself and Jessica here, far from Ted. Patrick started to speak, when Jessica interrupted.

"Rose is so worried about Nanny, and she doesn't even know what could happen with Ted. She sent me an e-mail, saying no one has seen Nanny in two days. It's not exactly easy to lose a white whale, but now she seems to be lost," Jessica said, and Patrick stopped dead in his tracks.

"Patrick?" Marisa asked. "Are you okay?"

"I am," he said, giving her a hug and a kiss. "I know you've got to get ready for your big moment, and I have to make a couple of calls. I just want you to know, I'll be here in the crowd when you take the stage, rooting for you with all I've got."

"And I want you to listen especially," she said, staring into his eyes as she grabbed his wrist, "to the last song in our set."

"The last song?"

She nodded, her green eyes glinting. And as he turned to go into the inn to call Liam, he knew that everything she wanted him to hear and everything he needed to know would be in that song, and he would be sitting right here on the stand he'd just built, listening.

Ghost Hills had all but died down. The only evidence that they had been there at all were the large swells rolling over the reef, the surfers waiting in vain for another killer wave breaking with a sixty-foot drop, the seabirds cruising the skies as if hoping for a resurgence of the rich marine life that had populated these waters this last summer month.

Only two trawlers remained to survey the area. One, operated by Captain Nick Olson out of Galilee, and the other, a rust red vessel from Cape Hawk, Nova Scotia, its nets and trawl doors hauled fast, to prevent any passing Coast Guard vessels or aircraft from suspecting it of fishing outside Canadian waters.

While the two fishing boats drifted hundreds of yards apart, the two skippers drove hard-bottom inflatable dinghies toward each other, to meet in what was basically the middle of the open ocean. Money was exchanged—twenty-five thousand U.S. dollars, in cash.

The two boat captains were nervous, but for different reasons. Captain Gerard Lafarge had a deadline to meet, and he was already several days behind. The big fancy resort was scheduled to open on Labor Day weekend, and he knew that many important people had booked their rooms, that the resort owners were planning to put on a show for them unlike anything they'd ever seen.

Captain Nick Olson was nervous because he had already gotten in trouble with Fish and Wildlife once this summer, and he had the feeling they were watching him. He'd made his crew stay extra vigilant, reporting to him any suspicious activity, or people asking questions about ship business. Not only that, but he wasn't all that thrilled about what Lafarge was doing. The waves rose and fell, and although he had never felt seasick a day in his life, he felt mighty queasy.

"So the place opens in what, a week?" he asked Lafarge.

"Yes. Just think of it, all those rich people having their last holiday of summer, swimming with marine mammals supplied by us."

"What do they have?" Nick asked. "A big tank with dolphins instead of a pool with a waterslide?"

"Basically," Gerry laughed. "Everyone wants the next thrill. People swim with sharks in Australia and South Africa, they dive with moray eels in Cancún. Now they don't even have to leave the Northeast. Instead of paying their hard-earned money to go on whale-watch cruises, they can actually swim with them."

"This place cost a lot to stay at?"

"It's a luxury resort," Gerry said. "As fancy as it gets. That's why I just paid you twenty-five grand. Sea Canyon thanks you."

Captain Nick grunted. He glanced over at *Mar IV.* He wondered how long the dolphins could last out of water. He wondered whether they'd catch the beluga, and if they did, what kind of drugs they'd give it to keep it calm for the voyage up the coast.

"Seriously," Lafarge said. "If you hadn't used your contacts to figure out where the thing was, we'd never have known where to start trailing her. It's perfect—swimming right in front of Neill's house. That know-it-all idiot. Treating me like shit since we were kids."

"Huh," Nick said. He had seen that look of derision in ocean-ographers' eyes before. They always thought they were the good guys, while Nick and Gerry were just fishermen trying to make a living. He tried to tell himself that now—so why did he feel so bad?

"Look," Gerry said. "My brother fucked up the seals we were supposed to deliver, so I'd better get going, catch the damn thing."

"Fine," Nick said, stowing the bag of money under his seat. "See you round."

"Yeah," Gerry said. "Call me next time Ghost Hills appear. This was great—we wouldn't have had a chance at the whale up home, that's for sure. She was the biggest tourist attraction Cape Hawk ever had, and if things go right, she'll do the same for Sea Canyon. And we'll be the richer for it."

Nick didn't even reply to that. He was remembering a time thirty years ago, when he was a boy. Whales had been rare in Rhode Island waters, then as now, but one winter a humpback whale had swum up Narragansett Bay, all the way north of the Newport Bridge. His grand-father had taken Nick on board his sturdy lobster boat, and they had followed the whale, trying to get it to turn around and swim out to sea.

"Why are we doing this, Grandpa?" Nick had asked, his fingers frozen inside his gloves.

"Because whales are mammals," his grandfather said, standing at the helm. "They are warm-blooded and breathe air, just like people."

"They're not like fish?"

"They swim like fish," his grandfather said. "But that's all. When whales lose their mates, they sing underwater until they find them again. If we don't help this one turn around, there might be another whale out there, singing and searching."

His grandfather told Nick to pound the surface with his oar, to make the biggest ruckus he could. They drove the lobster boat around and around the spot where they'd last seen the whale dive, where air bubbles came to the surface from her breath. His grandfather stared, driving the boat and following the whale, while Nick made noise—until they saw the whale make a wide turn, her shape a submarine-like shadow under the icy waves, and head back out to sea.

Nick remembered that now. He waved goodbye to Lafarge, then pushed the throttle open and drove across the open water to his fishing boat. Even though he made his living on salt water, hooking and netting and slicing open fish all day long, he'd never felt sicker about a catch. And the whale wasn't even caught yet. He imagined his grandfather looking down, ashamed of him.

He couldn't imagine her surviving the trip north. His stomach upset and churning, in a way he couldn't understand and couldn't quite believe, Nick Olson wheeled back to the ship, leaving *Mar IV* in his wake.

The day had seemed endless, waiting for the concert to begin. Jessica stared at the computer screen, knowing that she wanted to write to Rose, but not knowing what to say. What Patrick said had scared her a lot, as she thought of Ted in Rose's life. Jessica thought about Nanny, because it was easier than thinking about Ted. She knew how it felt to be so worried about an animal. Jessica had felt that way last year, when she'd watched Tally so hurt, lying on her mother's lap.

Petting Flora, Jessica looked into the Lab's dark, deep eyes. She felt the smooth fur under her hand, warm and soft. Flora dipped her head, edging closer to Jessica. Somehow it seemed as if the dog knew how much Jessica missed her puppy; or maybe it was Patrick who knew that. For some reason he had let Flora sleep here last night, instead of with him at the inn. Jessica knew it was partly because he had gone out with her mother—but she knew it was also because Patrick seemed to understand that Jessica needed Flora.

Walking into the living room, she found her aunt standing in front of the mirror, fixing her makeup. Jessica stood still, watching for a few seconds. Her heart skipped a beat—and she suddenly felt so happy, her heart almost hurt. She hadn't felt this way in a long time, since before Ted had come into their lives.

Back then, life had been different. She had missed her father, but she'd known that he was in heaven looking over them; she'd known that the world was good, and people loved each other. Her aunt would send postcards from all over the world, and sometimes she would come to visit—for Christmas or summer vacation, or to surprise Jessica's mother for her birthday. After Ted came along, he seemed to drive Aunt Sam away. And once he killed Tally, Jessica had stopped believing that the world was a good place after all.

"Who's that standing so quietly over there?" Aunt Sam asked, putting on her eye shadow.

"It's me," Jessica said, coming forward.

"Where's Flora? I've seen her around so much in the last two days, it seems as if I have another niece!"

"My sister Flora," she said.

"Oh, it's great having a sister," Sam said. "I don't know what I'd do without your mother."

"Even though you didn't come to visit us for a long time?"

Aunt Sam lowered her hands, turned to face Jessica. She was dressed for the ceili in black jeans and a black ballet top, with bright blue Incan beads around her throat and a green ribbon in her curly red hair.

"Even so."

"I thought you were mad," Jessica said. "It was so different than before, when you used to visit all the time."

Aunt Sam sat down on the loveseat, pulled Jessica to sit beside her. "You and your mother are the most important people in my life," she said. "Sometimes sisters have disagreements. Or one sees the other doing something she thinks might be bad for her . . . if she speaks up, there might be hurt feelings. And if she stays quiet, well—she worries that something bad will happen."

"Like Mom and Ted?"

Aunt Sam hesitated, and Jessica's stomach hurt. She didn't like it when adults didn't tell the whole truth, when they held back hard thoughts because they thought kids couldn't take them. But Aunt Sam made up her mind and nodded.

"Yes," she said. "But your mother was very brave to get away, come all the way up here to start a new life. I'm so proud of her. I like seeing her fight back."

"Thank you," Jessica's mother said, coming into the room.

"I heard what Patrick said," Aunt Sam said. "I don't like to see people like Ted get away with hurting others."

"I know," her mother said in a funny, thoughtful voice.

"Didn't Patrick say your friend has a court battle coming up?" Aunt Sam asked.

"He did say that."

Jessica looked from her mother to her aunt. They looked so much alike, yet were so different. Aunt Sam was tall and thin, with full, wavy red hair and fun-loving green eyes. Her mother was tall but not quite as thin, with straight dark hair cut chin-length. Her eyes were the same sea green as her sister's; for a long time, Jessica had wondered where the fun had gone. There had once been fire there, and mischief, and excitement—as if she believed that something wonderful was about to happen.

Her mother's eyes had lost that, for a long time. But now, watching the two sisters putting on their cowboy boots, gathering up their fiddles, Jessica could see the fun and fire coming back.

"You could go down to Connecticut after the concert," Aunt Sam said. "And help Lily in court. You have a few things you could tell the judge that would keep Edward out of Rose's life."

"About Tally!" Jessica said.

"And other things," her mother said.

"I want to go too," Jessica said. "To be with Rose."

"He would be there, Jess. We'd have to see him."

Jessica thought of Tally, and she thought of the baby seals, and she thought of Lily and Rose and Nanny—she would help them all if she could. "Mom," Jessica said, "they're our friends, and we love them. I want to go."

"So do I," her mother said.

"We could all go," Sam said. "I'd like to be there too."

"Oh, Sam . . ."

Jessica's mother was smiling so wide, and Aunt Sam looked so fierce and protective, sparks glistening in her eyes.

"First," Aunt Sam said, "we have a ceili festival to win."

"Look out," Jessica said. "Here come the Flying Angels."

"It's Fallen—" Aunt Sam started to say, but Jessica's mother stopped her.

"I think we need a new name," she said. "And I think Jessica just gave it to us."

The excitement had built all week, and now, on the last day of the ceili, the moment had come at last: for all finalists to take the stage and play the best music of their lives. The inn's lawn was completely packed, with not even an inch of grass to spare. Blankets were side-by-side, and people sat in beach chairs with their knees drawn up. The Nanouk Girls had commandeered a prime spot between the gazebo and the stage. The two grandstands were filled with dignitaries from the town and province, contest judges, and the Neill family—Camille, Jude, Anne, as well as some distant cousins.

Gazing down the long hillside, Marisa saw the sun's rays illuminating the wide blue bay. Mountain shadows turned the surface dark silver, rippling with the wakes of returning fishing boats. She listened to the band playing—a quartet from Ingonish, the uilleann pipes haunting and mystical, their notes hanging in the clear northern air.

Sam stood beside her, quietly tuning her fiddle. Although they hadn't played together publicly in years, they spent these minutes before taking the stage in perfect ease. Sam's way of dealing with any preconcert nervousness had always been to concentrate on her instrument. Marisa's was to search the crowd for the faces of the people she knew best.

There were the Nanouks, sipping wine and drinking in the beautiful music. Anne had to sit with her family, but Marisa knew that her heart was with the group of friends on their blankets by the gazebo. Marisa saw T.J. leaning against the rail fence.

And there, right in front of the stage, sitting side by side, were Patrick and Jess. Flora lay at their feet. Marisa's heart began to thump. She breathed in the clean air. For so long, she had never even imagined a night like this. Seeing her daughter with a man she trusted was more than she had let herself dream. She glanced at her sister, rosining her bow, and wondered what she'd say if Marisa told her she thought she was in love.

The band from Ingonish finished, and everyone clapped. Then Anne stood up from the grandstand and climbed the stairs to the stage. Marisa nudged Sam. She knew that they were about to get their cue. Anne smiled out at the crowd, thanked everyone for being there, and then turned toward the inn.

"We have a special entry in the contest," she said. "They are nurses, they are sisters, they are my friends. Please give a warm Cape Hawk welcome to—" Anne glanced down at Jessica, as if she needed a reminder of the new name, "to the Flying Angels!"

Marisa grabbed Sam's hand, and they ran down the path together. Their fiddles seemed to whistle in the wind blowing through their strings. How many times had they done this? Hurried along, on their way to somewhere important—school, a concert, a birthday party, a wedding—together, each one knowing that the other was there?

They climbed the makeshift stage. Sam looked at Marisa, and Marisa nodded. "One, two," Sam said, counting them in, and they began to play.

They both wore black. Sam's cowboy boots were scuffed yellow, and Marisa's were scuffed turquoise. They stood so close together that when the breeze blew Sam's hair, a few strands caught in Marisa's mouth. She barely noticed. Their bows moved in unison, fast and precise.

They played a jig, a reel, and a ballad—"O'er the Hills," their signature song. When they started that one up, a voice from the back of the crowd whooped—Marisa was tempted to look out, see if she might catch a face from the past, maybe an old fan from the Baltimore days. But the truth was, tonight she was playing for two people—the little girl out front, who had always had Marisa's heart, and the man next to her, who had begun to open it up again. She and Sam sang in harmony, playing along.

When it was time for the fourth song, Sam got ready to start, but Marisa lowered her bow. Surprised—her rhythm thrown off, Sam glanced over.

"Everything okay?" she whispered.

"Yes," Marisa said. She just had to look up for a minute. The sky was blue, just starting to darken. Soon the stars would appear, silver sparks, bursting in the velvet sky. Marisa imagined a cat's cradle, threads in the night, connecting the stars and holding everyone together. She thought of Lily, sent her love and hope, wished for her to hold on tight until help—Patrick, Marisa, Jessica, and Sam—arrived. Then she looked at Patrick and her daughter, sitting side by side.

"This is the last song," she said out loud, looking straight at Patrick. He nodded, and she suddenly had such a lump in her throat, she wasn't sure she could sing.

"Ready?" Sam asked, bow poised.

"Ready," Marisa said. She tapped her toe, one, two, three, four . . . And then the sisters began to sing.

> *There was a storm at sea,*
> *With killer waves,*
> *And my little boat,*
> *So far from shore,*
> *I couldn't see the land,*
> *Sea was so rough,*
> *I was sailing to you,*
> *In my storm-tossed boat,*
> *I'd forgotten that love*
> *Is the only thing,*
> *That can save a girl*
> *From drowning alone.*
> *You're my life preserver,*
> *You're my star in the sky,*

You're my port in the storm,
You're my light in the night. . . .

The sisters sang harmony. Everyone in the crowd was silent. Maybe they knew they were hearing a private love song, and maybe they didn't. Marisa played her fiddle, gazing down at one face in the crowd. His hair was red. His eyes were so blue. Even in the gently falling darkness, his eyes were so blue.

When the music ended, the silence was deafening—and suddenly the crowd erupted in thunderous applause. People jumped up, gave them a standing ovation. Marisa and Sam locked hands, took a deep bow.

Now the judges had to consult among themselves, to make their decision, but Marisa could barely think about that. This night had already given her everything she wanted. Still holding her sister's hand, she climbed down off the stage, into Patrick's and Jessica's embrace.

"You were great, Mommy!" Jessica said. "Aunt Sam too! You are definitely going to win."

"I don't know," Marisa heard Sam say. "We're such late entries, we're the festival's dark horse."

"Patrick," Marisa said, holding him and looking up into his clear blue eyes.

"You were amazing," he said.

"Thank you," she said.

"That song was the most beautiful I've ever heard. . . ."

Marisa gazed up at him. She wanted to tell him how *he* had made the words and notes flow.

But for now, they had something much more important to do. Singing the song, staring down the hill at Lily's shop, knowing that loyalty and friendship were what had saved Marisa and Jessica these last months—everything had built up like a tidal wave in Marisa's chest.

"Patrick," she said. "We have to go."

"What do you mean?"

"To Connecticut," Marisa said.

"To help Lily and Rose," Jessica said. "Is there room for all of us? Me, Mom, and Aunt Sam?"

"Of course," he said, his eyes glinting.

"We'll take my car. Let's leave right away, this minute—so we can get there in time," Marisa said.

Patrick kissed her, drowning out the roar of the crowd, letting her know that they were on their way.

Chapter 25

E arly Monday morning, Liam, Lily, and Rose went to stand on the rocks in front of the house. Liam and Lily were both dressed for court. Rose stood in front of them, then crouched by the edge of the bay. No one spoke for a few minutes, but they were all scanning the blue surface, rippled with the butterscotch light of the early-morning sun, looking for Nanny.

"She's not here again today," Rose said sadly.

"Not that we can see," Liam said.

"But if she was here," Rose said, "she'd have to come up for air."

"She might come up for air at the very minute you turn your back."

Rose peered over her shoulder at him for a long minute, taking him in. Then, as if in those seconds she feared she'd miss Nanny, she whipped her head back.

"Did I miss her?" Rose asked.

"No," Liam said.

"But she's *not* here, is she?" Lily asked, her voice low and worried. "If she were, she'd show up on your tracking screen, right?"

"Her transmitter might have gotten lost," Liam said, taking his eyes off the water just long enough to gaze into Lily's eyes. "The battery could have died; I've known that it was time to replace it, but I don't have my equipment here. It's all back in Cape Hawk."

"So she really could be right here?" Lily asked. "And we've somehow not seen her the last five—"

"Six," Rose interrupted.

"Six days?" Lily asked.

"It's possible," Liam said, scanning again.

He knew that other things were possible as well. Nanny was getting older. Her immune system could have become compromised, living so far from her native arctic waters. She could have picked up a parasite.

Her normal food source, capelin, was unavailable. The boat traffic in Long Island Sound was very busy, especially in near-shore areas. Perhaps she had been injured by a propeller. Her journey south from Nova Scotia, seeming to follow Rose along the way, had been an extraordinary one.

Liam prayed that Patrick was wrong.

He couldn't bear to think of the proud white whale in captivity—he hoped that Patrick was mistaken, that the Lafarge brothers had nothing to do with Nanny's disappearance. Liam had alerted John Stanley and Peter Wayland, the Fish and Wildlife officer, and by now he was sure that the Coast Guard and every oceanographic research vessel in the area were on the lookout for the *Mar IV.*

In spite of Patrick's suspicions, Liam continued to look out. Just like his ancestors, who had stood in the crow's nest of the *Pinnacle,* watching for whale spouts so they might kill the whales for profit, Liam stood on the rocks, scanning for Nanny, so he and his beloved Lily and Rose might continue their summer of faith. That's what it had been, he realized.

He knew that Ghost Hills—as amazing and unbelievable as they were—provided a scientific explanation for why Nanny had come south from Cape Hawk. Liam knew what his oceanographer colleagues would say. But deep down, he knew differently. Nanny had come to Connecticut out of love. Whales are mammals, and life is full of mystery. Not everything could be explained by logic and science. There had been nothing logical about Nanny's behavior this summer.

But looking down at Lily and Rose, Liam realized that there had been nothing logical about his, either. He had spent most of his life in a fortress of his own making. In a stone house on a hill, surrounded by boreal forest, surrounded by books and journals instead of people to love. He had lost his arm to the shark that had killed his brother Connor. And he'd spent every year since then trying to make sense of the loss, trying to understand tragedy with his mind.

From the minute Lily and Rose had entered his life, he had loved them. Yet because Lily was so protective and closed off, Liam had kept his feelings mostly to himself. He hadn't wanted to scare Lily or drive her away; he had understood that something terrible had happened to her, and that she needed to stay behind her walls as much as Liam had needed to stay behind his.

Over time, he began to realize that Lily was just like him. She had been attacked by a shark too. She had gone into the water one fine day, and after that, nothing would be the same. Liam suspected that she ran the same thoughts through her mind as he did through his: *What if I had been a minute earlier? A minute later?* Maybe the shark would have gone swimming by, and she wouldn't have been attacked.

Edward might not have noticed her. He might have set his sights on the next woman to walk by—someone else wearing expensive shoes, a cashmere coat. The shark might have swum on to other waters, to menace someone else. But then she wouldn't have had Rose. And Liam wouldn't have met either of them.

Liam put his arm around Lily now. As they scanned the bay for Nanny, he knew that she was worried about court. They had to be there in an hour. Life as Lily knew it was hanging in a very precarious balance; she was about to enter into the court system, where men in black robes would soon be making decisions that would affect the way she raised her daughter.

Although a respectable scientist, Liam was also a northern renegade. He was descended from Cape Hawk whalers—Arctic explorers who had sailed from the Gulf of St. Lawrence around Cape Horn and the Cape of Good Hope, had survived shipwrecks and subsisted on rainwater and vegetation. They had gone one-on-one with the sea, and lived to tell about it.

What Lily didn't know was, Liam would do anything for her and Rose. And "anything," to a man who'd had his arm ripped off by the shark that had killed his brother, was a big word. If Edward tried anything today—raised one hand to Lily . . . well, Liam would almost welcome it.

His cell phone rang, and he reached into his pocket to answer it.

"Hello?" he said.

"Liam, it's Pete Wayland."

"Hi, Pete," Liam said. Although he was on the way to court, immersed in all of that, he was grateful for the distraction. He stepped away from Lily and Rose to take the call. "Did John tell you what was going on? Patrick Murphy, a retired detective, thinks that maybe Gerard Lafarge is after a beluga—"

"Your friend's right," Pete said. The connection was terrible, but even through the static, Liam could hear the excitement in his voice. "You'll never believe who came through."

"Who?"

"Nick Olson—Captain Nick. He contacted me yesterday, told me that there was a beluga whale in the hold of—you guessed it—*Mar IV.* He gave us the ship's coordinates, and we went right out. Lafarge had a hold full of marine mammals—sick or dying dolphins."

"What about a beluga?" Liam asked, his heart falling.

"No," Peter said. "She wasn't on board. We're keeping an eye out for her, but there've been no sightings. If it's any consolation, Lafarge is in custody for violating the Marine Mammal Protection Act."

"Thanks," Liam said. "Let me know if you see her."

"I will," Pete promised, and they hung up.

Liam's heart kicked over. He hadn't realized how upset he felt about Nanny—even in spite of what was going on with the people he loved—until now. Rose stood on the rocks, pointing out to sea.

"That's a school of blues," he said as the seagulls began to wheel and dive on the slick of bluefish, silver and gleaming at the surface.

"It's so shiny, just like Nanny's head," Rose said, disappointed.

"Rose, try not to worry," Lily said, crouching beside her daughter, taking her hand. "You know that Nanny always takes care of herself. She found her way down here, to Hubbard's Point. I'm sure she's making her way somewhere else, right now. We'll hear about her soon."

"But I already miss her," Rose whispered.

"So do I," Lily said.

"Do you think she's swimming back to Cape Hawk?" Rose asked.

Lily and Rose both turned to look at Liam.

"I don't know, Rose," he said.

Worry lines creased her brow. Holding her mother's hand, she turned back toward the bay, gazing into the unknown.

Liam stared at the backs of their heads, this mother and daughter he loved so much. He and Lily were dressed in the dark, conservative clothes they had brought along from Cape Hawk. Although they hadn't discussed it, he knew they had brought them fearing that something would happen to Maeve—that her coma would prove to be irreversible. They had been prepared for the worst—and it hadn't happened. That could be true for Nanny too.

"Have faith, Rose," he said now.

"Faith?" she asked.

"We've got to trust that everything is going to work out," he said.

"For Nanny?" Rose asked.

"For everyone," Liam said, staring straight into Lily's blue, questioning, worried eyes.

Rose, her mother, and Dr. Neill were making their way up the hill, away from the rocks. Nanny hadn't shown up, and now it was time for the grownups to go to court. Rose was going to stay with Maeve and Clara. They had plans to plant four new rosebushes right beside the wishing well. Maeve had even bought Rose her own straw hat, trowel, and garden gloves. But the funny thing was, when Rose looked into the bag, she saw *two* new hats, *two* new trowels, and *two* new pairs of garden gloves.

"Who's the other one for?" Rose had asked, but Maeve had just smiled with that great-grandmotherly twinkle in her eye.

Now, coming around the side of the house, Rose saw Maeve and Clara by the wishing well, starting to dig. The garden smelled of fresh earth. Rose clung to her mother's hand. She didn't want her to leave.

"Stay," Rose said. "Maeve got new gloves for us, you and me."

"Honey," her mother said, bending down to look Rose in the eyes. "I have to go to court. I don't have a choice. But I want you to know—you don't have to worry about anything. You're here with Maeve and Clara, and I'll come home as soon as I can."

"I don't want you to go," Rose whispered, with a big lump in her throat. She knew that *court* was a place where important things happened. Gripping her mother's hand, she stared into her eyes for answers.

"I know you don't," her mother said. "But I'm going for *us*."

"What do you mean?"

"I'm going to tell the judge how much I love you."

"Really?" Rose asked.

"Really," her mother said. "There's nothing in the world more important than that."

"Why do you have my hospital records?" Rose asked, because she had seen her mother going through them on the table last night, putting them into a folder that she told Dr. Neill she was taking to court.

"Because I want to tell the judge how much you've been through . . ."

"Been through *together*," Rose emphasized.

"Yes, honey. I want him to understand that you have heart defects that have taken a lot of healing. A lot of time, and doctors' visits, and trips to the hospital."

"With you," Rose said. "You are always with me, Mommy."

"Yes," her mother said, her eyes gleaming as she smiled. "Always."

"Rose," Dr. Neill said now, his hand on her shoulder—almost as if he knew that Rose's heart had just started jumping and banging, going crazy inside her chest. She hadn't had any blue spells in a long time now—not since the last surgery. But right now she was getting breathless.

He picked her up. She put her arms around his neck, leaned her face against his cheek. It felt smooth but just a little scratchy, from his shave. He smelled like shaving cream and shampoo. His dark hair curled around his ears, and he had gray in his temples. She closed her eyes, let-

ting him hold her, calming her down. Even though he didn't say anything, she felt better.

"Rose," Maeve called, "will you come and help me and Clara plant
these rosebushes?"

Just then, a car pulled into the cul-de-sac. Still in Dr. Neill's arms,
Rose craned her neck to see who it was. The car was familiar, but she
wasn't sure. A door opened, and a black dog jumped out. The dog was
sweet and friendly, with a red collar and pink tongue hanging out—
Rose recognized her as belonging to Patrick, the red-haired policeman.

"Flora, darling!" Maeve said, sounding shocked and happy just as
the back door opened all the way, and Rose saw who was inside.

"Jessica!" she cried out, wriggling as Dr. Neill put her down. Rose
tore up the stone steps.

Her best friend jumped out of the car and came flying down the
road. They met halfway, hugging and laughing. Rose's heart was in her
throat, but in a good way—the best way ever. Jessica had tears in her
eyes, and so did Rose. She wiped them away, laughing so hard, feeling
all the sadness of missing her best friend melt into the summer sky.

"I can't believe you're here!" Rose said.

"I can't believe I am, either!" Jessica said.

Rose held her hand, tugged her down the steps into her great-grandmother's beautiful yard. She was so proud to show her friend where her
family came from—the cozy shingled cottage, the stone wishing well
with the magical arch spelling out *Sea Garden*, roses everywhere, and
the sparkling Sound spreading out from the long, sloping rock ledges.

"Hi, Dr. Neill," Jessica said.

"Hello, Jessica," he said. "It's nice to see a friend from Cape Hawk."

"It's nice to see *you*," she said.

And then Rose's mother came around the car with Marisa and
another woman—both as tall as Rose's mother was tiny. Patrick walked
beside Marisa, and Rose noticed that they were holding hands.

"Well, you must be Marisa," Maeve said.

"I'm so glad to meet you, Mrs. Jameson," Marisa said. She reached
out her hand, as if to shake Maeve's—but Maeve pulled her close in a
hug.

"This is my sister Sam," Marisa said.

"Hello," the redheaded woman said.

"Thank you both for coming," Maeve said. "It means so much to us."

"I wouldn't miss it," Sam said. "He did the same things to Marisa
and Jess as he did to your granddaughter. . . ."

"Jessica," Maeve said, turning toward her. "Do you like gardening?"

Jessica nodded. "I planted a rosebush in Cape Hawk. It's like the one we had in our garden back home, in Weston."

"Well, that's wonderful," Maeve said. "Clara and I thought Rose might like to help us plant these rosebushes while her mother takes care of business . . . would you like to help us?"

Jessica glanced at her mother a little anxiously. Rose knew that she was probably feeling the same way she felt about her mother's going to court, so she squeezed Jessica's hand. That made her friend smile.

"Sure," Jessica said. "I want to help."

Rose ran into the house and got the gardening gear her grand-mother had bought. Now she knew who it was for! She put one of the straw hats on her head, and stood on tiptoe to put the other on Jessica's. They waved their trowels, shiny silver spades with glossy wooden handles.

"Ready!" Rose said.

"I'm ready," Jessica piped in.

The adults all looked at each other. The two older women, dressed in their messy garden clothes and straw hats, and the five grownups in their court clothes—Patrick and Marisa and Sam, and Rose's mother and Dr. Neill.

"Are we ready too?" Patrick asked with his big Irish grin.

"Yes," Marisa said.

"You bet," Rose's mother said.

"Let's go get him," Dr. Neill said.

"I can't wait," Sam said.

Then Rose's mother and Dr. Neill leaned down to give Rose the biggest hug she'd ever had in her life—both of them looking at her with love and bravery in their eyes. She felt a giant swell, almost as if Nanny had just come up for air, sent a huge wave flooding over her. She closed her eyes, letting the wave and their hugs hold her aloft.

Rose watched as her mother stopped in front of Maeve. They looked at each other for the longest time, arrows of strength and love shooting from their eyes. Rose felt almost like crying, even though she didn't know why. Her great-grandmother's gaze was so ferocious—she looked charged up, ready for battle. She kissed Rose's mother. And then she did the oddest thing. She shook her hand—just as if they were in a business meeting instead of a rose garden.

"Godspeed, my darling," Maeve said. "You will prevail."

"Granny," Rose's mother said, her eyes huge and wide open, looking almost as if she were a very little girl, and in that second Rose could see her mother at Rose's age and even younger, turning to Maeve for everything.

"Right is might, darling," Maeve said. "He has gotten away with so much for so long. You're going to end that with the truth. Today . . ."

"What if he wins?"

"He won't," Maeve said, hands on Rose's mother's cheeks, gazing hard into her eyes. Her touch left two small streaks of dirt on her cheekbones, like war paint. Dr. Neill brushed them away, and Rose's mother turned, and she and Dr. Neill walked up the stone steps.

"I love you, Mommy!" Rose shouted out.

Her mother looked directly at Rose. Their eyes met and held—her mother's were as bright blue as the sky. They smiled at each other. Her mother held up a coin and threw it into the Sea Garden wishing well. It sparkled in the sunlight, turning as it flew through the air, jingling against the rocks inside.

Rose's mother had thrown the coin, but Rose made a wish anyway.

Chapter 26

Lily and Liam sat together in front, while Patrick, Marisa, and Sam rode in back. Marisa and Patrick seemed so happy and close, even though they had to be exhausted from their long drive. The conversation was quick and lively, catching up on the weeks since they'd first met in Cape Hawk, hearing about Patrick driving Sam up from Baltimore for the ceili, and it reminded Lily of good friends, out for a summer drive—instead of on the way to Family Court.

"You should have heard Marisa and her sister," Patrick said. "They were the best at the festival."

"Even though we came in third," Marisa said.

"Wait till next year," Sam said.

Talking with Marisa, listening to her calm voice and irrepressible laugh, made Lily forget the butterflies in her stomach for a minute or two. But then her mind would turn to what might happen next—and she'd feel cold and clammy and so nervous she couldn't think straight. Liam held her hand. She kept glancing across the seat, as if to make sure he was really there.

Pulling into Silver Bay, past the beach shops and children's museum, it was easy to think that this was just another summer day. The drugstore still had bins of beach balls and colorful rafts out front, along with signs for school supplies in the windows. Mothers and kids, shopping for school shoes, came out of Sutherland's in a hurry to get back to one of the last beach days.

When they got to the courthouse parking lot, Patrick spoke to the guard, who leaned into the car to shake his hand and asked him where he'd been.

The building itself was white brick, nondescript architecture from the sixties. Lily had driven past here countless times, on her way to the IGA, or the bookstore, or the record shop, or the garden center—life's little everyday journeys. How often had she come by, not even turning her head to watch the men and women on the way inside, to battle over the very things they each held most dear?

"I don't want to go inside," she said, grasping Liam's hand.

Everyone turned to look at her. Only Marisa spoke, reaching forward over the front seat to touch Lily's shoulder.

"You can do this," she said.

"I can't!" Lily said, filled with panic.

"Lily," Marisa said, their eyes meeting. "You've got to believe me. I know you can do this. You're my role model. You're going to go in there and stand tall, and you're going to be heard. And we're going to be right there rooting for you."

"All of us," Sam said.

Lily closed her eyes, feeling the world spin.

"Yes," Liam said softly. "All."

Something in the way he said the word . . .

Lily slowly opened her eyes. She looked out the window and saw her friends coming toward them: Tara and Joe, Bay and Danny. They surrounded the car. "Is he here?" she heard Patrick ask Joe.

"Oh yeah," Joe said. "All shiny and prepped."

"Creep," Patrick muttered.

Liam climbed out and reached back into the car for her. Lily stared at his hand. She knew that she could wait in here indefinitely, until the judge called and someone came to get her. She could stay till the court closed for the day, skip the proceedings entirely.

She'd tried flight already. Now it was time to fight. She grabbed Liam's hand, and let him pull her out of the car, into his embrace.

Joe's cell phone rang; he answered it, then covered the mouthpiece. "Excuse me," he said. "I'll see you inside."

Walking around the building, they heard radios squawking and the sound of a crowd. Emerging on the front sidewalk of the courthouse, she blinked as reporters rushed forward. They had microphones and cameras. She remembered to hold her head high.

"Lily," some of the reporters called. "Mara!" shouted others.

"The idiot called the press," she heard Patrick say.

"Well, isn't he in for a surprise?" she heard Tara retort with a chuckle.

Lily didn't know what she meant, but she was surprised by her friend finding humor in such a scene. She felt herself pushed and shoved, borne forward like someone at a warped Mardi Gras. There was a festive tone in the air, a feeling of anticipation yet at the same time resolution. When she raised her head, she saw many of the re-porters smiling at her.

"Go for it, Lily," one of them, a young woman with short blond hair, called. "Don't let him win!" called another, a man with dark glasses.

"We're right here rooting for you," said a print reporter, her note-book open, as Lily walked by. "Can I have a comment?"

Lily couldn't reply, but Marisa did. "We're together in this," she said.

"Ask her name," Lily heard Sam direct one of the TV anchors, the pretty dark-haired woman from the Hartford station. Lily turned, saw Sam pointing at Marisa.

"What's your name?" the anchor asked, microphone in Marisa's face.

"My real name is Patricia Hunter," Marisa said, standing tall and proud.

The crowd began to buzz, and then to roar. "It's his second wife!" someone called, and then they were all pressing forward, asking ques-tions, ready with their microphones. Lily looked at Sam, tears running down her cheeks, her throat tight with emotion and pride for her friend. She knew that Marisa had much more to say, but for right now it would have to wait.

The courthouse door swung open, and Joe stood there smiling—no, grinning—beckoning Lily and her entourage inside. And, glancing at Liam for strength, with her arm linked with Marisa's, Lily walked for-ward into the Silver Bay Family Courthouse, ready to meet her and Rose's destiny.

No cameras were allowed inside, so the hall was relatively empty. A cluster of state marshals stood off to the side, talking and watching. Like the guard out back, they waved at Patrick.

They made it through the line for the metal detector in just a few minutes. Walking down the corridor toward the courtroom, Lily and Marisa clasped hands. Coming around the corner, they saw Edward.

Or more importantly, he saw them.

In that moment, Lily watched the skies open up. The look in Ed-ward's golden-hazel eyes, when he saw his two ex-wives together, was a full-fledged thunderstorm. Dark clouds, torrential rains, thunder, and lightning. His face went bright red, looking ready to explode.

"Hello, Ted," Sam called.

"Oh boy," Tara said.

"Do you see that?" Lily whispered to Marisa.

"I'd almost forgotten what it was like to watch him lose it," Marisa said. "But now it's all coming back to me."

Liam put his arm around Lily's shoulders.

Edward's rage was so blatant, everyone saw it. Lily's stomach clenched. This is what Rose will face, she thought, if Edward wins today. She shook off her emotions and felt her spine stiffen.

"He called the press, but he didn't count on Marisa showing up," Patrick said.

"Hello, everyone," Lindsey Winship said, joining them.

"Lindsey," Lily said, and began making introductions. She saved Marisa for last. "This is my wonderful friend Marisa Taylor. She came all the way down from Nova Scotia to show up today."

"It's so good of you to be here," Lindsey said warmly to Marisa. "He might easily deny the allegations of one woman—but your story will make that much more difficult."

"I want to be called by my real name today," Marisa said. "So he doesn't figure out my alias. I want to be able to leave again, and not have him find me and Jessica. So it's Patricia Hunter."

"Patty," Sam said, putting her arm around her sister's shoulders.

"Good idea, Patty," Lindsey said, her eyes shining. "Although perhaps that won't be necessary."

"Heads up," Liam said, tightening his arm around Lily as Edward left his lawyer and walked over.

"Well," Edward said sharply, looking back and forth between Lily and Marisa. "Isn't this something? You couldn't win on your own, Lily, so you had to get another liar to help you?"

Lily and Marisa faced him together, Liam, Patrick, and Sam standing right there. Lily didn't know what the judge would say, or what the reporters would report, but she knew in that moment that she was the most blessed person ever—to have such wonderful friends.

"We don't lie, Edward," Lily said softly.

"No, Ted," Marisa said. "And you, of all people, know that . . ."

"We were good and loving and true," Lily whispered.

"And you just trashed them," Sam said.

"You're deluded," Edward said. "And I'm going to prove to the judge exactly that."

Lily just shook her head. Standing in the courthouse corridor, she felt her strength building, as if every angel in her life had come to earth, to be with her now. Her father and mother were here. Liam's brother Connor . . .

Lily felt the courage of her convictions. She felt the warmth of her humanity, and her big, loving heart. She felt the energy of being a woman. She felt the tenderness of Liam's love for her, and hers for him. She felt the flow of friendships, some old, some new. She felt the respect of strangers—the reporters who had come to witness, and the marshals who guarded the courthouse. She felt the strength that came from being Rose's mother.

A door opened, and Lily looked down the hall behind Edward. It was almost ten o'clock, the time court was scheduled to begin. Two women were coming down the hall, one of them with an armload of files. Court clerks, Lily thought. But Edward didn't turn around. He had eyes only for Lily. It was as if everyone, even Marisa, had just melted away. She was his opponent. He was here to defeat her and no one else.

The crowd began to rustle a little. Lily felt an electric buzz coming off Liam. She wanted to look at him, but she was mesmerized by Edward. She had loved him once; even now, she wanted to ask him, couldn't he just see reason and go away? They both knew that he cared nothing for their child. . . . His eyes were black holes, burning with hate.

Joe cleared his throat, and Lily's attention was torn away from Edward's eyes. Joe was grinning, and as Lily looked around, she saw that so were Patrick, Tara, Bay, and Danny. Marisa too. Lindsey. And even Liam.

"What is it?" Lily asked Liam.

The two women got closer, right behind Edward. As they approached, Lily saw Joe raise his eyebrow at one of the uniformed marshals, giving him the high sign. The marshal acknowledged it with a nod, but didn't move.

"Liam?" Lily asked, looking up at him.

"Getting nervous?" Edward asked, smiling.

"She has no reason to be," Patrick said.

Edward just stared him down.

"You know," Patrick said, "there's someone else that Joe and I thought Lily and Marisa should meet."

Edward just stood there, his face red and smug.

"Who's that?" Edward asked.

"Hi, Ed," said one of the two women behind him. Midway between Lily's and Marisa's height, she had the same dark brown hair. Her eyes were soft, warm, blue. She had a long thick scar all the way up the right side of her face.

Beads of sweat popped out on Edward's forehead. A few reporters pressed forward, and the other woman—younger, in a business suit, looking very much a lawyer—opened one of her files and handed them some photographs.

Lily saw the pictures flash by: a woman bruised and broken, head and face bandaged in some shots, cut and stitched in others, one with her broken-toothed mouth hanging open as if she had no jawbones.

Suddenly, Lily knew.

"Judy?" she asked, her eyes filling with tears.

Judy Houghton smiled and nodded, and with blue eyes gleaming stepped forward to give Lily a big hug.

Chapter 27

"Judy Houghton," Lily said. "The one before me.

"Yes," Judy said. "I'm so sorry for what you've been through."

"Judy, this is Patricia," Lily said, and the three women stared at each other, smiling and holding hands.

Edward had wheeled around back down the hall, where he was deep in conference with his lawyer, a tall, older, stooped man in a three-piece suit. The reporters were examining the photos. Lily's eyes were drawn to one photo in particular—a mummylike figure in a bed, hooked up to tubes.

"Is that you?" Lily asked.

"Yes," Judy said. "That was the night Edward beat me for coming home late. He accused me of being out with another man, even though I was at my sister's."

"I'm so sorry," Lily said, tears welling up with compassion for what Edward had done to her.

"He broke my nose and shattered my cheekbone," Judy said. "With just one punch, he broke my jaw in three places. All my front teeth, and the ones in back on the right, were broken. I went flying across the room and smashed into the window. That's how I got this." She touched the long scar on her cheek.

"Oh, Judy," Marisa whispered.

"He didn't hit us," Lily said.

Judy glanced down the hall, where Edward was hunched with his lawyer, talking and gesturing.

"No," she said. "He learned not to. The police came. He got arrested."

Lily remembered Edward telling her about hitting Judy. He had made it seem so long ago, a fleeting incident, almost unreal. She had been disturbed even then about his seeming lack of remorse. Looking back, of course, she knew that he had told her about his previous violence to put her on notice. But now, to meet this real woman, to know that he had disfigured her face and put her in the hospital, literally made Lily sick.

"We knew about Edward's record of assault," Patrick said, stepping forward. "It's one of the reasons we looked at him so hard when you went missing, Lily."

"And one of the reasons we went looking for Judy again now, for this hearing," Joe said.

"Liam really pushed us," Patrick said, and Lily glanced up, saw Liam blushing.

"Judy wasn't so easy to track down," Joe said. "It was touch and go, and we didn't say anything because we didn't want you to be disappointed, and you needed to be prepared to go forward without her if necessary."

"I left Hawthorne," Judy said. "After everything that happened. And after Ed, well, he wouldn't fulfill his obligations to me."

"Obligations?" Lily asked.

"I remember reading about your disappearance," Judy continued. "At first I was sure he'd killed you. But I always hoped that you'd just gotten away."

"I did get away," Lily said. "I ran for my life. And my baby's . . ."

"How is she?" Judy asked with a smile.

"She's wonderful," Lily told her, smiling back.

Just then, Edward came back over. He was pale and drawn, and his voice shook as he stood there, staring from Judy to Lily to Marisa, and he said, "You can't hurt me now."

"Hurt you?" Judy asked.

"I've paid my debt for those," he said, pointing at the photos. "You had me arrested, and I did all the time I had to do. You can't do anything more to me."

"Anything more to *you*?" Lily asked, incredulous, wanting to scream at him. Her heart was racing, and Judy had to put her hand on her wrist to gentle her down.

"He doesn't get it," Judy said calmly. "He never did. And he's certainly never paid his debts."

"I'll see you in court," Edward said to Lily.

❧

"He worked for my father," Judy said. "That's how I met him. My father had a seat on the New York Stock Exchange. Ed did maintenance work at my father's boatyard. But he was smart, and funny, and my father liked him. Ed used to read the *Wall Street Journal,* asking my father for

stock tips. My father was impressed with some of his picks, and he offered him a job as an assistant. That's how he got started."

"Your father gave him a job. . . ." Marisa said.

"Ed was smart. He made connections very fast and easily. He made
up an Ivy League background. It was the boom eighties, and he got a
job as a stockbroker right after I left him." Judy laughed lightly. "Unlucky, in some ways, for him."

"Why?"

"Well . . ." Judy began.

"Very unlucky for him," said the other young woman, and for the
first time, Lily turned to smile at her. She was obviously a lawyer—in
her gray striped suit and black patent leather pumps, her arms full of
files, her dark hair pulled back in a neat French twist. She and Lindsey
had had their heads together while Lily and Judy talked.

"I haven't met you yet," Lily said. "I'm Lily Malone. Are you Judy's
lawyer?"

"I'm Rebecca," the young woman said, laughing. "So sorry not to
have introduced myself first. But I've been a little mesmerized by this
whole thing. Yes, I consider myself her lawyer."

"And a very fine one," Judy said proudly.

Just then, the court doors swung open, and a marshal signaled
everyone to start filing in. Edward and his lawyer had started arguing
again. His lawyer was advising something, and Edward was shaking his
head with vehemence, shaking his finger. Lindsey came forward,
tapped Lily on the shoulder.

"Are you ready?" she asked.

"Yes," Lily said, smiling at Judy. "I am."

Liam and Marisa and Judy and everyone from Hubbard's Point were
right with her, and they all filed into the courtroom.

Liam watched Lily in action, and she was incredible. All through the
last days, he had wanted to tell her what Joe and Patrick were doing—
trying to put together a case for the judge, bringing together the other
two women in Edward Hunter's life—so that Lindsey Winship could
argue against forcing Rose to take the DNA test.

Now, as the courtroom filled up, he kissed Lily on the cheek as she
went up to the table. He felt the change in her mood. Having everyone's
support made such a difference—especially the support of Marisa and
Judy. He glanced at the two women, sitting between him and Sam, in
the row directly behind Lily, and wondered what kind of man could do
so much to destroy such wonderful spirits.

If there was one thing that made this moment almost pleasurable, it was seeing Edward Hunter squirm across the courtroom, at the plaintiff's table. He was still whispering insistently to his lawyer. The elderly lawyer's face was lined and gaunt, and he had a haunted, worried look.

Just then a marshal banged the gavel.

"Family Court of the State of Connecticut is in order, the Honorable Martha D. Porter presiding. Please be seated." The judge was in her mid-fifties, tall and slender, with frosted brown hair and a very slight tan. She gazed out over her courtroom with dark, wise eyes that had perhaps seen more than their share of pathos.

"Judge Porter is a woman?" he heard Bay whisper.

"Excellent," Tara whispered back.

"Hearing arguments in the matter of Hunter versus Malone," the court clerk read. "Motion to compel—"

"Excuse me," Lindsey Grant Winship said, rising from her seat. "If I may, Your Honor, I would like to address a matter of pressing urgency."

"Yes, Ms. Winship . . . you're attorney for the defense?"

"Yes, Your Honor. Until this moment, I have represented Lily Malone and the minor child Rose Malone in the aforestated action. However, I must recuse myself, due to conflict of interests."

Lily's gasp was horrible to hear.

Across the courtroom, Edward was alert and on guard. His lawyer whispered something, explaining what was happening, and a slow smile began to seep across Edward's face like molasses—it touched only the surface, didn't come from deep inside, as if there were no deep insides to come from. He was responding to the sound of pain. Liam saw, and felt revulsion.

Lily's face was a mask of confusion and anguish as Lindsey marshaled her papers and faced the judge. Lindsey leaned over, hand on Lily's shoulder, whispered something into her ear.

"Your Honor," Edward's lawyer said, "this is highly irregular, and I must object. To leave Ms. Malone without legal counsel at this moment is unacceptable. My client has waited nine years to meet his daughter."

Rebecca, Judy Houghton's lawyer, snorted and let out a wildly exuberant laugh.

"Judge Porter," Lindsey Winship said, "I wish to offer these affidavits and court orders in support of my new client. As you can see, there's already been a judgment entered in this matter, with a rather serious problem in terms of compliance. May I approach?"

"Yes," the judge said, and Lindsey stepped forward to lay one document on the clerk's table and another on the plaintiff's—directly in front of Edward.

Watching from the second row, Liam saw Edward blanch. He turned gray-white, the color of a shark's belly. Edward's lawyer fought him for the paper, which Edward clearly didn't want him to see. Once the old lawyer won the tug-of-war, he too turned shark-belly white.

"As you can see, Your Honor," Lindsey said as the clerk marked the document and handed it to the judge, "Mr. Hunter is already in serious arrears for child support."

"Your Honor," Edward's lawyer said in stentorian tones, "this order is many years old. It was entered for a minor child, who not only is not the concern of this court at this time, but is no longer even a minor!"

"I'm twenty-one," Rebecca said, standing up.

"Your Honor!" the old, stooped lawyer said as Edward inched lower in his seat and began to look for the exit sign.

"He was ordered to pay child support," Rebecca said, "beginning the day I was born, when my mother was still in the hospital. She'd been at my aunt's, making curtains for my nursery, and he thought she was having an affair instead, and beat her so badly, she went into early labor."

Liam saw Lily's mouth open and her eyes fill with tears. They were both remembering the day Rose was born and Lily's anguish.

"Too bad for him," Rebecca said, "I was born three months premature—three months more that he owes."

"Your Honor," Lindsey said, "Mr. Hunter was ordered to pay two thousand dollars a month child support for his daughter. To date, he has never willingly paid one cent. Ms. Houghton had his salary attached for a time, but she lost track of him when he moved nine years ago."

"That's a lot of unpaid child support, Mr. Hunter," Judge Porter said.

"Your Honor, the order states that the support ceases after the end of schooling," Edward's lawyer said feebly. "At twenty-one, the young lady must be finished with college, so I submit—"

"I'm in law school," Rebecca said. "He's never wanted to meet me, so he doesn't know that. But I've helped my mother file legal documents against him for so long . . ."

Liam smiled up at the young woman, fierce and bright and shining, facing the judge and her father. She was straight and tall, with dark hair—like Lily's, Marisa's, and her mother's. Liam suspected that if they were to track down Mrs. Hunter, Edward's mother, she might turn out to have dark hair too.

"And I want to become a Family Court lawyer," Rebecca said, staring straight at Edward. "I want to practice advocacy. For women who have been abused by men like my father."

The court erupted in applause. Liam looked around as Marisa, Sam,

Tara, Joe, Bay, Danny, Patrick, the reporters, and people sitting in the gallery joined in. His eyes met Lily's at the defense table, and he saw that she was clapping harder than anyone. The judge allowed the applause to go on for a few beats, and then she banged her gavel.

Edward and his lawyer were huddled, heads close together in conference. The judge stared at them with dispassion, waiting for a response.

"Your Honor," Lindsey said, "Mr. Hunter already has unfulfilled obligations to one daughter . . . and I submit that his reasons for maintaining to want to know Rose are a sham that go hand in hand with his proven history of abuse. Now, if he would like to pay child support to Rose Malone . . ."

"We withdraw our motion!" Edward's lawyer said hurriedly.

"The child, Rose Malone," the judge said, "has the right to know who her father is, as well as a right to parental support. Ms. Malone, if you would like me to enter an order compelling Mr. Hunter to take a paternity test . . ."

"No!" Lily said sharply. "I mean, thank you, Your Honor."

Edward spoke to his lawyer, stood up, and started down the aisle.

"Your Honor," the lawyer said, "Mr. Hunter asked to request a recess, so that he can—"

Joe Holmes stepped into the aisle, right in Edward's path. He spread his legs, flashed his badge. "FBI," he said. "And Mr. Hunter, you're under arrest, for violations of the Child Support Recovery Act."

"How's that for the wheels of justice?" Tara asked under her breath, catching Edward's eye as Joe snapped on the cuffs. "The local cops can get him for what he did to Maeve too." Across the aisle, reporters were scribbling madly in their pads, and courtroom artists were capturing the scene with sketch paper and charcoal for the afternoon news cycle.

The judge banged down her gavel, telling the marshals to clear the court. Lily was the first down the aisle, right into Liam's arms. Then he watched as she hugged everyone from Hubbard's Point, and everyone from Cape Hawk. She saved her biggest hugs for Judy and Rebecca.

"Thank you," Lily said, holding Rebecca. "How can I ever tell you how much it means to me, that you'd be so brave and stand up this way?"

"I'm so, so proud of you, sweetheart," Judy said as tears ran from her eyes, down her cheeks and the edge of her scar.

"I did it for us, Mom," Rebecca said, her hazel eyes gleaming. "And I did it for Rose."

"Rose?" Lily asked.

"My half-sister," Rebecca said.

Chapter 28

Maeve knew that the time for farewell was upon them. She wanted to have everyone over to the house for a big party and celebration, and to meet Judy and Rebecca. Clara agreed, so between the two of them, they arranged for caterers and a big yellow-and-white-striped tent, to be erected in the side yard between the two houses.

"You realize that that's exactly where Edward and I got married," Lily said to her grandmother.

"Of course," Maeve said. "We have to purge the ground. Is he really in jail?"

"He is," Lily said. "They're holding him on a federal warrant. Joe said that lots of deadbeat dads skate by every day, and that if they make even the simplest effort to set up a payment plan, they're allowed out. But Edward's arrogance was just so intense. Once they arrested him for the child support, they began investigating him for other things. Including hurting you."

"And there was that incident on the Internet," Maeve said. "That Marisa talked about."

"Edward was an equal opportunity predator," Lily said. "He never met a victim he didn't like. He's always been so arrogant about it all."

"Tara knew?"

"Everyone knew, I think," Lily said. "Tara was egging Joe on to get all the legal stuff in order, and Liam was pushing to make sure they brought Marisa and Judy back in time. And Patrick has never stopped trying to prove that he had something to do with poisoning you."

"Yes, that's a mystery," she said.

"When Judy told us that he used to work in a boatyard, Patrick decided to go talk to the owner. It turns out that Edward did lots of work on heating systems on boats. So he knows plenty about ducts and vents and fumes and all that."

"Well," Maeve said. "If he did it, I believe that Patrick will catch him. Life is long, and a person's character generally catches up to him."

"Is that another way of saying 'Right is might'?" Lily asked.

Her grandmother nodded. She sat on the loveseat, gazing out the window at the rippling blue bay. The light was reflected in her eyes, and a small smile played on her mouth. Outside, people's voices could be heard in the yard, on the rocks, everywhere. Workers preparing for the party were raising the tent, setting up the bar, tables, and dance floor. Liam and Patrick were down front with Rose, Jessica, Marisa, and Sam.

"Granny?" Lily asked. "You look lost in thought."

Maeve turned to gaze at her. Lily was struck, as she often was since returning to Hubbard's Point, by how much Maeve had aged. Nine years had passed since their last summer together, and the weight of every second hung heavy on Lily's heart.

"I'm thinking about you, my darling," Maeve said.

"What about me?"

"About how afraid I was, the day you went to court. Afraid that Edward would somehow pull off one of his magic tricks, by fooling the judge."

"Not Judge Porter," Lily said.

"She never heard the case, though," Maeve said. "I wonder how she would have decided, if Judy hadn't come forward."

"I know," Lily said.

"It's possible that she would have applied the law fairly," Maeve said. "But what does that even mean? I think that the judicial system in general, and men in particular, need to school themselves about the realities of emotional abuse."

"Rebecca will help see to that," Lily said.

"Oh, I can't wait to meet her at the party tonight," Maeve said. But her eyes were still so serious, Lily couldn't understand.

"What's wrong, Granny?"

Maeve sighed. She turned her head, but try as she might, she couldn't hide the tears in her eyes. "I want it to be enough," she whispered.

"What?" Lily asked. "What do you want to be enough?"

"This," Maeve said, waving her arm in a sweeping arc. "Having you back here again. Spending time with my darling Rose—and Liam. Seeing justice served, and Edward incarcerated. It's so much. But . . ."

"It's not enough," Lily said.

Maeve shook her head. She picked up her glasses case—the one Lily had needlepointed for her up in Cape Hawk, with the word NANOUK in big block letters, and a whale's tail curving in the background. "This was almost all I had of you for nine years," she said.

"The entire length of Rose's life," Lily said.

"You made it for me, sent it to me . . . I used to hold it against my heart," Maeve said, as she did now, clutching it tightly. "And pray for you and your little girl. I didn't even know her name!"

"I couldn't tell you," Lily said. "I was afraid he would somehow find out. And I think, also, I was afraid you'd want us as much as we wanted you. The more you knew about us, the more you'd miss us. It was the reason I couldn't let myself think about you, or home. Not consciously, anyway. But every night, my dreams . . ."

"Ah, dreams," Maeve said. "I had them of you too. Holding your hand."

"When I was a little girl, walking with you to the school bus," Lily said.

"We had the same dream," Maeve said.

"There were always roses in mine," Lily said. "Just like in your garden."

"Dublin Bays," Maeve said. "Scarlet Beauties, Garnet-and-Golds."

"And all the beach roses, between your yard and Clara's," Lily said.

"Do you suppose we'll dream the same dreams after you go again?" Maeve asked, reaching over to pull Lily closer.

"I don't think we'll have to," Lily said. "Because I'll never be gone long. And I want you to come up to Cape Hawk to visit—see our house and my shop, and walk Rose to school. We'll never miss another holiday together."

"Holidays were hard," Maeve whispered.

"For me too," Lily said, wiping her eyes as she remembered the terrible pain of missing home, especially the first few years.

The waves splashed up against the rocks, sending gentle music though the open windows. The reflection played upon the white ceiling, dancing with shadows and light. Seabirds called overhead. Rose's voice wafted up from the tidal pool, and Jessica's answered, both girls breaking into peals of laughter that couldn't help but make Lily and Maeve smile and dry their tears. Maeve handed Lily the glasses case.

"Your needlework is so beautiful," Maeve said.

"I can't wait for you to see my shop."

"What about those publishers? Do you think they'd like to know you're back and ready to create that magazine? *Lily's Home* has such a lovely ring to it."

Lily smiled sadly, shook her head. "I don't think so," she said.

"Another thing Edward stole from you?" Maeve said. "Don't you want to try to get it back?"

"I have a life I love, Granny," Lily said. "In a magical, amazing place. The only thing that was really missing in it was you. I sell my designs to women who really appreciate them. Rose . . . well, Rose takes up most of my creative time. Considering what she's been through, I'm not sure I'd ever have really been cut out for running a magazine. As flattering as it was."

"They loved the idea of your tapestries of life," Maeve said, smiling. "Creating them, designing them, and then selling them to all the women of America."

Lily hugged her grandmother. "When living them is really just about as much as I can handle."

Maeve hugged her back—hard, but not too hard, and tight, but not too tight. After all, Lily thought: her grandmother knew that Lily might be going away, but she also knew she'd be coming back. They broke apart and Maeve went to find Clara, and Lily went in search of Liam and Rose, to get ready for the party that night.

The band began to play just as the evening star came out. Venus glowing in the west, in the rose-violet twilight. The dark, rich colors shadowed the pine trees and rosebushes, and cast a mysterious net on the smooth bay. The air was balmy, without any hint of last week's chill. Just warm summer breezes for Lily's last night here in the south.

Friends from the beach and town arrived, greeted Maeve and Clara, standing at the wishing well. The two hostesses wore long dresses with shawls around their shoulders, and they directed everyone over to the tent for food and something to drink. When Lindsey Grant Winship arrived, Lily hurried over to meet her.

"Hi, Lily. How are you?" she asked.

"I'm fine, Lindsey," she said, giving her a hug, admiring her coral silk sheath dress.

"This is the first time I've really had the chance to tell you I'm sorry for dropping that bombshell on you in court. It's just that everything had happened so fast. Joe Holmes had just been filling me in on his plans to arrest Edward; he could have done that without my making that plea to the court, but I wanted the judge to see with her own eyes what kind of man Edward was."

"I was upset at the very moment you said you weren't my lawyer anymore," Lily said. "But after that, I couldn't have been happier."

Lindsey nodded. "I'd just met Judy and Rebecca, and I was interviewing them as our witnesses—when it occurred to me that the proceedings could be stopped before they even got started if I could get Rebecca on the record right away."

"Well, whatever you did, it worked," Lily said, smiling, and pointed her toward Tara and Joe.

And then Judy and Rebecca arrived. Scanning the crowd for Rose, Lily introduced them to Maeve and Clara.

"Our heroes," Maeve said, holding Rebecca's hands.

"We were happy to be there," Judy said. Her scar wasn't as apparent in the twilight, but just seeing a hint of it made Lily shiver. Leaving Rebecca with Maeve briefly, Lily pivoted Judy for a moment alone.

"I can't thank you enough," Lily said, gazing at Judy.

"There were so many times when I wanted to call you," Judy said. "Back when you first married him, and I saw the announcement in the paper. I remember looking at your picture, thinking you looked so happy. I thought, maybe he's different with her. Maybe it really was me—that I just made him so mad, we couldn't be together."

"It wasn't you," Lily said.

"No. But back then, I felt so terrible. Rebecca was nine then, and he'd never had one thing to do with her."

"Rose's age now . . ."

Judy nodded. "We had moved out of Hawthorne, up to Salisbury, where we live now. It's about as far from Edward as we could get in this state. At first, Rebecca used to wonder about her father, but then she stopped asking. It was as if he didn't really exist. But I would look in the mirror and know he did."

"I thought of calling you so many times," Judy continued. "I wanted you to find me. If you had, I would have said, 'I've been waiting for your call.' I knew, deep down, that Ed was doing the same kind of things to you. It's in him too deep to ever stop. I wanted you to know that you weren't alone."

"I know it now," Lily said, hugging Judy. Just then, Liam and Rose came over. They all stood there, and Lily's eyes roved back and forth between Rebecca and Rose.

Lily held out her hand to Rose.

"Honey," she said, "I want you to meet someone. Rose, this is Rebecca Houghton. Rebecca, my daughter Rose Malone. Rose," Lily said, "do you remember I told you about Rebecca? How you and she are related?"

Rose nodded. Rebecca crouched down, looking straight into her eyes.

"You're my sister," Rebecca said, holding Rose's hand. Their similarities were so great: they were both graceful, strong, beautiful brown-haired girls. Their eyes were hazel, green flecked with gold. Seeing them together, Rose's small hand in Rebecca's, brought a lump to Lily's throat.

"My mother told me," Rose said.

"Officially, we're half-sisters," Rebecca said. "But that doesn't sound right."

"Rebecca's not half anything," Judy said.

"Neither is Rose," Lily whispered, and Liam put his arm around her.

"We have the same father," Rebecca said. "So we can thank him for that—for each other. But other than that, we're fine without him. We have great mothers, and we have ourselves."

"Ourselves?" Rose asked.

"Yes," Rebecca said. "We're girls, and we're great. Don't ever forget that, Rose. When you get a little older . . ." She paused, and Lily had the sense of Rebecca remembering back to a younger version of herself, trying to figure out what she'd understood at nine. "You'll know what I mean. Girls who don't grow up with their fathers sometimes think they're not good enough. But you are, Rose."

"You are too, Rebecca."

"Rebecca is about to start law school," Judy said to Rose. "She graduated from college in May, and she took lots of pre-law classes. Now she's going to become a lawyer, and help women and kids. She's going to be their advocate."

"Advocate?" Rose asked.

"Someone who pleads a cause," Rebecca said. "I'm going to help everyone in the country understand that women and children have to be treated with respect. Especially judges and courts. Because so many people go there for help, and they don't get helped. I'm going to change that."

"That's good," Rose said. "I'll help you."

"She's going to end up on the Supreme Court," Judy said, her eyes shining as she faced Lily.

"I think you're right," Lily said as she stared down at Rose and Rebecca, the two bright and brilliant daughters of such a tarnished man.

After everyone had eaten, and the band got into full swing, Tara and Bay came dancing over to Lily and Liam. They tapped Liam on the shoulder, and he turned to look. At first Lily thought they were cutting in to dance with him—but no. They wanted Lily. "May we have the pleasure of this dance, madame?" Tara asked.

"But of course," Lily said, smiling up at Liam, kissing him as they spun her away.

They had all kicked off their shoes the minute they'd arrived, so the three of them danced barefoot. Lily began to notice that her two friends were easing her through the crowd, to the edge of the dance floor, and then out from under the tent.

"Let me guess," she said. "You want us to dance under the stars."

"No," Tara said, grabbing her and Bay's hands, starting to run toward the rocks. "I want us to dance underwater."

Suddenly they were fourteen again. Tara didn't have to say another word for Lily and Bay to know what she meant. They had left many parties right in the middle to do this very thing. End-of-summer nights, with music soaring through the air, were made for this. They climbed down the seawall and walked across the rock ledges. Lily knew she could do this blindfolded. Her bare feet knew every inch of the rocks—every ridge, every crevice.

When they got to the edge, the black zone of shore, where the rocks were wet and slippery, they pulled their dresses over their heads, dropped them in a heap, and dove in. The water was silky and warm. Lily stroked through, tasting salt, her fingertips brushing her friends' hands as they all swam underwater.

She came up for air, to a night sky painted with stars. Brushing water from her eyes, she floated on her back, looking up. This was her element. Salt water surrounding her, holding her afloat, with constellations all around. Her best friends were floating beside her, and her daughter and true love were up at the house, and her grandmother was fine, and Lily had never been so happy—and sad—in her life.

"I can't believe I'm leaving tomorrow," she said.

"Sssh," Bay said. "Let's pretend that's not happening."

"We have to face facts," Tara said. "Or else we'll be really, really upset when we realize she's left."

Lily's heart swelled. To have come all the way here, and to have had so many wonderful things happen, and then to have to leave again. Was this what life was all about? Comings and goings, needing to let go again and again, never able to hold on to the things she loved most? Because how could she have it both ways: her love for everyone here at Hubbard's Point, and her life with Liam and Rose up in Cape Hawk? And what about Nanny? Lily glanced around the darkness, looking for that big, beautiful flash of white. But Nanny was gone. . . .

"You know," Tara said, swimming over to lift a handful of Lily's wet hair. "I almost hoped you wouldn't want to come swimming with us."

"Why?"

"Because I was hoping that tonight you were going to surprise us. Bay and I both secretly thought you'd stage a wedding. That we were all being invited here for a supposed farewell bash—when in fact, you and Liam were going to tie the knot."

Lily smiled, treading water.

"Liam's the one, isn't he?" Bay asked.

Lily nodded. "He always was. It just took me a long time to figure it out." So long, she thought now. Through all the years alone with Rose up in Cape Hawk. Liam had always been there, waiting and helping. He had loved them every step of the way, and Lily had finally felt brave enough to love him back. Trusting a man after what had happened with Edward was no small feat. But now, with Liam, it seemed as easy and lovely as swimming on a summer night.

"We're so happy for you, Lily," Bay said. "We thought we'd lost you forever. Now that we have you back, it's going to be so hard to let you go. . . ."

"I thought you were the one who didn't want to talk about it," Tara said.

"You were right," Bay said to Tara as she joined hands with both friends. "We'd better face the truth tonight, or we won't be ready when she leaves again tomorrow."

"This time you know I'll be back," Lily said.

"Promise?" Tara asked.

"I promise," Lily said, and she had never meant a promise more.

Patrick stood with Marisa, listening to the music. The party swirled around them, and Patrick realized that he was standing in the place where it had all begun—Maeve's garden.

"What are you thinking?" Marisa asked.

"Right there," he said, pointing toward the wishing well. "That's where I found her watering can and yellow boots. Lily walked out of her life nine years ago, and I walked in."

"Thank God you did," Marisa said.

Patrick felt himself redden. "For all the good I did," he said. "I never found her, in all that time."

"You found me," Marisa whispered, holding him.

"I didn't even know I was looking for you," he said, staring into her green eyes.

"I know," she said. "Out of something so terrible has come more than I've ever imagined."

Patrick followed her gaze across the rose garden, to Sam, Jessica, and

Rose, playing with Flora. He thought of Tally, and held Marisa a little tighter.

He thought of the cases he had worked on, the crimes he had tried to solve. He thought of Edward Hunter's smug face, and he gazed into Marisa's luminous eyes.

"Sometimes you have to look at what's really bad," he said, "to see what's really good."

She reached up, touched his cheek. Her smile was still sad, just a little, so much less so than when he'd first met her.

"I'm looking," she said, fixed on his eyes, "at what's really good, right now."

"So am I," he said.

"The best," she whispered, standing on tiptoes to kiss him as the music played on in Maeve's rose garden.

When she'd dried off and toweled her hair, and gotten dressed again, Lily went to find Liam. He was sitting out a dance with Rose, on the four-seasons bench. They moved over to make room for her, and they all sat very still for a few minutes, just listening to the music, and enjoying the party, and knowing that they had so much to celebrate tonight.

"I'm glad Jessica and Marisa and Patrick and Sam are here," Rose said. Marisa and Sam were talking to Maeve, and Jessica and Patrick sat not far away, with Flora at their feet.

"Me too," Lily said.

"It wouldn't seem right, having this party without them," Liam said.

"No, you're right," Lily said, smiling. "Not *this* party."

"It's pretty special, right?" Rose said.

"Oh, I'd say so," Liam said.

"Why is it so special?" Rose asked. "I think I know, but tell me."

"Well," Lily said, "lots of reasons. It's both a reunion, and a farewell. We're getting together with my oldest friends in the world—Tara and Bay, and their families—and you got to meet Rebecca and Judy."

"Rebecca says we're going to be real sisters. She's going to come visit me, and I'm going to go visit her at law school."

"I'm so glad about that," Lily said, hugging Rose. She had come so close to losing her several times in her life; but the surgeries had worked, and her heart seemed as good as could be.

"Why else is the party so special?"

"We're celebrating Maeve getting well and you being so healthy. And all the roses you planted, and the ones from long ago . . . that bloom year after year, always reminding us that summer comes again."

"No matter how long the winter seems," Liam said.

"All those things," Rose said. "And the surprise . . ."

"Ah, the surprise," Lily said. She looked across Rose's head at Liam. His blue eyes twinkled, as if he'd never been so happy.

"I'd say it's an all-around perfect night," Liam said.

"Except for Nanny," Lily said, looking out over the water. "When I went swimming, I hoped she'd show up. But she didn't . . ."

The music played on. Lily's stomach tumbled a little. It was almost time. She, Rose, and Liam sat on the old bench depicting the four seasons. Winter, spring, summer, fall. The months and years roll on, but some things endure forever. True love, she thought. For people, but also for places. Hubbard's Point was in her heart, in her very blood.

Across the yard, a cell phone rang. Patrick answered it, looked up, and called out, "Marisa!"

"Who can that be?" Sam asked.

"I don't know," Marisa said, and ran over to Patrick to answer the call.

"Hurry," Rose called. "We're about to start the surprise." She smiled up at Lily and Liam, and went to get the basket she needed.

Alone with Liam, Lily leaned her head on his shoulder. If he minded her wet hair, he didn't complain. She felt his lips on her head, heard him chuckle.

"Salty," he said.

"I couldn't help myself," she said. "Swimming with the girls is a summer party tradition."

"All parties?" he asked.

"Yes."

"Even weddings?"

"Especially!" she said, and they laughed. He embraced her, pulling her close, and in the shadow of the cedars, they kissed. Lily melted into Liam, feeling liquid from her swim, and from the heady perfume of the rose garden. She was with him now, and she knew she'd be with him forever. Tonight was just one moment in their own private eternity. Their kiss was long and salty, and she tasted the sea on his lips.

Then Rose came walking back to them, holding a basket over one arm, filled with rose petals that she had gathered earlier—from pink, red, yellow, and white roses blooming all through the garden.

"Guess who that was?" Marisa asked, joining them.

"Who?" Lily asked.

"Anne! And guess who's back in Cape Hawk?"

"Not Lafarge," Lily said.

"Definitely not. Nanny's there!"

The news was so happy and welcome, Lily's eyes filled with tears. Nanny had been their family angel this summer, guiding them from one place to the next. From Cape Hawk, to Boston for Rose's surgery, down here to Hubbard's Point to see about Maeve, and now back to the northern waters of the Gulf of St. Lawrence and Nova Scotia.

"Back in her home waters," Liam said. "And guiding us back to ours."

"Our home waters," Rose said, jumping up and down. "Cape Hawk!" In her exuberance, she jostled a few rose petals out of her basket. She started to pick them up, but instead looked up at Lily and Liam. "Is it time?" she asked.

"To surprise the party?" Lily asked, smiling. "I think so."

Lily's eyes met her grandmother's. Alone of everyone else there, Maeve knew what was about to happen. She smiled her radiant grandmotherly smile, and gave a nod to let Lily know she was ready and waiting.

Then Liam bent down, reached under the four-seasons bench. He pulled out a basket a little bigger than Rose's. It was covered with a needlepoint canvas made by Lily many years ago—when she was a young girl, not much older than Rose was now. It depicted Sea Garden, with all its magical, mysterious roses, shades of pink, peach, scarlet, crimson, and white. The white roses were the most beautiful, and showed the most detail. Lily had made this canvas with a dream of her wedding day.

She had always wanted to be married right here in this yard. She had envisioned all the roses being in bloom, especially the white ones, just right for a bride. When she was a young teenager, dreaming of her future, she had stitched this canvas. And she had vowed to celebrate a summer wedding, amid her grandmother's roses.

"What will they think of the ice?" Liam asked.

"It won't matter," Rose said. "We'll tell them to wear warm clothes!"

"The ice can be the most beautiful part," Lily said, holding Liam's hand and gazing into his blue eyes. She thought of that old photo, of the whaling ship covered in ice, its spars and rigging black and glistening under layers of silver, the fjord's cliffs rising majestically behind, faced with ice and snow.

That was Lily's landscape now. She had traveled north to find ice and snow, the aurora borealis, white whales, and more warmth than she had ever dreamed possible. She had had her daughter there, and she had met her true love—the great-great-grandson of that dark ship's captain; just when she thought her winters would last forever, she had met Liam Neill.

Seasons change, she thought. And roses bloom all year round, somewhere in the world. Her Christmas wedding would be full of roses, regardless of the fact that it would take place in Cape Hawk. She'd order them from somewhere warm, where the sun was always shining. Her friends and family would gather round, on the shortest day of the year, and they would celebrate Lily and Liam's wedding.

As they walked through the crowd, Lily and Rose reached into the basket and gave each person an invitation. Tara tore hers open right away.

"December twenty-first," she cried. "The winter solstice!"

"My new life with Rose began on the summer solstice, the longest day of the year," Lily said. "So we thought we would bring some light to the shortest day . . ."

"In Cape Hawk," Bay added.

"We want you all to be there," Lily said. "Please say you'll come. We'll rent a bus, a motorcoach, do whatever it takes to get you there . . ."

"We'll be there if we have to swim," Tara promised.

"Marisa and Sam, will you please play at the wedding?" Lily said, smiling at her friends.

"Fallen Angels?" Liam asked.

"The Flying Angels," Sam said, with her arm around her sister. "My niece gave us a new name."

"I like it better," Jessica said.

"Names are important," Rose said.

Liam nodded, and Lily leaned her head against his shoulder. Around them, the moonlight sparkled on mica, ledge, and sea.

The waves were gentle now. They beat in rhythm against the rocks, the force of life that bound everyone together, the salt of blood and hearts and sea. Ghost Hills were gone; time and tide swept north to Cape Hawk.

Lily felt Rose's hand slip into hers. She tugged, and Lily and Liam bent down to pick her up. A breeze whispered, and so did Rose.

Lily watched her press her lips to Liam's ear. Overhead, seagulls flew, their cries sounding for all the world like expressions of love, of joy. She couldn't hear her daughter's words, but from Liam's smile, she thought maybe Rose had just called him by the name she had dreamed of calling him for so long.

"Daddy . . ."

About the Author

LUANNE RICE is the author of twenty novels, most recently *Summer of Roses, Summer's Child, Silver Bells, Beach Girls, Dance With Me, The Perfect Summer,* and *The Secret Hour.* She lives in New York City and Old Lyme, Connecticut. *Beach Girls* has been made into a six-hour television series by the Lifetime network for release in summer 2005; and *Silver Bells* will be a Hallmark Hall of Fame feature presentation during the 2005 holiday season.

Visit the author's website at www.luannerice.com.